# Katharine of Aragon

The trilogy covers the life of Katharine of Aragon from the time she left her native Spain to marry Prince Arthur until her death in Kimbolton Castle. In *Katharine, the Virgin Widow* she is seen coming to an alien land ruled over by her calculating father-in-law Henry VII; and when her brief marriage ended the question which was to overshadow her life arose: Was the marriage consummated? At the opening of *The Shadow of the Pomegranate* Katharine is married to Henry and the marriage seems ideal. Her device was the Pomegranate, the Arabic sign of fertility, and she believed she would give the King what he most desired: an heir to the throne of England; but she was disappointed in this and when Bessie Blount, the beautiful maid of honour, was seduced by the King and bore him a son, Katharine learned of the danger which threatened her. The third book of the trilogy, *The King's Secret Matter*, shows the King determined to rid himself of a wife of whom he had tired. These were the momentous years and the principal actors were the once-powerful Cardinal Wolsey, the martyrs Fisher and More, the tragic young Princess Mary, and the two chief protagonists: Henry, self-indulgent, self-deceptive, lusty and sanctimonious; and Katharine, lonely, brave, persecuted and humiliated, yet never failing to stand firm against all that was implied in the King's Secret Matter.

# JEAN PLAIDY HAS ALSO WRITTEN

BEYOND THE BLUE MOUNTAINS
(A novel about early settlers in Australia)
DAUGHTER OF SATAN
(A novel about the persecution of witches and Puritans in the
16th and 17th centuries)
THE SCARLET CLOAK
(A novel of 16th century Spain, France and England)

*Stories of Victorian England*
{ IT BEGAN IN VAUXHALL GARDENS
{ LILITH

THE GOLDSMITH'S WIFE
(The story of Jane Shore)
EVERGREEN GALLANT
(The story of Henri of Navarre)

*The Medici Trilogy*
    Catherine de' Medici
{ MADAME SERPENT
{ THE ITALIAN WOMAN } Also available in one volume
{ QUEEN JEZEBEL

*The Lucrezia Borgia Series*
MADONNA OF THE SEVEN HILLS
LIGHT ON LUCREZIA

*The Ferdinand and
Isabella Trilogy*
CASTILE FOR ISABELLA
SPAIN FOR THE SOVEREIGNS } Also available in one volume
DAUGHTERS OF SPAIN

*The French Revolution Series*
LOUIS THE WELL-BELOVED
THE ROAD TO COMPIEGNE
FLAUNTING EXTRAVAGANT QUEEN

*The Tudor Novels*
    Katharine of Aragon
{ KATHARINE, THE VIRGIN WIDOW
{ THE SHADOW OF THE POMEGRANATE } Also available in one volume
{ THE KING'S SECRET MATTER
MURDER MOST ROYAL
(Anne Boleyn and Catherine Howard)
THE SIXTH WIFE
(Katharine Parr)
ST THOMAS'S EVE
(Sir Thomas More)
THE SPANISH BRIDEGROOM
(Philip II and his first three wives)
GAY LORD ROBERT
(Elizabeth and Leicester)
THE THISTLE AND THE ROSE
(Margaret Tudor and James IV)
MARY, QUEEN OF FRANCE
(Queen of Louis XII)

*The Mary Queen of Scots Series*
ROYAL ROAD TO FOTHERINGAY
THE CAPTIVE QUEEN OF SCOTS

*The Stuart Saga*
THE MURDER IN THE TOWER
(Robert Carr and the Countess of Essex)

    Charles II
{ THE WANDERING PRINCE
{ A HEALTH UNTO HIS MAJESTY } Also available in one volume
{ HERE LIES OUR SOVEREIGN LORD
THE THREE CROWNS (William of Orange)
THE HAUNTED SISTERS (Mary and Anne)
THE QUEEN'S FAVOURITES (Sarah Churchill and Abigail Hill)

*The Georgian Saga*
THE PRINCESS OF CELLE
QUEEN IN WAITING
CAROLINE, THE QUEEN
THE PRINCE AND THE QUAKERESS
THE THIRD GEORGE
PERDITA'S PRINCE
SWEET LASS OF RICHMOND HILL
INDISCRETIONS OF THE QUEEN
THE REGENT'S DAUGHTER
GODDESS OF THE GREEN ROOM
VICTORIA IN THE WINGS

*The Queen Victoria Series*
CAPTIVE OF KENSINGTON PALACE
THE QUEEN AND LORD M
THE QUEEN'S HUSBAND
THE WIDOW OF WINDSOR

*General Non-fiction*
A TRIPTYCH OF POISONERS
(Cesare Borgia, Madame de Brinvilliers and Dr Pritchard)

*The Spanish Inquisition Series*
THE RISE OF THE SPANISH INQUISITION
THE GROWTH OF THE SPANISH INQUISITION
THE END OF THE SPANISH INQUISITION

# Katharine
# of Aragon

## JEAN PLAIDY

ROBERT HALE · LONDON

© *Jean Plaidy 1968*
*This omnibus volume first published 1968*
*Reprinted 1969*
*Reprinted 1970*
*Reprinted 1972*
*Reprinted 1975*

SBN 7091 0511 8

Robert Hale & Company
63 Old Brompton Road
London, S.W.7

PRINTED IN GREAT BRITAIN BY
LOWE AND BRYDONE (PRINTERS) LIMITED, THETFORD, NORFOLK

# CONTENTS

## *Katharine, The Virgin Widow*

## *The Shadow of the Pomegranate*

## The King's Secret Matter

*Katharine, The Virgin Widow*

# THE ARENA

THE SUN PICKED out sharp flints in the grey walls of the towers so that they glinted like diamonds. The heat was great, and the courtiers sweated beneath their stomachers over which their doublets were elegantly laced; they did not move even to throw back their long loose-sleeved gowns. Each man and woman among them was intent on what was going on in the arena before them, where a lion—one of the finest and fiercest in the King's menagerie —was engaged in a bloody fight with four English mastiffs. The dogs were sturdy and game; but this lion had never been beaten. He roared his contempt of the four dogs, and the spectators cheered him.

"Now, Rex, get to work," shouted a boy who was seated among the royal party. His cheeks were ruddy, his hair gleamed reddish gold in the sunlight; and his voice was shrill with excitement.

The girl who sat beside him, and who was a few years older, laid a restraining hand on his arm; and several people let their attention stray from the animals to the children. Many found themselves catching the boy's excitement, for there was something infectious about the vitality and gaiety of young Prince Henry.

As for Henry, he was aware of nothing but the fight in the arena. He wanted the mastiffs to win, yet he did not believe they could. Rex was the finest lion in the world, which was why he had been called Rex.

The King from his seat of honour was watchful. He sat erect, not so magnificently attired as many of his subjects, for he was a man who resented wasting money on outward show. Money, in his opinion, should be used to create more money. It had been his policy ever since Bosworth Field. And the result? A depleted treasury was now a full one, carefully watched over by the King's miserly eye, continually augmented by his clever schemes; although he would be the first to admit that he owed a great deal to those two able ministers of his—Richard Empson and Edmund Dudley—who now sat near the royal party, their lawyers' eyes alert.

The King's gaze rested briefly on his Queen—a beautiful woman of whom he was secretly proud. But he was not a man to show his feelings and would never allow Elizabeth of York to know how much he esteemed her. When a man's claim to the throne was doubtful, when there was the hint of bastardy among his forbears, he must be careful. Henry VII was a careful man.

Elizabeth had been a good wife and he had never regretted the marriage, even when he considered his early love for Maud Herbert and his more mature passion for Katherine Lee. He was not a man who would allow his emotions to interfere with his ambitions.

Once Richard III had been defeated, once Henry knew that the great ambition was about to be realized, he had ceased to think of Katherine Lee; he had known there was only one suitable bride for him, and that was Elizabeth of York, that the Houses of York and Lancaster might thus be united and bring peace to England. Henry VII would never wage war if he could help it, for to him it represented the loss of gold.

He looked at his family and allowed his feeling of pleasure temporarily to turn up the corners of his stern mouth. Two sons and two daughters.

"Fair enough, fair enough," he murmured to himself.

Elizabeth had been six times pregnant and they had lost only two so far, which, considering the fate of most children, was good fortune indeed.

It was true that Arthur, the eldest and Prince of Wales, who was not quite fifteen, was a sickly boy. He was handsome enough with his pretty pink and white complexion, but that was not in his case the sign of health. Arthur coughed too much; there were occasions when he spat blood; yet he lived.

Perhaps there would have been cause for anxiety if Arthur had not possessed such a brother as Henry. There was a Prince to delight the eyes of any parent. Glances were even now straying to this ten-year-old boy. It was the same when they went among the people. It was young Henry whom the people called for. It was for him they had their smiles. Fortunately, Arthur had the sweetest temper and knew no envy. But perhaps he was too tired to feel envy; perhaps he was grateful to this robust, vital brother who could appear so fresh at the end of a day's riding, who always knew how to respond to the people's applause.

Between the two boys sat Margaret, a dignified Princess, looking older than twelve, keeping a watchful eye on her exuberant brother Henry who, strangely, did not seem to resent this. It was pleasant to see such affection between a brother and sister. And on the other side of Henry sat Mary, an enchanting creature of five years, a little wilful, because she was so pretty perhaps and doubtless over-pampered because of it.

Four children, mused the King, and Arthur the only one whose health gives cause for anxiety. Edward's daughter has done her duty well.

The Queen turned to him and was smiling. She read his thoughts. She knew that he was studying the children and had been thinking: There's time for more.

Elizabeth of York stilled the sudden resentment which rose within her. The only real desire her husband would feel would be for the aggrandisement of the throne. She was dear to him, she knew, not because of any beauty or talents she might possess, but because she was the daughter of Edward IV, and when she married him the union had brought peace to England; she had also given him children, four of whom were living.

There was tension among the spectators, and the King's attention was now on the arena, where the battle was not going according to expectations. Rex was lying on his back while one of the mastiffs had him by the throat; the others were leaping on him, tearing his flesh, their jaws bloody.

Prince Henry had risen to his feet.

"They have beaten Rex," he cried. "Oh, bravo . . . bravo !"

The cry was taken up among the spectators, as the body of Rex lay lifeless and the dogs continued to worry it.

The Queen leaned slightly towards the King.

"I would not have believed that the dogs could defeat the lion."

The King did not answer, but beckoned to one of the keepers of his menagerie.

"Take the dogs away," he said; "remove the carcass of the lion and then return to me."

As the man bowed low and went off to obey the King's command, an excited chatter broke out among the children.

Henry was shouting: "Did you *see*? Arthur, did you see. . . ?"

Arthur was pale. He murmured: "I like not these sports."

Henry laughed at him. "I like sport better than anything in the world, and never have I seen such a battle."

Mary asked: "What has happened to the lion?" But no one took any notice of her.

Margaret gripped Henry's arm. "Be silent," she whispered. "Do you not see that our father is displeased?"

Henry turned to stare at the King. "But why . . ." he began. "I should have thought it was good sport. I . . ."

The King's stern eyes rested on his son. "Henry," he said, "one day you will learn that what *you* think is of far more interest to yourself than to others."

Henry looked puzzled, but it was impossible to check his exuberance.

The King signed to one of the keepers. "Let the bears and the ban-dogs be brought on," he said.

\*        \*        \*

The company stared aghast.

Before them in the arena scaffolds had been set up and on these hung the bodies of the four English mastiffs, the dogs which, but half an hour before, had conducted themselves so valiantly against the King's fiercest lion.

The King silently watched the assembly. His chief counsellors, Dudley and Empson, watched also.

The farce was ended, but everyone should have learned the lesson it was intended to convey.

The dogs had been sentenced to death for treason. They had dared to destroy Rex the lion. They were traitors.

The King had ordered the sentence to be read before the ropes were put about the animals' necks. Then he had said in his low sombre voice: "So perish all traitors!"

His subjects stared at the writhing dogs, but it was of the King they were thinking.

Indeed he must be a man beset by fears since he could not resist pointing out to them the fate of those who attempted to overcome the power of kings.

Henry rose suddenly and, as he left his seat, his family and immediate circle prepared to follow him.

The games were over for that day.

\*        \*        \*

The children had escaped to the privy garden. It was pleasant out of doors because a breeze was beginning to blow off the river.

They were unusually silent, for the hanging of the four mastiffs had subdued them. Here in this pleasant garden, in which the scent of roses was very strong, they often gathered when their parents were in residence at the Palace of the Tower of London. They delighted now in its familiarity because the scene they had witnessed had been unexpected, and it was comforting to be in a place they knew so well. This they looked upon as their own little garden; here they felt shut away from the ceremony which was such a large part of their lives. The great walls of the Cradle Tower and the Well Tower formed a bastion against too curious eyes. Here they could forget they were Princes and Princesses and be children.

Henry broke the silence. "But why!" he demanded. "Those four brave mastiffs . . . traitors! How could they be traitors?"

Mary began to cry. She loved dogs and she had been delighted when the four had beaten the cruel lion. Had she not been told so often that Princesses do not cry in public she would have burst into tears when she saw the ropes being put about their necks.

"Hush, Mary," said Margaret, stern Margaret, who kept them in order as though she were the eldest. Someone, Margaret often pointed out, had to keep the family in order, and Arthur was useless in that respect.

Mary obediently stopped crying, but it was clear that she could not forget the mastiffs.

Arthur turned to Henry. He looked almost as old as his father in that moment. "It is all so easy to understand," he said.

"But *I* do not understand," cried Henry hotly.

"That is because you are but a boy for all your arrogance," Margaret retorted.

"Do not call me a boy. I am as tall as Arthur."

"So you may be, but that does not make you grown up," Margaret told him.

Arthur said almost wearily: "Our father had the dogs hanged because they had used their strength against Rex. Rex was the king of my father's beasts, and Rex means King. Our father was showing all those people what happens to those who pit their strength against kings."

"But the dogs were sent into the arena to fight," persisted Henry. "It makes no sense."

"The ways of kings do not always appear to make sense," answered Arthur.

"But *I* would have good sense prevail always."

"I . . . I . . . I!" murmured Margaret. "You use that word more than any other, I do declare."

"Should not a King show his subjects that he is a man of good sense then?" Henry persisted.

"No," answered Arthur, "only that he is a King to be feared."

"I do not want the dogs to be dead," cried Mary, and began to sob loudly.

Margaret knelt down and, taking a kerchief from her pocket, wiped Mary's tears away. "Have you not been told that it is unseemly for a Princess to cry like a peasant?"

"But they killed the dogs. They put ropes round their necks. They killed . . ."

"I see," said Henry in his resonant voice, "that all traitors should be hanged, but . . ."

"Let us talk of something else," commanded Margaret. "I must stop this child making such a noise. Now, Mary, what will your new sister say when she comes here and finds you such a cry-baby?"

Mary stopped crying; it was obvious that she had forgotten the death of the dogs and was thinking of her new sister.

"Just think," went on Margaret, "she is coming all the way across the sea to be our sister. So instead of four of us there'll be five."

Arthur turned away from the group, pretending to examine one of the roses. He was embarrassed by this talk of his imminent marriage. He was a great deal more uneasy about it than he cared to admit.

"Will she be big like you?" asked Mary peering into Margaret's face.

"Bigger. She is older."

"As old as our father?"

"Do not be foolish. But she is older than Arthur."

"Then she must be very old."

"Arthur is not really very old," put in Henry. "I am nearly as old as Arthur."

"Nonsense," said Margaret, "you're five years younger."

"In five years then *I* shall have a marriage."

Margaret said sharply: "*You* are destined for the Church, Henry. That means that you'll have no marriage."

"I shall if I want one," retorted Henry; his small eyes narrowed suddenly in his plump, dimpled face.

"Don't talk so foolishly."

"Arthur may not either," went on Henry, who did not like the idea of his brother's having something which he could not. "It seems to me that his Spaniard is a long time coming."

Arthur turned to face them all. He said: "Her ships have met with disaster. It is a long and hazardous journey she has to make."

"Still," said Henry, "we heard a long time ago that she had set out . . . and still she does not come."

"There are storms in the Bay of Biscay," Margaret put in.

"Perhaps," cried Henry spitefully, "she'll be drowned. Then *you* won't have a marriage either."

Arthur nodded in his mild way; but he did not look in the least perturbed by this possibility.

Poor Arthur, thought the wise Margaret, he is not looking forward with any great pleasure to being a husband.

It occurred to her that the subject of the Spanish marriage was not really a very much happier topic than that of the mastiffs.

"I'm going to have a game of tennis," said Henry suddenly. That meant that he was leaving the family party,—because Arthur was not good enough to play with him. Henry would go and find the sprightliest of young boys, and doubtless he would win, not only because he hated to lose and his opponents knew this, but because he really did excel at all games. Arthur would shut himself into his own apartments to read or brood. Margaret would hand Mary over to her nurses, and she herself would do a little embroidery with some chosen companions, chatting lightly but thinking of Arthur's marriage with the Infanta of Spain and wondering what further marriages were being arranged. It was almost certain that her own would be the next. She would not be as fortunate as Arthur, who at least would stay at home. She believed she would have to go into the wild country beyond the border.

\*　　\*　　\*

The Queen took an early opportunity of retiring to her own apartments. The spectacle had disgusted and alarmed her. She was shocked that her husband should have so betrayed himself. She had not dared to glance at him, sitting there stonily staring ahead at those struggling bodies, but she knew exactly how he would be looking. His lips would be tightly compressed; his eyes narrow and calculating. She understood more of his nature than he would have believed possible. She had seen much, during her lifetime, of the terrible fascination a crown had for some men and women; she had seen them face disaster and death to win and then retain it.

Yet Henry, her husband, did not understand this. He did not understand her at all; he made no attempt to. He was a man shut in with his emotions, and shared them with none. For two things only did he betray an overwhelming passion: for the crown and for gold; and these she knew he loved with an intensity he would never feel for anything or anyone else.

She herself was no longer young, having last February passed her thirty-fifth birthday; and during those thirty-five years what she had lacked most was security.

Her handsome father had doted on her; he had planned a grand marriage for her, and when she was nine years old she had been affianced to Charles, who was the eldest son of Louis XI, and she remembered how at that time everyone had called her Madame la Dauphine. She remembered the French lessons she had taken at that time. It was imperative, her father had said, that she speak fluently the language of the country which would one day be her home. She had also learned to write and speak Spanish.

Thinking of those early days, she said to herself: "The latter will be useful when the Infanta arrives . . . if the Infanta ever does arrive."

Royal marriages! How could one be sure they would ever take place until one witnessed the actual ceremony itself! Her marriage to the Dauphin had certainly not; she remembered the occasion when the news had arrived at the Palace of Westminster that Louis was seeking the hand of Margaret of Austria for his son.

Elizabeth could recall her father's rage; the hot red blood rushing to his face and the whites of his eyes. He had died soon after—some said of the rage this news had aroused in him.

She had been afraid of such emotion ever since. For that was the beginning of trouble. Her father dead, her uncle taking the crown, herself with her mother and some other members of the family taking refuge in sanctuary, where her little brothers were taken from them to be lodged in the Tower—this Tower in which she now sat. Somewhere in this place were buried the bodies of those two young princes who had disappeared mysteriously from their lodgings. She could remember them so well, her little brothers whom she had loved so dearly. What had happened to them? They had stood in the way to the throne. In the way of her uncle Richard? In the way of her husband, Henry?

She dared not think of their fate.

It had all happened so long ago. Her uncle Richard, who had once thought of marrying her, had met his death at Bosworth Field; the Tudor dynasty had begun.

It was this matter of hanging the mastiffs which had made her brood on the past. It was this betrayal of her husband's fear, of his determination to show all those who might rise against him what they could expect at his hands.

It was thus that Henry found her. He had come to her, she knew, to discover her feelings regarding the affair in the arena, though he would not ask. He never asked her advice or opinion. He was determined that she should remain his consort only. This desire to preserve his own supremacy was always present. Elizabeth knew it for a weakness which he attempted to hide by a show of arrogance.

"You are resting?" he asked.

He had come to her unheralded. She, who remembered the pageantry of royalty with which her father had surrounded himself, even now was a little surprised by this.

She gave him her hand which he kissed without much grace.

"The heat in the arena was overpowering," she said. "At one time I was afraid Arthur would be overcome by it."

The King frowned. "The boy's health leaves much to be desired," he said.

The Queen agreed. She murmured: "But young Henry grows more and more like my father every day."

The King was not displeased; he liked to be reminded that his son's maternal grandfather was Edward IV. But he did not wish Elizabeth to realize the extent of his pride, so he said: "Let us hope he does not inherit your father's vices."

"He had many virtues," Elizabeth said quietly.

"His virtues gave him the strength to fight for the throne; they brought men rallying to his side; but it was his vices which killed him. Let us hope young Henry will not be so fond of good food and wine, and most of all, women."

"Henry will take care of himself. It is Arthur on whose account I am so concerned."

"Soon the Infanta will be here, the marriage celebrated." Henry rubbed his hands together and his grave face was illumined suddenly by a smile.

Elizabeth knew that he was contemplating the Infanta's dowry and congratulating himself that there could not have been a more advantageous match than this one with Spain.

Henry turned to his Queen. "I must be watchful of Ferdinand. I am not sure that he is to be trusted. He will try to arrange that all the advantages are on his side."

"You too are shrewd," his wife reminded him.

Henry nodded. "It has been very necessary for me to foster shrewdness. I shall be very pleased when the dowry is in my possession and the marriage ceremony has been performed."

"It would seem that what is delaying our Infanta is not her father's diplomacy but the weather."

"Ah, the weather. The winds of the Bay of Biscay are unaccountable, even in summer."

"What is the latest news of her journey?"

The King hesitated. He did not share such information with any, even his ministers. But there could be no harm in telling her of the Infanta's progress.

"I have heard that her squadron is still at Laredo to which port she was forced to return on account of the storms. It seems to me that Ferdinand and Isabella are deliberately keeping her there to delay her arrival in England."

"No doubt the Queen finds it hard for a mother to part with her daughter."

The King grunted impatiently. "This is a girl who is to become

Princess of Wales. I should have thought they would have been as distressed by the delay as we are."

There was a great deal he did not understand, thought Elizabeth; and never would. This husband of hers was without emotions except those of ambition.

"Yet," murmured the Queen, "I have heard that Queen Isabella is loth to lose her daughter."

"And she is said to be a great Queen!"

Henry was thoughtful; he was recalling the rumours he had heard concerning the relationship of the Spanish King and Queen with whom his own family would soon be linked in marriage. It was said that Isabella never forgot that she was the Queen of Castile and the senior in the royal partnership. Henry, glancing swiftly at his Queen, was once more grateful to the fate which had given him such a woman.

In an unguarded moment he said: "I think some of our subjects were a little shocked by the hanging of the traitors."

"The four dogs? I think many were."

"And you?"

He so rarely allowed a personal note to creep into their relationship that she was momentarily startled.

"I . . . I was surprised."

"It is not a pleasant death," said the King. "It is well to remind ambitious men of this now and then."

He was smiling but his smile was cold. He had been on the verge of telling her that he intended to send an English sailor to Laredo—a Devon pilot who could lead the fleet of the Spanish Infanta to England without delay; but he changed his mind.

Elizabeth was critical of his conduct and he would endure no criticisms from any man or woman living.

He said: "Matters of state demand my attention. Tonight I shall visit you."

She bowed her head in acquiescence, but she was afraid. Must there be another pregnancy, another child who, it was more than likely, would never grow to maturity?

It seemed such a short time ago that little Edmund had died. It was heart-breaking when they lived a little while and one grew to love them. A pretty child, Edmund, but to suffer such discomfort, such pain, and then to give birth to a sickly child over whom one watched with anxiety until one suffered yet another loss!

I am too old, too weak for more childbearing, she thought. But she said nothing. What use would it have been to complain to him

—to say: I have given you six children, four of whom are living. Do they not suffice?

His answer would be cool and to the point. A Queen must go on bearing children as long as possible. It is her duty.

Did he, she wondered, ever give a thought to Katherine Lee, her own maid of honour? If he did, not even Katherine would know it. She doubted whether Henry was ever unfaithful to herself even in thought.

She had married a strange man, a cold man; but at least she had a faithful husband. Henry would indulge in a sexual relationship for only one purpose: the procreation of children; and to procreate children with any other partner than his wife would in his opinion be an unnecessary act.

There were times when the Queen of England wanted to cast aside her dignity and laugh aloud; but that would be hysterical laughter and the Queen was no more given to hysterical outbursts than her husband was.

So she bowed her head and told herself that she must inform her women that this would be one of the nights which the King would spend in her bed.

# THE MARRIAGE OF ARTHUR, PRINCE OF WALES

THE INFANTA STOOD on deck and watched the Spanish coastline fade from view.

When would she see it again? she wondered.

Doña Elvira Manuel, the stern and even formidable duenna whom Queen Isabella had put in charge of the Infanta and her maids of honour, was also gazing at the land she was leaving; but Elvira did not share the Infanta's sorrow. When she left Spain her authority began, and Elvira was a woman who dearly loved power.

She laid her hand on the Infanta's arm and said: "You should not grieve. You are going to a new land whose Queen you will surely be one day."

The Infanta did not answer. How could she expect Elvira Manuel to understand. She was praying silently, praying for courage, that she would not disgrace her family, that she would be able to remember all that her mother had taught her.

It had been a mistake to think of her mother. The thought had conjured up an image of that stern yet loving face which had changed in recent years. The Infanta remembered Queen Isabella, always full of quiet dignity but at the same time possessed of a purposeful energy. Sorrow had changed her—that sorrow which had come to her through her great love for her children.

In Spain I was dearly loved, thought the Infanta. What will happen to me in England? Who will love me there? I am not even beautiful as my maids of honour are. I shall look plainer than ever, compared with them. It was not kind of my father-in-law to stipulate that my maids of honour should all be handsome.

"All will be different," she whispered.

Elvira Manuel said quickly: "Your Highness spoke?"

"I merely said that nothing will be the same, in this new land, as it has been in Spain. Even my name will be different. From now on I am no longer Catalina; I am Katharine. And they say there is little summer in England."

"It cannot be colder there than it is in some parts of Spain."

"But we shall miss the sun."

"When you have children of your own you will not care whether or not the sun shines."

The Infanta turned away and looked at the heaving waters. Yes, she thought, a son. Children would make her happy; she knew that. And she would have children. Her very device was the pomegranate, which to the Arabs signified fruitfulness. It reminded her of the pomegranate trees which grew so profusely, with the myrtle, in the gardens of the Alhambra. Whenever she saw her device, and she knew it would throughout her life be constantly with her, she would always remember the *patios* of Granada and the glistening waters in the fountains. She would think of her childhood, her parents and her brother and sisters. Would she always think of them with this deep yearning? Perhaps when she had children of her own she would overcome this desire to be back in her own childhood.

But it was long before she could expect children; and in the meantime she could only yearn for home.

"Oh, Mother," she whispered, "I would give everything I have to be with you now."

In the royal apartments in the Alhambra Queen Isabella would be thinking of her now. She could be certain of that. The Queen would pray for her daughter's safety at sea until she reached England; then she would pray that her Catalina's marriage with her English Prince might be fruitful, that Catalina might achieve a happiness which had been denied her sisters, Isabella and Juana, her brother Juan.

The Infanta shivered and Elvira said sharply: "A breeze is rising, Highness. You should retire to your cabin."

"I am warm enough," was the answer. She was unaware of the wind. She was thinking of early days in the nursery when they were all together. She felt almost unbearably sad to recall those days when she had sat at her mother's knee while her sisters, Isabella and Maria, had worked at their tapestry and Juan read aloud to them. Her sister Juana had neither sat at her needlework nor read, nor nestled quietly at their mother's feet—restless Juana who gave them all cause for such anxiety!

Her sister Isabella and her brother Juan were tragically dead; Maria had gone into Portugal recently to marry Isabella's widower, Emanuel, King of Portugal. She would be happy there, for Emanuel was a kindly gentle man and would cherish Maria for the sake of her sister whom he had dearly loved. And Juana? Who could say what was happening to Juana? Her life would never run smoothly. There had been rumours that all was not well with her marriage to the handsome Archduke Philip and that in the Brussels court there was many a stormy scene of jealousy which ended in outbursts of strange conduct on Juana's part.

All her life the Infanta had realized what a deep shadow her sister Juana cast over her mother's happiness.

But that was the family she was leaving. What of the new one to which she was going?

"Arthur, Margaret, Henry, Mary." She whispered their names. They would be her companions now; and to them she would be Katharine . . . no longer Catalina.

She was going into a new country. The King and Queen of England would be her father and mother now. "We shall regard the Infanta as our own daughter, and her happiness shall be our main concern. . . ." Thus wrote the King of England to her mother, who had shown her those words.

"You see," the Queen had said, "you will have a new family, so perhaps you will soon forget us all at home."

At that she had been unable to preserve the dignity which was considered necessary to an Infanta of Spain, and had flung herself into her mother's arms and sobbed: "I shall never forget you. I shall never cease to long for my return."

Her mother had wept with her. Only we, her children, know how gentle she is, thought the Infanta. Only we know that she is the best mother in the world and that necessarily our hearts must break to leave her.

It was different, saying goodbye to her father.

He embraced her affectionately, kissed her fondly, but his eyes gleamed, not with tears at the parting but with satisfaction at the marriage. If he had had his way she would have been despatched to England long before. He needed the friendship of England; he was eager for this marriage. He was fond of her, but the great loves of his life were power and money, and his feeling for his children was always second to the advantages they could bring him.

He had not attempted to hide his delight at the parting. There was little that was subtle about Ferdinand.

"Why, daughter," he had said, "you'll be Princess of Wales, and I'll warrant it won't be long before you're Queen of England. You'll not forget your home, my child?"

His meaning was different from that of her mother. The Queen meant: You will remember the love we bear each other, the happiness we have had together, all that I have taught you which will help you to bear your trials with fortitude. Ferdinand meant: Do not forget that you are a Spaniard. When you are at the Court of England be continually on the alert for the advantages of Spain.

"Write often," Ferdinand had said, putting his lips close to her ear. "You know the channels through which any secret information should be sent to me."

She closed her eyes now and looked at the grey waters.

It was true, a storm was rising. The hazards of the sea were all about her. What if she should never reach England?

She gripped the rail and thought of Isabella and Juan, both of whom had finished with earthly trials. How long would it be before her mother joined them?

Such thoughts were wicked. She, not yet sixteen, to long for death!

Only in that moment had she realized the depth of her fear.

This is cowardice, she told herself sharply. How do I know what awaits me in England?

\*     \*     \*

Sick from the rocking of the ship, cold and drenched with sea water, Katharine stood on deck watching the land which grew more and more distinct as she stood there.

England! The land in which she was destined to be Queen.

Elvira was at her side. "Highness, you should prepare yourself to meet the King."

"Do you think he will be at Plymouth to greet me?"

"Surely he will, and the Prince with him. Come! We must make you ready to receive them."

They went to her cabin where her maids of honour clustered round her. All so much prettier than I, she thought; and she imagined Arthur, looking at them and being disappointed because she was the Infanta and his bride.

"We are far from London," said Elvira. "I have heard that the journey to the capital will last three weeks."

Katharine thought: Three weeks! What did it matter what discomfort she had to endure if it meant postponing the ceremony for three weeks!

When she was ready to go on deck the ship already lay at anchor. A beautiful sight met her eyes; the sun had come out and was discovering brilliants on the blue water. Stretched before her was the lovely coast of Devon, the grass of which was greener than any she had ever seen; and the gorse was golden.

Before her was Plymouth Hoe, and she saw that many people had gathered there and that they carried banners on which were the words—she knew little English but they were translated for her: "Welcome to the Princess of Wales!" "God bless the Infanta of Spain!"

There was the sound of cheering as she came on deck with her ladies, and she found that her spirits were lifted. Then she heard the bells ringing out and she saw a small boat approaching the ship; in it was a company of splendidly dressed men.

The English pilot who had brought them safely to England came to Katharine's side and bowing to the veiled figure said: "Your Highness, you are safe from the sea. This is Plymouth Sound and the people of Devon are eager to show you how glad they are to have you with them. Here come the Mayor and his aldermen to give you formal welcome."

She turned to an interpreter who stood beside her and told him to ask whether the King and Prince of Wales were in Plymouth.

"I doubt they could make the journey to Plymouth, Your Highness," was the answer. "We are three weeks' journey from London. But they will have sent orders that all are to welcome you right royally until they can do so themselves."

She had a feeling that this was an apology for the absence of his King and Prince. It need not have been made to her. She was relieved that she could have a little respite before she met them.

She received the Mayor and his aldermen as graciously as even her mother could have wished.

"Tell them I am happy to be with them," she said. "I am grateful that I have escaped the perils of the sea. I see a church steeple there. I would first like to go to church and give thanks for my safe arrival."

"It shall be as Her Highness commands," was the Mayor's answer.

Then Katharine came ashore and the people of Plymouth crowded about her.

"Why," they said, "she is naught but a child." For although her face was veiled there was no doubt that she was young, and there was many a mother in the crowd who wiped her eyes to think of a young girl's leaving her home and going to a strange land.

How brave she was! She gave no sign of her disquiet. "She's a Princess," they said, "every inch a Princess. God bless her."

Thus Katharine of Aragon rode through the streets of Plymouth to give thanks for her safe arrival in England and to pray that she might give no offence to the people of her new country, but please them in every way.

Her spirits rose a little as she went through those streets in which the tang of the sea was evident. She smiled at the fresh faces which pressed forward to glimpse her. Their free and easy manners were strange to her; but they were showing her that they were pleased to see her, and that gave infinite comfort to a lonely girl.

*　　　*　　　*

The journey towards London had begun; it was inevitably a slow one, for the people of England had been commanded by their King to show a hearty welcome to the Princess from Spain. They needed no such injunctions; they were ever ready to accept an excuse for gaiety.

In the villages and towns through which the cavalcade passed the people halted its progress. The Princess must see their folk dances, must admire the floral decorations and the bonfires which were all in her honour.

They were attracted by this quiet Princess. She was such a child, such a shy, dignified young girl.

It was a pleasant journey indeed from Plymouth to Exeter, and Katharine was astonished by the warmth and brilliance of the sun. She had been told to expect mists and fog, but this was as pleasant as the Spanish sunshine; and never before had she seen such cool green grass.

At Exeter the nature of the journey changed. In that noble city she found more ceremony awaiting her than she had received in Plymouth, and she realized that thus it would be as she drew nearer to the capital.

Waiting to receive her was Lord Willoughby de Broke, who told her that he was High Steward of the King's household and that it was the express command of His Majesty that all should be done for her comfort.

She assured him that nothing more could be done for her than had been done already; but he bowed and smiled gravely as though he believed she could have no notion of the extent of English hospitality.

Now about her lodgings were ranged the men at arms and yeomen, all in the royal green and white liveries—and a pleasant sight they were.

She made the acquaintance of her father's ambassador to England and Scotland, Don Pedro de Ayala, an amusing and very witty man, whose stay in England seemed to have robbed him of his Spanish dignity. There was also Dr. de Puebla, a man whom she had been most anxious to meet because Ferdinand had warned her that if she had any secret matter to impart to him she might do it through Puebla.

Both these men, she realized, were to some extent her father's spies, as most ambassadors were for their own countries. And how different were these two: Don Pedro de Ayala was an aristocrat who had received the title of Bishop of the Canaries. Handsome, elegant, he knew how to charm Katharine with his courtly manners. Puebla was of humble origin, a lawyer who had reached his present position through his own ingenuity. He was highly educated and despised all those who were not; and Ayala he put into this category, for the Bishop had spent his youth in riotous living and, since he came of a noble family, had not thought it necessary to achieve scholarship.

Puebla's manner was a little sullen, for he told himself that if all had gone as he had wished he should have greeted the Infanta without the help of Ayala. As for Ayala, he was fully aware of Puebla's feelings towards him and did everything he could to aggravate them.

As they left Exeter, Don Pedro de Ayala rode beside Katharine, and Lord Willoughby de Broke was on her other side, while Puebla was jostled into the background and fumed with rage because of this.

Ayala talked to Katharine in rapid Castilian which he knew Willoughby de Broke could not understand.

"I trust Your Highness has not been put out by this outrageous fellow, Puebla."

"Indeed no," replied Katharine. "I found him most attentive."

"Beware of him. The fellow's an adventurer and a Jew at that."

"He is in the service of the Sovereigns of Spain," she answered.

"Yes, Highness, but your noble father is fully aware that the fellow serves the King of England more faithfully than he does the King and Queen of Spain."

"Then why is he not recalled and another given his position?"

"Because, Highness, he understands the King of England and the King of England understands him. He has been long in England. In London he follows the profession of lawyer; he lives like an Englishman. Ah, I could tell you some tales of him. He is parsimonious—so much so that he brings disgrace to our country. He has his lodgings in a house of ill-fame and I have heard that when he does not dine at the King's table he dines at this disreputable house at the cost of two pence a day. This, Highness, is a very small sum for a man in his position to spend, and I have heard it said that the landlord of this house is glad to accommodate him in exchange for certain favours."

"What favours?" demanded Katharine.

"The man is a lawyer and practises as such; he is on good terms with the King of England. He protects his landlord against the law, Highness."

"It seems strange that my father should employ the man if he is all you say he is."

"His Highness believes him to have his uses. It is but a few years ago that the English King offered him a bishopric, which would have brought him good revenues."

"And he did not accept?"

"He longed to accept, Highness, but could not do so without the consent of your royal parents. This was withheld."

"Then it would seem that they value his services."

"Oh, he has wriggled his way into the King's confidence. But beware of the man, Highness. He is a Jew, and he bears his grudges like the rest."

Katharine was silent, contemplating the unpleasantness of having to meet two ambassadors who clearly disliked each other; and she was not surprised when Puebla seized his opportunity to warn her against Ayala.

"A coxcomb, Highness. Do not put your trust in such a one. A Bishop! He knows nothing of law and has never mastered Latin. His manner of living is a disgrace to Spain and his cloth. Bishop indeed! He should be in Scotland now. It was for this purpose that he was sent to this country."

"It would not please my parents if they knew of this discord between their two ambassadors."

"Highness, they know of it. I should be neglectful of my duty if I did not inform them. And inform them I have."

Katharine looked with faint dislike at Puebla. Not only did he lack the charming manners of Ayala but she found him pompous, and she thought that his petty meanness, which was noticed by many of those who travelled with them, was humiliating for Spain.

"I used the fellow in Scotland," went on Puebla. "He was useful there in cementing English and Scottish relations which, Highness, was the desire of your noble father. War between England and Scotland would have been an embarrassment to him at this time, and James IV was harbouring the pretender, Perkin Warbeck, and seemed likely to support him."

"Warbeck has now paid the price of presumption," said Katharine.

"Your Highness most wisely has become informed of English politics, I see."

"Her Highness, my mother, insisted that I should know something of the country to which I was going."

Puebla shook his head. "There are bound to be such impostors when two young Princes disappear. So we had our Perkin Warbeck claiming to be Richard, Duke of York."

"How very sad for the Queen of England," said Katharine. "Does she still mourn for her two brothers who disappeared so mysteriously in the Tower of London?"

"The Queen is not one to show her feelings. She has children of her own, a good husband and a crown. The last certainly could not be hers had her brothers lived."

"Still she must mourn," said Katharine; and she thought of her own brother, Juan, who had died, young and beautiful, a few months after his wedding. She believed she would never forget Juan and the shock and tragedy of his death.

"Well, quite rightly Warbeck has been hanged at Tyburn," went on Puebla, "and that little matter has been settled. That would be satisfactory if it did not mean that Ayala has left the Scottish Court for that of England. London suits him better than Edinburgh. He is a soft liver. He did not like the northern climate nor the rough Scottish castles. So . . . we have him with us."

Ayala rode up beside them.

His smile was mischievous. "Dr. de Puebla," he said, "I do declare your doublet is torn. Is that the way to appear in the presence of our Infanta! Oh, he's a close-fisted fellow, Highness. If you would know why, look at the shape of his nose."

Katharine was horrified at the gibe and did not look at Ayala.

"Highness," cried Puebla, "I would ask you to consider this: Don Pedro de Ayala may have the nose of a Castilian but the bags under his eyes are a revelation of the life he leads. One is born with one's nose; that is not a result of dissipation, evil living. . . ."

Ayala brought his horse closer to Katharine's. "Let us heed him not, Highness," he murmured. "He is a low fellow; I have heard that he follows the trade of usurer in London. But what can one expect of a Jew?"

Katharine touched her horse's flanks and rode forward to join Lord Willoughby de Broke.

She was alarmed. These two men, who could not control their hatred of each other, were the two whom her parents had selected to be her guides and counsellors during her first months in this strange land.

*      *      *

Yet as the journey progressed she was attracted by the gaiety of Ayala.

She had discovered that he was amusing and witty, that he was ready to answer all her questions about the customs of the country and, what was more interesting, to give her little snippets of gossip about the family to which she would soon belong.

For much of the journey Katharine travelled in a horse litter, although occasionally she rode on a mule or a palfrey. October in the West country was by no means cold, but there was a dampness in the air and often Katharine would see the sun only as a red ball through the mist. Occasionally there were rain showers, but they were generally brief and then the sun would break through the clouds and Katharine would enjoy its gentle warmth. In the villages through which they passed the people came out to see them, and they were entertained in the houses of the local squires.

Here there was food in plenty; Katharine discovered that her new countrymen set great store by eating; in the great fireplaces enormous fires blazed; even the servants in the houses crowded round to see her—plump, rosy-cheeked young men and women, who shouted to each other and seemed to laugh a good deal. These people were as different from the Spaniards as a people could be. They appeared to have little dignity and little respect for the dignity of others. They were a vigorous people; and, having taken Katharine to their hearts, they did not hesitate to let her know this.

But for the ordeal she knew to be awaiting her at the end of the journey, she would have enjoyed her progress through this land of mists and pale sunshine and rosy-cheeked, exuberant people.

Ayala often rode beside her litter and she would ask him questions which he would be only too ready to answer. She had turned from the pompous Puebla in his musty clothes to the gay cleric, and Ayala was determined to exploit the situation to the full.

He made her feel that there was a conspiracy between them, which to some extent there was. For she knew that, when he rattled on in the Castilian tongue, none of those who were near could understand what was said.

His talk was gay and scandalous, but Katharine felt it was what she needed, and she looked forward to these conversations.

"You must be wary of the King," he told her. "Have no fear of Arthur. Arthur is as mild as milk. You will be able to mould that one to your way . . . have no fear of that. Now, had it been Henry, that might have been another matter. But, praise be to the saints, Henry is the second son and it is Arthur for Your Highness."

"Tell me about Arthur."

Ayala lifted his shoulders. "Imagine a young boy, a little nervous, pink and white and golden-haired. He is half a head shorter than you are. He will be your slave."

"Is it true that he does not enjoy good health?"

"It is. But he will grow out of that. And he seems the weaker because he is compared with robust young Henry."

Katharine was relieved; she was delighted with the idea of a gentle young husband. She had already begun to think of him as her brother Juan, who had been as fair as an angel and gentle in his manner.

"You said I must beware of the King."

"The King is quiet and ruthless. If he does not like you he will have no compunction in sending you back to Spain."

"That would not greatly distress me."

"It would distress your royal parents. And think of the disgrace to Your Highness and the House of Spain."

"Is the King very formidable?"

"He will be gracious to you but he will never cease to watch. Do not be deceived by his mild manners. He fears all the time that some claimant to the throne will appear, and that there will be supporters to say such a claimant has a greater right. It is not always comfortable to wear the crown."

Katharine nodded; she thought of the strife which had marred the earlier years of her parents' life together, when Isabella had been engaged in the bitter War of the Succession.

"There is a mystery surrounding the death of the Queen's two young brothers, the elder of whom was King Edward V and the younger the Duke of York. Many say they were murdered in the Tower of London by their wicked uncle, the crook-backed Richard, but their bodies were never discovered and there are many rumours concerning those deaths of which it would be unwise even to think, Highness."

Katharine shivered. "Poor children," she murmured.

"They are now past all earthly pain, and there is a wise King sitting on the throne of England. He married the Princes' sister, and so joined the two warring factions. It might be wise not to dwell on the past, Highness. There have been two pretenders to the throne: Perkin Warbeck and Lambert Simnel. Simnel, who pretended he was Edward Plantagenet, Earl of Warwick and nephew of Richard III, is now serving as a scullion in the King's household. He was obviously an impostor; therefore the King sent him to the kitchens—a sign of the King's contempt—but Warbeck was hanged at Tyburn. This King is fond of showing examples to his people, because he lives in perpetual terror that someone will try to overthrow him."

"I hope I shall find favour in his sight."

"Your dowry has already found favour with him, Highness. As for yourself, you will please him too."

"And the Queen?"

"Have no fear of the Queen. She will receive you kindly. She has no influence with the King, who is eager to show her that he owes no part of the throne to her. He is a man who takes counsel of none, but if he could be said to be under the influence of any, that one is his mother. You must please Margaret Beaufort Countess of Richmond if you will please the King—and all you need do is to provide the royal house with heirs, and all will go merrily."

"I pray that God will make me fruitful. That, it seems, is the prayer of all Princes."

"If there is aught else Your Highness wishes to know at any time, I pray you ask of me and ignore the Jew."

Katharine bowed her head. And so the journey progressed.

\*        \*        \*

The King set out from Richmond Palace. He had become impatient. He was all eagerness to see the Spanish Infanta who had taken so long in reaching his country.

Arthur had been on pilgrimage to Wales—as Prince of Wales he was warmly greeted there and the King wished his son to show himself now and then in the Principality. Arthur had received word from his father that he was to come with all speed to East Hampstead, where he would greet his bride.

Henry disliked journeys, for he was not a man of action and they seemed to him an unnecessary expense.

"But on the occasion of my son's wedding," he grumbled to Empson, "I daresay we are expected to lay out a little."

"That is so, Sire," was the answer.

"Let us hope that we shall have the revenues to meet this occasion," sighed the King; and Empson decided that he would raise certain fines to meet the extra expense.

Henry smiled wryly, but he was in fact delighted because his son was acquiring one of the richest Princesses in Europe. It was a good thing that this little island should be allied to the greatest power in the world, and what better tie could there be than through marriage?

Heirs were what were needed and, once this girl provided them, all well and good. But he was a little anxious about her. Her brother, the heir of Spain, had died shortly after his marriage. Exhausted by being a husband, it was said in some quarters. He hoped Katharine was of stronger health. And if *she* were . . . what of his own Arthur? Arthur's cough and spitting of blood denoted weakness. They would have to take great care of Arthur, and he

was not yet fifteen. Was it too young to tax his strength with a
bride?

He had not consulted his physicians; he consulted no one; he
and he alone would decide whether the marriage should be consummated immediately, or whether the royal couple should wait
for a few months, or perhaps a year.

Young people, he mused, might indulge unwisely in the act of
love. They might have no restraint. Not that he believed this
would be the case with Arthur. Had it been Henry, it would have
been another matter; but then there would have been no cause
for anxiety on that account where Henry was concerned. But
what of the Infanta? Was she a lusty young woman? Or was she
sickly like her elder sister who had recently died in childbirth?

The more the King pondered this matter, the more eager he
was to meet the Infanta.

\*          \*          \*

There was consternation in the Infanta's party.

A message had been brought to Ayala stating that the King was
on his way to meet his son's bride, who had stayed that night at
the residence of the Bishop of Bath in Dogmersfield and was some
fifteen leagues from London Bridge.

Ayala did not pass on the news to Puebla. Indeed he was
determined to keep it from the man—not only because he disliked
him and never lost an opportunity of insulting him, but because
he really did believe that Puebla was more ready to serve Henry
VII of England than Isabella and Ferdinand of Spain.

Instead he sought out Elvira Manuel.

"The King is on his way to meet us," he told her abruptly. "He
wishes to see the Infanta."

"That is quite impossible," retorted Elvira. "You know the
instructions of their Highnesses."

"I do. The Infanta is not to be seen by her bridegroom or anyone at the English Court until she is a wife. She is to remain
veiled until after the ceremony."

"I am determined," said Elvira, "to obey the commands of the
King and Queen of Spain, no matter what are the wishes of the
King of England."

"I wonder what Henry will say to that." Ayala smiled somewhat
mischievously, for he found the situation piquant and amusing.

"There is one thing that must be done," said Elvira. "To prevent discord, you should go ahead and explain to the King."

"I will leave at once," Ayala told her. "In the meantime you
should warn the Infanta."

Ayala set out on the road to East Hampstead; and Elvira, her lips pursed with determination, prepared herself to do battle.

She went to Katharine and told her that the King would make an attempt to see her, and that on no account must he succeed.

Katharine was disturbed. She was afraid that the King of England might consider her extremely discourteous if she refused to receive him.

\*         \*         \*

When Arthur joined his father at East Hampstead, Henry noticed that his son looked wan and worried.

No, the King decided, the marriage shall not be consummated for a year. In any case I doubt whether Arthur would be capable of consummating it.

"Put your shoulders back, boy," he said. "You stoop too much."

Arthur obediently straightened his shoulders. There was no resentment. How differently young Henry would have behaved! But of course there would have been no necessity to criticize Henry's deportment.

We should get more sons, thought the King anxiously.

"Well, my son," he said, "very soon now you will be face to face with your bride."

"Yes, Father."

"You must not let her think that you are a child, you know. She is almost a year older than you are."

"I know it, Father."

"Very well. Prepare yourself to meet her."

Arthur asked leave to retire and was glad when he reached his own apartment. He felt sick with anxiety. What should he say to his bride? What must he do with her? His brother Henry had talked slyly of these matters. Henry knew a great deal about them already. Henry ought to have been the elder son.

He would have made a good king, thought Arthur. I should have done better in the Church.

He let himself brood on the peace of monastic life. What relief! To be alone, to read, to meditate, not to have to take a prominent part in ceremonies, not to have to suffer continual reproach because a few hours in the saddle tired him, because he could never learn to joust and play the games at which Henry excelled.

"If only," he murmured to himself, "I were not the first-born. If only I could miraculously change places with my brother Henry, how happy I could be!"

\*         \*         \*

The next morning the King, with the Prince beside him, set out on the journey to Dogmersfield.

Almost immediately it began to rain, and the King looked uneasily at his son while Arthur squirmed in the saddle. His cough would almost certainly come back if he suffered a wetting, and although the rain was fine it was penetrating.

Arthur always felt that it was his fault that he had not been born strong. He tried to smile and look as though there was nothing he enjoyed so much as a ride in the rain.

When they were within a few miles of the Bishop's Palace the King saw a rider galloping towards his party, and in a very short time he recognized the Spanish Ambassador Ayala.

Ayala drew up before Henry and sweeping off his hat bowed gracefully.

"News has been brought to me that Your Grace is on the way to see the Infanta."

"That news is now confirmed," answered the King. "So impatient was our young bridegroom that, having heard that the Infanta was at Dogmersfield, he could wait no longer. He himself has come hot-foot from Wales. He yearns to see his bride."

Arthur tried to force his wet face into an expression which would confirm his father's words as the Spanish Ambassador threw a sly smile in his direction which clearly conveyed his knowledge of the boy's nervousness.

"Alas," said Ayala, "Your Grace will be unable to see the bride."

"I . . . unable to see the bride!" said the King in a cold, quiet voice.

"The King and Queen of Spain insist that their daughter should observe the customs of a high-born Spanish lady. She will be veiled until after the ceremony, and not even her bridegroom may see her face until then."

The King was silent. A terrible suspicion had come into his mind; he was the most suspicious of men. Why should he not look on the face of the Infanta? What had the Spanish Sovereigns to hide? Was this some deformed creature they were sending him? "Not until after the ceremony." The words sounded ominous.

"This seems a strange condition," said Henry slowly.

"Sire, it is a Spanish custom."

"I like it not."

He turned his head slightly and said over his shoulder: "We will form a council, my lords. Here is an urgent matter to discuss. Ambassador, you will excuse us. It will take us but a short time to come to a decision, I imagine."

Ayala bowed his head and drew his horse to the side of the road while the King waved a hand towards a nearby field.

"Come with us, Arthur," he said. "You must join our council."

Henry placed himself and his son in the centre of the field and his followers ranged themselves about him. Then he addressed them:

"I like this not. I am denied admittance to my son's bride although she is in my territory. I would not wish to go against the law in this matter. Therefore, the council must decide what should be done. The Infanta has been married to the Prince by proxy. What we must decide is whether she is now my subject; and, if she is my subject, what law could prevent my seeing her if I wished. I pray you, gentlemen, consider this matter, but make it quick for the rain shows no sign of abating and we shall be wet to the skin by the time we reach Dogmersfield."

There was whispering among those gathered in the field. Henry watched them covertly. He had as usual conveyed his wishes and he expected his councillors to obey them. If any one of them raised objections to what he wished, that man would doubtless find himself guilty of some offence later on; he would not be sent to prison; he would merely have to pay a handsome fine.

All knew this. Many of them had paid their fines for small offences. The King thought no worse of them, once they had paid. It was their money which placated him.

In a few seconds the council had made its decision.

"In the King's realm the King is absolute master. He need not consider any foreign law or customs. All the King's subjects should obey his wishes, and the Infanta, having married the Prince of Wales, albeit by proxy, is the King's subject."

Henry's eyes gleamed with satisfaction which held a faint tinge of regret. He could not, with justice, extract a fine from one of them.

"Your answer is the only one I expected from you," he said. "It is not to be thought of that the King should be denied access to any of his subjects."

He led the way out of the field to where Ayala was waiting for him.

"The decision is made," he said. Then he turned to Arthur. "You may ride on to Dogmersfield at the head of the cavalcade. I go on ahead."

He spurred his horse and galloped off; and Ayala, laughing inwardly, closely followed him.

The Sovereigns of Spain would learn that this Henry of England was not a man to take orders, thought the ambassador. He wondered what Doña Elvira was going to say when she was confronted by the King of England.

*    *    *

Katharine was sitting with her maids of honour when they heard the commotion in the hall below. It had been too miserable a day for them to leave the Bishop's Palace and it had been decided that they should remain there until the rain stopped.

Elvira burst on them, and never had Katharine seen her so agitated.

"The King is below," she said.

Katharine stood up in alarm.

"He insists on seeing you. He declares he *will* see you. I cannot imagine what their Highnesses will say when this reaches their ears."

"But does not the King of England know of my parents' wishes?"

"It would seem there is only one whose wishes are considered in this place and that is the King of England."

"What is happening below?"

"The Count of Cabra is telling the King that you are not to be seen until after the wedding, and the King is saying that he will not wait."

"There is only one thing to be done," said Katharine quietly. "This is England and when we are in the King's country we must obey the King. Let there be no more protests. We must forget our own customs and learn theirs. Go and tell them that I am ready to receive the King."

Elvira stared at her in astonishment; in that moment Katharine looked very like her mother, and it was as impossible for even Elvira to disobey her as it would have been to disobey Isabella of Castile.

*    *    *

She stood facing the light, her veil thrown back.

She saw her father-in-law, a man a little above medium height, so thin that his somewhat sombre garments hung loosely on him; his sparse fair hair, which fell almost to his shoulders, was lank and wet; his long gown which covered his doublet was trimmed with ermine about the neck and wide sleeves. There was mud on his clothes and even on his face. He had clearly travelled far on horseback in this inclement weather and had not thought it necessary to remove the stains of travel before confronting her.

Katharine smiled and the alert, crafty eyes studied her intently, looking for some defect, some deformity which would make her parents desirous of hiding her from him; he could see none.

Henry could not speak Spanish and he had no Latin. Katharine had learned a little French from her brother Juan's wife, Margaret of Austria, but Margaret's stay in Spain had been short and, when she had gone, there had been no one with whom Katharine could converse in that language. Henry spoke in English: "Welcome to England, my lady Infanta. My son and I have eagerly awaited your coming these many months. If we have rudely thrust aside the customs of your country we ask pardon. You must understand that it was our great desire to welcome you that made us do so."

Katharine attempted to reply in French but slipped into Spanish. She curtseyed before the King while his little eyes took in the details of her figure. She was healthy, this Spanish Infanta, more so than his frail Arthur. She was a good deal taller than Arthur; her eyes were clear; so was her skin. Her body was sturdy, and if not voluptuous it was strong. She was no beauty, but she was healthy and she was young; it was merely custom which had made her parents wish to hide her from him. Her only real claim to beauty was that abundant hair—thick, healthy hair with a touch of red in its colour.

Henry was well satisfied.

She was talking to him now in her own tongue, and, although he could not understand her, he knew that she was replying to his welcome with grace and charm.

He took her hand and led her to the window.

Then he signed to Ayala who had at that moment entered the apartment.

"Tell the Infanta," said Henry, "that I am a happy man this day."

Ayala translated, and Katharine replied that the King's kindness made her very happy too.

"Tell her," said the King, "that in a few minutes her bridegroom will be riding to the palace at the head of a cavalcade. They cannot be much more than half an hour after me."

Ayala told Katharine this; and she smiled.

She was standing between the King and Ayala, they in their wet garments, when she first saw her bridegroom.

He looked very small, riding at the head of that cavalcade, and her first feeling for him was: He is so young—he is younger than I am. He looks frightened. He is more frightened than I am.

And in that moment she felt less resentful of her fate.

She determined that she and Arthur were going to be happy together.

\*          \*          \*

It was later that evening. Katharine looked almost pretty in candlelight; her cheeks were faintly flushed; her grey eyes alight with excitement. Her maids of honour, all chosen for their beauty, were very lovely indeed. Only Doña Elvira Manuel sat aloof, displeased. She could not forget that the wishes of her Sovereigns had been ignored.

The Infanta had invited the King and the Prince to supper in her apartments in the Bishop's Palace; and in the gallery the minstrels were playing. The supper had been a prolonged meal; Katharine was continually being astonished at the amount that was eaten in England. At tonight's feast there had been sucking pigs and capons, peacocks, chickens, mutton and beef, savoury pies, deer, fish and wild fowl, all washed down with malmsey, romney and muscadell.

The English smacked their lips and showed their appreciation of the food; even the King's eyes glistened with pleasure and only those who knew him well guessed that he was calculating how much the feast had cost, and that if the Bishop could afford such lavish entertainment he might be expected to contribute with equal bounty to the ever hungry exchequer.

The Prince sat beside Katharine. He was an elegant boy, for he was fastidious in his ways and his lawn shirt was spotlessly clean as was the fine silk at collar and wristbands; his long gown was trimmed with fur as was his father's, and his fair hair hung about his face, shining like gold from its recent rain-wash.

His skin was milk-white but there was a delicate rose-flush in his cheeks and his blue eyes seemed to have sunk too far into their sockets; but his smile was very sweet and a little shy, and Katharine warmed to him. He was not in the least like his father, nor like her own father. Her mother had once told her of her first meeting with her father and how she had thought him the handsomest man in the world. Katharine would never think that of Arthur; but then before she had seen him Isabella of Castile had determined to marry Ferdinand of Aragon, and she had gone to great pains to avoid all the marriages which others had attempted to thrust upon her.

All marriages could not be like that of Isabella and Ferdinand, and even that marriage had had its dangerous moments. Katharine remembered the conflict for power between those two. She knew that she had brothers and sisters who were her father's children but not her mother's.

As she looked at gentle Arthur she was sure that their marriage would be quite different from that of her parents.

Arthur spoke to her in Latin because he had no Spanish and she had no English.

That would soon be remedied, he told her. She should teach him her language; he would teach her his. He thanked her for the letters she had written him and she thanked him for his.

They had been formal little notes, those letters in Latin, written at the instigation of their parents, giving no hint of the reluctance both felt towards their marriage; and now that they had seen each other they felt comforted.

"I long to meet your brother and sisters," she told him.

"You shall do so ere long."

"You must be happy to have them with you. All mine have gone away now. Every one of them."

"I am sorry for the sadness you have suffered."

She bowed her head.

He went on: "You will grow fond of them. Margaret is full of good sense. She will help you to understand our ways. Mary is little more than a baby—a little pampered, I fear, but charming withal. As for Henry, when you see him you will wish that he had been born my father's elder son."

"But why should I wish that?"

"Because you will see how far he excels me in all things and, had he been my father's elder son, he would have been your husband."

"He is but a boy, I believe."

"He is ten years old, but already as tall as I. He is full of vitality and the people's cheers are all for him. I believe that everyone wishes that he had been my father's elder son. Whereas now he will doubtless be Archbishop of Canterbury and I shall wear the crown."

"Would you have preferred to be Archbishop of Canterbury?"

Arthur smiled at her. He felt it would have sounded churlish to have admitted this, for that would mean that he could not marry her. He said rather shyly: "I did wish so; now I believe I have changed my mind."

Katharine smiled. It was all so much easier than she had believed possible.

Elvira had approached her and was whispering: "The King would like to see some of our Spanish dances. He would like to see you dance. You must do so only with one of your maids of honour."

"I should enjoy that," cried Katharine.

She rose and selected two maids of honour. They would show the English, she said, one of the stateliest of the Spanish dances; and she signed to the minstrels to play.

The three graceful girls, dancing solemnly in the candlelit apartment, were a charming sight.

Arthur watched, his pale eyes lighting with pleasure. How graceful was his Infanta! How wonderful to be able to dance and not become breathless as he did!

The King's eyes were speculative. The girl was healthy, he was thinking. She would bear many children. There was nothing to fear. Moreover Arthur was attracted by her, and had seemed to grow a little more mature in the last hour. Was he ready? What a problem! To put them to bed together might terrify this over-sensitive boy, might disclose that he was impotent. On the other hand, if he proved not to be impotent, might he not tax his strength by too much indulgence?

What to do? Wait? There could be no harm in waiting. Six months perhaps. A year. They would still be little more than children.

If Henry had only been the elder son!

Ayala was at the King's elbow, sly, subtle, guessing his thoughts.

"The Infanta says that she does not wish Your Grace to think that only solemn dances are danced in Spain; she and her ladies will show you something in a different mood."

"Let it be done," answered the King.

And there was the Infanta, graceful still, dignified, charming, yet as gay as a gipsy girl, her full skirts twirling in the dance, her white hands as expressive as her feet. Katharine of Aragon could dance well.

The King clapped his hands and the Prince echoed his father's applause.

"We are grateful to the ladies of Spain for giving us such enjoyment," said Henry. "I fancy our English dances are not without merit; and since the Infanta has danced for the Prince, the Prince should dance for the Infanta. The Prince of Wales will now partner the Lady Guildford in one of our English dances."

Arthur felt a sudden panic. How could he match Katharine in the dance? She would despise him. She would see how small he was, how weak; he was terrified that he would be out of breath and, if he began to cough, as he often did at such times, his father would be displeased.

Lady Guildford was smiling at him; he knew her well, for she was his sisters' governess and they often practised dancing together. The touch of her cool fingers comforted him, and as he danced his eyes met the grave ones of the watching Infanta, and he thought: She is kind. She will understand. There is nothing to fear.

The dance over he came to sit beside her once more. He was a little breathless, but he felt very happy.

*     *     *

This was her wedding day. She was waiting in the Bishop's Palace of St. Paul's to be escorted to the Cathedral for the ceremony. She would be led to the altar by the Duke of York, whom she had already met and who disturbed her faintly. There was something so bold and arrogant about her young brother-in-law, and an expression which she could not understand appeared on his face when he looked at her. It was an almost peevish, sullen expression; she felt as though she were some delicious sweetmeat which he desired and which had been snatched from him to be presented to someone else.

That seemed ridiculous. She was no sweetmeat. And why should a boy of ten be peevish because his elder brother was about to be married?

She had imagined this; but all the same she felt an unaccountable excitement at the prospect of seeing the Duke of York again.

She had ridden into London from Lambeth to Southwark by way of London Bridge, and her young brother-in-law had come to escort her.

He was certainly handsome, this young boy. He swept into the apartment as though he were the King himself, magnificently attired in a doublet of satin the sleeves of which were slashed and ruched somewhat extravagantly; there were rubies at his throat. His face was broad and dimpled; his mouth thin, his eyes blue and fierce, but so small that when he smiled they seemed to disappear into the smooth pink flesh. His complexion was clear, bright and glowing with health; his hair was shining, vital and reddish gold in colour. There could be no mistaking him for anyone but a Prince. She found it hard to believe that he was merely ten years old, for he seemed older than Arthur, and she wondered fleetingly how she would have felt if this boy had been her bridegroom instead of his brother.

They would not have married her to a boy of ten. But why not? There had been more incongruous royal marriages.

He had taken off his feathered hat to bow to her.

"Madam, your servant," he had said; but his looks belied the humility of his words.

He had explained in Latin that he had come to escort her into London. "It is my father's command," he said. "But had it not been I should have come."

She did not believe that, and she suspected him of being a braggart; but she was conscious of the fascination he had for her and she realized that she was not the only one who was conscious of his power.

He had stared at her thick hair which she was to wear loose for the journey into London, and had put out a plump finger to touch it.

"It is very soft," he had said, and his little eyes gleamed.

She had been aware that she seemed strange to him, with her hair flowing thus under the hat which was tied on her head with a gold lace; beneath the hat she wore a headdress of scarlet.

"Your hat," he had told her, "reminds me of that which Cardinals wear."

And he had laughed, seeming but a boy of ten in that moment.

He had ridden on one side of her as they came through the streets while on the other side was the Legate of Rome. The people had lined the streets to see the procession and she had noticed that, although many curious glances came her way, eyes continually strayed to the young Prince riding beside her. He had been aware of this and she had noticed that he lost no opportunity of acknowledging his popularity and, she suspected, doing all he could to add to it.

The citizens of London had organized a pageant to show their welcome for the Spanish Princess whom they regarded as their future Queen, and in the centre of this pageant had been Saint Katharine surrounded by a company of virgins all singing the praises of the Princess of Wales.

She had smiled graciously at the people and they had cheered calling: "Long live the Princess of Wales! God bless the Infanta of Spain! Long live the Prince of Wales! Long live the Duke of York!"

And the young Duke of York had lifted his bonnet high so that the light caught his golden hair, and Katharine admitted that he was indeed a handsome Prince.

When they had reached the Bishop's Palace, which was adjacent to the Cathedral, it had been the young Duke of York who took her hand and led her in.

That had happened some days before, and now this was her wedding day; and once again that young boy would walk beside her and lead her to the altar where his brother would be waiting for her.

She stood still in her elaborate wedding finery; indeed she found it not easy to move. Her gown stood out over the hoops beneath it, and on her head she wore the mantilla of gold, pearls and precious stones. The veil cascaded over her head and shielded her face. She was dressed as a Spanish Princess and the style was new to England.

Henry came to her and looked at her in blank admiration.

Then he spoke: "Why, you are beautiful!"

"And you are kind," she answered.

"I am truthful," he said. "That is not kindness, sister."

"I am glad that I please you."

His eyes narrowed suddenly in a manner which she already knew was a habit with him. "It is not I whom you wish to please," he said sullenly. "Is that not so? It is my brother."

"I wish to please every member of my new family."

"You please Arthur," he said, "and you please Henry. It is of no importance that you please the girls."

"Oh, but it is . . . it is of the greatest importance."

"You will please Margaret if you embroider." He snapped his fingers. "Your eyes are too beautiful to strain with needlework. As for Mary, she is pleased by everyone who makes much of her. But you please me because you are beautiful. Is that not a better reason?"

"To embroider means to have learned how to do so. There is great credit in that. But if I should be beautiful—which I do not think I am—that would be no credit to me."

"You will find that people in England admire your beauty more than your embroidery," he told her. He frowned. He wished that he could think of something clever to say, the sort of remark which his tutor, John Skelton, would have made had he been present. Henry admired Skelton as much as anyone he knew. Skelton had taught his pupil a great deal—and not only from lesson books. Henry liked Skelton's bold, swaggering speech, his quick wit, and had absorbed all that he had taught him about the way a gentleman should live and a good deal else besides; Skelton was not averse to repeating Court gossip and tales of the scandalous habits of some of the courtiers. Often certain information passed between them which was to be secret; Skelton had said: "You have to be a man, my Prince, as well as an Archbishop, and if by ill fate you should be forced to enter the Church then you will do well to sow your wild oats early." Henry knew a great deal about the kind of wild oats which could be sown and was longing to sow some. He pitied poor Arthur under the tutelage of Dr. Linacre, a solemn, wise old man who thought—and endeavoured to make Arthur agree with him—that the main object in life should be the mastery of Greek and Latin.

He wanted to tell Katharine now that although he was young he would doubtless make a better husband for her even at this stage than Arthur. But the precocious child did not know how to express such thoughts.

So he took her by the hand, this wondrously apparelled bride of his brother's, and led her from the Palace to the Cathedral; and the people cheered and said: "What a handsome bridegroom our Prince Henry will make when his time comes!"

Henry heard and was pleased; yet he was angry at the same time. Life had given him all but one important thing, he believed. Good health, handsome looks, vitality, the power to excel—and then had made him the second son.

In the Cathedral a stage had been erected; it was circular in shape and large enough to contain eight people, including Katharine in her voluminous wedding dress. It was covered with scarlet cloth and about it a rail had been set up.

To this dais Henry led Katharine; and there waiting for her was Arthur, dazzling in white satin adorned with jewels.

Henry VII and his Queen, Elizabeth of York, watched the ceremony from a box at the side of the dais.

The King thought how small Arthur looked beside his bride and wondered whether the unhealthy whiteness of his skin was made more obvious by the hectic flush on his cheeks. He was still undecided. To consummate or not consummate? To make an effort to get a grandson quickly and perhaps endanger his heir's health, or to let the pair wait a year or so? He had half the bride's dowry already; he could scarcely wait to get his hands on the other half. He would have to watch Ferdinand. Ferdinand was continually planning wars; he wanted to see the Italian states under Spanish control; he would make all sorts of excuses about that second half of the dowry.

But I'll keep him to it, thought Henry. If there were a child, that would make him realize the need to pay the second half quickly. He would be doubly pleased with the marriage if his daughter conceived and bore quickly.

And yet . . .

Elizabeth was conscious of her husband's thoughts. They are too young, she considered. Arthur at least is too young. Over-excitement weakens him. If only Henry would talk to me about this matter! But what is the use of wishing that, when he never consults anyone. There will be one person to decide whether the young Infanta is to lose her virginity this night—and that will be the King of England. And as yet he is undecided.

The Archbishop of Canterbury with nineteen bishops and abbots was preparing to take part in the ceremony. Now he was demanding of the young couple that they repeat their vows; their voices were only just audible in the hushed Cathedral. The Infanta's was firm enough; Arthur's sounded feeble.

I trust, his mother thought uneasily, that he is not going to faint. It would be construed as an evil omen.

Her eyes rested long on her white-clad firstborn and she remembered that September day in Winchester Castle when she had first heard the feeble cries of her son.

She had been brought to bed in her chamber which had been hung with a rich arras; but she had insisted that one window should not be covered because she could not endure the thought of having all light and air shut out. Her mother-in-law, Margaret Beaufort, Countess of Richmond, had been with her, and she had been grateful for her presence. Before this she had been considerably in awe of this formidable lady, for she knew that she was the only woman who had any real influence with the King.

The birth had been painful and she had been glad that she had only women to attend to her. Margaret had agreed with her that the delivery of babies was women's work; so she had said farewell to all the gentlemen of the Court when her pains had begun and retired to her chamber, with her mother-in-law in charge of the female attendants.

How ill she had been! Arthur had arrived a month before he was expected, and afterwards she had suffered cruelly from the ague; but she had recovered and had tried not to dread the next confinement, which she knew was inevitable. A Queen must fight, even to the death, if necessary, to give her King and country heirs. It was her mission in life.

And there he was now—that fair, fragile baby, her firstborn—having lived precariously enough through a delicate childhood, preparing now to repeat the pattern with this young girl from Spain.

There was a tear in her eye and her lips were moving. She realized she was praying: "Preserve my son. Give him strength to serve his country. Give him happiness, long life and fruitful marriage."

Elizabeth of York feared that she was praying for a miracle.

*     *     *

After mass had been celebrated, the young bride and groom stood at the door of the Cathedral, and there the crowds were able to see them kneel while Arthur declared that he endowed his bride with a third of his property.

The people cheered.

"Long live the Prince and Princess of Wales!"

The couple rose, and there beside the bride was young Prince Henry as though determined not to be shut out from the centre of attraction. He took the bride's hand and walked with her and his brother to the banqueting hall in the Bishop's Palace where a feast of great magnificence had been set out for them.

There Katharine was served on gold plate which was studded with precious gems; but as she ate she was thinking with trepidation of the night which lay before her, and she knew that her bridegroom shared her fears. She felt that she wanted to hold back the night; she was so frightened that she longed for her mother, longed to hear that calm, serene voice telling her that there was nothing to fear.

The feasting went on for several hours. How the English enjoyed their food! How many dishes there were! What quantities of wine!

The King was watching them. Was he aware of their fear? Katharine was beginning to believe that there was little the King did not understand.

The Queen was smiling too. How kind she was—or would have been if she had been allowed to be. The Queen would always be what her husband wished, thought Katharine; and there might be times when he wished her to be cruel.

Katharine had heard of the ceremony of putting the bride to bed. In England it was riotous and ribald . . . even among royalty. It could never have been so for her mother, she was sure. But these people were not dignified Spaniards; they were the lusty English.

She turned to Arthur who was trying to smile at her reassuringly, but she was sure his teeth were chattering.

*　　　*　　　*

The moment had come and they were in the bedchamber. There was the bed, and the curtains were drawn back, while it was being blessed; Katharine knew enough English now to recognize the word fruitful.

She dared not look at Arthur, but she guessed how he was feeling.

The room was illuminated by many candles and their light

shone on the scarlet arras, on the silk bed curtains and the many faces of those who had crowded into the bedchamber.

The King came to them and, laying a hand on the shoulder of each, he drew them towards him.

He said: "You are very young. Your lives lie before you. You are not yet ready for marriage, but this ceremony shall be a symbol, and when you are of an age to consummate the marriage then shall it be consummated."

Katharine saw the relief in Arthur's face and she herself felt as though she wanted to weep for joy. She was no longer afraid; nor was Arthur.

They were led to the bed and the curtains were drawn while their attendants stripped them of their clothes; and when there was nothing to cover their white naked bodies and they knelt side by side, still they were not afraid.

They prayed that they might do their duty; they prayed as all married people were expected to pray on the night of their nuptials. But this was no ordinary wedding night because it was the King's express command that they were too young to consummate the marriage.

A cup of warm, sweet wine was brought to them and they drank as commanded. Then an attendant came and wrapped their robes about them. The ceremony was over.

The people who had crowded into the bedchamber departed; the servants of Katharine and Arthur—Spanish and English—remained in the ante-chamber; the door of the nuptial chamber was locked, and the bride and bridegroom were together.

Arthur said to her: "There is nothing to fear."

"I heard the King's command," she answered.

Then he kissed her brow, and said: "In time I shall be your husband in truth."

"In time," she answered.

Then she lay down in the marriage bed still wearing the robe which her attendant had wrapped about her. The bed was big. Arthur lay down beside her in his robe.

"I am so tired," said Katharine. "There was so much noise."

Arthur said: "I am often tired, Katharine."

"Goodnight, Arthur."

"Goodnight, Katharine."

They were so exhausted by the ceremonies and their attendant fears that soon they slept; and in the morning the virgin bride and groom were ready to continue with their wedding celebrations.

ALL LONDON WAS eager to celebrate the marriage of the Prince of Wales and the Infanta; the King was wise enough to know that his people must have some gaiety in their lives, and that if he allowed them to celebrate the marriage of his son, they might for a time forget the heavy taxes with which they were burdened.

"Let them make merry," he said to Empson. "A fountain of wine here and there will be enough to satisfy them. Let there be plenty of pageantry. The nobles will provide that."

Henry was even ready to contribute a little himself, for he was very anxious that his subjects should express their loyalty to the new Tudor dynasty. There was nothing the people loved so much as a royal wedding; and as this was the wedding of the boy who was destined to become their King, it was the King's wish that the celebrations should continue.

Katharine felt a little bewildered by them. Arthur was tired of them, but young Henry revelled in them. Margaret uneasily wondered when *her* marriage would be celebrated, and as for little Mary, she was delighted whenever she was allowed to witness the pageantry.

The greatest pageant of all was staged at Westminster, to which the royal family travelled by barge. After the night following the wedding day, Katharine had been sent to Baynard's Castle where she had been placed under the strict surveillance of Doña Elvira. The King had made it clear to the duenna that the marriage was not yet to be consummated; and as Elvira considered her Infanta as yet too young for the consummation she was determined that the King's wishes should be respected.

So, by barge, came the Infanta with her duenna and lovely maids of honour.

Katharine sometimes wished that her maids of honour were not so beautiful. It was true that she was always dazzlingly attired, and her gowns were more magnificent than those of the girls, but beauty such as that possessed by some of these girls did not need fine clothes to show it off.

The people lined the river banks to cheer her on her way to Westminster and as she smiled and acknowledged their cheers she temporarily forgot her longing for home.

Alighting from her barge she saw that before Westminster

Hall a tiltyard had been prepared. On the south side of this a stage had been erected; this was luxuriously hung with cloth of gold; and about the open space other stages, far less magnificent had been set up for the spectators.

This, Katharine discovered, was the joust, the Englishman's idea of the perfect entertainment. Here the nobility of England would gather to tilt against each other.

On this, the occasion of the most important wedding in England, the great houses were determined to outshine each other, and this they endeavoured to do with such extravagance that, as the champions entered the arena, there were continual gasps of wonder and wild applause.

Katharine was led on to the stage amid the cheers of the people; and there she seated herself on cushions of cloth of gold. With her were the King, the Queen and all the royal family. But she herself occupied the place of honour.

She thought how pleased her parents would be if they could see her now.

Beside her sat Arthur, looking pale and tired; but perhaps that was because Henry was also there, radiant and full of health. He had seated himself on a stool at the bride's feet and sat clasping his hands about his knees in a manner which was both childish and dignified.

Margaret, of whom Katharine felt a little in awe, was seated with her mother, but Katharine noticed how she kept her eyes on young Henry. Little Mary could not resist bouncing up and down in her seat now and then with excitement. No one restrained her, for her childish ways found such favour with the people.

The King was pleased. At such moments he felt at ease. Here he sat in royal panoply, his family all about him—two Princes and two Princesses to remind any nobles, who might have disloyal thoughts concerning his right to the throne, that he was building the foundations of his house with firmness.

"Look," said Henry. "There's my uncle Dorset coming in."

Katharine looked and saw the Queen's half-brother entering the arena beneath a pavilion of cloth of gold which was held over him by four riders as he came. He looked magnificent in his shining armour.

"And," cried Henry, "there's my uncle Courtenay. Why, what is that he is riding on? I do declare it is a dragon!"

He gazed up at Katharine, eager to see what effect such wondrous sights were having upon her. Her serenity irritated him mildly. "I'll warrant you do not see such sights in Spain," he challenged.

C

"In Spain," said Arthur, "there is the great ceremony of La Corrida."

"I'll warrant," boasted Henry, "that there are no ceremonies in Spain to compare with those in England."

"It is well," Arthur replied, "that Katharine does not understand you or she would not admire your manners."

Henry said: "I wish she would learn English more quickly. There is much I would say to her."

Katharine smiled at the boy, whose attention was now turned back to the arena, where Lord William Courtenay, who had married Queen Elizabeth's sister, came lumbering in astride his dragon.

Katharine was being introduced to English pageantry; she thought it a little vulgar, a little simple, but she could not help but marvel at the care which had gone into the making of these symbols; and the delight which they inspired was infectious.

Now came the Earl of Essex whose pavilion was in the form of a mountain of green on which were rocks, trees, flowers and herbs; and on top of the mountain sat a beautiful young girl with her long hair loose about her.

The spectators applauded wildly, but many of the nobles present whispered that Essex was a fool thus to display his wealth before the King's avaricious eyes. His "mountain" was clearly very costly indeed and the days when nobles flaunted their wealth so blatantly were no longer with them.

So Katharine sat back in her place of honour and watched the jousting. She listened to the cheers of the people as their favourites rode into the arena; and she found her attention fixed not so much on those whose skill with the lance gave such pleasure to the company, but on the two brothers—her husband and Henry.

Henry's eyes were narrow with concentration; his cheeks were flushed. It was clear that he longed to be down there in the arena and emerge as the champion. As for Arthur, he seemed to shrink into his golden seat, closing his eyes now and then when disaster threatened one of the combatants. He knew that death could easily result from these jousts and he had never been able to accept such accidents with equanimity.

That day there were no serious casualties and he was glad that it was November so that the dusk fell early and it was necessary to leave the tiltyard for the hall of the Palace, where the banquet and further entertainments were awaiting them.

At the centre of the table on an elevated dais the King took his place, and on his left were seated Katharine, the Queen and the King's revered mother, the Countess of Richmond. On the King's right hand sat Arthur. Margaret and Mary were next to their grandmother on the Queen's side, and on the King's side next to Arthur, in order of precedence, were the nobility of England.

The monumental pies with their golden pastry, the great joints, the dishes of flesh and fowl, were brought in with ceremony; the minstrels played and the feasting and drinking began.

But there must be pageantry, and in the space made ready before the banqueting table the dancing and spectacle began.

Katharine looked on at the ship, the castle and the mountain, which in their turn were wheeled into the hall to the cries of admiration of the guests. The ship, which came first, was manned by men dressed as sailors who called to each other in nautical terms as their brilliantly painted vehicle trundled round and round the hall. On the deck were two figures which were intended to represent Hope and Desire, and suddenly there appeared beside them a beautiful girl dressed in Spanish costume.

Henry called to Katharine from his place at table: "You see, this is all in your honour. You are the hope and desire of England."

It was very flattering and Katharine, guessing what her young brother-in-law implied, graciously acknowledged the compliment with smiles which she hoped expressed her great pleasure and appreciation.

The mountain came next, and here again were allegorical figures all intended to pay homage to the new bride.

The most splendid of all the pageants was the castle which was drawn into the hall by lions of gold and silver; there was much whispering and laughter at the sight of these animals, for it was well known that inside each of the lion's skins were two men; one being the front part, the other the hindquarters. The spectators had seen these animals perform before, as they were a feature of most pageants; but they slyly watched Katharine to see her astonishment, for it was believed that she must be wondering what strange animals these were.

Seated on top of the castle was another beautiful girl in Spanish costume, and she, like the other, was being courted by Hope and Desire.

And when the ship, the mountain and the castle were all in the hall, the minstrels began to play; then beautiful girls and handsome men stepped from them, and as there was an equal number of both sexes they were most conveniently partnered for a dance, which they performed in the space before the banqueting table.

When this dance was over the performers bowed low and, to great applause, slipped out of the hall.

Now the company must join in, but first the royal bride and groom must dance followed by other members of the royal family.

Katharine and Arthur did not dance together. Many present thought this meant that the marriage was not yet to be consummated. So Katharine chose her maid of honour Maria de Rojas, and together they danced a *bass* dance, which was stately and more suitable, she thought, to the occasion than one of those dances known as *la volta* and which involved a good deal of high stepping and capering.

Katharine was at her best in the dance, for she moved with grace and she was an attractive figure in spite of the superior beauty of Maria de Rojas.

Two gentlemen at the table watched Maria as she danced. One was the grandson of the Earl of Derby, who thought her the most beautiful girl he had ever seen; but there was another watching Maria. This was Iñigo Manrique, the son of Doña Elvira Manuel, who had accompanied the party to England in the role of one of Katharine's pages.

Maria was conscious of these looks as she danced, and deliberately she gave her smile to the young Englishman.

But although Maria's beauty attracted attention there were many who closely watched the young Infanta. The King and Queen were delighted with her; she was healthy and whether or not she was beautiful was of no great moment. She was fresh and young enough not to be repellent to a young man. They were both thinking that when the time came she would be fertile.

Arthur watched her and found pleasure in watching her; now that he knew he need not fear the consummation of their marriage he was very eager to win the friendship of his wife.

Henry could not take his eyes from Katharine. The more he saw of her the more his resentment rose. The precocious youth enjoyed occasions such as this, but he was never completely happy unless he was the centre of attraction. If only he had been the bridegroom! he was thinking. If only he were the future King of England!

The dance was over, the applause rang out while Katharine and Maria returned to their places. Arthur then led out his aunt, the Princess Cecily, and the dance they chose was a grave and stately one. Henry, watching them through sullen eyes, was thinking that so must Arthur dance, because the high dances made him breathless. But that was not the English way of dancing. When the English danced they threw themselves wholeheartedly into the affair. They should caper and leap and show that they enjoyed it. He would show them when his turn came. He was impatient to do so. When it came he and his sister Margaret stepped into the centre of the hall; there was immediate applause, and all sullenness left Henry's face as he bowed to the spectators and began to dance. He called to the minstrels to play more quickly; he wanted a gayer air. Then he took Margaret's hand and the colour came into their faces as they danced and capered about the hall, leaping into the air, twirling on their toes; and when Margaret showed signs of slackening Henry would goad her to greater efforts.

The company was laughing and applauding, and Henry, the sweat running down his face, threw off his surcoat and leaping and cavorting in his small garments continued to divert the company.

Even the King and Queen were laughing with pleasure, and when the music eventually stopped and the energetic young Prince with his sister returned to the table, congratulations were showered on them from every corner of the hall.

Henry acknowledged the cheers on behalf of himself and Margaret, but his small eyes rested on Katharine. He knew that his father was wishing his first-born were more like his other son.

Henry realized then that he was hoping Katharine was making a similar comparison of himself and Arthur.

\*　　　\*　　　\*

Doña Elvira Manuel, that most domineering of duennas, was delighted with the state of affairs in England, for while Katharine had her separate household she remained in charge of it, and she knew well that once Katharine became in truth the wife of Arthur she would cease to maintain the power which was now hers.

As duenna to a virgin bride she was supreme, for Katharine herself, on the instructions of Queen Isabella, must bow to her wishes.

Doña Elvira had never been chary of expressing her opinions, and it was inevitable that other ambitious people in the Spanish entourage should find her intolerable and seek to undermine her power.

There was one who held great influence with Katharine. This was Father Alessandro Geraldini who had been her tutor for many years and who now was her chief chaplain and confessor.

Since he had been in England Geraldini had become increasingly aware of the important role which was his and what a different matter it was to be adviser and confidant of the Princess of Wales after being merely tutor to the Infanta of Spain.

Not only was Katharine the most important lady in England next to the Queen, but she was also more important to her parents' political schemes than she had ever been before. And he, Geraldini, was her confessor. Was he going to allow a sharp-tongued woman to dominate him!

He sought for means of destroying her power. He asked permission to speak to Don Pedro de Ayala confidentially.

The ambassador shut the door of the ante-room in which the interview took place and begged Geraldini to state his business.

Geraldini came straight to the point. "Doña Elvira Manuel has become insufferable. One would think she was the Princess of Wales."

"In what way has she offended you, my friend?"

"She behaves as though she has charge of the Infanta's very soul. And that happens to be my duty."

Ayala nodded. He was secretly amused; he liked to contemplate strife between the domineering duenna and the ambitious priest.

"The sooner our Infanta is free of such supervision the better, I say," continued Geraldini. "And the sooner this marriage becomes a real marriage the better pleased will be our Sovereigns."

"I see that you are in their Highnesses' confidence," said Ayala with a smile.

"I think I know my duty," answered Geraldini sharply. "Could not their Highnesses be persuaded that it is dangerous to Spanish policy if the marriage remains unconsummated?"

"Tell me how you see such danger in our Infanta's virginity."

The priest grew pink. "It is . . . not as it should be."

"I will pass on your comments to the Sovereigns," Ayala told him.

Geraldini was not satisfied. He went to Puebla. Like most of the Infanta's household he had come to despise Puebla, who was often disparagingly referred to as the *marrano*. Christianized Jews were people of whom the Inquisition had taught Spaniards to be wary.

As for the English, they had found Puebla parsimonious and, although this was a trait they had to accept in their King, they did not like it in others. Therefore Geraldini was less careful of offending Puebla than of offending Ayala.

"The marriage should be consummated," he said at once. "It is our duty as servants of their Catholic Highnesses to see that this unsatisfactory state of affairs is ended."

Puebla eyed the priest speculatively. He knew of Geraldini's influence with Katharine.

"It is the wish of the Infanta?" he asked.

Geraldini made an impatient movement. "The Infanta is innocent. She expresses no opinion. How could she, knowing little of such matters? Yet she holds herself willing to obey the command of her parents."

Puebla was thoughtful, wondering how best he could ingratiate himself with the English King. He believed that England was to be his home for a long time, and that pleasing the King of England was as important a matter—if not more so—as pleasing the Spanish Sovereigns. Yet the consummation of the Infanta's marriage seemed to him of small importance compared with the matter of her dowry.

Even as he listened to Geraldini he was wondering what he could do to please the King of England in this matter without displeasing the Spanish Sovereigns. The dowry had been agreed on as two hundred thousand crowns, one hundred thousand of which had been paid on the wedding day. Fifty thousand more were due in six months' time and another fifty thousand within the year. The plate and jewels, which Katharine had brought with her from Spain and which were to form part of the payment, were valued at thirty-five thousand crowns. This was important to Henry because the plate and jewels were actually in England. For the remainder of the dowry he had only the word of Isabella and Ferdinand to rely on. Why should not Henry take the plate and jewels *now*? They were in England, so protests from Spain would be fruitless. Henry had already shown when he had seen the Infanta before her wedding that in England he was determined to have his way.

So Puebla was of the opinion that the consummation of the marriage was of far less importance than the Infanta's dowry.

"It is always the King of England who will decide," he said.

"Then I think we should let it be known that the Sovereigns of Spain *expect* consummation without delay."

Puebla lifted his shoulders and Geraldini could see that, like Ayala, he was indifferent.

But the fact that Geraldini had approached both ambassadors in the matter was brought to the notice of Doña Elvira, and she immediately realized that the officiousness of the priest was directed against her own authority.

Doña Elvira was never a woman to consider whether or not she offended others.

She asked Geraldini to come to her apartments and, when he arrived, she went straight into the attack.

"It appears, Father Geraldini, that you choose to forget that *I* am in charge of the Infanta's household!"

"I did not forget."

"Did you not? Then it seems strange that you should go about explaining that it is the wish of their Catholic Highnesses that the marriage should be consummated."

"Strange, Doña Elvira? It is common sense."

"You are in the Sovereigns' confidence?"

"I . . . I am the Infanta's confessor, and as such . . ."

Doña Elvira's eyes narrowed. And as such, she thought, you enjoy too much of her confidence. I shall remedy that.

She interrupted coldly: "Queen Isabella put me in charge of her daughter's household, and until she removes me from that position, there I shall remain. It is for the good of all that as yet the marriage shall remain unconsummated. Our Infanta is as yet too young and her husband even younger. I will thank you, Father, not to meddle in affairs which are no concern of yours."

Geraldini bowed to hide the hatred in his eyes, but Doña Elvira made no attempt to hide that in hers.

There was war between them, and Doña Elvira would not be satisfied until she had arranged for the insolent priest's recall to Spain.

\*　　　\*　　　\*

Henry came running into his brother's apartments, his eyes blazing with excitement.

Arthur was stretched out on a couch looking very pale.

"Are you sick, Arthur?" asked Henry, but he did not wait for an answer. "I have just seen a strange thing, brother. Our father has done to death his best falcon, and for no other reason than that it was not afraid to match itself with an eagle."

"Is that so?" said Arthur wearily.

"Indeed it is so. Our father ordered the falconers to pluck off its head, and this was done."

"I understand why," said Arthur, "because I remember how he hanged the mastiffs."

"Yes," said Henry. "I remembered too. Our father said: 'It is not meet for any subject to attack his superior.' "

"Ah," mused Arthur, "our father is fond of these little parables, is he not?"

"But his best falcon! And all because the bird was game enough to show no fear of the mighty eagle. I should have treasured that falcon. I should have been proud of him. I should have used him continually. *I* should not have plucked off his head for bravery."

"You are not King."

"No—that is not for me." Arthur noticed the sullen lines about the little mouth.

"It is unfortunate. You would have made a much better King than I, Henry."

Henry did not deny this. "But you are the elder. It is the Church for me. And you already have a wife."

Arthur flushed. He was a little ashamed of being a husband and yet no husband. It was embarrassing to know that there was a great deal of talk about whether or not the marriage should be consummated. It made him feel foolish.

Henry was thinking of that now. His face was as usual expressive, and Arthur could always guess at his thoughts.

Henry strutted about the apartment, imagining himself as the husband. There would be no question of the consummation then.

"You find her comely?" he asked slyly.

"She is very comely," answered Arthur.

"And she brings you much enjoyment?"

Arthur flushed. "Indeed yes."

Henry rocked on his heels and looked knowledgeable. "I have heard that the Spaniards are a passionate people, for all their solemn dignity."

"Oh, it is true . . . it is true . . ." said Arthur.

Henry smiled. "It is said that you and she are not husband and wife in truth. I'll warrant those who say that do not know the real truth."

Arthur began to cough to hide his embarrassment; but he did not deny Henry's suggestion.

Henry began to laugh; then suddenly he remembered the falcon. "If I were King," he said, "I do not think I should have to hang my bravest dogs and destroy my most gallant falcon to warn my subjects that they must obey me."

Henry was looking into the future, and once more Arthur guessed his thoughts. Do I look so ill then? he wondered. And he knew that he did, and that the chances were that he would not live, nor beget children, to keep Henry from the throne.

\*     \*     \*

It was time that Arthur returned to the Principality of Wales and the question had arisen as to whether Katharine should accompany him.

The King was undecided. Each day it seemed to him that Arthur looked weaker.

Puebla had been to him and, in an endeavour to assure Henry that he, Puebla, in reality served the King of England even though he was supposed to be the servant of the Spanish

Sovereigns, he suggested that Henry should immediately take possession of Katharine's plate and jewels.

"They will, of course, be Your Grace's at the end of the year, but why should you not take them now?"

Henry considered the value of the plate and jewels—some thirty-five thousand crowns, according to the valuation made by the London goldsmiths—and when he contemplated such wealth his fingers itched to take possession of it. A year was a long time to wait. Anything could happen in a year, particularly as Arthur was not strong. But once the plate and jewels were in his possession there they should remain.

He sent therefore to Katharine's treasurer, Don Juan de Cuero, and asked that the plate and jewels be handed to him.

This Don Juan de Cuero refused to do.

"Nay," he told Henry's messenger, "I am in charge of the Infanta's revenues, and it was the express command of the Sovereigns of Spain that the plate and jewellery should remain the property of their daughter until the time was ripe for the payment of the second half of the dowry."

Henry was irritated when he received this reply, but he had no intention of upsetting the Spanish Sovereigns at this stage and was ready to abandon the idea of laying his hands on the plate and jewels until the appointed time.

Puebla came to him with a suggestion. Puebla had made up his mind that it would be to Spain's advantage if the marriage were consummated, and he was determined to do everything in his power to bring this about.

He had Henry's confidence. More than once he had shown the King of England that he worked with an eye to England's advantages, and now he had a suggestion to make.

"If the Infanta could be induced to wear her jewellery and use her plate it could then be called second-hand and you could decline to accept it as part payment of the dowry. Ferdinand and Isabella would then be bound to pay you thirty-five thousand crowns instead of the plate and jewels—which would remain in England so that you could always take them if you wished."

This seemed a good idea to Henry's crafty mind. But he pointed out: "Her treasurer keeps a firm hand on the plate and jewels which he knows are to come as part payment of the dowry. He would never consent to her using them."

Puebla appeared to be thoughtful. He knew Isabella and Ferdinand well and he was convinced that the fact that the plate and jewels had been used by their daughter would have no effect whatsoever on the bargain they had made. They needed money too desperately to consider lightly parting with it. But Puebla's desire was not to work against Spain for the sake of Henry but only to give Henry the impression that he was doing so.

Then Puebla said: "If the Infanta accompanied the Prince to Wales, they could set up a small court there, and the Infanta's plate could be used by them both. She would want to wear her jewels in her own little court."

The King nodded.

"The Princess of Wales shall accompany her husband to Ludlow," he said.

\*       \*       \*

The journey westwards was pleasant enough. Arthur seemed happy to escape from his father's notice. He rode at the head of the cavalcade and Katharine was close to him, riding on a pillion behind her master of horse; and when this mode of travel tired her she took to her litter which was borne between two horses.

The people came out in the villages to welcome her and Arthur, and she was delighted that Arthur always considered the pleasure of the people and would stop and speak to them, always gentle, always with a smile, no matter how tired he was—and he was so often tired.

She was glad that his father had sent a council of men with him, headed by Sir Richard Pole, which meant that Arthur had no decisions to make which would have caused him anxiety; he travelled as the representative of the King, and could always call in his councillors if action was necessary, and should it not be carried out in accordance with the King's pleasure, it would be Sir Richard and the council who would be blamed, not Arthur.

With Katharine rode her own household headed by Doña Elvira, whose son, Don Iñigo Manrique, was among Katharine's pages. Don Iñigo strove to ride beside Maria de Rojas, who did her best to keep close to Katharine. Alessandro Geraldini was also a member of the party, and the strife between him and Doña Elvira increased as the days passed.

Many of Katharine's entourage who had accompanied her from Spain had now been sent back to their own country; and as Katharine rode towards Wales she felt a sudden desolation because she had said goodbye to the Archbishop of Santiago and many others. She envied them their return to Spain and she let herself wonder what was happening in the Madrid Alcazar or the great Alhambra. How happy she would have been if she could have burst into her mother's apartments and thrown herself into those loving arms!

I shall never cease to long for her, she thought sadly as she lay back in her litter.

They rested for a night in the royal Manor at Bewdley in Worcestershire, and it was here that Arthur showed her the chapel in which their marriage had been performed by proxy.

"Puebla stood as your proxy," said Arthur, wrinkling his nose with disgust.

Katharine laughed. "At least you prefer me to him!" she slowly answered in English which he was teaching her and at which she was making good progress.

"I like him not," answered Arthur. "And you I like so much."

As they went back to the Manor and their separate apartments there, Katharine thought that she was fortunate indeed to have a husband as kind and gentle as Arthur.

"You are smiling," said Arthur, "and you look happier than I have seen you look before."

"I was thinking," she answered, "that if my mother were here with us I should be completely happy."

"When I am in truth King," Arthur told her, "we will visit your mother and she shall visit us. You love her so dearly, do you not? Your voice is different when you mention her."

"She is the kindest mother anyone ever had. She is the greatest of Queens and yet . . . and yet . . ."

"I understand," said Arthur, touching her arm gently.

"Others did not understand her always," went on Katharine. "They thought her cold and stern. But to us, her children, she was always gentle. Yet none of us, not even my sister Juana, would have dared disobey her. Sometimes I wish she had not been perfect; then it would have been easier to have said goodbye to her."

They were silent, but during that stay at Bewdley she realized that she could easily love Arthur. As for Arthur, he was happy with his bride.

He was thinking: In a year or so I shall be her husband in very truth. Then we shall have children, and she will be such a mother to them as Queen Isabella was to her.

Arthur could look forward to the future with a serenity and pleasure he had rarely known before.

And so they came to Ludlow.

*     *     *

The castle rose from the point of a headland, and its bold grey towers appeared to be impregnable.

"There are no better views in all England than those to be seen from the castle," Arthur told Katharine. "From the north side there is Corve Dale, and from the east you can see Titterstone Clee Hill. And stretched out beyond is the valley of the Teme with the Stretton Hills forming a background. I have a great affection for Ludlow. It is on the very borders of the Welsh country which I have always felt was my country."

Katharine nodded. "The people here love you," she said.

"Am I not the Prince of Wales? And do not forget that you are the Princess. They will love you too."

"I fervently hope so," answered Katharine.

Katharine never forgot her first nights in Ludlow Castle. There in the large hall fires had been lighted; cressets shone their light from the walls, and as she sat beside Arthur while the chieftains of Wales came to the castle to pay homage to their Prince, she felt that she was farther from the halls of the Alhambra than she had ever been.

Never had she seen such fierce men as those who came in from the Welsh mountains. She could not understand their melodious speech; some looked like mountain brigands, others appeared in odd finery, but all spoke like poets and entertained her with such sweet singing that she was astonished.

The first of the chieftains of Wales, Rhys ap Thomas, came to pay his homage and to swear to Arthur that he accepted him as his Prince and would fight for him whenever and wherever it should be necessary.

Arthur was a little in awe of the fierce chieftain who he knew hoped for much, now that there was a Tudor king on the throne. Perhaps he was a little disappointed. Perhaps the Tudor was more English than Welsh. But at least he sent his son to forge friendships with the people of Wales, and in the mountains they continued to hope that one day the Tudors would remember Wales.

With Rhys ap Thomas came his son, Griffith ap Rhys, a beautiful young boy who, said his father, sought service in the household of the Prince and Princess of Wales; and when the boy was brought forward to kneel and kiss the hands of Arthur and Katharine, he assured Arthur in the Welsh tongue of his loyalty and will to serve.

"Now speak the other tongues you know, boy," said his father proudly; and Griffith ap Rhys began to speak in a language which Katharine recognized as French.

This delighted Katharine, because here was someone with whom she might be able to converse. She answered Griffith in French, and to her pleasure he was able to understand; and although their accents and intonations were so different they could chat together.

"I wish to make Griffith my gentleman usher," she told Arthur, and there was nothing she could have said which would have given the boy's father more delight.

There was no doubt in the minds of any that Wales was pleased with its Princess.

\*          \*          \*

A few weeks passed, weeks which afterwards seemed to Katharine like a dream. She was happier than she had been since she left Spain. She, Arthur and Griffith ap Rhys rode together; she found great pleasure in talking in French to Griffith, and Arthur liked to listen to them. They were like two brothers and a sister— constantly discovering interests in common. In the long evenings by the blazing fires and the lights of the torches there would be singing and dancing in the great hall; and those who watched said: "Before long this marriage will be consummated. The Prince and the Princess are falling in love."

They would sit side by side, and Griffith would be seated on a stool at their feet, strumming on his harp and singing songs, the favourite of which was one about a great King Arthur who had once reigned in Britain.

One day, it was said, there would be another great King Arthur to rule over England and Wales; he would be this Arthur who now sat in the hall of Ludlow Castle. He was young yet; he was a little pale and seemed weak; but he was leaving boyhood behind him, he was becoming a man, and he had the fair young Princess from Spain beside him.

\*          \*          \*

March had set in and the snow gave place to rain. For days the mist hung about the draughty rooms of the castle; the damp seeped into the bones of all and even the great fires which blazed on the hearths could not drive the mist from Ludlow Castle.

Katharine longed for the cold, frosty weather; then she and Arthur could have gone riding together. She dared not suggest that they go out in the driving rain, for Arthur had begun to cough more persistently since they had come to Ludlow.

One day Griffith ap Rhys burst somewhat unceremoniously into their presence.

They were sitting by the fire in one of the smaller apartments of the castle and a few of their suite were with them.

Doña Elvira looked sternly at the young Welshman and was

preparing to reproach him for forgetting the respect he owed to the Prince and Princess of Wales, when Griffith burst out: "I have ill news. The sweating sickness has come to Ludlow."

A horrified silence fell on the company. The sweating sickness was considered to be one of the greatest calamities which could befall a community. It spread rapidly from one to another and invariably ended in death, although if the patient could survive the first twenty-four hours of the disease, it was said that he usually recovered.

Questions were fired at Griffith, who said that several of the townsfolk were stricken and that he had himself seen people in the streets sinking to the ground because the fever had overcome them before they could reach their homes.

When this was explained to Elvira she began giving rapid orders. The castle was to be closed to all visitors; they were to consider themselves in a state of siege. At all costs the sweating sickness must not be allowed to enter Ludlow Castle while the Infanta of Spain was there.

The news had cast a gloom on the company, but Katharine was eager to know more about the dreaded disease, and Griffith sat beside her and told her and Arthur how it began with a fever and that many died before the sweating stage began. Then they sweated profusely and, if they could cling to life long enough, they stood a chance of recovery; for in sweating they cast off the evil humours of the body and thus recovered.

Arthur was disturbed; he told Katharine: "The disease broke out soon after my father won the throne. I think some looked upon it as an evil omen. It is strange that it should have broken out here in Ludlow now we are come. It would seem that there is a blight on our House."

"No," replied Katharine fiercely, "this sickness could happen anywhere."

"It started in the army which landed at Milford Haven with my father."

Katharine endeavoured to disperse his gloom, but it was not easy; and that night the singing ceased in Ludlow Castle.

\*     \*     \*

Katharine awoke in the night. She was conscious of a curious burning sensation in her limbs; she tried to call out but her mouth was parched.

She lay still, thinking: So it has come to Ludlow Castle and I am its victim. Yet if I am to die, then I shall be with my sister Isabella and my brother Juan, and I think I should be happy.

There was another thought which came to her and which she would not voice. It was that her mother might not be long for this world, and if she too were going to pass from the Earth to be with Isabella and Juan, then Katharine would long to join them.

She felt lightheaded; she had forgotten she was in grim Ludlow Castle; she thought she was back behind the rose-tinted walls of the Alhambra; she thought that she lingered in one of the *patios*, trailing her hot fingers in the cool fountains; but the fountains were not cool; they were hot as fire and she believed she had put her fingers in the fires in which the heretics were burned, mistaking them for fountains.

She was tossing from side to side in her bed when Maria de Rojas came to bid her good morning.

Maria took one look at her mistress and was terrified. She ran screaming to Doña Elvira.

*　　*　　*

So Katharine lay a victim of the dreaded sickness. All through the day and night which followed Elvira was in the sick-room. Angrily she ordered possets and herbal drinks to be prepared in case they might be of some use to her Infanta. She cursed those who had dared bring infection into the castle. She had no thought of anything but the health of her mistress.

Katharine had passed into the sweating period. Elvira hovered anxiously about her bed. If she sweated profusely the evil humours would be thrown off; and she *was* sweating.

"The Sovereigns will never forgive me," cried Elvira, "for letting their daughter face such infection. She *must* recover. It is unthinkable that she should die . . . her dowry not even paid, her virginity intact."

The energy of Doña Elvira affected all who came in contact with the sick-room.

News was brought for Katharine, but Elvira would not admit the messenger.

So the Prince was sick? Well, was not the Prince always ailing? The Infanta, who was never ill, was now laid low with their miserable sweating sickness!

It was twenty-four hours since Katharine had been taken ill. She lay limp and exhausted on her bed; but she still lived.

Doña Elvira busied herself with making a brew of aromatic herbs, laurel and juniper berries which the physicians had recommended; and when Katharine had drunk it she opened her eyes and said: "Doña Elvira, bring my mother to me."

"You are in your bed in Ludlow Castle, Highness. You have been very ill but I have nursed you back to health."

Katharine nodded her head slightly. "I remember now," she said; and there were tears in her eyes which would never have appeared but for her bodily weakness. She wanted her mother now, even more than ever. She knew that, if only she could feel that cool hand on her brow, see those serene eyes looking into hers, commanding her to bear whatever ill fortune God had seen fit to send to her, she could have wept for joy; as it was she could not prevent herself from weeping in sorrow.

"The worst is over," said Elvira. "You will get well now. I have nursed you with my own hands, and shall do so until you are completely recovered."

"Thank you, Doña Elvira."

Elvira took Katharine's hand in hers and kissed it. "Always I am at your service, my dearest Infanta," she said. "Do you not understand that?"

"I understand," said Katharine; and she closed her eyes. But try as she might she could not prevent the tears seeping through.

If I could see her but once . . . she thought. She turned her head that Doña Elvira might not see the tears.

"Does my mother know of my illness?" she asked.

"She will hear of it and of your recovery in the same message."

"I am glad of that. Now she will not be grieved. If I had died that would have been her greatest sorrow. She loves me dearly."

Now the tears were flowing more freely, and it was no use trying to restrain them. These were the tears which had been demanding to be shed for so long, and which in her strength she had withheld. Now she was too weak to fight them and she wept shamelessly.

"For she loves me so," she whispered, "and we are parted. There will never be another to love me as my mother loved me. All my life there will never be love for me such as she gave me."

"What nonsense is this?" said Elvira. "You must keep well covered. It may be that you have not sweated enough. There may be more humours to be released. Come, what would your mother say if she saw those foolish tears?"

"She would understand," cried Katharine. "Did she not always understand?"

Elvira covered her up sharply. The Infanta's tears shocked her.

She is very weak, she thought. But the worst is over. I have nursed her through this. She is right when she says the Queen dotes on her. I shall have Isabella's undying gratitude for nursing her daughter through this illness.

*          *          *

There was a muffled silence throughout the castle. People were speaking in whispers. Griffith ap Rhys sat with his harp at his knees, but the harp was silent.

There was death in the Castle of Ludlow. Disease had struck where it could not be defeated.

In the chamber of the Prince of Wales the candles were lighted by the bed and the watchers kept their vigil. Sir Richard Pole's courier was on his way to Greenwich, to break the news to the King and Queen.

In the whole of Ludlow Castle Katharine, lying on her sick bed, was the only one who did not know that this day she had become a widow.

As soon as Queen Elizabeth received the message that she was to go with all haste to the King's chamber, as soon as she looked into the face of the messenger, she knew that some dire tragedy had befallen her House. And when she learned that the couriers had come from Ludlow she guessed that what she had been dreading so long had at last taken place.

She steeled herself for the ordeal.

Henry was standing in the centre of the chamber; his usually pale face was grey and his eyes looked stricken. He did not speak for a moment, and the Queen's glance went from her husband to the Friar Observant who was the King's confessor.

"My son?" whispered the Queen.

The Friar bowed his head.

"He is . . . ill?"

"He has departed to God, Your Grace."

The Queen did not speak. For so many years she had waited for this news, dreading it. The fear of it had come to her in the days when she had held Arthur in her arms, a weak baby who did not cry but lay placid in his cradle, not because he was contented, but because he was too weak for aught else. It had come at last.

The King said: "Pray leave the Queen and myself. We will share this painful sorrow alone."

The Friar left them and even when the door shut on them they did not move towards each other; and for some seconds there was silence between them.

It was the King who broke it. "This is a bitter blow."

She nodded. "He was never strong. I always feared it. Now it has befallen us."

She lifted her eyes to her husband's face and she was suddenly aware of a deep pity for him. She looked at the lean face, the lines etched by the sides of his mouth; the eyes which were too alert. She read the thoughts behind that lean and clever face. The heir to the throne was dead, and there was only one male child left to him. There was also a nobility which he would never trust and which was constantly on the alert to shout that the Tudors had no legitimate claim to the throne. All her life Elizabeth had lived close to the struggle to win and keep a crown. It was painful to her now that her husband should not think of Arthur as their dear son, but as the heir.

He would never know what it was to love, to feel acute sorrow such as she was feeling now. Should she feel envious of him because he did not suffer as she did through the loss of their son? No, even in this bitter moment she felt sorry for him because he would never know the joy of loving.

"Why does God do this to us?" demanded Henry harshly. "The Friar has just said that if we receive good at the hands of God, we must patiently sustain the ill He sends us."

"It is true," said Elizabeth. She went to the window and looked out on the river as it flowed peacefully past this Palace of Greenwich. "We have much for which to thank God," she added.

"But this was my eldest son . . . my heir!"

"You must not grieve. You must remember that you have your duty to do. You have other children."

"Yet the plague could carry off our children in a few hours."

"Arthur was not strong enough to withstand the attack. The others are stronger. Why, Henry, your mother had but you, and look to what you have come. You have one healthy Prince and two Princesses."

"Henry is my heir now," mused the King.

Elizabeth had left the window and was walking towards him. She had to comfort him.

"Henry," she said, "we are not old. Perhaps we shall have more children. More sons."

The King seemed somewhat pacified. He put his arm about her and said with more feeling than he usually displayed: "You have been a good wife to me. But of course we shall get ourselves more sons."

She closed her eyes and tried to smile. She was thinking of the nights ahead which must be dedicated to the begetting of children. She longed for peace at night. She was growing more and more aware of her need for rest. She thought of the weary months of pregnancy, which must precede a birth.

But it was the duty of Queens to turn their backs on sorrow, to stop grieving for the children who were lost to them, and to think of those as yet unborn.

Henry took her hand and raised it to his cold lips.

He said as he released it: "I see trouble ahead with regard to Katharine's dowry. If only Arthur had lived another year it should all have been paid over, and perhaps by that time Arthur would have got her with child."

The Queen did not answer; she fancied that her husband was reproving their delicate son for dying at a time most inconvenient to his father's schemes.

Poor Henry! she mused. He knows nothing of love. He knows little of anything but statecraft and the best methods of filling the coffers of his treasury.

Why should she say Poor Henry! when he was quite unaware of any lack in his life? Perhaps she should say Poor Katharine, who at this time lay sick at Ludlow, her dowry half paid, her position most insecure. What would happen to Katharine of Aragon now? The Queen of England would do all in her power to help the poor child, but what power had the Queen of England?

\* \* \*

Before the burnished mirror in his apartment young Henry stood.

He had received the news with mingled feelings. Arthur . . . dead! He had known it must happen, but it was nevertheless a shock when the news came.

Never to see Arthur again! Never to show off his superior prowess, never to strut before the delicate brother. It made him feel a little sad.

But what great avenues were opening out before him. To be Prince of Wales when one had been Duke of York! This was no trifling title, for one who had been destined to become Archbishop of Canterbury would one day be King of England.

King of England! The little eyes were alight with pleasure; the smooth cheeks flushed pink. Now the homage he received would be doubled, the cries of the people in the streets intensified.

No longer Prince Henry—but Henry, Prince of Wales, heir to the throne of England.

"Henry VIII of England!" There were no sweeter words in the English language.

When he contemplated them and all they meant he could cease to grieve for the death of his delicate brother Arthur.

\* \* \*

In a litter, covered with black velvet and black cloth, Katharine travelled from Ludlow to Richmond. How different was this journey from that other which she had taken such a short time before with Arthur!

The weather had changed, but Katharine was unaware of all the beauty of an English spring. She could think only of the husband whom she had lost, the husband who had been no husband.

And then there came a sudden blinding flash of hope as she remembered the fate of her sister Isabella, which was so like her own. Isabella had gone into Portugal to marry the heir to the throne, and shortly after their marriage he had died in a hunting accident. The result was that Isabella had returned to Spain.

Now, thought Katharine, they will send me home. I shall see my mother again.

So how could she be completely unhappy at that prospect? She believed that this time next year her stay in England would be like a distant dream. She would wander through the flagged corridors of the Alhambra; she would look through her windows on to the Courtyard of Lions; she would stray into the Court of Myrtles, and her mother would be beside her. The pomegranate would no longer merely be a device; it would be all about her—growing in the gardens, pictured on the shields and the walls of her parents' palace. Happiest of all, her mother would be beside her. "You did your duty," she would say. "You went uncomplaining to England. Now, my Catalina, you shall stay with me for ever."

Katharine of Aragon would again become Catalina, Infanta, beloved daughter of the Queen.

So, as she went on her way to Richmond, she thought tenderly of Arthur who had been so kind to her in life, and who in death would, she believed, bring her relief from bondage.

\*    \*    \*

Queen Elizabeth was waiting to receive the young widow.

Poor child! she thought. She will be desolate. How will she feel, alone in a strange land? Does she realize how her position has changed? She, who was Princess of Wales, is now merely a Spanish Princess, who has been married in name only. If there had been an heir on the way the circumstances would have changed considerably. But now . . . what is her position? How sad that girls should be used thus by ambitious men.

The King came to her apartment. He gave her that cool appraising look which she knew meant that he was looking for some sign of pregnancy.

She said: "The Infanta should arrive at Richmond tomorrow, I believe."

A wary look replaced the speculative one in the King's eyes.

"I will keep her with me for a while," went on the Queen. "This is a terrible shock for her."

"It would not be wise for her to remain at Richmond," said the King quickly.

The Queen did not answer, but waited for his commands.

"She should be installed with her household outside the Court," went on the King.

"I thought that, so soon after her bereavement . . ."

The King looked surprised. It was rarely that the Queen sought to question his orders.

"This is a most unsatisfactory state of affairs," he said. "Our son dead within a few months of his marriage, and that marriage never consummated—or at least so we believe."

"You have reason to suspect that it was consummated?" asked the Queen sharply.

The King shrugged his shoulders. "I ordered that it should not be, but they went to Wales together—two young people, not displeased with each other. It would not have been impossible for them to be together . . . alone."

"If this happened," said the Queen excitedly, "if Katharine should be with child . . ."

"Then she would be carrying the heir to the throne. Our son Henry would not be pleased, I'll swear."

"Henry! He is so like my father sometimes that I do not know whether to rejoice or tremble."

"I thank God we have our son Henry, but I am not an old man myself, and I should have some years left to me . . . enough that Henry may be of age before his turn comes to take the throne. But, as you say, what if Katharine should be carrying a child? It *is* possible, although I doubt Arthur would have gone against my expressed wish. If only he had lived a few months longer. You may be sure there will be difficulty with those Spaniards."

"They will be more inclined to meet your demands if we treat their daughter well."

"I shall treat her as her dignity warrants. She shall stay with you at Richmond for a day or so, until she has had time to overcome her grief. Then she shall take up residence in the house opposite Twickenham Church. She shall live there with her own suite. Remember, she has no claim on us now and it would be as well that she shall not be at Court until we have negotiated with her parents as to what is to become of her."

The Queen bowed her head. It was no use pleading with her husband. She would not be able to comfort the young girl, to treat her as she would a sorrowing daughter. The King would have the Sovereigns of Spain know that the death of the Prince of Wales had put their daughter in a precarious position.

\*       \*       \*

Katharine was sorry that she could not stay with the Court at Richmond, but she believed this to be only a waiting period, for she was certain that, as soon as her parents heard the news, they would give orders that she return to Spain. But it would take a little time for the message to reach Spain and for the Sovereigns' orders to be sent to England.

It would have been pleasant to have had the company of Henry and Margaret. Margaret herself was in need of comfort, for she was soon to depart to Scotland as a bride.

But this could not be and, after a brief stay at Richmond, Katharine and her household were removed to a turreted house with the church opposite, and Doña Elvira took charge of all household arrangements.

It was soon decided that the palace of the Bishop of Durham, which was situated on the Strand, would be a more suitable dwelling for the Infanta; and so to Durham House she went.

Elvira was delighted with this seclusion because it meant that, removed from the Court as they were, she was in charge of the entire household. Her husband, Don Pedro Manrique, and her son, Don Iñigo, held high posts in Katharine's household and Elvira was ambitious for them. She had determined that Maria de Rojas should be betrothed to Iñigo; she believed that Maria's dowry would be a large one.

Elvira often thought of her brother, Don Juan Manuel, whose service to the Sovereigns should not go unrewarded. Isabella, she knew, thought highly of him and he should have had more honours than he had so far received. Elvira guessed that it was Ferdinand who barred his way to success, for Ferdinand was constantly seeking favours for his illegitimate children and, although the Queen insisted on having her way, Ferdinand was full of cunning and often scored in spite of his wife.

If there were no King Ferdinand, Elvira often thought, Juan would receive his dues.

She wished sometimes that she were in Spain; she felt sure that she would have been able to expedite Juan's rise to favour in the same efficient way in which she was able to look after Iñigo's in London.

But for the moment she was contented. The Infanta had reverted to her care, and as she was now a widow in a difficult situation, she relied on Elvira. Isabella would soon be sending instructions, and those instructions would come to Elvira.

So life in Durham House took on the pattern of that of a Spanish Alcazar. The English tongue was rarely heard; the English nobles who had held places in the entourage of the Prince and

Princess of Wales disappeared, and their places were taken by Spaniards. Don Pedro Manrique was once more the first Chamberlain; Don Juan de Cuero was treasurer; Alessandro Geraldini remained the Infanta's confessor; and Don Iñigo was at the head of her pages. Elvira ruled the household; but that did not mean that the animosity, which she had engendered in the heart and mind of Geraldini, was abated. Rather it had intensified.

Puebla remembered insults which the duenna did not cease to heap upon him.

Ayala watched mischievously, fearing that soon he might be recalled to Spain and so miss the fun which, he felt sure, must be lurking in such a delicate situation.

\*       \*       \*

As the party rode towards Richmond, people stopped to stare at it.

"Spaniards!" they whispered. They knew, for they had seen Spaniards in plenty since the Infanta had come to England.

Something was afoot. Perhaps the gentleman who rode at the head of that party of foreigners had come to take the widowed Infanta back to Spain.

The party was riding towards the Palace where the King was in residence.

Hernan Duque de Estrada was thoughtful; he did not notice the attention he and his party attracted. He had a difficult task before him, which he did not relish; and it was going to be made doubly difficult because of his imperfect knowledge of the English language.

Beside him rode Dr. de Puebla—a man whom he could not like. How was it possible for an Asturian nobleman to have a fondness for a *marrano*! The fellow might be clever—it was clear that the Sovereigns thought so—but his appearance and his manners were enough to make a Spanish nobleman shudder.

Ayala was of a different kind. A nobleman to his fingertips, but light-minded. Hernan Duque was not very happy with his two colleagues.

"There lies the Palace of Richmond," said Ayala, and Hernan Duque saw the line of buildings, the projecting towers, the far from symmetrical turrets. He, who had come hot-foot from the Alhambra, was not impressed by the architecture of the country, and he forgot momentarily that the beautiful building with which he was comparing this Palace was a masterpiece of Arabic, not Spanish, architecture.

"The King is often at Richmond," Ayala explained. "He has

a feeling for the place. It may well be that he likes to be near the river, for Greenwich is another favourite residence."

Puebla put in: "And so we are to obey you without question."

"The express orders of the Sovereigns," Hernan Duque replied.

"It seems strange," grumbled Puebla. "We, who have been here so long, understand the situation so much better than anyone in Spain possibly could."

"I have their Highnesses' instructions. It would go ill with you if you did not do all in your power to help me carry them out."

Puebla tossed his head. "I do not envy you your task. You will find the Tudor is not an easy man with whom to drive a bargain."

"It is so unfortunate that the death of the Prince occurred at this time."

"What is your first move?" Ayala asked.

Hernan Duque looked over his shoulder.

"Let us ride on ahead," said Ayala. "It is better to be absolutely sure. Although it is doubtless safe enough to talk. The English cannot learn the languages of others. Their secret belief is that all who do not speak English are barbarians and that foreigners deserve the name in any case."

"An insular people," murmured Duque. "I pity our Infanta."

"Why should you? Do you not carry orders from their Highnesses that she is to return to Spain?"

"I brought three documents with me. You have seen the first . . . that which commanded you to obey me in all matters concerning this affair. The second and third are for the eyes of the King. But he will not see the third until he has digested the second. Nor shall he know at this stage that it exists."

"And the second?" asked Puebla.

"It demands the return of the hundred thousand crowns, the first half of the dowry, which has already been paid."

"Do you wish to break the heart of the King of England?" demanded Ayala.

"He will not relish this, I know."

"Relish it!" screamed Ayala. "The King loves those hundred thousand crowns more than he loved his son. You cannot deal him another blow—one so close on the other."

"I shall do more. I shall demand those revenues which the Prince of Wales promised to his wife on the day of their marriage."

"The King will never consent to that."

"I shall then ask for the return of the Infanta to Spain."

"With the spoils," put in Ayala, laughing. "Not so bad—the dowry, one third of the revenues of Wales, Chester and Cornwall, and our Infanta, virginity intact. A pleasant little adventure for the Infanta, and a remunerative one for the Sovereigns. Ah, do you think the King of England will agree?"

"He will not like this, I know," said Duque. "He will refuse, for I doubt not that he will never be induced to part with the money. Yet what alternative has he—except to incur the displeasure of the Sovereigns of Spain? That is why the second document is of such great importance."

"And this second document?" Puebla asked eagerly.

Duque looked once more over his shoulder. "The King has a second son," he said quietly.

"Ah!" whispered Ayala.

"Dangerous!" Puebla put in. "He is her brother by marriage. Are we not told in Leviticus that a man is forbidden to marry his brother's widow?"

"The Pope would give the dispensation. He gave it to Emanuel of Portugal when he married the Infanta Maria on the death of her sister Isabella."

"That was the dead wife's sister."

"The situation is similar. There will be no difficulty if the Pope will give the necessary dispensation. And as it is said that the marriage was never consummated, that should simplify matters."

"I should like to make sure on that point," said Puebla. "It is important."

Ayala looked scornfully at the Jew. "Your lawyer's mind boggles at unimportant details. Rest assured that if the Sovereigns want the dispensation they will get it. Spain is great enough to make sure of that."

"At first I shall say nothing of this suggested marriage. I wish to alarm the King by demanding the return of the dowry and the transfer of the goods which the Infanta has inherited by her marriage. That will put him into a mood to agree to this second marriage—and it is the wish of the Sovereigns that it should take place."

"I thought," said Ayala, "that the Queen would have wished to have her daughter back."

"She wishes it most fervently, but duty comes before her own personal desires as always. There is another matter. Her health has declined rapidly during the last months. You, who have not seen her for so long, would scarcely know her. I do not think Isabella of Castile is long for this world. She knows it, and she wishes to see her youngest daughter happily settled, with a crown in view, before she departs this life."

"She need have no fear. Henry will agree to this marriage,"

smiled Ayala. "It is the way out for him. He would never allow anyone to take one hundred thousand crowns from him."

They had reached the gates of the Palace.

With Puebla on one side and Ayala on the other, Hernan Duque rode in; and shortly afterwards Puebla and Ayala presented him to the King, who was very ready to conduct him to a small chamber where they might discuss this matter of the Infanta's future in private.

\*     \*     \*

In the seclusion of Durham House, Katharine had no idea that her parents' envoy had arrived in England with such important documents affecting her future.

She felt at peace, for she was certain that very soon now she would be preparing to make the journey back to Spain. In her apartments, the windows of which overlooked the Thames, she could almost believe she *was* back in Spain. Here she sat with three of her maids of honour, all of whom were dear to her, and they stitched at their embroidery as they would in their own country.

She could almost believe that at any moment there would be a summons for her to go to her mother's apartment in this very palace, and that if she looked from the window she would not see the lively London river with its barges, its ferries, its watermen all shouting to each other in the English tongue, but the distant Sierras of Guadarrama or the crystal-clear waters of the Darro.

In the meantime she could live in Durham House as though she were in a Spanish Alcazar and wait for the summons to return home.

Maria de Rojas had grown even prettier in recent weeks. Maria was in love with an Englishman. Francesca de Carceres was only pretending to sew, because she hated to sit quietly and was not fond of the needle; she found life at Durham House irksome, longed for gaiety, and it was only the thought that soon they would be returning to Spain that made it possible for her to endure it. Maria de Salinas worked quietly. She too was happy because she believed they would soon be leaving for Spain.

Francesca, who could never contain her thoughts for long, suddenly burst out: "Maria de Rojas wishes to talk to Your Highness."

Maria de Rojas flushed slightly, and Maria de Salinas said in her quiet way: "You should not hesitate. Her Highness will help you, I am sure."

"What is this?" asked Katharine. "Come along, Maria, tell me."

"She is in love," cried Francesca.

"With Don Iñigo?" Katharine asked.

Maria de Rojas flushed hotly. "Indeed no."

"Ah, then it is with the Englishman," said Katharine. "He returns your affection?"

"He does indeed, Highness."

"And you wish to marry him?"

"I do, Highness; and his grandfather is willing that we should marry."

"The consent of the King of England would be necessary," said Katharine, "and of my parents."

"Maria is thinking," Maria de Salinas said, "that if Your Highness wrote to the King and Queen of Spain, telling them that the Earl of Derby is a great English nobleman and his grandson worthy of our Maria, they would readily give their consent."

"And her dowry also," put in Katharine. "You may depend upon it, Maria, that I shall write immediately to my parents and ask them to do what is necessary in the matter."

"Your Highness is good to me," murmured Maria gratefully. "But it will then be necessary to have the consent of the King of England as well."

"That will easily be obtained," answered Francesca, "if the Countess of Richmond is approached first. Her opinion carries more weight with the King of England than anyone else's."

"You must ask your lover to arrange the English side of the project," said Katharine. "As for myself, I will write to my parents without delay."

Maria de Rojas sank to her knees and taking Katharine's hand kissed it dramatically.

Francesca laughed and Maria de Salinas smiled.

"What a wonderful thing it is to be in love," cried Francesca. "How I wish it would happen to me! But there is one thing I should welcome more."

"And that?" asked Katharine, although she already knew the answer.

"To return home, Highness. To leave this country and go home to Spain."

"Ah yes," sighed Katharine. "Which of us does not feel the same—except Maria, who has a very good reason for wishing to stay here. Prepare my writing table. I will write at once to my parents and ask for their consent."

Maria de Rojas obeyed with alacrity, and the three maids of honour stood about Katharine's table as she wrote.

"There!" said Katharine. "It is ready. As soon as the messenger leaves for Spain he shall take this with him among other important documents."

"None is as important as this, Highness," cried Maria de Rojas, taking the letter and kissing it.

"So when we leave for Spain we shall leave you behind," said Katharine. "We shall miss you, Maria."

"Your Highness will be so happy to return home—and so will the others—that you will all forget Maria de Rojas."

"And what will she care?" demanded Francesca. "She will be happy with her English lord whom she loves well enough to say goodbye to Spain and adopt this country as her own for ever more."

"That," answered Katharine soberly, "is love."

\*        \*        \*

Dr. de Puebla called at Durham House. The Infanta had no wish to see him. She found him quite distasteful, and although she was always pleased to see Ayala the little *marrano* irritated her, and because she knew that he was ridiculed throughout the English Court she felt ashamed of him.

Puebla was well aware of this, but he was not unduly put out; he was accustomed to being scorned and he had an idea that he would remain at his post longer than Don Pedro de Ayala, for the simple reasons that he was more useful to the Sovereigns and that the King of England believed he was as good a friend as any foreign ambassador could be.

His lawyer's outlook demanded that he know the truth concerning the Infanta's marriage. Whether or not the marriage had been consummated seemed of enormous importance to him because, if it had not been, it would be a far simpler matter to get the dispensation from the Pope. He was determined to find out.

And who would be more likely to know the truth than Katharine's confessor? So when Puebla arrived at Durham House it was not to see Katharine that he came, nor yet Doña Elvira, but Katharine's confessor—Father Alessandro Geraldini.

Geraldini was delighted to be sought out by Puebla. He pretended, with everyone else, to despise the man, but he knew the power of Puebla and he felt, when the ambassador came to see him, that he was becoming of great importance. Had not Torquemada begun as confessor to a Queen? And look what power he had held! Ximenes de Cisneros was another example of a humble Friar who became a great man. Ximenes was reckoned to be the most powerful man in Spain at this time—next to the Sovereigns, of course.

So Geraldini was proud to receive Puebla.

The cunning Puebla was well aware of the feelings of the Friar, and decided to exploit them.

"I would ask your opinion on a very delicate matter," Puebla began.

"I shall be delighted to give it."

"It is this matter of the Infanta's marriage. It seems a very strange thing that two young people should be married and not consummate."

Geraldini nodded.

"As the King forbade consummation it is almost certain that the Infanta would have mentioned in her confessions to her priest if she and her husband had defied the King's wish."

Geraldini looked wise.

"A confessor is the one confidant to whom it is possible to tell that which one keeps secret from the world. Is that not so?"

"It is indeed so."

"Therefore if anyone knows what happened on the Infanta's wedding night, that person is most likely to be yourself." The little priest could not hide the pride which showed in his eyes. "In the name of the Sovereigns, I ask you to tell me what happened."

Geraldini hesitated. He knew that if he told the truth and said he did not know, he would cease to be of any importance to Puebla; that was something he could not endure. He wanted to see himself as the Infanta's confidant, as a man destined to play a part in Spanish politics.

"You see," went on Puebla, noticing the hesitancy, "if the marriage *was* consummated and this fact was kept hidden the bull of dispensation from the Pope might not be valid. It is necessary to lay all the facts before his Holiness. We must have the truth, and you are the man who can give it. You know the answer. Your peculiar position enables you to have it. I pray you give it to me now."

As it was more than Geraldini could bear to admit ignorance, why should he not make a guess? The young couple had spent the wedding night together according to custom. Surely they must have consummated their marriage. It was but natural that they should.

Geraldini paused only one second longer, then he leaped.

"The marriage has been consummated," he said. "It is likely that it will prove fruitful."

Puebla left Durham House with all speed. He first despatched a letter to the Sovereigns and then sought out members of the King's Council.

This was what he had hoped. He liked clean-cut facts. If the Infanta carried the heir of England in her womb then there could be no more doubt of her position in Henry's realm.

The belief that the marriage had not been consummated was highly dangerous. It was a matter about which there would continue to be conjecture.

Puebla was therefore very happy to let it be known that Arthur and Katharine had cohabited and that there might be a hope that their relationship would be a fruitful one.

\*        \*        \*

Doña Elvira was holding in her hand a letter which she had taken from a drawer of her table, where a short while before she had hastily placed it.

The courier had left and was now well on his way to the coast with the letters he was carrying from England to Spain.

"And this," said Elvira to herself, "will not be one of them."

She was going to burn it in the flame of a candle as soon as she had shown it to Iñigo, and made him aware that he would have to move faster. He was evidently slow in his courtship if he had allowed Maria de Rojas to prefer this Englishman to himself.

How had the Englishman been in a position to pay court to Maria de Rojas, she would like to know! Clearly there were traitors in the household. She, Doña Elvira Manuel, and she alone, should rule; and if her rule had been absolute, Maria de Rojas would never have exchanged anything but glances with her Englishman.

She suspected three people of seeking to wean Katharine from her. The first was that pernicious little priest, who recently had given himself airs; the second was Don Pedro Ayala whose cynicism and riotous living had earned her disapproval; and of course, like everyone else of noble blood, she disliked Puebla.

She would send for Iñigo. She would show him the letter in Katharine's handwriting, asking for a dowry for Maria de Rojas; and she would have him know that a son of hers must not allow others to get ahead of him.

She called to one of the pages, but even as she did so the door was flung open and her husband Don Pedro Manrique came into the room. He was clearly distraught, and temporarily Doña Elvira forgot Maria de Rojas and her love affair.

"Well," she demanded, "what ails you?"

"It is clear that you have not heard this rumour."

"Rumour! What is this?"

"It concerns the Infanta."

"Tell me at once," demanded Doña Elvira, for she expected immediate obedience from her husband as she did from the rest of the household.

"Puebla has told members of the Council that the marriage was consummated and that there is every hope that the Infanta may be with child."

"What!" cried Elvira, her face growing purple with rage. "This is a lie. The Infanta is as virgin as she was the day she was born."

"So I had believed. But Puebla has told members of the Council that this is not the case. Moreover he has written to the Sovereigns to tell them what, he says, is the true state of affairs."

"I must see Puebla at once. But first . . . let the courier be stopped. It is a lie he is carrying to the Sovereigns."

"I will despatch a rider to follow him immediately, but I fear we are too late. Nevertheless I will see what can be done."

"Hurry then!" Doña Elvira commanded. "And have Puebla brought to me immediately. I must stop the spread of this lie."

Her husband retreated in haste, leaving Doña Elvira to pace up and down the apartment.

She was certain that Katharine was still a virgin. She would have known if it had been otherwise. There had been only the wedding night when they had been together, and they were both too young, too inexperienced . . . Besides, the King had made his wishes known.

If what that miserable Puebla was saying was true, if Katharine carried a child within her, then she would no longer be exiled to Durham House; she would be at Court, and that would be the end of the rule of Doña Elvira.

"She *is* a virgin," she cried aloud. "Of course she is. I would swear to it. And if necessary there could be an examination."

\*　　　\*　　　\*

Dr. Puebla stood before Doña Elvira and her husband. He was a little disturbed by the fury of the woman. She was formidable, and moreover he knew that Queen Isabella regarded her highly.

"I want to know," she shouted, "why you have dared to tell this lie to members of the Council here, and write it to the Sovereigns."

"What lie is this?"

"You have declared that the marriage was consummated. Where were you on the wedding night, Dr. de Puebla? Peering through the bed curtains?"

"I have it on good authority that the marriage was consummated, Doña Elvira."

"On whose authority?"

D

"On that of the Infanta's confessor."

"Geraldini!" Elvira spat out the word. "That upstart!"

"He assured me that the marriage had been consummated and that there was hope of issue."

"How had he come into possession of such knowledge?"

"Presumably the Infanta had confessed this to him."

"He lies. One moment." Elvira turned to her husband. "Send for Geraldini," she commanded.

In a few minutes the priest joined them. He was a little pale; like everyone in the household he dreaded the fury of Doña Elvira.

"So," cried Elvira, "you have informed Dr. de Puebla that the marriage between our Infanta and the Prince of Wales was consummated, and that England may shortly expect an heir."

Geraldini was silent, his eyes downcast.

"Answer me!" shouted Elvira.

"I . . . I did verily believe . . ."

"You verily believed indeed! You verily guessed. You fool! Do you dare then dabble in matters which are so far above you! You should be in your monastery, babbling your prayers in your lonely cell. Such as you have no place in Court circles. Confess that the Infanta never told you that the marriage was consummated!"

"She . . . she did not tell me, Doña Elvira."

"Yet you dared tell Dr. de Puebla that you knew this to be so!"

"I thought . . ."

"I know! You verily believed. You knew nothing. Get out of my sight before I order you to be whipped. Begone . . . quickly. Idiot! Knave!"

Geraldini was relieved to escape.

As soon as he had gone Elvira turned to Puebla. "You see what this meddling has done. If you wish to know anything concerning the Infanta, you must come to me. There is only one thing to be done. You agree now that this man Geraldini has led you completely astray?"

"I do," said Puebla.

"Then you should write to the Sovereigns immediately, telling them that there is no truth in the news contained in your previous document. If you are quick, you may prevent that first letter from reaching their Highnesses. Let us pray that the tides are not favourable for a few hours. Go at once and set right this matter."

Although Puebla resented her high-handed manner, he could not but agree that he must do as she said; and he was indeed eager to write to the Sovereigns, rectifying his mistake.

He bowed himself out and set about the task immediately.

When she was alone with her husband Doña Elvira sat at her table and began to write. She addressed her letter to Her Highness Queen Isabella, and she told of the mischief Father Alessandro Geraldini had wrought against the Infanta. She added that she believed Don Pedro de Ayala's presence in England to be no longer necessary to the welfare of Spain. She hesitated, considering Puebla. He had been docile enough and ready to admit his mistake. She decided that she might be served worse by any other ambassador the Sovereigns saw fit to send. Too many complaints could give the impression that she was hard to please. If because of this matter she could rid the household of Geraldini she would be satisfied.

As she sealed the letter, she remembered that other letter which had angered her before she heard of Geraldini's gossip.

She took it up and thrust it into her husband's hands.

"Read that," she said.

He read it. "But you had decided . . ." he began.

She cut him short. "I wish Iñigo to see this. Have him brought here immediately, but first have this letter despatched to the Sovereigns. I should like it to reach them if possible before they receive Puebla's."

Don Pedro Manrique obeyed her as, during their married life, he had grown accustomed to; and in a short time he returned to her with their son.

"Ah, Iñigo," she said, "did I not tell you that I had decided a match with Maria de Rojas would be advantageous to you?"

"You did, Mother."

"Well then, perhaps you would be interested to read this letter which the Infanta has written to her parents. It is a plea that they should give their consent to the marriage of Maria de Rojas with an Englishman and provide her with a dowry."

"But, Mother, you . . ."

"Read it," she snapped.

Young Iñigo frowned as he read. He felt himself flushing. It was not that he was so eager for marriage with Maria, but that he feared his mother's wrath, and it seemed as though she were ready to blame him—though he could not quite understand why.

"You have finished it?" She took it from him. "We must not allow others to step ahead of us and snatch our prizes from under our noses, must we?"

"No, Mother. But she wishes to marry the Englishman, and the Infanta supports her."

"It would appear so." Elvira was thoughtful. "We shall do nothing yet."

"But in the meantime the Sovereigns may provide the dowry and the consent."

"Why should they," said Elvira, "if they do not know it has been asked for?"

"But it is asked for in the Infanta's letter," her husband pointed out.

Elvira laughed and held the letter in the flame of the candle.

THE LONG DAYS of spring and summer passed uneventfully for Katharine. Always she was awaiting the summons to return home.

This did not come, although others had been summoned back to Spain. One was Father Alessandro Geraldini; another was Don Pedro de Ayala.

Doña Elvira had explained their departure to Katharine. Don Pedro de Ayala, she said, was unworthy to represent Spain in England. He led too carnal a life for an ambassador, and a bishop at that. As for Geraldini, he had whispered slander against the Infanta herself, and for such she had demanded his recall.

"Her Highness your mother declares that he is indeed unworthy to remain a member of your household. I thank the saints that I was shown his perfidy in time."

"What did he say of me?" Katharine wanted to know.

"That you were with child."

Katharine flushed scarlet at the suggestion, and Elvira felt very confident that, if it should ever come to the point when there must be an examination, her pronouncement would be vindicated.

"I had hoped my mother would send for me," said Katharine mournfully.

Elvira shook her head. "My dear Highness, it is almost certain that there will be another marriage for you in England. Had you forgotten that the King has another son?"

"Henry!" she whispered; and she thought of the bold boy who had led her to the altar where Arthur had been waiting for her.

"And why not?"

"He is but a boy."

"A little younger than yourself. When he is a little older that will be of small account."

Henry! Katharine was startled and a little afraid. She wanted to escape from Elvira, to think about this project.

That night she could not sleep. Henry haunted her thoughts and she was not sure whether she was pleased or afraid.

She waited for more news of this, but none came.

It was so difficult to know what was happening at home. There were only fragments of news she heard now and then. The war for

Naples, in which her parents were engaged against the King of France, was not going well for them. That, she believed, was why the King of England was hesitating over her betrothal to his son. If the Sovereigns were in difficulties he could make a harsher bargain with them. He did not forget that only half her dowry had been paid.

So the months went by without much news. She found that she had very little money—not even enough to pay her servants. She was worried about Maria's dowry, for there was no news from Spain about this.

The King of England said that she had no right to a third of the property of her late husband, because the second half of her dowry had not been paid. She needed new dresses, but there was no money to buy any. There was her plate and jewels, which represented thirty-five thousand crowns; could she pawn these? She dared not do so because she knew that they had been sent from home as part of her dowry; but if she had no money, what could she do?

There were times when she felt deserted, for she was not allowed to go to Court.

"She is a widow," said the King of England. "It is well that she should live in seclusion for a while."

Henry had his eyes on the Continent. It might be that, as the French seemed likely to score a victory over the Spaniards, a marriage for his son with France or with the House of Maximilian might be more advantageous than one with Spain.

Meanwhile, living in England was the daughter of Isabella and Ferdinand—a Princess, but penniless, a wife but no wife, virtually a hostage for her parents' good behaviour.

It was no concern of his that she suffered poverty, said the King. He could not be expected to pay an allowance to the woman whose dowry had not been paid.

Puebla came to see her, shaking his head sadly. He also had received no money from Spain. It was fortunate that he had other means of making a living in England.

"They are using every *maravedi* for the wars, Highness," he said. "We must perforce be patient."

Katharine sometimes cried herself to sleep when her maids of honour had left her.

"Oh, Mother," she sobbed, "what is happening at home? Why do you not send for me? Why do you not bring me out of this . . . prison?"

*　　*　　*

It was almost Christmas. A whole year, thought Katharine, since she had come to England, and during that time she had married and become a widow; yet it seemed that she had been a prisoner in Durham House for a very long time.

She was not to join the Court at Richmond for the Christmas celebrations: She was a widow, in mourning. Moreover the King of England wished the Spanish Sovereigns to know that he was not showering honours on their daughter, since half her dowry was still owing to him and he was not very eager to make a further alliance with their House.

Maria de Rojas was fretful. "No news from home?" she was continually demanding. "How strange that the Queen does not answer your request about my marriage." Maria was anxious, for shut up in Durham House she had no opportunity of seeing her lover. She wondered what was happening to him and whether he was still eager for the marriage.

Francesca declared that she would go mad if they had to remain in England much longer; even gentle Maria de Salinas was restive.

But the days passed, all so like each other that Katharine almost lost count of time except that she knew that with each passing week she owed the members of her household more and more, and that Christmas was coming and they would have no money for celebrations, for gifts or even to provide a little Christmas cheer for their table.

It was in November that Queen Elizabeth came to Durham House to call on Katharine.

Katharine was shocked when she saw Elizabeth, because she had changed a great deal since they had last met. The Queen was far advanced in pregnancy and she did not look healthy.

The Queen wished to be alone with Katharine, and as they sat together near the fire, Elizabeth said: "It distresses me to see you thus. I have come to tell you how sorry I am, and have brought food for your table. I know how you have been placed."

"How kind you are!" said Katharine.

The Queen laid her hand over the Infanta's. "Do not forget you are my daughter."

"I fear the King does not think of me as such. I am sorry the dowry has not been paid. I am sure my parents would have paid it, if they were not engaged in war at this time."

"I know, my dear. Wars . . . there seem always to be wars. We are fortunate in England. Here we have a King who likes not war, and I am glad of that. I have seen too much war in my life. But let us talk of more pleasant things. I could wish you were joining the Court for Christmas."

"We shall do well enough here."

"I envy you the quiet of Durham House," said the Queen. "Tell me when your child is expected."

"In February." The Queen shivered. "The coldest month."

Katharine looked into the face of the older woman and saw there a resigned look; she wondered what it meant.

"I trust you will have a Prince," Katharine murmured.

"Pray that I may have a healthy child. I have lost two at an early age. It is so sad when they live a little and then die. So much suffering . . . that one may endure more suffering."

"You have three healthy children left to you. I have never seen such sparkling health as Henry's."

"Henry, Margaret and Mary . . . they all enjoy good health, do they not. My life has taught me not to hope for too much. But I did not come to talk of myself, but of you."

"Of me !"

"Yes, of you. I guessed how you would be feeling. Here you live almost a prisoner, one might say, in a strange country, while plans are made for your future. I understand, for I have not had an easy life. There has been so much strife. I can remember being taken into the Sanctuary of Westminster by my mother. My little brothers were with us then. You have heard that they were lost to us . . . murdered, I dare swear. You see, I have come to tell you that I feel sympathy for you because I myself have suffered."

"I shall never forget how kind you are."

"Remember this: suffering does not last for ever. One day you will come out of this prison. You will be happy again. Do not despair. That is what I have come to say to you."

"And you came through the cold to tell me that?"

"It may be my last opportunity."

"I hope that I may come and see you when the child is born." The Queen smiled faintly and looked a little sad.

"Do not look like that," Katharine cried out in sudden panic. She was thinking of her sister Isabella, who had come back to Spain to have her child, the little Miguel who had died before he was two years old. Isabella had had some premonition of death.

She expected some reproof from the Queen for her outburst, but Elizabeth of York, who knew what had happened to the young Isabella, understood full well the trend of her thoughts.

She stood up and kissed Katharine's brow. That kiss was like a last farewell.

*          *          *

It was Candlemas-day and the cold February winds buffeted the walls of the Palace of the Tower of London, although the Queen was unaware of them.

She lay on her bed, racked by pain, telling herself: It will soon be over. And after this, should I live through it, there cannot be many more. If this could be a son . . . if only this could be a son!

Then briefly she wondered how many Queens had lain in these royal apartments and prayed: Let this be a son.

It must be a son, she told herself, for this will be the last.

She was trying to shake off this premonition which had been with her since she knew she was to have another child. If her confinement could have taken place anywhere but in this Tower of London she would have felt happier. She hated the place. Sometimes when she was alone at night she fancied she could hear the voices of her brothers calling her. She wondered then if they called her from some nearby grave.

This was a sign of her weakness. Edward and Richard were dead. Of that she was certain. The manner of their dying could be of little importance to them now. Would they come back to this troublous Earth even if they could? For what purpose? To denounce their uncle as a murderer? To engage in battle against their sister's husband for the crown?

"Edward! Richard!" she whispered. "Is it true that somewhere within the grey walls of these towers your little bodies lie buried?"

A child was coming into the world. Its mother should not think of the other children—even though they were her own brothers—who had been driven out of it before their time.

Think of pleasant things, she commanded herself: Of rowing down the river with her ladies, with good Lewis Walter, her bargeman, and his merry watermen; think of the Christmas festivities at Richmond. The minstrels and the reciters had been more engaging than usual. She smiled, thinking of her chief minstrel who was always called Marquis Lorydon. What genius! What power to please! And the others—Janyn Marcourse and Richard Denouse—had almost as much talent as Lorydon. Her fool, Patch, had been in great form last Christmas; she had laughed lightheartedly at his antics with Goose, young Henry's fool.

How pleased Henry had been because Goose had shone so brilliantly. It had pleased the boy because his fool was as amusing as those of the King and Queen.

Henry must always be to the fore, she mused. "Ah well, it is a quality one looks for in a King."

There had been a pleasant dance too by a Spanish girl from Durham House. Elizabeth had rewarded her with four shillings and fourpence for her performance. The girl had been indeed grateful. Poor child, there were few luxuries at Durham House.

The Queen's face creased into anxiety. Where will it all end? she asked herself. She thought of her son Henry, his eyes glistening with pride because his fool, Goose, could rival the fools of his parents. She thought of the lonely Infanta at Durham House.

The fate of Princes is often a sad one, she was thinking; and then there was no time for further reflection.

The child was about to be born, and there was nothing left for the Queen but her immediate agony.

\* \* \*

The ordeal was over, and the child lay in the cradle—a sickly child, but still a child that lived.

The King came to his wife's bedside, and tried not to show his disappointment that she had borne a girl.

"Now we have one son and three bonny girls," he said. "And we are young yet."

The Queen caught her breath in fear. Not again, she thought. I could not endure all that again.

"Yes, we are young," went on the King. "You are but thirty-seven, and I am not yet forty-six. We still have time left to us."

The Queen did not answer that. She merely said: "Henry, let us call her Katharine."

The King frowned, and she added: "After my sister."

"So shall it be," answered the King. It was well enough to name the child after Elizabeth's sister Katharine, Lady Courtenay, who was after all the daughter of a King. He would not have wished the child to be named Katharine after the Infanta. Ferdinand and Isabella would have thought he was showing more favour to their daughter, and that would not have been advisable.

The bargaining had to go on with regard to their daughter; and he wanted them to know that it was they who must sue for favours now. He was still mourning for that half of the dowry which had not been paid.

He noticed that the Queen looked exhausted and, taking her hand, he kissed it. "Rest now," he commanded. "You must take great care of yourself, you know."

Indeed I must, she thought meekly. I have suffered months of discomfort and I have produced but a girl. I have to give him sons . . . or die in the attempt.

\* \* \*

It was a week after the birth of the child when the Queen became very ill. When her women went into her chamber and found her in a fever they sent a messenger at once to the King's apartments.

Henry in shocked surprise came hurrying to his wife's bedside, for she had seemed to recover from the birth and he had already begun to assure himself that by this time next year she might be brought to bed of a fine boy.

When he looked at her he was horrified, and he sent at once for Dr. Hallyswurth, his best physician, who most unfortunately was at this time absent from the Court in his residence beyond Gravesend.

All through the day the King waited for the arrival of Dr. Hallyswurth, believing that, although other physicians might tell him that the Queen was suffering from a fever highly dangerous after childbirth, Dr. Hallyswurth would have the remedy which would save her life.

As soon as the doctor was found and the King's message delivered he set out for the Court, but dusk had fallen when he came, lighted by torches into the precincts of the Tower.

He was taken at once to the Queen's bedchamber, but, even as he took her hand and looked into her face, Elizabeth had begun to fight for her breath and the doctor could only sadly shake his head. A few minutes later Elizabeth sank back on her pillows. The daughter of Edward IV was dead.

Henry stared at her in sorrow. She had been a good wife to him. Where could he have found a better? She was but thirty-seven years of age. This dolorous day, February 11th of the year 1503, was the anniversary of her birth.

"Your Grace," murmured Dr. Hallyswurth, "there was nothing that could have been done to save her. Her death is due to the virulent fever which often follows childbirth. She was not strong enough to fight it."

The King nodded. Then he said: "Leave me now. I would be alone with my grief."

*       *       *

The bells of St. Paul's began to toll; and soon others joined in the dismal honour to the dead, so that all over London the bells proclaimed the death of the Queen.

In the Tower chapel she lay in state. Her body had been wrapped in sixty ells of holland cloth and treated with gums, balms, spices, wax and sweet wine. She had been enclosed by lead and put into a wooden coffin over which had been laid a black velvet pall with a white damask cross on it.

She had been carried into the lying-in-state chamber by four noblemen. Her sister Katharine, the Earl of Surrey and the Lady Elizabeth Stafford led the procession which followed the coffin; and when mass had been said, the coffin remained in the lighted chamber while certain ladies and men-at-arms kept vigil over it.

All through the long night they waited. They thought of her life and her death. How could they help it if they remembered those little boys, her brothers, who had been held in captivity in this very Tower and had been seen no more?

Where did their bodies lie now? Could it be that near this very spot, where their sister lay in state, those two little boys were hidden under some stone, under some stair?

\*        \*        \*

A week after the death of Queen Elizabeth, the little girl, whose existence had cost the Queen her life, also died.

Here was another blow for the King, but he was not a man to mourn for long. His thoughts were busy on that day when his wife was carried to her tomb.

It was the twelfth day after her death and, after mass had been said, the coffin was placed on a carriage which was covered with black velvet. On the coffin a chair had been set up containing an image of the Queen, exact in size and detail; this figure had been dressed in robes of state and there was a crown on its flowing hair. About the chair knelt her ladies, their heads bowed in grief. Here they remained while the carriage was drawn by six horses from the Tower to Westminster.

The people had lined the streets to see the cortège pass and there were many to speak of the good deeds and graciousness of the dead Queen.

The banners which were carried in the procession were of the Virgin Mary, of the Assumption, of the Salutation and the Nativity, to indicate that the Queen had died in childbirth. The Lord Mayor and the chief citizens, all wearing the deepest mourning, took their places in the procession; and in Fenchurch Street and Cheapside young girls waited to greet the funeral carriage. There were thirty-seven of them—one for each year of the Queen's life; they were dressed in white to indicate their virginity and they all carried lighted tapers.

When the cortège reached Westminster the coffin was taken into the Abbey, ready for the burial which would take place the next morning.

The King asked to be left alone in his apartments. He was genuinely distressed, because he did not believe that he could ever find a consort to compare with the one he had lost. She had had everything to give him—royal lineage, a right to the crown of England, beauty, docility and to some extent fertility.

Yet, there was little time in the life of kings for mourning. He was no longer a young romantic. That was for youth, and should never be for men who were destined for kingship.

He could not prevent his thoughts from going back to the past. He remembered now how, when Edward IV's troops had stormed Pembroke Castle, he had been discovered there, a little boy five years old, with no one to care for him but his old tutor, Philip ap Hoell. He could recall his fear at that moment when he heard the rough tread of soldiers mounting the stairs and knew that his uncle, Jasper Tudor, Earl of Pembroke, had already fled leaving him, his little nephew, to the mercy of his enemies.

Sir William Herbert had been in charge of those operations, and it was well that he had brought his lady with him; for when she saw the friendless little boy she had scolded the men for daring to treat him as a prisoner, and had taken him in her arms and purred over him as though he were a kitten. That had been the strangest experience he had ever known until that time. Philip ap Hoell would have died for him, but their relationship had never been a tender one.

He recalled his life in the Herbert household. Sir William had become the Earl of Pembroke, for the title was taken from Uncle Jasper Tudor and bestowed on Sir William for services rendered to his King.

It had been strange to live in a large family; there were three sons and six daughters in the Herbert home, and one of these was Maud. There had been fighting during his childhood—the continual strife between York and Lancaster; and, when Lancastrian victory brought back the earldom and castle of Pembroke to Jasper Tudor, Henry was taken from the Herberts to live with his uncle once more.

He remembered the day when he had heard that Maud had been married to the Earl of Northumberland. That was a sad day; yet he did not despair; he had never been one to despair; he considered his relationship with Maud, and he was able to tell himself that, although he had loved her dearly, he loved all the Herberts; and if marriage with Maud was denied him he could still be a member of that beloved family by marrying Maud's sister, Katharine.

And then fortune had changed. A more glorious marriage had been hinted at. Why should not the Tudor (hope of the Lancastrian House) marry the daughter of the King, for thus the red and white roses could flower side by side in amity?

He had then begun to know himself. He was no romantic boy —had never been a romantic boy. Had he wished to marry Maud that he might become a member of a family which had always seemed to him the ideal one, because from loneliness he had been taken into it by Lady Herbert and found youthful happiness there? Perhaps, since it had seemed that Katharine would do instead of Maud.

But the match with Elizabeth of York had been too glorious to ignore and he was ready to give up all thoughts of becoming a member of his ideal family, for the sake of a crown.

Life had never been smooth. There had been so many alarms, so many moments when it had seemed that his goal would never be reached. And while he had waited for Elizabeth he had found Katherine Lee, the daughter of one of his attendants—sweet gentle Katherine, who had loved him so truly that she had been ready to give him up when, by doing so, he could be free to marry the daughter of a King.

He was a cold man. He had been faithful to Elizabeth even though Katherine Lee had been one of her maids of honour. He saw her often, yet he had never given a sign that she was any more to him than any other woman of the Palace.

Now Elizabeth was dead, and she left him three children. Only three! He must beget more children. It was imperative.

Forty-six! That is not old. A man can still beget children at forty-six.

But there was little time to lose. He must find a wife quickly. He thought of all the weary negotiations. Time . . . precious time would be lost.

Then an idea struck him. There was a Princess here in England —she was young, personable and healthy enough to bear children.

What time would be saved! Time often meant money, so it was almost as necessary to save the former as the latter.

Why not? She would be agreeable. So would her parents. This half-hearted betrothal to a Prince of eleven—what was that, compared with marriage with a crowned King?

His mind was made up; his next bride would be Katharine of Aragon. The marriage should be arranged as quickly as possible; and then—more sons for England.

The next day Queen Elizabeth was laid in her grave; but the King's thoughts were not with the wife whom he had lost but with the Infanta in Durham House who should take the place of the dead woman.

# BAD NEWS FROM SPAIN

KATHARINE WAS HORRIFIED.

She sat with her maids of honour, staring at the embroidery in her hands, trying in vain to appear calm.

They tried to comfort her.

"He will not live very long," said the incorrigible Francesca. "He is old."

"He could live for twenty years more," put in Maria de Rojas.

"Not he! Have you not noticed how pale he is . . . and has become more so? He is in pain when he walks."

"That," Maria de Salinas said, "is rheumatism, a disease which many suffer from in England."

"He is such a cold man," said Francesca.

"Hush," Maria de Salinas reproved her, "do you not see that you distress the Infanta? Doubtless he would make a kind husband. At least he was a faithful one to the late Queen."

Francesca shivered. "Ugh! I would rather such a man were unfaithful than show me too much attention."

"I cannot believe that my mother will agree to this match," Katharine exclaimed anxiously, "and unless she does, it will never take place."

Maria de Salinas looked sadly at her mistress. There was no doubt that Queen Isabella loved her daughter and would be happy if she returned to Spain, but she would certainly give her blessing to the marriage if she considered it advantageous to Spain. Poor Infanta! A virgin widow preserved for an ageing man, whose rheumatism often made him irritable; a cold, dour man, who wanted her only because he wanted to keep a firm hand on her dowry and believed that she could give him sons.

\*     \*     \*

There was no news from Spain. Each day, tense and eager, Katharine waited.

She knew that the affairs of her parents must be in dire disorder for them so to neglect their daughter. If only they would send for her. If she could sail back to Spain the treacherous seas would have no menace for her. She would be completely happy.

Never, she believed, had anyone longed for home as she did now.

Maria de Rojas was restive. Why did she never hear from the Sovereigns about their consent to her marriage? Why was there no reply regarding her dowry? Katharine had written again because she feared her first letter might not have reached her mother; but still there was no reply to the questions.

Francesca gave loud voice to her grievances; Maria was filled with melancholy. Only Maria de Salinas and Inez de Veñegas alternately soothed and scolded them. *They* were unhappy, but what of the Infanta? How much harder was her lot. Imagine, it might well be that she would have to submit to the will of the old King of England.

*        *        *

At last came the news from Spain. Katharine saw the messengers arrive with the despatches and had them brought to her immediately.

Her mother wrote as affectionately as ever, and the very sight of that beloved handwriting made the longing for home more intense.

Isabella did not wish her daughter to marry the King of England. She was eager for a match between Katharine and the young Prince of Wales. She was writing to the King of England suggesting that he look elsewhere for a bride.

Katharine felt limp with relief, as though she had been reprieved from a terrible fate.

Unless some satisfactory arrangement could be made for Katharine's future in England, Isabella wrote, she would demand that her daughter be returned to Spain.

This made Katharine almost dizzy with happiness and, when her maids of honour came to her, they found her sitting at her table smiling dazedly at the letter before her.

"I am not to marry him," she announced.

Then they all forgot the dignity due to an Infanta and fell upon her, hugging and kissing her.

At last Maria de Rojas said: "Does she give her consent to *my* marriage?"

"Alas," Katharine told her, "there is no mention of it."

*        *        *

Henry sat for a long time listening to Puebla's account of his instructions from Spain. So the Sovereigns did not want him for a son-in-law. He read between the lines. They would be delighted if their daughter became the Queen of England, but he was old and she was young; they believed that he could not live for a great number of years and, when he died, she would be merely the Dowager Queen, who would play no part in state affairs. Moreover even as Queen, she would have no power, for Henry was not the man to allow a young wife to share in his counsels.

Isabella was emphatic in her refusal of this match.

"Her Highness," Puebla told the King, "suggests that it might be well if the Infanta returned to Spain."

This was high-handed indeed. Henry had no wish to send the Infanta back to Spain. With their daughter living in semi-retirement in England he had some hold over the Sovereigns. He wanted the rest of her dowry, and he was determined to get it.

"These are matters not to be resolved in an hour," replied Henry evasively.

"Her Highness suggests that, since you are looking for a wife, the Queen of Naples, now widowed, might very well suit you."

"The Queen of Naples!" Henry's eyes were momentarily narrowed. It was not a suggestion to be ignored. Such a marriage should give him a stake in Europe; so if the widow were young and handsome and likely to bear children, she would be a good match; and Henry, ever conscious of his age, was eager to marry soon.

He therefore decided to send an embassy to Naples immediately.

It was rather soon after his wife's death and he did not wish to appear over-eager.

Puebla was whispering: "The Infanta might write a letter to the Queen of Naples, to be delivered into her hands and hers alone. This would give some messenger on whom you could rely the opportunity of looking closely at the Queen."

Henry looked with friendship on the Spaniard who had ever seemed a good friend to him.

It was an excellent idea.

"Tell her to write this letter at once," he said. "You will find me a messenger on whom I can rely. I wish to know whether she be plump or lean, whether her teeth be white or black and her breath sweet or sour."

"If Your Grace will leave this matter with me I will see that you have a description of the lady which shall not prove false. And, Your Grace, you will remember that it is the hope of the Sovereigns that there should be a betrothal between their daughter and the Prince of Wales."

"The Prince of Wales is one of the most eligible bachelors in the world."

"And therefore, Your Grace, well matched to the Infanta of Spain."

Henry looked grave. "The wars in Europe would seem to be

going more favourably for the French than the Spaniards. It might be well if the Infanta did return to Spain."

Puebla shook his head. "If she returned, the Sovereigns would expect you to return with her the hundred thousand crowns which constituted half of her dowry."

"I see no reason why I should do that."

"If you did not, Your Grace, you would have a very powerful enemy in the Sovereigns. Where are your friends in Europe? Do you trust the French? And who in Europe trusts Maximilian?"

Henry was silent for a few moments. But he saw the wisdom of Puebla's advice.

He said: "I will consider this matter."

Puebla was jubilant. He knew that he had won his point. He would soon be writing to the Sovereigns to tell them that he had arranged for the betrothal of their daughter with the Prince of Wales.

\*     \*     \*

Prince Henry came in, hot from the tennis court. With him were his attendants, boys of his own age and older men, all admiring, all ready to tell him that they had never seen tennis played as he played it.

He could never have enough of their praises and, although he knew they were flattery, he did not care. Such flattery was sweet, for it meant they understood his power.

Each day when he awoke—and he awoke with the dawn—he would remember that he was now his father's only son and that one day there would be a crown on his head.

It was right and fitting that he should wear that crown. Was he not a good head taller than most of his friends? It was his secret boast that, if anyone had not known that he was the King's heir, they would have selected him from any group as a natural leader.

It could not be long before he was King. His father was not a young man. And how he had aged since the death of the Queen! He was in continual pain from his rheumatism and was sometimes bent double with it. He was growing more and more irritable and Henry knew that many were longing for the day when there would be a new King on the throne—young, merry, extravagant, all that the old King was not.

Henry had no sympathy for his father, because he who had never felt a pain in his life could not understand pain. The physical disabilities of others interested him only because they called attention to his own superb physique and health.

Life was good. It always had been. But during Arthur's lifetime there had been that gnawing resentment because he was not the firstborn.

He made his way now from the tennis court to the apartments of his sister Margaret. He found her there and her eyes were red from weeping. Poor Margaret! She was not the domineering elder sister today. He did feel a little sorry. He would miss her sorely.

"So tomorrow you leave us," he said. "It will be strange not to have you here."

Margaret's answer was to put her arms about him and hug him tightly.

"Scotland!" she whimpered. "It is so cold there, I hear. The castles are so draughty."

"They are draughty here," Henry reminded her.

"There they are doubly so. And how shall I like my husband, and how will he like me?"

"You will rule him, I doubt not."

"I hear he leads a most irregular life and has many mistresses."

Henry laughed. "He is a King, if it is only King of Scotland. He should have mistresses if he wishes."

"He shall not have them when he has a wife," cried Margaret fiercely.

"You will make sure of that, I'll swear. So there will only be one sister left to me now. And Mary is little more than a baby."

"Always look after her, Henry. She is wayward and will need your care."

"She will be my subject and I shall look after all my subjects."

"You are not yet King, Henry."

"No," he murmured reflectively, "not yet."

"I wish that the Infanta might be with us. It is sad to think of her in Durham House, cut off from us all. I should have liked to have had a sister of my own age to talk to. There would have been so much for us to discuss together."

"She could tell you little of the married state," said Henry. "Unless rumour lies, our brother never knew his wife. What a strange marriage that was!"

"Poor Katharine! I suffer for her. She felt as I feel now. To leave one's home . . . to go to a strange country . . ."

"I doubt your James will be as mild as our brother Arthur."

"No, it may be that he will be more like my brother Henry."

Henry looked at his sister through narrowed eyes.

"They say," went on Margaret, "that Katharine is to be *your* bride."

"I have heard it."

He was smiling. Margaret thought: He must have everything.

Others marry, so he must marry. Already he seems to be contemplating his enjoyment of his bride.

"Well, what are you thinking?" Henry asked.

"If you are like this at twelve, what will you be at eighteen?"

Henry laughed aloud. "Much taller. I shall be the tallest English King. I shall stand over six feet. I shall outride all my subjects. I shall be recognized wherever I go as the King of England."

"You do it as much as ever," she said.

"What is that?"

"Begin every sentence with *I*."

"And why should I not? Am I not to be the King?"

He was half laughing, but half in earnest. Margaret felt a new rush of sadness. She wished that she need not go to Scotland, that she could stay here in London and see this brother of hers mount the throne.

\*          \*          \*

Puebla brought the news to Katharine. The little man was delighted. It seemed to him that what he had continued to work for during many difficult months was at last achieved. In his opinion there was only one way out of the Infanta's predicament: marriage with the heir of England.

"Your Highness, I have at last prevailed upon the King to agree to your betrothal to the Prince of Wales."

There had been many occasions when Katharine had considered this possibility, but now she was face to face with it and she realized how deeply it disturbed her.

She had at once to abandon all hope of returning home to Spain. She remembered too that she had been the wife of young Henry's brother, and she felt therefore that the relationship between herself and Henry was too close. Moreover she was eighteen years old, Henry was twelve. Was not the disparity in their ages a little too great?

Yet were these the real reasons? Was she a little afraid of that arrogant, flamboyant Prince?

"When is this to take place?" she asked.

"The formal betrothal will be celebrated in the house of the Bishop of Salisbury in the near future."

Katharine said quickly: "But I have been his brother's wife. The affinity between us is too close."

"The Pope will not withhold the Bull of Dispensation."

There was no way out, Katharine realized, as she dismissed Puebla and went to her own apartment. She wanted to think of this alone, and not share it even with her maids of honour as yet.

She had escaped the father to fall to the son. She was certain that the King filled her with repugnance, but her feelings for young Henry were more difficult to analyse. The boy fascinated her as he seemed to fascinate everyone. But he was too bold, too arrogant.

He is only a boy, she told herself; and I am already a woman.

There came to her then an intense desire to escape, and impulsively she went to her table and sat down to write. This time she would write to her father, for she was sure of her mother's support, and if she could move his heart, if she could bring him to ask her mother that she might return, Isabella would give way immediately.

How difficult it was to express these vague fears. She had never been able to express her emotions. Perhaps it was because she had always been taught to suppress them.

The words on the paper looked cold, without any great feeling.

"I have no inclination for a second marriage in England . . ."

She sat for some time staring at the words. Of what importance were her inclinations? She could almost hear her mother's voice, gentle yet firm: "Have you forgotten, my dearest, that it is the duty of the daughters of Spain to subdue their own desires for the good of their country?"

What was the use? There was nothing to be done. She must steel herself, become resigned. She must serenely accept the fate which was thrust upon her.

She continued the letter:

"But I beg you do not consider my tastes or convenience, but in all things act as you think best."

Then firmly she sealed the letter and, when her maids of honour came to her, she was still sitting with it in her hands.

She turned to them and spoke as though she were awakening from a dream. "I shall never again see my home, never again see my mother."

\*　　　\*　　　\*

The hot June sun beat down on the walls of the Bishop's house in Fleet Street.

Inside that house Katharine of Aragon stood beside Henry, Prince of Wales, and was formally betrothed to him.

Katharine was thinking: It is irrevocable. When this boy is fifteen years old, I shall be past twenty. Can such a marriage be a happy one?

Henry studied his fiancée and was aware that she was not overjoyed at the prospect of their marriage. He was astounded, and this astonishment quickly turned to anger. How dared she not be overjoyed at the prospect! Here he was, the most handsome, the most popular and talented of Princes. Surely any woman should be overjoyed to contemplate marriage with him.

He thought of some of the girls he had seen about the Court. They were a constant provocation; they were very eager to please him and delighted when he noticed them. John Skelton was amused at such adventures, implying that they were worthy of a virile Prince. And this woman, who was not outstandingly beautiful, who had been his brother's wife, dared to appear doubtful.

Henry looked at her coldly; when he took her hand he gave it no warm pressure; his small eyes were like pieces of flint; they had lost something of their deep blueness and were the colour of the sea when a storm is brewing.

He was annoyed that he must go through with the betrothal. He wanted to snatch his hand away and say: "You do not care to marry me, Madam. Well, rest assured that affects me little. There are many Princesses in the world who would count you fortunate, but since you are blind to the advantage which is yours, let us have no betrothal."

But there was his father, stern, pale, with the lines of pain etched on his face, and while he lived Prince Henry was only Prince of Wales, not King of England. It was doubly humiliating to realize that he dared not flout his father's orders.

As for the King, he watched the betrothal with satisfaction. He was to keep the hundred thousand crowns which he had already received as the first payment of Katharine's dowry and another hundred thousand crowns would be paid on her marriage. Meanwhile she would receive nothing of that third of the revenues of Wales, Chester and Cornwall, which was her right on her marriage to Arthur; although when she married Henry she would receive a sum equal to that.

This was very satisfactory, mused the King. Katharine would remain in England; he would keep the first half of the dowry; she would not receive the revenues due to her; and the betrothal was merely a promise that she should marry the heir to England; so that if the King should change his mind about that before the Prince reached his fifteenth birthday—well, it would not be the first time that a Prince and Princess had undergone a betrothal ceremony which was not followed by a wedding.

Yes, very satisfactory. Thus he could keep what he had, maintain a truce with the Sovereigns of Spain, and shelve the marriage for a few years.

Now he was only waiting to hear from Naples. His own marriage was of more urgency than that of his son.

Out into the June sunshine of Fleet Street came a satisfied King, a sullen Prince and an apprehensive Princess.

\*  \*  \*

Now that Katharine was formally betrothed to the Prince of Wales, she could not be allowed to live in seclusion at Durham House, and life became more interesting for her.

The maids of honour were delighted by the turn of events because it meant that now they could go occasionally to Court. There was activity in their apartments as they hastily reviewed their wardrobes and bewailed the fact that their gowns were shabby and not of the latest fashion.

Katharine was upset. Badly she needed money. Her parents had written that they could send her nothing, because they needed everything they could lay their hands on to prosecute the war, and military events were not going well for Spain. Katharine must rely on the bounty of her father-in-law.

It had been uncomfortable having to rely on the bounty of a miser. And it was the fact that she was unable to pay her servants that had upset Katharine most.

But now that she was betrothed to his son, the King could no longer allow her to live in penury, and grudgingly he made her an allowance. This was relief, but as it was necessary to maintain a large household, and debts had been steadily mounting, the allowance was quickly swallowed up, and although the situation was relieved considerably, comparative poverty still prevailed at Durham House.

Doña Elvira was the only one who resented the change. She was jealous of her power and was becoming anxious to settle the matter of Maria de Rojas and Iñigo.

It was all very well to prevent letters, concerning Maria's hoped-for marriage to the grandson of the Earl of Derby, from reaching the Sovereigns, but this was not arranging a match between Maria and Iñigo.

She had given Iñigo full power over the pages and he was continually seeking the company of the maids of honour—Maria de Rojas in particular. He was not popular however and Hernan Duque complained of his insolent manner.

This infuriated Elvira, who promptly wrote off to Isabella declaring that, if she were to be responsible for the Infanta's household, she could not have interference from their Highnesses' ambassadors and envoys.

Isabella, who put complete trust in Elvira as her daughter's guardian, wrote reprovingly to Hernan Duque; and this so delighted Elvira that she became more domineering than ever.

Katharine was growing weary of Elvira's rule. She was no longer a child and she felt that it was time that she herself took charge of her own household. She began by commanding Juan de Cuero to hand over some of her plate and jewels, which she pawned in order to pay her servants' wages.

When Elvira heard of this she protested, but Katharine was determined to have her way in this matter.

"These are my jewels and plate," she said. "I shall do with them as I will."

"But they are part of the dowry which you will bring to your husband."

"I will use them instead of the revenues I was to have received from my late husband," answered Katharine. "The jewels and plate will not be needed until I am married to the Prince of Wales. Then I shall receive an amount similar to that which I have had to renounce. I shall redeem the jewels with that."

Doña Elvira could not believe that her hold on Katharine was slackening, nor that it was possible for her to be defeated in any way.

So she continued, as determined as ever to govern the household, not realizing that Katharine was growing up.

\*     \*     \*

Katharine found Maria de Rojas in a state of despondency.

"What ails you, Maria?"

Maria blurted out that she had met her lover at the Court and that he was less ardent.

"What could one expect?" demanded Maria. "All this time we have waited, and your mother ignores your requests on my behalf."

"It seems so very strange to me," said Katharine. "It is unlike her to ignore such a matter, for she would clearly see it as her duty to look to the welfare of my attendants."

Katharine pondering the matter remembered that Iñigo was hoping for Maria, and that Doña Elvira approved of his choice. That was certain, for he would never have dared show it if that had not been so.

Katharine said slowly: "I will write to my mother again, and this time I will send the letter by a secret messenger—not through the usual channels. It has occurred to me, Maria, that something—or someone—may have prevented my mother from receiving those letters."

Maria lifted her head and stared at her mistress.

Understanding dawned in Maria's eyes.

\* \* \*

The letter was written; the secret messenger was found. A few days after he had left—far too soon to hope for a reply to that letter—Katharine, seated at her window, saw a courier arrive and knew that he brought despatches from Spain.

It was six months since her betrothal to Henry in the Bishop of Salisbury's house in Fleet Street, and now that she had become accustomed to the idea that she must marry young Henry she had come to terms with life. The slight relief which the new turn of affairs had brought to her living standards was welcome, and life was far more tolerable.

She found that she could speak English fairly fluently now, and as she grew accustomed to her country of adoption she was even growing fond of it.

News from Spain always made her heart leap with hope and fear; and this message was obviously an important one. There was an urgency about the courier as he leaped from his saddle and, not even glancing at the groom who took his horse, hurried into the house.

She did not wait for him to be brought to her, but went down to meet him. She was determined now that letters should come direct to her, and that they should not first pass through the hands of Doña Elvira.

She came into the hall and saw the courier standing there. Doña Elvira was already there. The courier looked stricken, and when she saw that Doña Elvira had begun to weep, a terrible anxiety came to Katharine.

"What has happened?" she demanded.

The courier opened his mouth as though he were trying to speak but could not find the words. Doña Elvira was holding a kerchief to her eyes.

"Tell me . . . quickly!" cried Katharine.

It was Doña Elvira who spoke. She lowered her kerchief and Katharine saw that her face was blotched with tears, and that this was no assumed grief.

"Your Highness," she began. "Oh . . . my dearest Highness . . . this is the most terrible calamity which could befall us. How can I tell you . . . knowing what she meant to you? How can I be the one?"

Katharine heard her own voice speaking; she whispered: "Not . . . my mother!"

There was no answer, so she knew it was so. This was indeed the greatest calamity.

"She is sick? She is ill? She has been sick for so long. If she had not been sick . . . life would have been different here. She would never have allowed . . ."

She was talking . . . talking to hold off the news she feared to hear.

Doña Elvira had recovered herself. She said: "Highness, come to your apartment. I will look after you there."

"My mother . . ." said Katharine. "She is . . ."

"God rest her soul!" murmured Elvira. "She was a saint. There will be rejoicing in Heaven."

"It is so then?" said Katharine piteously. She was like a child pleading: Tell me it is not so. Tell me that she is ill . . . that she will recover. What can I do if *she* is not there? She has always been there . . . even though we were parted. How can I live with the knowledge that she is gone . . . that she is dead?

"She has passed peacefully to her rest," said Doña Elvira. "Her care for you was evident right at the end. The last thing she did was to have the Bull of Dispensation brought to her. She knew before she died that an affinity with Arthur could not stand in the way of your marriage with Henry. She satisfied herself that your future was assured and then . . . she made her will and lay down to die."

Katharine turned away, but Elvira was beside her.

"Leave me," said Katharine. "I wish to be alone."

Elvira did not insist and Katharine went to her room. She lay on her bed and drew the curtains so that she felt shut in with her grief.

"She has gone," she said to herself. "I have lost the dearest friend I ever had. No one will ever take her place. Oh God, how can I endure to stay in a world where she is not?"

Then she seemed to hear that voice reproving her—stern yet kind, so serene, so understanding always. "When your time comes, my daughter, you will be taken to your rest. Until that time you must bear the tribulations which God sees fit to lay upon you. Bear them nobly, Catalina, my dear one, because that is what I would have you do."

"I will do all that you wish me to," said Katharine.

Then she closed her eyes and began to pray, pray for courage to bear whatever life had to offer her, courage to live in a world which no longer contained Isabella of Castile.

# MARIA DE ROJAS

THE KING OF ENGLAND was furious.

His envoy had returned from Naples with reports that the Queen of Naples was plump and comely; she had remarkably beautiful eyes and her breath was sweet.

Henry cared nothing for this, since he had discovered that the Queen of Naples had no claim whatsoever on the crown of Naples and was nothing more than a pensioner of Ferdinand.

He had been deceived. The Sovereigns had tried to trick him into marriage. Much valuable time had been lost and he was no nearer to getting himself sons than he had been at the time of his wife's death.

One could not trust Ferdinand. There was not a more crafty statesman in the whole of Europe.

Moreover what was Ferdinand's position since the death of Isabella? All knew that the senior in the partnership had been the Queen of Castile. What was Aragon compared with Castile? And although the marriage of the Sovereigns had united Spain the Castilians were not prepared to accept Ferdinand as their King now that Isabella was dead.

Isabella's daughter Juana had been declared heiress of Castile, which meant that her husband Philip was the King. He was in a similar position to that which Ferdinand had occupied with Isabella. And Ferdinand? He was merely relegated to be King of Aragon . . . a very different rank from King of Spain.

Ferdinand was sly; he was unreliable. He would feel little anxiety concerning his daughter in England. All that had come from Isabella.

There was another matter which had upset the King of England. He had made a treaty with the Spanish Sovereigns to the effect that English sailors should have the freedom of Spanish ports and that they should be able to do business there on the same terms as Spaniards. He had just received news from certain merchants and sailors that this agreement had not been respected, and that they who had gone to Seville in good faith had found the old restrictions of trading brought against them, so that, unprepared as they were, they had suffered great losses.

"So this," Henry had said, "is the way Ferdinand of Aragon keeps his promises."

He sent for Puebla, and demanded an explanation.

Puebla had none. He was bewildered. He would write with all speed to Ferdinand, he had said, and there should be just restitution for the Englishmen.

This he had done, but Ferdinand was in no position to refund what had been lost. His authority in Castile was wavering and he was deeply concerned about the accession of his daughter Juana, for he feared the duplicity of her husband.

"And here am I," raged the King, "giving an allowance to Ferdinand's daughter. It shall be immediately stopped."

His eyes were speculative. Was the daughter of the King of Aragon such a prize? Was she worthy to mate with one of the most desirable *partis* in Europe?

Maximilian might be unreliable, but then so was Ferdinand; and as events were turning out it seemed that very soon the Hapsburgs would be the most influential family in Europe. Young Charles, the son of Juana and Philip, would be heir not only to Isabella and Ferdinand but to his paternal grandfather's dominions. Surely the greatest catch in Europe was little Charles.

His aunt Margaret, Maximilian's daughter, had married the heir of Ferdinand and Isabella—Juan, who had died a few months after the marriage, and had again become a widow on the decease of the Duke of Savoy.

Henry began to consider an alliance with the Hapsburgs. Margaret for himself; she was both comely and rich. Young Charles for his daughter Mary; and Eleanor, daughter of Juana and Philip, for Henry Prince of Wales. His betrothal to Katharine of Aragon? What of that? Isabella of Castile was dead, and what did he care for Ferdinand, now merely King of Aragon, who was almost certain to find trouble with his son-in-law Philip and his daughter Juana when they came to claim the crown of Castile!

Henry had made up his mind. He sent for a certain Dr. Savage, a man in whose ability he believed.

He said to him: "I want you to prepare to leave for the Court of Brussels. Don Pedro de Ayala is the Spanish ambassador at that Court and I believe him to be well disposed towards me, for we became friends during his term in England. I wish you to make it known to the Archduke Philip that I seek his friendship. As for his Archduchess, now Queen Juana of Castile, you need only to win her husband's friendship to make sure of hers. Ayala will help you, I am sure."

Henry then began to lay before Dr. Savage his plans for an alliance between his family and the Hapsburgs.

"Proceed," he said, "with all speed, for although my son and daughter can wait for their partners, there is not a great deal of time left to me. Do your work well and I doubt not that before long the Duchess Margaret will be on her way to England."

Dr. Savage declared his desire to serve his King in all ways.

He would prepare to leave for Brussels at once.

\* \* \*

How different had life at Durham House become!

Katharine's presence was no longer required at Court; there was no money coming in; poverty and boredom had returned.

The maids of honour grumbled together and despaired of ever returning to Spain. They used their jewelled brooches to pin their torn gowns together; their food consisted of stale fish and what little could be bought at the lowest prices in the street markets. It was small consolation that such food was served on plates of gold and silver.

Katharine rarely saw the Prince to whom she was supposed to be affianced; she heard gossip that he was going to marry her little niece, Eleanor. Life was even worse than it had been in previous times of neglect, because then she could always write to her mother.

In desperation she wrote to Ferdinand.

"I pray you remember that I am your daughter. For the love of our Lord help me in my need. I have no money to buy chemises of which I am in great need. I have had to sell some of my jewels to buy myself a gown. I have had but two dresses since I left Spain, for I have been wearing those which I brought with me. But I have very few left and I do not know what will become of me and my servants unless someone helps me."

Ferdinand ignored such pleas. He had too many troubles of his own to think about his daughter's chemises.

So the weeks passed.

Dr. Savage made little progress in Brussels; this was largely because of circumstances which were unknown to Henry. Since Isabella's death there had arisen certain factions which were determined to oust Ferdinand from Castile; and at the Court of Brussels there were two rival factions from Spain, one working for Ferdinand, one for Philip, his son-in-law. The head of Philip's faction was Juan Manuel, brother of Doña Elvira, who had worked for the Sovereigns when Isabella was alive because of his admiration for the Queen. He had never admired Ferdinand; and now that the Queen was dead he was determined to force him out of Castile by supporting his son-in-law, Philip. Ferdinand's supporters were his ambassador to Brussels, Don Gutierre Gomez de

Fuensalida, and Don Pedro de Ayala. Ayala, to whom Dr. Savage presented himself, was certainly not going to bring Philip and the doctor together, because an alliance between Philip and England would be to Ferdinand's detriment.

Thus, although Ayala received Dr. Savage with a show of friendship, he was secretly working all the time to avoid bringing the doctor to Philip's notice. Negotiations hung fire, and this was very irritating to the English King, who knew little of the intricacies of politics at the Brussels Court.

The delays did not endear his daughter-in-law to him, and as his rheumatism was growing gradually more painful he became more irascible than ever and quite indifferent to the hardship which Katharine was suffering.

Katharine began to pawn more and more of her jewels, and she knew that when the time came for them to be valued and handed over to the King, as part of her dowry, they would be very much depleted. But what could she do? Her household had to eat even if they had received no payment for many months.

The entire household was becoming fretful, and one day Katharine came upon Maria de Rojas sobbing in distress, so deep that it was some time before Katharine could understand what had happened.

At length the sad little story was wrung from Maria.

"I have had news that he has married someone else."

"My poor Maria!" Katharine sought to comfort the forlorn maid of honour. "But since he could not remain faithful, surely he would have made a bad husband."

"It was all the waiting," cried Maria. "His family insisted. They believed we should never have the consent of the Sovereigns and that there would be no dowry. Why, only half of your own was paid, and consider the poverty in which your father allows you to live!'"

Katharine sighed.

"Sometimes," she said, "I wonder what will become of us all."

Maria continued to weep.

*     *     *

It was a few days later when Doña Elvira called Maria de Rojas to her.

Maria, who had been listless since she had heard the news of her lover's marriage, was not apprehensive as she would ordinarily have been by a summons from Doña Elvira. She simply did not care. Whatever Doña Elvira did to her, she said to Maria de

Salinas, whatever punishment she sought to inflict, she would not care. Nothing could hurt her now.

With Doña Elvira was her son, Iñigo, who looked sheepishly at Maria as she entered.

Maria ignored him.

"Ah, Maria," said Doña Elvira smiling, "I have some good news for you."

Maria lifted her leaden eyes to Elvira's face, but she did not ask what the good news was.

"You poor girl!" went on Elvira. "If the Prince of Wales had not died, good matches would have been found for all of you. You must have suffered great anxiety as to your future."

Maria was still silent.

"You however are going to be very fortunate. My son here wishes to marry you. His father and I are agreeable to this match. I see no reason to delay."

Maria spoke then, recklessly, for the first time in her life not caring what Doña Elvira could do to her: "I do not wish to marry your son, Doña Elvira," she said.

"What!" screeched the duenna. "Do you realize what you are saying?"

"I am perfectly aware of what I am saying. I mean it. I wished to marry but was prevented from doing so. Now I do not wish to marry."

"You wished to marry!" cried Elvira. "You persuaded the Infanta to plead with the Sovereigns for their consent and a dowry. And what happened, eh? Did you get that consent? I have seen no dowry."

Elvira was smiling so malevolently that Maria suddenly understood. Did not Elvira see all the letters which were despatched to the Sovereigns? Katharine must have realized this, because that last letter she wrote—and she must have written it at the very time when Isabella lay dying—was to have been delivered by a secret messenger, which meant, of course, that it should not pass through Elvira's hands.

Maria knew then that this woman had wrecked her hopes of happiness; she hated her, and made no attempt to control her emotion.

"So it was you," she cried. "You have done this. They would have given what I asked. I should have married ·by now, but you . . . you . . ."

"I fear," said Doña Elvira quietly, "that this cannot be Maria de Rojas, maid of honour to the Infanta. It must be some gipsy hoyden who looks like her."

Iñigo was looking at Maria with big pleading eyes; his look was tender and he was imploring her: Maria be calm. Have you forgotten that this is my mother, whom everyone has to obey?

Maria gave him a scornful look and cried out in anguish: "How could you do this, you wicked woman? I hate you. I tell you I hate you and will never marry your stupid son."

Doña Elvira, genuinely shocked, gripped Maria by the shoulders and forced her on to her knees. She took her long dark hair and, pulling it, jerked the girl's head backwards.

"You insolent little fool," she hissed. "I will show you what happens to those who defy me." She turned to Iñigo. "Do not stand there staring. Go and get help. Call my servants. Tell them to come here at once."

She shook Maria, whose sobs were now choking her and, when her servants came, Doña Elvira cried: "Take this girl into the ante-room. Lock the door on her. I will decide what is to be done with her."

They carried the sobbing Maria away, and Elvira, her mouth firm, her eyes glittering, said to her son: "Have no fear. The girl shall be your wife. I know how to make her obedient."

Iñigo was shaken. It had hurt him to see Maria so ill treated. He was certain that she would be his wife, because his mother had said she would, and whatever Doña Elvira decreed came to pass.

*        *        *

Katharine was deeply disturbed by what had happened to Maria de Rojas. Doña Elvira had kept her locked away from the other maids of honour, and they all knew that Doña Elvira was determined that Maria should be forced to accept Iñigo as her betrothed.

Katharine considered this matter and asked herself why she allowed her household to be dominated by Doña Elvira. Was she herself not its head?

She remembered her parting from her mother. She could almost hear that firm voice warning her: "Obey Doña Elvira in all things, my dearest. She is a strong woman and a wise one. Sometimes she may seem harsh, but all that she does will be for your good. Always remember that I trust her and I chose her to be your duenna."

Because of that Katharine had always sought to obey Doña Elvira, and whenever she had felt tempted to do otherwise she remembered her mother's words. But what duplicity Elvira had used in not allowing Katharine's requests on Maria's behalf to reach Isabella!

Katharine asked Elvira to come to her apartment and, as soon as the duenna entered, saw that her mouth was set and determined and that she was going to do fierce battle in this matter of Maria's marriage.

"You have removed my maid of honour from my service," Katharine began.

"Because, Highness, she has behaved in a most undignified manner, a manner of which your dear mother would heartily disapprove."

That was true. If Maria had sobbed and wept and declared her hatred of Elvira, as Katharine had heard she had, Isabella would certainly have disapproved.

"Doña Elvira, I wrote some letters to my mother and I believe she never received them."

"Storms at sea," murmured Elvira. "It invariably happens that some letters do not reach their destination. If I wish to send important news I send two couriers, and not together. Did you take this precaution?"

Katharine looked boldly into the face of her duenna. "I believe these letters never left this house."

"That is an accusation, Highness."

"I meant it to be."

"Your mother put me in charge of your household, Highness. I never forget that. If I believe that I should sometimes act boldly on any matter, I do so."

"Even to destroying letters which were meant for my mother?"

"Even to that, Highness."

"So you were determined that Maria should marry Iñigo, and not the man of her choice."

"Indeed that is so, Highness. She wished to marry an Englishman. There are many matters which are hidden from Your Highness. It is only seemly that it should be so. Your mother instructed me that I must be careful of those who would spy against you. I must not too readily trust the English. What an excellent opportunity for spying an Englishman would have if he were married to one of your own maids of honour!"

"But this was not a case of spying. They loved . . ."

"So dearly did he love her that he married someone else . . . not so long after plighting his troth to her."

"They were kept apart."

"And this great love could not endure against a little absence? Nay, Highness, trust your duenna, as your mother did. Always remember that it was our dearest Queen who put me in this position of trust. She will be looking down from her place in

Heaven now—for who can doubt that such a saint is now in Heaven?—and she is imploring me—can you not sense her? I can —she is imploring me to stand firm, and you to understand that all I do is for your good."

Any mention of her mother unnerved Katharine. Merely to say or hear her name brought back so clearly an image of that dear presence that she could feel nothing but her bitter loss.

Doña Elvira saw the tears in Katharine's eyes; she seized her opportunity: "Come, Highness, let me take you back to your apartments. You should lie down. You have not recovered from the terrible shock of her death. Who of us have? Do not distress yourself about the love affairs of a lighthearted maid of honour. Trust me . . . as *she* always wished you to."

Katharine allowed herself to be led to her apartments, and there she lay on her bed continuing to think of her mother.

But when her grief abated a little she thought with increasing distrust of Doña Elvira, and although there was nothing she could do now to bring Maria's love back to her she determined from that moment that in future she was going to take a firmer hand in the management of her own household.

\*       \*       \*

Iñigo scratched at the door. Maria heard him but she took no notice.

"Maria," he whispered.

"Go away," she answered.

"I will when I have spoken to you."

"I do not wish to see you."

"But you can hear me as I speak to you through the key-hole."

She did not answer.

"I know you can," he went on. "I have come to say that I am sorry."

Still she was silent.

"My mother is determined that we shall marry. She always has been. It is no use fighting against my mother, Maria. Maria, do you hate me so much?"

"Go away," she repeated.

"I shall always be kind to you. I will make you love me. Then you will forget what my mother has done."

"I shall never forget what she has done."

"Do you wish to remain locked up here?"

"I do not care what becomes of me."

"You do, Maria. When you marry me I will take you back to

Spain. Just answer one question: Do you want to go back to Spain, Maria?"

"To Spain!" the words escaped her. She thought of her home, of being young again. If she were ever going to forget her faithless lover she might do so at home.

"Ah," he said, "you cannot deceive me. It is what you long for. If you marry me, Maria, I will take you home as soon as it can be arranged."

She was silent.

"Can you hear me, Maria? I want to please you. I will do anything you ask."

"Go away. That is what I ask. That is the way to please me."

He went away, but he returned a little later. He came again and again; and after a few days she began to look for his coming.

He was always gentle, always eager to please her.

She found that she was able to laugh as she said: "You are not overmuch like your mother, Don Iñigo Manrique."

He laughed with her; and from that moment their relationship changed.

It was a few days later when she rejoined the maids of honour. She was subdued and sullen.

"I have agreed to become betrothed to Don Iñigo Manrique," she told them.

# THE PROTEST OF THE PRINCE OF WALES

THE PRINCE OF WALES was approaching his fourteenth birth-day, and he was determined that it should be celebrated with all the pomp due to his rank.

He would have masques and pageants such as had never been seen during his father's reign. Fourteen was an age when one left childhood behind and became a man.

He was already taller than most men and had the strength of two. People often said that he was going to be a golden giant. He liked to hear that.

He refused to do lessons and commanded John Skelton to plan a masque.

"The kind I like best," declared the Prince, "are those in which masked men appear at the joust and beg leave to be able to take part. One of them, taller than the rest and clearly noble, in spite of his disguise, challenges the champion."

"And beats him," whispered Skelton.

"Yes, and beats him; and then there is a cry of 'This is a god, for no man on Earth could beat the champion'. Then the ladies come forward and there is a dance. . . ."

"And the masked hero will allow only the most beautiful lady to remove his mask," added Skelton.

"That is so, and when the mask is removed . . ."

"The god is revealed to be His Grace the Prince of Wales!" cried Skelton. "Fanfares."

"Why, but that is exactly what I had planned," cried Henry in surprise.

"Does it not show that our minds are in unison, Your Grace?"

"It would seem so."

"But then we have had these pageants before, and methinks the unmasked hero has already made his debut. But, there is no reason I can see why he should not appear again . . . and again and again."

Henry was never quite sure whether or not Skelton was laugh-ing at him, but because he admired the man and believed he had much to learn from him, he preferred to think he was not, and invariably laughed with him.

"Fourteen," he mused. "In another year I shall be betrothed."

"A year will pass like a day, in the full life of Your Royal Highness."

"It is indeed so, my good John. And have you heard that I am now to marry Marguerite d'Angoulême? They say she is very beautiful."

"All high-born ladies are said to be beautiful," answered John.

"It is not true, though their jewels and clothes often make them seem so."

"I did not speak of what they are but what they are said to be."

The Prince was thoughtful. Then he said: "They say that Marguerite adores her brother Francis. They say he is handsome and excels at all sports; that there is none like him in the whole of France and, if ever he comes to the throne, he will make a great King."

"So there are two such paragons—one in England, one in France."

The Prince drew himself up to his full height. "I believe him not to be as tall as I, and he is dark."

"A minor paragon," murmured Skelton.

"And," went on the Prince, "there is no doubt that I shall one day be King. But Francis will only ascend the throne if old Louis dies childless. He must be beside himself with terror."

"Why, my Prince, it is not easy for old men to beget children."

"But for his future to hang on such a thread! His mother and sister call him Caesar. I hope Marguerite is soon brought to England."

"Your Grace will have much to teach her, and not least of the lessons she will learn will be that there is a Prince more handsome, more excellent, more god-like than her brother."

The Prince did not answer. His eyes were narrowed in the characteristic way; his small mouth was set. What a King he will make! thought Skelton. His ministers will have to learn to pander to his wishes, or it will go hard with them. Our golden god will be a despot, and heads will doubtless fly like tennis balls.

Henry was thinking of Marguerite. Surely she must come soon. He was going to insist on marrying this girl. Many had been offered to him, and then the offers had been withdrawn. He wanted Marguerite. She was beautiful, he had heard, and it was all very well for Skelton to say that all high-born ladies were beautiful; he did not believe it. Look at Katharine of Aragon in her faded gown, and her face pale and stricken with mourning. He rejoiced that it was Marguerite who had been chosen for him and not Katharine.

While he sat with Skelton a messenger from the King arrived

and told the Prince that his father wished to see him without delay.

Skelton watched the Prince as he immediately obeyed the summons. There is one person alone who can deflate our great Prince, mused Skelton—his Royal Father. When he is no longer there, what an inflated King we shall have.

As soon as Henry came into his father's presence the King waved his hand to those attendants who were with him, indicating that he wished to be alone with his son.

He looked at Henry sternly. The boy's glowing health could not but give him the utmost satisfaction, yet he was afraid that young Henry had extravagant tastes. He must have a serious talk with him in the very near future; he must make him realize how carefully his father had built up a firm exchequer. It would be terrible if the wealth of the country and the Tudors were frittered away in useless pageants.

But he had not summoned the boy to talk of extravagance. That could wait. There was a matter which he considered more urgent.

"My son," said the King, "one day you will be married, and that day is not far distant."

"I hear, Sire, that a new bride is being suggested now. I like what I hear of Marguerite."

"Yes, Marguerite," said his father. "Do you remember that when you were thirteen you were betrothed to another in the house of the Bishop of Salisbury?"

"I remember it well—a hot day. The people cheered me as I came into Fleet Street!"

"Yes." Henry's tone was curt. "We know full well that the people cheer you wherever you go. Katharine of Aragon is not the match today that she was at that time. Circumstances change. Now that her mother is dead, her father's position is not what it was. I do not trust her father. I feel sure that were a marriage to take place there would still be difficulty about getting the remainder of the dowry. In other words, I do not favour the marriage with Katharine."

"No, Sire. I . . ."

The King lifted his hand. "We will not discuss your wishes because they are at this time of no moment."

The blood flamed into young Henry's face. A protest rose to his lips; then he remembered that this was his father; this was the King. One did not argue with Kings. He tried to suppress his anger. His mouth was tight and his eyes a blazing blue.

"According to what was arranged in the Bishop of Salisbury's house a year ago, when you are fifteen you would marry Katharine. That is in a year's time. I now desire you to make a formal protest. You are to meet Archbishop Warham here in the Palace. He is waiting now. You will solemnly protest that you have no wish for this marriage with Katharine of Aragon."

"But . . ." began Henry.

"You will do as you are told, my son. The Archbishop is waiting to see you now."

All the egoism in the Prince's nature was rising in protest—not against marriage with Katharine but against his father's management of what he considered to be his personal affair. Young Henry knew that royal marriages were usually arranged, but he was no ordinary Prince. He was old enough to have a say in his own affairs.

If he, of his own free will, decided against marrying Katharine, all well and good. But to be told to make such a protest offended his *amour propre*, which was extremely sensitive.

His father said testily: "This is what you will say: 'The betrothal was contracted in my minority. I myself was not consulted in the matter. I shall not ratify it when the time comes, and it is therefore null and void.'"

"I should like time to consider this matter," said Henry boldly.

"That is enough," his father retorted; "you do as you are told. Come . . . say those words after me."

For a few seconds Henry's blazing eyes looked into his father's. But he knew he must obey. He was only a boy not yet fourteen, and this man, whose face was lined with suffering, was the King. He murmured the words he had been told to repeat.

"Again," said his father.

It was humiliating. Why should I? he asked of himself. Then a cunning thought came into his mind. It would not always be as it was now. One day he would be King, and the man who was now commanding him would be nothing but a mouldering corpse. What did words matter? When young Prince Henry was King Henry, then he would have his way and, if he wished to marry Katharine of Aragon, there would be none to deny him his wish.

He repeated the words sullenly.

"Come," said the King. "I dare swear Warham has arrived already."

So, in the ground floor apartment in Richmond Palace, young Henry repeated the words which were his formal protest against a marriage with Katharine of Aragon.

Words, thought Henry as he went back to his own apartments.

He would never allow a few words to stand between himself and what he wanted.

After that he thought of Katharine of Aragon more frequently. He remembered her as she had been when he had led her to the Palace after her wedding ceremony.

His father had made up his mind that he should never have Katharine, yet his father himself had wanted to marry her. Katharine was now out of reach. She represented a challenge. She had suddenly become quite attractive—more so than Marguerite, who was so enamoured of her own brother that she thought him the handsomest boy in the world.

# THE TREACHERY OF ELVIRA

DOÑA ELVIRA WAS in very secret conference with her husband, Don Pedro Manrique. She spoke quickly and quietly, for she was very eager that what she was saying should reach no other ears but those of her husband.

"Juan is certain of it," she was saying. "If this meeting can be arranged, it will teach Ferdinand the lesson he needs."

Don Pedro was alarmed. It was true that his wife was a woman who always had her way; but the domestic politics of the Infanta's household were a very different matter from those of Europe. She had become more confident than ever, since she had successfully arranged the betrothal of Iñigo and Maria de Rojas. But Don Pedro wished she would leave intrigue to her brother.

Elvira's great aim was to bring power to the Manrique and Manuel families. Therefore she was going to stand firmly behind her brother, Don Juan Manuel, who at the Court of Brussels represented the Castilian faction, the aim of which was to oust Ferdinand from power and support Philip.

"He is asking your help in this matter?" asked Don Pedro.

Elvira nodded proudly. "Why not? I hold an important position here in England. There is a great deal I could do."

"What do you propose? Are you going to consult Puebla?"

"That little fool! Indeed I am not. This is a matter which I shall trust to no one."

"But how do you propose to bring about a meeting between Henry and Philip? And what would Ferdinand's reaction be if this were done?"

"I do not think we should concern ourselves with Ferdinand's reactions. Ferdinand is growing old. He is like a lion whose teeth have been drawn. He understands now that he owed much to Isabella. He is going to realize that it was more than he suspects, even now. Ferdinand's days as a power in Europe are numbered. Once I have arranged this meeting . . ."

"Elvira, have a care."

"Oh you are a fool, Pedro. You are too timid. If it had been left to you, Iñigo would still be looking for a bride."

"All I ask is that you should go warily."

"Can you not trust me to do that?"

"You are clever, Elvira; you are shrewd. But this is dangerous politics. Tell me what you propose to do."

She looked at him with a scornful smile, made as though to speak and then paused. "No," she said, "I think I will tell you afterwards. You are too timid, my dear Pedro. But have no fear. I know exactly how to handle this matter."

\*      \*      \*

Katharine's maids of honour were helping her to dress when Elvira came to them.

"Is that the best gown you can find for Her Highness?" she demanded, staring at the stiff brocade skirt which had been mended in several places.

"It is the least shabby of Her Highness's gowns," said Inez de Veñegas.

Elvira clicked her tongue and murmured as though to herself: "A pretty pass . . . a pretty pass . . ."

She watched while the maids dressed Katharine's hair, then she waved her hands in a gesture they knew well, shooing them away as though they were chicken.

When they had gone Elvira said: "It distresses me, Highness. I often wonder what your mother would have said if she could see what has befallen you in England."

"She knew how I was placed, even before she died, yet there was nothing she could do. Had it been possible she would have done it."

"An Infanta of Spain to be so shabby! I feel it should not be allowed to continue."

"It has gone on so long that one grows accustomed to it."

"There is a new Queen of Spain now. I wonder what she would say if she could see her sister."

"Ah . . . Juana!" murmured Katharine, and thought of that wild sister who laughed and cried too easily. "It is strange to think of her as Queen in our mother's place."

"How would you like to see her again?"

Katharine did not speak. To see Juana! It would be the next best thing to seeing her mother.

"I do not see," whispered Elvira, watching her closely, "why it should not be arranged."

Katharine turned to her swiftly. "But how?"

"Suppose you wrote to her, telling her of your desire to see her. Do not forget, she is the Queen now. Suppose you told her of your homesickness, your longing to see a member of your family; I feel sure she would be as eager to see you as you are to see her."

"You mean that I should leave England . . . ?"

"Why not? They could come to the coast to meet you. The King might accompany you; it would be an opportunity for him to meet the new Queen and her husband."

"Doña Elvira, do you really think . . . ?"

How young she is, thought Elvira. How innocent. How easily she is deluded!

Elvira turned away as though to hide an emotion of which she was ashamed because it showed a weakness.

"I think it is worth trying. Why should you not write a note to your sister, suggesting such a meeting. What harm could that do?"

"I can see no harm in it. I should so rejoice to hear from Juana."

"Then write the note and we will send it by special courier to Brussels. He shall wait there and bring back your sister's answer to you."

Katharine rose and went to her table. Her fingers were trembling with excitement as she took up her pen.

\*　　　\*　　　\*

Katharine looked at the note. It brought back memories of Juana.

How wonderful for them to be together, to exchange experiences, to give themselves up to the joy of "Do you remember?" It would be almost like living those days of childhood again.

We *should* be together, thought Katharine; there are so few of us left now.

Juana had written that she would be delighted to see her sister, that there was nothing she wanted more. Why should not the two parties meet half way?

If King Henry and Katharine would cross to Calais and travel to Saint-Omer, which was but eight leagues away, there Juana and her husband, Philip, would be waiting to meet them.

Katharine showed the letter to Doña Elvira, who was overjoyed. Juan had been clever to get the unbalanced Juana to write the letter exactly as he wished, so the strategy had succeeded even beyond her hopes.

There was now of course the difficulty of persuading the King to enter into the plan, but Elvira did not think that would be difficult, since Henry desperately needed a bride and was desirous of linking up with the Hapsburgs. He was feeling his age, it was true, and a sea journey would not be very comfortable, but he was ever a man to put diplomacy before comfort. Elvira had little doubt that he would accept the invitation.

She was jubilant. She would have achieved for her brother that which he had been working hard to bring about: A meeting between Henry and Philip which could only work out to the detriment of Ferdinand and the Aragonese faction.

"You should write to the King at once," said Elvira, "showing him this invitation from your sister. If you will do it now, I myself will give the order for your chamberlain to prepare to take it to Richmond with all speed."

"I will write at once. Tell Alonso de Esquivel to make ready. He rides faster than any, and I can scarcely wait for the King's answer. I will take it down to him myself when I have written it, with special instructions that it is to be put into no hands other than those of the King."

Elvira nodded, well pleased, and went off at once to tell the chamberlain to make ready.

Katharine carefully wrote her letter to the King, sealed it and was making her way down to the courtyard when she came face to face with Dr. de Puebla.

She felt so happy that she could not resist confiding in the ambassador, and said almost childishly: "I have had an invitation from my sister. She has invited me . . . and the King . . . to see her. I am asking the King to agree to this."

Puebla put his hand out to the wall to steady himself. He knew at once what this meant. Katharine would not go alone. There would be a royal party and the King would most certainly be at the head of it. The enemies of Ferdinand had been working long and secretly to bring about such a meeting. This was direct treachery towards Katharine's father.

He took the letter from her and she, unthinking, let it go.

Katharine said sharply. "Give me back that letter."

The little ambassador continued to clutch it tightly.

"Highness," he began, "this could be a matter of policy . . ."

Katharine's habitual calm deserted her. She thought of the months of loneliness, boredom, poverty and humiliation. She did not trust Puebla, whom she had never liked, and Elvira had lost no opportunity of poisoning her mind against him. She snatched the letter from the ambassador and went past him.

His ambassadorial duties had accustomed Puebla to quick thinking. He guessed that Elvira was behind these arrangements, for he was well aware that her brother, Juan Manuel, was working in Brussels for the Castilian party against the Aragonese.

It was useless to follow Katharine. Glancing hastily through a window he saw the chamberlain, ready for his journey, standing by while his horse was being saddled. There were a few moments left to him in which to act. He sped along to Elvira's apartment and on his way there met her returning from the courtyard.

"This is treachery," he cried, "treachery against our Sovereign master."

Elvira was too much taken off her guard to feign surprise. "If the Infanta wishes to see her sister, why should she be prevented?"

"This meeting has been arranged at the instigation of your brother, who is a traitor to Ferdinand. We are Ferdinand's servants. Your brother is a traitor, and you know that full well. If that letter of invitation is sent to the King I shall have no alternative but to acquaint Ferdinand with *your* treachery. It is one thing for your brother to work against the King of Aragon in Brussels, but quite another for you to do so here in the household of Ferdinand's daughter. He could recall you to Spain, and he will do so. I do not think your fate would be a very happy one if that should happen."

"I do not understand . . ." began Elvira, but for once she was trembling. The success of her venture depended entirely on its seeming innocence. The meeting for which she had planned must appear to have been brought about through Katharine and Juana. She understood her danger if Ferdinand were informed that she had played a part in it.

"There is little time to lose," said Puebla. "In less than five minutes Esquivel will be on his way to Richmond."

Doña Elvira made a quick decision. "I will go down at once and tell him that he must not take the letter to the King."

Puebla, who was sweating with the excitement and dismay of those moments, now relaxed.

She undersood the danger to herself and her family. She had not only her own but her family's future to think of. She would not want it known that Juan Manuel had played his part in this; and although Ferdinand had been weakened by the death of Isabella, he was still a power in Spain, and it might be that he would act as Regent for Juana and Philip, who must necessarily spend a certain time in their other dominions.

Elvira knew very well that she was playing a dangerous game.

She went down to the courtyard, while Puebla watched from a window. Katharine had given the chamberlain her letter with instructions to ride to Richmond with all speed, and had returned to the house.

That made Elvira's task more easy. Puebla watched her take

the letter from the chamberlain; he saw the look of surprise on the man's face as the horse was led back to the stables.

The ambassador sighed with relief. A chance meeting with the Infanta had diverted a catastrophe. He felt exhausted. He would return immediately to his lodgings in the Strand and there rest awhile.

I am too old for such alarms, he told himself.

As he came out of Durham House his servant, who had been waiting for him, came hurriedly to his side, surprised to see his master so weary.

Puebla was about to start on his way when he stopped abruptly. "Wait here," he said. "If you should see Don Alonso de Esquivel ride off in some haste towards Richmond lose no time in coming straight to me."

He then made his way to his lodging. He did not trust Elvira. He had always known that the woman sent adverse reports of him to Isabella, and was doubtless doing so to Ferdinand. He had an inkling that she might attempt to thwart him even now that he was aware of her duplicity.

He was right.

He had not been in his lodgings very long when his servant came panting into his presence, to tell him that the chamberlain had, very soon after the departure of Dr. de Puebla from Durham House, set off in the direction of Richmond, riding at great speed.

Puebla was horrified. He should have foreseen this.

The mischief was done. The King was being offered what was tantamount to an invitation to meet Philip and Juana; if he accepted, months of diplomacy were ruined.

He could not prevent Katharine's letter from reaching the King, but he could at least warn Katharine of the part she had been inveigled into playing. Then perhaps he could warn the King of the unreliable character of the Archduke Philip.

He had no time to form elaborate plans. He must act with speed. Of one thing he could be certain: The Infanta was completely loyal to her own family; if she knew that she had been used in a plot against her father, she would be horrified.

He lost no time in returning to Durham House, and there burst unceremoniously into the presence of the Infanta.

Katharine was with some of her maids of honour and, when he stammered out the plea that he speak to her alone, she was so shocked by his distress that she immediately agreed that he should do so.

As soon as they were alone he said: "Highness, you are the victim of a plot against your father." He then explained how for months the Castilian faction in Brussels had been working to bring about a meeting between Henry of England and her brother-in-law, Philip.

"You must understand, Highness, that your brother-in-law is no friend of your father. He seeks to take from him all the power he has in Castile and relegate him solely to the affairs of Aragon. You know how distressed your mother would be if she could know what is happening now. In her will she asks that in the absence or incapacity of your sister Juana, your father should be sole regent of Castile until the majority of her grandson Charles. Philip is determined to increase the discord and distrust between your father and the King of England. He will seek to make a pact with him against your father. Doña Elvira's brother, Don Juan Manuel, is the leader in this plot. It is for this reason that she has urged you to help bring about this meeting."

Katharine was staring at the ambassador in horror. She was remembering how Doña Elvira had commiserated with her, how she had urged her to write to Juana. So she and Juana were being used by their father's enemies! Katharine thought of her mother, who had always stood firmly beside her father. How shocked and horrified she would be at the idea of her daughters' working with their father's enemies.

She was trembling as she said: "I believe what you say. I see that I have been their dupe. What can I do now?"

Puebla shook his head sadly, for he had realized that there was nothing now to be done. The King would receive the letter from his daughter-in-law, enclosing that from Juana. It was entirely in his hands whether or not that invitation would be accepted.

"At least, Highness," he said, "you know your duenna for the scheming woman she is. With your leave I will retire now. I shall go with all speed to Richmond, and there I shall try to use my influence with the King to avoid this meeting."

\*　　　\*　　　\*

Henry was studying the letter from Katharine and that from Juana.

To cross to Saint-Omer, to meet the heir of Isabella and her husband! Perhaps to make the arrangements for those alliances which he coveted? Philip would have the backing of his father, Maximilian, and if they could come to some agreement it might mean that he would have his bride in England soon. Maximilian's daughter, a beautiful young woman, though twice widowed. . . . They could get children. He was very eager to have a bride for himself and those alliances for his family. Charles, the heir of the

Hapsburgs and of Isabella and Ferdinand, would be the richest monarch in Europe when he came of age. Little Mary was the bride for him. And Eleanor, the daughter of Philip and Juana, would do very well for young Henry. All this could be arranged if he met Philip and Juana.

They would want something in exchange—promises of help, doubtless, against Ferdinand, because there would certainly be trouble in Castile between Ferdinand and Philip. It was easy to make promises.

A meeting was desirable, but it would be expensive; a King could not travel abroad in modesty; that gave an impression of poverty and would not be wise. He did not like travel; he was getting too old, and his limbs were often so stiff when he arose in the mornings that he could scarcely put his feet to the ground. Yet those alliances were what his family needed.

Puebla was announced, and the ambassador, when he entered and stood before the King, was clearly distraught.

"You look disturbed," said Henry.

Puebla, feeling the situation to be too dangerous for subterfuge, explained in detail how Doña Elvira had used Katharine to suggest this meeting.

"Well, are the means so important?"

"Your Grace, the Spanish situation is fluid . . . very fluid. There is so much treachery involved in this that it is difficult to know who is one's friend, who one's foe. There are the two rival factions in Brussels. How can you know who it is who have arranged this meeting? Is it your friends? Is it your enemies? A King is vulnerable when he leaves his own shores. Philip is as wayward as thistledown. He will sway this way and that. He does not keep his promises if the whim takes him to break them. You would be ill advised to take this suggestion of a meeting seriously."

The King was thoughtful. There was spying and counter-spying in all countries, he knew, but the Spanish situation at this time was certainly dangerous.

He knew Philip for a pleasure-loving young man whose political ambitions waxed and waned. Ferdinand he looked upon as a rogue, but at least he and Ferdinand were of a kind.

"I will consider this matter," he said, and Puebla's spirits rose.

He did not believe that Henry would make that journey. Clearly he was dreading it. Crossing the Channel could be hazardous, and if he suffered even a slight wetting he could be sure that his rheumatism would be the worse for it.

Henry was thinking that this meeting, plotted by women, was perhaps not the wisest course at this time. What if Philip had no wish to see him? What if it should turn out to be a reunion of Katharine and her sister merely? He shuddered to think of the expense that would be involved, the money wasted.

"I will ponder on this," he said.

\*      \*      \*

At the window of her apartments at Durham House Katharine sat for a long time looking out. Puebla had gone to Richmond and would now be with the King.

Katharine was deeply shocked. She could not free her mind of the memory of her mother's face. Isabella had been at her happiest when she had her family about her. Katharine could remember those occasions when the family sat with her, the girls at their needlework, Juan reading to them; then perhaps Ferdinand would join them, and her mother's face would take on that look of serene contentment she loved to recall.

Now they were scattered. Her brother Juan and sister Isabella were dead, Maria was the Queen of Portugal, Juana the wife of Philip and she herself in England; and here in England she had become involved in a plot against her father.

Her horror gave place to anger. She forgot that her father had never loved her in the same tender way in which her mother had; she forgot how pleased he had been to send her to England. She thought of him only as the father who had joined their family group and added to her mother's happiness. Ferdinand was her father. Her mother would always have her remember that. There had been times when Isabella deferred to Ferdinand; that was when she was reminding them all that he was their father. At such times she forgot that she was the Queen of Castile and he merely the King of Aragon. Where the family was concerned he, Ferdinand, was the head.

And Doña Elvira had tricked her into working against her own father!

Katharine stood up. She could not see her reflection or she would have noticed that a change had come over her. She held her head higher, and her shabby gown could not hide the fact that she was a Princess in her own household. She had ceased to be the neglected widow; she was the daughter of Isabella of Castile.

She called to one of her maids and said: "Tell Doña Elvira that I wish to see her without delay."

Her tone was peremptory and the girl looked at her in astonishment; but Katharine was unaware of the glance. She was thinking of what she was going to say to Doña Elvira.

Elvira came in, gave the rather curt little bow which was her custom, and then, as she looked into the Infanta's face, she saw the change there.

"I sent for you," said Katharine, "to tell you that I understand full well why you persuaded me to write to my sister."

"Why, Highness, I knew you wished to see your sister, and it seemed shameful that you should live here as you do . . ."

"Pray be silent," said Katharine coldly. "I know that your brother, Don Juan Manuel, plots against my father in Brussels and has persuaded you to help him here in Durham House."

"Highness . . ."

"Pray do not interrupt me. You forget to whom you speak."

Elvira gasped in amazement. Never before had Katharine spoken to her in that manner. She knew that Puebla had betrayed her to Katharine, but she had been confident that she could continue to rule Durham House.

"I do not wish," said Katharine, "to have here with me in England servants whom I do not trust."

"What are you saying . . . ?" Elvira began in the old hectoring manner.

"That I am dismissing you."

"You . . . dismissing me! Highness, your mother appointed me."

It was a mistake. Elvira realized it as soon as she had mentioned Isabella. Katharine's face was a shade paler, but her eyes flashed in a new anger.

"Had my mother known that you would plot against my father, you would have spent these last years behind prison walls. It is where you should be. But I will be lenient. You will prepare to leave Durham House and England at once."

"This is quite impossible."

"It shall be possible. I will not send you back to my father with an explanation of your conduct. I will spare you that. But since you are so eager to help your brother in Brussels you may go there."

Elvira tried to summon all the old truculence, but it had deserted her.

"You may go now," continued Katharine. "Make your preparations with all speed, for I will not suffer you for a day longer than I need under this roof."

Elvira knew that protest was useless. If she attempted to assert her authority, Katharine would expose the part she had been playing in her brother's schemes.

It was hard for a proud woman to accept such defeat.

She bowed and, without another word, left the presence of the Infanta.

Katharine was shaken, but she felt exultant.

For so long she had been, not so much the prisoner of Durham House, as the prisoner of Doña Elvira. Now she was free.

# JUANA IN ENGLAND

**K**ATHARINE HAD BEGUN to wonder whom she could trust, for when her anger against Doña Elvira had subsided she realized how shocked she had been by the duenna's duplicity.

Maria de Rojas was steeped in melancholy. Yet another marriage which had been planned for her was not to take place because Iñigo had departed with his mother.

It was true that the household was free of the tyranny of Doña Elvira, but poverty remained.

Katharine summoned Puebla to her, and he came limping into her presence. He was growing old and shocks such as that which he had sustained seemed to add years to his age in a few weeks.

In her newly found independence Katharine spoke boldly.

"This situation cannot go on. I must have some means of supporting my household. I am the daughter-in-law of the King of England and I think that you, as my father's ambassador, should bestir yourself and do something about it."

Puebla spread his hands helplessly.

"You should go to the King," went on Katharine, "and speak boldly to him. Tell him that it is a disgrace to his name that he allows me to live in this way."

"I will do my best, Highness," answered Puebla.

He shuffled out of the apartment, not relishing his task and yet agreeing with Katharine that she could not continue in such penury for much longer.

He sought audience with the King.

Henry was still brooding on the suggested meeting with Philip and Juana. Perhaps in the spring or the summer . ... he had been thinking, for the prospect of the damp seeping into his bones alarmed him. It would be disastrous if he became completely crippled. It seemed so ridiculous that he could not get himself a bride. Yet it was not easy for Kings to find suitable partners. So many qualifications were necessary in a Queen.

He frowned at Puebla as he came in, but he listened quietly while the ambassador laid before him Katharine's complaint.

Henry nodded gravely. "It is true," he said, "that Durham House must be an expensive household to manage. I am sorry for the Infanta. I will help her."

Puebla's face lighted up with pleasure.

"She shall give up Durham House," went on Henry, "and come to Court. I am sure, when she no longer has such a large establishment to support, she will live more comfortably."

Puebla thanked the King, but he was dubious as he went back to Durham House, being unsure how Katharine would receive this news. He knew that with an adequate allowance and without Doña Elvira life at Durham House might be quite pleasant; and it was this allowance for which Katharine had hoped; but if she went to Court she would be under supervision as strict as that of Doña Elvira.

He was right. Katharine was far from pleased.

She looked at the shabby little man and was filled with disgust. This man . . . an ambassador from that country which she had always been taught was the greatest in the world! How could she hope to be treated with respect, how could she possibly retain her dignity when her father's representative in England was this little *marrano*!

She spoke coldly to him. "I see that my position has changed very little for the better. Sometimes I wonder whether you work more for the King of England than for the King of Spain."

Puebla was deeply wounded. How could she understand the intricacies of state policies? How could she realize the dangerous and difficult game he must continually play?

It seemed to be his fate in life to be misunderstood, to be scorned by those to whom he gave his services.

Katharine was thinking as he left her: Was Doña Elvira really spying for her brother, or did Puebla, with diabolical cunning, contrive the whole situation in order to have Elvira removed? Was the King of England behind the scheme? Did he wish to close Durham House, to bring her to Court where many might gloat over her poverty and the indignity of her position? Whom could one trust?

\*     \*     \*

There was news from Spain which shocked Katharine.

Her father was proposing to marry again.

Katharine was so disturbed that she shut herself in her apartments and told her maids of honour that she must be left alone. Kings remarried speedily when they lost their Queens; she knew that. It was a continual need of Kings to get heirs. But this seemed different. There would be someone to take the place of Isabella of Castile, and in Katharine's eyes this was sacrilege.

Moreover her father proposed to marry a young girl of eighteen. She was very beautiful, rumour said; and that hurt Katharine even more. She thought of her father, showering caresses on a beautiful young girl, and she pictured her mother, looking down from Heaven in sorrow.

Nonsense! she admonished herself. It is a political marriage.

It was true that Ferdinand was anxious to make an alliance with the French King, Louis XII. The situation had changed. The French had been driven from Naples, for a too easy success had made them careless; and Ferdinand had Gonsalvo Cordova, the Great Captain, to fight for him.

In the circumstances, Louis was delighted to see the trouble between Ferdinand and his son-in-law Philip. Philip or his son Charles was going to be the most powerful man in Europe. There would be Maximilian's dominions to come to him, including Austria, Flanders and Burgundy; but that was not all; for from Juana would come the united crowns of Spain, and in addition all the overseas dependencies.

To Louis alliance with Ferdinand seemed advisable, even though Louis' daughter had been promised to young Charles.

Louis laid down his conditions. He would relinquish his claim to Naples, which he would give to the young bride as her dowry. Germaine de Foix was the daughter of Jean de Foix, Viscount of Narbonne; this viscount's mother had been Leonora, Queen of Navarre, half sister to Ferdinand, and she had poisoned her sister Blanche to win the Crown of Navarre. The Viscount had married one of the sisters of Louis XII, so Germaine was therefore not only related to Louis but to Ferdinand.

Ferdinand also agreed to pay Louis a million gold ducats during the course of the following ten years to compensate Louis for what he had lost in the Naples campaign.

This was the news which came to Katharine and which seemed to her such an insult to her mother. It was not merely that her father had taken a young wife in her mother's place, but, as she realized, this marriage could result in destroying that policy for which Isabella had worked during the whole of her reign: the unity of Spain. It had been Isabella's delight that when she married Ferdinand she united Castile and Aragon; and when together they drove the Moors from the kingdom of Granada they had made a united Spain. But if this new marriage were fruitful, if Germaine bore Ferdinand a son, that son would be the heir of Aragon, while Juana and her heirs—and she already had sons— would be rulers of Castile. Thus by his selfish action—perhaps to have a beautiful young wife, but more likely to grasp the somewhat empty title of King of Naples—Ferdinand was showing his indifference to the lifelong wishes of Isabella.

This treaty between Ferdinand and Louis had already been signed in Blois.

Katharine, no longer a child, no longer ignorant of state politics and the overwhelming greed and pride of ambitious men and women, wept afresh for her mother.

\*　　\*　　\*

It was bleak January and there were storms all along the coast; the wind swept up the Thames and not even the great fires which blazed in Windsor Castle could keep out the cold. Katharine sat huddled about the fire with some of her maids of honour. They were very gloomy and rarely ceased talking of their desire to return to Spain.

Francesca de Carceres, who was impulsive and never could control her tongue, blamed the various members of Katharine's household in turn. First she blamed Puebla, then Juan de Cuero. They were all in league with the King of England, she declared, and their desire was to keep them all in this island until they grew crippled with rheumatism.

Maria de Rojas was sunk in gloom. As she had mourned for her Englishman, now she mourned for Iñigo Manrique

Katharine was dipping into her store of plate and jewels, and often wondered what would happen when the time came for the remainder of them to be valued.

There was no news from Spain. Ferdinand rarely had time to write to his daughter. He was too busy, she supposed bitterly, thinking of his new marriage which would shortly take place.

As they sat thus they heard the clatter of horses' hoofs and shouts from without, and Francesca ran to the window.

"There is some excitement below," she said. "It is evidently important news."

"News from home?" asked Katharine quickly.

"No," answered Francesca, as the others came to the window to stand beside her. "That is no Spanish courier."

Katharine who had risen sat down listlessly.

"There is never news from Spain . . . never news that one wishes to hear."

The other girls turned from the window, and Maria de Salinas said: "It must change soon. It cannot go on like this. Perhaps when there is a new King . . ."

"He will marry Her Highness," cried Francesca.

Katharine shook her head. "No, he is promised to Marguerite of Angoulême."

"Oh, he has been promised to so many," Francesca said.

"That happens to most of us," put in Maria de Rojas bitterly.

Katharine was silent; she was thinking of the Prince of Wales, whom she saw occasionally. It was a strange position; she did not know whether she was still affianced to him or not. It was true there had been a formal betrothal in the Bishop of Salisbury's house, but ever since then there had been rumours of other brides who had been chosen for him.

He was growing up quickly, for he seemed much older than his years. When they were together she would often find his eyes fixed on her broodingly. It was a little disquieting; it made her wonder what the future would hold for her when the old King died and Henry VIII was King of England.

Someone was at the door, begging to be allowed to see the Infanta, and Inez de Veñegas came bursting unceremoniously into the apartment. She was clearly excited.

"Highness," she stammered. "There is great excitement below. Ships broken by the storm have sought refuge here in England."

Francesca said impatiently: "That's to be expected in such weather."

"But these are the ships of Her Highness the Queen of Castile."

Katharine had risen; she grew pale and then flushed scarlet.

"Juana . . . my sister . . . in England!"

"Highness, she is here . . . seeking refuge from the storm. Her fleet of ships has met with disaster oñ their way from Flanders to Spain. And she and her husband and their suite . . ."

Katharine clasped her hands across her breast; her heart was leaping with excitement.

Juana here . . . in England!

This was the happiest news she had heard for years.

\*     \*     \*

Juana, Queen of Castile, was happy at last. She was on a ship bound for Castile, and her husband was with her; and while they sailed together it was impossible for him to escape her.

She was wildly gay; she would stand on deck, her face held to the wind while it loosened her hair and set it flying about her head. Her attendants looked at her anxiously, then covertly; as for her husband, sometimes he jeered at her, sometimes he was ironically affectionate—so much depended on his mood.

Philip was a man of moods. He changed his plans from day to day, as he changed his mistresses. If he had held a place less prominent in world politics this would have been of less importance; as it was he was becoming noted for his inconsequential ways, and this was dangerous in a son of Maximilian. There was no ruler in Europe who did not view him with disquiet. Yet, he was one of the most powerful men in Europe on account of his position; he knew it. It delighted him. He loved power, whether it was in politics or in his affairs with women.

He came on deck to stand beside his wife.

How mad she looks! he thought, and he was exultant. He would exact complete obedience or he would have her put away. It would be no lie to say: "I must keep her in safe custody. Alas, my wife is a madwoman."

Yet there were times when it was necessary to say: "Oh no, she is not mad. A little impulsive, a little hysterical, but that is not madness."

This was one of the latter occasions, because he was going to claim her Crown of Castile. The people of Spain would never accept the son of Maximilian as their ruler; they would only accept the husband of their Queen Isabella's daughter, Juana, who was now herself Queen of Castile.

Juana turned to look at him, and that soft, yearning look, which sometimes amused, sometimes sickened him, came into her eyes.

How beautiful he is! she thought. The wind had brought a richer colour to his cheeks, which were always rosy; his long golden hair fell to his shoulders; his features were like those of a Greek god; his blue eyes sparkled with health and the joy of living. He was not tall, nor was he short; he was slim and he moved with grace. The title of Philip the Handsome, by which he was known, had not been given out of idle flattery.

"The wind is rising," she said, but her expression said something else, as it always did when he was near her. It implored him to stay with her every hour of the day and night, it betrayed the fact that she was only happy when he was with her.

Philip turned to her suddenly and gripped her wrist. She felt the pain of this, but he was often cruel to her and she welcomed his cruelty. She was happier when he laid his hands on her—no matter how brutally—than when he reserved his affection or anger for others.

"I anticipate trouble with that sly old fox, your father."

She winced. She was, after all, Isabella's daughter, and Isabella had taught her children the importance of filial duty. Even in wild Juana, besotted as she was by her desire for this cruelly wayward husband, the influence of the great Isabella still persisted.

"I doubt not that he will be pleased to see us," she began.

"Pleased? I'll tell you what, my dear wife: He's hoping we shall perish at sea. He's hoping that he can take our son Charles under his guidance and rule Castile and Aragon as the boy's Regent. That's what Ferdinand hopes. And we are in his way."

"It cannot be so. He is my father. He loves me."

Philip laughed. "That's your foolish woman's reasoning. Your father never loved anything but crowns and ducats."

"Philip, when we are in Castile, don't put me away. Let me stay with you."

He put that handsome head on one side and smiled at her sardonically. "That depends on you, my dear. We cannot show a madwoman to the people of Castile."

"Philip, I am not mad. . . . I am not mad . . . not when you're kind to me. If you would only be affectionate to me. If there were no other women . . ."

"Ah," Philip mocked. "You ask too much." Then he began to laugh and laid an arm about her shoulder. Immediately she clung to him, her feverish fingers tearing at his doublet. He looked at her with distaste and, turning from her to stare at the heaving water, he said: "This time, you will obey me. There shall be nothing like that Conchillos affair again, eh?"

Juana began to tremble.

"You have forgotten that little matter?" went on Philip. "You have forgotten that, when your father sought to become Regent of Castile, you were persuaded by that traitor, Conchillos, to sign a letter approving of your father's acts?"

"I did it because you were never with me. You did not care what became of me. You spent all your time with that big Flemish woman . . ."

"So you turned traitor out of jealousy, eh? You said to yourself, I will serve my father, and if that means I am the enemy of my husband, what do I care?"

"But I did care, Philip. If you had asked me I would never have signed it. I would have done everything you asked of me."

"Yet you knew that by signing that letter you went against my wishes. You set yourself on the side of your father against me. You thought you would take a little revenge because I preferred another woman to you. Look at yourself sometimes, my Queen. Think of yourself, and then ask yourself why I should prefer to spend my nights with someone else."

"You are cruel, Philip. You are too cruel. . . ."

He gripped her arm, and again she bore the pain. She thought fleetingly: it will be bruised tomorrow. And she would kiss those bruises because they were the marks made by his fingers. Let him be cruel, but never let him leave her.

"I ask you to remember what happened," said Philip quietly.

"Conchillos was put into a dungeon. What became of him there I do not know. But it was just reward, was it not, my cherished one, for a man who would come between a husband and his wife. As for my little Queen, my perfidious Juana, you know what happened to her. I had her put away. I said: My poor wife is suffering from delusions. She has inherited her madness from her mad grandmother, the old lady of Arevalo. It grieves me that I must shut her away from the world for a while. Remember. You are free again. You may be a sane woman for a while. You may go to Castile and claim your crown. But take care that you do not find yourself once more shut away from the world."

"You use me most brutally, Philip."

"Remember it," he murmured, "and be warned by it."

He turned then and left her, and she looked after him longingly. With what grace he walked! He was like a god come to Earth from some pagan heaven. She wished she could control her desire for him; but she could not; it swamped all her emotions, all her sense. She was ready to jettison pride, dignity, decency—everything that her mother had taught her was the heritage of a Princess of Spain—all these she would cast aside for a brief ecstatic hour of Philip's undivided attention.

\*     \*     \*

There was disaster aboard. A few hours before, when they had sailed into the English Channel, there had been a strange calm on the sea and in the sky which had lasted almost an hour; then suddenly the wind rose, the sky darkened and the storm broke.

Juana left her cabin; the wind pulled at her gown and tore her hair from the headdress. She laughed; she was not afraid. There was no one on board who feared death less than she did.

"We shall die together," she shouted. "He cannot leave me now. I shall be by his side; I shall wrap my arms about him and we shall go to meet Death together . . . together at last."

Two of her women came to her; they believed that a fit of madness was about to take possession of her. It seemed understandable. Everyone on board ship was terrified and fearful that they would never reach Castile.

"Highness," they said, "you should be at your prayers."

She turned to them, her eyes wide and wild. "I have prayed so much," she said quietly, "and my prayers have rarely been answered. I prayed for love. It was denied me. So why should I pray for life?"

The women exchanged glances. There is no doubt, said those looks, the madness is near.

One of them whispered: "Your mother would wish you to pray if she were here."

Juana was silent and they knew that she was thinking of Queen Isabella.

"I must do what she would wish," she murmured as though to herself. Then she shouted: "Come, help me dress. Find my richest gown and put it on me. Then bring me a purse of gold pieces."

"Your richest dress, Highness," stammered one of the women.

"That is what I said. My richest dress and gold which shall be strapped to my body. When I am washed up on some distant shore I would not have them say: 'Here is a woman done to death by the sea' but 'Here is a Queen!' That is what my mother would wish. I will write a note to say that the money is for my burial . . . a Queen's burial. Come, why do you stand there? There may be little time left. We can scarcely hear ourselves speak now. We can scarcely keep upright. My dress . . . the purse . . ."

She was laughing wildly as they went to obey her.

\*          \*          \*

In her ceremonial gown, her purse strapped firmly to her waist, Juana stumbled to her husband's cabin. She scarcely recognized Philip the Handsome in the pale-faced man who shouted orders in a high voice cracked with fear, while his attendants helped him into an inflated leather jacket. Where was the swaggering heir of Maximilian now? The fair hair was in disorder, there were smudges of fatigue under the blue eyes, and the beautiful mouth was petulant and afraid.

"Come," screamed Philip. "Is this thing safe? Fasten it. Do you think we have hours to waste. At any minute . . ."

Even as he spoke there was a sudden cry of "Fire!" and an ominous flickering light rapidly lightened the darkness.

Juana, standing serene now in her rich garments, said in a voice much calmer than usual: "The ship is on fire."

"On fire!" shouted Philip. "Put out the fire. Put out the fire. What will become of us!"

Don Juan Manuel, who was accompanying the royal party to Spain, said quietly: "All that can be done is being done, Highness."

"Where are the rest of the ships? Are they standing by?"

"Highness, we have lost the rest of the ships. The storm has scattered them."

"Then what is to be done? We are doomed."

No one answered, and then Philip turned and looked into the

face of his wife who stood beside him. They seemed in that moment to take measure of each other. She in her rich gown with the purse tied to her waist was calmly awaiting death. Philip, in his inflated leather garment which his attendants swore would keep him afloat in a rough sea, was afraid.

She laughed in his face. "We are together now, Philip," she cried. "You cannot leave me now."

Then she flung herself at his feet and embraced his knees.

"I will cling to you," she went on. "I will cling so closely that Death will not be able to separate us."

Philip did not answer; he remained still, looking down at her; and it seemed to some who watched them that he found comfort in her arms which were about him.

She became tender and astonishingly calm, as though she realized that his fear made it necessary for her to be the strong one now.

"Why, Philip," she said, "whoever heard of a King's being drowned? There was never a King who was drowned."

Philip closed his eyes as though he could not bear to contemplate the signs of impending disaster. His hand touched the leather garment on which the words "The King, Don Philip" had been painted in huge letters. He who had been so vital had never thought of death. He was not yet thirty years of age, and life had given him so much. It was only Juana whose mind often led her into strange paths, only Juana, who had suffered deeply, who could look death in the face with a smile which was not without welcome.

He heard her voice shouting amid the tumult: "I am hungry. Is it not time we ate? Bring me a box with something to eat."

One of the men went off to do her bidding while she remained smiling, her arms about her trembling husband's knees.

*　　　*　　　*

The fire was now under control, thanks to the almost superhuman efforts of the crew. The ship was listing badly, and with the coming of day it was seen that land was close at hand.

Philip cried out in relief, shouting that they must make for dry land with all speed.

Don Juan Manuel was at his side. "This is England," he said. "If we land, we put ourselves in the hands of the Tudor."

"What else could we do?" demanded Philip. "Is the Tudor more to be feared than a grave in the ocean bed?"

Don Juan admitted that until their ship was repaired they would have little hope of reaching Spain.

Philip spread his hands. The sight of land had restored his good spirits, because in his youthful arrogance he believed himself capable of handling the Tudor King; and it was only death that terrified him.

"We'll make for the shore with all speed," he said.

So at last into the shallow harbour of Melcombe Regis came the battered ship carrying Juana and Philip. The people all along the coast as far as Falmouth had seen that a fleet of ships was in distress, and they were unsure as to whether these ships belonged to friends or enemies.

They gathered on the beaches, brandishing bows and arrows and their farming implements; and when Philip and Juana came into Melcombe Regis harbour they found a crowd of uncertain English men and women waiting for them.

The ship's company had gathered on the deck, and for some moments the people ashore believed that the strangers had come to attack them, for their pleas for help were unintelligible.

Then a young man, obviously of the gentry, pushed himself to the front of the crowd on the quay and shouted to the people on deck in French: "Who are you? And why do you come here?"

The answer came: "We are carrying The Archduke and Duchess of Austria, King and Queen of Castile, who were on their way to Spain and have been wrecked on your shores."

That was enough. A stout, red-faced man came to stand beside the young man who had spoken in French.

"Tell them," he said, "that they must accept my hospitality. Let them come ashore and rest awhile in my house while I inform the King's Grace of their arrival."

Thus Philip and Juana landed in England, and while they were given a sample of lavish English hospitality in the manor house of Sir John Trenchard in Melcombe Regis, close by Weymouth, couriers rode to Court to inform the King of the arrival of the royal pair.

\*       \*       \*

How pleasant it was to be on dry land, and how generous was the hospitality bestowed upon the party by Sir John Trenchard and his household.

Juana and Philip were introduced to the comforts of an English manor house. Fires roared in enormous open fireplaces; great joints of meat turned on the kitchen spits and from the kitchens came the smell of baking.

Philip was happy to relax, and so delighted to be on *terra firma* that, for a few days, he was kind to Juana, who was accordingly filled with bliss.

News came that other ships of their fleet had found refuge along the coast as far west as Falmouth. Some were not damaged beyond repair and could in a short time put to sea again.

This was comforting news, for when the storm had abated the weather was mild and the seas so calm that Don Juan Manuel was eager to continue with the journey.

Sir John Trenchard was bluffly indignant when this was suggested.

Nay, he declared. He'd not allow it. He would not be denied the honour of offering a little more entertainment to his distinguished guests. Why, his King would never forgive him if he let them go. It would seem churlish.

Don Juan Manuel understood.

"He is waiting for instructions from Henry," he told Philip. "I doubt that the King of England will allow you to go until there has been a meeting."

"I see no reason why there should not be a meeting," retorted Philip. "Although if I wished to go, nothing would deter me."

"The King of England might. Who knows, there might be an army approaching now to detain you."

"Why should he do that?"

"Because you are in his country, and here he is all-powerful. It would be easier if you stayed here awhile as a guest rather than as a prisoner."

"I should like to see my sister Catalina," said Juana. "How strange that a little while ago she wanted to arrange a meeting. Now the storm may have done that for us."

Philip studied his wife. She was in one of her sane periods at this time. The ordeal at sea had calmed her while it had distressed others. None would guess now that the seed of madness lurked in her.

"Then," said Philip, "we must perforce enjoy English hospitality a little longer. And I have no fears of a meeting with the King of England. Indeed there is much I would like to discuss with him."

Juan Manuel lowered his eyes. There were times when he was afraid of and for his reckless master.

Philip was aware of Juan Manuel's apprehension, and it amused him. He was going to make all his servants understand that he and he alone would make decisions as to policy. Seeing Juana quite normal now, Queen of Castile, Philip made up his mind that when he met Henry he would do so in his own right.

He would meet him as the Archduke Philip, heir to Maximilian, not as the consort of the Queen of Castile, although of course it was Castile he wished to discuss with Henry. He was going to attempt to win Henry's support against Ferdinand; and as Juana, in her sudden return to sanity, might remember that Ferdinand was her father, it would be well for him to go on ahead of Juana to meet the King of England.

\*     \*     \*

News from Henry came quickly to Melcombe Regis. He would not allow his guests to leave England until they had talked together. He was delighted to have such august visitors, and he was sending an escort to bring them to Windsor, where he and the Prince of Wales would be waiting to receive them.

Philip was delighted when he saw the magnificence of the cavalcade which had been sent to take him to Windsor, but Don Juan Manuel and his more sober advisers were apprehensive. They knew that it was useless to caution their headstrong master. To do so might make him more reckless than ever.

Juana came to her husband as he stood by a window looking out on the brilliantly caparisoned horses which were waiting below.

"And they say," cried Philip, "that Henry is a mean man."

"He has certainly treated my sister with great meanness," replied Juana.

Philip looked pleased. The King of England was mean to the daughter of Ferdinand but eager to shower honours on the son of Maximilian.

Then he remembered that part of this show was for another of Ferdinand's daughters, and that this was his wife, the Queen of Castile.

"I look forward to the journey," went on Juana. "It will be pleasant to see this country which is now Catalina's. And what joy to see her at the end of the journey! My poor Catalina, her letters were often sad."

"Juana," said Philip, "I am most solicitous for your comfort."

A smile of happiness touched her lips and she gazed at him ardently. "Oh Philip," she murmured, "you need have no fear for me. I only have to be with you to be happy."

He gently unlaced her clinging fingers which were on his arm.

"I must travel with all speed to Windsor," he said. "You shall follow at a slower pace."

"You mean . . . you will go without me!" Her voice was shrill.

"I would not submit you to the hazards of rapid travel. You shall come slowly and with dignity."

"Why, why?" she screamed. "I have faced the dangers of the sea with you. What hazards would there be on the road? You shall not be rid of me. I know full well why you seek to escape me. There is that woman . . ."

"Be silent," he said sharply. "You weary me with your eternal jealousies."

"Then remove the cause of my jealousy."

"I should die of boredom, which I believe would be more tiresome than death by drowning."

"You are so cruel," she complained pathetically.

"You will do as I say," he told her.

"Why should I? Am I not the Queen? But for me, Castile would never be for you."

"So you boast once more of the titles you have brought me. Have I not paid dearly for them? Do I not have to endure you also?"

"Philip, I shall come with you."

"You will do as I say. Do you want me to have you put away again?"

"You cannot do it."

"Can I not? I did it before. Why should I not do it again? All know that you are mad. You make no secret of the fact. You shall say a wifely farewell to me and I will go on ahead of you. You will be calm and follow me. You will travel the same road, but some days after me. Is that such hardship?"

"It is always hardship not to be with you."

He took her cheek between his fingers and pinched hard.

He said: "If you do as I say, I will promise to be a loving husband to you this night."

"Philip . . ." She could not quench the longing in her voice.

"Only if," he went on, "you promise to say a nice, pleasant, calm farewell to me on the morrow."

"It is bribery," she said. "It is not the first time. You give me as a concession that which is mine by right, and always you demand a price for it."

He laughed at her. He was so sure of his power over her. He would spend his last night at Melcombe Regis with her, and in the morning he would leave her behind while he rode on to Windsor to meet the King of England.

\*          \*          \*

F

Windsor looked pleasant to Katharine that winter's day. She was pleased now that she had left Durham House and was at Court. It would be wonderful to see Juana again, to whisper confidences, to recall the old days and perhaps to explain the difficulties of her position here in England.

With her maids of honour ranged about her she was at the window, waiting for the first signs of the cavalcade.

"I wonder if I shall recognize her," murmured Katharine. "She will have changed since I saw her, doubtless."

"It is long since she went to Flanders," Maria de Salinas reminded her.

Katharine thought of that day, nearly ten years ago, when Juana had set out for Flanders. She remembered the sadness of her mother who had accompanied Juana to Laredo, and how Isabella had returned to find that her own mother—so like Juana in her wildness—was dying in the Castle of Arevalo.

It was all so long ago. What resemblance would Juana, Queen of Castile, bear to that high-spirited, wayward girl who had gone into Flanders to marry Philip the Handsome?

She looked at her maids of honour, but their expressions were blank and she knew that they were thinking of the wild stories they had heard of her sister—how she had bound one of her husband's mistresses and cut off her long golden hair, how she had thought herself to be a prisoner at Medina del Campo and had escaped from her apartments and refused to return, spending the bitterly cold night out of doors in her night attire. Uneasy rumours of Juana's conduct continued to come from Flanders.

When I see her, thought Katharine, she will talk to me of her life; I shall be able to comfort her as she will comfort me.

So there she waited, and when the fanfares of trumpets heralded the arrival of the cavalcade, and the King and the Prince of Wales went down to the courtyard to receive the guests, Katharine saw the fair and handsome Philip, but she looked in vain for her sister.

She stood at her window watching the greetings between the royal parties. Surely Juana must be there. She was in England with Philip. Why was she not with him now?

Soon she herself would be expected to descend and greet the guests of the King; but she must wait until summoned; she must remember that there were many at the Court of greater importance than she was.

She gazed at her brother-in-law. He was indeed a handsome man. How haughty he looked, determined to stand as the equal of the King of England; and as he greeted him, by very comparison Henry VII of England seemed more aged and infirm than usual.

But there was the Prince of Wales—already taller than Philip himself—the golden Prince, even more arrogant than Philip, even more certain of his right to the centre of the stage.

Katharine could never look upon the Prince of Wales unmoved, and even at such a time as this she temporarily forgot Juana, because she must wonder whether or not that disturbing boy would eventually be her husband.

She heard her maids of honour whispering together.

"But how strange this is! What can have happened to the Queen of Castile?"

\*          \*          \*

Those were uneasy days at Windsor for Philip's followers—not so for Philip; he was determined to enjoy the lavish hospitality. It was a pleasure to show his skill at hunting and hawking in the forests of Windsor; he liked to ride through the straggling street which was the town of Windsor, and to see the women at their windows, or pausing in the street, as he passed, all with those looks and smiles which he was accustomed to receive from women everywhere. He liked to sit in the great dining hall on the King's right hand and sample the various English dishes, to listen to the minstrels, to watch the baiting of bears, horses and mastiffs.

He did not know that the King of England only entertained on such a lavish scale when he hoped to profit from doing so.

Glorious days these were, and Philip was in no hurry to leave for Spain. He had met his sister-in-law, poor little Katharine, who seemed to be somewhat ill-used by this wily old Tudor. The girl was dull, he thought; too melancholy, lacking in the gaiety which he liked to find in women. She was shabby compared with the other Court ladies; he had little interest in her.

On the rare occasions when they met she persistently questioned him about Juana. Why was Juana not with him? Why did they not travel together?

"Ah," he had replied, "I came with all speed on the King's express desire. I did not wish to subject Juana to such a tiring journey."

"Would she not have preferred to travel with you?"

"I have to be firm with her. I have to consider her health."

Katharine did not trust him, and more than ever she longed to see her sister.

Meanwhile the King was making headway with Philip.

There was, sheltering in Burgundy under the protection of

Maximilian, a cousin of that Earl of Warwick whom Henry had
executed because of his claim to the throne; this cousin was
Edmund de la Pole who called himself Duke of Suffolk; and,
while such a man lived, Henry could not feel entirely secure. His
great aim was to eliminate all those who laid claim to the throne
and, with Edmund de la Pole skulking on the Continent, he could
never be sure when the man might land in England and seek to
take the Crown from him. He remembered his own days of exile
and how he had lain in wait for the opportune moment to rise
and snatch the throne for himself.

He was subtle in his dealing with Philip, and Philip had not
learned subtlety. It was gratifying to the King of England that
he had such an arrogant young man to deal with, for this made
the way so much easier than if it had been necessary to bargain
with Philip's wiser ministers.

He knew what Philip wanted from him: help against Ferdinand.
Well, reasoned the King of England, that sly old fox Ferdinand
was ever an enemy of mine.

Henry was finding Philip's visit stimulating, and he was enjoying it as much as his rheumatism would allow him to enjoy anything.

Henry was eager that there should be a commercial treaty with
Flanders and this he obtained—making sure that it should be very
advantageous to England.

It was not so easy to bring about the expulsion of Edmund de la
Pole, but slyly and subtly Henry reminded Philip that he was held
a prisoner in England—by the weather. But Philip knew that
there was a veiled threat in the words; and even he did not see
how they could leave England if Henry did not wish them to
do so.

So de la Pole was thrown to the King, and Henry blessed that
storm which had cast this incautious young man upon his shores.

"This is indeed a happy day," he cried. "See, we have come to
two agreements already. We have a commercial treaty between
our two countries, and you have agreed to give me the traitor,
de la Pole. It was a happy day when you came to visit us."

Happy for England, thought Juan Manuel; and he was already
wondering how soon the fleet of ships, which were now assembling
at Weymouth, could be ready to put to sea. He hoped it would be
before the rash Philip had made more concessions to his wily host.

"Let us make even happier arrangements," went on the King
of England. "It is the maxim of your House that it is better to wed
than to war. If you will give me your sister Margaret I shall be
a happy man."

"There is none to whom I would rather give her," answered Philip.

"And the Emperor?"

"My father and I are of one mind in this matter."

"A speedy marriage would please me greatly."

"A speedy marriage there shall be," answered Philip. He did not mention that his sister had loudly protested against a match with the old King of England and that, since she had been twice married and twice widowed and was now Duchess of Savoy, she could not be forced against her will into a marriage which was unattractive to her.

But Philip would say nothing of this. How could he, to a man who might be his host but was also to some extent his jailer?

To discuss the marriage of the King's daughter Mary to Charles was a pleasant enough occupation. That marriage, if it ever took place, would occur far in the future when Philip would be miles away from England. The Prince of Wales' marriage to Philip's daughter Eleanor would not, if it ever came about, be so far distant. It was very pleasant to discuss it, although Henry was on dangerous ground, thought Philip, when he talked of marrying to Juana's daughter a son who had already been promised to her sister.

Well, Juana had no say in these matters.

*       *       *

Katharine in her apartments in the Castle was being prepared by her ladies for the entertainment in the great hall.

They were sighing, all of them, because they had no new gowns, and even the one Katharine must wear had been mended.

"How shall we look?" wailed Francesca. "The Archduke will be ashamed of us."

"Perhaps he will be sorry for us," put in Maria de Salinas.

"I do not think he would ever be sorry for anyone," Maria de Rojas countered.

Katharine listened to their chatter. Poor Juana, she thought. How strange that you are not here with us!

She watched them putting the jewels in her hair.

"This brooch will cover the thin part of the bodice," said Maria de Salinas.

It was incongruous to have a great ruby covering a threadbare bodice. But then, thought Katharine, my whole life has been incongruous since I came to England.

"I wonder if the Prince of Wales will dance," said Francesca, "and with whom."

Katharine felt their eyes upon her and she tried not to show her embarrassment; the strangest part of all was not to know whether she was seriously affianced to the Prince of Wales. He would soon be fifteen and it was on his fifteenth birthday that they were to have been married.

If that day comes and goes, and I am still a widow, Katharine pondered, I shall know that Henry is not intended for me.

The Princess Mary came into the apartment, carrying her lute, at which she had become very skilful.

"I hope," she said, "that I shall be able to play to the company tonight."

How eagerly they sought the attention of the crowd, these Tudors, mused Katharine.

Mary was a beautiful girl, now about ten years old, wilful, wayward but so fascinating that even the King's face softened when he looked at her; and, when he was irritable with her, all knew that his rheumatism must be particularly painful.

"They will surely ask you to do so," Katharine assured her.

"I hope I may play while Henry dances. I should like that."

"Doubtless you will if you ask that you may."

"I shall ask," said Mary. "Did you know that we are to return to Richmond on the eleventh?"

"Indeed no. I had not heard."

"You are to return with me. It is my father's order."

Katharine felt numb with disappointment. Each day she had waited for the arrival of Juana. It was now the eighth of the month, and if she left on the eleventh she had only three more days in which to wait for her sister—and even if she came now they would have only a short time together.

She said nothing. It was no use protesting. At least she had learned the folly of that.

Oh, let her come soon, she prayed. Then she began to wonder why Juana was not with them and what mystery this was surrounding her sister who was Queen of Castile and yet was lacking in authority. Why, Juana had taken the place of their mother, and none would have dared dictate to Isabella what she must do—not even Ferdinand.

In the great hall that day there was feasting, and Katharine danced the Spanish dances with some of her women. The women enjoyed it; and Francesca in particular was very gay. After this, thought Katharine, they will long more than ever to return to Spain.

Mary played the lute while her father watched her fondly, and Prince Henry danced vigorously to loud applause. When he returned to his seat his eyes were on Katharine. Was she applauding as loudly as the rest?

He seemed satisfied; and Katharine noticed throughout the evening that his eyes were often fixed upon her, brooding, speculating.

She wondered what he was thinking; but she soon forgot to wonder. Her thoughts continually strayed to Juana and she was asking herself: What is this mystery in my sister's life? Is she deliberately being kept from me?

*    *    *

On the tenth of February, one day before that on which, at the King's command, Katharine was due to leave with the Princess Mary, Juana arrived at Windsor.

She was carried into the castle in her litter, and Katharine was among those who waited to receive her.

Katharine looked in dismay at the woman her sister had become. Could that be young Juana, the gay—too gay—girl who had left Spain to marry this man who now obsessed her? Her hair was lustreless, her great eyes were melancholy; it seemed that all that vitality which had been so much a part of her had disappeared.

She was received with ceremony. First the King took her hand and kissed it; then the Prince of Wales bowed low in greeting.

"We have missed you at our revels," said Henry.

Juana could not understand, but she smiled graciously.

Then Katharine was face to face with her sister. She knelt before her not forgetting, even at such a moment, that she was in the presence of the Queen of Castile.

Then the sisters looked into each other's faces and both were astonished at what they saw. Juana's little sister had become a tragic woman, no less than she had herself.

"Juana . . . oh, how happy I am to see you at last!" whispered Katharine.

"My sister! Why, you are no longer a child."

"I am a widow now, Juana."

"My poor, sweet sister!"

That was all. There were others to be greeted; there were the formalities to be considered; but even while these were in progress Katharine noticed how hungrily her sister's eyes followed the debonair figure of her husband, and she thought: What torture it must be to love a man as Juana loves him!

How brief was the time they could spend together. Had it been arranged, Katharine wondered, that her sister should arrive the day before she was to leave for Richmond, so that they might have a glimpse of each other and nothing more?

Yet at last when they were alone together Katharine was conscious of the rapid passing of time. She wanted to hold it back. There was so much to say, so many questions to ask that she, in fear of not having time to say half, was temporarily unable to think of any of them.

Juana was not helpful; she sat silent as though she were far away from the Castle at Windsor.

"Juana," cried Katharine desperately, "you are unhappy. Why, my sister? Your husband is in good health and you love him dearly. You are Queen of Castile. Are you unhappy, Juana, because you can only be Queen of Castile since our mother is no more?"

"He loves me," said Juana in a low melancholy voice, "because I am Queen of Castile." Then she laughed, and Katharine was filled with uneasiness by the sound of that laughter. "If I were not Queen of Castile he would throw me out into the streets to beg my bread tomorrow."

"Oh, Juana, surely he is not such a monster."

She smiled. "Oh yes, he is a monster . . . the handsomest, finest monster that the world ever knew."

"You love him dearly, Juana."

"He is my life. Without him I should be dead. There is nothing in the world for me . . . except him."

"Juana, our mother would not have you say such things, or think such thoughts. You are the Queen even as she was. She would expect you to love Castile, to work for Castile, as she did. She loved us dearly; she loved our father; but Castile came first."

"So it would be with Philip. He will love Castile."

"He is not master in Castile. Even our father was not that. You know how our mother always ruled, never forgetting for one moment that she was the Queen."

"It is the women," sighed Juana. "How I hate women. And in particular golden-haired women . . . big-breasted, big-hipped. That is the Flanders women, Catalina. How I loathe them! I could tear them all apart. I would throw them to the soldiers . . . the lowest of the soldiers . . . and say: They are the true enemies of the Queen of Castile."

"Our father was not always faithful to our mother. It grieved her, I know. But she did not let it interfere with the affection she bore him."

"Our mother! What did she know of love?"

"She knew much of love. Do you not remember her care for

us? I verily believe that, when we left her, she suffered even more than we did."

"Love!" cried Juana. "What do you know of love? I mean love like this which I have for him. There is nothing like it, I tell you." Juana had stood up; she began beating her hands against her stiffly embroidered bodice. "You cannot understand, Catalina. You have never known it. You have never known Philip."

"But why are you so unhappy?"

"Do you not know? I thought the whole world knew. Because of those others. They are always there. How many women have shared his bed since he came to England? Do you know? Of course you do not. Even he will have forgotten."

"Juana, you distress yourself."

"I am in continual distress . . . except when he is with me. He says he does his duty. I am often pregnant. I am happiest when I am not, because he always remembers that I should become so."

Katharine covered her face with her hands. "Oh, Juana, please do not talk so."

"How else should I talk? He went on in advance of me. Can you guess why? Because there were women with whom he wished to amuse himself. I tell you, I hate women . . . I hate . . . hate . . . hate women."

Juana had begun to rock herself to and fro, and Katharine was afraid her shouts would be heard in those apartments of the Castle near her own.

She tried to soothe her sister; she put her arms about her, and Juana immediately clung to her, rocking Katharine with her.

"Why, Juana," whispered Katharine, "you are distraught. Would you like to lie on your bed? I would sit beside it and talk to you."

Juana was silent for a while, and then she cried out: "Yes. Let it be so."

Katharine took her sister's arm and together they went to Juana's bedchamber. Some of her attendants were waiting there, and Katharine knew from their expression that they were prepared for anything to happen.

"The Queen wishes to rest," said Katharine. "You may go. I will look after her."

The women retired, leaving the sisters together, and Katharine realized that Juana's mood had changed once more. Now she had sunk into melancholy silence.

"Come," said Katharine, "lie down. Your journey must have been very tiring."

F*

Still Juana did not answer but allowed herself to be led to the bed and covered with the embroidered coverlet.

Katharine sat by the bed and reached out for the white ringed hand. She held it, but there was no response to her tenderness from the hand which lay listlessly in hers.

"There is so much we have to say to each other," said Katharine. "You shall tell me your troubles and I shall tell you mine. Oh, Juana, now that I have seen you I know how wretched I have been in England. Imagine my position here. I am unwanted. When our mother was alive I longed to return to Spain. Now that she is gone I do not know what I want. I do not understand the King of England. His plans change abruptly, and a marriage is planned one day and forgotten the next. You must see how poor I have become. Look at this dress. . . ."

She stood up and spread her skirt, but Juana was not even looking at her.

She went on: "I suppose my only hope is marriage with the Prince of Wales. If that should take place, at least I should be accorded the dignity due to my rank. But will it ever take place? He is much younger than I and they say he is to marry Marguerite of Angoulême, but the King has arranged something other with your husband."

At the mention of Philip a faint smile touched Juana's lips.

"They say he is the handsomest man in the world, and they do not lie."

"He is indeed handsome, but it would have been better if he had been kind," said Katharine quickly. "While you are here, Juana, cannot you do something to alleviate my poverty? If you would speak to King Henry . . ."

The door opened and Philip himself came into the room. He was laughing and his fair face was slightly flushed.

"Where is my wife?" he cried. "Where is my Queen?"

Katharine was surprised at the change which came over Juana. She had leaped from the bed, all melancholy gone.

"Here I am, Philip. Here I am."

Without ceremony she flung herself into his arms. It nauseated Katharine to see her sister clinging to this man, who stood, his arms limp at his sides, while he looked over Juana's head at Katharine.

"I see," said Philip, "that you have an august visitor."

"It is Catalina . . . only my little sister."

"But I disturb you. And it is so long since you have met. I must leave you together."

"Philip, oh Philip . . . do not go. It is so long since we have been alone together. Philip, stay now . . ."

Katharine stood up. She could bear no more.

"Pray give me leave to retire," she said to her sister.

But Juana was not looking at her; she was breathless with desire and completely unaware of her sister's presence.

Philip smiled at her sardonically; and she saw that he was not displeased. Was he showing her how abject the Queen of Castile could become in her need for the comfort only he could give? Was he telling her that the present King of Castile would be very different from the previous one? Ferdinand had been a strong man, but his wife had been stronger. Juana would never be another Isabella of Castile.

Katharine went swiftly to her own apartments. What will become of her? she asked herself. What will become of us all?

So this was the meeting for which she had longed. There would be no time for more meetings, because she was to leave Windsor for Richmond tomorrow. There were no concessions for Katharine from the King of England, any more than there were for Juana, Queen of Castile, from her cruel careless husband, Philip the Handsome.

She did not even listen to what I was telling her, thought Katharine. She completely forgot my existence, the moment he entered the room.

\*        \*        \*

There was little to do, with the Court at Richmond, but sit and embroider with her maids of honour and listen to their laments for Spain. The Princess Mary was with her often. She would sit at Katharine's feet playing her lute, listening to her comments and being instructed by them, for Katharine herself excelled with the lute. Sometimes they sang together the old songs of Spain, but more often the songs of England. "For," complained Mary, "your songs are sad songs."

"They sound sad," Katharine told her, "because I sing them in a strange land."

Mary scarcely listened; she was too absorbed by her own affairs; but Katharine enjoyed the company of this light-hearted, beautiful child who was the favourite of everyone at Court.

She had seen nothing of the King or the Prince since she had left Windsor; she knew that the fleet of ships which had been in difficulties in the Channel were now being refitted and made ready for the journey to Spain. With the coming of spring they would sail away again.

I shall never see Juana again, thought Katharine. And if I did, what could we have to say to each other?

In April, Philip and Juana embarked at Weymouth and on a calm sea they set out for Spain.

Katharine remembered all the hopes that had come to her when Doña Elvira had first suggested such a meeting. How different the reality had been!

She knew, as she had never known before, that she was alone, and her future lay not with her own people but the English rulers.

# PHILIP AND FERDINAND MEET

NEWS WAS BROUGHT to Ferdinand that his son-in-law had landed at Corunna.

This was disquieting news. Ferdinand knew he had good reason to mistrust Philip and that his son-in-law's intention was to drive him out of Castile, become King himself and reduce Ferdinand to nothing but a petty monarch of Aragon.

This Ferdinand would fight against with all his might.

He was not an old man, he reminded himself. He felt younger than he had for many years. This was doubtless due to the fact that he had acquired a new wife, his beautiful Germaine.

Many eyebrows had been raised when Germaine had arrived at Dueñas, close by Valladolid, for there, thirty-seven years before, he had come in disguise from Aragon for his marriage to Isabella.

There were many people in Castile who looked upon Isabella as a saint, and they were deeply shocked that Ferdinand should consider replacing her; and to do so by a young and beautiful girl seemed double sacrilege; moreover as any fruit of the union might result in the breaking up of Spain into two kingdoms, this was not a popular marriage.

Ferdinand was realizing how much of his popularity he had owed to Isabella. Yet he had lost none of his ambition; and he was ready enough to end his six weeks' honeymoon with the entrancing Germaine in order to go forward and meet Philip, to match his son-in-law's rashness with his own experience and cunning.

There was one man in Spain whom he heartily disliked but who, he knew, was the country's most brilliant statesman. This man was Ximenes, whom, against Ferdinand's advice, Isabella had created Archbishop of Toledo and Primate of Spain. Ferdinand summoned Ximenes to his presence and Ximenes came.

There was a faint contempt in the ascetic face, which Ferdinand guessed meant that the Archbishop was despising the bridegroom. This was a marriage which would seem unholy to Ximenes, and when he received him Ferdinand was conscious of a rising indignation. But he calmed himself. Ferdinand had learned to subdue his hot temper for the sake of policy.

"You have heard the news, Archbishop?" 'he asked when the Archbishop had greeted him in his somewhat superior manner, which Ferdinand thought implied that he, Ximenes, was the ruler.

"I have indeed, Highness."

"Well?"

"It will be necessary to walk carefully. There should be a meeting between you and the Archduke, and it should be a peaceful one."

"Will he agree to this?"

"He will if he is wise."

"He is young, Archbishop. Wisdom and youth rarely go together."

"Wisdom and age mate almost as rarely," replied the Archbishop.

That allusion to the marriage made the hot blood rush to Ferdinand's cheeks. He had often advised Isabella to send the insolent fellow back to his hermit's cell. But he was too useful. He was too clever. And he was ready to devote that usefulness and cleverness to Spain.

"What in your opinion should be done in the matter?" asked Ferdinand shortly.

The Archbishop was silent for a while; then he said: "As husband of the *Reina Proprietaria*, Philip has a stronger claim to the Regency than Your Highness. Yet since you are a ruler of great experience and this is a young man who has had a greater experience of light living than of serious government, it might be that the grandees of Spain would prefer to see you as Regent rather than your son-in-law."

"And you would support my claim?"

"I would consider Your Highness the more likely to do good for Spain, and for that reason I would give you my support."

Ferdinand was relieved. Much depended on the Archbishop. It was fortunate that Philip's reputation for licentious behaviour had travelled ahead of him; it would not serve him well with Ximenes.

"Philip is now in Galicia," said Ferdinand. "It will take a little time for us to meet; and in the meantime, I understand that many of the grandees are flocking to him, to welcome him to Spain."

Ximenes nodded. "I fear the recent marriage has not endeared Your Highness to many of the late Queen's subjects."

"She would not have wished me to remain unmarried."

"One of her most proud achievements was the union of Castile and Aragon under one crown."

Ferdinand's brows were drawn together in a frown and he needed a great deal of restraint not to send this insolent fellow about his own business. But this *was* his business. Ximenes was Primate of Spain and he was not a man to diverge from what he considered his duty, no matter whom he upset by doing it. Such a man would go cheerfully to the stake for his opinions.

One should rejoice in him, thought Ferdinand grudgingly. He seeks no honours for himself. He thinks only of Spain; and because he believes I shall make a better Regent than Philip he will support me.

"There must be a speedy meeting between Your Highness and your son-in-law."

"Should I go cap in hand, across a country which I have ruled, to implore audience of this young man who has no right to be here except for the fact that he is married to my daughter?"

Ximenes was silent for a few seconds; then he said: "I myself could go to him as your emissary. I could arrange this meeting."

Ferdinand studied the gaunt figure of the Archbishop in those magnificent robes of office which he wore carelessly and under protest. It was only an order from the Pope which had made him put on such vestments, and Ferdinand knew that beneath them he would be wearing the hair shirt, and the rough Franciscan robe. Such a man would surely overawe any—even such as Philip the Handsome.

Ferdinand knew he could trust this affair in such hands. He was greatly relieved and it occurred to him in that moment that Isabella had been right when she had insisted on giving this man the high office of Archbishop of Toledo, even though Ferdinand had wanted it for his illegitimate son.

It seemed that, now she was dead, Ferdinand was continually discovering how right Isabella had so often been.

\* \* \*

In the village of Sanabria, on the borders of Leon and Galicia, Ferdinand met Philip. Philip came at the head of a large force of well-armed troops, but Ferdinand brought with him only some two hundred of his courtiers riding mules. On the right hand of Philip rode Juan Manuel, but on the right hand of Ferdinand rode Ximenes.

The meeting was to take place in a church and, when Philip entered, only Juan Manuel accompanied him; and Ximenes was the sole companion of Ferdinand.

Ximenes studied the young man and found that he did not despise him as he had thought he would. Philip was not merely a philanderer and seeker after pleasure. There was ambition there also. The mind of this extraordinarily handsome young man was light, and he had never learned to concentrate on one subject for long. He had been born heir to Maximilian; and consequently all his life he had been petted and pampered. But there was material there, mused Ximenes, which could be moulded by such as himself; once this young man had realized the brief satisfaction which the indulgence of his sensuality could bring him, a ruler of significance might emerge.

As for Ferdinand, he and Ximenes had never been friends. It was the Queen whom Ximenes had served from the time Isabella had brought him from his hermit's hut until her death, when he had occupied the highest position in Spain; and although Ximenes had not—so he assured himself—ever sought such honours, since they were thrust upon him he had done all in his power to deserve them. The welfare of Spain was of the utmost importance to him. He would serve Spain with his life; and now he was ranged on the side of Ferdinand, and his great desire was to prevent civil strife between these two.

He did not like Juan Manuel—a trouble-maker and a self-seeker, decided Ximenes. His presence would hamper the proceedings greatly, for it was clear to Ximenes that Philip relied on the man.

Ximenes turned to Juan Manuel and said: "Their Highnesses wish to speak in private. You and I should leave them for a while. Come."

He took Juan Manuel's arm and with him went from the church.

Juan Manuel was so overcome by the personality of this strange man that he obeyed without question; and when they were outside the church, Ximenes said: "Ah, but there should be someone to guard the door. It would not be well if their Highnesses were interrupted. As a man of the Church I will undertake this task. Return to your army and I will send for you immediately your presence is required."

Juan Manuel hesitated, but when he looked into those deep-set eyes he felt that he was in the presence of a holy man and dared not disobey. So he left Ximenes, who returned to the church, which he entered, thus joining Philip and Ferdinand.

Ferdinand was asking Philip why his daughter had not accompanied her husband to this meeting place, for she was in truth the ruler of Castile; and Philip was explaining that his wife, alas, was not always in her right mind. There were occasions when she was lucid enough, but there were others when it was necessary to put her under restraint.

Ferdinand accepted this. It suited him, no less than Philip, that

Juana should be at times sane and at others insane. Her unbalanced state was a matter which men such as her husband and father would use according to their needs.

It soon became clear that the advantages were all in Philip's hands and he was not going to relinquish them. Juana was Queen of Castile; her son Charles was heir to the crowns both of Castile and Aragon. Therefore as husband of Juana and the father of the heir he had a greater right to govern Castile as Regent.

There was nothing Ferdinand could do about that and Ximenes was aware of this. Ferdinand must sign those documents required of him; he must surrender the entire sovereignty of Castile to Philip and Juana, and all that was left to him were the grand masterships of the military orders and those revenues which Isabella had left to him in her will.

Thus Ferdinand, in the village of Sanabria, lost all that he had so longed to hold. He was merely King of Aragon; and there was a Regent of Castile. It seemed as though the provinces were once more divided and Isabella's dream of a united Spain might be in danger of destruction.

Ximenes agreed that this was the only course. In any case to have refused to accept it would have meant civil war in Spain, and that was unthinkable. The Archbishop therefore decided that it was his duty to attach himself to Philip. He did not trust the young man and he felt a great desire to guide him. Moreover, as Archbishop of Toledo his place was with the ruler of Castile. But he knew how Isabella would have been saddened by this scene in the church; and Ximenes was determined that he would watch the interests of Isabella's husband.

As they came out of the church Ferdinand's expression was enigmatic. Yet he did not look like an ambitious man who has signed away a kingdom.

# THE MYSTERIOUS DEATH OF PHILIP

**P**HILIP WAS TRIUMPHANT. Now he would ride into Valladolid and all should proclaim him as the ruler of Castile. As for Juana, he had determined to shut her away. He had long been wearied by her passion and possessiveness; Ferdinand had surrendered Castile. So why should he hesitate to go forward and take it; and since Juana was an encumbrance, why not rid himself of her by shutting her away as her grandmother had been shut away before her?

Philip usually acted on impulse, and he immediately called together the most influential noblemen of Castile, and when they were assembled he told them how concerned he was regarding his wife's mental state.

"I have pondered this matter deeply, as you may well imagine," he went on, "and it is my considered judgment that the Queen's interests could best be served if she were allowed to live in retirement. My greatest desire is to do what is best for her, and on this account I ask you all to sign a declaration agreeing to her retirement into seclusion."

There was silence among the nobles. They could not forget that the Queen was the daughter of the great Isabella and that this young man's only claim to the crown was through his marriage with Juana and the fact that he was the father of Charles, the boy who would immediately become their King should Juana die.

Was it not possible, they asked themselves, that cunning men might trick them? Could they be sure that Juana was mad?

The Admiral of Castile, who was Ferdinand's cousin, spoke for that faction which was in doubt.

"It would seem that, although the Queen's mind is said to be at times deranged, there are many who declare her to be sane; and we must all remember that she is the true Queen of Castile and heir of Isabella. Before agreeing to such measures I should wish to have an interview with the Queen."

Philip was nonplussed. He had no wish for Juana to come face to face with these men. How could he be sure of what she would say to them? He might threaten Juana or bribe her with offers of his company as he had on other occasions; but Juana was growing suspicious. If she were mad she was not without cunning. She guessed that he was considering putting her away, and that was something against which she would fight with all her strength.

But he dared not refuse to allow the Admiral to see the Queen.

\*      \*      \*

Juana lifted leaden eyes to the Admiral's face. He was regarding her with kindness; he was trying to tell her that he was her cousin; that it grieved him to see Castile ruled by one who was not related to them except by his marriage to her.

"You have recently seen my father?" asked Juana at length.

"Yes, Highness. I said farewell to him but yesterday. That was at Tudela. He is now on his way to Aragon."

"It seems so strange. I did not see him. It is so many years since I have seen him; yet I, his daughter, did not see him."

"That is strange, Highness, and sad."

Her eyes were melancholy.

"So much that is strange would seem to happen to me now," she said sadly. "I should have been so happy to see my father, even though he has a new wife now and I cannot understand how he could have replaced my mother. But I should dearly have liked to see him again. God guard him always."

"Highness, we of Castile wish to see you govern side by side with your husband."

She nodded.

"That is the wish of us all. Our great Queen Isabella appointed you her heir. It was her wish that you should govern Castile with your husband beside you. But, as her daughter, *you* are our Queen."

At the mention of her mother Juana's expression lightened a little.

"It was her wish," she said. "Here in Castile I recall the past so much more readily than I did in Flanders. It was her wish, was it not? And it is true that I am Queen of Castile."

"It is true, Highness," answered the Admiral.

When he left her he went to his friends and gave them his opinion.

"She seemed as lucid as one could wish. We must guard against ambitious men."

\*      \*      \*

The knowledge came to Juana one morning when she awoke after a restless night which she had spent alone.

He wants to be rid of me, she thought. He is planning to put me away.

L

Where had he spent the night? With one of his women doubtless. He had never considered her feelings, and he wanted her out of his sight. It was not because she was in the way of his having other women, but because he wanted her crown. He did not wish to be merely her consort. He wanted to rule alone.

She would not part with her crown. It was the one possession which made her desirable to him.

The dull melancholy had left her eyes. They sparkled with purpose. She would show him now that she was ready to fight, that she was not as stupid as he thought.

He came to her apartments, all smiles.

They were to make a solemn entry into Valladolid, and he dared not go without her. The people were suspicious of him; they wanted to see their Queen. They would not accept his word for her madness, but wanted to judge for themselves.

Ah, Philip, she thought, you may be master of Castile's Queen but you are not yet master of Castile.

He took her hand and kissed it; how gracious he could be, how charming! She yearned to throw herself into his arms, but she was able to restrain herself because she kept thinking of the castle of Arevalo where her grandmother had lived out her clouded days.

Not for me! she wanted to shout. I am Queen of Castile and I will not allow you to put me away.

"Are you ready for the ceremony?" he asked.

"Ready," she countered, "and determined to accompany you."

"I am glad to hear it."

"Are you, Philip? I thought you were hoping that you would go alone."

"But why should you have such an idea?"

She smiled, saying nothing, and the quietness of her smile alarmed him. Could it be that he was losing his hold over her?

"I thought that in your condition . . ."

"But three months' pregnant. That is nothing, Philip."

He could scarcely bear to look at her, he was so dismayed. Now that he wished her to show her madness she was being perfectly restrained. She did not cling to him as he had become accustomed to her doing. She seemed almost aloof. It was that Admiral of Castile who had put notions into her head. He would have to go a little warily where she was concerned.

He put his arms about her and held her against him. "I am concerned for your health," he said, and when he felt her body quiver a triumphant smile curved his lips. The old power was still there. She was fighting a desperate battle to resist it, but he was determined it should be a losing battle.

"Your concern is appreciated," she said, "the more so because it is rare."

"Oh come, Juana, you know how fond I am of you."

"I did not know. Perhaps because your ways of showing it are so strange."

"You have allowed yourself to be jealous . . . unnecessarily."

"That was foolish of me," she said. "Now that I am in Castile I remember so much my mother taught me. I hear that there are two banners. I should like to see them."

"They shall be brought to you," said Philip, hiding his chagrin. This new calmness, this undoubted sanity, was more disturbing than her madness, and he was going to strain every effort to have her put away because, if she persisted like this, he would find himself in a similar position to that endured by Ferdinand in his relationship with Isabella. That was something Philip would never endure.

But for the time he must act cautiously.

The banners were brought and Juana studied them. "But it would seem," she said, "that there are two rulers of Castile. There is only one; that is the Queen."

"Have you forgotten that I am your husband?" demanded Philip hotly.

"In the past *you* have forgotten that more readily than I have. My husband you are indeed; that is why you ride beside me as my consort. But there is only one ruler of Castile."

What could he say? He was surrounded by strong men who would be ready to fly to her support against him. Philip had not believed this situation possible; but when they came to Valladolid, Juana rode as the Queen of Castile, and her companion was not the King but merely her consort.

Mounted on her white jennet, dressed in the sable robes of royalty, Juana delighted the people of Valladolid. They remembered that this was the daughter of their own Isabella; and their cheers were for their Queen.

\*        \*        \*

Philip was dissatisfied. The Cortes had declared its allegiance to Queen Juana and had stated its willingness to accept Philip only as her consort.

Philip fumed with rage.

"The Queen is mad!" he cried. "She is not in the least like her mother. Sometimes I wonder who is the madder—the Queen or the people who insist on making her their ruler."

The Admiral of Castile stood firm.

"I and many others with me will not allow this iniquitous deed to be done," he said. "We shall never stand aside and see our Queen sent into seclusion that others may rule in her stead."

Philip saw that it was no use expecting help from the Castilian nobles; he turned to his own supporters, the chief of whom was Juan Manuel, who saw that with Philip as ruler many rich pickings would fall into his hands. He was continually at Philip's side and he assured him that in good time they would achieve their end, and Juana would be forced into retirement leaving the field clear for Philip.

Philip was lavishly generous to those whom he considered to be his friends, and recklessly he distributed revenues to them which should have gone to the maintenance of the state. Juan Manuel, on whom he relied as on no other, was becoming richer every week; but Juan was rapacious; he had been led to Philip's side because he believed that Ferdinand had denied him the honours due to him, and he could not grasp enough.

He greatly desired the Alcazar of Segovia which was in the charge of the Marquis and Marchioness of Moya—the latter was that Beatriz de Bobadilla who had been Isabella's greatest friend —and Philip, deciding that the Alcazar should be given to Juan Manuel as a reward for his fidelity, sent orders to the Marquis and Marchioness to leave the Alcazar immediately.

The command was delivered into the hands of the intrepid Beatriz de Bobadilla, who retorted that the Alcazar should be handed over to one person only, and that was Isabella's daughter, Queen Juana.

Philip was furious when he heard this and sent troops ahead to take the Alcazar, while he himself prepared to follow them, Juana with him.

Juana's resistance was beginning to break down. The effort of remaining calm had been too much for her. If she could have overcome her passionate need of Philip she could have continued in her calm restraint; but he was always there, always taunting her, understanding how she needed him and enjoying baiting her in this way. He was luring her to display her hysteria before the nobles of Castile who had declared her to be sane. She knew this, but she could not always fight against it. And when he mocked her, she wanted to throw herself into his arms, as she had done on so many previous occasions, and implore him to be a good and faithful husband to her.

"Philip," she said, "why are you so eager to take the Alcazar of Segovia?"

"Because that insolent woman has denied it to us."

"She is a formidable woman. I remember her in my childhood. She would even advise my mother."

"She will see that we will brook none of her insolence."

"Yet she was a good friend. Should you not leave her in peace out of respect to my mother?"

"I leave no one in peace to insult me."

His mouth tightened and the newly realized fear came back to her.

"Why do you want the Alcazar of Segovia?"

He did not answer. "I know," she cried. "It is because you want to make me a prisoner there. Segovia will be for me what Arevalo was to my grandmother. You are going to shut me away . . . away from the world. You are going to make them believe I am mad."

Still he did not answer.

She went on wildly: "I will go no further. I will not be put away. I am not mad. I am the Queen. You wish to take my crown from me, but you shall not."

Philip laid a hand on her jennet's bridle, but she hit him. She heard his low, devilish laugh.

Now she was really alarmed; now she was certain that her premonition was true. He was going to imprison her in Segovia and announce to the world that she was no longer capable of living among ordinary people.

She slid down from her jennet and lay on the ground.

"I will not go a step farther towards Segovia," she announced.

The cavalcade had halted and Philip was delighted. Now there was going to be one of those scenes which surely must convince all who saw it of her madness.

"Mount your jennet," he said quietly. "They will be waiting for you at Segovia."

There seemed to be a grave threat behind his words which terrified her, and she lay writhing on the ground.

Philip leaped from his horse and bent over her with a show of tenderness.

"Juana," he said audibly, "I pray you remount. Do you want everyone to say that you are mad?"

She looked into his eyes and she was afraid of him; and yet she knew that her great fear was not that she would be shut away from the world but that she would be shut away from him.

She rose obediently and mounted her jennet; then she turned away from the party and cried: "I shall not enter Segovia, because I know that you plan to lock me away in the Alcazar there."

Then she galloped ahead of them across country and back

again, refusing to ride towards Segovia or back the way they had come.

Dusk had fallen and night came; and Juana continued to ride back and forth over the country round Segovia, determined not to enter the town.

Philip thought: If ever anyone doubted her madness, can they do so any longer?

Nothing could have pleased him more.

Such conduct in the Queen of Castile could scarcely be called sanity.

\*         \*         \*

Philip's troops had driven Beatriz de Bobadilla from Segovia, and the Alcazar was now in the possession of Juan Manuel.

There was a certain discontent throughout Castile that this foreigner should come among them and take their castles with their revenues and distribute them among his friends. Soon, it was said, all the strongholds of Castile would be in the hands of Philip's followers, and the old Castilian nobility would have no power in the land.

Philip had decided against going into Segovia, as Juana showed such fear of the place, and had gone instead to Burgos where he, Juana and their party lodged at the palace of the Constable of Castile, who belonged to the Enriquez family and was related to Ferdinand.

In view of Juana's strange conduct on the way to Segovia Philip felt justified in putting guards outside her apartments, so that she was to some extent under supervision.

The Constable's wife, who was the hostess to the party, expressed her concern that the Queen should be treated so, and as a result Philip ordered her to leave the palace.

This seemed the utmost arrogance, and the whisperings against the Queen's consort intensified; but Philip cared little for this and laughed with Juan Manuel at the Castilians. He had the troops and they would enforce his wishes. He did not doubt that before long he would have Juana put right away finally and he himself would be accepted as ruler in very truth.

"In the meantime," he said, "we should celebrate our victories, my dear Juan. The Alcazar of Segovia has fallen into our hands; and now we might say that the same has happened to this palace of Burgos. Once we have rid ourselves of that interfering woman the place is ours. Do you not think that that is worthy of a little celebration?"

"Very worthy, Highness," agreed Juan.

"Then see to it. Arrange a banquet, a ball; and I will show these Spaniards how the Flemings can beat them at all sport."

"It shall be done."

While they talked together a page arrived to tell Philip that an envoy from Ferdinand had arrived at Burgos.

"Let him be brought to me," said Philip; and when the page had gone he smiled at Juan Manuel.

"What despatches are these my worthy father-in-law sees fit to send me, I wonder?"

"Oh, there is nothing to fear from him. The old lion has had his teeth drawn. He will find it a different matter being merely King of Aragon instead of Spain."

"My mother-in-law kept the fellow in his place. She must have been a strong-minded woman."

Juan Manuel looked serious for a moment. When he remembered the great Queen Isabella he could not help wondering what she would say if she could see him now, a traitor to her husband.

He shrugged aside the thought; Ferdinand's conduct would not have pleased her either, he reflected. It seemed to him that if the great Queen could come alive again she would be so saddened by her husband's conduct that she would have little thought to spare for Juan Manuel.

Philip was his master now, and it was Philip whose interests were his own.

"It will be interesting to see what despatches this fellow has brought," went on Philip. "You may remain, and we will study them together."

A few minutes later the page returned with Ferdinand's envoy.

"Don Luis Ferrer," he announced.

And Ferdinand's envoy was bowing before the man who was certain that before long he would be sole ruler of Castile.

*          *          *

The celebrations were magnificent. Juan Manuel had arranged them to appeal to his master. He wished to show his gratitude for all the benefits which had come his way since he had entered Philip's service; he wished him to know that he would continue to lay all his skill at his master's feet.

Juana was allowed to partake in the celebrations.

Juan had said: "It would be unwise at this stage to shut her away completely. Wait until more fortresses have come into our hands."

"Rest assured," said Philip, "there will be others as important as Segovia and Burgos."

"Let her show the people that she is truly mad. Then they cannot complain."

Philip agreed with this. But he had made up his mind that he was going to put her away in as complete a seclusion as that in which her grandmother had passed the last years of her life.

Juana joined in the feasting. There were days when she was very gay, and others when she was overcome by her melancholy. There were times when she calmly received the homage of all; there were others when she shut herself away in her apartments.

She called her father's envoy, Luis Ferrer, to her and demanded to hear news of her father, of whether he spoke often of her or any of her sisters; of how he lived with his new wife.

Luis Ferrer was eager to talk to her of Ferdinand, and Manuel was afraid that he was trying to bring about a meeting between father and daughter which, he was sure, could only result in harm to Philip.

"We should watch this Luis Ferrer," he said to Philip. "It is my belief that the fellow is here for no good purpose."

The peak of the celebrations was planned to take place on a warm September day. There was to be a banquet more lavish than any of those of the last few days, and afterwards there would be ball games, because Philip excelled at these and he was very eager to show the Castilians what he called his superior Flemish skill.

Juana was present at the banquet. She had rarely seen her husband so gay, and she thought how beautiful he was and how in comparison all others—men and women—seemed ugly and lacking in grace.

Beside her at the table was Luis Ferrer, and she was glad of this because she knew that it disturbed Philip to see them together, and that meant that, while she was with Ferrer, at least Philip was thinking of her.

As soon as the banquet was over the ball games began and here Philip certainly did excel, for he beat all his opponents. Yet how could one be sure, Juana wondered, whether his opponents felt it would be wise to let him win? Nevertheless he played with great skill and she was momentarily happy to see him flushed and taking a boyish pride in his achievements.

He was very hot when the game was won, and he called for a drink. No one was quite sure afterwards who gave him that drink; one thing was certain: he drank deep.

During the dancing and pageantry which followed, several people noticed that he seemed a little tired. But then it had been a strenuous ball game.

When she retired that night Juana lay in her bed hoping he

would come to her, although she knew he would not; in four months' time she could expect the birth of a child, so he would not come—unless of course he wished to placate her, which he seemed nowadays inclined to do at certain times.

There in the quiet of her apartment Juana began to think of the sadness of her life and to ask herself if there was not a curse on the House of Spain. She had heard such a legend at the time of her sister's death. Her brother, Juan, was dead and his heir had been still-born; her sister, Isabella, had died in childbed and her child had followed her to the grave. That left Juana, Maria and Catalina. Maria might be happy in Portugal, but Catalina certainly was not so in England. As for herself surely none was as unhappy as she was.

She thought sadly of Catalina's woes. Her sister had talked of them.

"But I did not listen," whispered Juana. "I could only think of my own miseries which I know are far greater than hers. For what greater tragedy could befall a woman than to have a husband whom she adores with a passionate intensity which borders on madness, but who cares so little for her that he is planning to declare her mad and put her from him?"

There were strange noises in the palace tonight. She could hear the sound of footsteps and whispering voices.

"Shall I wake the Queen?"

"She should know."

"She would want to be with him."

Juana rose from her bed and wrapped a robe about her.

"Who is there?" she called. "Who is whispering there?"

One of her women came in, looking startled.

"The doctors have sent word, Highness . . ." she began.

"Doctors!" cried Juana. "Word of what?"

"That His Highness is in a fever and a delirium. They are bleeding him now. Would Your Highness care to go to his bedside?"

Juana did not wait to answer; she sped through the apartments to those of Philip.

He was lying on his bed, his fair hair made darker with sweat, and his beautiful blue eyes looked blankly at her. He was murmuring, but none understood what he said.

She knelt by the bed and cried: "Philip, my dearest, what has happened?"

Philip's lips moved, but his glassy eyes stared beyond her.

"He does not know me," she said. She turned to the physicians. "What does this mean? What has happened?"

"It is a chill, Highness. Doubtless His Highness became too hot during the ball game and drank too much cold water. That can produce a fever."

"A fever! So it is a fever. What are you doing for him?"

"We have bled him, Highness. But the fever persists."

"Then bleed him again. Do not stand there doing nothing. Save him. He must not die."

The physicians smiled knowledgeably. "Your Highness is unduly disturbed. This is but a slight fever. His Highness will soon be playing another ball game to delight his subjects."

"He is young," said Juana, "and he is healthy. He will recover."

She was calm now, because she felt exultant. It was his turn now to be at her mercy. She would let no one else nurse him. She would do everything herself. Now that he was ill she was indeed Queen of Castile and mistress of this palace. Now she would be the one to give the orders and, no matter whom she commanded, they must obey.

*  *  *

All through the rest of the night she was with him, and in the morning he seemed a little better.

He opened his eyes and recognized her sitting there.

"What happened?" he asked.

"You had a little fever." She laid a cool hand on his brow. "I have been sitting by your bed since they told me. I am going to nurse you back to health."

He did not protest; he lay looking at her, and she thought how defenceless he seemed, with the arrogance gone from him, and his usually ruddy cheeks pale. She felt very tender towards him, and she said to herself: "How I love him! Beyond all things. Beyond my children, beyond my pride."

He was aware of her feelings, and even now, weak as he was, he relished his power over her.

"I shall nurse you until you are quite recovered. I shall allow no other woman in the room."

His lips twitched faintly in a smile, and she thought he was remembering the early days of their relationship when he had found her more desirable than he did now.

He tried to raise himself but he was very weak and, as he moved, he grimaced with pain.

"It is in my side," he said in answer to her question and, as he sank back, she saw the beads of sweat which had broken out on his smooth brow and across the bridge of his handsome nose.

"I will call the physicians," she said. "I will send for Dr. Parra. I believe him to be the best in the country."

"I feel safe . . . with you," said Philip, and there was a wry twist to his lips.

"Ah, Philip," she said gently, "you have many enemies, but you need not fear while I am here."

That seemed to comfort him and she told herself exultantly: He rejoices that I am here. My presence comforts him. He knows I will protect him. For a time he loves me.

She smiled almost roguishly. "You do not think me mad now, Philip?"

She took his hand which was lying on the coverlet, and he returned the pressure feebly because he felt so weak.

She thought: When you are strong and well you will mock me again. You will try to convince them that I am mad. You will try to put me in prison because you want my crown all for yourself. But now . . . you need me and you love me, just a little.

She was smiling. Yes, he had taken all her pride. He loved her once for her crown; and now he loved her for the safety he could feel in her presence.

But I love him with all my being, she reminded herself, so that I care not for what reason he loves me, if only he but will.

She rose and sent at once for Dr. Parra.

No one else should come near him. She would nurse him herself. She would forbid all other women to come into this sickroom. She would give the orders now. Was she not the Queen of Castile?

\*     \*     \*

It was four days before Dr. Parra reached Burgos, and by that time Philip's fever had increased. He was now quite unaware of where he lay or who tended him. There were days when he did not speak at all but lay in a coma, and others when he muttered incoherently.

Juana remained in the sick-room, clinging to her determination that no one but herself should wait on him. He took no food but occasionally sipped a little drink, and Juana would allow no one to offer this but herself.

None could have been more calm than she was at that time. Gone was all the hysteria; she moved about the sick-room, the most efficient of nurses, and all the time she was praying that Philip would recover.

But after seven days of fever his condition grew rapidly worse, and Dr. Parra ordered that cupping glasses be applied to his shoulders and purgatives administered. These instructions were carried out, but the patient did not rally.

He had now fallen into a lethargy from which it was impossible to waken him; only now and then would he groan and put a hand to his side, which indicated that he suffered pain.

On the morning of the 25th September of that year, 1506, black spots appeared on his body. The doctors were baffled, but there were strong suspicions now throughout the palace that Philip had drunk something more than water on that day when, overheated by the sport, he had asked for a drink.

There were whispers now of: "Who brought the drink?" None could be sure. Perhaps Philip remembered, but he was too weak to say.

Philip had many enemies, and the greatest of these was Ferdinand, who had been forced to surrender his rights in Castile. Ferdinand was far away, but men like Ferdinand did not do such deeds themselves; they found others to do the work for them.

It was remembered that, shortly before Philip had been taken ill, Ferdinand's envoy, Luis Ferrer, had come to Burgos. But it was well not to talk too much of this, for, if Philip died and Juana were proved mad, then Ferdinand would undoubtedly become the Regent of Castile.

So it was only in secret that people asked themselves who had poisoned Philip the Handsome. In public it was said that he was suffering sorely from a fever.

\*        \*        \*

He was dead. Juana could not believe it. The doctors had said so, but it must not be.

He was so young, only twenty-eight years of age, and he had been so full of vigour. It was not possible.

They were surrounding her, telling her of their sorrow, but she did not hear them; she saw only him, not as he was now, drained of all life, but young, handsome, mocking, full of the joy of being alive.

He is not dead, she said to herself. I will never believe that. I will never leave him. He shall stay with me always.

Then she thought: I can keep him to myself now. I can send them all away. I am the ruler of Castile, and there is none to stand beside me and try to snatch my crown from me.

They were weeping; they were telling her they suffered with her. How foolish they were! As if they could suffer as she suffered!

She looked regal now. There was no sign of wildness in her face. She was calmer than any of them.

"He shall be carried to the hall, and there he shall lie in state," she said. "Wrap him in his ermine robes and put a jewelled cap on his head. He will be beautiful in death as he has been in life."

They obeyed her. They wrapped him in his ermine robe, which was lined with rich brocade; they placed the jewelled cap on his head and they laid a diamond cross on his breast. He was put on a catafalque covered with cloth of gold and carried down to the hall. There a throne had been set up and he was seated upon this so that he looked as though he were still alive. Then the candles were lighted and the friars sang their dirges in the hall of death.

Juana lay at his feet, embracing his legs; and there she remained through the night.

And when the body was embalmed and placed in its lead coffin she refused to leave it.

"I shall never leave him again," she cried. "In life he left me so often; in death he never shall."

Then it seemed that the madness was with her once more.

\*          \*          \*

They carried her to her apartment from which all light was shut out. She was exhausted, for she would neither sleep nor eat. It was only because she was weak that they were able to remove her from the coffin. For several days she sat in her darkened room, refusing all food; she did not take off her clothes; she spoke to no one.

"Assuredly," said all those of her household, "her sanity has left her."

While she remained thus shut away, the coffin was taken from the hall of the Palace of Burgos to the Cartuja de Miraflores and, when she heard that this had been done, she hurriedly left her darkened room.

Now she was the Queen again, preparing to follow the coffin with all speed, giving orders that mourning should be made and that this was to resemble the garb of a nun, because she would be remote for ever from the world which did not contain her Philip.

When she arrived at the church she found that the coffin had already been placed in a vault, and she ordered that it should immediately be brought out.

She would have no disobedience. She reminded all that she was the Queen of Castile and expected obedience. So the coffin was brought from the vault.

Then she cried: "Remove the cerecloths from the feet and the head. I would see him again."

And when this was done, she kissed those dead lips again and again and held the feet against her breast.

"Highness," whispered one of her women, "you torture yourself."

"What is there for me but torture when he is no longer with me?" she asked. "I would rather have him thus than not at all."

And she would not leave the corpse of her husband, but stayed there, kissing and fondling him, as she had longed to during his life.

She would only leave after she had given strict orders that the coffin should not be closed. She would come again the next day and the next, and for as long as the coffin remained in this place she would come to kiss her husband and hold his dead body in her arms.

And so she did. Arriving each day from the Palace of Burgos, there she would remain by the coffin, alternately staring at that dead figure in the utmost melancholy, and seizing it in her arms in a frantic passion.

"It is true," said those who watched her. "She is mad. . . . This has proved it."

AFTER HER MEETING with Juana, Katharine realized that she could hope for no help from her own people. Her father was immersed in his own affairs, and indeed was far less able to help her by sending the remainder of her dowry than he had been when her mother was alive. As for Juana, she had no thought of anything but her own tragic obsession with her husband.

That month had arrived during which, Katharine believed, she would know what her fate in England was to be.

Her maids of honour chatted together about that important day, the twenty-ninth; she listened to them and did not reprove them. She knew they would talk in secret if not before her.

"He will be fifteen on the twenty-ninth."

"It is the very month, this very year."

"Then we shall see."

"When they are married it will make all the difference to our state. Oh, would it not be wonderful to have a new gown again!"

Katharine broke in on their conversation. "You are foolish to hope," she said. "The Prince was betrothed to me, but that was long ago. Do you not realize that if we were to be married we should have heard of it long ere this? There would surely be great preparations for the marriage of the Prince of Wales."

"It may be that the marriage will be announced," said Francesca. "Mayhap they are saving the announcement, that it may be made on his fifteenth birthday."

Katharine shook her head. "Does the King of England treat me as his future daughter-in-law?"

"No, but after the announcement he might."

"You are living in dreams," said Katharine.

She looked at those faces which had been so bright and were now often clouded by frustration and disappointment.

She knew that the betrothal of herself and Henry would be forgotten, as so many similar betrothals had been, and that his fifteenth birthday would pass without any reference to the marriage which was to have taken place on that day.

Katharine caught the despair of her maids in waiting, and she sent for Dr. de Puebla.

The doctor arrived, and the sight of him made her shudder

with disgust. He looked so shabby; he seemed to wear a perpetually deprecating expression, which was probably due to the fact that he was continually apologizing to Henry for Ferdinand, and to Katharine for his inability to improve her lot. He was infirm nowadays and almost crippled; he could not walk or ride the distance from his humble lodgings in the Strand to the Court, so travelled in a litter. He was in constant pain from the gout and, since he had received no money from Ferdinand for a very long time, he was obliged to live on the little which came in from his legal business. This was not much, for Englishmen were not eager to consult a Spaniard and he had to rely on Spaniards in England. He dined out when he could and, when he could not, he did so as cheaply as possible; and he was a great deal shabbier than Katharine and her maids of honour.

He was unfortunate inasmuch as he irritated Katharine; she was by nature serene and compassionate, but the little Jew, perhaps because he was her father's ambassador in a Court where she needed great help, exasperated her almost beyond endurance and she began to feel—wrongly—that, if only she had a man more worthy to represent her father and to work for her, her position would not be so deplorable as it was and had been for most of her stay in England.

"Dr. de Puebla," said Katharine, as he shuffled towards her and kissed her hand, "have you realized that the fifteenth birthday of the Prince of Wales has now come and gone and there has been no mention of the marriage which was once proposed between us?"

"I fear I did not expect there would be, Highness."

"What have you done about this matter?"

Puebla spread his hands in a well-remembered gesture. "Highness, there is nothing I can do."

"Nothing! Are you not here to look after the interests of my father, and are they not mine?"

"Highness, if I could persuade the King of England to this marriage do not doubt that I should do so."

Katharine turned away because such bitter words rose to her lips, and the sight of the sick little man made her feel ashamed of her anger towards him.

"Is nothing ever going to happen?" she demanded. "How do you think I live?"

"Highness, it is hard for you. It is hard for me. Believe me, I am well acquainted with poverty."

"It goes on and on and on," she cried. "There is no way out. If I could return to Spain . . ."

She stopped. In that moment she had made a discovery. She did not want to return to Spain, because all that she had wished to return to was no more. She had longed for her mother, but Spain no longer contained Isabella. Did she want to be with her father? There had never been any great tenderness between them, because his affection for his children had always been overlaid with hopes of what they could bring him. Maria was in Portugal. Juana had grown strange. Did she want to go to Spain then to be with Juana and her husband, to see their tempestuous relationship, did she want to see that handsome philanderer gradually driving her sister over the edge of sanity?

Spain had nothing for her. What had England? Nothing apart from the dazzling prospect of marriage with the Prince of Wales.

Katharine realized in that moment that she must marry the Prince or remain all her life an outcast from Spain, the unwanted stranger in a foreign land.

She needed brilliant diplomacy to bring about the marriage, and all she had was this shabby, gouty Jew.

He was saying now: "Highness, I have done everything I can. Believe me, I will not spare myself . . ."

Katharine shook her head and murmured: "Mayhap you do your best, but I like not the way these matters go. You may retire now. Should you become further acquainted with the King's mind, I pray you come to me, for I am anxious."

Puebla shuffled out, and he was surprised, when he had left her presence, to find his cheeks were wet.

I am worn out, he said to himself, with all the work which has come to nothing. I suffer pain; I can no longer amuse and entertain. I have outlived my usefulness. That is why old men shed tears.

And, left alone, Katharine wrote to her father. She told him that his ambassador in England was no longer able to work for her good or the good of Spain. She implored him to give this matter his attention and appoint a new ambassador to the Court of the Tudor King, for the sake of Spain and for his daughter, who was beside herself with misery.

*          *          *

Eagerly she awaited news from her father. Each day during that summer seemed more trying than the last. The maids of honour did not attempt to hide their dissatisfaction. They were continually longing to be back in Spain.

There were perpetual quarrels in the household, and Katharine almost wished that Doña Elvira was back with them to keep them all in order. Francesca was more restless than the others and she seemed to find a wicked delight in accusing each member of the household of intriguing to keep them in England. There could be no greater sin in the eyes of Francesca.

The fact is, thought Katharine, they need to be married. If Arthur had lived, they would all have worthy husbands now, and rich, full lives.

It seemed to her that each month it was necessary to rifle her store of jewels and plate. She felt guilty when she sold or pawned these pieces, but what could she do? Her expenses had to be met, and disposing of her plate and jewellery was the only means of doing this.

At last news came from Spain, and when she read of the death of Philip she could not help but rejoice.

He was my father's enemy, she told herself; he turned him from Castile and he would have taken the crown from Juana. She is miserable now, but it is a good thing that he has gone.

She imagined her father's secret delight, for if Juana were incapable of ruling it was certain that Ferdinand would come back to Castile and the Regency.

She realized what this would mean. Ferdinand would be of more account in Europe than previously, and the manner in which the King of England treated her depended largely on what was happening to her father.

So could she consider this sudden and mysterious death of her handsome brother-in-law good news? She believed she could.

There was a letter from her father in answer to that which she had sent asking for a new ambassador.

"Why should you not be my ambassador?" wrote Ferdinand. "You have been at the English Court for some years. You know their ways; you speak their language. In due course I will send you an ambassador, but in the meantime you may consider yourself as such. Listen to Puebla; he is a clever man, perhaps cleverer than you realize. Be guided by him. He has worked well for Spain and will, I hope, continue to do so."

When Katharine had stopped reading there was a faint colour in her cheeks. She felt more cheered than she had for a long time. Now she would have an interest in life; now she would have more power, and she would try to serve her father faithfully and at the same time bring about a happier state for herself. And how could she achieve such a state? There was one answer: Only by marriage to the Prince of Wales.

*       *       *

The King of England requested the pleasure of her company. She went to his apartments, her hopes high, wondering what news he had to impart to her.

He was alone and he received her with graciousness, as though, she believed, he considered her of greater importance than he had when they had last met.

When she had been formally greeted she was allowed to sit in his presence and, cupping his face in his hands, the King said: "This is a matter which I believe I can entrust to your hands more readily than I could to any other."

"Your Highness delights me," she answered.

Henry nodded, his lower lip protruded, his expression more pleasant than usual.

"I shall never forget the day when your sister, the Queen of Castile, arrived at Windsor. What grace was hers! What charm!"

Katharine was puzzled. She too would never forget that day, but had been struck more by Juana's melancholy than her grace and charm.

"I have not forgotten her from that day to this," said the King. He paused and then went on: "You now act as your father's ambassador, so I am going to entrust this matter to you. I want you to tell your father that I am asking for the hand of the Queen of Castile."

Katharine caught her breath in astonishment. Juana . . . the wife of the King of England! She, who had adored that handsome, golden-haired philanderer, to become the wife of this ageing man with the cold, hard face and the uncertain temper! It was impossible.

But was it? Royal marriages could be incongruous. And if this one were to become fact, she would have her sister in England, the Queen of England. Surely the sister of the Queen of England could not be humiliated. Surely she would be able to live in a state worthy of her relationship to the Queen.

And what joy to have her own sister in England!

Katharine's busy thoughts were halted suddenly. But to be married to the King. She remembered her own feelings when it had been suggested that he should be her next bridegroom. She had shuddered with distaste, and yet she had felt delighted at the thought of Juana's taking the place she despised.

But this could not be. Juana was mad. She had begun to believe that there was little doubt of this, since she had heard further rumours of her sister's strange behaviour.

The King was watching her intently. She must learn to guard

her expression. She hoped that she had not allowed distaste to show itself.

He seemed not to have noticed and was smiling almost vacuously, as a country yokel might smile at the prospect of a bride. It was almost as though he had fallen in love with Juana. Oh no, no! Henry VII could never fall in love . . . except with a crown. That was the answer. He was falling in love with the crown of Castile.

She must be wily. She must not tell him that she thought this marriage would be quite distasteful because he was an old man and her sister was mad.

If she listened to his plans, if she worked with him, he might be prepared to reward her in some way. She was not a foolish young girl any more. She was a woman who had suffered great hardship and deep humiliation, and there was little that could make an Infanta of Spain suffer more.

She said calmly: "I will inform my father of your request."

Henry nodded, still smiling that smile which sat so oddly on his harsh features.

"You should write to your sister and tell her of the delights of the English Court. Tell her that I have been a faithful husband to one Queen and would be so to another. You will plead my cause; and from whom could that plea come more effectively than from her sister?"

So Katharine, in her new role of ambassadress, prepared herself to open the courtship between that incongruous pair—Henry Tudor, King of England, and Juana, Queen of Castile, who was now becoming known as Juana the Mad.

# THE STRANGENESS OF JUANA

WHEN JUANA RECEIVED the invitation to state her views as to a marriage with Henry Tudor she shrugged her shoulders and immediately dismissed the matter from her mind. She was concerned only with one thing, which was to keep Philip with her now that he was dead.

She would sit for hours alone in her darkened room, wearing the mourning garments which were like a nun's and included a great cowl, the purpose of which was to hide as much of her face as possible.

She would mutter to herself: "Women . . . Let no women come near me. They are seeking now to take him from me. It was always so. Wherever he went they sought him. He could not escape from them even had he wished . . . but of course he did not wish. Now they shall not take him from me."

Sometimes her attendants heard wild laughter coming from her apartments. They never heard sobs. She had not shed a tear since his death. When the melancholy moods were with her she would sit silent for hours at a time.

She ate scarcely anything and her body was pitiably thin beneath the flowing nun's robes. But there were times when she would have musicians play to her, for only music could soothe her. She would send for her minstrels and they would play to her in the darkened room until she tired of them and sent them away.

There were no women now in her household, except one, her washerwoman.

"And even that one, I must watch," she often murmured to herself. Then she would send some of her men-servants to see what the washerwoman was doing, and have her summoned to her presence.

"Wash the clothes here," she would cry, "that I may see what you are about."

And water and tubs would be brought to the royal apartments while the poor bewildered washerwoman washed the clothes under the suspicious eye of the Queen.

It was small wonder that rumours of her madness were growing.

She was heavy with her child now, and sometimes she would talk of it.

"It is not so long since he was here," she would say, putting her hands on her body that she might feel the movement of the child. "He was happy to see his family growing. I hope I shall be able to tell him soon that we have another boy."

There were occasions when certain grandees came to her and implored her to take an interest in state matters, reminding her that she was the Queen.

But she only shook her head. "I shall do nothing more, until I die, but pray for the soul of my husband and guard his dead body," she said. "There is time for nothing else."

They could only shake their heads and wait for the return of Ferdinand.

The year was passing and December came. In January her child would be born, and those who wished her well told themselves that with the coming of the child she would forget this obsession with her husband's dead body.

It was one cold December day when she set out to hear mass at the Cartuja where Philip's body lay. Soon, it was said, she would be unable to make even the short journey from the palace, encumbered as she was with her pregnancy. She went through the usual ceremony of kissing the lips of her husband and embracing his feet; and then suddenly she announced: "It was his wish that he should be buried in Granada. He has tarried long enough here. I shall take him to Granada. Pray prepare to leave at once."

"Your Highness," she was told, "this is winter. You could not cross the steppes of Castile at this time of the year."

She drew herself up to her full height and her eyes flashed wildly. "It was his wish that he should go to Granada, and it is my desire to take him there."

"With the coming of the spring . . ."

"Now," she said. "We leave today."

This was indeed madness. She proposed to cross the snowy wastes between Burgos and Granada in the bitterly cold weather, and she herself in her eighth month of pregnancy!

The monks did their best to dissuade her. She grew angry; she reminded them that she was their Queen.

"He shall stay no longer in this place," she cried. "It is unworthy of him. Prepare at once, I say."

"But the weather, Highness . . ."

"He will not feel the weather. He never cared for the heat. He loved the open air. The cold winds invigorated him, he said." Then she suddenly screamed: "Why do you hesitate? Do not dare disobey me. If you do it will be the worse for you. Prepare at once. We are taking him to Granada this day."

*       *       *

Across the snowly tablelands the procession slowly made its tortuous way. The wind penetrated the garments of the bishops, the choristers, the men of the Church and the men-servants. The only person who did not feel the cold was the Queen who, in her nun's robes, was carried over the rough land in her litter.

There was not a person in the retinue who did not hope that the Queen's child would be born before the middle of January when it was expected. They prayed for anything which could put an end to this nightmare journey.

Beside the litter, and covered with a velvet pall, was the hearse, so that it should never be out of the Queen's sight. As they walked it was the duty of the choristers to chant their mournful dirges.

At dusk the Queen reluctantly allowed the cortège to halt at an inn or a monastery, and there each night the coffin must be opened that the Queen might throw herself upon the dead body, kissing those silent lips again and again.

Those who looked on at this ritual asked themselves how long they could expect to be at the mercy of a madwoman's whims.

One night the coffin was carried into what was believed to be a monastery; and there, before entering the buildings, by the light of torches the coffin was opened and the gruesome ceremony began.

While it was in progress a figure appeared from the building followed by two others.

One of the bishops said: "We come, with the Queen, to rest here a night."

"I will make ready to receive Her Highness," was the answer. But at the sound of that high, musical voice Juana leaped to her feet, her eyes suddenly blazing.

"That is a woman!" she cried. "Come here, woman. No . . . no. Stay where you are. I will come to you. You shall not come near him."

"I am the Abbess, Highness," said the woman.

Juana screamed at her bishops: "How dare you bring me here! There are women here. That place is full of women. You know I will let no woman come near him."

"Highness, these are nuns . . ."

"Nuns are women," she retorted. "I trust no women. Close the coffin. We are going on."

"Highness, the night is cold and dark."

"Close the coffin!" She turned to the Abbess. "And you . . . go back into your convent. Do not dare to set foot outside until we have gone. No woman shall come near him, I tell you."

The Abbess bowed and retired, thankful that the mad Queen was not to be her guest.

The coffin was closed; the procession left the convent precincts and went on, in the hope that the next place of refuge would be a monastery.

So the dreary journey continued with painful slowness.

It was a great relief when it reached the village of Torquemada, for here Juana's warning pains began, and even she realized that she could not go on. They had come only thirty miles in some three weeks.

The coffin was set up where she might see it and make sure that no woman came near it; and on the 14th January in that year 1507 her child was born.

It was a girl and she called her Catalina after her sister, about whom now and then her conscience troubled her. She was unhappy, even as I am, she thought; and yet I did not listen to her tale of suffering.

She lay in melancholy silence, the child in her arms, while she kept continual watch over all that was left to her of her gay and heartless Philip.

\*　　　\*　　　\*

In England Henry was waiting impatiently for news of his proposed match with Juana.

He sent for Puebla, and the gouty old man was carried to Richmond in his litter.

"I hear nothing from Spain concerning my proposals," he began. "It would seem that they are unwelcome."

"Nothing, Your Grace, would be more welcome to Spain than a match between Your Highness and Queen Juana."

"Then why do I hear nothing?"

"My master is still in Naples, and there is much to occupy him."

"And the Queen of Castile herself?"

"Has been so recently widowed, so recently brought to bed of a child . . ."

Those words increased Henry's impatience. There was a woman who had borne several children. If she were his wife he need have no doubt that he could beget many boys. She had already borne two healthy boys and she was only twenty-eight. Certainly she was capable of bearing more. She had given proof of her fruitfulness. Had not her husband left her pregnant when he died? And it was said that he had given the greater part of his attention to other women.

Puebla, accustomed now to Henry's irritable temper, reminded him that Juana was considered to be somewhat unstable of mind.

"I saw her here in England, and I was impressed by her charm and beauty," said the King. "I did not see any signs of insanity. And yet . . . if it should be that she is insane I should not consider that an obstacle to marriage, for she has proved that this mental illness does not prevent her from bearing children."

"I will tell my master what Your Grace has said."

Henry nodded, and a familiar grimace of pain crossed his face as he moved in his chair.

"There is one other little matter," he went on. "His Highness Ferdinand may well return to the position he occupied immediately after the death of Queen Isabella. He will return to power as Regent of Castile and ruler of Spain—that is if his daughter is indeed unfit to take her place on the throne. He has made no effort to pay the remainder of his daughter's dowry. Say this to him when you write: If he does not soon pay this long overdue account there will be only one course open to me. I shall be obliged to consider the match between his daughter Katharine and the Prince of Wales broken off."

Puebla felt a lifting of his spirits. This was an indication that a match between Katharine and young Henry was still possible. Henry's terms were: the rest of the dowry which had not been paid after Arthur's death, and marriage with Juana.

\*       \*       \*

Juana did not recover quickly from the birth of her daughter Catalina. Those who had accompanied her on the thirty-mile trek from Burgos hoped that when she was well again her interests would be concentrated on the child, and she would give up this mad project of taking her husband's corpse to Granada in this way.

While Juana lay in her apartments, the cradle of her daughter beside her, and the coffin placed in the room so that she could gaze at it at any hour of the day or night, one of her servants came to tell her that a friar, who had heard she was in Torquemada, had travelled far to see her. He had important news for her.

Juana was not interested in any news which could be brought to her; but she agreed to see the Friar, and when the man stood before her she looked at him with melancholy eyes clearly showing her indifference.

The man was travel-stained; his eyes were wild. As he bowed, his gaze went at once to the coffin and stayed there; and watching him, Juana lost her listlessness and found herself gripped by excitement.

"Highness," cried the Friar, "I have had a vision."

"Of whom?"

The Friar indicated the coffin.

"I saw him rise from it. He came out, all shining and beautiful."

Juana sat up in her bed that she might see the Friar's face more clearly.

"He rose from the dead!" she whispered.

"Yes, Highness. He threw off the cerecloths and there he was, whole and well; and there was great rejoicing."

"This came to you in a dream?"

"As a vision, Highness. I had fasted many days and spent many more on my knees in humble seclusion. Then this vision came to me. He left his coffin and walked from this place into the streets. I saw him clearly in these very streets . . . and I knew that it was in Torquemada that the Queen's consort had risen from the dead."

"Here in Torquemada!" cried Juana, clasping her hands together in ecstasy. "Then it was by divine will that we left Burgos . . . that we came here and were forced to rest at Torquemada. Oh, glory be to God and all His saints! Here in Torquemada my Philip will rise from the dead."

"I came with all haste to tell Your Highness."

"I thank you with all my heart. You shall be well rewarded."

The Friar closed his eyes and bowed his head.

Excitement gripped the village of Torquemada. All were waiting for a miracle. Outside the house in which Juana lodged people gathered; they were coming in from the neighbouring villages to wait for the miracle.

Juana had changed completely; all her melancholy was thrown aside; she was gay—not hysterically so, but with a quiet contentment. She was certain that the Friar was a holy man and that Philip was about to return to life.

She kept her vigil by the coffin, determined that she would be the first to welcome him back to life. He would hear then how she had kept him with her, and he would be so much happier to awaken from the dead by her side than he would have been to awaken in the gloom of some dismal vault that he would be grateful to her. If ever he had needed proof of her love he would have it now.

The Friar, well rewarded, left Torquemada, but the sightseers continued to come in. The summer was hot and the village had never contained so many people; and as the houses were filled, many were forced to sleep in the street and the fields.

In the heat of the afternoon one of the sightseers collapsed suddenly and lay groaning in a high fever. He died almost immediately, and that very day three more people were stricken in the same manner. Before the next day came, the crowds in and about Torquemada realized that someone had brought the plague among them, and were terrified.

News was brought to Juana that there was plague in Torquemada.

"Highness," said one of her bishops, "we should prepare to leave this place with all speed."

"Leave it!" she screamed. "But it is here that my Philip will come to life again."

"Highness, every hour you delay you put yourself and the child in danger."

"Our faith is being tried," she answered. "If I leave Torquemada now there will be no miracle."

Again and again efforts were made to persuade her. Juana remained stubborn.

So, while the plague raged in Torquemada, Juana stayed there with her newly born daughter and the remains of her husband, waiting for a miracle.

\*　　　\*　　　\*

All through the summer Juana remained in Torquemada. The plague abated with the passing of the hot weather, and still Juana watched over the coffin, waiting for a miracle.

There were occasions when she believed that Philip had indeed risen from the dead, and her servants would hear her murmuring endearments or loudly upbraiding him for his infidelities. It was a strange household that rested in the village of Torquemada. There was the Queen of Castile, living humbly with no women in her household except the washerwoman, a young Princess who thrived in spite of the conditions in which she lived, and the remains in the coffin which were regularly kissed and embraced.

Then one day there was great rejoicing in Torquemada. The news spread rapidly, and all in that grim household knew that the days of waiting were over.

Ferdinand had arrived in Valencia. Now there would be some law and order throughout Castile.

\*　　　\*　　　\*

"I must go to meet my father," declared Juana. "He will expect it of me."

She had either forgotten the Friar's prophecy or given up all hope of its coming true, for it was almost with relief that she prepared to go.

She had no wish to see the sun, she said. She was a widow and her life would therefore in future be lived in darkness. She would travel only by night and by the light of torches, and wherever she went there would her husband go with her.

In vain did those who cared for her comfort seek to dissuade her; any opposition to her will sent her into paroxysms of rage. She would be obeyed. She would have them remember that, although she was the most unfortunate widow in the world, she was their Queen, and from them she expected obedience.

So once more the cortège set out. Beside her went the hearse so that she never lost sight of Philip's coffin. They travelled by the light of torches and the going was rough and very slow. The choristers sang their dismal funeral dirges as they went; and Juana, riding or carried in her litter, travelled always in melancholy silence.

It was at Tortoles that Ferdinand and his daughter came face to face.

When Ferdinand saw her, he was horrified. It was years since they had met, but the lapse of time did not entirely account for the great change. It was almost impossible to believe that this sad woman, with the melancholy eyes in which madness lurked, was his gay daughter who had often shocked her mother by her wildness.

Juana also was not unmoved. She found herself in those first moments of reunion remembering the days of her childhood, when she, her brother, sisters, father and mother had all been together.

She went on her knees and gripped her father's hands, while Ferdinand, astonished at his emotion, knelt too and, putting his arms about her, held her tenderly.

"My daughter, my daughter," he murmured, "what has happened to bring you to this?"

"Oh, my father," she murmured, "I have suffered as few are called upon to suffer. I have lost all that I love."

"There are your children. They can bring great comfort."

"They are his children too," she said, "but when he died the sun went from life. Now there is only darkness, for it is perpetual night."

Ferdinand rose from his knees, his emotion evaporating. If

Juana was really as mad as she seemed, then the way would be easy. He could now be sure of taking the Regency.

"I will care for you now," he said, and she did not notice the glint in his eyes; nor did she see any hidden meaning in his words.

"It is a joy to me that you have come," she said.

Ferdinand pushed back the black hood and kissed her brow.

He thought: She is indeed mad. There can be no doubt of it. Regent of Castile until Charles is of age! There were many years of government ahead of him.

"We cannot stay here in Tortoles," said Ferdinand. "We should travel to a place where we can live and discuss matters of state in comfort."

She did not demur and he was delighted that she appeared ready to agree with everything he said; but he soon discovered how stubborn she could be.

"I only travel by night," she told him.

He was astonished.

"Travel by night! But how is that possible? The journey would take four times as long."

"That may be so, but I am in no hurry. I am shut away from the sun and the light of day. My life from now on will be lived in darkness."

"Certainly we cannot travel by night. You must end this foolishness."

Then he saw it, the flash of obstinacy, and he remembered that she was Isabella's daughter. Similar conflicts came to his mind; he remembered how often his will had pulled against that of Isabella, and how Isabella had invariably won because she was the Queen of Castile and he but her consort. Now here was Isabella's daughter reminding him that she was the Queen of Castile and he but her father.

Ferdinand determined then that all Castile must know that Juana suffered from periodic insanity, that she could not be relied upon; and the only way in which Castile could be satisfactorily ruled was by a Regent while the Queen spent her life in seclusion.

Let her travel by night. Let her carry the coffin of her husband about with her; let her fondle the corpse when she liked. All this would enable the people to understand that the Queen was in truth a madwoman.

So Ferdinand travelled by day, and Juana by night; and when Juana realized that they were taking the route to Burgos, that town full of the most poignant memories—for it was there that Philip had died—she refused to travel further.

She stopped at Arcos and took up her residence there. In vain did her servants protest that she had chosen the most unhealthy spot in Spain. She retorted that she did not care for the weather. The cold meant nothing to her; she no longer felt anything but sorrow.

Ferdinand made no protest. He could wait.

She was making it easy for him to convince the people that their Queen was mad, and then he would cease to fear anything she might do. With great vigour he set about putting his affairs in order.

He read the despatches from Puebla. Puebla was growing old; he would send a new ambassador to England; he must try once more to bring about the marriage of his youngest daughter with the Prince of Wales.

# FUENSALIDA AT THE KING'S COURT

IT WAS A bleak February day and a chilly mist enveloped the countryside. The elegant foreigner clearly found the weather distasteful, and his retinue, being fully aware of his choleric temper and his habit of speaking his mind, whispered together that it was to be hoped the weather improved before they reached London.

The journey from the coast had taken them several days and they had come to rest for the night in an inn still some miles from the capital. Their coming had aroused a certain flutter of excitement within the hostelry, for it was known that the party must be on their way to the King's Court, and there was speculation even among the scullions as to whether this meant a marriage for the Prince of Wales with his brother's widow, and perhaps a bride for the King.

This was not the first party of Spaniards they had seen; but the nobleman who was clearly the most important member of the party was certainly a very touchy gentleman. He complained of this and that, and although he was too haughty to speak to them they were fully aware of his fastidiousness.

Don Gutierre Gomez de Fuensalida was however in far from an ill mood. The weather might be distasteful and he hated the discomforts of travel, but he was quite certain that he was going to complete a mission, over which that fool Puebla had been stumbling for so many years, and complete it to such satisfaction to his master that great honours would be showered upon him.

The futility, he said to himself, of allowing such a man as Puebla to handle these delicate matters! A Jew of no standing! Diplomacy should be conducted only by members of the nobility.

Don Gutierre was complacent. He himself belonged to a family which could trace its glorious ancestry back through the centuries; he was wealthy; he was not in the diplomatic service of his country for financial gain but for honours. He had recently come from the Court of Philip the Handsome, and previously he had represented Ferdinand at that of Maximilian. He was fully aware of the intrigues of traitors such as Juan Manuel and he had never swerved from the cause of Ferdinand. Now that Philip was dead and Juana recognized almost universally as mad, Gutierre Gomez de Fuensalida was coming into his own; his would be the rewards of fidelity and, when he had satisfactorily arranged the marriage between Ferdinand's daughter and the Prince of Wales, Ferdinand would indeed be grateful to him.

While he mused thus a visitor arrived at the hostelry; he came riding in with a few servants and asked immediately of one of Gutierre's servants if he might be taken to his master.

"I have ridden from London," he said, "for the sole purpose of greeting Don Gutierre Gomez de Fuensalida and that I might have the pleasure of returning with him to the capital."

Gutierre, delighted when he heard that a gentleman of distinction had called to see him, although it was no more than courtesy demanded and it was certainly what he expected, ordered that the visitor should be brought to him immediately.

"I am Dr. Nicholas West, Bishop of Ely," Gutierre was told. "I heard that you had arrived and have come to usher you into Court circles, on the express command of His Highness the King."

"It gives me great pleasure to meet you," answered Gutierre.

The innkeeper, a little flustered by such distinguished guests, provided a private room in which refreshment was served to the two gentlemen.

And when they had talked of the perils of sea journeys and the weather in England, they reached the real purpose of the meeting.

"The King has not enjoyed such good health during this winter as he has hitherto," explained Dr. West. "Indeed, his physicians are in constant attendance."

"What ails His Grace?"

"He has been plagued by pains in his body for some years, and his limbs have become so stiff that it is often painful for him to put foot to the ground. These pains are always more severe during the winter months. But this winter he has suffered more than usual. He has had rheums and coughs which have kept him to his bed for many weeks. His physicians do not allow him to spend long at a time with his ministers, and there are days when they implore him not to see them at all."

"I understand," said Gutierre. "This will mean that there may be some delay in his receiving me?"

"It may well be so."

"Then I must perforce wait until he commands me to his presence. In the meantime I will call on the Infanta. I doubt not she will be eager to have news of her father."

"That is something of which I must warn you. It is the etiquette of the Court that ambassadors should not visit anyone belonging to the royal household until they have been received by the King."

"Is that so? That is going to make my position somewhat difficult . . . unless I have an early interview with the King."

"You may rest assured that as soon as His Grace's health has improved he will receive you. He is eager to have news of his friend and brother, King Ferdinand."

"He cannot be more eager for these negotiations than my master is."

"Had you any plans as to where you would lodge?"

"Yes. I thought of staying awhile in the house of Francesco Grimaldi, who, as you know, is the London agent of the Genoese bank."

Dr. West nodded. He understood that this was significant. There was no doubt in his mind that Ferdinand was now preparing to pay the remainder of Katharine's dowry and that Grimaldi would be called in to conduct the business.

"I cannot think of a more satisfactory arrangement," he said.

The conversation continued in the pleasantest manner. Dr. West informed the new Spanish ambassador of affairs at Court. He spoke of the popularity and charm of the Prince of Wales, who was becoming more and more important to the people as his father grew more infirm.

The eyes of the Spanish ambassador glinted with pleasure.

There could be no doubt that his main purpose in coming to London was to bring about the marriage of his master's daughter and the Prince of Wales.

* * *

Francesco Grimaldi was delighted to welcome the Spanish ambassador. Grimaldi was well past middle-age, but he lived well and he was fond of gaiety, and any form of excitement was welcome. He was an astute business man who had built up a considerable fortune, and was therefore able to entertain Don Gutierre Gomez de Fuensalida in a manner to which even he was accustomed.

Excellent food and wines were served at Grimaldi's table, and Gutierre was not the most discreet of men.

So the dowry which had brought so much trouble to the Infanta was at last to be paid? How many years was it since she had arrived in England a hopeful bride? It must be nearly seven. And what a sad life the poor lady had led since the death of Prince Arthur!

Gutierre found Grimaldi not only entertaining but useful, for he was able to supply that kind of Court gossip which never appeared in the state papers.

He did not see why he should change his lodgings since he was perfectly comfortable in the house of Grimaldi, which was within easy reach of the Court.

On the day of his arrival in the banker's house a young man called to see him. He humbly announced himself as the son of Dr. de Puebla, who deeply regretted that he was unable to call on the ambassador as he was confined to his bed with an attack of gout.

Gutierre looked down his long aristocratic nose at the humble son of a humble father. He was eager to show these people that he, Knight Commander of the Order of Membrilla, scion of an ancient house, was quite determined not to listen to the babbling of upstarts, who were of humble origin and *marranos* at that.

"Give your father my regrets and wishes for his speedy recovery," he said coldly.

"My father hopes you will call on him at the earliest time Your Excellency finds agreeable. He wishes me to say to you that this matter, which is the reason for your coming to England, is a very complicated one and, as the English are extremely shrewd, he would like to make you acquainted with all details as soon as possible."

Gutierre bowed his head and murmured that he would bear the matter in mind.

He would make no appointment to call at the residence of his fellow ambassador, and the young man was forced to retire in some bewilderment.

When he had gone, Gutierre let his anger burst forth.

Does that Jew think that he can teach me Court manners? he asked himself. He would show Dr. de Puebla—and their master, Ferdinand—that the only ambassadors worthy of the name were those of noble blood.

\*　　　\*　　　\*

The news was brought to Katharine that her father's ambassador was in England, and she rejoiced. She was optimistic. Her father's affairs were becoming prosperous once more and she knew that, on the rise and fall of her father's power, her own future prospects would fluctuate.

She wept bitterly when she heard the news of Juana's strange conduct and of how she kept the dead body of her husband with her and refused to relinquish it. She had become accustomed to hearing her sister referred to as the mad Queen; but she was still endeavouring to bring about a marriage between Juana and Henry because Henry so desired it and, she told herself, if Juana were to come to England, I could help to look after her; and surely she could not bring the body of her dead husband here. Katharine believed that once Juana could be persuaded to bury Philip, she would begin to regain her sanity.

She was not unconscious of the fact that, as a result of Juana's madness, Ferdinand was a greater power in Spain than he would be if Juana were sound in mind and able to rule; and, since it was due to the rising power of Ferdinand that she herself was treated with more respect, she could not help reflecting sadly that they appeared to be a house divided against itself, since Juana's misfortune could work to her, Katharine's, good.

She was all eagerness to meet Gutierre Gomez de Fuensalida, for she would be delighted to dispense with the services of Puebla.

Her maids of honour—and Francesca de Carceres in particular —were continually complaining about the little man. They were sure it was due to his mismanagement of affairs that they were still living in this unsatisfactory way, while the years passed, they grew older, and no husbands were found for them.

Francesca was particularly bitter, as she loved gaiety more than did the others. Maria de Salinas and Inez de Veñegas were resigned, and she believed these two very dear friends of hers suffered more on her account than on their own.

Katharine lost no time in telling them of the arrival of the new ambassador.

Francesca was frankly delighted. "And Don Gutierre Gomez de Fuensalida!" she cried. "He is a very grand gentleman. He will know how to deal with your father-in-law, Highness."

"I do not believe my father-in-law will care whether he has to deal with the nobleman or the lawyer Jew. His great concern will be the payment of the dowry."

"I shall make our sad state known to the new ambassador," declared Francesca. "Something must be done for us before we are too old to be married at all."

Poor Francesca! thought Katharine. How she longed for marriage! She should be the mother of several children by now.

"I am a little anxious," she said. "I am wondering what will happen when my plate and jewels are valued. The value will be found to be a great deal less than when I arrived. And these were to be part of the dowry."

"But what could Your Highness do?" demanded Maria de Salinas. "You had to live."

"There are times," Katharine murmured, "when I believe that kings and ambassadors do not think that it is necessary for a princess and her household to eat. She is merely a figure to be used when the state needs her. She can marry. She can bear children. But eat! That is not considered at all necessary."

Maria de Salinas was startled to hear the bitterness in Katharine's voice. It was well, she reflected, that the new ambassador was here and that it was possible he would bring the negotiations, which had been going on for so many years, to a satisfactory end.

\*　　　\*　　　\*

When Henry received the Spanish Ambassador, the King was wrapped in a long robe and sat huddled near a blazing fire.

"My dear Ambassador," said Henry with more warmth than he usually displayed. "You find me in ill health. I cannot move easily, so you must sit beside me and give me news of my dear brother, the King of Aragon."

"My master sends his greetings to Your Grace," answered Fuensalida, bowing with courtly grace.

"I pray you be seated," said Henry; and, his alert eyes looking out from the wrinkles which pain had set about them, he summed up the character of the new ambassador. Here was one of the Spanish grandees, a man with a great opinion of himself. That was not displeasing. Henry liked weakness in the ambassadors of other countries.

When Fuensalida was seated, Henry said: "I know that you have come to see me on two matters of great importance and interest to me. They are also matters of great happiness: marriages. How much better it is for Kings to unite through such alliances than to quarrel together! What news do you bring me of Queen Juana?"

"There is no King to whom Ferdinand would rather see his daughter married than yourself."

"Then why delay . . . why delay?"

"It is on account of the strangeness of the Queen of Castile."

Henry frowned. "I have heard of this strangeness, but what does it mean? She has recently been brought to bed of a fine daughter. She has borne sons. I would ask nothing more of a wife than that."

"It is said that the Queen of Castile is insane."

"Insane! Bah! She is fertile. We in England would have no objection to a little insanity if a Queen were fertile, as I have already explained."

"Then the negotiations should go forward."

"And with speed," cried the King. "You see me here . . ."

He did not finish, and Fuensalida spoke for him: "Your Grace is no longer in your first youth. A speedy marriage is a necessity for you that you might get sons before it is too late."

Henry was astonished. No one had ever dared refer to the fact that it was possible he would not be long for this world. And here was this stranger calmly telling him so. He felt very angry, the more so because he knew the truth of the statement. Had they told Juana that he was an old man and that his eagerness for their marriage was not his regard for her but the immediate and desperate need to beget a son before the grave claimed him?

Surely this ambassador must be the most tactless man Ferdinand could possibly have sent him.

"And there is a matter of great importance to us both," went on Fuensalida who, since he never considered the feelings of others, was never conscious of wounding them, "and that is the marriage of the Infanta and the Prince of Wales."

Impudence! thought Henry. He dares to change the subject! Where are his manners? Or does he think that a Spanish grandee takes precedence over a King of England?

Henry did not show his anger when dealing with foreign diplomats. He said calmly: "I have a great regard for the daughter of the King of Aragon. I find her gracious, charming and beautiful. It has grieved me that she must live so long in such uncertain state."

"Your Grace remembers that he promised that she should marry the Prince of Wales?"

"I do not forget it and I see no reason why this marriage should not take place, providing certain questions can be amicably settled between my friend the King of Aragon and myself."

"It is precisely that such matters should be settled that I am here with Your Grace."

"Is that so?"

Still Henry showed no sign of the fury he felt. It was not the marriage of Katharine and the Prince of Wales he was eager to discuss, but his own marriage with Juana.

"Why," he went on, "I remember full well that these two were betrothed. I am not a man to break my word. I should tell you that the Prince of Wales has had many offers . . . many brilliant offers of marriage."

"There could scarcely be a more brilliant marriage, Your Grace, than with a daughter of Spain."

Insolent fellow! thought Henry. He would see that Ferdinand realized his folly in sending such a man to England. Henry greatly preferred little Dr. de Puebla—a man who lacked this arrogance and certainly realized that the best way to serve his master was not to antagonize those with whom that master wished to make new friendships.

"I am weary," he said. "My doctors warned me. You will be received by my councillors, and you can lay the terms of the King of Aragon before them." The King closed his eyes. Gutierre Gomez de Fuensalida was dismissed.

\*        \*        \*

The Council were far from helpful. Fuensalida did not know that the King had already told them of his dislike for the new ambassador, and had hinted that no concessions should be made to him.

As for Fuensalida, he was afraid that certain members of this Council were not of sufficient nobility to be on equal terms with him, and he was disgusted that the King was not present that he might address himself to him.

The Bishop of Winchester, who with the Bishop of Ely and the Earl of Surrey formed part of the Council, showed no grace or finesse in dealing with this delicate matter of Katharine's dowry. They wanted to know how the money was to be paid.

"As previously arranged," said Fuensalida. "There will be sixty-five thousand crowns and the remainder in plate and jewellery."

"You have presumably brought the plate and jewels with you?" one of the members of the Council enquired.

"You know full well that the Infanta brought her plate and jewels with her when she arrived in this country."

"That," said Surrey, "was in the year 1501; quite a long time ago."

"You knew that this plate and these jewels were intended for her dowry?"

"How could that be," asked Winchester, "when the Infanta has been wearing the jewels and using the plate?"

"And disposing of them if my information is correct," added Surrey.

The Bishop of Ely added slyly: "On the marriage of a husband and wife, the wife's property becomes that of the husband. Therefore it would seem that the Infanta's jewels became the property of Prince Arthur and consequently the property of the King."

"Does Don Gutierre Gomez de Fuensalida then seek to pay the King the remainder of the Infanta's dowry with the King's own plate and jewels?" Ely wanted to know.

"This is monstrous!" cried Fuensalida, who had never learned to control his temper.

Winchester was delighted, for he knew that the best way of scoring over the Spaniard was to make him lose his temper.

He went on: "This is the King's property, into which over a number of years the Infanta has been breaking, selling a piece here, and a piece there, so that much of that which should be in the King's coffers is now in those of the Lombard Street merchants!"

"This is a matter for your shame!" shouted Fuensalida. "You have treated the Infanta as a beggar. You have dared behave so to a daughter of Spain."

"Whose dowry was never paid in full," put in Winchester.

"I shall not remain to hear more of such insolence!" cried Fuensalida; and he left the council chamber to the delight of the English.

# IN THE HOUSE OF GRIMALDI

FRANCESCA DE CARCERES was determined on action. Something had to be done, and she guessed that the marriage negotiations of the Infanta and the Prince of Wales were as far as ever from reaching a satisfactory conclusion.

Until the Infanta was married, none of her maids of honour would be.

And thus, thought Francesca, the years will pass until we are all dry old spinsters whom no one would take in marriage even if we had big dowries.

Francesca was never one to wait for opportunity; she went out to seek it.

She had met Don Gutierre Gomez de Fuensalida and recognized in him a nobleman such as Puebla could never be. Being suspicious of Puebla and believing that he worked for the King of England rather than for Ferdinand, she wished that he should be recalled to Spain; it seemed that he never would be, because Ferdinand for some strange reason trusted him. And in any case the old fellow was now so infirm that he would be of no use in Spain. It was characteristic of Ferdinand that he should not recall him. It was so much easier to keep the ailing old man in England, pay him no wages and let him work for Spain.

Francesca pinned her hopes on Fuensalida.

She decided therefore that she would see him in private. This was not an easy thing to do at Court because when he came he was not alone; and in any case what chance had a maid of honour of a private interview without calling a great deal of attention to herself to obtain it?

There was plenty of freedom now in Katharine's entourage, so Francesca had planned that she would slip away one afternoon and call on the ambassador at his lodgings, which she knew to be in the house of the banker, Francesco Grimaldi.

She wrapped herself in a cloak, the hood of which did much to conceal her face, and set out. When she reached the banker's house she was taken into a small room and the servant who had brought her in went away to discover whether the Spanish ambassador was in his apartment.

While Francesca waited she examined the rich hangings and the fine furniture in this small room. She had been struck by the grandeur of the house as soon as she entered it. Perhaps this appreciation was the more forceful because she thought of the poverty in which she and the Infanta's maids of honour had lived for the last few years.

Banking must be a profitable business, she reflected; and it was brought home to her that people such as bankers must live in more affluent circumstances than many a Prince or Princess.

The door was opened and a rather plump man stood in the doorway. Francesca noticed at once that his jacket was made of rich velvet and that his stomacher was most elegantly embroidered. His hanging sleeves were somewhat exaggeratedly long and there were jewels at his throat and on his fingers. He gave an impression of elegance and wealth and his corpulence and air of general well-being indicated a man who lived most comfortably. His eyes were warm brown and very friendly.

When he bowed low over Francesca's hand on which his lips lingered slightly longer than Court etiquette would have considered necessary, she discovered that she was not displeased.

"I am happy to see you in my house," he said. "But alas, Don Gutierre Gomez de Fuensalida is not here at this time. If there is anything I could do to help you, depend upon it I should be greatly honoured."

"That is very kind of you," Francesca replied, and she told him who she was.

"This is a happy day for my house," answered the banker, "when one of the Infanta's ladies call. And that she should surely be the most beautiful adds to my pleasure."

"You are very gracious. Will you be so kind as to tell Don Gutierre Gomez de Fuensalida that I called? I should have told him I was coming."

"Pray do not leave so soon. I cannot say when he will return, but it is possible that he may do so within the hour. If in my humble way I could entertain you during that time, I should be most happy."

Francesca said: "Perhaps I could linger for a little while." And she was gratified to see the look of bemused pleasure in the face of the banker.

"Allow me to offer you refreshment," he said.

Francesca hesitated. This was most unconventional, but she was known to be the most adventurous of the Infanta's maids of honour and she thought how she would enliven them all when she returned by telling them of her adventures at the home of the Genoese banker; so she succumbed to temptation and sat down; whereupon Grimaldi summoned a servant and gave his orders.

Half an hour later Francesca was still in the banker's company; she was amusing him with stories of Court life, and he was amusing her equally with stories of his own world. When she expressed her admiration for his beautiful furniture he insisted on showing her some of his more elaborate pieces, which resulted in a tour of this very fine house of which he was clearly—and justly—proud.

Fuensalida had not returned when Francesca decided that she really must leave; Grimaldi wished to escort her back, but she refused to allow this.

"We should be seen," she said. "And I should doubtless be severely reprimanded."

"What a mischievous young lady you are!" murmured the banker rapturously.

"One must bestir oneself in some ways," retorted Francesca. "I do admit the others are somewhat prim."

"I shall never cease to bless the day you came to see Don Gutierre Gomez de Fuensalida, and I feel grateful to him for not returning, thus allowing me to enjoy your company and have it all to myself."

"Are bankers always so gallant?" asked Francesca almost archly.

"Even bankers cannot fail to be in the presence of such overwhelming beauty," he told her.

It was all very pleasant and Francesca had enjoyed the encounter; and when he said goodbye his lips lingered even longer on her hand. We are so unused to such attentions, she told herself; and even when they do not come from the nobility they are not without their attractions.

"If you should ever desire to do me this honour again," he said earnestly, "I should rejoice in my good fortune."

She did not answer, but her smile was provocative.

She hurried back to the palace, telling herself how she would enjoy explaining her little adventure to the others; she imagined herself imitating the banker's voice as he paid her the most extravagant compliments. How they would laugh! And who among them had ever had such an adventure?

Then suddenly she decided she would say nothing. What if she were forbidden to visit the banker's house again? Not that she intended to go again; but suppose she wanted to, it would be most irritating to be forbidden to do so.

No, for the present her encounter with Francesco Grimaldi should remain her secret.

*        *        *

When Katharine heard that Fuensalida had quarrelled with the Council she was disturbed and commanded Puebla to come to her at once.

The old man sent for his litter and, as he was carried from his lodging to the palace, he reflected that he would not make many more such journeys, for he was well aware that the end was in sight for him. It was sad that he had worked so hard and unfailingly to bring about this marriage without success, and now that Ferdinand had sent his new ambassador the position had rapidly worsened.

He did not expect to be appreciated. When had he ever been appreciated? He was a Jew by birth, and he had become a Christian. Such as he must become accustomed to injustice. He should think himself lucky that he was not in Spain, where he might so easily commit some mild indiscretion and be taken before the tribunal of the Inquisition and charged with heresy.

At least, he thought, I shall die in my bed; and the reward for my services will be merely neglect and general ingratitude.

As he dragged himself painfully into the Infanta's apartment Katharine felt an immediate pity for him.

"Why, you are ill !" she said.

"I grow old, Highness," he murmured.

She called for a chair that he might sit in her presence, and for this he was grateful.

She came straight to the point. "I had hoped," she said, "that my dowry was to be paid and that I should be able to claim the fulfilment of my marriage treaty. It seems this is not to be so. When I came here it was understood that my plate and jewels were to form part of my dowry, and now Don Gutierre Gomez de Fuensalida informs me that the King will not accept this."

"He must accept it," said Puebla. "It was part of the marriage treaty."

"But Don Gutierre says that the Council refuse to admit this."

"Then they must be made to admit it. I fear he has offended the Council with his quick temper and high-handed manners. He forgets that he is in England; and he will never bring matters to a satisfactory conclusion if he is going to offend the people whom it is necessary to placate."

"You think that they can be made to accept the plate and jewels?"

"I am sure they will. But the jewels and plate are much depleted, I believe."

"I have found it necessary to have some money to live, and I have pawned or sold a considerable amount of the plate and jewels."

"Highness, if your father will make up the discrepancy I feel sure we can come to an arrangement with the King."

"Then you must see Fuensalida and make him understand this."

"I will. And Your Highness should have no fear. The King will wish to come to this arrangement. He is eager for a match between your nephew, Charles, and the Princess Mary. He is even more eager to enter into marriage with your sister, Her Highness Queen Juana. I believe that a little diplomacy will settle these matters amicably."

"Then I pray you go to Fuensalida with all speed. And, Dr. de Puebla, I am concerned for your health. I am going to send my physician to see you. You must act on his advice."

"Your Highness is gracious," murmured Puebla.

He felt resigned. He knew that Fuensalida was the last man to handle this delicate situation with the right amount of tact and shrewdness. He knew also that when Katharine's physician saw him, he would be told to keep to his bed. That he knew was tantamount to receiving his death warrant.

\* \* \*

Katharine was frustrated. She was aware that the King disliked the Spanish ambassador and made continual excuses not to grant the interviews he asked.

Puebla, who alone might have made some progress now that Ferdinand really seemed desirous of settling his daughter's affairs, had now taken to his bed. Too late Fuensalida learned how useful the little man could be.

The matter dragged on. Henry, who was beginning to see that he would never get Juana, was growing angry. He did not trust Ferdinand. Henry was becoming increasingly difficult to deal with because he was now in acute pain and the calmness which had been characteristic of him was deserting him. His skin was turning yellow and he was rapidly losing weight. There were whole days when he was invisible to any but his doctors.

Katharine was so eagerly watching the progress of her own affairs that she failed to notice the change in one of her maids of honour. Francesca had seemed to grow younger; she had come into possession of some beautiful pieces of jewellery. She did not flaunt these before the eyes of the others, it was true, but on one occasion when Maria de Rojas had called attention to a handsome ruby ring which she was wearing, Francesca had shrugged her shoulders, murmured, "Have you not seen it before?" and hastily changed the subject.

Francesca was the only member of the Infanta's household who was not depressed by the way things were going; each day she contrived to slip away, and remained absent for several hours.

Fuensalida was making himself unpleasant to various members of the Infanta's household. He had quarrelled with Puebla many times, and only the little man's humility and desire to bring about a successful solution of the troublesome matter of the dowry made their association possible. His chief enemy in the household was Fray Diego Fernandez, who was Katharine's confessor and whose position gave him especial influence over her. This friar seemed to Fuensalida an arrogant young man because he did not show sufficient respect to the ambassador, and he had threatened to write to Ferdinand to the effect that Fernandez was not only incompetent but dangerous, as the Infanta placed too much trust in him.

Katharine was desperate, realizing that when she needed as much support as she could get, her affairs were continually being obstructed by strife within her own circle.

One day Fernandez came to her in a state of great indignation. He had had a narrow escape, he told her. Fuensalida had made an attempt to have him arrested and shipped out of the country.

Katharine was angry, but there was nothing she could do. Puebla was confined to his bed and clearly was dying; now she reproached herself for not appreciating that little man before. It was only now that she could compare him with Fuensalida that she realized how admirable he had been. She could not ask her father to recall Fuensalida and send her another ambassador. The situation was too involved and, by the time a new man arrived, who could say what might have happened?

So she prayed constantly that her ill luck would change and that soon her affairs might be put in order.

*        *        *

What joy it was to escape to the house of the Genoese banker! thought Francesca. How merry that man was, and how delighted that Francesca de Carceres should deign to visit him. It was true, of course, that she was of a most noble family and he was merely a banker; but how much more extravagantly he lived, and what great comfort he enjoyed!

She could not recall how many times she had been to his house, ostensibly to visit the ambassador, and how she arranged her

visits to fall at those times when she knew Fuensalida would not
be present.

She had meant to implore him to do something for Katharine's
maids of honour, who should have marriages arranged for them,
but she had found no opportunity of speaking of this matter to
the ambassador.

There was so much of interest to see in the house, and her
banker delighted in showing her. She had only to admire something, and he implored her to accept it. He was surely the most
generous man in the world!

So it was fun to slip on her cloak and hasten to his lodgings.

On this occasion he was waiting for her, and he seemed more
serious; as it was unusual to see him serious, she wondered what
had happened.

They took wine together with some of those excellent cakes
which his cooks made especially for her, and as they sat together
he said suddenly: "How strange that I should be Francesco, and
you Francesca. It seems yet another link between us."

"Yes," she smiled, "it is certainly strange."

Then he became even more serious and said: "How long can
this continue?"

"You mean my visits? Oh, until the Court moves, or until I am
discovered and forbidden to come."

"That would stop you . . . if you were forbidden?"

"I might be tempted to disobey."

He leaned towards her and took one of her hands. "Francesca,"
he said, "would you consider becoming mistress of this house?"

She grew a little pale, realizing the enormity of what he was
suggesting. She . . . marry him! But her marriage was one which
would have to be approved by the Infanta, by the Queen of
Castile or by Ferdinand, and by the King of England. Did he not
understand that she was not a little seamstress or some such
creature to make a match on the spur of the moment?

"The suggestion is repulsive to you?" he said wistfully.

"No . . . no!" She was emphatic. She was thinking of how dull
her life had been before these visits; and how it would seem even
more dull if she were forced to give them up. She went on:
"Marriages are arranged for people in my position. I should never
be allowed to marry you."

"You have been neglected," he argued. "To whom do you
owe loyalty? As for myself, I am no subject of the King of England. If I wish to marry, I marry. If you decided you did not
want to go back to the palace one day, I would have a priest here
who should marry us. I would place all my possessions and myself

at your service. I love you, Francesca. You are young, you are beautiful, you are of noble birth, but you are a prisoner; and the only one of these attributes which can remain to you is your noble birth. Francesca, do not allow them to bury you alive. Marry me. Have we not been happy together? I will make you happy for the rest of your life."

Francesca rose. She was trembling.

She must go quickly. She must be alone to think. She was terrified that she would commit some indiscretion which would decide the whole of her future life.

"You are afraid now," he said gently. "Make no mistake. It is not of me, Francesca, that you should be afraid. You would never be afraid of me. You are bold and adventurous. Not for you the palace prison. Come to me, Francesca, and I will make you free."

"I must go," she said.

He did not attempt to detain her.

"You will think of what I have said?" he asked.

"I cannot stop thinking of it," she answered. Then he took her face in his hands and kissed her forehead tenderly. She knew that she was going to feel cheated if she did not see him again. Yet how could she?

# JUANA AT TORDESILLAS

JUANA IN THE town of Arcos knew nothing of the negotiations which had been going on to marry her to the King of England. She had settled in this most unhealthy climate, but she was quite unaware of the cold winds which penetrated the palace. Her little Catalina had become a lively little girl who seemed readily to accept the strangeness of her mother. Juana had also insisted that her son Ferdinand should be brought to live with her, and this wish had been granted. But little Ferdinand, who was nearly six years old, did not take kindly to his mother's household. He did not like the coffin which was always prominently displayed; nor did he care to look on his dead father and to see his mother fondling the corpse.

Juana went about the palace dressed in rags, and she did not sit at table but ate her food from a plate on the floor like a cat or a dog. She never washed herself, and there were no women-servants in the house except the old washerwoman.

Music could sometimes be heard being played in the Queen's apartment; otherwise there was almost continuous silence.

Young Ferdinand was very happy when his grandfather came to Arcos and took him away, although his mother screamed and shouted and had to be held by attendants while he rode away with his grandfather. Ferdinand loved his grandfather, who made much of him.

"We are both Ferdinands," said the elder Ferdinand, and that delighted the boy, who decided that he would be exactly like his grandfather when he grew up.

Juana might have gone on in this state at Arcos but for the fact that revolt broke out in Andalusia, and it immediately occurred to Ferdinand that the rebels might plan to use her as a figurehead. He decided then that he was going to remove her to the isolated castle of Tordesillas, where it would be so much easier to keep her under restraint.

He came to the Palace of Arcos one day and went straight to those apartments where Juana was sitting, staring moodily at the coffin of her husband. Her hair, which had not been dressed for many months, hung about her haggard face; her face and hands were dirty, and her clothes hung in filthy rags about her gaunt figure.

Ferdinand looked at her in horror. There was indeed no need to *pretend* that she was mad.

Undoubtedly she must be removed to Tordesillas. He knew that there was a plot afoot to displace him and set up young Charles as King. As Charles was now nine, this arrangement would give certain ambitious men the power they needed; but Ferdinand was determined that the Regency should remain in his hands, and he would be uneasy until Juana was his prisoner in some place where he could keep her well guarded.

"My daughter," he said as he approached her—he could not bring himself to touch her. As well touch a beggar or gipsy; they would probably be more wholesome—"I am anxious on your account."

She did not look at him.

"Last time I was here," he went on, "I did not please you. But you must realize that it is necessary for the people to see little Ferdinand; and what I did was for the best."

Still she did not answer. It was true then that, although she had raged when he had taken her son, a few days later she had completely forgotten the boy. There was no real place in that deranged mind for anyone but the dead man in the coffin.

Ferdinand went on: "This place is most unhealthy. You cannot continue to live here in this . . . squalor. I must insist that you leave here. The castle of Tordesillas has been made ready to receive you. It is worthy of you. The climate is good. There you will recover your health."

She came to life suddenly. "I shall not go. I shall stay here. You cannot make me go. I am the Queen."

He answered quietly: "This place is surrounded by my soldiers. If you do not go of your own free will, I shall be obliged to force you to go. You must prepare to leave at once."

"So you are making me a prisoner!" she said.

"The soldiers are here to guard you. All that is done is for your good."

"You are trying to take him away from me," she screamed.

"Take the coffin with you. There is no reason why you should not continue to mourn in Tordesillas, as you do in Arcos."

She was silent for a while. Then she said: "I need time to prepare myself."

"A day," he said. "You can wash yourself, have your hair dressed, change into suitable clothes in a day."

"I never travel by day."

"Then travel by night."

She sat still, nodding.

And the next night she left Arcos. She had been washed; her wild hair had been set into some order; she wore a gown suited to her rank; and, taking little Catalina in her litter, she set out with her followers; as usual, beside the Queen's litter, so that it was never out of her sight, went the hearse drawn by four horses.

Through the nights she travelled and, as the third day was beginning to break, the party arrived at the old bridge across the Douro. There Juana paused to look at the castle which was so like a fortress. Immediately opposite this castle was the convent of Santa Clara, and in the cloisters of this convent she allowed the coffin to be placed. Then from the windows of her apartments she could look across to the coffin, and she spent the greater part of her days at her window watching over her dead. Each night she left the castle for the convent, where she embraced the corpse of Philip the Handsome.

So dragged on the long years of mourning, and each day she grew a little more strange, a little more remote from the world; only in one thing was she constant—her love for the handsome philanderer who had played such a large part in making her what she was.

K ATHARINE HAD NOW lost all hope. Her affairs were in the direst disorder. Fuensalida had quarrelled openly with Henry, and when the ambassador had gone to Court he had been told that the King had no wish to see him.

Fuensalida, haughty, arrogant and tactless, had even tried to force an entry, with the result that he had suffered the extreme indignity of being seized by guards and put outside the Palace precincts.

Never had an ambassador been submitted to such shame, which clearly indicated that Henry had no respect for Ferdinand's suggestions. Indeed Henry was boasting that he would marry Mary and Charles without the help of Spain.

Katharine was with her maids of honour when the news was brought to her of Puebla's death. This, she had at last come to realize, was one of the greatest blows which could befall her, for now there was no one to work for her in England but the incompetent Fuensalida.

"This is the last blow," she said. "I fear now that there is no hope.".

"But what will become of us?" asked Maria de Salinas.

"Doubtless we shall be sent back to Spain," put in Maria de Rojas hopefully.

Katharine said nothing. She realized that to be sent back to Spain was the last thing she wanted. She would go back, humiliated, the unwanted Infanta, the widow who was yet a virgin. Had ever any Princess of Spain been so unfortunate as she was? There was only one dignified course left to her, and that was marriage with the Prince of Wales.

That was hopeless, for the King had shown so clearly that he would not allow the marriage to take place. Whenever she saw the Prince he had kindly smiles for her, which was comforting, for his importance grew daily, one might say hourly.

Katharine noticed that Francesca was not with them.

"Where is Francesca?" she asked.

"I have not seen her, Highness," answered Maria de Salinas.

"Now that I recall it," pursued Katharine, "she seems to absent herself often. What does she do when she is not with us?"

No one could answer that; which was strange because Francesca had been inclined to talk a great deal—often it seemed too much—of her personal affairs.

"I shall ask her when she returns," said Katharine; and then they fell to discussing what would happen when Ferdinand learned that his ambassador had been refused admittance to the Palace.

Nothing would happen, thought Katharine wretchedly. Looking back over the years since Arthur's death, she saw that her position had changed but little. She could go on living in penury and uncertainty for the rest of her days.

*          *          *

"Highness!" It was Maria de Rojas, and her voice was trembling with excitement.

Katharine had left her maids of honour an hour before because she wished to be alone; she had felt she could no longer endure their chatter, which alternated between the desire to raise her hopes by improbable changes of fortune and sighing for their native land.

She looked at Maria quickly, eager to know what had happened to change her mood.

"This has been delivered at the Palace. It is for you."

Katharine took the letter which Maria was holding out to her. "It is in Francesca's handwriting," said Maria.

"Francesca!"

Katharine's heart began to beat fast as she opened the letter, and she hastily scanned the words without taking them in the first time. Then she read it again. It was brief and to the point.

Francesca would never return. She had married Francesco Grimaldi, the banker from Genoa.

"It is . . . impossible!" breathed Katharine.

Maria was at her side; forgetting all ceremony, all discipline as she looked over Katharine's shoulder and read the words which the newly married bride had written.

"Francesca . . . married! And to a banker! Oh, how could she? How could she! A banker! What will her family say? Highness, what will *you* do?"

"It must be some joke," murmured Katharine.

But they both knew that it was no joke; Maria's horror changed momentarily to envy. "At least she *married*," she whispered; her lips quivered and there came to her eyes the frantic look of a prisoner who has heard of another's escape, but sees no way out for herself.

"So this is where she has been," went on Katharine. "It is the man with whom Fuensalida had his lodgings. How could she, a Carceres, so far forget the honour due to her rank as to marry a banker!"

Maria was speaking as though to herself: "Perhaps she fell in love with him. But it is more likely to be because he is very rich and we have been so poor. Francesca did not have an offer all the time we were here . . . perhaps she thought she never would have one."

Katharine remembered her dignity. "Leave me now," she said. "If she has left us we should make no effort to bring her back. She has chosen the way she wishes to go."

"Your Highness will allow this?"

Katharine smiled bitterly. "You do not blame her, Maria. I can remember, when I came to England, how eager you all were to come with me. It seemed such a glorious future, did it not? But how differently it turned out! Francesca has escaped . . . that is all. As you would escape, Maria, if the opportunity offered itself. Go now. Break this news to the others. I'll warrant they will share your envy of Francesca."

Maria left her mistress and Katharine re-read the letter. Francesca was happy, she said. She had married the man of her choice. There was excitement in every line. Francesca had escaped.

It seemed to Katharine in that moment that she touched the depth of hopelessness. Gay Francesca had risked the displeasure of kings and a powerful noble family to escape from the dreary existence which she had been forced to share with the daughter of Ferdinand and Isabella.

\*          \*          \*

It was the month of April. The birch and willow were in flower; the stitchwort threw a silvery sheen on the green hedges; and the meadows were bright with deep yellow cowslips.

In the Palace of Richmond, Henry VII lay dying, and in the streets the people rejoiced furtively. The old reign was passing and the new one would soon begin. People forgot that their King had brought peace to England. To most he had seemed unkingly because he hated war—not because of the misery it brought, it was true, but because of the waste of good money and lives which could be used to make the country prosperous. He had never spent lavishly on pageants for the people's pleasure, and there had only been rich ceremonies when there had been the need to impress other rulers with England's powers.

To the people he was a miserly King, insignificant in appearance; he had imposed cruel taxes on his subjects; he had shown little affection even to his family. They forgot that from 1485, when he had come to the throne, to this year of 1509 the country had lived in peace, and in place of a bankrupt state he had built up a rich treasury. They did not tell themselves that this was the first King who had lived within his income, who had laid the foundations on which could be built a major Power. They said: "The old miser is dying. Old Henry is passing; this is the day of young Henry." And when they thought of their laughing, golden Prince, they said: "Now England will be merry."

The excitement throughout the Court was growing to a feverish pitch. Courtiers gathered in little groups waiting for the cry of "The King is dead."

That young Henry should marry almost immediately was a matter on which all seemed to agree. Such a Prince needed a Queen. Who should it be?

There were many who favoured alliance with France. Let it be Marguerite of Angoulême, they said. There were others who believed that alliance with the Hapsburgs would be more advantageous. Let it be Eleanor, the daughter of Juana and Philip. Was Eleanor too young for their golden Prince? Well then, Duke Albert of Bavaria had a daughter. Maximilian would be delighted to sponsor such a match.

There was no mention of Katharine of Aragon, who had gone through a betrothal ceremony with the Prince of Wales some years before.

When Fuensalida came to visit Katharine he was gloomy. He was shut out from the Palace; he was useless as an ally. He told her that he was making arrangements to have her plate and jewels secretly shipped back to Spain.

He could not have said more clearly: The game is over, and we have lost.

*        *        *

The Prince of Wales waited in his apartments. Soon he would hear the stampede. They would come to acclaim him as their King. They, no less than he, had been waiting for this day.

He would tower above them all; none could mistake him, with his great height and his crown of fiery hair; his big, beaming and benign countenance was known throughout the country.

His eyes narrowed as he thought of the years of restraint when he, the beloved of the people, had been forced to obey his father.

He was no longer a boy, being in his eighteenth year. Surely this was the threshold of glorious manhood. He could not be merely a man; he was a god. He had so much beauty, so much strength. There was none at Court who could compare with him; and now, as though not content with the gifts which had been showered on him, fate was putting the crown of yellow gold on that red-gold head.

From his window he could see the courtiers. They were whispering together . . . about him. Of course it was about him. The whole country was talking about him. They were saying he should marry soon, and marry soon he would, for he had a fancy for a wife.

Marguerite from France, who thought her brother the most wonderful man in the world? Little Eleanor who was but a child? They were daring to choose his bride for him!

He could scarcely wait for the moment when they would proclaim him King. One of his first acts would be to show them that he was their King in truth, and that, whether it was a bride or a matter of policy, it was the King who would decide.

They were coming now. So it was all over. The long-awaited moment was at hand.

He was ready for them as they came into the apartment. His eyes gleamed with appreciation, for he quickly sensed the new respect, the subtle difference in the way a King was greeted.

They were on their knees before him.

"Then it is so?" he said. "Alas, my father!"

But there was no time for sorrow. There was only triumph for the cry had gone up: "The King is dead. Long live the King! Long live King Henry VIII!"

*         *         *

Katharine had come to pay homage with the rest, and kneeling before him, she looked appealing in her humility.

The young King turned to those who stood about him and said: "You may leave us. I have something to say to the Infanta which she must know before all others."

When they were alone he said: "You may rise, Katharine."

He was smiling at her with the expression of a boy who has prepared, for a friend, a wonderful surprise, in which he is going to find as much pleasure—or even more—than the one for whom it is intended.

"Doubtless," he said, "you have heard of many plans afoot to marry me to Princesses of Europe."

"I have, Your Grace."

"And I venture to think they have caused you some disquiet."

H*

Henry did not wait for confirmation of that which he considered to be obvious. "They need concern you no more. I have chosen my own bride. Do you think, Katharine, that I am the man to allow others to decide such a matter for me?"

"I did not think you would be, Your Grace."

"Then you are right, Kate. I have chosen." He took both her hands in his and kissed them. "You are to be my bride. You are to be Queen of England."

"I . . . I . . ." she stammered.

He beamed. No speech could have been more eloquent in his ears. She was overwhelmed by the honour; she was overcome with joy. He was delighted with her.

"I'll brook no refusal!" This was a joke. How could any woman in her right senses refuse the most glorious offer that could possibly be made? "I have made up my mind. You *shall* be my bride!"

How handsome he was; his face creased in that happy, sunny smile. Yet behind it there remained the shadow of the sullen boy who had said: Nobody shall tell me what I must do. I make my own decisions.

For a brief moment Katharine asked herself what would have become of her if this boy had been told he must marry her instead of having been forbidden to.

Then she refused to consider such a thought.

Of what importance was what might have been, when she was being offered freedom from poverty and the humiliating position in which she had lived for so many years?

She knew the waiting was over. The neglected Infanta was about to become the most courted woman in England, the Queen, the bride of the most handsome, the most kingly ruler in Christendom.

# QUEEN KATHARINE

KATHARINE RODE BESIDE the King through the streets of London.

A few days earlier they had been married in the Palace of Greenwich, for Henry, once having made up his mind, was eager for the marriage to be celebrated.

He was attentive to his bride; he was affectionate; he, who had never made a secret of his feelings, announced to his councillors that he loved her beyond all women.

So they must proceed from Greenwich to the Tower, and with them rode the flower of the nobility; through the streets they went, past the rich tapestries which hung from the windows to welcome them; and Cornhill, proud that all should know it was the richest street in the city, hung cloth of gold from its windows. The route was lined with young girls in white to indicate their virginity; all sang praises of their King and Queen.

There was Henry, and even he had never looked quite so magnificent as he did on that day; his enormous figure ablaze with jewels, his open countenance shining with good intentions and pleasure in his people and himself. The handsomest King ever to ride through the city of London, not excepting his maternal grandfather, Edward IV.

And there was the Queen looking radiant, with her beautiful hair streaming over her shoulders, on her head a coronal set with jewels of many colours. She was dressed as a bride in white satin exquisitely embroidered, and she rode in a litter of cloth of gold drawn by two white horses.

It was not easy to recognize in this dazzling bride the neglected Infanta of Durham House.

Happiness had brought beauty to her face.

She could only say to herself: It is over . . . all the humiliation, all the misery. Who would have believed it possible that it could have happened so quickly?

And there was another matter for rejoicing. She was in love. What woman could help but fall in love with the gay and handsome King who had rescued her from all her misery? He was the Prince of legend, and no such Prince had ever been so handsome as this young Henry VIII of England.

The people cheered her. They were ready to cheer anyone

whom their King honoured, for they told themselves, the old days of parsimony and taxation were over; a gay young King was on the throne.

There were some in the crowd who remembered the day the Queen had married Arthur. Was a brother's widow the happiest choice? Was there not some allusion to this in the Bible which stated that such marriage was illegal?

But the sun was shining. The dour reign of Henry VII was over, and England was about to grow merry.

Away with such thoughts! This was the occasion of their King's wedding. He had married the woman of his choice. He was a radiantly happy bridegroom and a dazzling King.

"Long live King Henry VIII and his bride!" shouted the people of London.

And so from the pleasant Palace of Greenwich came the dazzling cavalcade, through the gaily decked streets into the precincts of the Tower of London.

The grey fortress looked grim, the stone towers menacing; but Katharine only saw the golden beauty of her bridegroom, only heard the shouts of the people: "Long live the King's bride! Long live our Queen, Katharine of Aragon."

*The Shadow of the Pomegranate*

## CHAPTER I

## "SIR LOYAL HEART"

IN THE ROYAL bedchamber at the Palace of Richmond the Queen of England lay alone. "She should rest now," the doctors said. "Leave her to sleep."

Yet, tired as she was, Queen Katharine, who was known to the people as Katharine of Aragon although it was ten years since she had left her native land to come to England, had no desire to sleep. It was long since she had known such happiness. She had come through humiliation to enjoy the greatest esteem; she who had once been neglected was now courted and treated with great respect. There was no woman in England who was accorded more homage than the Queen. During the month just past she had celebrated her twenty-fifth birthday; she was reckoned to be handsome and, when she was dressed in her jewelled garments and her lovely hair with its tints of reddish gold fell loose about her shoulders, the looks of admiration which were bestowed upon her were those given to a beautiful woman, whether she were Queen or beggarmaid.

Her husband was devoted to her. She must share in all his pastimes; she must be present to watch his prowess at the joust; she must applaud his success at tennis; and it was to her he presented the spoils of the hunt. She was the luckiest of women because her husband was the King—five years her junior, it was true, but an open-hearted boy, generous, passionate, loving, who, having escaped from the tiresome restrictions of a miserly parent, was determined to please his people and asked only adoration and admiration from those surrounding him.

Katharine smiled thinking of this big handsome boy whom she had married, and she was glad that she was older than he was; she was even glad that she had suffered such poverty and humiliation when she had lived in England as the widow of Henry's brother Arthur and had been used by her father-in-law, Henry VII, and her father, Ferdinand of Aragon, as a counter in their game of politics.

All that was over. Henry, headstrong, determined to make his own decisions, had chosen her as his bride; and as a result he, like some sixteenth-century Perseus, had rescued her, had cut her free from the chains of poverty and degradation and had declared his intention of marrying her—for she pleased him better than any other woman—and setting her beside him on the throne of England.

How could she ever show enough gratitude? She smiled. *He* was never tired of her gratitude; his small blue eyes, which seemed to grow more blue with emotion, would glisten like aquamarines when he looked back into the not very distant past and compared her state then with what it was now.

He would place a heavy arm about her shoulders and give her one of those hugs which took her breath away; she was not sure whether he was unaware of his strength or liked to pretend he was, and so make others the more aware of it.

"Ah, Kate," he would cry; Kate was his name for her; he liked to be thought bluff and blunt, a King who could talk on equal terms with his humblest subject. Kate was a good old English name. " 'Tis not so long, eh, since you were languishing in Durham House, patching your gowns. A different story now, eh, Kate!" And he would burst into that loud laughter which brought tears to those blue eyes and made them brighter than ever. Legs apart he would survey her, head on one side. "I brought you up, Kate. Never forget that. I . . . the King . . . who would let no other choose my woman for me. 'You shall not marry Katharine,' they said. They made me protest against the betrothal. That was when I was but a child and powerless. But those days are past. Now it is my turn to decide, and none shall say me nay!"

How he revelled in his power . . . like a boy with new toys! He was twenty, strong and healthy; he was well nigh perfect in the eyes of his subjects, and quite perfect in his own.

And Katharine, his wife, loved him; for who could help loving this golden boy?

"How happy you make me," she had told him once.

"Ay," he had answered proudly. "I have, have I not, Kate? And you shall make me happy too. You shall give me sons."

The blue eyes looked complacently into the future. He was seeing them all—boys, big boys, with red in their hair and their cheeks; with eyes as blue as aquamarines, boys strong and healthy, all made in the image of their glorious sire.

She had determined that he should not be denied his desires. He should have sons; and within a few weeks of their marriage she had become pregnant. She had been very unhappy when her still-born daughter had been born. She, who had suffered in dry-eyed silence for so many years, wept at the sight of Henry's disappointment. But he could not long believe in failure. The gods were smiling on him even as his Court and subjects did. All Henry desired must be his.

But she had quickly become pregnant again, and this time she had given him all that he needed to make his contentment complete.

In the cradle lay their son. What a happy omen that he should have been born on New Year's Day!

Henry had stood by her bed, his eyes ablaze with triumph.

"Here lies Your Grace's son and heir," she had said. "My New Year's gift to you."

Then Henry had fallen on his knees beside her bed and kissed her hand. She had thought that he was but a boy himself, for all his joy, all his pleasure in her and his son, was in his face for everyone to see.

"I would ask a boon of you," Katharine had whispered.

"Name it, Kate," he had cried. "You have but to name it . . . and it is yours."

He was ready to give her anything she asked because he wanted her to know how he felt; he wanted the whole Court, the whole world, to know of his gratitude to the Queen who had given him his son.

"It is that this Prince shall be called Henry after his most noble, his most beloved Sire."

Henry's eyes had been moist for a moment; then he had leaped to his feet.

"Your wish is granted!" he cried. "Why, Kate, as if I could deny you aught!"

She smiled, remembering. Almost at once he had been impatient to leave her, because he was planning the christening ceremony which he had decided must be more magnificent than any such ceremony had ever been before.

This was his first-born son, the heir to the throne, who was to be called Henry. He was the happiest of Kings; so she, in whom love for him had grown out of her great gratitude, was the happiest of Queens.

It was small wonder that she had no wish to slip into the world of sleep, when waking she could savour such happiness.

\*          \*          \*

The King smiled with affection at his opponent in the game of tennis which they had just finished. It had been a close game, but there had never been any doubt in the mind of the King that he would be the victor. There had been no doubt in the mind of Charles Brandon either. He was not such a fool as to think of beating the King, although, he was ready to admit, it was questionable whether he would have been able to. Henry excelled at the sport.

Now Henry slipped his arm through that of his friend with the familiarity which was so endearing. They were almost the same height, but not quite; Charles Brandon was tall but Henry was taller. Charles was handsome but he lacked the pink and golden perfection of his King; he was wily and therefore he always saw to it that, although he jousted as a champion and excelled at all sports, he just failed to reach the perfection of his master.

"It was a good game," murmured Henry. "And I thought at one time you would beat me."

"Nay, I am no match for Your Grace."

"I am not sure, Charles," answered the King, but his expression showed clearly that there could be no doubt whatsoever.

Brandon shook his head with feigned sorrow. "Your Grace is . . . unrivalled."

The King waved a hand. "I would talk of other matters. I wish to plan a masque for the Queen as soon as she is able to rise from her bed, and to show in this my pleasure in her."

"Oh fortunate Katharine to be Queen to such a King!"

Henry smiled. Flattery delighted him and the more blatant it was the better he liked it.

"I fancy the Queen is not displeased with her state. Now, Charles, devise some pageant which will please me. Let us have a tournament in which we shall appear disguised so that the Queen will have no notion who we are. We will surprise the company with our daring and then, when we are acknowledged the champions, let us throw off our disguise."

"That would give Her Grace much pleasure, I am sure."

"You remember how I surprised her at the Christmas festivities in the guise of a strange knight, and how I astonished all with my skill. And how surprised she was when I unmasked and she found in the strange knight her own husband?"

"Her Grace was delighted. She had been wondering how it was possible for any to rival her husband and when she had seen one who showed the same skill it was only to discover that it was the King in disguise!"

Henry burst into loud laughter at the memory. "I remember a time when I, with my cousin Essex, forced my way into her apartments dressed as Robin Hood and his men," he mused.

"And there was that occasion when, with Essex and Edward Howard and Thomas Parr . . . there were others also . . . we appeared dressed as Turks and we blacked the faces of our attendants so that they looked like blackamoors."

"I remember the occasion well. Your Grace's sister, the Princess Mary, danced disguised as an Ethiopian Queen."

"She did well," said the King fondly.

"It was a goodly sight though her pretty face was veiled."

" 'Twas well that it should be." Henry's mouth was a little prim. "My sister grows too fond of her pretty face."

"Is that so?" murmured Brandon.

"She is a witch who can twist me about her finger," murmured the King fondly. "But what would you? She is my only sister now that Margaret is away. It may be that I am over-indulgent."

"It is difficult not to indulge one so charming," agreed Brandon.

Henry was faintly impatient. "But the masque, man. I would have you devise some pageant which will amuse the Queen."

"I will give the matter my earnest attention."

"And remember that there must be little delay. The Queen cannot lie abed much longer."

It was on the tip of Brandon's tongue to remind the King that the Queen had, in less than two years of marriage, twice been brought to bed for the purpose of bearing a child. But one only reminded the King of that which he wished to remember. He himself enjoyed perfect health; those who did not he considered to be rather tiresome.

"I'll swear Her Grace is all impatience to join the revels," said Brandon.

"It is so. So let us give her a worthy spectacle, Charles."

"Your Grace commands, and it is my pleasure to obey. There shall be a spectacle such as none of your courtiers have ever seen before."

"Then I shall go to the Queen and bid her hasten her convalescence."

As they approached the Palace they were joined by many of the courtiers who hastened to pay compliments to the King.

"Listen," commanded Henry, "I would have the Queen know our pleasure. There is to be a pageant. . . ."

They listened, all eager to join in the fun. The new King was a complete contrast to his father, and in this new reign to be young gay, witty, to excel at the jousts, could lead the way to fortune.

There was not a courtier, as there was not a man or woman in the street, who did not rejoice in the accession of Henry VIII.

They were joined by the King's sister, the young Princess Mary, said by many to be the loveliest girl at Court. Henry's eyes glistened with affection as they rested on her. She was now fifteen, full of life as became a Tudor, inclined to take liberties with her brother which no one else would dare; and he seemed to like it.

"Well, sister," he said, "are you ready to join in our fun?"

Mary swept a deep curtesy and smiled at her brother. "Always ready to be at Your Grace's side."

"Come here to me," said Henry.

She came and he slipped his arm through hers. She was a beauty, this little sister. Tudor, all Tudor. By God what a handsome race we are! thought Henry; then he remembered his father's somewhat sere, sour face, and laughed.

"It will be necessary for you to show a little decorum, my child," said Henry.

"Yes, Your Grace. I live but to please Your Grace."

She was laughing at him, imitating his sycophantish courtiers, but he did not object. He took her cheek between his fingers and pinched it.

Mary cried out. "Too much pressure of the royal fingers," she explained, taking those fingers and kissing them.

"I shall miss you, sister, when you leave us."

Mary frowned. "It will be years yet."

Henry looked at her; he could see the shape of her breasts beneath her bodice. Fifteen! She was a woman. It could not be long before she left England for Flanders to marry Charles, grandson of Maximilian and Ferdinand of Aragon, and heir to great dominions. He did not want to lose Mary, but, as he told himself sadly, a King must not think of his own feelings.

She guessed his thoughts and pouted. She was going to raise difficulties when the time came for her to go.

"It may be," she said suddenly, and her lovely face was radiant, "that Your Grace will discover he cannot bear to part with his little sister—and Charles will then not get his bride."

There was an appeal in the lovely eyes; they had strayed to Brandon's face and rested there. Fifteen! thought Henry. She has the provocation of a girl some years older. He must warn her not to look at men like Brandon in that way. Charles Brandon had not lived the life of a monk. That was something Mary was as yet too young to understand; he should warn her, for he was not only her King but, since she had neither father nor mother, he must be her guardian too.

"Enough, enough," he said. "Come turn your wits to the pageants. I expect you to give the Queen a goodly spectacle."

The King's thoughts had gone to the Queen and his son and purposefully he made his way through the Palace to her apartments.

In her bedchamber the Queen was awakened by the fanfares which announced the King's coming. Her doctors had said that she must rest, but the King did not know this, or had forgotten.

She spread her hair about her pillows, for he liked it in that way and her hair was her one real beauty.

He burst into the apartment, and she saw him standing on the threshold with Mary on one side of him and Brandon on the other. Behind him were other friends and courtiers.

"Why, Kate," he cried advancing, "we come to see how you are. Are you not weary of bed? We plan a great entertainment for you. So get well quickly."

"Your Grace is kind to me," answered the Queen.

"Your King takes pleasure in pleasing you," replied Henry.

The courtiers were surrounding her bed, and she felt very tired but she smiled, because one must always smile for the King, that golden boy whose strict upbringing under his father's rule had been perhaps a little too severe for his exuberant nature.

He was a little irritated by the sight of her. She must lie a-bed, and he was impatient with all inactivity. He was urging her to shorten the period of rest, but she dared not. She had to preserve her strength; she had to remember that this was one of many births which must follow over the coming years.

The baby in his cradle cried suddenly as though he came to his mother's aid.

The King immediately swung round and the procession, with him at its head, went towards the cradle.

Henry took the child in his arms, and he looked at it with wonder.

"Do you realize," he said, to those who crowded about him, "that this infant could one day be your King?"

"We trust not until he is an old greybeard, Your Grace."

It was the right answer. The King laughed. Then he began to walk up and down the Queen's bedchamber, the child in his arms.

The Queen watched smiling.

He is but a boy himself, she thought.

\*　　　　\*　　　　\*

As soon as Katharine left her bed she prepared to leave Richmond for Westminster. The King had gone on before her; impatient and restless he had already journeyed to Walsingham, there to give thanks for his son at the Shrine of the Virgin.

But he had now returned to Westminster and was there waiting to receive the Queen.

Katharine who still felt weak would have enjoyed some respite, perhaps a few weeks of quiet at Richmond; but she knew that was too much to hope for because Henry begrudged every day he spent hidden from the public gaze. So did the people. Wherever he went they crowded about him to bless his lovely face and express their pleasure in him.

The people would not be excluded from the festivities at Westminster. One of the reasons why they loved their new King was because he showed them with every action, every gesture, that he was determined to be a very different King from his father. One of his first acts had been the public beheading of his father's ministers, Dudley and Empson, those men whom the people had regarded as the great extortioners of the previous reign. Nothing could have been more significant. "These men imposed great taxes on my beloved people; they have brought poverty and misery to thousands. Therefore they shall die." That was what the young King was telling his people. "England shall now be merry as she was intended to be." So they cheered themselves hoarse whenever they saw him.

It seemed fitting to them that their handsome young King should be covered in glittering jewels, that his satin and velvet garments should be more magnificent than anyone had ever worn before. And because he was always conscious of the presence of the people, always determined to extract every ounce of their affection, he constantly won their approval.

They were now looking forward to the festivities at Westminster almost as eagerly as Henry was himself. Therefore there could be no delay merely because the Queen would have liked a little longer to recover from giving the King and country an heir.

All along the route the people cheered her. She was Spanish and alien to their English ways, but their beloved King had chosen her for his wife and she had produced a son; that was enough to make the people shout: "Long live the Queen!"

Beside Katharine rode her beautiful and favourite lady in waiting, Maria de Salinas, who had been with her ever since she had left Spain. It was significant that even when they were alone together she and Maria spoke English nowadays.

"Your Grace is a little weary?" asked Maria, anxiously.

"Weary!" cried Katharine faintly alarmed. Did she look weary? The King would be hurt if she did. She must never show him that she preferred to rest rather than to frolic. "Oh no . . . no, Maria. I was a little thoughtful, that was all. I was thinking how my life has changed in the last few years. Do you remember how we suffered, how we patched our gowns and often had to eat fish which smelt none too good because it was the cheapest that could be bought in the market, how we wondered whether my father would send for us to return ignobly to Spain, or whether the King of England would ever pay me an allowance?"

"After such humiliation Your Grace can now enjoy all the fine gowns that you wish for, all the good food that you care to order for your table."

"I should be ungrateful indeed, Maria, if I allowed myself to be tired when so much is being arranged for my pleasure."

"Yet weariness is something over which we have no control," began Maria.

But Katharine laughed: "We must always have control over our feelings, Maria. My mother taught me that, and I shall never forget it."

She smiled, inclining her head as the people called her name. Maria had guessed that she was weary; no one else must.

\*      \*      \*

The Queen was seated in the tiltyard for the tournament would soon begin. All about her were signs of the King's devotion. His enthusiasm was such that when he was gratified the whole world must know it. This woman whom his father had tried to withhold from him, but whom he had insisted on marrying, had proved his wisdom in marrying her, for she had quickly given him a son. He wanted everyone to know in what esteem he held her, and everywhere Katharine looked she could see those entwined initials H and K. They were on the very seat on which she sat—gold letters on purple velvet.

If my mother could see me now, she would be happy, thought Katharine. It was nearly seven years since her mother had died and ten since she had seen her, yet she still thought of her often and when something happened which was particularly pleasing, it was almost as though she shared her pleasure with her mother. Isabella of Castile had been the greatest force in her daughter's life and when she had died it seemed to Katharine that something very beautiful and vital had gone from her life. She believed that perhaps in the love she would bear towards her own children she would find some consolation for this aching loss; but that was in the future.

The ordinary people were crowding into the arena. They seemed always to be present. Henry would be pleased; he would triumph of course at the tournament and he liked his people to see him victorious. He would seem like a god to them in his glittering armour, with his looks which were indeed unrivalled, and his great height—no one at Court was taller than Henry. Katharine wondered what chance of favour a man would have who happened to be an inch taller than the King.

She suppressed such thoughts. They came to her now and then but she constantly refused to entertain them. Her Henry was a boy and he had the faults of a boy. He was young for his years, but she must always remember that he had been repressed during his boyhood by a father who had always feared he might be spoiled by others, and who was eager that the eighth Henry should rule in a manner similar to that of the seventh.

All about her was the glittering Court. Henry was not present so she knew that he would appear later in the guise of some wandering king, perhaps a beggar, or a robber, some role which would make the people gasp with surprise. He would either tilt in his new role and as the conqueror disclose who he really was, or show himself before the joust and then proceed to conquer. It was the old familiar pattern, and every time Katharine must behave as though this were the first time it had happened. Always her surprise that the champion was in truth the King must appear to be spontaneous and natural.

What is happening to me? she asked herself. There had been a time when she was happy enough to enter into his frolics. Was that because in the first year of their marriage she had felt as though she were living in a dream? The period of humiliation had been so close in those days; now that it was receding, was she less grateful?

A hermit was riding into the arena and there was a hush in the crowd. He wore a grey gown and tattered weeds.

No, thought Katharine, he is not quite tall enough. This is not the great masquerade.

The hermit was approaching her throne and, when he was before her, he bowed low and cried aloud: "I crave the Queen's Grace to permit me to tilt before her."

Katharine said as was expected: "But you are no knight."

"Yet would I ask your royal permission to test my skill, and it shall all be for Your Grace's honour."

"A hermit . . . to tilt in my honour!"

The crowd began to jeer, but Katharine held up her hand.

"It is strange indeed to find a hermit in the tiltyard, and that he should wish to tilt stranger still. But our great King has such love for all his subjects that he would please them each and every one. The lowliest hermit shall tilt before us if it is his wish. But I warn you, hermit, it may cost you your life."

"That I would willing give for my Queen and my King."

"Then let it be," cried Katharine.

The hermit stepped back, drew himself to his full height, threw off his grey tattered robe, and there was a Knight in shining armour—none other than Charles Brandon himself.

The Princess Mary, who was seated near the Queen, began to clap her hands, and all cheered.

Brandon now asked the Queen's permission to present to her a knight of great valour who was desirous, like himself, of tilting in her honour.

"I pray you tell me the name of this knight," said Katharine.

"Your Grace, his name is Sir Loyal Heart."

"I like well his name," said Katharine. "I pray you bring him to me."

Brandon bowed and there was a fanfare of trumpets as Sir Loyal Heart rode into the arena.

There was no mistaking that tall figure, that gold hair, that fresh fair skin which glowed with health and youth.

"Sir Loyal Heart!" shouted the ushers. "Who comes to tilt in honour of the Queen's Grace."

Before the Queen's throne Henry drew up, while the people roared their approval.

Katharine felt that her emotions might prevent her in that important moment making the right gesture. Sir Loyal Heart! How like him to choose such a name. So naïve, so boyish, so endearing.

Surely I am the most fortunate of women, she thought; Mother, if you could but see me now, it would make up for all you have suffered, for my brother Juan's death, for my sister Isabella's death in childbirth, for Juana's madness. At least two of your daughters inherited what you desired for them. Maria is the happy Queen of Portugal, and I am happier still, as Queen of England, wife of this exuberant boy, who shows his devotion to me by entwining my initials with his, by riding into the arena as Sir Loyal Heart.

"How happy I am," she said in a voice which was not without a tremor of emotion, "that Sir Loyal Heart comes hither to tilt in my honour."

There was nothing she could have said which would have pleased Henry more.

"The happiness of Sir Loyal Heart equals that of Your Grace," cried Henry.

He had turned—ready for the joust.

The tournament was opened.

\*       \*       \*

Darkness came early in February, and the Court had left the tiltyard for the whitehall of Westminster. This did not mean that the festivities were over. They would go on far into the night, for the King never tired and, until he declared the ball closed, it must go on.

He had scored great success in the tiltyard to the delight of the people. But none was more delighted than Henry. Yet now that the party had entered the Palace he had disappeared from Katharine's side.

This could only mean one thing. Some pageant or masque was being planned in which he would play a major part. Several of his friends had crept away with him, and Katharine, talking to those who remained about her, tried to compose her features, tried to display great expectation while she hoped that she would be able to register that blank surprise when she was confronted with some denouement which she had guessed even before the play had begun.

One must remember, she reminded herself, that he has been brought up in a most parsimonious fashion. She knew that his father had ordered that his doublets must be worn as long as they held together and then turned if possible; he and the members of his household had been fed on the simplest foods and had even had to save candle ends. All this had been intended to teach him the ways of thrift. The result? He had rebelled against thrift. He was ready to dip into his father's coffers to escape from the parsimony, which had been anathema to him, in order to satisfy his extravagance. His nature was such that he must passionately long for all that was denied him—so for him the scarlet and gold, the velvet and brocade; for him the rich banquets, the pomp and the glory. It was fortunate that the thrift of Henry VII had made it possible for Henry VIII to indulge his pleasure without resorting to the unpopular methods which his father had used to amass his wealth.

Katharine looked about the hall, which had been so lavishly decorated, and tried to calculate the cost to the exchequer. The English love of pageantry was unquestionable. What great pains had been taken to turn this hall into a forest. There were artificial hawthorns, maples and hazels, all so finely wrought that they looked real enough. There were the animals, a lion, an antelope, and an elephant all cleverly made. She did not know the price of the commodities necessary to make these things but she guessed it was high, for clearly no expense had been spared. There were beautiful ladies to roam the mock forest and they, with the wood-woos, who were wild men of the forest, had to be specially apparelled. The maids of the forest wore yellow damask, and the wood-woos russet sarcenet; she knew the high cost of these materials.

Should she remonstrate with the King? Should she point out that such pageants were well enough when there was some great event to celebrate—as there was at this time the birth of their son—but this was one among many. Since Henry had come to the throne feasting had followed feasting, and pageant, pageant.

She imagined herself saying: "Henry, I am older than you . . . and I had the advantage of spending my early years with my mother who was one of the wisest women in the world. Should you not curb these extravagances?"

What would be his response? She pictured the brows being drawn together over those brilliant blue eyes, the pout of a spoiled boy.

Yet was it not her duty?

One of the courtiers was at her elbow. "Your Grace?"

"You would speak with me?"

"Your Grace, I know of an arbour of gold, and in this arbour are ladies who would show you their pastime in the hope that they might please your Grace. Would you wish to see this arbour?"

"I greatly desire to see it."

The courtier bowed, and then, drawing himself to his full height, he declaimed: "Her Grace Queen Katharine wishes to see the arbour of gold."

A curtain which had been drawn across one end of the hall was then pulled back to disclose a pavilion in the form of an arbour. This was composed of pillars about which artificial flowers made of silk and satin climbed naturalistically. There were roses, hawthorn and eglantine, and the pillars had been decorated with ornaments of pure gold.

This arbour was carried by stout bearers and placed close to the Queen's throne. She saw that in it were six of the most lovely girls, and that their dresses were of white and green satin which appeared to be covered with gold embroidery; but as they came closer she realized that what she had thought was embroidery were two letters entwined—the familiar H and K. She stared in admiration, for it was indeed a pretty sight, and as she did so six men dressed in purple satin which, like the gowns of the girls, was adorned with the entwined letters, sprang forth to stand three on either side of the arbour.

Each of these knights had his name on his doublet in letters of real gold; and there was one among them who stood out distinguished by his height and golden beauty; and across his doublet were written the words Sir Loyal Heart.

The ordinary people who revelled in these antics of the Court had pressed into the hall and now cheered loudly, calling "God bless his Grace! God bless the Queen!"

Henry stood before her, his face expressing his complete joy. Katharine applauded with her ladies, and the King clapped his hands—a signal for the ladies to step from the arbour.

Each of the six ladies was taken as a partner by one of the six men.

"Make a space for us to dance!" commanded Sir Loyal Heart. And the bearers wheeled the arbour back through the forest to the end of the hall where the people who had crowded into the Palace from the streets stood agog watching all this splendour.

"Come," cried the King to the musicians, and the music began.

Henry danced as he loved to dance. He must leap higher than any; he must cavort with greater verve. Katharine watching him thought: He seems even younger now than he did the day we married.

"Faster! Faster!" he commanded. "Who tires? What you, Knevet?" The glance he threw at Sir Thomas Knevet was scornful. "Again, again," he commanded the musicians, and the dance continued.

So intent were all on the dancing of the gay young King that they did not notice what was happening at the other end of the hall.

One man, a shipmaster whose trade had brought him to the port of London, murmured: "But look at the trimmings on this arbour. These ornaments are real gold!"

He put up his hand to touch one, but another hand had

reached it before him. A gold ornament was taken from the arbour, and several crowded round to look at it.

In a few moments many of the spectators had plucked a gold ornament from the arbour; and those at the back, who saw what was happening, determined not to be left out, pressed forward and in the space of a few minutes that arbour was denuded of all the gold ornaments which had made it such a thing of beauty.

Meanwhile the King danced on, smiling at the ladies, now and then glancing in the Queen's direction. Was she watching? Was she marvelling?

Katharine was ready every time his eyes met hers; and she had managed to infuse that look of wonder into her expression which he constantly demanded.

At last the music stopped, and Henry stood smiling benignly at the company.

"You see," he announced, "that the dresses of the performers are covered in gold letters. These form my own initial and that of the one who is most dear to me. I now invite the ladies to come and help themselves to these entwined letters and I trust they will treasure them and when their time comes to marry they will endeavour to live in perfect harmony and follow the example set by their Queen and . . . Sir Loyal Heart."

The ladies rushed forward. There were many, Katharine noticed, to gaze coquettishly at the King, and then she was grateful to him for his loyalty and ashamed of her criticisms. He is but a boy, she told herself; a boy who wishes to be good.

There was a sudden shout from the back of the hall, where the once golden arbour had been transformed into a few sticks of wood. The populace who, as custom demanded, were permitted to see their King at his meals, at his dancing and games, rushed forward.

The ladies had been invited to strip the King of his ornaments; well, so they should; and the men would help them in the game.

There was a startled cry of surprise from the dancers as they found themselves surrounded. The King himself was in the hands of half a dozen laughing men and women, but in their eyes there was something more than laughter. They had looked on at the luxury of Westminster and had compared it with their own homes; they had seen men and women whose garments were covered in glittering jewels and gold ornaments, one of which would keep them in luxury for a very long time.

This was their King and their beloved King, but the mob stood together against its rulers and when the call came it was invariably ready. But this was merely a masque; and the people had caught the spirit of the masque. They would not have harmed their handsome King; but they wanted his jewels.

Listening to the cries of protest of his friends, being aware of the people—who smelt none too fresh—pressing close to him, Henry ceased to be a pleasure-loving boy. He was a man at once —shrewd and cunning. He knew no fear; he had always felt himself to be capable of dealing with any situation and, because it had been his pleasure to go among his people as often as possible, he was able to understand them; and of all the noblemen and women in that hall there was none more calm, more wise than the King.

There was no sign of anger in those blue eyes which could so easily grow stormy at a courtier's careless word. They were purposely full of laughter. He had played his own game; now he must play the people's game; but he did not forget that he was still the central player.

He smiled into the eyes of a pretty young seamstress who had snatched a gold button from his doublet.

"May it continue to make your pretty eyes shine," he said.

She was startled, flushed scarlet, then she turned and ran.

They had stripped him of all his jewels; they had torn his cloak from his shoulders so that he was wearing nothing but his doublet and his drawers. He laughed aloud being aware that his courtiers were being more roughly handled than he was himself while they were being stripped of their valuables. Moreover he saw too that the guards had rushed into the hall, halberds raised, and were doing their duty. They had taken several of the people and were hustling them into a corner of the hall, from where they were loudly abusing the guards.

Henry glancing quickly round the company saw that the dishevelled ladies looked bewildered and that Sir Thomas Knevet who had climbed up one of the pillars was clinging there stark naked. Sir Thomas had protested so vigorously that the mob had denuded him not only of his jewels but of all his clothes.

Looking at Knevet clinging to the pillar Henry burst into sudden loud laughter; it was the signal. Clearly the King intended to treat the affair as part of the masque and everyone was expected to do the same. Those of the people who had been muttering now joined in the laughter. "God Save the King!" they cried, and they meant it. He had not disappointed them. He was a true sportsman and they had nothing to fear from such a king.

He was shouting to his courtiers: "Why do you look so glum? My people have helped themselves to largesse. Let us leave the matter at that, for I confess to a hunger which must be appeased, and I am thirsty too."

The people were not loth to be hustled from the hall grasping the spoils they had snatched. The sound of their laughter came floating back to the hall. They were delighted. They loved their King. Now when he rode through the streets they would cheer him more loudly than ever.

Katharine, who had watched the incident with rising horror, had been much astonished by the attitude of the King. She had expected him to roar his anger, to summon the guard, to have the people punished; yet she, whose eyes had not left him, had seen no sign of anger in the bright flushed face.

He was not merely a boy, she realized now. He was a King. And his crown was more dear to him than all the jewels in the world; he was more than a feckless boy, because he knew that he kept that crown by the will of the people. He would rage against his courtiers; he would without hesitation send them to the block; but when he came face to face with the mob he would have nothing for them but smiling tolerance.

Then she did not know this man she had married as she had believed she did, and the knowledge that this was so filled her with faint misgivings.

He was at her side, mischievous in his doublet and drawers.

"Come, Kate," he said. "I starve. Let us lead the way to the banquet that awaits us."

He took her hand and led her into his own chamber where the feast awaited them; and seated at the place of honour at that table with Katharine on his right hand, he was very merry as he surveyed his courtiers in their tattered garments; nor would he allow any to leave the banquet except Sir Thomas Knevet who, he said, for dear decency's sake must find himself some garments.

"My friends," said Henry, "your losses are largesse to the commonalty. That is an end of the matter. Now to work!"

And laughing he tackled the good red meat which he loved.

\*　　　\*　　　\*

The Countess of Devonshire came unceremoniously to the Queen's apartment. Katharine received her husband's favourite aunt graciously but she was quick to see that the Countess was alarmed.

"It is the Prince, Your Grace," she burst out. "He has had an uneasy night and seems to find breathing difficult."

Katharine was filled with apprehension.

"I must go to him at once," she said.

The Countess looked relieved. "I have called the physicians to look at him. They think his Royal Highness has caught a chill, and may be better in a few days."

"Then I will not tell the King . . . as yet."

The Countess hesitated; then she said: "It might be well that the King is told, Your Grace. He will wish to see his son."

Katharine felt sick with fear. So the child was worse than they pretended. They were trying to spare her, to break bad news gently.

"I will tell the King," she said quietly, "and I am sure he will wish to make all speed with me to Richmond."

\*       \*       \*

It could not be true; Henry would not believe it. This could not happen to him. The son, of whom he had been so proud, little Henry his namesake, his heir—dead! The child had lived exactly fifty-two days.

He stood, his face puckered, his legs apart, looking at the Queen. The courtiers had left them together, believing that one could comfort the other and thus make their grief more bearable.

Katharine said nothing; she sat in the window seat looking out over the river, her body drooping, her face drawn. She looked like an old woman. Her eyes were red, her face blotched, for she had shed many bitter tears.

"We should have taken greater care of him," she whispered.

"He had every care," growled Henry.

"He caught a chill at the christening. He was robust until then."

Henry did not answer. It had been a splendid christening, with the Archbishop of Canterbury officiating and the Earl of Surrey and the Countess of Devonshire standing as sponsors; he had enjoyed every minute of it. He remembered thinking, as he watched the baby being carried to the font, that this was one of the happiest moments of his life. He had thanked God for His grace. And now . . . the baby was dead.

He felt the anger bubbling within him. That this should happen to him! What he wanted more than anything in the world, he told himself, was a son—strong and healthy like himself—a boy whom he could watch grow up and teach to be a King.

He felt bewildered because Fate had dared take from him his greatest prize.

"It was well that he was christened, since he is now dead," he said sullenly.

She could not be comforted. She longed for children; she needed them even as he did.

He thought how old she looked, and he felt angry with her because he wanted to feel angry with someone. He had been so grateful to her because she had given him a son; and now he was no longer grateful.

Katharine glancing up suddenly saw his eyes upon her—small, narrowed, cruel.

She thought: Dear God. Holy Mother, does he then blame me?

And her sorrow was tinged with an apprehension so faint that it was gone before she realized fully what it meant.

Even as he gazed at her his expression softened. He said: "This is a bitter blow, Kate. But I am no greybeard and you are young yet. We'll have more children, you see. We'll have a son this time next year. That's the way to chase away our sorrow, eh?"

"Oh Henry," she cried and held out her hand.

He took it.

"You are so good to me," she told him. "I only live to please you."

He kissed her hand. He was too young, too sure of himself, to believe that ill luck awaited him. This was an unfortunate accident. They would have more sons; so many that the loss of this one would cease to matter.

I

## CHAPTER II

## THE KING'S INDISCRETION

THE KING SAT in the window seat strumming his lute and trying out a song of his own composition; there was a dreamy expression in his eyes and he did not see the courtyard below; he was picturing himself in the great hall, calling for his lute and surprising all present with the excellence of his song.

They would say: "But who is the composer? We must bring him to Court. There are few who can give us such music."

He would put his head on one side. "I do not think it would be an *impossible* task to bring this fellow to Court. In fact I have a certain suspicion that he is with us now."

They would look at each other in surprise. "But, Sire, if such genius were among us surely we could not be so blind as to be unaware of it. We pray Your Grace, summon him to your presence and command him to continue to delight us."

"I doubt he would obey my command. He is a rash fellow."

"Not obey the command of the King!"

Then he would laugh and say: "Now I will play you one of my own songs. . . ." And he would play and sing the very same song.

They would look at each other in amazement—but not too much surprise. They must not run the risk of implying that they did not believe him capable of writing such music. They would quickly allow their bewilderment to fade and then it would be: "But how foolish of us. We should have known that none but Your Grace could give us such a song."

In a little while the song would be sung throughout the Court. The women would sing it, wistfully, and with yearning in their eyes and voices. There were many women who looked at him with longing now. He knew he had but to beckon and they would be ready for anything he should suggest whether it was a quick tumble in a secluded garden or the honour of being the recognized mistress of a King.

His mouth was prim. He intended to be virtuous.

He sang quietly under his breath:

"The best I sue,
The worst eschew:
My mind shall be
Virtue to use;
Vice to refuse
I shall use me."

He would sing that song, and as he did so he would look at those wantons who tried to lure him into sin.

Of course, he told himself often, I am a King, and the rules which are made for other men are not for Kings. But I love my wife and she is devoted to me. She will bear me children in time, and to them and to my people will I set an example. None shall say of me: There was a lecher. It shall be said: There goes the King who is strong, not only in battle, not only in state councils, but in virtue.

So his little mouth was prim as he sat playing his lute and practising the song with which, later that day, he would surprise the Court.

And watching at the window he saw her. She was neither tall nor short, and she was very beautiful. She looked up and saw him, and she dropped a curtsey. There was invitation in the way she lifted her skirts and lowered her eyes. He knew her. Her name was Anne and she was Buckingham's younger sister who had recently married her second husband. Images of Anne Stafford with her two husbands came into his mind. The primness left his mouth which had slackened a little.

He bowed his head in acknowledgment of her curtsey and his fingers idly strummed the lute, for he had momentarily forgotten the song.

Anne Stafford went on her way, but before she had taken more than a few steps she turned to look again at the window.

This time she smiled. Henry's lips seemed to be frozen; he did not acknowledge the smile but after she had disappeared he went on thinking of her.

He found that one of the grooms of the bedchamber was standing beside him. He started and wondered how long the man had been there.

"So 'tis you, Compton," he said.

"'Tis I, Your Grace," answered Sir William Compton. "Come to see if you have work for me to do."

Henry strummed on the lute. "What work should I have for which I should not call you?"

"I but seek excuses to speak awhile with Your Grace."

Henry smiled. There were times when he liked to live informally among his friends; and Sir William Compton, a handsome man some ten years older than himself, amused him. He had been Henry's page when he was Prince of Wales and they had shared many confidences. When he had become King, Henry had given Compton rapid promotion. He was now chief gentleman of the bedchamber, as well as Groom of the Stole and Constable of Sudeley and Gloucester castles.

"Well, speak on," said Henry.

"I was watching Lady Huntingdon pass below. She's a forward wench."

"And why did you think that?"

"By the glance she threw at Your Grace. If ever I saw invitation it was there."

"My dear. William," said Henry, "do you not know that I receive such invitations whenever I am in the company of women?"

"I know it, Sire. But those are invitations discreetly given."

"And she was not . . . discreet?"

"If she seemed so to Your Grace I will say that she was."

Henry laughed. "Ah, if I were not a virtuous married man. . . ."
He sighed.

"Your Grace would seem to regret that you *are* a virtuous married man."

"How could I regret my virtue?" said Henry, his mouth falling into the familiar lines of primness.

"Nay, Sire. You, being such a wise King, would not; it is only the ladies who are deprived of Your Grace's company who must regret."

"I'll not say," said the King, "that I would ask for too much virtue in a man. He must do his duty, true, duty to state, duty to family; but when that is done. . . ."

Compton nodded. "A little dalliance is good for all."

Henry licked his lips. He was thinking of Anne Stafford; the very way she dipped a curtsey was a challenge to a man's virility.

"I have heard it said that a little dalliance away from the marriage bed will often result in a return to that bed with renewed vigour," murmured Henry.

"All are aware of Your Grace's vigour," said Compton slyly, "and that it is in no need of renewal."

"Two of my children have died," said the King mournfully.

Compton smiled. He could see how the King's mind was working. He wanted to be virtuous; he wanted his dalliance, and yet to be able to say it was virtuous dalliance: I dallied with Anne Stafford because I felt that if I strayed awhile I could come back to Katharine with renewed vigour—so powerful that it must result in the begetting of a fine, strong son.

Compton, who had lived many years close to Henry, knew something of his character. Henry liked to think of himself as a deeply religious man, a man devoted to duty; but at heart he had one god and that was himself; and his love for pleasure far exceeded his desire to do his duty. Moreover, the King was not a man to deny himself the smallest pleasure; he was a sensualist; he was strong, healthy, lusty like many of his friends; but, whereas some of them thoughtlessly took their pleasures where they found them, Henry could not do this before he had first assured himself that what he did was the right thing to do. He was troubled by the voice of his conscience which must first be appeased; it was as though there were two men in that fine athletic body: the pleasure-seeking King and the other, who was completely devoted to his duty. The former would always be forced to make his excuses to the latter, but Compton had no doubt of the persuasive powers of one and the blind eye of the other.

"There are some ladies," mused Compton, "who are willing enough to give a smile of promise but never ready to fulfil those promises."

"That is so," agreed Henry.

"There are some who would cling to their virtue even though it be the King himself who would assail it."

"A little wooing might be necessary," said Henry implying his confidence that if he were the wooer he could not fail to be successful.

"Should the King woo?" asked Compton. "Should a King be a suppliant for a woman's favours? It seems to me, Your Grace, that a King should beckon and the lady come running."

Henry nodded thoughtfully.

"I could sound the lady, I could woo her in your name. She has a husband and if her virtue should prove overstrong it might be well that this was a matter entirely between Your Grace, myself and the lady."

"We speak of suppositions," said Henry laying a hand on Compton's shoulder. He picked up his lute. "I will play and sing to you. It is a new song I have here and you shall tell me your opinion of it, good Compton."

Compton smiled and settled himself to listen. He would sound the lady. Kings were always grateful to those who arranged their pleasures. Moreover Anne Stafford was the sister of Edward Stafford, Duke of Buckingham, an arrogant man whom Compton would delight in humiliating; for such was the pride of the Staffords that they would consider it humiliation for a member of their family to become any man's mistress—even the King's.

So, while Henry played his lute and sang his song, Sir William Compton was thinking of how he could arrange a love affair between the sister of the Duke of Buckingham and the King.

\*        \*        \*

Anne Stafford was bored. She was of the Court, but it was her sister Elizabeth who had found favour with the Queen; and this was because Elizabeth was of a serious nature which appealed to Katharine.

The Queen, thought Anne, was far too serious; and if she did not take care the King would look elsewhere for his pleasure.

Anne laughed to herself; she had very good reason to believe that he was already looking.

Anne had had two husbands and neither of them had satisfied her. In a family such as theirs there had been little freedom. They would never forget, any of them, their closeness to the throne, and they were more conscious of their connection with royalty than the King himself. Through her father Anne was descended from Thomas of Woodstock, a son of Edward III; and her mother was Catharine Woodville sister of Elizabeth Woodville who had been Edward IV's Queen.

Anne's father had been an ardent supporter of the House of Lancaster, and Richard III had declared him a traitor and the "most untrue creature living." He was beheaded in the market-place at Salisbury, thus dying for the Tudor cause, a fact which had endeared his family to Henry VII; and Henry VIII carried on his father's friendship for the Staffords.

And what was the result? Anne had been married twice without being consulted, and given a place at Court; but there she was merely a spectator of the advancement of her elder sister.

Being a Stafford, Anne was not without ambition, so she thought how amusing it would be to show her family that the way to a King's favour could be as effectively reached in the bedchamber as on the battlefield. How amusing to confront that arrogant brother of hers, that pious sister, with her success!

Once she and Henry were lovers, neither brother nor sister would be able to prevent the liaison's continuance, and then they would have to pay a little attention to their younger sister.

One of her maids came to tell her that Sir William Compton was without and would have speech with her.

Sir William Compton! The King's crony! This was interesting; perhaps the King had sent for her.

"I will see Sir William," she told the maid, "but you should remain in the room. It is not seemly that I should be alone with him."

The maid brought in Sir William and then retired to a corner of the room, where she occupied herself by tidying the contents of a sewing box.

"Welcome, Sir William," said Anne. "I pray you be seated. Then you can comfortably tell me your business."

Compton sat down and surveyed the woman. Voluptuous, provocative, she certainly was. A ripe plum, he thought, ready enough to drop into greedy royal hands.

"Madam," said Compton, "you are charming."

She dimpled coquettishly. "Is that your own opinion, or do you repeat someone else's?"

"It is my own—and also another's."

"And who is this other?"

"One whose name I could not bring myself to mention."

She nodded.

"You have been watched, Madam, and found delectable."

"You make me sound like a peach growing on a garden wall."

"Your skin reminds me—and another—of that fruit, Madam. The peaches on the walls are good this year—warm, luscious, ripe for the plucking."

"Ah yes," she answered. "Do you come to me with a message?"

Compton put his head on one side. "That will come later. I would wish to know whether you would be prepared to receive such a message."

"I have an open mind, Sir William. I do not turn away messengers. I peruse their messages; but I do not always agree to proposals."

"You are wise, Madam. Proposals should always be rejected unless they are quite irresistible."

"And perhaps even then," she added.

"Some proposals would be irresistible to any lady; then it would be wise to accept them."

She laughed. "You keep company with the King," she said. "What is this new song he has written?"

"I will teach it to you."

"That pleases me." She called to her maid and the girl put down the box and hurried forward. "My lute," said Anne. And the girl brought it.

"Now," went on Anne.

Compton came close to her and they sang together.

When they stopped he said: "I shall tell the King that you sang and liked his song. It may be that His Grace would wish you to sing for him. Would that delight you?"

She lowered her eyelids. "I should need some time to practise. I would not wish to sing before His Grace until I had made sure that my performance could give the utmost satisfaction to him . . . and to myself."

Compton laughed.

"I understand," he murmured. "I am sure your performance will give the utmost pleasure."

\*          \*          \*

Anne was passing through an ante-room on her way from an interview with her sister. She was feeling annoyed. Elizabeth had been very severe. She had heard that Sir William Compton had visited Anne on several occasions and such conduct, she would have Anne know, was unseemly in a Stafford.

"I was never alone with him," Anne protested.

"I should hope not!" retorted Elizabeth. "Do behave with more decorum. You must keep away from him in future. The Queen would be displeased if she knew; and what of your husband? Have you forgotten that you are a married woman?"

"I have been twice married to please my family, so I am scarcely likely to forget."

"I am glad," replied Elizabeth primly.

Anne was thinking of this as she hurried through the rooms. The Queen would be displeased! She laughed. Indeed the Queen would be displeased if she knew the true purpose of Sir William's visits. Perhaps soon she would be ready for that encounter with the King, and once that had taken place she was sure that Queen Katharine's influence at Court would be a little diminished. There would be a new star, for Anne Stafford, Countess of Huntingdon, would be of greater importance even than her brother, the Duke of Buckingham.

As she came into an ante-room a woman rose from a stool and came hurriedly towards her.

"My lady Huntingdon," the voice was low and supplicating,

and vaguely familiar. The accent was foreign and easily recognizable as Spanish since there had been so many Spaniards at
Court. This was a very beautiful woman. "You do not know me,"
she said.

"I know your face. Were you a lady in waiting to the Queen?"

"I was, before she was Queen. My name is Francesca de
Carceres and I am now the wife of the Genoese banker, Francesco
Grimaldi."

"I do remember," said Anne. "You ran away from Court a
few months before the Queen's marriage."

"Yes," said Francesca and her lovely face hardened. She
had schemed for power; she had imagined that one day she
would be the chief confidante of the Queen; but the Queen had
been surrounded by those whom Francesca looked upon as her
enemies, and in despair Francesca had run away from Court to
become the wife of the rich and elderly banker.

Her banker was ready to lavish his fortune upon her, but it
was not jewels and fine garments which Francesca wanted; it
was power. She realized that fully, now that she had lost her
place at Court; and she cursed herself for a fool because she had
run away two months before Henry had announced his intention
to marry Katharine. Had she waited two months longer, as one
of Katharine's ladies in waiting, as a member of one of the
noble families of Spain, she would have been given a husband
worthy of her background; she would have remained in the
intimate circle of the Queen.

Having lost these things Francesca now realized how much
they meant to her, and she presented herself at Court in the
hope of getting an audience with Katharine, but Katharine had
so far declined to see her. Francesca had been a trouble-maker;
she had quarrelled with Katharine's confessor, Fray Diego
Fernandez; she had intrigued with Gutierre Gomez de Fuensalida who had been the Spanish ambassador at the time and
whose arrogance and incompetence had aroused Katharine's
indignation and had resulted in his being sent back to Spain.

Moreover in Katharine's eyes Francesca had committed the
unforgivable sin of marrying a commoner, and she wished her
former maid of honour to know that there was no longer a place
at Court for her.

But Francesca was not one to give way lightly; and she was
constantly to be seen in ante-rooms, hoping for a glimpse of the
Queen that she might put her case to her and plead eloquently
for that for which she so much longed.

Francesca now said eagerly: "I wonder if you could say a word in my favour to Her Grace the Queen."

"You mistake me for my sister," Anne answered. "It is she who is in the service of Her Grace."

"And you . . . are in the service of . . . ?"

Anne smiled so roguishly that Francesca was immediately alert.

"I am the younger sister," said Anne. "My brother and sister think me of little account."

"I'll warrant they're wrong."

Anne shrugged her shoulders. "That may well be," she agreed.

"The Queen has changed since her marriage," went on Francesca. "She has grown hard. There was a time, when she lived most humbly at Durham House and I waited on her. Then she would not have refused an audience to an old friend."

"She disapproved strongly of your marriage; she is very pious and surrounds herself with those of the same mind."

Francesca nodded.

"My sister is one of them. I have just received a letter on the lightness of my ways, when all I did was to receive a gentleman— one of the *King's* gentlemen—in the presence of my maid."

"It is natural," said Francesca slyly, "that the Queen's friends should be disturbed when a gentleman of the King's household visits a lady as beautiful as yourself . . . on the King's orders."

"But I did not say . . ." began Anne, and then she burst into laughter. She went on incautiously: "She is indeed so much older than he is, so much more serious. Is it to be wondered at?"

"I do not marvel," replied Francesca. "And, Lady Hunting- ton, if ever you should find yourself in a position to ask favours, would you remember that I have a desire to return to Court?"

Anne's eyes gleamed. It was a glorious thing to be asked such favours; the power of the King's mistress would be infinite.

She bowed her head graciously.

"I would be your friend for evermore," murmured Francesca.

Anne laughed lightly and said: "I shall not forget you."

She walked on as though she were a Queen instead of a potential King's mistress.

Little fool! thought Francesca. If she ever does reach the King's bed she will not stay there long.

There was a constricted feeling in Francesca's throat which was the result of bitterness. She was the most unfortunate of women. She had endured all the years of hardship as Katharine's friend; and then two months before the coming of power and glory she had run away to Grimaldi—she, who longed to live her life in an atmosphere of Court intrigue, whose great delight was to find her way through the maze of political strategy.

She went back to the luxurious house where she lived with her rich husband.

He watched her with a certain sadness in his eyes. To him she was like some gorgeous bird which had fluttered into the cage he had prepared for her and was now longing to escape.

She was so young and so beautiful, but lately the lines of discontent had begun to appear on her brow.

"What luck?" he asked.

"None. When do I ever have luck? She will not receive me. She will never forgive me for marrying you. I have heard that she thinks I did it to cover up a love affair with Fuensalida. Our Queen cannot understand a noblewoman's marrying a commoner except to avoid a great scandal. Fuensalida was of a family worthy to match my own."

"And I am a vulgar commoner," sighed Grimaldi.

Francesca looked at him, her head on one side. Then she smiled and going to him she took his head in her hands and laid her lips lightly on the sparse hair. She loved power and he gave her power over him. He would do anything to please her.

"I married you," she answered.

He could not see her mouth, which had twisted into a bitter line. I married him! she thought. And in doing so I brought about my exile from the Court. It was so easy to offend. She thought of the frivolous Anne Stafford who was hoping—so desperately hoping—to begin a love affair with the King.

Then she smiled slowly. Such a woman would never keep her place for more than a night or two. Francesca would not place herself on the side of such a woman; and if it was going to be a matter of taking sides there would be another on which she could range herself.

If Katharine were grateful to her, might she not be ready to forgive that unfortunate marriage?

\* \* \*

Katharine was on her knees praying with her confessor, Fray Diego Fernandez, and the burden of her prayer was: Let me bear a son.

Fray Diego prayed with her and he comforted her. He was a young man of strong views and there had been certain rumours, mainly circulated by his enemies, the chief of whom was the ambassador Fuensalida with whom he had clashed on more than one occasion; and another was Francesca de Carceres who had been convinced, first that he was preventing her returning to Spain and, now that she was married and exiled from Court, that he was preventing her being received again.

The pugnacious little priest was the kind to provoke enemies; but Katharine trusted him; indeed in those days, immediately before her marriage, when she had begun to despair of ever escaping from the drab monotony of Durham House, and had discovered the duplicity of her duenna, Doña Elvira and the stupidity of her father's ambassador, Fuensalida, she had felt Fray Diego to be her only friend.

Katharine was not likely to forget those days; her memory was long and her judgment inflexible. If she could not forgive her enemies, she found it equally difficult to forget her friends.

Fuensalida had been sent back to Spain; Francesca had proved her treachery by deserting her mistress and escaping to marriage with the banker; but Fray Diego remained.

She rose from her knees and said: "Fray Diego, there are times when I think that you and Maria de Salinas are the only part of Spain that is left to me. I can scarcely remember what my father looks like; and I have almost as little esteem for our present ambassador as I had for his predecessor."

"Oh, I do not trust Don Luis Caroz either, Your Grace," said the priest.

"I cannot think why my father sends such men to represent him at the English Court."

"It is because he knows his true ambassador is the Queen herself. There is none who can do his cause more good than his own daughter; and none more wise or understanding of the English."

Katharine smiled tenderly. "I have been blessed in that I may study them at the closest quarters . . . singularly blessed."

"The King is full of affection towards Your Grace, and that is a matter for great rejoicing."

"I would I could please him, Fray Diego. I would I could give him that which he most desires."

"And is there any sign, Your Grace?"

"Fray Diego, I will tell you a secret, and secret it must be, for it is as yet too soon to say. I believe I may be pregnant."

"Glory be to the saints!"

She put her fingers to her lips. "Not a word, Fray Diego. I

could not endure the King's disappointment should it not be so. You see, if I told him he would want to set the bells ringing; he would tell the entire Court . . . and then . . . if it were not so . . . how disappointed he would be!"

Fray Diego nodded. "We do not wish Caroz to prattle of the matter."

"Indeed no. Sometimes I wonder what he writes to my father."

"He writes of his own shrewdness. He believes himself to be the greatest ambassador in the world. He does not understand that Your Grace prepared the way for him. He does not know how you continually plead your father's cause with the King."

"I do not see it as my father's cause, Fray Diego. I see it as friendship between our two countries. I would have perfect harmony between them, and I believe we are working towards it."

"If Caroz does not ruin everything, it may well be. He is such an arrogant man that he does not know that Your Grace's father sent him to England because he had sufficient wealth to pay his own way."

"Ah, my father was always careful with the gold. He had to be. There were so many calls upon it."

"He and the late King of England were a pair. The King, your husband, is of a different calibre."

Katharine did not say that her husband's extravagance sometimes gave her anxiety; she scarcely admitted it to herself. Henry VII had amassed a great fortune, and once his successor had had a surfeit of pleasure he would shoulder his responsibilities and turn his back on it. Katharine often remembered his behaviour when the people had robbed him of his jewellery so unexpectedly; and she believed that when he was in danger he would always know how to act. He was a boy as yet—a boy who had escaped from a parsimonious upbringing. He would soon grow tired of the glitter and the gold.

Fray Diego went on: "Your Grace, Francesca de Carceres was at the Palace today, hoping for an audience."

"Did she ask it?"

"She did and I told her that Your Grace had expressed no desire to see her. She abused me, telling me that it was due to me that you had refused, that I had carried evil tales about her. She is a dangerous woman."

"I fear so. She is one who will always scheme. I do not wish to see her. Tell her I regret her marriage as much as she evidently does; but since she made it of her own free will I should admire her more if she were content with the station in life which she herself chose."

"That I will do, Your Grace."

"And now, Fray Diego, I will join my ladies. And remember I have not even told Doña Maria de Salinas or Lady Elizabeth Fitzwalter of my hopes."

"I shall treat it as a secret of the confessional, Your Grace; and I shall pray that ere long the whole Court will be praying with me that this time there may be an heir who lives."

*        *        *

Francesca de Carceres was furiously angry as she left the Palace. She had always hated Fray Diego Fernandez but never quite so much as she did at this time. She had persuaded herself that it was due to his influence that Katharine would not receive her; and she decided to seek the help of the Spanish ambassador, Don Luis Caroz.

This was not difficult to arrange, because her husband transacted business for Caroz as he had done for Fuensalida, and the ambassador was a frequent visitor to the Grimaldi household.

So on his very next visit Francesca detained him and told him that she had news of an intrigue which was taking place at Court and of which she felt he should not be kept in ignorance.

She then told him that she believed that the King was either conducting, or preparing to conduct, a love affair with Lady Huntingdon.

The ambassador was horrified. It was essential to Spanish interests that Katharine should keep her influence with the King, and a mistress could mean considerable harm to those interests.

"The affair must be stopped," he said.

"I doubt whether it has begun," answered Francesca. "The King has been a faithful husband so far, in spite of temptations; but I think he is eager to subdue his conscience and take a mistress. I believe therefore that we should take some action . . . quickly. The Queen will not see me. Could you approach her, tell her that *I* have discovered this and am sending the news to her through you? You might hint that if she would see me I could tell her more."

The ambassador shook his head. "It would be dangerous to approach the Queen. We cannot be sure what action she would take. She might reproach the King, which could have disastrous results. Nay, this woman has a sister who is in the service of the Queen. We will approach the sister, Lady Fitzwalter. She will almost certainly call in the help of her brother the Duke and I am sure that the proud Staffords would not wish their sister to become the mistress even of the King. They will doubtless realize that the relationship with this rather foolish woman would be of short duration."

Francesca was silent. She did not see how this was going to help her win the Queen's favour, which was her sole object; but she had grown wise since making her fatal mistake. Her most powerful friend was the ambassador, and if she wished to keep his friendship she must fall in with his wishes.

"You are right," she said at length. "The important thing is to prevent the Queen from losing her influence over the King."

Caroz smiled slowly. "I think you might ask for an audience with Lady Fitzwalter. Tell her what you know. We will then watch how the Staffords receive the news. If things do not work out as we wish, we might take other action."

"I shall do exactly as you say," Francesca assured him.

He answered: "You are a good friend to Spain, Doña Francesca."

She felt more hopeful than she had for a long time. Perhaps previously she had been wrong to count so much on getting an audience with the Queen. She must work her way back through more devious paths. The Spanish ambassador might even report to Ferdinand her usefulness. It was possible that Katharine's father would command his daughter to take such a useful servant of Spain back into her service.

\* \* \*

Edward Stafford, third Duke of Buckingham, looked at his elder sister in dismay which was quickly turning to anger.

Buckingham's dignity was great. Secretly he believed that he was more royal than the King himself, for the Tudor ancestry could not bear too close a scrutiny; but the Staffords had royal blood in their veins and the present Duke could never forget that he was directly descended from Edward III.

Buckingham was a member of the King's most intimate circle, but Henry had the Tudor's suspicion of any who had too close a connection with the throne, and would never have the same affection for the Duke as he had for men like Sir William Compton.

In spite of his ambition Buckingham could not overcome his

pride. Because he himself could never forget his royal descent he could not help making others aware of it on every conceivable occasion. Often his friends had warned him to beware; but Buckingham, although being fully conscious of possible danger, could not curb his arrogance.

As yet the danger was not acute. Henry was young with a boy's delight in sport and pageantry. He enjoyed perfect health and his bursts of ill temper, although liable to occur suddenly, were quickly over and forgotten. So far he was sure of his popularity with his people and therefore inclined to be a little careless of the ambitions of others. But there were times when those suspicions, which had been so much a part of his father's character, made themselves apparent.

Buckingham's reactions to the news his sister was telling him were so fierce that he forgot that the King was involved in this matter.

He burst out: "Has the woman no family pride! Does she forget she is a Stafford?"

"It would seem so," answered Elizabeth Fitzwalter. "I am informed that it can only be a matter of days before she surrenders."

"She is such a fool that she would not hold the King's attention more than a night or so," growled Buckingham. "Moreover, the King is still too enamoured of the Queen for a mistress to have any chance of making her position really secure."

Elizabeth bowed her head. She was deeply shocked that a sister of hers should be ready to indulge in such immorality, but she was after all an ambitious Stafford and did know that the families of King's mistresses rarely suffered from their connection with royalty. But she, like her brother, realized that Anne's triumph would be short-lived; therefore it was advisable to stop the affair before it went too far.

"I suppose the whole Court is gossiping of this matter!" said Buckingham.

"I do not think it is widely known as yet; but of course as soon as she has shared the King's bed for one night it will be known throughout the Court. So far Compton is acting as go-between, and the final arrangements have not yet been made. Our sister is behaving like a simpering village girl—clinging to her chastity with reluctant fingers."

"And likely to let go at any moment. Well, she shall not do so. I trust that we may rely on our informants."

"I am sure of it. You remember Francesca de Carceres?

She is a clever woman and very eager to return to Court. She is anxious to show the Queen that she is still her humble servant. Anne—the little fool—allowed this woman to wheedle her secret from her; and I believe that Carceres feels that if she can prevent our sister's becoming the King's mistress she will have earned the Queen's gratitude. She makes a good spy, that woman."

The Duke nodded. "There is one thing to be done. I will send immediately for Huntingdon. He shall take his wife away to the country with all speed."

"I was sure you would know what should best be done, Edward." She looked anxious. "And the King? I am a little worried concerning his feelings when he knows that she has been whisked away from him."

"He will have to understand," said Buckingham haughtily, "that if he wants to take a mistress he must not look for her among the Staffords, whose blood is as royal as his own."

"Edward, do not let anyone hear you say that."

Buckingham shrugged his shoulders. "It does not need to be said. It is known for the truth by any who care to look into the matter."

"Still, have a care, Edward. I shall be so pleased when her husband has taken her out of danger."

\* \* \*

Anne's maid came to tell her that Sir William Compton was begging an audience.

"Then bring him to me," said Anne, "and do not forget to remain in the room."

He came in and once again the maid set about tidying the sewing box.

"I declare you grow more beautiful every time I have the pleasure of seeing you."

"You are gracious, sir."

"I come to tell you that impatience is growing strong in a certain breast."

"And what should *I* do about that?"

"It is only yourself who can appease it. I come to ask you if you will allow me to arrange a meeting between you and this impatient one."

"It would depend. . . ."

"On what, Madam?"

"On when and where this meeting should take place."

Compton came closer and whispered: "In one of the royal

apartments. None would see you come to it. It should be a matter between you and him who bids me tell you of his impatience."

"Then it seems this would be a command rather than a request."

"It could seem so," agreed Compton.

She smiled, her eyes gleaming. "Then I have no alternative but to say, Tell me when . . . tell me where. . . ."

The door opened suddenly. The Countess of Huntingdon gave a little cry of alarm, and the maid dropped her sewing box as the Duke of Buckingham strode into the room.

"Why, brother, is it indeed you?" stammered Anne.

"Whom else did you expect? Your lover! Or is this one he? By the saints, Madam, you forget who you are! This is conduct worthy of a serving wench."

"My lord Buckingham," began Compton sternly, "I come on the King's business."

"Neither the King nor anyone else has business in the private apartment of a married woman of my family."

"The King, I had always believed, might have business with any subject, an he wished it."

"No, sir, you are mistaken. This is my sister, and if she has forgotten the dignity due to her name, then she must be reminded of it." He turned to Anne. "Get your cloak at once."

"But why?"

"You will understand later, though it is not necessary for one so foolish to understand, but only to obey."

Anne stamped her foot. "Edward, leave me alone."

Buckingham strode forward and seized her by the arm. "You little fool! How long do you think it would last for you? Tonight? Tomorrow night? This time next week? No longer. And what to follow? Disgrace to your name. *That* you are ready to bear. But, by God and all the saints, I'll not suffer disgrace to mine. Come, you would-be harlot, your cloak." He turned to the maid. "Get it," he shouted, and the girl hurried to obey.

Compton stood looking at the Duke. He wondered how long such arrogance could survive at Court. But Buckingham was no youngster; he was well past his thirtieth birthday; he should be able to look after himself, and if he valued his family pride more than his life, that was his affair.

Compton shrugged. He was faintly amused. It would be interesting to see how the spoiled golden boy responded to this.

Buckingham snatched the cloak from the maid's trembling hands and roughly threw it about his sister's shoulders.

"Where are you taking me?" she asked.

"To your husband who, if he takes my advice, will place you this night in a convent. A pallet in a cell for you, sister; that is what your lust shall bring you."

Compton plucked the sleeve of the Duke's doublet.

"Do you realize that His Grace will not be pleased with you?"

"I," retorted Buckingham haughtily, "am far from pleased with His Grace's attempt to seduce my sister. Nor do I care for pimps —even though they be the King's own—to lay hands on me."

"Buckingham," murmured Compton, "you fool, Buckingham!"

But Buckingham was not listening; he had taken his sister by the shoulders and pushed her before him from the room.

\*          \*          \*

"And so, Your Grace," said Compton, "the Duke burst into his sister's apartment, bade her maid bring her cloak, and thereupon hustled her from the apartment with threats that he was taking her to her husband, and that the pair of them would see that this night she would lie in a convent."

The King's eyes were narrow and through the slits shone like pieces of blue glass; his fresh colour was heightened.

"By God and our Holy Mother!" he cried.

"Yes, Sire," went on Compton. "I warned the Duke. I told him of Your Grace's pleasure."

"And what said he?"

"He cared only for his sister's honour."

"I planned to honour the woman."

"'Tis so, Sire. The Duke has another meaning for the word."

"By God and his Holy Mother!" repeated the King.

Anything can happen now, thought Compton. The frisky cub is a young lion uncertain of his strength. He will not be uncertain long. Soon he will know its extent, and then it will go ill for any who oppose him.

Compton tried to read the thoughts behind those pieces of blue flint.

Frustrated desire! Now the lady seemed infinitely desirable. Out of reach in a convent! Could he demand her release? Could he have her brought to his apartments, laid on his bed? But what of the people, the people who adored him, who shouted their approval of their golden boy? They had seen him embrace his wife whom he had married because he said he loved her more than any woman. The people wanted their handsome King to be a virtuous husband. What would they say if they heard the story of the King and Buckingham's sister? They would laugh; they would snigger. They might say: Well, he is a King, but he is a man as well. They would forgive him his frailty; but he wished to have no frailty in their eyes. He wished to be perfect.

His eyes widened and Compton saw that they were the eyes of a bewildered boy. The cub was not yet certain of his strength; he had not yet grown into the young lion.

Now there was anger on the flushed face . . . vindictive anger. He would not send for the woman and there would be no scandal. Yet he would not lightly forgive those who had frustrated him.

He turned on Compton. "How did Buckingham discover this?"

"It was through his sister—Your Grace may recollect that the the Duke has two sisters—Anne, your Grace's . . . friend, and Elizabeth, Lady Fitzwalter."

"I know her," growled Henry. "She is with the Queen."

"A lady of high virtue, Your Grace. And much pride, like her brother."

"A prim piece," said Henry, and his eyes were cruel. Then he shouted: "Send for Buckingham."

Compton left him, but Buckingham was not at Court. He, with Anne and Lord Huntingdon, were on their way to the convent which Buckingham had ordered should be made ready to receive his erring sister.

*         *         *

The King's anger had had time to cool by the time Buckingham stood before him; but Henry was not going to allow anyone to interfere in his affairs.

He scowled at the Duke.

"You give yourself airs, sir Duke," he said.

"If Your Grace will tell me in what manner I have displeased you I will do my best to rectify my error . . . if it be in my power."

"I hear you have sent your sister into a convent."

"I thought she needed a little correction, Your Grace."

"You did not ask our permission to send her there."

"I did not think Your Grace would wish to be bothered with a family matter."

The King flushed hotly; he was holding fast to his rising temper. The situation was delicate. He was wondering how much of this had reached the Queen's ears and hoping that he could give vent to his anger in such a manner that Katharine would never hear of it.

"I am always interested in the welfare of my subjects," he grumbled.

"Her husband thought she was in need of what the convent could give her."

"I could order her to be brought back to Court, you know."

"Your Grace is, by God's mercy, King of this realm. But Your Grace is a wise man, and knows the scandal which would be bruited about the Court and the country itself, if a woman who had been sent by her husband into a convent should be ordered out by her King."

Henry wanted to stamp his feet in rage. Buckingham was older than he was and he knew how to trap him. How dared he stand there, insolent and arrogant! Did he forget he was talking to his King?

For a few moments Henry told himself that he would send for Anne; he would blatantly make her his mistress and the whole Court—ay, and all his subjects too—must understand that he was the King, and when he ordered a man or woman to some duty they must obey him.

But such conduct would not fit the man his subjects believed him to be. He was uncertain. Always he thought of the cheering crowds who had come to life when he appeared; he remembered the sullen looks which had been thrown his father's way. He remembered too the stories he had heard of his father's struggle to take the throne. If he displeased the people they might remember that the Tudor ancestry was not as clean as it might be—and that there were other men who might be considered worthy to be Kings.

No. He would remain the public idol—perfect King and husband; but at the same time he would not allow any subject of his to dictate to him what should be done.

"My lord Buckingham," he said, "you will leave Court. And you will not present yourself to me until I give you leave to do so."

Buckingham bowed.

"You may go," went on the King. "There is nothing more I have to say to you. I should advise you to be gone in an hour, for if I find you lingering after that I might not be so lenient."

Buckingham retired, and the King paced up and down like a lion in a cage.

He summoned one of his pages to him and said: "Send for Lady Fitzwalter. I would have immediate speech with her."

The page rushed to do his bidding and soon returned with Elizabeth Fitzwalter.

She looked disturbed, Henry was pleased to notice. A prim woman, he thought, with none of her sister's voluptuousness. The sight of her reminded him of Anne, and he was furious once more to contemplate what he had lost.

"Lady Fitzwalter," he said, "you are, I believe, one of the Queen's women."

She was bewildered. Surely he knew. He had seen her so often when he was in the Queen's company.

"Did I say you *are* one of Her Grace's women? It was a mistake, Lady Fitzwalter. I should have said you *were*."

"Your Grace, have I offended . . .?"

"We do not discuss why we banish from our Court those who do not please us, Lady Fitzwalter. We merely banish."

"Your Grace, I beg to . . ."

"You waste your time. You would beg in vain. Go back to your apartment and make all haste to leave Court. It is our wish that you are gone within the hour."

The startled Lady Fitzwalter curtseyed and retired.

Henry stared at the door for a few minutes. He thought of voluptuous Anne and realized suddenly how urgently he desired a change, a new woman who was as different from his wife as could be.

Then he began to pace up and down again . . . a lion, not sure of his strength, but aware of the cage which enclosed him. The bars were strong, but his strength was growing. One day, he knew, he would break out of the cage. Then there would be nothing—no person on Earth to restrain him.

\*    \*    \*

Elizabeth Fitzwalter came unceremoniously into the apartment where the Queen sat sewing with Maria de Salinas.

Katharine looked with surprise at her lady in waiting, and when she saw how distraught Elizabeth was she rose quickly and went to her side.

"What has happened to disturb you so?" she asked.

"Your Grace, I am dismissed from the Court."

"You, dismissed! But this is impossible. None has the authority to dismiss you but myself. Why. . . ." Katharine paused and a look of horror spread across her face. There was one other who had the power of course.

Elizabeth met Katharine's gaze, and Katharine read the truth there.

"But why?" demanded the Queen. "On what grounds? Why should the King dismiss you?"

"I find it hard to say, Your Grace. I am to leave at once. I have been told to make ready and go within the hour. I pray you give me leave to make ready."

"But surely the King gave you a reason. What of your brother?"

"He has already gone, Your Grace; and my sister also."

"So the King is displeased with all your family. I will go to see him. I will ask him what this means. He will keep nothing from me."

Maria de Salinas, who loved Katharine sincerely and with a disinterested devotion, laid her hand on the Queen's arm.

"Well, Maria?"

Maria looked helplessly at Elizabeth as though asking for permission to speak.

"What is it?" asked Katharine. "If it is something I should know, it is your duty to tell me."

Neither of the women spoke, and it was as though each was waiting for the other to do so.

"I will go to the King," said Katharine. "I will ask him what this means, for I see that you both know something which you believe you should keep from me."

Maria said: "I must tell Her Grace. I think she should know."

Katharine interrupted sternly: "Come Maria, enough of this. Tell me at once."

"The Countess of Huntingdon has been taken away from Court by her husband and brother because they . . . they feared the King's friendship."

Katharine had grown pale. She was almost certain now that she was with child and had been wondering whether she could tell the King. She had looked forward to his pleasure and had told herself how thankful she should be to have such a faithful husband.

She looked from Maria to Elizabeth and her gaze was bewildered. The King's friendship for a woman could surely mean only one thing.

But they must be mistaken. They had been listening to gossip. It was not true. He had always been faithful to her. He had firm notions on the sanctity of marriage: he had often told her so.

She said quietly: "Pray go on."

"Sir William Compton acted as His Grace's emissary in the matter," said Elizabeth. "Francesca Carceres discovered what was happening and warned me. I told my brother and, as a result, my sister has been sent to a convent. But the King was displeased with my brother and myself."

"I cannot believe this to be true."

"Your Grace, pray sit down," whispered Maria. "This has been a shock."

"Yes," said the Queen, "it has been a shock, a shock that such rumours can exist. I believe it all to be lies . . . lies. . . ."

Maria looked frightened. Elizabeth whispered: "Your Grace, give me leave to retire. I have to prepare with all speed to leave Court."

"You shall not go, Elizabeth," said Katharine. "I will speak to the King myself. There has been some terrible mistake. What you believe has happened is . . . an impossibility. I will go to him now. You will see, he will give me the explanation. I will tell him that I wish you to remain. That will suffice."

Katharine walked from the apartment, while Maria looked after her sadly; and Elizabeth, sighing went to make ready to leave.

* * *

It seemed to Henry that he saw his wife clearly for the first time.

How sallow her skin is! he thought comparing her with Anne Stafford. How serious she was! And she looked old. She was old of course, compared with him, for five years was no small matter.

She seemed distasteful to him in that moment, because he felt guilty, and he hated to feel so.

"Henry," she said, "I have heard some disturbing news. Elizabeth Fitzwalter comes to me in great distress and says that you have commanded her to leave Court."

"It is true," he said. "She should be gone within an hour of our giving her the order to leave."

"But she is one of my women, and I do not wish her to go. She is a good woman and has given me no offence."

The colour flamed into his face. "We will not have her at Court," he shouted. "Mayhap it escapes your notice, but our wishes here are of some account."

Katharine was afraid, yet she remembered that she was the daughter of Isabella of Castile, and it ill became any—even the King of England—to speak to her in such a manner.

"I should have thought I might have been consulted in this matter."

"No, Madam," retorted Henry. "We saw no reason to consult you."

Katharine said impetuously: "So you had the grace to try to keep it from my notice."

"We understand you not."

She realized then that he was using the formal "we", and she guessed he was attempting to remind her that he was the King and master of all in his dominions, even his Queen. She saw the danger signals in his eyes, for his face always betrayed his feelings, but she was too hurt and unhappy to heed the warning.

"It is true then," she burst out, "that the woman was your mistress. . . ."

"It is not true."

"Then she was not, because Buckingham intervened in time.'

"Madam, if the King wishes to add to his friends it is no concern of any but himself."

"If he has sworn to love and cherish a wife, is it not his wife's concern if he takes a mistress?"

"If she is wise and her husband is a King, she is grateful that he is ready to give her children . . . if she is able to bear them!"

Katharine caught her breath in horror. It is true then, she thought. He blames me for the loss of our two children.

She tried to speak but the words would not pass the lump of misery in her throat.

"We see no reason to prolong this interview," said Henry.

Her anger blazed suddenly. "Do you not? Then I do! I am your wife, Henry. You have told me that you believe that husbands and wives should be faithful to each other; and as soon as a wanton woman gives you a glance of promise you forget your vows, you forget your ideals. The people look upon you as a god—so young, so handsome, so model a king and a husband. I see now that your vows mean nothing to you. You think of little but seeking pleasure. First it is your pageants, your masques . . . now it is your mistresses!"

He was scarcely handsome in that moment. His eyes seemed to sink into his plump red face. He hated criticism and, because he was so deeply conscious of his guilt, he hated her.

"Madam", he said, "you should do your duty. It is what is expected of you."

"My duty?" she asked.

"Which is to give me sons. You have made two attempts and

have not been successful. Is it for you to criticize me when you
have failed . . . so lamentably?"

"I . . . failed? You would blame *me* then. Do you not know
that I long for sons as much as you do? Where have I failed?
How could I have saved the lives of our children? If there is a
way, in the name of the saints tell it to me."

Henry would not look at her. "We lost them both," he
mumbled.

She turned to him. She was about to tell him that she had
hopes of bearing another child; but he looked so cruel that she
said nothing. She was bewildered, wondering if this man who
was her husband was, after all, a stranger to her.

Henry felt uneasy. He hated to know that Katharine had
become aware of his flirtation with Anne Stafford. Looking back
it was such a mean little affair—it had not even approached its
climax. He felt small, having sent Compton to do his wooing
for him, and taking such a long time to make up his mind whether
he should or shouldn't, and so giving Buckingham time to whisk
his sister away.

He was angry with everyone concerned in the affair and, as
Katharine was the only one present, he gave vent to his venom
and let it fall upon her.

"It may be," he said coldly, "that the difference in our ages is
the cause. You are five years older than I. I had not realized
until today how old you are!"

"But," she stammered, "you always knew. I am twenty-five,
Henry. That is not too old to bear healthy children."

Henry looked past her, and when he spoke—although he did
so more to himself than to her—she felt a cold terror strike at
her.

"And you were my brother's wife," was what he said.

She could bear no more. She turned and hurried from his
presence.

Before Lady Fitzwalter had left Court the news was circulating.
"The King and Queen have quarrelled bitterly. This is the first
quarrel. Perhaps there will be fewer of those entwined initials.
Perhaps this is the end of the honeymoon."

*       *       *

Maria de Salinas helped the Queen to her bed. Never had
Maria seen Katharine so distraught; for even in the days of
humiliating poverty she had never given way to her grief but
had stoically borne all her trials.

"You see, Maria," said Katharine, "I feel I did not know him. He is not the same. I have glimpsed the man behind my smiling happy boy."

"He was angry," said Maria. "Perhaps Your Grace should not have spoken to him on the matter yet."

"Perhaps I should never have spoken to him on the matter. Perhaps the love affairs of Kings are to be ignored by all, including their wives. My father was not entirely faithful to my mother. I wonder if she ever complained. No, she would be too wise."

"You are wise too. Perhaps your mother had to learn also to curb her jealousy."

Katharine shivered. "You speak as though this is but a beginning, the first of many infidelities."

"But he was not unfaithful, Your Grace."

"No, the lady's brother and her husband intervened in time. It is naught to do with the King's virtue. I think that is why he is so angry with me, Maria . . . because he failed."

"He is young, Your Grace."

"Five years younger than I. He reminded me of it."

"It will pass, dearest lady."

"Oh, Maria, I am so tired. I feel bruised and wounded. I have not felt so sad . . . so lost . . . since the old days in Durham House when I thought everyone had deserted me."

Maria took the Queen's hand and kissed it. "All did not desert Your Grace."

"No. You were always there, Maria. Oh, it is good to have staunch friends."

"Let me cover you. Then you should try to sleep. When you are rested you will feel stronger."

Katharine smiled and closed her eyes.

*       *       *

It was later that night when she was awakened by pains which gripped her body and brought a sweat upon her skin.

She stumbled from her bed, calling to her ladies as she did so; but before they could reach her she fell groaning to the floor.

They put her to bed; they called her physicians; but there was nothing they could do.

On that September night Katharine's third pregnancy ended. It had been brief, but the result was no less distressing.

Once more she had failed to give the King the son for which he longed.

She was ill for several days, and during that time she was tormented with nightmares. The King figured largely in these— an enormous menacing figure with greedy, demanding hands which caressed others, but when he turned to her, held out those hands, crying: "Give me sons."

## CHAPTER III

# THE SECRET LIFE OF THOMAS WOLSEY

As THE DAYS passed they took some of Katharine's sorrow with them, and she began to look at her life in a more philosophical way. Through the ages Kings had taken mistresses who bore them children, but it was the children who were born in wedlock who were heirs to their father's crown. She must be realistic; she must not hope for impossible virtue from her lusty young husband.

More than ever she thought of her mother, who had borne the same tribulations before her; she must endeavour as never before to emulate Isabella and keep the memory of her as a bright example of how a Queen should live.

As for Henry, he was ready enough to meet her half way. Reproaches would only result in sullen looks; and the pout of the little mouth, the glare of the little eyes in that large face implied that he was the King and he would do as he wished. But any signs of a desire on her part to return to the old relationship brought immediate response; dazzling smiles would light up his face; he would be boisterously affectionate, sentimental, calling her his Kate—the only woman who was of any real importance to him.

So Katharine set aside her illusions and accepted reality; which was, she assured herself, pleasant enough. If she could have a child—ah, if she could have a child—that little creature would make up to her for all else. That child would be the centre of her existence; and her husband's philandering would be of small importance compared with the delight that child would bring her.

In the meantime she would concern herself with another important matter.

Since she had become Queen of England she had been in close contact with her father. She waited for his letters with the utmost eagerness, forgetting that, when she had been living in neglected seclusion at Durham House, he had not written to her for years.

"What a joy it is to me," Ferdinand assured her, "that you, my daughter, are the Queen of England, a country which I have always believed should be my closest ally. I am beginning to understand that a father can have no better ambassador than his own daughter."

Ferdinand in his letters to her artfully mingled his schemes with his news of family affairs. His daughter was the beloved wife of young Henry, and if the King of England was occasionally unfaithful to his marriage bed, what did that matter as long as he continued to regard his wife with affection and respect!

"If your dear mother could know what a comfort to me you have become, what a clever ambassadress for her beloved country, how happy she would be."

Such words could not fail to move Katharine, for the very mention of her mother always touched all that was sentimental in her nature.

After receiving her father's letters she would put forward his ideas to Henry, but never in such a manner that it would appear she was receiving instructions from Spain.

"The King of France," Ferdinand wrote, "is an enemy to both our countries. Singly we might find it difficult to subdue him. But together. . . ."

Henry liked to walk with her in the gardens surrounding his palaces. When he felt particularly affectionate towards her he would take her arm and they would go on ahead of the little band of courtiers, and occasionally he would bend his head and whisper to her in the manner of a lover.

On such an occasion she said to him: "Henry, there are certain provinces in France which are by right English. Now that there is a young King on the throne, do you think the people would wish to see those provinces restored to the crown?"

Henry's eyes glistened. He had always longed for the conquest of France. He was beginning to think he had had enough of empty triumphs at the jousts and masques. He wished to show his people that he was a man of war no less than a sportsman. Nothing could have given him greater pleasure at that time than the thought of military conquest.

"I'll tell you this, Kate," he said. "It has always been a dream of mine to restore our dominions in France to the English crown."

"And what better opportunity could we have than an alliance with my father who also regards the King of France as his enemy?"

"A family affair. I like that. Your father and I standing together against the French."

"I believe my father would be ready enough to make a

treaty in which you and he would agree to attack the French."

"Is it so, Kate? Then write to him and tell him that, having such regard for his daughter, I would have him for my friend."

"You have made me happy, Henry . . . so happy."

He smiled at her complacently. "We'll make each other happy, eh Kate?" His eyes were searching her face. There was a question in them which he did not need to put into words. It was the perpetual question: Any sign, Kate? Any sign yet that we may expect a child?

She shook her head sadly. He did not share her sadness today. The thought of war and conquest had made him forget temporarily even the great need for a son.

He patted her arm affectionately.

"Have no fear, Kate. We'll not suffer ill luck for ever. I have a notion, Kate, that England and Spain together are . . . invincible! No matter what they undertake."

She felt her spirits rising. It was a great pleasure to see that his thoughts were turned for a while from the matter of childbearing; and it was equally gratifying that he was so willing to fall in with her father's desires. Thus she could please them both at the same time. And surely her next pregnancy must result in a healthy child!

*       *       *

Richard Fox, Bishop of Winchester and Lord Privy Seal, was deeply disturbed, and he had asked Thomas Howard, Earl of Surrey, and William Warham, Archbishop of Canterbury, to call upon him.

Fox, some sixty-four years of age, was as much a politician as a man of the Church. He had stood staunchly by Henry VII and had worked in co-operation with the King since the victory at Bosworth, receiving from that monarch the offices of Principal Secretary of State and Lord Privy Seal. When he had died Henry VII had recommended his son to place himself under the guidance of Richard Fox, and this young Henry had been prepared to do, particularly when Warham had declared himself against the marriage with Katharine.

Fox, the politician, had supported the marriage because he believed that an alliance with Spain was advantageous. Warham, as a man of the Church, had felt that a more suitable wife than the widow of his brother might have been found for the King. The fact that Fox had supported the marriage had placed him higher in the King's favour than the Archbishop of Canterbury;

but Fox was now becoming disturbed to see that the country's wealth, which he so carefully had helped Henry VII to amass, was being extravagantly squandered by the young King.

But that was not the matter he intended to discuss with his two colleagues at this time—something of even greater importance had arisen.

William Warham, who was perhaps a year or two younger than Fox, had also served the Tudors well. Henry VII had made him Lord Chancellor and he had held the Great Seal for some nine years. Although he disagreed with Fox on certain matters they both felt deeply the responsibility of guiding a young king who lacked his father's caution and thrift.

The third member of the party was the choleric Thomas Howard, Earl of Surrey, who was the eldest of the three by some five years.

His record was not one of loyalty to the Tudors for he and his father had both fought at Bosworth on the side of Richard III. At this battle Surrey had been taken prisoner and his father killed. There had followed imprisonment in the Tower and forfeiture of his estates; but Henry VII had never been a man to allow desire for revenge to colour his judgment; he realized the worth of Surrey who believed in upholding the crown and the nobility, no matter who wore the first and whatever the actions of the latter, and it seemed to the crafty King that such a man could be of more use to him free than a prisoner. It cost little to restore his titles—but Henry kept the greater part of his property, and sent him up to Yorkshire to subdue a rebellion against high taxation.

The King proved his wisdom when Surrey turned out to be a first-class general and as ready to work for the Tudor as he had for Richard III. For his services he was made a member of the Privy Council and Lord Treasurer.

When Henry VII had died, Surrey, on account of his age and experience, had become the chief of the new King's advisers; and recently, to show his appreciation, young Henry had bestowed upon his faithful servant the title of Earl Marshal.

As soon as these three men were together Fox told them of his concern.

"The King contemplates war with France. I confess that the prospect does not please me."

"The expense would be great," agreed Warham, "and what hope would there be of recovering that which we laid out?"

They were looking at Surrey, the soldier, who was thoughtful.

The prospect of war always thrilled him; but he was becoming too old to take an active part in wars and therefore could consider them, not in terms of adventure and valour, but of profit and loss.

"It would depend on our friends," he said.

"We should stand with Spain."

Surrey nodded. "Spain could attack from the South; we from the North. It does not sound a pleasant prospect for the French."

"The late King," said Fox, "was against wars. He always said that it was a sure way of losing English blood and gold."

"Yet, there could be riches from conquest," mused Surrey.

"Victory," put in Warham, "is more easily dreamed of than won."

"The King is enamoured of the prospect," Fox declared.

"Doubtless because the Queen has made it sound so attractive to him," added Warham. "Can it be that Ferdinand has placed an ambassador nearer to the King than any of his own advisers could hope to be?"

He was looking ironically at Fox, reminding him that he had been in favour of the marriage while he, Warham, had seen many disadvantages—of which this could be one.

"The King is pleased with his Queen as a wife," put in Fox. "Yet I believe him to be wise enough to look to his ministers for advice as to how matters of state should be conducted."

"Yet," Surrey said, "he would seem eager for war."

"How can we know," went on Warham, "what has been written in Ferdinand's secret despatches to his daughter? How can we know what the Queen whispers to the King in moments of intimacy?"

"It always seemed to me that the young King must tire of his sports and pageants in time," said Fox. "Now the time has come and he wishes to turn his energies to war. This was bound to happen, and the conquest of France is a natural desire."

"What course do you suggest we should take in this matter?" Warham asked.

"Why," Fox told him, "I believe that if we advised His Grace to send a few archers to help his father-in-law in his battles, that would suffice for the time."

"And you think the King will be satisfied with that?" demanded Surrey. "Young Henry is yearning to place himself at the head of his fighting men. He wishes to earn glory for his country . . . and himself."

"His father had turned a bankrupt state into one of some

K

consequence," Warham reminded them. "He did it through peace, not through war."

"And," put in Surrey, remembering the confiscation of his own estates, "by taxes and extortions."

"I was not speaking of the method," Fox told him coldly, "but of the result." He went on: "I have asked the King's almoner to join us here, for there are certain matters which I feel we should lay before him; and he is such an able fellow that he may help us in our counsels."

Surrey's face grew purple. "What!" he cried. "That fellow, Wolsey! I will not have the low-born creature sharing in my counsels."

Fox looked at the Earl coldly. "He has the King's confidence, my lord," he said. "It would be well if you gave him yours."

"That I never shall," declared Surrey. "Let the fellow go back to his father's butcher's shop."

"Ah," said Warham, "he has come a long way from that."

"I'll admit he has sharp wits," conceded Surrey. "And a quick tongue."

"He also has the King's ear, which is something we should not forget," Fox told him. "Come, my lord, do not allow your prejudices to affect your judgment of one of the ablest men in this country. We have need of men such as Thomas Wolsey."

Surrey's lips were tightly pressed together and the veins in his temples stood out. He wanted them to know that he was a member of the aristocracy and that he supported his own class. If there were honours to be earned they should be earned by noblemen; to his bigoted mind it was inconceivable that a man of humble origin should share the secrets of the King's ministers.

Fox watched him ironically. "Then, my lord," he said, "if you object to the company of Thomas Wolsey, I can only ask you to leave us, for Wolsey will be with us in a very short time."

Surrey stood undecided. To go would mean cutting himself off from affairs; he was growing old; he believed that Fox and this upstart of his would be delighted to see him pass into obscurity. He could not allow that.

"I'll stay," he said. "But, by God, I'll stand no insolence from a butcher's cur."

\*      \*      \*

Thomas Wolsey had taken time from his duties to visit his family. This was one of the pleasures of his life; not only did he enjoy being a husband and father but the fact that he must do so with secrecy gave his pleasure an added fillip.

He was a priest but that had not prevented his being un-canonically married; and when he had fallen in love with his little "lark", and she with him, it became clear that their relation-ship was no light matter of a few weeks' duration and must there-fore be set on as respectable a basis as was possible in the circumstances.

So he had gone through a form of marriage with Mr. Lark's daughter; he had made a home for her which he visited from time to time, leaving his clerical garments behind, and dressed so that he could pass through the streets as an ordinary gentleman return-ing to his home.

It was a rather splendid little home, for he enjoyed ostentation and could not resist the pleasure of making his family aware that he was rising in the world.

As he entered the house he called: "Who is at home today? Who is ready to receive a visitor?"

A serving maid appeared and gave a little cry of wonder. She was followed by a boy and a girl who, having heard his voice, rushed out to greet him.

Thomas Wolsey laid his hand on the boy's shoulder and put an arm about the girl. The smile on his face made him look younger than his thirty-seven years. The alertness in the eyes almost disap-peared; Thomas Wolsey briefly looked like a man who is contented.

"Why, my son, my little daughter, so you are pleased to see your father, eh?"

"We are always pleased to see our father," said the boy.

"That is as it should be," answered Thomas Wolsey. 'Now Tom, my boy, where is your mother?"

There was no need to ask. She had started to come down the stairs, and as Thomas looked up she paused and for a few seconds they gazed at each other. The woman, thought Thomas, for whom I was ready to risk a great deal. Not everything, and per-haps what he had risked was not very much—for why should not a priest have a wife as long as he did not prate of it—but the fact that he was ready to risk anything, that he was ready to pause in his journey up the steep and difficult slopes of ambition to spend a little time with this woman and their children, was an indication of the extent of his feelings for her.

"Thomas, had I known . . ." she began; and she came down the stairs slowly, almost reverently, as though she marvelled yet again that this great man should have time to spare for her.

He took her hand and kissed it.

"Well met, Mistress Wynter," he said.

"Well met, Master Wynter."

It was the name behind which they sheltered from the world. She longed to boast that she was the wife of the great Thomas Wolsey, but she knew well the folly of that. He had given so much; he could not be expected to give more. She was happy enough to be plain Mistress Wynter, with a husband whose business frequently called him away from home but who was now and then able to visit his family.

The future of her children was secure. Thomas was rising rapidly in the service of the King; he was proud of the children; he would not forget them, and their way would be easier than his had been. Honours, riches would come to them—that would be when they were of an age to receive them—and by that time Thomas would be the most important man in the realm. Mistress Wynter believed that, for Thomas had determined it should be so; and Thomas always achieved his ends.

The children stood aside while their parents embraced.

"How long will you stay, Thomas?" she asked.

"Naught but a few hours, my lark." Even as he uttered the endearment he wondered what certain members of the King's entourage would say if they could see and hear him now. Fox? Warham? Surrey? Lovell? Poynings? They would snigger doubtless; and the wise among them would not be displeased. They would tell themselves that he had his weaknesses like all other men, and such weaknesses were not to be deplored but encouraged, for they were as a great burden hung upon the back to impede the climb to the heights of success.

There are some who are afraid of Thomas Wolsey, thought Thomas, and the thought pleased him; for when men began to fear another, it meant that that one was high upon the ladder since others could see him mounting.

But I must take care, he thought as he stroked his wife's hair; no one however dear must prevent my taking every opportunity; the road to disaster and failure is one of lost opportunities.

But for a few hours he was safely hidden from the Court, so for that time he would be happy.

"Why, Mistress Wynter," he said, "you were not warned of my coming, but I smell goodly smells from your kitchen."

The children began to tell their father what was for dinner. There was a goose, capon and chicken; there was a pastie which their good cook had made in the shape of a fortress; there was pheasant and partridge.

Thomas was pleased. His family lived as he would have them live. It made him happy to think that he could pay for their comforts; and the sight of the rosy cheeks and plump limbs of his children was an immense satisfaction to him.

Mistress Wynter in a flurry of excitement went off to the kitchen to warn the servants that the master was in the house; and there the cook harried the lower servants to do their best and prove that, although the master of the house was often absent on his important business, the house was so well managed that he need have no fears.

So Thomas sat at table and watched the food brought in, while his wife sat facing him and on either side of the table was a child.

It was very humble compared with the King's table, but here was contentment; and in such moments he deeply wished that he was not a priest and that he might take this charming family with him to Court and boast of the health of the boy and the good looks of the girl.

He now wished to know how young Tom was getting on with his studies, and he put on a sternly paternal expression when he discovered that the boy was not quite so fond of his studies as his tutor would wish.

"That must be remedied," said Thomas, shaking his head. "Doubtless you think that you are young yet and that there is always time. Time is short. It is hard for you to realize it at your age, but soon you must understand that it is so, for when you do you will have learned one of the first lessons of life. It is those who dally by the wayside, my son, who never reach the end of the road."

There was quiet at the table, as there always was when he spoke; he had a melodious voice and a way of driving home his points which demanded attention.

And as they sat eating their way through meat and pies to the marchpane and sugar-bread he told his family how he himself had once defeated time in such a way that he had convinced the King that he had a little more than ordinary men to offer in his service.

"It was when I was in the service of the old King . . ." He did not tell them that he had been the King's chaplain; children often talked freely in the hearing of servants, and he must keep secret his connection with the Church. "This was not the King you have seen riding through the streets. This was the old King, his father, a King with a very serious mind and one who had learned the value of time.

"He called me to him and he said: 'I wish you to go on a journey to Flanders as a special envoy to the Emperor Maximilian. Prepare to leave as soon as possible.' So I took the message which I was to deliver and I set out for my lodgings. My servant said: 'You will leave tomorrow, my lord?' And I answered: 'Tomorrow! Nay, I shall leave today . . . at this very hour.' He was astonished. He had thought I should need time to prepare for such a journey; but I was conscious of time and I knew that the message I carried was of great importance. It might be that if it arrived a day later than I intended to deliver it, the answer to that letter would not be the same favourable one that I was determined to get. Circumstances change . . . and it is time which changes them.

"The message I carried was the King's request for the hand of Maximilian's daughter in marriage. If I could bring a favourable reply from Maximilian, the King would be happy, and that would make him pleased with me; and if that reply came quickly, the better pleased he would be.

"I crossed the water. I rode hot foot to Flanders; I saw the Emperor, delivered the King's message and received his reply; then back to the coast and home. It had been three days since I left England. I presented myself to the King, who frowned in anger when he saw me. He said: 'I had thought you received orders to take a message to Flanders. I expected you would have left by now. I like not dilatory service.' Then my heart leaped in exultation and I waited a few seconds for the King's anger to grow, for the greater it grew the more surprised he must be when he heard the truth. 'Your Grace,' I told him, 'I left for Flanders within an hour of receiving your instructions to do so. I have now returned and bring you the Emperor's reply.' The King was astonished. Never had he been served with such speed. He grasped my hand and said: 'You are a good servant.' "

"And that was all, Father?" demanded young Thomas. "It seems a small reward to shake your hand and tell you you were a good servant."

"He did not forget me," said Thomas.

No, indeed he had not. Thomas Wosley had become Dean of Lincoln and, had Henry VII lived longer, doubtless more honours would have come his way. But the old King had died; yet that was not a matter for mourning, because the new King was as interested in his servant Wolsey as the old one had been.

From this young King Thomas Wolsey hoped for much. He understood the eighth Henry. Here was a young man, lusty, sensual, far less interested in matters of state than in pleasure. He was the sort of King who is always beloved of ambitious ministers. Henry VII had conducted all state business himself; he had indeed been head of the state. But the joust, tennis, dancing, possible fornication and adultery gave no pleasure to his rheumaticky body. How different was his young and lusty son! This King would wish to place at the helm of the ship of state a man with capable hands; there was every opportunity for ambitious ministers to rule England under such a King.

The King's almoner saw great possibilities ahead.

He smiled at the eager faces about the table—flushed with good food and drink. This was his oasis of pleasure, of humanity; here it was possible to stray from the road of heated ambition to dally in a cool green meadow.

He saw Mistress Wynter through a veil of gratitude and desire, and she seemed fairer to him than any Court lady.

He said to the children: "You will leave your mother with me for a while. We have matters to speak of. I shall see you again before I leave."

The children left their parents together, and Thomas took Mistress Wynter in his arms and caressed her body.

They went through to her sleeping chamber and there made love.

As she lay in his arms she thought: It is like a pattern, always the same. Will it remain so? What when he is the first minister at the King's Court? This he would be, for in a moment of confidence he had told her so.

If it were not so, she thought, if he lost his place at Court, he might come home to us.

It was a wicked thought. He must not lose his place. It meant more to him than anything . . . more than this, his home, more than her and their children.

When he had dressed in that precise manner of his, he said: "I will see the children before I go."

He noticed that she looked a little sad but he did not mention this. He knew that she was wishing they lived a normal married life, that they did not have to go to bed in the middle of the day because it was the only time they had. She was picturing him, being there every day—a merchant, a lawyer, a goldsmith . . . a man of some profession such as those of her neighbours. She thought of cosy conversations over the table, of discussions as to what should be planted in the garden, about the education of the children; she pictured them retiring to bed each night by the light of candles, the embrace that had become almost a habit, the slipping into sleep afterwards. It was normality she craved.

Poor little Mistress Wynter, he thought, she can only share one very small portion of my life and she wants to share the whole.

It was unfortunate for her that she loved not a man of ordinary ability, but one who had risen from a humble Ipswich butcher's shop to his present position and was determined to go to the very heights of ambition.

He said: "Let us go to the children. I have little time left to me."

He kissed her once more, but this time he did not see the sadness in her eyes. He saw only Wosley, going higher and higher. He saw the Cardinal's hat, but that of course was not the end. There was still the Papal Crown; and since even he must realize that he could never be the King of England, his ultimate ambition was that he should be head of the Church.

He went to his children, smiling happily, for his ambition did not seem an impossible one to achieve. Thomas Wosley, who had learned so many lessons from life, believed that all that which he desired would eventually be his.

\*     \*     \*

As soon as he returned to Court a messenger informed him that the Archbishop of Canterbury and the Bishop of Winchester with the Earl of Surrey requested his presence.

He donned his clerical garments and washed his hands before making his way to their presence, for this was one of those occasions when time should be used to create an impression of his own power and importance.

They were waiting rather impatiently when he arrived.

"My lords," he said, "you requested my presence."

Surrey looked with distaste at Thomas Wosley. He reeks of vulgarity, thought Surrey. That coarse skin, that over-red complexion—they proclaim him the vulgarian he is.

Surrey was scarcely pale himself, nor was his skin extra fine, but he was determined to find fault with Wolsey and looked for opportunities to remind him that he was not of noble blood and was only admitted to their counsels as a special privilege for which he should be perpetually grateful.

Fox welcomed him with a smile of pleasure. Fox had believed in his exceptional powers from the first and was determined to be proved right.

"We have been discussing the possibility of war with France," Warham told him.

Wolsey nodded gravely.

"You, Mr. Almoner, should know how much we could put into the field," Surrey pointed out, implying by his tone that it was as a lower servant of the King's that Wolsey had been invited and that his opinion must be confined only to questions of goods and gold.

"Ah," said Wolsey ignoring Surrey and turning to Fox and Warham, "it would depend on what scale the war was to be carried on. If the King should put himself at the head of his men that could be costly. If we sent a small force under the command of some noble gentleman . . ." Wolsey glanced at Surrey. . . . "that would be well within our means."

"I see you are of our opinion," Fox put in. "At the moment any action should be kept on a small scale."

"And," continued Wolsey, "I dare swear we would not move until we had an assurance from the King of Spain that he also would take action."

"Any alliance with the King of Spain," Surrey interrupted hotly, "should surely be no concern of Mr. Almoner."

"My lord is mistaken," Wolsey said coolly. "That the alliance should be made and adhered to is of the utmost importance to every subject in this land, including the King's Almoner."

The veins seemed to knot in Surrey's temples. "I cannot see that matters of state policy are the concern of every *Tom*, Dick or Harry."

"Might it be that there is much that the noble lord fails to see?" retorted Wolsey. "But since he is now aware of his blindness he may seek a cure for it."

Surrey lifted his fist and brought it down on the table.

"This is insolence!" he shouted. He glared at Fox and Warham. "Did I not tell you that I had no wish to consort with . . . trades-men!"

Wolsey looked round the apartment in astonishment.

"Tradesmen?" he said, but the hot resentment was rising within him. "I see no tradesmen present." He was fighting his anger because his very love of ostentation grew out of his desire to live as the nobility lived—and a little more richly—that he might leave behind him the memory of the butcher's shop.

K*

"No," sneered Surrey, "how could you? There is no mirror in this room."

"My lord," said Wolsey almost gently, "I am not a tradesman. I graduated at Oxford and was elected Fellow of Magdalen College. Teaching was my profession before I took Holy Orders."

"I pray you spare us an account of your achievements," sneered Surrey, "which I admit are remarkable for one who began in a butcher's shop."

"How fortunate," retorted Thomas, "that you, my lord, did not begin in such an establishment. I fear that if you had you would still be there."

Warham lifted a hand. "I pray you, gentlemen, let us return to the point of discussion."

"I prefer not to continue with it," Surrey shouted. "There is scarce room for myself and Master Wolsey in this council."

He waited for Warham and Fox to request Wolsey to retire. Wolsey stood still, pale, but smiling; and both Fox and Warham looked beyond the now purple-faced Earl. Surrey! Fox was thinking. With his inflated ideas of his own nobility he was scarcely likely to continue in favour with the King. Wolsey, with his quick and clever mind, his ability to smooth out difficulties, and make easy the King's way to pleasure, was by far the better ally. Moreover, Fox had always looked upon the almoner as one of his protégés. Let Surrey stomp out of the apartment. They could well do without him.

As for Warham, he also recognized the almoner's brilliance; he had no love for Surrey either. Surrey belonged to the old school; the days of his youth had been lived in that period when valour in battle brought glory; but Henry VII had taught his people that the way to make a country great was by crafty statesmanship rather than through battles, even if they should be victorious.

With an exclamation of disgust, Surrey flung out of the room.

Wolsey smiled in triumph. "The atmosphere, gentlemen, is now more conducive to thoughtful reasoning," he said.

Fox returned his smile in a manner implying that they were well rid of Surrey.

"And your opinion?"

Wolsey was ready. He was not going to say that he was against sending an army to France, because it might well be that the King wished to send one; it was almost certain that the Queen did, because that was the desire of her father, and the Queen was naturally working for her father's interests. If a decision was made which was contrary to the King's wishes, let Fox and Warham make it.

"As my lord of Surrey pointed out," he said almost demurely, "matters of state are scarcely the concern of the King's Almoner. Should His Grace decide to go into battle I will see that all available armaments are made ready for him; but it is only reasonable to suppose that the mustering of arms to equip a small force, say under some nobleman, would be a simpler matter and one which would give us practice in this field before embarking on the great campaign."

"I see," said Fox, "that you are of our opinion."

They discussed the matter in detail, and, although he seemed outwardly calm, inwardly Thomas Wolsey felt his pride to be deeply bruised. He could not forget the scorn in Surrey's eyes when he had referred to the butcher's shop. Would he ever escape such slights?

They could not be forgotten; therefore they could not be forgiven. Surrey's name was on that list he kept in his mind of those who must one day pay for the indignity they had made Thomas Wolsey suffer.

## CHAPTER IV

## SPANISH INTRIGUE

KATHARINE REJOICED TO see the change in her husband. She was sure that the irresponsible boy had been left behind and the King was growing to maturity.

He had forgotten their differences and talked with her of his ambitions; this made her very happy; he had even ceased to ask questions as to whether or not she had conceived again.

She had said to him: "It may be that the fact that we concern ourselves so constantly with my pregnancies is the reason that I am not with child. I have heard that constant anxiety can make one sterile."

He may have taken this to heart, but on the other hand the prospect of war may have been entirely responsible for turning his interest into other channels.

One day he swept into her apartments, and she was aware that instead of glancing appreciatively at the prettiest of her women with that glazed look in his eyes which she had noticed with some alarm on previous occasions, he waved his hands for their dismissal.

"Ah, Kate," he cried when they were alone, "I chafe at this delay. I would I could set out this day for France. These ministers of mine think the time is not meet for me to leave the country."

"I have heard from my father," she told him. "He writes that he knows that you would be welcomed in Guienne. The people there have never taken kindly to French rule, he says, and have always considered the English their true rulers. He says that once they see Your Grace they would rally to your banner."

Henry smiled complacently. He could well believe that. He was certain that the wars with France should never have been allowed to die out while the position was so unsatisfactory for England. England had been torn by her own Wars of the Roses—which was a matter he could not regret as out of that had come the victorious conclusion which had set the Tudors on the throne; but now that there was peace within England and there was a King on the throne who was as strong and eager for conquest as Henry V had been, why should not the struggle be continued?

But Guienne! His ministers were a little anxious. It would have been so much simpler to have attacked nearer home. Calais was the natural starting point.

He would of course be near his ally if he attacked in the south; delay galled him. He could not imagine defeat, so he longed to set forth, to show the people his conquests.

"It would please me, Kate," said Henry, "to lead my army and join up with that of your father. Together we should be invincible."

"I am sure that you would. My father is considered one of the greatest soldiers in Europe."

Henry frowned. "You would imply, Kate, that I should find it necessary to learn from him?"

"He is a man of great experience, Henry."

Henry turned from her. "There are some who are born to be conquerors. They are endowed with the gift. They do not need lessons in bravery."

She went on as though she had not heard him. "He and my mother had to fight for their kingdoms. She often said that without him she would have been lost."

"I like to hear of a wife who appreciates her husband."

"She appreciated him . . . although he was often unfaithful to her."

"Ha!" cried Henry. "You have no such complaint."

She turned to him smiling. "Henry, never give me cause for such complaint. I swear to love and serve you with all my might. I picture us growing old together with our children about us."

His eyes were misted with sentiment. The thought of children could always produce this result. Then his face puckered suddenly.

"Kate, I do not understand. We have been unfortunate, have we not?"

"Many are unfortunate, Henry. So many children die in infancy."

"But three times. . . ."

"There will be many times, Henry."

"But I cannot understand. Look at me. See my strength. My good health is something all marvel at. And yet . . ." He was looking at her almost critically.

She said quickly: "I too enjoy good health."

"Then why . . . I could almost believe that some spell has been cast upon us . . . that we have offended God in some way."

"We cannot have done that. We are devout worshippers,

both of us. No, Henry, it is natural to lose children. They are dying every day."

"Yes," he agreed. "One, two, three or four in every family. But some live."

"Some of ours will live."

He stroked her hair, which was her claim to beauty, and as he watched the sun bring out the red in it he felt a sudden rush of desire for her.

He laughed and taking her hand he began to dance, twirling her round, releasing her to caper high in the air. She watched him, clapping her hands, happy to see him so gay.

He grew excited by the dancing and he seized her and hugged her so tightly that she could not breathe.

"A thought comes to me, Kate," he said. "If I go to France with my armies, you must stay behind. We shall be apart."

"Oh Henry, that will make me very sad. I shall miss you so sorely."

"Time will pass," he assured her "and while we are separated how can I get you with child?" Then he began to laugh afresh. "And we squander our time in dancing!"

Then with a swift gesture—eager even in this moment of excitement that she should marvel at his strength—he swung her into his arms and carried her across the apartment to the bed-chamber.

*        *        *

Ferdinand, King of Aragon and Regent of Castile until his grandson Charles should come of age, was eagerly awaiting despatches from England.

His great desire at the moment was for the conquest of Navarre. He had made Naples safe and this left him free to make new conquests. It had always been one of his ambitions that Navarre should be under Spanish dominion; his great concern now was to persuade the Archbishop of Toledo and Primate of Spain, Francesco Ximenes de Cisneros, of the justice of this.

He had summoned Ximenes to his presence with the sole purpose of winning his approval of the project. Ximenes came, but from the moment he entered the King's apartments in the Alhambra he showed his reluctance to be torn from his beloved University of Alcalá, which he himself had built and where he was now finishing that great work, his polyglot bible.

Ferdinand felt a surge of resentment as Ximenes entered the apartment. Whenever he saw the man he remembered how his first wife, Isabella, had bestowed the Archbishopric of Toledo on this recluse when he, Ferdinand, had so deeply desired it for his illegitimate son. He had to admit that Isabella's trust in Ximenes had not been ill-founded; the man was a brilliant statesman as well as a monk; yet the resentment lingered.

Even now, thought Ferdinand, I must make excuses for my conduct to this man. I must *win* him to myself, because he wields as much power as I do, since while I am Regent for my grandson, he is Primate in his own right.

"Your Highness wished to see me," Ximenes reminded Ferdinand.

"I am concerned about the French, and the dilatory ways of the English."

"Your Highness is eager to make war on the French for, I believe, the purpose of annexing Navarre."

Ferdinand felt the warm blood rushing to his face.

"Your Eminence has forgotten that I have a claim to Navarre, through my father's first wife."

"Who was not Your Highness' mother."

"But I claim through my father."

"Through his marriage into the royal house of Navarre," Ximenes reminded Ferdinand, "it would seem that Jean d'Albret is the rightful King of Navarre."

Ferdinand said impatiently: "Navarre is in a strategic position. It is necessary to Spain."

"That is scarcely a reason for making war on a peaceful state."

You old fool! thought Ferdinand. Go back to your university and your polyglot bible. Leave me to fight for my rights.

But he said craftily: "How can we be sure that their intentions are peaceful?"

"We have no evidence to the contrary, and it is scarcely likely that such a small kingdom would seek to make war on Spain."

Ferdinand changed the subject.

"The English are eager to take Guienne."

"A foolish project," said Ximenes, "and one doomed to failure."

Ferdinand smiled slyly. "That is a matter for them to decide."

"Your Highness has doubtless roused these ambitions in the mind of the young King of England."

Ferdinand lifted his shoulders. "Should it be my concern if the King of England becomes ambitious to regain territories in France?"

"It could well be," retorted Ximenes, "since the English could harry the French, leaving you free to walk into Navarre."

The sly old fox! thought Ferdinand. There was little he did not know of European affairs. There he sat in his gloomy cell in his grim old university, scratching away with his scholars at their polyglot bible. Then he took one look at affairs and saw the position as clearly as those did who studied it hourly.

The man had genius. Trust Isabella to discover it and use it. If I could but lure him to my side, the conquest of Navarre would be as good as achieved.

But the Primate was not with him; it was against his principles to make war on a peaceful state. Ximenes did not wish for war. He wanted peace, that he might make a great Christian country, a country which was the strongest in the world, and in which no man could live and prosper unless he was a Christian. The Inquisition was dear to his heart; he was eager that every Spaniard should be as devout as himself and he was ready to torture them to make them so—for he was a man who did not hesitate to torture himself. Ferdinand knew that, beneath the grand robes of his office—which he wore only because he had been ordered to do so by the Pope—was the hair shirt and the rough serge of the Franciscan habit.

We shall always pull one against the other, thought Ferdinand. It was inevitable that he, the ambitious, the sensuous, the avaricious, should be in continual conflict with the austere monk.

Yet, he thought, he shall not hold me back. I must lure the English to France, and this I shall do for I have the best ambassador a man could have at the Court of England. My daughter is the Queen, and the King cherishes her, and as the King is young, inexperienced and inordinately vain, it should not be difficult.

He began to talk of other matters because he saw it was useless to try to convince Ximenes of the need to take Navarre. But all the time he was thinking of the instructions he would give to Katharine and Luis Caroz in London. With the English as his ally he would do without the approval of Ximenes.

He hid his resentment and feigned such friendship for his Primate that he accompanied him to his apartments. A faint sneer touched his lips as he saw the elaborate bed—worthy of the Cardinal, Inquisitor General and Primate of Spain—because he knew that Ximenes used it only for ceremonial occasions and spent his nights on a rough pallet with a log of wood for a pillow. It was incongruous that such a man should hold such a position in a great country.

Ferdinand, however, lost no time in returning to his own apartments and writing to his ambassador in London.

The King of England must be persuaded to join Spain in the war against France without delay. The Queen of England must influence her husband. It would not be good policy of course to let her know how, in inducing England to make war, she was serving Spain rather than England; but she must be made to use all her power to persuade the King. It was clear that certain of the King's ministers were restraining him. Those ministers should be promised bribes . . . anything they wished for . . . if they would cease to dissuade the King of England from war. But the most important influence at the Court of England was the Queen; and if Caroz could not persuade her to do what her father wished, he should consult her confessor and let the priest make Katharine see where her duty lay.

Ferdinand sealed the despatches, called for his messengers and, when they had gone, sat impatiently tapping his foot. He felt exhausted, and this irked him for it was yet another indication that he was growing old. He thought with regret of those days of glowing health and vitality; he was a man of action and he dreaded the thought of encroaching old age.

If he could not be a soldier leading men into battle, a statesman artfully seeking to get the better of his opponents, a lusty lover of women, a begetter of children, what was left to him? He was not one who could enjoy the quiet pleasures of old age. He had always been a man of action, first and foremost.

And now there was grey in his beard, pouches beneath his eyes and a stiffness in his limbs. He had a young and beautiful wife, yet his pleasure in her was spoilt by the contrast in their ages; he could not forget his age when he was with her, but rather was more conscious of the years.

He longed for sons, because he was feeling a growing animosity towards his young grandson Charles, a boy who was being brought up in Flanders and who could inherit not only the dominions of his grandfather, the Emperor Maximilian, but those of Isabella and Ferdinand and all the Spanish dependencies . . . unless Ferdinand's wife Germaine gave him a son to whom he could leave Aragon.

So much! thought Ferdinand. For one young boy who has done nothing to win it for himself!

He thought of the early struggles he and Isabella had endured in order to win Castile, and he longed afresh for his youth. With mingled feelings he remembered Isabella—a great Queen but at times an uncomfortable wife. His Germaine was more pliable; there was no question of her attempting to use her authority in defiance of his—she had none in any case. And yet . . . those days of struggle and triumph with Isabella had been great days.

But she was gone these many years, and her daughter Juana, Queen of Spain in name only, passed her tragic days in seclusion at the Castle of Tordesillas, roaming from room to room, her mentality so clouded that she talked to those who had died years before, or fell into silences which lasted for weeks; ate her meals from the floor like an animal, never cleaned herself, and constantly mourned the dead husband who had been noted for his infidelity and his beauty.

Tragic for her of course, but not so for Ferdinand, since it was due to Juana's insanity that he ruled Castile. But for that he would be merely a petty ruler of Aragon realizing how much he owed to his marriage with Isabella.

But the past was done with, and the once active, lusty man was feeling his age.

Unless he got Germaine with child, young Charles could inherit everything his maternal and paternal grandparents had to leave. But his younger brother, Ferdinand, should not be forgotten. His grandfather and namesake would see to that. All the same he longed for a son of his own.

He had thought at one time that his wish was to be fulfilled. Germaine had two or three years before given birth to a son; but the little boy had died only a few hours after birth.

Ferdinand sat musing on the past and the future, and after a while he rose and went through the main apartments to a small chamber in which he kept certain important documents.

He opened a cabinet in this room and took out a small bottle which contained certain pills, which he slipped into his pocket.

Unobtrusively he would take one half an hour before retiring. He had proved the efficacy of these pills and would reward his physician if the desired result were achieved.

Germaine would be surprised at his powers.

He smiled; yet at the same time he felt a little sad that a man who had once been noted for his virility should be forced to resort to aphrodisiacs.

\*　　　　\*　　　　\*

Don Luis Caroz, waiting in an ante-chamber of the Queen's apartments at Westminster, chafed against this mission which he felt to be an indignity to a man of his position. Don Luis flicked at the elaborate sleeve of his doublet; it was an unnecessary gesture; there was no dust on his sleeve; but it conveyed his fastidiousness and his contempt for the streets through which he had passed.

His garments were more magnificent than those of most ambassadors at the King's Court; indeed he vied with the King and he assured himself that it was merely because Henry favoured the brightest colours that he appeared to be more dazzling. It was a matter of English vulgarity against Spanish good taste. Don Luis had a very high opinion of himself; it seemed to him that his diplomacy succeeded brilliantly; he lost sight of the fact—if it ever had occurred to him—that it was the Queen who made it easy for him, not only to gain an audience with the King whenever he wished to do so, but, receiving hints of her father's desires, by preparing the King's mind favourably towards them before Caroz appeared.

Vain, immensely rich—which was the reason why Ferdinand had chosen him to be his ambassador in England since he could pay his own expenses and thus save Ferdinand's doing so—Don Luis was determined that his suite should be more grand than that of any other ambassador, and that the Court should not forget that his position was a specially favourable one on account of the Queen's being the daughter of his master.

It was therefore galling for such a grand gentleman to be kept waiting—and by a humble priest at that. At least he should have been humble; but Caroz had reason to know that there was nothing humble about Fray Diego Fernandez.

Katharine, who was almost as pious as her mother had been, naturally placed great confidence in her confessor, and the friar who held such a position was certain to wield an influence over her.

Don Luis paced up and down the ante-room. How dare the priest keep the ambassador waiting! The vulgar fellow. It was the ambassador's belief that the little priest was itching to get a finger into the political pie. Let him keep to his post and the ambassador would keep to his.

But Fray Diego's task was to be the Queen's confessor—and a woman such as Katharine would consider her actions always a matter of conscience.

Don Luis made a gesture of impatience. "The saints preserve us from saintly women," he murmured.

At length the priest appeared. Don Luis looked at him—

uncouth, he thought, in his priestly robes, a smug satisfaction on his young but clever face.

"Your Excellency wished to see me?"

"I have been waiting this last half hour to do so."

"I trust you have not found the waiting tedious."

"I always find waiting tedious."

"It is because you are a man of such affairs. I pray you therefore let me know your business."

Don Luis went swiftly to the door; he opened it, looked out, then shut it and stood leaning against it. "What I have to say is for you alone . . . for Spanish ears, you understand me?"

The priest bowed his head in assent.

"Our master is eager that the King of England should declare war on France without delay."

The priest lifted his hands. "Wars, Excellency, are beyond my sphere."

"Nothing is beyond the sphere of a good servant of Spain. That is what our master thinks. And he has work for you."

"I pray you proceed."

"King Ferdinand believes that the Queen could help us. She has much influence with King Henry. Indeed her influence must surely be of greater account than that of his ministers."

"I doubt that, Excellency."

"Then it must become so. If it is not, mayhap it is because the Queen has not worked hard enough to obey her father's wishes."

"Her Grace wishes to please her father and her husband. Her father is far away and did little to succour her when she needed his help. Her husband is here at hand; and I doubt he could be led too far from his own desires."

"What do you know of these matters? He is young and ardent. If the Queen used skill, the utmost tact . . . she could win his promise immediately."

"It is my opinion that this would not be so."

"Your opinion was not asked. And how can you, a celibate, understand that intimacy which exists between a man and woman in the privacy of the bedchamber? My dear Fray Diego, there are moments, I assure you, which if chosen with skill can be used to great advantage. But you do not know of these matters —or do you?"

There was a sneer behind the words, a suggestion that the rumours of a secret life, attributed to Fray Diego, might be true. If such rumours were proved to be true they could cost him his position, Fray Diego knew; for Katharine herself would be so shocked that, much as she relied on him, she would let him go if she discovered his secret.

The priest knew that the ambassador was not his friend; but he had triumphed over enemies before. He remembered with relish his battle with Francesca de Carceres; she had hated him and had schemed for his recall to Spain. But look what had happened to her! Now married to the banker Grimaldi she was desperately trying to regain her position at Court, whereas he was higher in the Queen's favour than he had ever been, and so important that the ambassador was forced, though much against his will, to seek an interview with him.

Fray Diego, was young; he was somewhat arrogant. He really did not see why he should take orders from Caroz. It was Ferdinand's wish that he should do so, but he no longer regarded Ferdinand as his master. His influence seemed slight from such a great distance. Ferdinand had neglected his daughter during the years of her widowhood; it was only now that he wrote to her so frequently and so affectionately. Katharine remembered this; and in Fray Diego's opinion she was more Queen of England than Infanta of Spain.

He was determined therefore that he was not going to allow his fear of Ferdinand to rob him of the ascendancy he felt he possessed over Ferdinand's ambassador, towards whom the Queen did not feel as affectionate as she did towards her friend and confessor.

"It is true," he said, "that I have not your experience, Don Luis, of these matters. But what you ask is for the Queen's conscience, and for Her Grace to decide."

"Nonsense!" retorted Caroz. "It is a confessor's duty to guide those who are in his spiritual care. A few careful words, spoken at the appropriate moment, and the Queen will realize her duty."

"You mean her duty to her father, I am sure. But there is the possibility that Her Grace might also realize the duty to her husband."

"Do you mean that you refuse to obey our master's commands?"

"I mean," said Fray Diego with dignity, "that I will give the matter my consideration and if, after meditation and prayer, I can convince myself that what you ask is good for the soul of Her Grace, I shall do as you say."

"And if not . . . ?" burst out Caroz, fuming with indignation.

"This is a matter for my conscience as well as the Queen's. That is all I can say."

Caroz curtly took his leave and went away fuming. The arrogance of that upstart! he was thinking. A vulgar fellow. It was a great mistake that any but the highest nobility should be entrusted with state matters—and the Queen's confessor should have been a man of highest integrity and that noble birth which would have kept him loyal to his own kind.

Caroz soothed his anger by thinking of the account he would send to Ferdinand of this interview.

You will not long remain in England, my little priest, he prophesied.

His next call was on Richard Fox, Bishop of Winchester—a man who, he knew, had great influence among the King's ministers.

Promise them anything, Ferdinand had said, but get in exchange for your promise theirs to work for the English invasion of France.

Here was a man, thought Luis, who could surely be bribed because as an ambitious man he must be eager for the prizes of power and fame.

Caroz was proud of his ingenuity, for he had made up his mind what he was going to promise Richard Fox.

Fox received him with seeming pleasure, but beneath that calm expression of hospitality there was an alertness.

"I pray you be seated," said Fox. "This is indeed both an honour and a pleasure."

"You are kind, my lord Bishop, and I thank you. I have come here today because I believe it is in my power to do you some service."

The Bishop smiled rather ambiguously. He knew that it was a bargain the ambassador would offer rather than a gift.

"Your kindness warms my heart, Excellency," he said.

"It would not be an easy matter to achieve," admitted Caroz, "but I would ask my master to work for this with all his considerable power—and he has great power."

The Bishop was waiting, now almost unable to curb his eagerness.

"His Holiness plans to create more Cardinals. There are two French Cardinals and it has been suggested that he will present the hat to more Italians and Spaniards. My master is of the opinion that there should be some English holders of the office. I think he would be prepared to consider those for whom he felt some . . . gratitude."

The Bishop, who had been sceptical until this moment, could

scarcely hide the great excitement which possessed him. The Cardinal's hat! The major step towards the highest goal of all churchmen—the Papal Crown.

Fox had assured himself that he was a man of integrity; he would work for the good of England—but what an honour for England if one of her bishops became a Cardinal; what great glory if one day there should be an English Pope!

Caroz, exulting inwardly, knew of the conflict which was going on behind the immobile features of the Bishop. What a stroke of genius on his part to think of hinting at a Cardinal's hat! It was the irresistible bribe. No matter if there was no possibility of the offer's ever being made; promises such as this were all part of statecraft. How delighted Ferdinand would be with his ambassador when he heard of his ingenuity. It was worthy of Ferdinand himself.

"I agree with His Highness, King Ferdinand, that there should be a few English Cardinals," said Fox. "It will be interesting to see if the Pope shares that opinion."

"There are few whom I would consider for the office," said Caroz. "But there are some . . . there is one. . . ."

The Bishop said fervently: "That man would never cease to be grateful to those who helped him to attain such office, I can assure you."

"I will pass on your words to my master. As you know, since the alliance of his daughter and the King he has had a great affection for your countrymen. It is something which he does not bear towards the French. Nothing would please him more than to see our two countries set out side by side to conquer our mutual enemy."

The Bishop was silent. The terms had been stated. Withdraw your opposition to the project of war, and Ferdinand will use all his considerable influence with the Pope to win you a Cardinal's hat.

Was it such a great price? Fox asked himself. Who could say? It might well be that those territories which had once been in English hands would be restored. Surely a matter for rejoicing. And his help might mean that an English Cardinal would be created, and English influence would be felt in Rome.

Caroz wanted to laugh aloud. It has succeeded, he thought. And why not? What bishop could turn aside from the glory of receiving his Cardinal's hat?

He took his leave of the Bishop and went to his own apartments, there to write to his master.

He wrote that he believed he had found a means of breaking down the opposition to the beginning of military operations. He added a footnote: "It would seem to me that the Queen's confessor, Fray Diego Fernandez, works more for England than for Spain, and I would recommend his recall to Spain."

## CHAPTER V

## MURDER IN PAMPLONA

JEAN D'ALBRET, THAT rich nobleman who owned much of the land in the neighbourhood of the Pyrenees, had become King of Navarre through his marriage to Catharine, the Queen of that state.

It was an ambitious marriage and one which had pleased him at the time he had made it, and still did in some respects. But to possess a crown through a wife was not the most happy way of doing so, and Jean d'Albret, a man who was more attracted by pleasure than ambition, by a love of literature than of conquest, was far from satisfied.

The times were dangerous and he saw himself caught between two great and militarily minded powers. His was a small state but it was in a strategic position and could be of importance to both France and Spain. Jean knew that Ferdinand had long cast acquisitive eyes on his and Catharine's crown; and that Louis was determined to keep Navarre as a vassal state.

It was tiresome. There were so very many interesting matters to occupy a man. War seemed to Jean senseless; and he knew that, if there should be war over Navarre, the Spanish and French sovereigns would see that it took place on Navarrese soil.

Jean began to think that had he made a less ambitious marriage, say with the daughter of a nobleman as rich as himself, their possessions could have been joined together and they would have remained happily French; and moreover lived the rest of their days in comfort without this perpetual fear of invasion of their territory.

His wife Catharine came to him, and he saw by the anxious expression on her face that she was even more worried than he was. She was pleased for once to find him alone; usually the fact that he preferred to live as an ordinary nobleman with as little royal style as possible, irritated her; but today she had something of importance to say to him.

"My agents have brought news of negotiations which are going on between Ferdinand and Henry of England. It is almost certain that the English will invade France."

Jean shrugged his shoulders. "Louis will laugh at their puny efforts."

"You have missed the point as usual," she told him tartly. "Ferdinand's plan is not to invade France but to take Navarre. As soon as the English engage the French he will march on us."

Jean was silent. He was watching the sun play on a fountain and thinking of a poem he had read a short while ago.

"You are not listening!" she accused. Her eyes flashed. "Oh, what a husband I have!"

"Catharine," said Jean gently, "there is nothing we can do. We live in this beautiful place . . . at least we live here for the time being. Let us enjoy it."

"To think that I could have married such a man! Does your kingdom, your family, your crown mean nothing to you?"

"The crown, as you have so often told me, was your wedding gift to me, my dear. It is not always comfortable to wear and if it were to be taken from me . . . well, then I should be plain d'Albret. It was the name I was born with."

Catharine narrowed her eyes. "Yes," she said, "you were Jean d'Albret from the time you were born, and it seems that so you may well die plain Jean d'Albret. Those who are not prepared to fight for their crowns would not arouse much sympathy if they lose them."

"But you, my dear, wish to fight for yours . . . fight an enemy ten times your size . . . fight to the death . . . and in death, my dear, of what use would the crown of Navarre be to you?"

Catharine turned from him in exasperation. Her grandmother Leonora, who had been Ferdinand's half-sister, had poisoned her own sister, Blanche, in order that she might take the crown of Navarre; Leonora had not lived long to enjoy that for which she had committed murder, and on her death her grandson, Catharine's brother, had become the King of Navarre.

Catharine now thought of her golden-haired brother Francis Phoebus, who had been so called on account of his wonderful golden hair and great beauty.

They had been a proud family, for Leonora's son, Gaston de Foix, had married Madeleine, the sister of Louis XI, and thus they were closely related to the royal house of France, and it was natural that they should look for protection to that monarch.

What an unlucky family we were! thought Catharine. My father, wounded by a lance in a tourney at Lisbon and dying long before his time. Francis Phoebus died only four years after he attained the crown, and so it had passed to Catharine, his only sister.

Ferdinand had desired a marriage between Catharine and his

son Juan; that would have been one way—and by far the simplest—of bringing the Navarrese crown under Spanish influence, for then Ferdinand's grandchildren would have been the future kings and queens of Navarre; but Catharine's mother, the Princess of France, was determined that she would do nothing to aid the aggrandisement of Spain. So Juan had married Margaret of Austria and had died a few months after the marriage leaving Margaret pregnant with what had proved to be a still-born child.

And Catharine had been married to Jean d'Albret—a match of her mother's making—because Jean was a Frenchman and the Princess Madeleine had been determined to keep Navarre a vassal state of France.

So this man is my husband! thought Catharine. And he does not care. All he wishes is that we should live in peace, that he may dance and make merry with those of the court, ride through the country and speak with the humblest of his subjects, asking tenderly after the state of the vines, like the commoner he still is.

But the granddaughter of the murderess, Leonora, was not going to allow her crown to be taken from her if she could help it.

She cried out: "We must make the position known to the King of France. We must lose no time. Cannot you see how important that is, Jean, or are you still dreaming? Send for one of your secretaries and he shall prepare a letter for the King with all speed. Do you think Louis will allow Ferdinand of Aragon to walk into Navarre and take what is ours? He will see the folly of it. He will make a treaty with us which will let Ferdinand know that, if he should attempt to attack us, he will have to face the might of France as well as that of Navarre."

Jean rose and went to the door. Catharine watched him as he gave an order to one of the pages. His manner even towards the page lacked dignity. She felt exasperated beyond endurance because she was so afraid.

In a short time the secretary appeared.

He was a tall young man, with bold black eyes, a little over-dressed; Catharine guessed that he could on occasions be somewhat bombastic. He was a little subdued as he entered the apartment, she was pleased to notice, and that was due to the fact that the Queen was present.

Jean was very much mistaken in behaving in a free and easy manner with his subjects. It might make him popular, but it certainly did not make him respected.

"The King and I wish you to draft a letter to the King of France."

The Secretary bowed his head. It was as though he wished to hide his eyes, which were always lustful when he was in the presence of a woman; he could not help himself now, as a connoisseur of the female body, studying the Queen and estimating the amount of pleasure the King derived from the relationship. He dared not allow the Queen to guess his thoughts, though it did occur to him that the King might. But the King would understand; he was easy-going and he would realize that a man of his secretary's virility could never keep the thought of sexual relationships out of his mind.

Jean was thinking exactly this. Poor young man, he pondered, women plague him. If he were not perpetually concerned with plots and schemes to go to bed with this one and that, he would be a very good secretary.

The Queen was not thinking of the young man as a man; to her he was merely a scribe. He would draft the letter to the King of France and it should be sent off with all speed.

Navarre was in serious danger from Spain. Louis must come to their aid.

*     *     *

The Secretary, hurrying through the streets of the poorer quarter of Pamplona, slipped through an alley and, coming to a hovel there, stopped, looked over his shoulder and tried the door. It was open.

Before entering the house, he glanced once more over his shoulder to make sure that he was not being followed. It would never do for one of the King's confidential secretaries to be seen entering such a place.

Ah, thought the Secretary, who can say where love will strike?

He had a host of mistresses—some court ladies, some peasants. He was a man of wide experience and not one to go into the matter of birth and rank before embarking on a passionate love affair.

But this one . . . ah, this one . . . she was the best of them all.

He suspected her of being a gipsy. She had dark, bold eyes and thick crisply curling hair; she was wildly passionate and even he had felt a little overwhelmed and lacking in experience when they indulged in their love-making.

She would dance with her castanets, more Spanish than

French; her skin was brown, her limbs firm and voluptuous; she was a cornucopia of pleasure. By a mere gesture she could rouse him to a frenzy of passion; a look, a slackening of the lips, were all that was necessary. She had said that he must come to this house, and he had come, although for anyone else he would have not done so. *He* would have decided the place of assignation.

He called her Gipsy. She called him Amigo. That was because he had accused her of being Spanish. A Spanish Gipsy, he called her, and she had slapped his face for that. He smiled now to think how he had leaped on her then, how they had rolled on the ground together—with the inevitable conclusion.

He was pleased enough to be Amigo to her. A confidential secretary to the King of Navarre should not disclose his real name.

He called to her as he stood in the darkness of the house. "Gipsy. . . ."

There was a short silence and he was aware of the darkness. A feeling of foreboding came to him then. Had he been unwise to come? He was the King's secretary; he carried important documents in his pockets. What if he had been lured to this place to be robbed of those papers? What a fool he was to have brought them with him. He had not thought to clear his pockets. When he was on the trail of a woman he never thought of anything else but what he intended to do with that woman; and if that woman was one such as Gispy, then the thoughts were all the more vivid, and completely all-absorbing, so that there was no room for caution or anything else.

Then as he hesitated he heard a voice say: "Amigo!" and his fears vanished.

"Where are you, Gipsy?"

"Here!" she was close beside him and he seized her hungrily.

"Wait, impatient one!" she commanded.

But there was to be no waiting. Here! Now! his desires demanded; and there and then it was, there in the darkness of this strange hovel, in one of the least salubrious byways of the town of Pamplona.

"There! Greedy one!" she cried pushing him away from her. "Could you not wait until I get a light?"

"I'll be ready again when you get the light, Gipsy."

"You . . ." she cried impatiently, "You want too much."

By the flickering light of a candle he saw the dark little room. So this was her home. He had seen her first near the castle, and he guessed that she came from the vineyards. There had been little time to discover much about each other, and all he knew was that she was a peasant girl who worked with the vines. All she knew was that he was employed at the Court. That made him rich in her eyes.

They had met many times in the vineyards at dusk; and even in daylight it had been easy enough to find a secluded spot. She knew that he carried papers in his pockets for they rustled when he threw off his doublet; he knew she carried a knife in the belt she wore about her waist.

"What is that for?" he had asked.

"For those who would force me against my will," she told him.

He had laughed triumphantly. She had never attempted to use the knife on *him*.

He was growing restive with passion again.

"Come up the stairs," she told him. "There we can lie in comfort."

"Come then," he said. "I pray you, lead the way."

She went before him carrying the candle. He caressed her bare thighs beneath her tattered skirt as they went.

She turned and spat at him: "Your hands stray too much."

"And how can I help that when I am near you?"

"And near others too!"

"What! You suspect me of infidelity to you?"

"I know," she answered. "There is one who works with me in the vineyards. She is small and fair and comes from the North."

He knew to whom she referred. The girl was a contrast to Gipsy; small, fair, almost reluctant, with a virginal air which was a perpetual challenge to him. It had challenged him only yesterday and he had succumbed.

"I knew her once," he said.

"You knew her yesterday," she told him.

So the girl had told! Foolish creature! Yet he was not displeased. He liked the women to boast of their connections with him.

Gipsy set down the candle. The room made him shudder. It was not what he was accustomed to. But there was always pleasure in novelty. And when Gipsy carefully unstrapped the belt containing the knife and laid it almost reverently on the floor and then began to take off all her clothes, he saw nothing but Gipsy.

"You also," she said.

He was more than willing to obey.

Naked she faced him, a magnificent Juno, her hands on her hips.

"So you deceive me with that one!" she spat out.

"It was nothing, Gipsy . . . over and done with . . . quickly forgotten."

"As with me?"

"You I will remember all my life. We shall never be parted now. How could any man be satisfied with another after Gipsy?"

"So you would marry me?"

He hesitated for half a second, and he could not help his mouth twitching slightly at the incongruity of the suggestion. Imagine Gipsy at Court—perhaps being presented to King Jean and Queen Catharine!

"Certainly, I would marry you," he said glibly.

"I told you once that if you went with another woman I would make you sorry for it."

"Gipsy . . . you couldn't make me anything but happy. You're too perfect. . . ."

He seized her; she eluded him; but he laughed exultantly; this was merely lover's play. He sensed her lassitude even as she struck out at him; in a matter of moments he forced her on to the straw.

Afterwards she lay supine beside him. He felt relaxed, the conqueror. She could not resist him, even though she was so frenziedly jealous.

He need not even bother to cover up his peccadilloes. He had been wrong to imagine that he would have to go carefully with Gipsy. Gipsy was like all the others—so filled with desire for a man of his unusual capabilities that she could not resist him.

She bent over him tenderly. "Sleep," she whispered. "Let us both sleep for ten minutes; then we will be wide awake again."

He laughed. "You're insatiable," he said . . . "even as I. Ah, they're a well matched pair, my Gipsy and her Amigo."

She bit his shoulder affectionately. And he closed his eyes.

Gipsy did not sleep, although she lay still beside him with her eyes closed. She was picturing him with that other one, and not only that one. There were many others. This faithful lover! she thought contemptuously.

She had told him that he would be sorry if he were not true to her. She had been true to him, yet he considered her so far beneath him that there was no need to keep his promises to her.

She was passionate; she had revelled in their intercourse;

but he was only a man, and there were many like him in Pamplona who would be ready to come to Gipsy's bed when she beckoned.

She listened to his breathing. He was asleep. Perhaps he slept lightly. Perhaps he would wake if she stirred.

She moved quietly away from him. He groaned and vaguely put out a hand, which she avoided, carefully watching the flickering candlelight on his face as she did so.

His hand dropped; his eyes remained shut.

Gipsy stood for a second, watching him; then she picked up her belt. From it she took the knife.

"No man betrays me," she whispered. "Not even you, my fancy court gentleman. I warned you, did I not. I said you'd be sorry. But you'll not be sorry . . . because you'll not be anything after tonight."

Her eyes blazed as she lifted the knife.

He opened his eyes a second too late; he saw her bending over him; he saw her blazing eyes, but this time they shone with hate instead of love, with revenge, not with passion.

"Gipsy . . ." He tried to speak her name, but there was only a gurgle in his throat. He felt the hot blood on his chest . . . on his neck, before the darkness blocked out her face, the sordid room in candlelight, and wrapped itself about him, shutting out light, shutting out life.

\*        \*        \*

Gipsy washed the blood from her naked body and put on her clothes. Then she blew out the candle and went down the stairs and out to the street.

She ran swiftly through the alley and through several narrow streets until she came to the house she wanted.

She knocked urgently on the door. There was no answer and again she knocked. At length she heard the sound of slow footsteps.

"Quickly, Father," she cried. "Quickly!"

The door was opened and a man stood peering at her; he was struggling into the robes of a priest.

She stepped inside and shut the door.

"What has happened, my child?" he asked.

"I need your help. I have killed a man."

He was silent in horror.

"You must help me. Tell me what to do."

"This is murder," said the priest.

"He deserved to die. He was a liar, a cheat and a fornicator."

"It is not for you to pass judgment, my child."

"You must help me, Father. It does not become any of us to prate of the sins of others."

The priest was silent. He had sinned with the woman, it was true. But what a provocation such a woman was, particularly to one who led the celibate's life on and off.

"Who is the man?" he asked.

"He is of the Court."

The priest drew a deep breath. "Fool! Fool! Do you imagine that murder of a noble gentleman can go unnoticed? If it had been one of your kind I might have helped. But a gentleman of the Court! There is nothing I can do, my child, but hear your confession."

"You will do more," she said. "Because you are wise, Father, and you have been my friend."

The priest fidgeted in his robes. He looked at her face in the candlelight. It was pale, and the eyes were enormous; there was no contrition there, only a contentment that vegeance had been wreaked on the faithless, only the determination that he who had shared in her sin should now share in her crime. She was a dangerous woman.

"It may well be that he was not in truth a gentleman of the Court," said the priest. "It may be that that was a story he told you."

"He was well dressed and he carried papers in his pockets."

"That's what he told you."

"I felt them . . . tonight. They were papers."

"Take me to where he lies."

They hurried back to the house wherein the murdered man lay. The girl took the priest up to the room; it was not the mutilated body nor the blood-soaked straw which claimed the priest's attention, but the papers which were in the pockets of the man's garments.

"Hold the candle nearer," he commanded.

She did so and, as he read, the priest's hand shook with excitement, for what he held in his hand was the draft of a secret treaty between the Kingdoms of Navarre and France.

"Well?" said the girl.

"This could be worth a fortune," he said.

"You mean . . . papers? How so? But I shall sell his clothes. They should fetch something."

"Yes, they should. But these papers are worth more than

L

clothes, I'll be ready to swear. I believe there are some who would pay highly for them."

"Who would?"

"The Spaniards." The priest's mind became alert. Priests were so poor in Pamplona—perhaps as they were all over the world—and there were some who could not help being attracted by riches even as they were by the voluptuous charms of a woman.

The situation was full of danger. The man who lay on the straw was one whose kind rarely came their way. His death must not be traced to this house. The priest was now an accomplice of the woman and it was imperative to him to cover up this murder.

"Listen carefully," he said. "I will leave at once on a journey. I am going to Spain, and there I shall endeavour to see the secretary of the King. He will, if I am not mistaken, be interested in this paper. But speed is essential. If what is written here comes to his knowledge before I reach him, then he will not be ready to pay me for what he already knows. But if he does not know . . . then he will be willing to pay me highly for what I can tell him."

"What is on the paper?" asked the girl.

"Matters of state. This man did not lie. He *was* one of the secretaries of the King. Now listen to me. There is one thing we must do before I leave. We must get him out of this house. And when he is gone you must clean away all signs of his having been here. Let us waste no time."

They worked feverishly. The priest had cast off his robes to prevent their being marked by blood, and worked in nothing but his drawers. The girl took off her clothes and put on only a light loose robe which could be washed immediately she had rid herself of her victim.

They carried the body out of the house and through the alley. They then placed it against a wall and hurried back to the house, where the priest put on his robes and carefully secreted the papers about his person.

"I shall set out at once," he said, "for there is little time to lose. You must tell people that I have been called away to see my sick brother. As for you, wash the house so that there are no signs of blood, wash your clothes and do not try to sell his until at least three months have passed."

She caught his arm. "How do I know that when you have the money for the papers, you will come back?"

"I swear by my faith that I will."

She was satisfied. He was after all a priest.

"If you do not . . ." she said.

He shook his head and smiled at her. "Have no fear. I shall never forget you."

He would not. She knew too many of his secrets; and she was a woman who did not hesitate to plunge a knife into the body of a man who had deceived her.

And while the priest set out on his journey for Spain, the girl cleaned the house and her garments, so that when the sun rose there was no sign there that the King's secretary had ever been her guest.

\* \* \*

Cardinal Ximenes arrived in Logroño on the banks of the river Ebro at the spot which marked the boundary between Castile and Navarre.

Ferdinand received him with such pleasure that the Cardinal guessed something unusual had happened to cause this. He dismissed all, so that they were alone together.

Ferdinand said: "Cardinal, you were opposed to my plans for attacking Navarre. The English are sending a force under the command of the Marquis of Dorset. It is my desire that they shall hold the French while I march on Navarre, which you have wished to leave untouched because you say it is a peaceful state."

The Cardinal nodded and then looked deep into Ferdinand's glowing eyes.

Smiling, Ferdinand reached for some papers which lay on the table at which he sat. He thrust them at Ximenes.

"Your Excellency should read this."

The Cardinal did so, and Ferdinand who was watching closely saw that almost imperceptible tightening of the thin lips.

"So you see," cried Ferdinand triumphantly, "while you were seeking to protect this *innocent* little state, its King and Queen were making a treaty with our enemy against us."

"So it would seem," replied Ximenes.

"Is it not clear? You see those papers."

"A rought draft of the treaty, yes. But how did they fall into your hands?"

"They were sold to me by a priest of Pamplona. I paid a high price for them—but not too high for their worth."

"A priest! Like as not this person was masquerading as such."

Ferdinand laughed slyly. "There are priests who do not regard their duty as highly as does your Eminence."

"I should distrust this person."

"So should I have done, but I am informed that one of the King of Navarre's confidential secretaries was found stabbed to death in a byway of Pamplona—stripped of all his clothes. It is reasonable to suppose that he would carry such papers in his pocket."

Ximenes nodded. He had no doubt of the authenticity of the documents. And since the state of Navarre was making such a treaty with France, there was only one course open to Spain: attack.

Ferdinand leaned across the table. "Am I to understand that Your Eminence now withdraws his opposition, and stands firmly behind the attack on Navarre?"

"In view of these documents," answered Ximenes, who never allowed personal pride to stand between him and his duty, "I think we are justified in going forward against Navarre."

## CHAPTER VI

# THE FRENCH DISASTER

AT THE HEADQUARTERS of his army in San Sebastian Thomas Grey, second Marquis of Dorset, felt sick, dizzy and decidedly uneasy. He had long regretted the day when his King had put him in charge of ten thousand archers and sent him to Spain as the spearhead of an army which, when the country was ready would, with the King at its head, join Dorset.

From the first he had been bewildered. The help he had been led to expect from his Spanish allies did not come. Ferdinand's army had done little to help him. There had been scarcely any fighting except a few clashes with isolated French troops; and his men roamed the countryside, drinking too much Spanish wine, eating too much garlic to which they were unaccustomed and which did not agree with them, catching diseases and vermin from the gipsy girls.

If, thought Dorset, I were not so ill myself that I fear I shall never leave this accursed country, I should feel alarmed, very alarmed.

Home seemed far away. The wrath of the King unimportant. The flies here were such a pest and the sight and smell of men, suffering from the continual dysentery, so repellent, that what was happening in England was of little importance.

He felt listless; that was due to the dysentery; he had ceased to long for home, only because he felt so tired. He believed that he had bungled his commission and that there would be trouble if he ever reached England; but he was too weary to care.

He had been chosen for this honour not because of his military skill but because the King had a fondness for him. Dorset excelled at the jousts and that was enough to make the King admire him. He had enough skill to come near to rivalling the King without quite matching him—a state which endeared Henry to a man and made him his friend.

"Why, Dorset," he had said, "I see no reason why you should not take the first contingent to Spain. These ministers of mine have now decided that they are in favour of war. Fox has given in at last—though the fellow was obstinate for so long. But you shall go, my friend, and show these Frenchmen the valour of our English archers."

The rosy cheeks had glowed and the eyes sparkled. "Would I were in your shoes, Dorset. Would I were going to lead an army into battle. But they tell me the time is not ripe for me to leave yet. In a year mayhap I'll be ready."

So it was Dorset who came to Spain, and Dorset who now lay sick of the maladies which sprang from a foreign land.

Life had not been easy for him; indeed he had lived in uneasy times. He was closely related to the royal family, and to the York branch, not that of Lancaster. His grandfather had been Sir John Grey, heir to Lord Ferrers of Groby and first husband of Elizabeth Woodville, Queen of Edward IV. Such a connection would be regarded somewhat cautiously by the Tudors; and although he had been received at Court he had quickly fallen under the suspicion of Henry VII and been confined to the Tower.

Dorset remembered now those days of imprisonment when he had lain in his cell and hourly expected the summons to the executioner's block. It would certainly have come had not Henry VII died; but, in those first months of power, his son had desired to show that he had escaped from the influence of his father. He had taken the heads of Dudley and Empson, his father's favourites, and given a pardon to Dorset.

The Marquis had done well in the service of the golden boy. Bluff, hearty, the young sportsman had given his father's prisoner the wardenship of Sawsey Forest; he made Dorset one of his companions, for such a figure was an ornament in the tilt-yard.

And after that, greater honours had been bestowed. How happy Dorset would have been if he had been allowed to confine his battles to the tiltyard!

He was lying in his tent, turning from side to side, feeling too ill to care what happened to him, when one of his men entered to tell him that the English ambassador to Spain was without.

"Bring him in," said Dorset.

And the ambassador entered. Dorset made an attempt to rise but he was too weak to do so.

"Sir John Still," he said, "you find me indisposed."

"I am grieved that this should be so." The ambassador was frowning as though he too shared the uneasiness of all who were connected with this campaign. "I have come to see if there is anything you need beyond the two hundred mules and asses which I had sent to you."

Dorset smiled wryly: "What we need is a means of getting back to England," he said grimly.

Sir John Still looked startled, and Dorset went on: "The mules and asses which you sent were unable to work. They had been starved and many of them were dying when they arrived. Those which survived had never been exercised and were unable to work for us."

"But I paid the Spaniards a great price for those animals."

"Ah, another Spanish trick."

"A trick?"

"Sir John, surely you know why we are here. The Spaniards have no intention of being our allies and helping us to regain our territories in France. We are here that the French may be uncertain of our numbers and, expecting that we might be a great army, must needs protect their land. Thus they are kept occupied while the Duke of Alva, at Ferdinand's command, walks into Navarre."

"You mean . . . that we English have been tricked!"

"Do not look so surprised, ambassador. All are tricked when they attempt to deal with Ferdinand of Aragon."

"I bring you instructions from England," said the ambassador. "The army is to remain here throughout the winter. Next year the King will be ready to join you."

"Stay here during the winter!" cried Dorset. "It's impossible. Those men out there are half dead now with the sickness from which you see me suffering. They'll not endure it."

"These are the orders from England."

"They in England can have no notion of what is happening here. We are given garlic . . . garlic all the time. There is more garlic than real food. The men are unused to this; they suffer from it. The wines overheat their bodies. Eighteen hundred men have already died; if we stay here many more weeks there will not be a healthy man among us."

"You cannot return. To do so would mean you had failed. What have you achieved since you have been here?"

"Ferdinand has conquered Navarre. We have served the purpose for which we came."

"You speak like a traitor, my lord Dorset."

"I speak truth. These men will die if they stay here. If disease does not finish them, the French will. No good can come of their staying."

"Yet the King's order is that they should."

Dorset staggered to the door of the tent. "Come with me," he said. "I will tell these men of the King's command that they are to stay in Spain."

The fresh air seemed too much for Dorset. He swayed uncertainly like a man intoxicated, and the ambassador had to hold him to steady him. Bent double with the pain which distorted his yellow face, Dorset tried to shout, but his voice was feeble. "Men! News from home."

The word *home* acted on the camp like magic. Men crawled out of tents, dragging with them those who could not walk. There was a feverish joy in their faces. They believed that the horror was over, and their commander had summoned them to tell them to prepare to leave for home.

"The King's orders," said Dorset. "We are to stay here through the winter."

There was a growl of discontent.

"No!" cried a voice; and others took up the cry. "Home! We are going home!"

"The orders of our most Gracious Sovereign. . . ."

"To the devil with our most Gracious Sovereign. Let him fight his own wars. Home! England! We're going home to England."

Dorset looked at the ambassador.

"You see," he said; and he staggered wearily back into his tent.

Now he was afraid. He saw that he was caught between the desires of his King and those of his men. He was faced either with disobedience to the King or wholesale desertions.

"I must write to His Grace," he said. "I must make him aware of the true state of affairs."

The ambassador waited while he wrote; but meanwhile outside in the camp the cries of rebellion grew louder. Dorset knew, and the ambassador knew, that even the King's order to remain in Spain would carry no weight with those men out there.

\*        \*        \*

The King was watching the return of his troops. He stood, legs apart, hands clenched at his side, his eyes so narrowed that they were almost lost in the flesh of his face.

Beside him stood the Queen, and she was ready to weep at the sorry plight of these men. They were in rags and many were still suffering from the fever; some had to be carried ashore. Yet as they came they were shouting with incoherent joy because the soil they trod was English, and the tears showed clearly on their poor sunken cheeks.

"What a sad sight," murmured the Queen.

"It sickens me!" the King growled.

But he did not see this return as Katharine did. He felt no pity. He had only room for anger. This was the army which he had sent to France and of which he had been so proud. "I have never seen a finer army!" he had written to John Still. And now . . . they looked like a party of vagabonds and beggars.

How dared they do this to him! He was the golden king, the darling of fortune. So far he had had everything he desired, except a son. He remembered this fleetingly and glared distastefully at his wife. There were tears in her eyes. She could weep for that band of scarecrows when she should be weeping because she had failed him and, although she could become pregnant, could not give birth to a healthy boy.

Katharine turned to him. "There is my lord Dorset, Henry. Oh, poor Dorset. How sick he is. See him. He cannot walk. They are carrying him on a litter."

The King followed her gaze and strode over to the litter on which lay the emaciated figure of the man who had once been a champion of the jousts. The sight of such sickness disgusted Henry.

"Dorset!" he cried. "What means this? I sent you out with an army and an order to fight for victory. You return with these . . . scarecrows . . . and dishonourable defeat."

Dorset tried to see who was towering over him, shouting at him.

He said: "Where am I? Is it night?"

"You are in the presence of your King," roared Henry.

"They'll mutiny," murmured Dorset. "They'll endure no more. Is it morning yet?"

"Take him away," cried the King. "I never want to see his treacherous face again."

The bearers picked up the litter and were passing on.

"He is sick, very sick,' Katharine ventured to point out.

Henry looked at her, and she noticed that characteristic narrowing of the eyes.

"He will be far sicker when I have done with him!"

"You can't blame him for what has happened."

"Then whom else!" snarled Henry. He looked about him impatiently. "Put me up a gallows," he shouted. "Not one, but twenty . . . a hundred! By God and all his saints, I'll show these paltry cowards what I do to those who fail to carry out my orders."

His face was suffused with rage. The tyrant was bursting his

L*

bonds. The metamorphosis was taking place before the eyes of the Queen. The vain good-natured boy was showing signs of the brutal egocentric man.

Katharine, watching him, felt an apprehension which was not only for the men whom he had so carelessly condemned to death.

\*            \*            \*

Katharine knelt before the King. The terrible rage which she had seen on his face had not altogether disappeared. There were signs of it in the over-flushed cheeks, the brilliant blue of the eyes.

He was watching her with interest, and she suddenly knew that she could change this tragedy into one of those situations which so delighted him in a masque.

"Henry," she cried, "I implore you to spare these men."

"What!" he growled. "When they have disgraced England! When our enemies are laughing at us!"

"The odds against them were too great. . . ."

It was a mistake. The faint geniality which she had perceived to be breaking through was lost, and the blue eyes were dangerous. "You would seek to enter our state counsels, Kate? You would tell us how to conduct our wars?"

"Nay, Henry. That is for you and your ministers. But the climate . . . and that disease which attacked them . . . how could you or your ministers know that such a catastrophe would befall them? That was ill luck."

"Ill luck," he agreed, somewhat mollified.

"Henry, I beg of you, show your clemency towards them. For this time forget the sneers of your enemies. Instead prepare to show them your true mettle. Let them know that England is to be feared."

"By God, yes!" cried the King. "They shall know this when I myself go to France."

"It will be so. Your Grace will go with an army, not as Dorset went, with only his archers. You will make great conquests . . . and so, in your clemency and your greatness, you can afford to laugh at your enemies and . . . spare these men."

"You have friends among them, Kate. Dorset is your friend."

"And a friend also to Your Grace."

He looked down at her head. Her hair fell about her shoulders —that beautiful hair; her eyes were lifted to his in supplication.

She was playing her part in the masque, but he did not know it; his masques were always real to him.

So he was pleased to see her thus, humble, begging favours. He was fond of her. She had failed so far but she was young yet. He would forgive her those miscarriages when she gave him a bonny son. In the meantime there was this game to be played.

"Kate," he said, his voice slurred with emotion, "I give you the lives of these men. Rise, my dear wife. They deserve to die for their treachery to me and to England, but you plead . . . and how could such as I deny a fair lady what she asked!"

She bowed her head, took his hand and kissed it. It was alarming when the masque had to be played out in stark realities.

## CHAPTER VII

# THE PERFIDY OF FERDINAND

IN HIS HEADQUARTERS at Logroño, Ferdinand was in gleeful conference with Cardinal Ximenes. It appeared that the King had cast off his infirmities; he was as a young man again. Perhaps, thought the Cardinal, watching him, he congratulates himself that, although his body may be failing him, his mind is as shrewd and cunning as it ever was—and indeed, it may be more so, for his experience teaches him further methods of double-dealing, of plotting against his friends while he professes his regard for them.

Ximenes could have felt sorry for the young King of England if he had not been convinced that what had happened to him was due to his own folly. The King of England was clearly a braggart, seeking easy glory. He had certainly not found it in Spain; and one of the first lessons he would have to learn was that none but the foolish would enter into alliance with the most avaricious, double-dealing monarch in Europe—Ferdinand of Aragon.

Henry was as yet over-sentimental; he believed that because he was Ferdinand's son-in-law he would be treated with special consideration. As if Ferdinand had ever considered anything but his gold and his glory.

"So, Excellency, the campaign is over; it merely remains to consolidate our gains. Jean d'Albret and Catharine have fled to France. Let them remain there. As for me . . . I have no further wish for conflict, and I do not see why, if Louis is agreeable, I should not make a truce with him."

"And your son-in-law?"

"The young coxcomb must fight his own battles . . . if he can, Excellency. If he can!"

"He received little help from his allies, Highness."

Ferdinand snapped his fingers. "My son-in-law will have to learn that if he hopes to win battles he should not send an army into a foreign land without the means to maintain it."

"He relied too strongly on the promised help of his ally."

"It was not promised, I do assure you. But we waste our time. I hear he tried his gallant officers and that they were forced to give evidence on their knees! That must have been a sight, eh!

He was trying them for the incompetence and lack of foresight of himself and his ministers. And it was my daughter who saved them from the gallows."

"It would seem that the Queen of England has not forgotten the teachings of her mother."

Ferdinand was sobered by the mention of Isabella; then he shrugged off the memory with the reminder that Isabella had worked unsparingly for Spain. She would surely have realized the importance of Navarre and have understood that the means of acquiring it were not so important as long as the deed was accomplished with the minimum of bloodshed and expense to Spain.

"I am sending despatches to my son-in-law, Excellency. Here they are. Glance through them and give them your approval!"

Ximenes took the proffered documents.

In these Ferdinand explained to Henry that the incompetence of Dorset's army had made conquest of Guienne impossible. He was not suggesting that Dorset was a true example of an Englishman; and it was his belief that English soldiers, if properly trained and armed, would make fair enough soldiers; perhaps then they would not show up so badly against those of Europe. At this time he could not ask Henry to send more men into Spain, even though he himself should lead them. He had been forced to conclude a six months' truce with Louis, as he feared that, if he had not, the French might feel—in view of the sad spectacle they had recently witnessed of English troops in action—that it would be an act of folly not to invade England, where they might—as they had seen a sample of English valour and fighting prowess—expect an easy victory. It was a great regret to Ferdinand that the English had failed to achieve their object—the conquest of Guienne—and if it was still the desire of his dear son-in-law that the province should be won for England, he, Ferdinand would, at the conclusion of the six months' truce, win it for England. He would need ten thousand German mercenaries to help him, for his dear son-in-law would readily understand that, in view of their recent capers, he could not ask for Englishmen. The cost of the mercenaries would be great, but it was not *money* his son-in-law lacked but men of valour and fighting spirit. Ferdinand would be hearing more of this through his ambassador, Don Luis Caroz, and more importantly and more intimately from his dearly beloved daughter who was also the wife of that dear and honoured son, the King of England.

Ximenes glanced up after reading the document.

"This will act as an irritant rather than balm to your dear son-in-law for whom you have such an affection," he said.

"It is what I intend," answered Ferdinand. "Do you not see, the young coxcomb will be so incensed that he will immediately plan to make war on Louis. It is exactly what we need to keep Louis engaged while we rest from battle and enjoy the spoils of victory."

Ximenes thought of Ferdinand's daughter. He could scarcely remember what she looked like as it was many years since he had seen her. Her mother had felt tenderly towards her, too tenderly, he had often said; for her devotion to her family had often come between herself and her duty to God.

Yet he was sorry for Isabella's daughter. He saw her as a helpless barrier between the youthful follies of her husband and the cruel ambition of her father.

How could he complain when Ferdinand was working for the glory of Spain? There could be no doubt that the recent conquest had brought glory to the country.

Ximenes handed the papers back to Ferdinand. He must approve; but how he longed for the peace of Alcalá, for that room in which the scholars sat with him working on the polyglot bible.

Ximenes believed then that he would have been a happier man if he had lived his hermit's life, free from power and ambition.

Happy! he reproved himself. We are not put on this Earth to be happy!

Smiling complacently, Ferdinand sealed his documents, forgetting as he did so encroaching old age, the pains which beset his body, the constant needs of ointments and aphrodisiac potions that he might in some measure wear the semblance of youth.

He could win battles; he could outwit his enemies, with even more cunning than he had shown in the days of his youth. Experience was dearly bought; but there were moments such as this one when he valued it highly and would not have exchanged it for the virility of his young son-in-law of England.

\*        \*        \*

Katharine was seated before her mirror and her women were dressing her hair. Her reflection looked back at her and she was not displeased with it. Henry admired her hair so much; he liked her to wear it loose by night—which tangled it; but often she compromised by having it plaited into two heavy ropes.

Henry was ardent again. They were full of hope, he and she; the next time there was the sign of a child she was to take especial care, he had commanded. It was clear to him that he was dogged by ill luck. Witness the campaign in Spain for instance. Their inability to produce a child who could live was merely another example of their bad luck.

She smiled. If only I had a child, a son, she thought, I could be completely happy.

"Maria," she said to her maid of honour, Maria de Salinas, "you have a happy look today. Why is that?"

Maria was confused. "I, Your Grace? But I did not know. . . ."

"It is a look of contentment, as though something for which you longed has come to pass. Does it concern my Lord Willoughby?"

"He intends to speak for me, Your Grace."

"Ah Maria, and since this has brought that look of happiness to your eyes, what can my answer be but yes?"

Maria fell to her knees and kissed Katharine's hand. When she lifted her face to the Queen's there were tears in her eyes.

"But you weep," said Katharine, "and I thought you were happy."

"It will mean that I can no longer remain in the service of Your Grace."

"He will wish to leave Court and take you away to the country then?"

"It is so, Your Grace."

"Well, Maria, we must accept that." And she thought: How I shall miss her! Of all the girls who came with me from Spain, Maria was the best, the most faithful. It was Maria whom I could trust as I could trust no other. Now she will be gone.

"I myself feel like shedding tears. Yet this must be a happy occasion, for you love this man, Maria?"

Maria nodded.

"And it is a good match. I know the King will willingly give his consent with mine, so there is naught to make us sad, Maria. Why, Lord Willoughby will not carry you off to a strange country. There will be times when you will come to Court, and then we shall be together."

Maria dried her eyes with her kerchief and Katharine, looking into the mirror, did not see her own reflection, but herself arriving in England, after saying an infinitely sorrowful farewell to her mother, with her the duenna Doña Elvira Manuel, who had proved treacherous, and her maids of honour who had all been chosen for their beauty. Maria had been one of the loveliest even of that lovely band. They were scattered now, most of them married. . . . Inez de Veñegas to Lord Mountjoy, and Francesca de Carceres, most unsuitably, to the banker Grimaldi.

"Maria, tell me, have you seen Francesca recently?"

"She still waits for an audience. Does Your Grace wish to see her? Perhaps, now that I am going. . . ."

Katharine's face hardened. "She left me once, because she felt it was to her advantage to do so. I would never take back one who has proved her disloyalty to me and to her family."

"I have heard, Your Grace, that the banker loves her truly."

"Then if she is so loved she should be content with that state of life which she deliberately chose. There will never be a place for her in my household."

When Katharine spoke as firmly as that Maria knew that her mind was made up.

Katharine changed the subject. "I hope that you do not intend to leave me at once, Maria."

Maria knelt once more at the Queen's feet and buried her face against Katharine's skirts.

"It is my only regret that I cannot be in constant attendance on Your Grace."

There was sudden commotion outside the apartment. The door was flung open and the King stalked in. His face was a deeper red than usual and his anger was apparent from the manner in which he strutted. In his hand he carried papers, and a quick glance at those papers, as she swung round from the mirror, told Katharine that it was news from Spain which had angered her husband.

Maria rose to her feet and dropped a curtsey with the other women in the apartment. The King did not bestow his usual smile of appreciation on some particular beauty who caught his eye. Henry was always single-minded and now his thoughts were on the papers he carried.

He waved his hand in an imperious gesture. It was eloquent. It meant: "Leave us." The women hastened to obey, and Maria's heart sank seeing those signs of anger in the King's face, because she, who was closer to Katharine than any of her companions, knew that the Queen was beginning to fear the King.

When they were alone Henry stood glaring at his wife, for the first few seconds too angry to speak. She waited, having learned from experience that when the King was in such a mood a carelessly spoken word could fan the flame of anger.

Henry waved the papers as though they were banners and he were advancing on an enemy.

"News from your father!" he spat out. "He seems determined to insult me."

"But Henry, I am sure this cannot be so. He has the utmost regard for you."

"So it would seem. He tells me here that my armies are useless. He is offering to fight my battles for me if I will pay him to provide mercenaries!"

"This cannot be so."

"You have eyes. Read this," he roared.

She took the papers and glanced at them. She could only see her father as her mother had taught her to look at him. Isabella had never complained to their children of Ferdinand's conduct; she had always represented him as the perfect King and father. Katharine had only heard by chance that her father had on many occasions been unfaithful to Isabella and that there were children to prove it. And even though she must accept him as an unfaithful husband—in her opinion to the greatest and most saintly woman who had ever lived—still she could not believe that he was anything but honourable; and she accepted in good faith what he had written.

"Well?" demanded Henry harshly.

"My father considered what happened to our men in Spain. He wishes to help you."

"So he casts a sneer at me and my armies."

"You read into this what is not intended, Henry."

"I . . . I? I am a fool, I suppose, Madam. I lack your perception. There is something you and your father forget." He came close to her, his eyes narrowed, and she shrank from the malice she saw in his face. "But for me, what would have happened to you? I brought you up to your present position. It would be wise not to forget that. There were many who were against our marriage. What were you then? A miserable outcast. Your father would not support you . . . you were living in poverty." Henry folded his arms behind his back and scowled at her. "I was told that a monarch such as I might choose my wife from all the greatest heiresses in the world. And what did I do? I chose you. You, Madam, who had been the wife of my brother, who were neglected by your father, who was living in miserable poverty in Durham House. I raised you up. I set you on the throne. And this is my reward. . . ."

She tried to fight the terror which such words inspired. She had grown pale and her twitching fingers caught at the cloth of her gown.

"Henry," she said, "this I know well. Even if I did not love you for your many qualities . . . I would be grateful and wish to serve you until the end of my life."

He was slightly mollified. She thought: Oh God, how easy it is to placate him, how easy to anger him.

" 'Tis as well you are aware of your debts," he growled. "And your father! What have you to say for him? He too should be grateful for what I did for you. This is an example of his gratitude!"

"Henry, he is offering to help you. . . ."

"With German mercenaries! Because we English are unable to fight our own battles!"

"He does not mean that, Henry. I am sure of this."

"Not mean it! Then why does he say it?"

"Because he believes you to be suffering a keen disappointment, because he is sorry our army did not achieve its end."

"He does not want English troops on Spanish soil! By God, would I had hanged the traitor Dorset. Would I had not listened to your woman's pleading for a worthless life."

"Nay, Henry, you must not blame Dorset." She was suddenly overwhelmed by her tenderness for this big man who, it seemed to her, at times had the heart and mind of a child. "Let us face the truth. We failed. We failed because we had not enough food for our men, and we sent them out ill-equipped. Certainly you cannot accept my father's offer—though he makes it in friendship; I do assure you of that. But there is an answer to those who have jeered at our failure. There is an answer to my father."

"What is this answer?"

"That you should prepare an army that will be invincible, that you should place yourself at the head of it and attack the French, not from the South but from the North. There you would find a climate not unlike our own; there would not be the same difficulties in feeding an army that was separated from England only by twenty-one miles of sea. And with you at the head of it. . . ."

A slow smile was spreading across the King's face. He did not speak for a few seconds; then he burst out: "By God, Kate, we have the answer there. That is it. We shall start from Calais . . . and go on from there. And this time it will not be a Marquis who commands, but a King."

All ill humour had disappeared. He seized her in his arms and hugged her, but already his thoughts were far away from her; he was leading his men into triumphant battle. This would be a masque to outdo those merry exercises that had charmed the courtiers and the people at Windsor, Richmond and Westminster.

He was content—content with life, content with Kate.

He danced round the apartment with her, lifting her in his arms, pausing so that she should marvel at his strength, which she did—running his fingers through her hair and over her body.

"There's one thing that will not please me. I shall be separated from my Kate. And what will she be doing while she awaits the return of the conqueror, eh?" The little eyes were alight with laughter and confidence. "Mayhap she will be nursing the heir of England . . . the heir to all those lands which I shall bring back to the English crown!"

Katharine was laughing in his arms. The danger was over for a while; the King was happy again.

\*          \*          \*

So it was to be war. Katharine was eager to show Henry how she could work for him and that he could rely on his Queen's being always at his side.

Henry was in high spirits. He was certain that he was going to win fresh honours and was already regarding the coming war as a glorified masque. It was a comfort to know that he could safely leave those matters of minor importance to Katharine, and he was pleased with her because she was so eager to be made use of.

He spent all his nights with her.

"There is one thing only I long for, Kate, and that is to leave you pregnant on my departure. What joy for me! I go forth to win honour for England, knowing you are at home nursing my seed within this comely belly of yours. I'll give England new dominions, Kate, and together we'll give her heirs. How's that?"

"Henry, if only it could be so I'd be the happiest woman on Earth."

"Of course it shall be so." He had no doubt.

Katharine summoned Thomas Wolsey to her presence; she was impressed by his efficient handling of his duties which now included the assembling of the materials to be used in the war.

She was glad one day when in conference with the almoner that the King joined them.

Henry's face glowed with bluff good humour.

"Ha, Master Wolsey," he cried. "Her Grace tells me that you are of great use to us."

"I do my humble best, Sire," answered Wolsey. "My regret is that I have not four pairs of hands and four heads with which to serve Your Grace the better."

Henry laughed and laid a great hand on Wolsey's shoulder. "We are well pleased with those two hands and that head, my friend. The Queen has shown me the value of your work. She regards you highly, and the Queen and I are of one mind on all matters."

"There is great joy in serving such a master . . . and such a mistress."

"And we are fortunate in our servant. Show me the list of supplies you have prepared."

"They are here, Your Grace."

"Fox tells me that you work with the vigour of two men. He too has a high opinion of you."

"The Bishop has always been a good friend to me."

"It pleases us. We like our ministers to work well together. Too often we hear of discord, so that it is pleasant to hear of harmony. Now, let me see. So many victuals, eh? So much conduct money. And you can raise it, Master Wolsey?"

"I have no doubt of it, Sire. I can explain in detail how I propose to make these arrangements."

"Enough, enough. We trust you. Bother us not with the how and the why and the where. Let us find that we have what we need. That is all we ask of you."

"It shall be so, Sire."

Henry once more patted Wolsey's shoulder and the almoner, who had always been a man to seize his opportunities, said with an air of impulsiveness which concealed a perfected rehearsal: "Your Graces, have I your permission to speak to you on a . . . somewhat delicate matter?"

Henry tried to look shrewd; Katharine was faintly alarmed. She was always afraid that someone whom she regarded highly would, by a carelessly spoken word, anger the King and so ruin a promising career.

"Speak," said Henry.

Wolsey lowered his eyes. "This is bold of me, Your Grace, but I was bold in the service of your most noble and honoured father, and thus found favour with him. I would serve Your Grace with all the zeal I gave to your father's cause."

"Yes, yes," said Henry impatiently.

"It concerns my lord of Surrey."

"What of my lord of Surrey?"

"I have noticed of late that he is failing. He plans to go to France with Your Grace. This is rash of me . . . but I shall not think of my own recklessness in speaking my mind—only of the service I could do Your Grace. Sire, the Earl of Surrey is too old to accompany Your Grace to France, and such men can do much to impede an expedition. If it is Your Grace's wish that the Earl of Surrey should accompany you to France, then it is my wish also, but . . ."

Henry nodded. "He speaks truth," he said. "Surrey is an old man. Do I want greybeards to march with me!"

The thought occurred to Katharine that the only reason he could want them would be to call attention to his own radiant youth.

But they were going into battle. Henry wanted young men beside him. He also wished to show this man that he appreciated what he had done. Bishop Fox, who looked upon Wolsey as his protégé, had informed the King that the energy of Wolsey astonished even him. He had taken control of tanneries and smithies, of bakeries and breweries; so that they were all working for the state to enable Master Wolsey to provide everything that was needed for the expedition. He worked all hours of the day and far into the night; he scarcely stopped to eat; he was determined to please the King by his diligence, determined that this time the war should not fail through lack of equipment.

I like this Thomas Wolsey, the King told himself.

To throw Surrey to him in exchange for all his labours was a small thing. Surrey was old and arrogant and had passed from the King's favour. And Wolsey asked it, Henry believed, not out of enmity towards the old man, but in his zeal for the success of the cause.

"When we leave for France," said Henry, "Surrey shall stay behind."

Wolsey bowed his head in such humble gratitude that he might have been receiving a great honour for himself.

"I am greatly relieved, Your Grace; I feared my importuning . . ."

Henry slapped the almoner's back with a blow which made him stagger a little.

"Have no fear, Master Wolsey. Serve us well and you will find us a good master."

Wolsey took the King's hand and kissed it; there were tears

in the eyes which he raised to Henry's face. "And the greatest, Sire," he murmured. "A master whom all men must delight to serve."

Henry's pleasure was apparent. He was thinking: When this war is won, I'll not forget Master Wolsey. Mayhap I'll keep him near me. He's a useful man, and a wise one.

\*       \*       \*

Wolsey, coming from the royal apartment was smiling to himself.

This war was serving him well, for it had brought him closer to the King's notice. He was going to impress the young monarch with his worth, as he had his father on that occasion when the old King had believed he had not begun a mission and had then found it completed with efficiency and success.

"The way is clear for me," he whispered to himself. "There is nothing to fear."

He felt faintly regretful that he could not share his triumphs with his family. He would have liked to see Mistress Wynter and the boy and girl at Court. He would have liked to put honours in their way. Of course he *would* do so. Both his children would be well looked after. Yet it saddened him that they must remain hidden.

He wondered what the King would say if he knew that Wolsey escaped from Court now and then to a woman who had borne him two children. He could guess. The little eyes would show a shocked expression; the royal mouth would be prim. Henry would expect celibacy in his priests; and he would be harder than less sensual men on those who were incontinent. *There* was a man, thought Wolsey, who lusted after the personable women whom he encountered. Yet he did not know it perhaps. He feigned to have a kingly interest in his subjects; but the interest was greater when the subject was a woman and a fair one.

No, the matter must be kept secret; his enemies must never discover the existence of Mistress Wynter. And he had enemies— many of them. They were an essential part of a man's life when that man had determined to rise from humble beginnings to greatness.

There was one of them approaching him at this moment.

The Earl of Surrey was pretending not to see him, but Wolsey decided that he should not pass.

"Good day, my lord."

Surrey gave him a haughty stare.

"You did not see me," went on Wolsey. "My lord, is your sight failing then?"

" 'Tis as good as it was the day I was twenty."

"A long, long time ago, my lord. You were deep in thought; mayhap that was why you did not see me. You were thinking of the campaign in France."

Surrey's curiosity overcame his contempt for one of such humble origin.

"You have been with the King?" he asked. "What news of our leaving? Are the stores ready yet?"

"They will be by the time the King is ready to leave. There will be work for us who go with him to France, and for those of you who stay behind."

"I am prepared to leave whenever His Grace gives the word," said Surrey.

"*You* are prepared to leave, my lord?"

"Indeed I am."

"You are certain then that you are to serve with the King in France?"

"Of a surety I am certain. Am I not the King's general?"

Wolsey smiled knowledgeably and in a manner which replaced Surrey's bombast with fear.

He could have struck the man, but he did not wish to soil his hands by touching a tradesman's son. Wolsey murmured: "A merry good day to you, my lord," and passed on.

*          *          *

Surrey stood for a few seconds looking after the almoner; then as his rising rage smothered his good sense, he hurried to the royal apartments.

"I wish to see the King at once," he demanded.

The guards looked astonished; but this was after all the great Earl of Surrey, and it might well be that he had news of importance to impart to the King.

He strode past them and threw open the door of the King's apartment. Henry was leaning against a table where Wolsey had recently left him; Katharine was seated, and the King was twirling a lock of her hair in his fingers.

"Sire, I must have immediate speech with you!"

Henry looked up, rather peevishly. He did not expect people to burst in unannounced. Could it be that Surrey considered that he was of such nobility that he need not observe the laws of ordinary courtiers?

Henry let fall the lock of hair and fixed his gaze on Surrey. The Earl should have been warned by the glitter in the King's eye, but he was too alarmed to take notice of anything.

"Sire, I have just met that butcher's son, coming from your apartments. The insolence of the fellow is beyond endurance."

"If you speak of my good friend Wolsey," said Henry sharply, "I should warn you, my lord, to do so with more respect."

"Your Grace, the fellow hinted that I am too old to follow you in battle. The impertinent butcher's cur. . . ."

"Your face is an unhealthy purple, Surrey," said Henry, "and it would seem that you are forgetful of your manners." He turned to Katharine. "Could that be his age, do you think?"

Katharine said nothing. She dreaded such scenes. She wanted to warn Surrey, but there was no restraining the irate nobleman.

"The impudent jackanapes! I'd have his tongue cut out. I'd cut off both his ears. . . ."

"Which shows what a fool you are and how unfit for our counsels," retorted Henry. "You would rob us of the man who is doing more than any to make the expedition into France a success."

"He has bemused Your Grace with his sly ways."

There was nothing he could have said to rouse Henry's anger more certainly. To suggest that he, the astute and brilliant leader, was a dupe!

Oh Surrey, you *fool*! thought Katharine.

Henry stood up to his full height and his voice rumbled like thunder when he shouted: "Nay, my lord Earl, there is no room for you in my army. There is no room for you in my Court. You will leave it at once. Do not let me see you until I send for you."

"Your Grace. . . ."

"Are you so old then that you have lost your hearing!" roared Henry cruelly. "You heard me, sir. Go! At once. Leave the Court. You are banished from our sight. Will you go, or shall I have to call the guard?"

Surrey crumpled suddenly, so that he did indeed look like an old man.

He bowed stiffly and left the King's presence.

\*            \*            \*

From a window of the Palace Wolsey watched the departure of Surrey. He wanted to laugh aloud in his triumph.

"Such disgrace shall befall all the enemies of Thomas Wolsey," he told himself. "No slight shall be forgotten."

He remembered then a certain gentleman of Limington in Somerset, a Sir Amias Paulet. In the days when Thomas had been rector of Limington he had not shown what Paulet considered adequate respect to this local bigwig; and Paulet had, on some flimsy pretext, caused Thomas Wolsey to be set in the stocks.

Even now Thomas could remember the indignity, and he told himself that when the time was ripe Paulet should deeply regret the day he had Thomas Wolsey set in the stocks.

An eye for an eye, a tooth for a tooth. Nay, thought Thomas, I am no ordinary man, and any who robs me of one tooth shall pay with two of his own.

So Surrey, who had called the King's almoner a butcher's cur, had lost his chance of following the King to France; he had also lost his place at Court.

That was meet and fitting, thought Thomas, smiling. There would be many scores to settle on the way up, and they should be settled . . . settled in full.

\* \* \*

It was some time since Ferdinand had felt so full of vigour. Hourly despatches were reaching him. He was playing the double game of politics which was so dear to his heart, and he never enjoyed it so much as when he was deluding those who thought themselves to be his allies, and coming to secret terms with those whom his allies thought to be a mutual enemy.

There was only one matter of moment to Ferdinand: the good of Spain. Spain's desire at this moment was for peace. She had Navarre and, with the acquisition of that important little state, she was ready to consolidate her triumphs.

The English were clamouring for action. Katharine wrote naïvely from England. His dear innocent daughter, did she think that politics were arranged like rules in a convent? She was eager to please that handsome young husband of hers and her father at the same time.

She was invaluable.

Through her, it seemed, Ferdinand could set the young monarch dancing to his tune. He could let England work for Spain. What an excellent state of affairs it was when one had docile children to work for one.

He was a little sad, thinking of his lost youth and his inability to get Germaine with child. The times when he could go to bed with several women in one night were over. But he was still the sly fox of Europe.

He would forget the fear of impotence; forget the delights of love and think of wars instead.

He would allow Caroz to make a treaty for him in London with his son-in-law. He would give his promises . . . although he had no intention of keeping them. Promises were counters used in a game. If it was worth while redeeming them, you did so; if not, you forgot you had ever made them.

He sat down and wrote to Caroz. ". . . my armies to invade Guienne while the English are to attack from the North. I doubt not that the present Henry will be about to repeat the success of that other Henry in France, and we shall soon be hearing news of another battle of Agincourt. Let there be a treaty between our two countries, and assure my son-in-law that I am in this matter with him, heart and soul. . . ."

While he was writing a page entered to tell him that the friar for whom he had sent had arrived.

"Bring him to me," said Ferdinand.

And the man was brought.

Ferdinand was pleased with his appearance. He looked like a wandering friar; he could pass from Spain to the Court of France without attracting a great deal of notice.

"I have work for you," he said. "You are to leave immediately for France. Seek out King Louis and tell him from whom you come. Tell him that the English are preparing to make war on him and that I, through my daughter, have information of where they will attack and in what force they will come. Sound him well. Let him know that I am ready to make peace with him for a consideration . . . terms which we can later discuss if he is ready to consider this matter."

The friar listened eagerly to Ferdinand's instructions and, when he had left, Ferdinand returned to the letter which he was writing to Caroz.

"I would have my son-in-law know that France is the enemy of us both and that we must stand together to crush her. Let me know how far preparations have proceeded, and we will sign our treaty so that all the world shall know that we are of one family and together in this matter."

Ferdinand sealed his letters and sent for his messengers.

He stood at the window watching their departure, laughing inwardly.

I am no longer young, he chuckled, I cannot satisfy a wife, let alone a mistress. Yet I am still the slyest fox in Europe.

\*　　　\*　　　\*

On a bright April day the King presided over the ceremony of signing the treaty with his father-in-law.

Luis Caroz, whose magnificence of person was only slightly less than that of the King, stood with Henry and Katharine; and a cheer went up from all those assembled, because they believed that with the help of Ferdinand they could not but be victorious against France.

The great days of conquest were about to begin. The triumphs of the warlike Henry V would be repeated. They looked at the glowing face of their twenty-two-year-old King and they told themselves that he would bring England to a new greatness.

Katharine felt content.

One of her dearest dreams was to make strong the friendship between her husband and father; that she believed she had achieved.

Surely that other—the bearing of a healthy son—must follow.

\*　　　\*　　　\*

Katharine stared at the letters in consternation. This could not be true. Her father could not have made a truce with the King of France a few days before Caroz was signing one on behalf of his master with the King of England.

There had been some confusion, a mistake somewhere.

She sent at once for Caroz. The ambassador came to her in complete bewilderment. As he passed through to her apartments he met her confessor, Fray Diego Fernandez. Fray Diego greeted the ambassador without much respect, and Caroz was quick to notice the quirk of satisfaction about the priest's mouth.

Laugh, my little man, thought Caroz. Your days here are numbered. I am beginning to make Ferdinand understand that you work more for England than for Spain.

But Caroz had little time to spare for the impudent priest on this day, and hurried to the apartment where Katharine was eagerly waiting to receive him.

"You have heard this news?" she asked.

"Yes, Your Grace."

"There has been some mistake."

Caroz shook his head. He knew his master better than the Queen knew her father, and it seemed to him that such an act was characteristic of Ferdinand. What worried him was the action Ferdinand would take next, for Caroz guessed that he had already settled on a scapegoat, and that would very likely be his ambassador in England.

"It cannot be that my father was making an agreement with France while the treaty of alliance was being signed here in England!"

"It would seem so, Your Grace."

"How could such a terrible misunderstanding come about?"

"Doubtless your father will offer some explanation."

Henry strode into the apartment. He was in a violent rage.

"Ha!" he cried. "Don Luis Caroz! So you are here. What news is this I hear from Spain? Someone has lied to me. How could your master give his name to two such agreements at the same time!"

"Sire, I can no more understand than you can."

"Then it is time you did. I want an explanation of this conduct." Henry turned to Katharine. "It would seem, Madam, that your father has been mocking us."

Katharine shivered, for Henry looked as though he were ready to destroy all things Spanish, including Caroz and herself.

"It cannot be so," she answered as calmly as she could. "This news *must* be false."

"It's to be hoped so," growled Henry.

Caroz said: "Sire, have I Your Grace's permission to retire, that I may despatch a letter to my master with all speed?"

"Retire!" cried Henry. "It would be well for you to retire, Sir Ambassador. If you stay I may do to you what those who betray my trust deserve."

The ambassador hurried away with all speed, leaving Katharine alone with her husband.

Henry stood in his favourite position, legs apart, fingers playing with his dagger hilt, eyes glinting blue fire between the lids which almost met.

"My ally!" he shouted. "So this is Spanish honour! By God, I have trusted you Spaniards too much. And what has it brought me? An alliance which is no alliance . . . a barren wife."

"No . . . Henry."

"No! What of this treaty your father has signed with France? France! Our enemy! His and mine! I have served you royally. I brought you from your poverty and set you on a throne. And how do you repay me? Three births and not a child to show for it. It would seem that Spaniards seek to make a mock of the King of England."

"Henry, it is no more my fault than yours that we have no child. That matter has nothing to do with this treaty it is said my father has made with France."

"Has it not, Madam. Has it not!"

"Henry, how could I be blamed because our children did not live?"

"Perhaps," said Henry more quietly, "it is because it is not the will of God that you should bear children. Perhaps because you were my brother's wife. . . ."

"The Pope gave us the dispensation," she said, her voice trembling with a vague terror.

"Because he believed that you were a virgin when you married me."

"As I was."

While he looked at her the rage in his face subsided and it was replaced by a look which might have been one of speculation. "As you tell me, Madam," he said.

And with that he turned and left her—bewildered, unhappy, and numbed by a fear which was as yet vague and shadowy.

\* \* \*

Ferdinand wrote to Henry and his daughter.

There had been a terrible misunderstanding. He was desolate because he feared he had been misrepresented. He had given no firm instruction that Caroz was to sign a treaty on his behalf with Henry. He was afraid that this matter had cast a slur on his honour; for even though he knew himself to be blameless, would others understand the truth?

It was a humiliating thing for a King to admit, but he feared that his ambassador in England was an incompetent fellow. He had misunderstood instructions . . . not deliberately. He would not believe that Don Luis was a rogue—but merely a fool.

"My dear daughter," he wrote, "you who were brought up in our Court know well the piety of your mother and that it was her wish that all her family should share that piety. I am a sick man, daughter. You would not recognize me if you saw me now. I believe myself to be very close to death. My conscience troubled me. When death is near, those of us who have striven to lead a religious life have an urgent desire to set our affairs in order. Make peace with your enemies—that is one of God's laws. So I looked about me and thought of my greatest enemy. Who could that be but Louis XII of France? So, believing that there should be reconciliation between Christians, I signed the truce with him. This was my reason. You, who are your mother's daughter, will understand my motives."

When Katharine read that letter her attitude towards her father began to change.

What loyalty do I owe to him now? she asked herself. It was the memory of her mother which had until this time made her wish to serve him; but her mother would never have agreed to the signing of these two treaties within a few days of each other.

It was not easy for one who had been brought up with the strictest regard for filial duty, to criticize a parent's action, but Katharine was beginning to do so.

The letter which Ferdinand had written to Henry was in the same strain.

He did not wish his son-in-law to think that he put friendship with the King of France on the same level with that which he bore to the King of England, he wrote. Nay, he had made peace with France because he feared he had but a short time to live and wished to die at peace with his enemies. But out of his love for his son-in-law, he would be ready to break the truce with France if necessary. There was a way in which this could be done. The province of Béarn was not included in the treaty and, if Ferdinand attacked Béarn and the King of France came to its defence—as he most assuredly would—then he would attack the Spanish, which would be breaking the treaty. And so it would be France which had broken faith, not Spain.

Henry scowled when he read this. He was beginning to believe that he was a fool to put any trust in such a double dealer. But it did not mean that he was not going forward with his plans for war.

*      *      *

Maria de Salinas came to the Queen's side and whispered: "Caroz is without. He is in a sorry state. An attempt has been made on his life."

Katharine, who had been sitting at her embroidery with two of her ladies, rose immediately and went with Maria into the adjoining ante-room.

"Bring him to me here," she said.

Maria returned in a short time with Caroz. His fine satin doublet was torn, and there was blood on his arm.

"Your Grace," he panted, "I was set upon in the street. I was attacked, but by a stroke of good fortune my attacker slipped just as he was about to thrust home his sword. It caught my arm and I ran . . . I ran for my life."

"Bring me water and bandages," said Katharine to Maria. "I will bind up the wound. I have a special unguent which is a wonderful healer."

As she spoke she cut the sleeve away from the wound and saw to her relief that it was not deep.

"I am submitted to insults on all sides." Caroz was almost sobbing. "Everyone here blames me for the treaty His Highness has made with the King of France. They have determined to kill me. It is unsafe for me to go abroad in the streets."

"You are distraught, Don Luis," said Katharine. "Pray calm yourself. This may have been nothing but the action of a cutpurse."

"Nay, Your Grace. The people are infuriated with me. They blame me, although Your Grace well knows. . . ."

Katharine said: "This may make you feel a little faint. Lie back and close your eyes."

As she washed the wound and applied the unguent, she thought: Poor Don Luis. He is the scapegoat. I must do all in my power to save him. I should not forgive myself if he, bearing the blame for my father's action, should also suffer the death wound which would be his should these people lay their hands upon him.

She bound the wound and made Don Luis lie down, setting two of her pages to watch over him.

Then she went to the King's apartment.

Henry frowned at her. He was still displeased with the Spaniards and he wished her to know that she was included in that displeasure. But she faced him boldly. She was certain that some of his friends had set an assassin to attack Don Luis, and she believed that Henry alone could save the ambassador from another attack. She felt sickened with humiliation because of her father's conduct and, although she had no great regard for Don Luis, she was determined that his death should not be placed to her family's account.

"Henry," she said, "Don Luis has been attacked."

Henry growled his indifference.

"His murder would help us not at all."

"Us?" he demanded. "For whom do you work, Madam? Do you set yourself on the side of your father or your husband?"

Katharine drew herself to her full height and in that moment she looked magnificent, with her eyes flashing and the colour in her cheeks.

"I have made my vows to love, cherish and honour my husband," she said distinctly. "*I* do not break my vows."

Then Henry laughed exultantly. His Kate was a handsome woman. She was telling him clearly that she recognized her father's duplicity and that she was ranging herself on her husband's side against him. The woman adored him. That was easy to see.

"Why, Kate," he said, "I knew it well."

She threw herself into his arms and clung to him.

"Oh Henry, I am fearful that you should go to war."

He stroked her hair gently. "No harm will come to me, Kate. I'll give a good account of myself."

"Yet I shall fret if you are away."

"You are a good wife to me, Kate. But have no fear for me. I'll go to France and I'll come back . . . in triumph . . . and you shall share those triumphs with me."

"Come back safely . . . that is all I ask."

"Bah! You speak like a woman." But he was not displeased that she should.

It was then that she asked him to forbid further attacks on Caroz.

"The man is a fool," she said, "but no knave. Rest assured that he signed the treaty on my father's behalf in good faith."

"I'll order it, Kate . . . since you ask me. Caroz can live on without fear of losing his life. And if your father does not recall him, he shall keep his position at Court." His eyes narrowed. "The man is a fool. But sometimes it is not a bad thing when those who are set to work against us are fools."

Katharine did not answer. She had shown clearly that she would never completely trust her father again. Henry was satisfied.

And so the life of Caroz was saved.

\*         \*         \*

The June sun shone on the walls of Dover Castle. From a window in the keep Katharine looked down on the fleet in the harbour, waiting to set sail. She knew most of the ships by name for she had taken the greatest interest in the preparations for this war. There lay the *Peter Pomegranate*—named in deference to her, whose device of the pomegranate had become so well known at the Court. There was the *Anne of Greenwich* side by side with the *George of Falmouth*; there was the *Barbara*, the *Dragon* and the *Lion*.

It had been a magnificent cavalcade which had passed along the road to Dover. The people had come out to cheer their King, and when they had seen him, so richly clad, so handsome, they had declared he was more like a god that a man. He was preceded by his Yeomen of the Guard in the Tudor colours, green and white; and the knights in armour and the gaily caparisoned horses were a colourful sight.

But it was the King who stood out in that glittering assembly. He was not in armour, but dressed as Supreme Head of the Navy of which he was very proud. There were four hundred ships waiting to set sail from Dover harbour, and he himself had superintended a great deal of the preparation for the journey. Thomas Wolsey was with him; he had learned more and more the value of that man.

And there rode Henry in his vest of gold brocade, his breeches of cloth of gold and his hose of scarlet. About his neck on a thick gold chain hung a whistle—the biggest any of the spectators had ever seen—and this was set with jewels which flashed in the sunlight. He blew on the whistle from time to time to the delight of all those who heard it.

Of all the pageants in which he had played his joyful parts there was not one which had delighted him as did this new game of going to war.

Katharine rode with him, applauding, admiring; and the glances he threw her way were full of love and tenderness.

There was a reason for this. As though to crown his happiness she had been able to give him, some few weeks before, the news which he had so wished to hear.

"Henry," she had said, her eyes alight with happiness, "there can be no doubt that I am with child."

Then he had embraced her and told her that there was only one regret in his life; that to make this holy war on France he must leave her.

"You must take care of yourself, Kate," he had said. "Remember in this fair body lies the heir of England."

She had sworn to take the utmost care.

Then he had requested her to be present at the meeting of the Council, and there he had announced that since he must go away he must appoint a Regent to govern the land in his absence.

"I have given this matter great thought. I have prayed for guidance, and I am leaving you the best and only possible Regent." There was the pause for dramatic effect; then the little eyes, shining with sentiment, were on Katharine.

M

"Gentlemen of the Council, your Regent during my absence will be Her Grace the Queen."

She had been overcome with joyful emotion, and she thought, as she did on all such occasions, If only my mother could be with me now!

So she was to be Regent during his absence. She was to have a Council to help her, should she need their help. The King had chosen the Archbishop of Canterbury, Thomas Lovell, and the Earl of Surrey. The Earl had been allowed to return to Court for Henry was in a mellow mood. Many of his most able statesmen were accompanying him to France, and Surrey who, in spite of his arrogance, was a man of experience, could be more useful at Court than skulking in the country, perhaps planning mischief. So back to Court came the Earl—although Thomas Wolsey had discreetly tried to advise the King against the old man's recall. Henry did not accept Wolsey's advice, and Wolsey was too clever to press it.

So they had ridden into Dover, up the steep hill to the Castle, there to rest awhile until the expedition was ready to sail.

\*　　　\*　　　\*

The King was now ready to embark. Beside him were the most courageous of his knights, men such as Brandon, Compton, Sir John Seymour, Sir Thomas Parr and Sir Thomas Boleyn. There was the indefatigable Thomas Wolsey determined to keep a wary eye on food supplies and equipment, not forgetting to glance with the faintest hint of triumph at the Earl of Surrey who was with those who remained behind.

There on Dover strand the King had decided a ceremony should take place. He wanted all his subjects to know in what affection he held his Queen; and when before them all he took her into his arms and kissed her loudly on both cheeks, a cheer went up, for the people never loved their King so much as when he, sparkling with the glitter of royalty, showed them that he was at heart an ordinary family man.

Then he took Katharine's hand and addressed the assembly.

"My subjects, my friends, you see me about to depart on a holy war. I grieve to leave my country but it is God's will that I should cross the sea to bring back to you that of which the French have robbed us. On this fine day you can see the coast of France; my town of Calais lies across the sea and I am now about to set out for that town. From there I shall seek to win back my rights and your rights. But while I am engaged on this duty I do not forget my people at home, so I leave you one who, I hope, is almost as dear to you as she is to me—my wife, your Queen. My friends, when I go aboard, when I set sail, Queen Katharine becomes the Governor of this Realm and Captain General of the forces for home defence."

As he took Katharine's hand and kissed it, another cheer went up.

He looked into her face and his eyes were glazed with tenderness and the pleasure he felt in scenes such as this.

"Farewell, my Kate. I will return with rich conquests. Guard yourself well . . . and that other."

"I will, my King," she answered.

A last embrace, and to the fanfares of trumpets he went abroad.

Katharine stood, with those who were remaining behind, on Dover strand, watching the glittering fleet as it set sail for France.

She was praying for Henry's safety, for divine guidance that she might carry out her duties in a manner worthy of the daughter of Isabella of Castile.

She determined to surprise the King with her ability to govern; she was going to show him that if at one time she had sought to win advantages for Spain, she no longer did so; for there was only one country which she now called her own; and that was England.

Yet the real reason for her exultation lay within her own body. The child! This child must come forth from her womb, strong and healthy; and when he did come he must not be allowed to die.

There must not be another disaster. If such a calamity should befall her, all the affection of the last weeks, all the love and devotion which the King had sworn he bore her, would be as lightly swept away as the gaudy paper decorations after a masque.

## CHAPTER VIII

## HENRY AT WAR

BY THE TIME the King's fleet had reached Calais the rain had begun to fall. This was disappointing as the cloth of gold and rich brocade trappings lost some of their dazzle in the downpour.

Henry was cheerful, however, determined to show his men that he was ready for any adversity, so certain of success that he was not going to be downcast by a little rain.

Then tents were set up; the army encamped; and on that first night, the King, his garments soaked, made the rounds of the camp like a practised commander. He laughed at the rain and he made his men do the same.

"We are not the men to let a wetting disturb our spirits. We'll snap our fingers at the weather as we will at that old rogue, the King of France."

The men were cheered by the sight of him—pink cheeked, ruddy haired and full of health and high spirits.

Nor was this the end of his endeavours for when he returned to his tent he did not take off his clothes.

"If this rain continues to fall," he told his companions, "the Watch will be in poor spirits as the night progresses. I have heard how Henry V before Agincourt went among his men to comfort them. I will show my soldiers that they have as good a leader in me as the victors of Agincourt had in that other Henry."

It was three o'clock when the King, still in his damp clothes, made the rounds of the camp.

He found the Watch disconsolate. In the darkness they did not recognize the figure on horseback immediately and Henry heard them, cursing the weather and talking of the warm beds in England which might have been theirs.

"Ay," said the King, "warm English beds sound even more inviting than they are in reality—when remembered under the rain of other lands."

"Your Grace!"

"Have no fear," said Henry. "I myself was thinking of my own bed and the comforts and pleasures I might have been enjoying there. We are of a kind, my friends. Men, all of us. It is understandable that our thoughts turn to the comforts of home. But be of good cheer. You see, I, like you, am damp from the rain. I suffer all that you suffer. That is how I would have it. My men and their King are together in this war. He never forgets it; nor should you; and if we have been made to suffer in the beginning, fortune promises us better things, God willing."

"Amen," murmured the men. And then: "God bless Your Grace!" Smiling Henry rode back to his own tent. He was not displeased with the rain which had enabled him to show his men that he was with them to take part in their misfortunes and give them a share in his triumphs.

\* \* \*

In the morning the rain was over and the sun shone brilliantly. The King was in high spirits and he told himself that he could not leave his good people of Calais before he had made them gay with certain masques and joustings, so that they might see something of the skill which their King and his men would display in battle.

So there in Calais there was jousting and tilting; and the King won the admiration of all by his skill with the bow.

Henry, however, was impatient to be done with mock battles and begin the real fighting, but it was necessary to await the arrival of his ally against the French, the Emperor Maximilian.

There was much talk of Maximilian who was known as one of the greatest soldiers of Europe. Henry was delighted to have him as a friend in this struggle against the French. With the help of Maximilian he could afford to snap his fingers at that other dubious ally, Ferdinand.

It was while he was showing his skill at archery that a message came to him from Maximilian.

He discarded his bow and read it immediately.

The Emperor believed that the first steps in the conquest of France should be the taking of those two towns, Thérouanne and Tournai. Once these were in the hands of the allies, Maximilian pointed out, there would be no difficulty in pouring men in from Flanders. He wanted the King of England to know that he merely proffered the advice of an old campaigner and he was the happiest general in Europe to serve under the banner of the King of England.

Henry, whose plans had been not to go so far from the main object—Paris—as towns on the Flemish border, was so charmed by the Emperor's last words that he succumbed immediately to his suggestions and set out for Thérouanne.

\* \* \*

The Emperor Maximilian—that hardened old campaigner—had been in communication with Ferdinand concerning the aspirations of the King of England.

"This young colt will become a menace to all if he is not curbed," wrote Maximilian. "I am mindful of his recent expedition as your ally. He has a conceit which makes it unnecessary to deceive him because he so obligingly is ever ready to deceive himself."

The Emperor had no great desire to make war on the King of France, but rather to make an alliance with him as Ferdinand had done; he was, as was Ferdinand, in secret negotiations with Louis.

The three great European rulers—Louis, Ferdinand and the Emperor—did not take very seriously the cavortings of the young King of England, who had too much money to squander; but they were all ready to make use of him, and Maximilian had been offered a bargain which was irresistible. His treasury was empty and he desperately needed to fill it; therefore he was eager to come to terms with the English King. He would place at Henry's service the cavalry of Burgundy and as many German *Lanzknechts* as he wanted. It would be necessary of course for Henry to pay for the hire of these men, because, while the Emperor had the men, he had not the means to keep them on the battlefield.

As for the Emperor himself, he would place himself under the command of Henry. "I shall be honoured to serve under such a banner. . . ." were words calculated to bring such satisfaction to the King of England that he would leap at the bargain without considering the cost. Such a general as the Emperor Maximilian must be paid for, and the King of England must understand that his personal expenses would be considerable. But all he would ask was a hundred crowns a day; and the King would naturally be expected to shoulder the expenses of the Emperor's household guards.

"We are invincible," Henry had cried, "now we have one of the greatest soldiers in Europe fighting under our banner."

The three experienced old warriors now prepared to watch the antics of the young cockerel who believed that war was a superior —though more expensive—kind of masque.

Cynically Ferdinand waited. Louis was preparing to make peace with Maximilian and Ferdinand. Maximilian was telling himself that the conquest of Thérouanne and Tournai were all he needed, and he saw no reason why Henry should not pay him for winning them for himself.

Louis had given his instructions that his soldiers were to avoid battle with the English. They were merely to harry them and make their stay in France mildly uncomfortable.

Dorset's campaign was remembered; so nobody took the English seriously . . . except themselves.

\* \* \*

What a glorious moment when the Emperor, simply dressed in black—because he was mourning the death of his second wife —rode into the camp to pay homage to the dazzling young King.

Henry embraced the Emperor and would not let him kneel; but the glitter of triumph was in his eyes for all to see.

Maximilian, who cared not at all for cloth of gold but only for making his Empire great, was quite ready to kneel if by so doing he could deceive this young man.

There were tears in Henry's eyes. "This is the greatest moment of my life," he declared, "to fight side by side with your Imperial Highness."

"Who is happy at this time to be your general," answered the Emperor glibly.

"The capture of these towns should be an easy matter," Henry told him. "And then . . . to Paris!"

"My daughter Margaret has written to me urging me to insist on your visiting her before you leave this land. She has heard of your fame and says that she will hold it hard against me if I allow you to depart without being her guest for a while."

Henry smiled. He had heard that Margaret of Savoy was not uncomely, and the thought of shining in feminine company was very attractive.

"I desire to see the lady as much as she does to see me," he declared.

"Then we must insist on that visit. My grandson has also heard of you. Charles—as you know he is being brought up by his aunt, my daughter Margaret—has said he wishes to see the King of England because he has heard that he is a young King possessed of all the virtues; and as he himself will be a ruler over great dominions he feels that to study the grace and prowess of great Harry of England would be a lesson to him."

"I have heard excellent reports of that boy."

"Ay, he'll make a good King. He's a serious young fellow."

"I can scarce wait to see him . . . and his aunt. But first there is a war to be won."

The Emperor agreed, and turned the conversation to plans for the first battle.

\*       \*       \*

The battle was of short duration. The French, who had not taken their enemy seriously and had been ordered by Louis not to join in a pitched battle, put into effect a mock retreat before Thérouanne; but the English were very serious; and for that matter, so was Maximilian, as this town, with Tournai, was at a strategic point on the border of the Netherlands, and Maximilian's object in joining this campaign was to win them.

The mock retreat soon became a retreat in real earnest; the small French forces were put to flight; and because they had been instructed not to fight, they were overcome by panic when they saw the weight of English and German forces; they galloped from the battlefield with the cavalry of the enemy in hot pursuit.

Henry was exultant; he had taken as prisoner the famous Chevalier Bayard, that knight who was known to be *sans peur et sans reproche*, and he felt that he was indeed making up for the disgrace which Dorset's army had brought upon his country.

The battle was derisively called by the French: The Battle of the Spurs; and shortly afterwards, with the Emperor beside him, Henry had taken Tournai.

When these two towns, the taking of which had been his reason for entering the war, were in his hands, Maximilian had had enough of war. Not so Henry.

He burst into Maximilian's tent and cried: "Now the way is clear. Now it is for us to go straight through to Paris to complete the victory."

Maximilian was thinking quickly. The date was August 22nd. It was hot but the summer was almost at its end and in a few weeks the rains would start. Henry could have no notion what the Flanders mud could be like.

The idea of marching on Paris, even if it was possible to defeat Louis, would only mean, if they were successful, that this conceited young man would become more overbearing than ever. The English were becoming too powerful already, and Maximilian had no intention of helping them at the expense of Louis, who was already preparing to make a treaty with him as he was with Ferdinand.

He must be kept in Flanders until the winter set in; then he would have to return to England, for he could not stay where he was through the winter. He could spend the winter in England preparing for a fresh onslaught next spring if he liked; that was of little concern to Maximilian since he had achieved what he wanted: These two towns which jutted into the Hapsburg dominions and which were therefore a menace to Netherlands trade.

"Have I your permission to speak frankly to Your Grace?" he asked.

Henry was always so delighted when the Emperor addressed him in humble fashion that he was ready to give what was asked even before the request was made.

"You have indeed."

"I am an old man. I have fought many battles. If we marched on Paris now, we could be defeated."

"Defeated! Standing together as we do. Impossible!"

"Nay, Your Grace, if you will forgive my contradiction. Louis has not put all his forces into the field for the protection of these two insignificant towns. He would fight to the death for Paris. Our men need rest, and a little gaiety. It is always wise in war to consolidate one's gains before one passes on to fresh conquests. I am under your command but it is my duty to give you the benefit of my experience. My daughter Margaret is impatient to see you. She is eager that the proposed marriage between Charles and your sister Mary may be discussed more fully. We have won these towns from the French. Let us fortify them and then go to my daughter's court. There she will entertain you right royally . . . the King of England, conqueror of Thérouanne and Tournai."

Henry wavered. He longed for conquest, yet the thought of being entertained and flattered by Margaret was growing more and more inviting.

\*        \*        \*

When Maximilian had left him Henry sent for Thomas Wolsey.

He looked affectionately at the almoner, of whose worth he had become daily more and more aware. When he needed anything, it was Thomas Wolsey who always seemed to be at his side to supply it. The Emperor had congratulated him on the excellence of his equipment. All this he owed to Wolsey.

He had even come to the point when he spoke to him of matters far beyond the man's duty; and, moreover, listened to his advice which had always seemed to him sound.

When Wolsey came to the King he saw at once the indecision in the King's eyes and he was alert. It was his policy to give the

King the advice he hoped for and then allow him to think that he had taken his, Wolsey's.

The King put his arm through that of Wolsey and proceeded to walk with him about the tent . . . a habit of Henry's when he was deep in thought and with one whom he wished to favour.

"Friend Thomas," he said, "we have won a victory. These two towns are in our hands. The Emperor is of the opinion that this victory should be consolidated and that we should now proceed to his daughter's court at Lille, there to rest awhile. Now you are in charge of our supplies. Is it your opinion that we need this time to make ready for further attacks?"

Wolsey hesitated. He could see that the King was torn between two desires and he was not certain which course the King had made up his mind to follow. Wolsey must be on the right side.

"Your Grace is tireless," he said. "I know full well that it would be no hardship for you to continue in fierce battle." He paused significantly. Then went on: "For others, who lack Your Grace's powers. . . ."

"Ah!" said the King, and it was almost a sigh of relief. "Yes, I owe something to my men, Thomas. I need them beside me when I ride into battle."

Wolsey went on triumphantly now that he had received his cue. The King wished to go to the court of the Duchess of Savoy, but it must be a matter of duty not of pleasure.

"Therefore, Sire," Wolsey continued, "I would say, since you command me to give you my humble advice, that for the sake of others—though not your august self—it would be desirable to rest awhile before continuing the fight."

Wolsey's arm was pressed; the King was smiling.

"I must perforce think of those others, Thomas. Much as it irks me to leave the field at this stage . . . I must think of them."

"Your Grace is ever thoughtful of his subjects. They know this, and they will serve you with even greater zeal remembering Your Grace's clemency towards them."

The King sighed deeply but his eyes were glittering with delight.

"Then, my friend, what must be, must be. We shall be leaving ere long for Lille."

Wolsey felt gratified; he had once more gracefully leaped what might have been a difficult hurdle.

The King was also gratified, for he went on: "The bishopric of Tournai has fallen vacant, I hear. Louis has put forward a new Bishop. I venture to think, now that Tournai is no longer in

French hands, it is not for Louis to appoint its Bishop and my nomination will more readily receive the blessing of His Holiness."

"Sire!" Wolsey's gratitude shone from his eyes as he knelt and kissed his sovereign's hand.

Henry beamed on him. "It is ever our wish," he said, "to reward a good servant."

Bishop of Tournai! pondered Wolsey. A further step along the road.

Bishop! he thought, and he kept his head lowered over Henry's hand lest his eyes should betray the ambition which he felt was so strong that it must be obvious.

Bishop! Cardinal? And then: Pope himself!

## CHAPTER IX

# THE FLOWERS OF THE FOREST

AT HOME IN England Katharine took her responsibilities very seriously. She was eager that when he returned Henry should be satisfied with the manner in which she had governed the realm during his absence. She attended meetings of her Council and impressed them with her good sense; she spent any time she could spare from these duties with her ladies who were busily working, stitching standards, banners and badges. She prayed each day for the strength to do her duty and that the child she carried would not suffer because of her activities.

She felt well and full of confidence. The news from France was good. Henry was in high spirits; she had heard of the successful conclusion of the Battle of the Spurs; and she wondered now and then whether Henry was learning soldiers' habits, for she knew that there would be women to haunt the camp. Would he remain faithful? She must remember how stoically her own mother had accepted Ferdinand's infidelities; and Isabella had been a Queen in her own right. Ferdinand had ruled Castile as her consort, and Isabella never forgot that; and yet she meekly accepted his unfaithfulness as something which women, whose husbands are forced to spend long periods from their marriage beds, must regard as inevitable.

She was thankful that there was so much with which to occupy herself. There was always the child to comfort her, and she thanked God daily that she had become pregnant before Henry had left.

This one must live, she told herself again and again. It would not be possible to go on having such disappointments.

One day, when she sat stitching with her women, Surrey came into the apartment without ceremony.

"Your Grace," he cried, "forgive this intrusion. You will understand when you hear the news. The Scots are gathering and preparing to swarm over the Border."

She stared at him in horror. "But the King made a treaty with his brother-in-law . . ." she began.

Surrey snapped his fingers. "Treaties, Your Grace, it would seem are made to be broken. This is no surprise to me. When the English army is overseas the Scots always attack."

"We must meet this attack," said Katharine quickly.

"Ay, Your Grace. I've men enough to meet the beggarly Scots."

"Then go to it. There's little time to waste."

Katharine went with him to the Council chamber. The time for stitching was over.

As she did so she was aware of the child moving within her and she felt exultant because of its existence and a certain apprehension because of the anxieties to come.

She thought of Margaret, Henry's sister, who was wife to James IV of Scotland, and it saddened her because sister must surely be working against brother.

She listened to Surrey, addressing the Council. His eyes gleamed and he seemed to have thrown off twenty years. It was as though he were saying, I was considered too old to join the French frolic. Now the King and the butcher's cur shall see how real victories are won.

I pray God that Surrey may succeed, thought Katharine. His victory would be hers, and if they could defeat the Scots Henry would be well pleased with her.

And yet . . . nothing would please him long, she knew, unless she brought forth a healthy son.

She spoke to the Council.

"There is little time to lose," she said. "Let us gather all our available forces and move at once to the Border. The Scottish King has broken his treaty and seeks to strike us in the back while the King with our armies is on foreign soil. Gentlemen, we must defeat him. We must show His Grace that there are as good men in England this day as there are in France."

"We'll do it," cried Surrey; and everyone in the Council chamber echoed his words.

But this was no occasion for words only. Action was needed. No one and nothing must be spared in the great endeavour.

*          *          *

The days were filled with a hundred anxieties. How could she raise the money to supply an army in France and another on the Border? There was only one answer: New taxes must be levied. Surrey was already in the North, fortifying the Border, raising an army to subdue the Stuart, and she herself was in continual correspondence with Wolsey. The amount of money and goods which were needed for the French war was staggering; yet somehow she must raise it.

There was no time now to indulge in those restful hours of sewing with her ladies. Disastrous news came from the North, where James had mustered an army of, some said, one hundred thousand men and was crossing the Tweed determined on battle.

She saw panic in certain faces about her. The King abroad on his French adventure, his country undefended and only a woman in control. Was this to be the end of the Tudor dynasty? Were the Stuarts going to do what they had longed to do for generations—join the two countries under Stuart rule?

It was unthinkable. She was riding about the country rousing the people to a realization of their danger because that army must be raised somehow. Surrey could not be expected to drive back a hundred thousand warlike Scots unless he had an army to match them.

But she knew she should rest more. There were times when she threw herself on her bed too exhausted to take off her clothes. In this national danger she forgot even the child because there seemed only one goal: to save England.

As she passed through the various towns and villages she stopped to talk to the people who flocked to see her. She looked magnificent on her horse, her eyes alight with purpose.

"God's hand is over those who fight for their homes," she cried. "And I believe that in valour the English have always surpassed all other nations."

The people cheered her and rallied to her banner, and when she reached Buckingham she had raised a force of sixty thousand men.

"I will lead them to York," she said, "and there join up with Surrey."

When she dismounted she could scarcely stand, so exhausted was she. But she was triumphant because she had achieved that which had seemed impossible and had surely proved herself to be a worthy Regent.

Tired as she was she found time to write to Henry before she slept. She also sent a note to Wolsey—that most able man—who in the midst of all his exertions never failed to find time to write to the Queen, although often Henry was too busy to do so.

She feared that Henry might be too rash on the battlefield; she was worried about his tendency to catch cold; she was having new linen sent for him as she knew how fastidious he was in such matters; and she asked good Master Wolsey, on whom she relied, to look after the King and keep him well, and advise him against over-rashness.

She sealed the letters and sent them off before she dropped into a deep sleep.

In the morning she was unable to leave her bed; her limbs were cramped, and there were frightening pains in her womb.

She felt sick with apprehension but she said to Maria de Salinas: "I rode too long yesterday. My condition is making itself felt."

"Your Grace should abandon the idea of riding North, and stay here for awhile," said Maria anxiously. "You have raised the men. They can join Surrey and his army while you rest a little."

She protested but even as she did so she knew that however much she wished to ride on she would be unable to do so.

She spent that morning in bed after giving orders that the army was to march on without her. And as she lay, racked by periodic pains, she remembered how her mother had told her that she had once sacrificed a child to win a war.

\*       \*       \*

That night her pains had increased and she could no longer feign not to understand the cause. The time had not come and the child was about to be born.

"Oh God," she murmured, "so I have failed again."

Her women were about the bed. They understood.

"Why, Maria," she said, her mouth twisted bitterly, "it has come to be a pattern, has it not. Why . . . why should I be so forsaken?"

"Hush, Your Grace. You need your strength. You are young yet. All your life is before you."

"It is the old cry, Maria. Next time . . . next time. . . . And always this happens to me. Why? What have I done to deserve this?"

"You have exhausted yourself. You should never have left Richmond. It is easy to understand why this has happened. My dearest lady, rest now. Do not take it too hard. There will be another time. . . ."

Katharine cried out in pain, and Maria called to those who were waiting: "The child is about to be born."

\*       \*       \*

It had been a boy. She turned her face into the pillows and wept silently.

She would meet Henry on his return and her arms would be

empty. He would look at her with those blue eyes, cold and angry. So you have failed once more! those eyes would say. And a little more of his affection would be lost.

They brought news to her as she lay in bed mourning for the lost boy.

"Your Grace, the Scots attacked Surrey's men six miles south of Coldstream. They fought there on Flodden Hill and it is victory, Your Grace, with the King of Scots dead and his men slain or in retreat. It is such a victory that warms the heart. They can never rally after this."

She lay still. So her efforts had not proved in vain. She had helped to save England for Henry, and she had lost him his child.

But how could she rejoice whole-heartedly? A Kingdom for the life of a child! Her mother had paid the same price. But how different had been the position of Isabella of Castile from that of Katharine of Aragon!

*       *       *

In the streets they were singing of victory. The battle of Flodden Field would be remembered down the ages, because it would be years before the Scots would be in a position to rise again. And this had been achieved with the King away from home and the Queen in control of the Kingdom.

"Long live Queen Katharine!" cried the people.

And she smiled and thought: How happy I should have been if I could have stood at the windows holding my child in my arms.

The people were singing Skelton's song:

> "Ye were stark mad to make a fray,
>   His Grace being then out of the way.
>   Ye wanted wit, sir, at a word
>   Ye lost your spurs and ye lost your sword. . . ."

And on the other side of the Border they were mournfully bewailing their dead.

But it was victory, thought Katharine, even though the child was lost. Had the Scots triumphed the kingdom might have been lost. As for the child—she was telling herself what so many others had told her: You are young yet. There is still time.

She sat down to write to Henry.

"Sir,

My lord Howard hath sent me a letter open to Your Grace

within one of mine by which you shall see the great victory which our Lord hath sent your subjects in your absence. . . . To my thinking this battle hath been to Your Grace and all your realm, the greatest honour that could be and more than should you win all the crown of France. Thanked be God for it and I am sure Your Grace forgetteth not to do so."

She went on to say that she was sending him the coat of the King of Scotland for his banner. She would have sent the body of the King of Scots himself, but those about her had persuaded her against this. She wished to know how the dead King's body should be buried and would await Henry's instructions on this matter.

"I am praying God to send you home shortly, for without this no joy here can be accomplished. I am preparing now to make my journey to our Lady of Walsingham."

She did not mention the death of the child. As yet she could not bring herself to do so.

## CHAPTER X

## BESSIE BLOUNT

As HENRY RODE with Maximilian to the court of the Duchess of Savoy in the town of Lille he felt completely happy.

The townsfolk had come out to see him and, as he rode among them, they shouted greetings; and when he asked Maximilian what they said, the Emperor answered him: "But this is not a King, this is a God."

His own subjects could not have been more appreciative and, when some of the beautiful women placed garlands about his neck, he took their hands and kissed them and even went so far, when the girls were pretty, to kiss their lips.

He came as a conqueror and he could never resist such homage.

Margaret of Savoy greeted him with pleasure. He thought her fair enough but she seemed old to him, twice widowed, or one might say three times if her first betrothal to the Dauphin of France were counted. Henry found some of the pretty girls of Lille more to his taste.

As for Margaret herself, she seemed mightily taken with that seasoned charmer, Brandon, and Henry, amused, made a point of bringing them together on all occasions.

So this was Charles, he mused, studying the fourteen-year-old boy, who was to be his brother-in-law. He could not help feeling complacent at the sight of him for, when Ferdinand and Maximilian died, this boy could be heir to their dominions which constituted a great part of Europe not to mention those lands overseas which their explorers had discovered and brought under their sway.

This boy would therefore be one of the rivals with whom Henry would juggle for power in Europe. It was an amusing thought. The boy's somewhat bulging eyes suggested that he needed great concentration to understand what was being said; he seemed to find difficulty in closing his mouth; his hair was yellow and lustreless; his skin so pale that he looked unhealthy.

His mother's mad, thought Henry. And, by God, it seems that the boy too could be an idiot.

Charles, however, greeted his grandfather and the King of England in the manner demanded by etiquette and he appeared to be endeavouring to take in everything that was being said.

He's far too serious for a boy of that age, Henry decided. Why, when I was fourteen, I looked eighteen. I was already a champion at the jousts and I could tire out a horse without a hint of fatigue to myself.

So it was comforting to discover that this future ruler was such a puny, slow-witted young fellow.

"My grandson," said Maximilian, "may well inherit the dominions on which the sun never sets. 'Tis so, is it not, Charles?"

Charles was slow in replying; then he said: " 'Tis so, Imperial Highness, but I trust it will be long ere I do so."

"And what's your motto, Grandson? Tell the King of England that."

Again that faint hesitation as though he were trying very hard to repeat a lesson. " 'More Beyond', Grandfather."

"That's right," said Maximilian.

Then he put an arm about the boy and held him against him, laughing.

"He's a good fellow, my grandson. He's a Fleming all through. None of your mincing Spaniard about Charles. And he works hard at his lessons. His tutors are pleased with him."

"We're all pleased with him," said Henry, laughing at his own subtlety.

*          *          *

Those weeks spent at Lille were delightful ones for Henry. He had changed since coming to France. Previously he had been more or less a faithful husband. Often he wished to stray, and in the case of Buckingham's sister had been prepared to do so; but he had always had to fight battles with his conscience. He was possessed of deep sensual appetites and at the same time wished to see himself as a religious and virtuous man. He wanted to be a faithful husband; but he desperately wanted to make love to women other than his wife. The two desires pulled him first in one direction, then in another; and always it seemed that he must come to terms with his conscience before indulging in his pleasures.

He had persuaded himself that when he was at war and far from home, he could not be expected to eschew all sexual relationships. The same fidelity must not be expected of a soldier as of a man who was constantly beside his wife. He reckoned that all the monarchs of Europe would have laughed at what they would call his prudery.

He is young yet, they would say. He believes it is possible to remain faithful to one woman all his life. What a lot he has to learn!

His conscience now told him that it was no great sin, while he was abroad, to make a little light love here and there.

The women expected it.

"By God," he told himself on the first lapse. "I could not so have disappointed her by refusing to grant that which she so clearly desired."

And once the first step was taken, others followed and thus the King of England was finding the life of a soldier a highly interesting and exhilarating one.

With each new love affair he thought less kindly of Katharine. She was his wife; she was the daughter of a King; but, by God, he thought, she knows less of the arts of loving than the veriest tavern wench.

Brandon was his closest companion, and Brandon's reputation, he had always known, was a none too savoury one.

He watched Brandon with the women and followed his example even while he shook his head over the man and was shocked by his conduct.

I am King, he excused himself. The woman will remember all her life, what she and I have shared. It was but a kindness on my part. But Brandon!

Always Henry saw his own acts shrouded in mystic glory. What he did was right because he was the King; it was entirely different if another did the same thing.

He was a little worried about Brandon because his sister Mary was so fond of the fellow, and he was afraid that one day she would be so foolish as to ask to be allowed to marry him. What would she say if she could see that bloodless boy to whom she was betrothed—and side by side with handsome, wicked Brandon!

Brandon was now even daring to carry on a flirtation with the Duchess Margaret; and such was the fascination of the man that Margaret seemed nothing loth.

He had watched the exchange of glances, the hands that touched and lingered.

By God, he thought, that fellow Brandon now has his eyes on the Emperor's daughter.

He thought about the matter until some hot-eyed wench sought him out in the dance and, when they had danced awhile, found a quiet room in which to explore other pleasures.

Each new experience was a revelation.

What did we know—Katharine and I—of making love? he asked himself. Was our ignorance the reason for our lack of children?

It behoved him to learn all he could.

There must be children, so what he did was really for England.

\* \* \*

Charles Brandon was hopeful. Was it possible that he could marry Margaret of Savoy? The prospects were glittering. He could look into a future which might even lead to the Imperial crown, for this crown was never passed to a hereditary heir. The Empire was composed of vassal states and Emperors were elected from a few chosen candidates.

The Emperor's grandson was a feeble boy who, Brandon was sure, would never win the approval of the electors. But Margaret was powerful and rich. Votes were won through bribery and the husband of Margaret would stand a very fair chance.

It was a dizzy prospect, and he brought out all his charm to dazzle the woman. He did not even have to make a great effort for she was attractive and he could feel real affection for her. Poor woman, she had been unfortunate first to have her betrothal to the Dauphin ruthlessly terminated by an ambitious King of France; then her marriage to the heir of Spain was shortlived, her child, which came after her husband's death, still-born; then had followed the marriage with the Duke of Savoy who had soon left her a widow.

Surely she was in need of such solace as one of the most glittering personalities of the English Court—or any Court for that matter—could give her.

Brandon had for some time been thinking a great deal of another Princess who he was sure would be delighted to be his wife. This was none other than the King's own sister, young Mary. Mary was a girl of great determination and too young to hide her feelings; Brandon had been drawn to her, not only because of her youthful charms and the great glory which would surely come to the King's brother-in-law, but because there was an element of danger in the relationship, and he was always attracted by danger.

But Mary was betrothed to the pale-eyed anaemic Charles, and she would never be allowed to choose her husband; but Margaret of Savoy was a widow, and a woman who would make her own decisions.

That was why he was growing more and more excited and

blessing the fate which had brought him to Lille at this time.

He was elated because he believed that the King was not ill-disposed to a marriage between himself and Margaret. Henry knew how his sister felt towards him, and Henry was fond of young Mary. He would hate to deny her what she asked, so it would be helpful to have Brandon out of her path, to let Mary see she had better be contented with her fate, because Brandon, married to the Duchess Margaret, could certainly not be the husband of the Princess of England.

So Brandon made up his mind that he would take an opportunity of asking Margaret to be his wife.

When they walked in the gardens, Margaret allowed herself to be led aside by Brandon, and, as soon as they were out of earshot of their companions, Brandon said to her familiarly: "You spoil that nephew of yours."

Margaret's eyes dwelt fondly on young Charles who was standing awkwardly with his grandfather and Henry, listening earnestly to the conversation.

"He is very dear to me," she answered. "I had no children of my own so it is natural that I should care for my brother's son."

"It is sad that you never had children of your own. But you are young yet. Might that not be remedied?"

Margaret saw where the conversation was leading and caught her breath in amazement. Would this arrogant man really ask the daughter of Maximilian to marry him as unceremoniously as he might—and she was sure did—invite some peasant or serving woman to become his mistress?

She was amazed and fascinated at the project; but she sought to ward it off.

"You have not a high opinion of my young nephew," she said. "I see that your King has not either. You do not know my Charles; he is no fool."

"I am sure that any child who had the good fortune to be under your care would learn something to his advantage."

"Do not be deceived by his quiet manners. There is little he misses. He may seem slow of speech, but that is because he never makes an utterance unless he has clearly worked out what he is going to say. Perhaps it would be well if others followed his example."

"Then there would never be time to say all that has to be said in the world."

"Perhaps it would not be such a tragedy if much of it was left unsaid. Charles' family life has been very tragic. As you know his father died when he was so young, and his mother. . . ."

Charles Brandon nodded. Who had not heard of the mad Queen of Spain who had so mourned her unfaithful husband that she had taken his corpse with her wherever she went until she had been made more or less a prisoner in the castle of Tordesillas where she still remained.

But Brandon did not wish to talk of dull Charles, his philandering father or his mad mother.

He took Margaret's hand in his. Reckless in love had always been his motto, and he was considered a connoisseur.

"Margaret," he began, "you are too fair to remain unmarried."

"Ah, but I have been so unfortunate in that state."

"It does not mean you always will be."

"I have had such experiences that I prefer not to risk more."

"Then someone must try to make you change your mind."

"Who should that be?"

"Who but myself?" he whispered.

She withdrew her hand. She was too strongly aware of the potent masculinity of the man for comfort.

"You cannot be serious."

"Why not? You are a widow who can choose your husband."

She looked at him. He was indeed a handsome man; he had the experience of life which was so missing in his young King.

Margaret asked herself: Could I be happy again with him?

He saw her hesitation and, taking a ring from his finger, slipped it on hers.

She stared at it in astonishment.

They were then joined by Henry, Maximilian and young Charles, and as the young boy stared at the ring on his aunt's hand there was no expression in his pallid eyes, but Margaret, who knew him so much better than everyone else, was aware that he understood the meaning of that little scene which he had witnessed from afar—understood and disapproved.

\*　　　\*　　　\*

By the beginning of October Henry, tired of play, now hoped to win fresh laurels; but the rainy season had started and when he sought out Maximilian and demanded to know when they would be ready to start on the march to Paris, the Emperor shook his head sagely.

"Your Grace does not know our Flanders mud. It would be impossible to plan an offensive when we have that to contend with."

"When then?" Henry wanted to know.

"Next Spring . . . next summer."

"And what of all the troops and equipment I have here?"

"That good fellow Wolsey will take charge of all that. You can rely on him to get them safely back to England for you."

Henry hesitated. He remembered the disaster which Dorset had suffered when he had stayed a winter in Spain.

He saw now that this was the only course for him to take. He was disappointed, for he had hoped to return to England, conqueror of France. All he had to show was the capture of two French towns and certain prisoners, whom he had sent home to Katharine, and who were causing her some anxiety because she had to feed them and treat them as the noblemen they were, because as the war with Scotland had proved costly and the war with France even more so, there was little to spare for the needs of noble prisoners.

Katharine had the victory of Flodden Field to set side by side with the conquest of Thérouanne and Tournai, and Henry felt piqued because he had to admit that she had scored the greater victory.

He felt angry towards her, particularly as he had now heard of the loss of the child. "Lost, that your kingdom might be held, Henry." Grudgingly he agreed that all she had done had been necessary. But, he had said to himself, it seemed that God's hand was against them; and since he had known many other women in France his satisfaction with Katharine had diminished.

Oh, it was time he went home; and he could go as a conqueror. The people of England would be eager to welcome him back.

He sent for Brandon.

"How goes the courtship?" he asked slyly.

Brandon shook his head. "I need time."

"And that is something you cannot have. We are returning to England."

Brandon was downcast. "Have no fear," said Henry, "we shall return and then ere long I doubt not you'll have swept the Duchess Margaret into marriage."

"She has returned my ring and asked for the one I took from her," said Brandon.

"Is that so? The lady is coy."

"One day she seems willing enough, and the next she holds back. She talks of previous marriages and says that she is afraid she is doomed to be unfortunate in that state. Then she talks of her duty to her nephew. 'Tis true that young fellow looks as though he needs a keeper."

Henry laughed. "I rejoice every time I look at him," he said. "Max can't last for ever. Nor can Ferdinand . . . and then . . . it will not be difficult to dupe that little fellow, what think you? And who will take over from old Louis . . . for he too must be near his death-bed? Francis of Angoulême." Henry's eyes narrowed. "I hear he is a young braggart . . . but that he excels in pastimes."

"A pale shadow of Your Grace."

Henry's mouth was prim suddenly. "That fellow is a lecher. His affairs with women are already talked of . . . and he little more than a boy! Brandon, have you thought that one day, and that day not far distant, there will be three men standing astride Europe . . . three great rivals . . . the heads of the three great powers? There will be Francis, myself and that young idiot Charles." Henry laughed. "Why, when I think of those two . . . and myself . . . I have great reason for rejoicing. God will not favour a lecher, will He, against a virtuous man? And what hope has young Charles, whose mother is mad and who seems to have been born with half his wits? Oh, Brandon, I see glorious days ahead of me and I thank God for this sojourn in Europe where my eyes have been opened to all that, with His help, may come to me."

"Your Grace stands on the threshold of a brilliant future."

Henry put his arm about Brandon's shoulder. "In which my friends shall join," he said. "Why, Charles, I might even win for you the hand of Margaret, eh, in spite of the fact that she returns your ring and demands hers back; in spite of the snivelling little nephew who doubtless cries to his aunt that her duty lies with him."

The two men smiled, drawn together by a joint ambition.

Henry was placated. He sent for Wolsey and told him to make arrangements to return to England.

\*     \*     \*

Katharine was deep in preparations for the return of the King.

Surely, she thought, he cannot but be pleased with me. It is true I have lost the child but, much as he longs for an heir, he must be satisfied with what I have done.

She had Margaret, widow of dead James IV, remain Regent of Scotland; after all, was she not the King's sister? It would have been too costly to have taken possession of the Scottish crown. She trusted Henry would approve of what she had done.

She had recovered from the last miscarriage, and felt well in body if a little uneasy in mind.

Maria de Salinas, now married to Lord Willoughby, was not at this time separated from her, and she talked to her about the masque she was planning to celebrate the King's return.

"It must be colourful," said Katharine. "You know how the King loves colour. Let there be dancing, and we will have the King's own music played. That will delight him."

While they sat thus Maria ventured: "Your Grace, Francesca de Carceres, realizing that there is no hope of regaining her place in your household, now has hopes of joining that of the Duchess of Savoy. She believes that if Your Grace would speak a word of recommendation to the Duchess on her behalf she would have her place."

Katharine was thoughtful. It would be pleasant to be rid of Francesca's disturbing proximity. While she was in England she would continue to haunt the ante-chambers, hoping for an interview with the Queen. Any mention of the woman brought back unpleasant memories . . . either of the old days when she had suffered such humiliation, or of that other unfortunate affair of Buckingham's sister.

Francesca was an intriguer. Was it fair to send her to the Court of the Duchess with a recommendation?

It was not just, she was sure of it.

No, much as she longed to be rid of Francesca she was not going to send her with a recommendation to someone else.

"No," said Katharine, "she is too perilous a woman. I shall not give her the recommendation she requires. There is only one thing to be done for Francesca; that is that she should be sent back to her own country. When Thomas Wolsey returns I will put this matter before him, and I doubt not he will find some means of having her sent back to Spain."

"It is where she longed to go in the past," said Maria. "Poor Francesca! I remember how she used to sigh for Spain! And now . . . when she does not want to return, she will go back."

"My dear Maria, she is an adventuress. She wanted to go to Spain because she thought it had more to offer her than England. Remember how she wanted to come to England, when I left Spain, because she thought England would have greater opportunities for her. Such as Francesca deserve their fate. Waste no sorrow on her. You have achieved happiness, my dear

Maria, with your Willoughby, because you did not seek to ride over others to reach it. So be happy."

"I shall be so," said Maria, "as long as I know that Your Grace is too."

The two women smiled at each other then. Their gaiety was a little forced. Each was thinking of the King—on whom Katharine's happiness depended. What would happen on his return?

\* \* \*

Henry came riding to Richmond.

As soon as he had disembarked, he had called for a horse, declaring that he was not going to wait for a ceremonial cavalcade.

"This is a happy moment," he cried. "Once more I set foot on English soil. But I cannot be completely happy until I am with my wife. So a horse . . . and to Richmond where I know she eagerly awaits me."

He had been unfaithful a score of times in Flanders but that made him feel more kindly towards Katharine. Those affairs had meant nothing to him, he assured himself. They were not to be given a moment's thought. It was Katharine, his Queen, whom he loved. There was no other woman who was of any importance to him.

Such peccadilloes were to be set at naught, merely to be mentioned at confession and dismissed with a Hail Mary and a Paternoster.

Katharine heard the commotion below.

"The King is here."

"But so soon!" Her hands were trembling, as she put them to her headdress. Her knees felt as though they were giving way beneath her.

"Oh Maria, how do I look?"

"Beautiful, Your Grace."

"Ah . . . you say that!"

"In my eyes Your Grace is beautiful."

"That is because you love me, Maria."

And how shall I look to him? she wondered. Will he, like Maria, look at me with the eyes of love?

She went down to greet him. He had leaped from his steaming horse. How dramatic he was in all he did.

His face was as smooth as a boy's, flushed with exercise, his blue eyes beaming with good will. Thank God for that.

"Kate! Why Kate, have you forgotten who I am?"

She heard his laughter at the incongruity of such a suggestion, saw the glittering arms held out. No ceremonial occasion this. Now he was the good husband, returning home, longing for a sight of his wife.

He had swung her up in his arms before those who had come riding ahead of the cavalcade, before those who had hastened from the Palace to greet him.

Two audible kisses. "By God, it does my heart good to see you!"

"Henry . . . oh my Henry . . . but you look so wonderful!"

"A successful campaign, Kate. I do not return with my tail between my legs like some licked cur, eh! I come as conqueror. By my faith, Kate, this time next year you'll be with me in Paris."

"The news was so good."

"Ay, the best."

He had his arm round her. "Come," he said, "let's get within walls. Let's drink to conquest, Kate. And later you and I will talk together . . . alone, eh . . . of all that has been happening there and here."

His arm about her they went into the great hall where the feast was waiting.

He ate while he talked—mainly of those great victories, Thérouanne and Tournai—and from his talk it would appear that he and he alone had captured them. Maximilian had been there, yes . . . but in a minor role. Had he not placed himself under Henry's banner; had he not received pay for his services?

"And you looked after our kingdom well in our absence, Kate. You and Surrey together with the help of all those good men and true I left behind me. So Jemmy the Scot is no more. I wonder how Margaret likes being without a husband. 'Tis a sad thing, Kate, to be without a husband. You missed me?"

"Very much, Henry."

"And we lost the child. A boy too. Alas, my Kate. But you lost him in a good cause. I have heard how you worked for England . . . when you should have been resting. . . ." His eyes were slightly glazed; he was remembering past experiences in Flanders. That sly court Madam, lady to the Duchess; that kitchen girl. By God, he thought, I have profited more than my Kate realizes by my Flanders campaign.

"Well, Kate, it grieves me. But we are young yet. . . ."

She thought: He has learned soldiers' ways in Flanders.

His eyes were warm, his hands straying to her thigh. But she was not unhappy. She had been afraid that he would blame her for the loss of the child as he had on other occasions.

He was drinking freely; he had eaten well.

"Come," he said, " 'twas a long ride to Richmond. 'Tis bed for us, Kate."

His eyes were warm; so that all knew that it was not to rest he was taking her.

She did not object; she was filled with optimism.

There would be another time, and then it should not fail.

\* \* \*

The Court was gay that Christmas. There was so much to celebrate. Henry was looking forward to the next year's campaign. His sister Margaret was looking after his interests in Scotland; and at the Palace of Richmond masques, balls and banquets were arranged for Henry's delight.

One day Lord Mountjoy, when talking to the Queen, mentioned a relative of his whose family were eager that she should have a place at Court.

William Blount, Lord Mountjoy, was one of Katharine's greatest friends. He was her chamberlain and one of the few seriously inclined men of the Court; Katharine had a great regard for him and had tried to influence the King in favour of this man. Mountjoy's friends were the learned men on the fringe of the Court—men such as Colet, Linacre, Thomas More.

So far the King had shown little interest in the more serious-minded of his subjects. His greatest friends were those men who danced well or excelled at the joust, men such as William Compton, Francis Bryan, Nicholas Carew, Charles Brandon.

But it sometimes seemed to Katharine that Henry grew up under her eyes. He had remained a boy rather long, but she was convinced that eventually the man would emerge and then he would take an interest in the scholars of his Court.

"I'm thinking of this relative of mine," Mountjoy was saying. "She is fifteen or sixteen . . . a comely child, and her parents would like to see her enjoy a place in Your Grace's household."

"You must bring her to me," said Katharine. "I doubt not we shall find room for her here."

So the next day Mountjoy brought little Bessie Blount with him to the Queen's presence.

The girl curtseyed, and blushed at Katharine's scrutiny, keeping her eyes modestly downcast. A pretty creature, thought

Katharine, and one who, if she could dance, would fit well into the Christmas masque.

"Have you learned the Court dances?" asked Katharine.

"Yes, Your Grace."

"And you wish to serve in my household. Well, I think that can be managed."

"Thank you, Your Grace."

"Can you play a musical instrument or sing?"

"I play the lute, Your Grace, and sing a little."

"Then pray let me hear you."

Bessie Blount took the instrument which one of Katharine's women offered her and, seating herself on a stool, began to pick out notes on the lute and sing as she did so.

The song she sang was the King's own song:

> "Pastance with good company
> I love, and shall until I die.
> Grudge who will, but none deny;
> So God be pleased, this life will I
> For my pastance
> Hunt, sing and dance."

And as she sat there singing, her reddish gold hair falling childishly about her shoulders, the door was burst open and the King came in.

He heard the words of the song and the music; he saw the child who sang them; and the words he was about to utter died on his lips. He stood very still, and those who were with him, realizing the command for silence in his attitude, stood very still behind him.

When the song came to an end, the King strode forward.

"Bravo!" he shouted. " 'Twas well done. And who is our performer?"

Bessie had risen to her feet and the flush in her cheeks matched her hair.

She sank to her knees, her eyes downcast, her long golden lashes, a shade or two darker than her hair, shielding her large violet-coloured eyes.

"Ha!" cried Henry. "You should not feel shame, my child. 'Twas worthy of praise." He turned to the company. "Was it not?"

There was a chorus of assent from those who stood with the King, and Katharine said: "This is little Bessie Blount, Your Grace, Mountjoy's relation. She is to have a place in my household."

"I am right glad to hear it," said Henry. "An she sings like that she will be an asset to your court, Kate."

"I thought so."

Henry went to the girl and took her chin in his hands. She lifted her awestruck eyes to his face.

"There is one thing we must ask of you, Mistress Bessie, if you belong to our Court. Do you know what it is?"

"No, Your Grace."

"Then we'll tell you, Bessie. 'Tis not to be afraid of us. We like our subjects who play our music and sing it well, as you do. You've nothing to fear from us, Bessie. Remember it."

"Yes, Your Grace."

He gave her a little push and turned to the Queen.

Mountjoy signed to the trembling girl that she should disappear. She went out quickly and with relief, while Henry began to talk to the Queen about some item of the pageantry. But he was not really thinking of that; he could not dismiss the picture of that pretty child sitting on the stool, so sweetly singing his own music.

\* \* \*

Never had the King seemed so full of vigour as he did that Christmas. That year the pageants were of the gayest, the banquets more lavish than ever before. Katharine hid her weariness of the continual round of pleasure which lasted far into the night, for it seemed that the King never tired. He would hunt through the day, or perhaps joust in the tiltyard, a splendid figure in his glittering armour inlaid with gold which seemed not to hamper him at all. His laughter would ring out at the splintering of lances as one by one his opponents fell before him.

Often he tilted in what was meant to be a disguise. He would be a strange knight from Germany, from Flanders, from Savoy, even from Turkey. The massive form would enter the tiltyard in a hushed silence, would challenge the champion, and, when he had beaten him would lift his visor; then the people would go wild with joy to recognize the well-known features, the crown of golden hair.

Katharine never failed to display a surprise which she was far from feeling. He would come to her, kiss her hand and tell her that his exploits were all in her honour. At which she would kiss him in return, thank him for the pastance, and then chide him a little for risking his life and causing her anxiety.

Henry enjoyed every moment. There was nothing he desired more than to be the popular, dazzling, god-like King of England.

It seemed, thought Katharine, that he had become a boy again. But there was a difference.

On occasions he would sit pensively staring before him; the music he played on his lute was plaintive. He was kinder, more gentle than he had ever been to Katharine and seemed to take great pains to please her.

Henry was changing subtly because he was falling in love.

She was a slip of a girl of sixteen with hair of that red gold colour not unlike his own; but shy and innocent as she was, she could not remain long in ignorance of his interest and its significance. In the dances which were arranged for the Queen's pleasure she would often find herself as his partner; their hands would touch and a slow smile would illumine the royal features. Bessie smiled shyly, blushing; and the sight of her, so young, so different from the brazen members of his Court, increased the King's ardour.

He watched her at the banqueting table, at the masques, in the Queen's apartments, but he rarely spoke to her.

He was surprised at his feelings. Previously he had believed that, if he desired, it was for him to beckon and the girl to come willingly. It was different with Bessie. She was so young, so innocent; and she aroused such tender feeling within him.

He even began to question himself. Should I? It would be so easy . . . like plucking a tender blossom. Yet she was ready for the plucking. But she was fragile and strangely enough he would not be happy if he hurt her.

Perhaps he should make a good match for her and send her away from Court. It was astonishing that he, who desired her so ardently, should think of such a thing; but it was his conscience which suggested this to him, and it was significant that it should never have worried him so insistently as it did over this matter of Elizabeth Blount.

During the masque they danced together.

He was dressed in white brocade of the Turkish fashion and he wore a mask over his face, but his stature always betrayed him, and everyone in the ballroom paid great deference to the unknown Turkish nobleman.

The Queen was seated on a dais with some of her women about her, splendidly clad in cloth of silver with many coloured jewels glittering about her person. She was easily tired, although she did not admit this: so many miscarriages were beginning to take their toll of her health. Often after supper she would make an excuse to retire and in her apartments her women would undress her quickly so that she might sink into an exhausted sleep. She was aware that meanwhile Henry capered and danced in the ballroom. It was different for him. He had not suffered as she had from their attempts to get children; she was nearly thirty; he was in his early twenties, and she was beginning to be uncomfortably aware of the difference in their ages.

Now she watched him leaping, cavorting among the dancers. Did he never tire? He must always remind them of his superiority. She imagined the scene at the unmasking; the cries of surprise when it was seen who the Turkish nobleman really was— as if everyone in the ballroom was not aware of this. She herself would have to feign the greatest surprise of all, for he would surely come to her and tell her that it was all in her honour.

How much more acceptable would a little peace be to me, she thought.

Henry wound his way among the dancers because he knew that she was there and he must find her. No mask could hide her from him. She was as delicate as a flower and his heart beat fast to think of her.

He found and drew her towards an embrasure. Here they could feel themselves cut off from the dancers; here Katharine could not see them from her dais.

"Mistress Bessie," he began.

She started to tremble.

His big hand rested on her shoulder then strayed down her back.

"Your Grace . . ." she murmured.

"So you have seen through the mask, Bessie."

"Anyone must know Your Grace."

"You have penetrating eyes. Can it be because you have such regard for your King that you know him, however he tries to hide himself?"

"All must know Your Grace. There is none like you."

"Ah . . . Bessie."

He seized her hungrily and held her against him for a few seconds.

He put his face close to her ear and she felt his hot breath on her neck. "You know of my feelings for you, Bessie. Tell me, what are yours for me?"

"Oh . . . Sire!" There was no need for more; that was enough.

His pulse was racing; his desire shone in the intense blue visible through the slits of the mask. He had abandoned all

N

thought of restraint. Only this evening he had been thinking of a good match for her. A good match there should be, but this was for afterwards.

"I have sought to restrain my ardour," he said, "but it is too strong for me, Bessie."

She waited for him to go on, her lips slightly parted so that she appeared breathless; and watching her, his desire was an agony which demanded immediate satisfaction.

But they were here in the ballroom, barely hidden from the rest of the company.

Tonight? he thought. But how could he leave the ball? Oh, the restraint set upon a King! All his actions watched and commented upon; too many people were too interested in what he did.

There must be no scandal, for Bessie's sake as well as his own.

He made a quick decision. For the sake of propriety his desire must wait . . . for tonight.

"Listen, Bessie," he said. "Tomorrow I shall hunt, and you must join the hunt. You will stay close beside me and we will give them the slip. You understand?"

"Yes, Sire."

He let his hand caress her body for a few seconds, but the emotions this aroused startled him, so he gave her a little push and murmured: "Back to the dance, girl." And she left him to stand there in the embrasure, trying to quell the rising excitement, trying to steel himself to patience.

\*  \*  \*

He rode with Compton and Francis Bryan beside him, the rest falling in behind. He had caught a glimpse of her among the party. She rode well, which was pleasing.

He said to Compton: "We must not forget this day that we have ladies with us. The hunt must not be too fierce."

"Nay," answered Compton, "since Your Grace is so considerate of the ladies, so must we all be."

It was impossible to keep secrets from Compton. He was one of those wise men who seemed to read the King's secrets before Henry had fully made up his mind to share them. Bryan was such another. His friends had often hinted that the King should live less virtuously. "For," Compton had said, "if Your Grace sinned a little the rest of us would feel happier about our own sins."

He could rely on their help and, as they already guessed his feelings towards Bessie and were waiting for the culmination of that little affair, Henry decided that he would use their help.

"When I give the sign," he said, "I wish you to turn aside from the rest of the party with me . . . keep about me to cover my retreat."

Compton nodded.

"And see that Mistress Blount is of our party."

Compton winked at Bryan knowing Henry could not see the signal. There was scarcely a man in the party who would not understand. But Henry always believed that those about him only saw that which he wished them to see.

"Your Grace," said Compton, "I know of an arbour in the woods which makes an excellent shelter."

"He has dallied there himself," put in Bryan.

"Well, Sire, it is an inviting arbour. It calls out to be of use."

"I would like to see this arbour and perhaps show it to Mistress Blount."

"Your humble servants will stand guard at a goodly distance," said Compton. "Near enough though to prevent any from disturbing Your Grace and the lady."

Henry nodded. Alas, he thought, that love must be indulged in thus shamefully. If I were but a shepherd, he thought, and she a village maid!

The thought was entrancing. To be a shepherd for an hour's dalliance one afternoon! And such was his nature—he who was more jealous of his rank and dignity than any man—that when he sighed to be a shepherd he really believed that it was his desire.

He saw her—his village maiden—among the women. Gracefully she sat her horse; and her eyes were expectant. It is a great honour I do her, Henry assured himself. And I'll make a goodly match for her. It shall be a complaisant husband who will be happy to do this service for his King.

It was easily arranged under the skiful guidance of Compton and Bryan; and even the sun shone its wintry light on the arbour; and the lovers did not feel the chill in the air. They were warmed by the hunt—not only of the deer but for the quenching of their desire.

Henry took her roughly into his arms; kissed her fiercely; then expertly—for he had learned of these matters in Flanders— he took her virginity. She wept a little, in fear and joy. She was overcome with the wonder that this great King should look her way. Her modesty enchanted him; he knew too that he would teach her passion and was amazed by the new tenderness she discovered in his nature.

He wanted to dally in the arbour; but, he said, even a King cannot always do as he wishes.

He kissed his Bessie. He would find means of coming to her apartments that night, he promised. It would not be easy, but it must be done. He would love her for ever; he would cherish her. She had nothing to fear, for her destiny was the King's concern and she would find him her great provider.

"Nothing to fear, my Bessie," he said running his lips along the lobe of her ear. "I am here . . . I your King . . . to love you for evermore."

*          *          *

During the weeks that followed Henry was a blissful boy. There were many meetings in the arbour; and scarcely anyone at Court did not know of the King's love affair with Elizabeth Blount, except Katharine. Everyone contrived to keep the matter from her, for as Maria de Salinas, now Lady Willoughby, said on her visits to Court, it would only distress the Queen, and what could she do about it?

So Katharine enjoyed the company of a gentler Henry during those weeks; and she told herself that his thoughtfulness towards her meant that he was growing up; he had come back from Flanders no longer the careless boy; he had learned consideration.

He was a gentler lover; and he frequently said: "Why, Kate, you're looking tired. Rest well tonight. I shall not disturb you."

He even seemed to have forgotten that desperate need to get a child. She was glad of the rest. The last miscarriage together with all the efforts she had put into the Scottish conflict had exhausted her more than anything that had gone before.

One day the King seemed in a rare quiet mood, and she noticed that his eyes were over-bright and his cheeks more flushed than usual.

She was sewing with her ladies when he came to her and sat down heavily beside her. The ladies rose, and curtseyed, but he waved his hand at them, and they stood where they were by their chairs. He did not give them another glance, which was strange because there were some very pretty girls among them, and Katharine remembered how in the past he had been unable to prevent his gaze straying towards some particular specimen of beauty.

"This is a charming picture you're working," he said, indicating the tapestry, but Katharine did not believe he saw it.

He said after a slight pause: "Sir Gilbert Taillebois is asking for the hand of one of your girls, Kate. He seems a good fellow, and the Mountjoys, I believe, are eager enough for the match."

"You must mean Elizabeth Blount," said Katharine.

"Ah yes . . ." Henry shifted in his seat. "That's the girl's name."

"Your Grace does not remember her?" said Katharine innocently. "I recall the occasion when Mountjoy brought her to me and you came upon us. She was singing one of your songs."

"Yes, yes; a pretty voice."

"She is a charming, modest girl," said Katharine, "and if it is your will that she should make the match with Taillebois, I am sure we shall all be delighted. She is after all approaching a marriageable age, and I think it pleasant when girls marry young."

"Then so be it," said Henry.

Katharine looked at him anxiously. "Your Grace feels well?"

Henry put his hand to his brow. "A strange thing . . . Kate, when I rose this morning I was a little dizzy. A feeling I never remember before."

Katharine rose quickly and laid a hand on his forehead.

"Henry," she cried shrilly, "you have a fever."

He did not protest but continued to sit slumped heavily on his chair.

"Go to the King's apartments at once," Katharine commanded the women who were still standing by their chairs. "Tell any of the gentlemen of the King's bedchamber . . . any servant you can find, to come here at once. The King must go to his bed and the physicians be called."

\*     \*     \*

The news spread through the Palace. "The King is sick of a fever."

The physicians were about his bedside, and they were grave. It seemed incredible that this healthy, vital young King of theirs could be so sick. None knew the cause of his illness, except that he was undoubtedly suffering from high fever. Some said it was smallpox; others that it was another kind of pox which was prevalent in Europe.

Katharine remained in his bedchamber and was at his side through the day and night; she refused to leave it even when her women told her that she would be ill if she did not do so.

But she would not listen. It must be she who changed the cold compresses which she placed at regular intervals on his burning forehead; it was she who must be there to answer his rambling questions.

It was clear that his mind wandered. He did not seem to be sure whether he was at the court of Lille or in some arbour in a forest—presumably, thought Katharine, some place he had seen when he was on the Continent. Patiently she sat beside his bed and soothed him, superintending his food, making special healthgiving potions, conferring with his physicians and keeping everyone else from the sickroom; and in less than a week his magnificent health triumphed over the sickness and Henry was able to sit up and take note of what was going on.

"Why, Kate," he said, "you're a good wife to me. It was not such an unhappy day, was it, when I said I'd marry the King of Spain's daughter, in spite of the fact that they were all urging me not to."

That was her reward. But as she sat beside his bed smiling she did not know that he was thinking how old and pale she looked, how wan, how plain. That was because he was comparing her with one other, whom he dared not ask to be brought to his sick room, but who was nevertheless continually in his thoughts.

He had come near death, he believed, and he was a little alarmed to contemplate that he might have died at a time when he was actually in the midst of an illicit love affair, committing what the priests would tell him was a cardinal sin.

But was it so? He began to wrestle with his conscience, a pastime which, since the affair with Bessie, he had indulged in with greater frequency.

But, he mused, she was so enamoured of me, that little Bessie. She would have broken her little heart if I had not loved her. It was for Bessie's sake, he assured himself. And I found her a husband.

Taillebois would be a good match for her, and she would have reason to be grateful to her King. As for himself, how far had he wronged his wife? She was ageing fast. There were dark shadows under her eyes; her once firm cheeks and neck were sagging; all the red seemed to have gone out of her hair and it was growing lustreless and mouse-coloured. She needed rest; and while he had Bessie abed Katharine could rest, could she not? She was grateful for the respite. Let her recover her health before they tried for more children.

So he had done no harm. How could he when he had made Bessie happy and Katharine happy? It was only himself who must fight this persistent conscience of his. He was the one who suffered.

He said: "My good Kate, you have nursed me well. 'Tis something I shall not forget. Now tell me. Before I went to bed with this sickness I had given my consent to Taillebois' marriage with that girl of yours. What's done about it?"

Katherine looked shocked. "There could be no marriage while Your Grace lay so ill."

"But I'm well again. I'll not have my subjects speaking of me as though I'm about to be laid in my coffin. Tell them to go on with that marriage. Tell them it is their sovereign's wish."

"You must not bother about weddings, Henry. You have to think about yourself."

He took her hand and fondled it. "I am a King, Kate, and a King's first thoughts must be for his subjects."

She kissed him tenderly, and in that moment of happiness she seemed to regain much of her lost youth.

He could not ask for Bessie to be brought to him, so he determined to be out of his sickroom within a day or so. He could, however, receive his old friends; and Bryan, Compton, Brandon and Carew all visited the sickroom and there were soon sounds of laughter coming from it.

Henry had become interested in illness for the first time in his life, and wanted to try his hand at making potions. During his sickness he had been tormented by certain ulcers which appeared on various parts of his body and that one which was on his leg had not healed like the others. This was treated with liniments and pastes, and he took a great interest in the preparation of these; something which, Katharine knew, he would have laughed to scorn a few months previously.

Compton disclosed a similar ulcer of his own and this made an even greater bond between those two. One day Katharine came into the sickroom to find Compton with his bare leg stretched out on the King's bed while Henry compared his friend's affliction with his own.

Under the treatment Henry's ulcer began to heal and he, full of enthusiasm, determined to heal Compton's. To take his mind from Bessie, he made ointments with Compton, into which he believed that if he added ground pearls he could construct a cure. He was determined to wait until he was strong before he returned to public life, because at the balls, and the masque, and banquets he must be as he had ever been; the King must leap higher in the dance; he must never tire.

So passed those days of recuperation, and during them Henry continued to think longingly of his Bessie who had become Lady Taillebois.

\*         \*         \*

Spring had come and, now that the King was well again, he had two great desires: to be with Bessie and to prepare for the war against France.

He had sent Charles Brandon over to Flanders—after bestowing upon him the title of Duke of Suffolk—for two purposes: to continue with his wooing of Margaret of Savoy and to make plans for the arrival of the army in spring or early summer.

Henry was relieved to see Charles out of the way, for the infatuation of young Mary for that man was beginning to alarm him. Mary must be prepared to accept that other Charles, Maximilian's and Ferdinand's grandson, and when Henry thought of that pale-faced youth with the prominent eyes and the seemingly sluggish brain, he shuddered for his bright and beautiful sister. But he would have to remind her that royal marriages were a matter of policy. I married my wife because she was the daughter of Spain, he often reminded himself, and he relished the thought because it was another excuse for infidelity. How could Kings be expected to be faithful when they married, not for love, but for state policy? He had already forgotten that it was he himself who had determined to marry Katharine, and that he had done so in spite of opposition.

It was a sad augury—but as yet Katharine continued in ignorance.

The days were full of pleasure and Henry's kindness and gentleness towards his Queen continued.

Often he and Bessie met, and their favourite meeting place was a hunting lodge which Henry called Jericho. This was in Essex near New Hall Manor which belonged to the Ormonde family. Henry stayed occasionally at New Hall, which pleased him because of its proximity to Jericho. Thomas Boleyn, who was eager for the King's favour, was the son of one of the Earl of Ormonde's daughters, and the ambitious Boleyn was always ready to make arrangements for the royal visit and to ensure secrecy for the King's visits to Jericho with Lady Taillebois.

So the days passed pleasantly and, when Katharine was able to tell Henry that she was once more pregnant, he declared that he was full of joy and there must be a masque to celebrate this happy news.

## CHAPTER XI

## THE FRENCH MARRIAGE

IN THE BED, about which the elaborate curtains had been drawn, Thomas Wolsey felt shut away from the world with Mistress Wynter.

He talked to her more freely than he could to any other person because he trusted her completely. It was his pride—that integral part of his nature which in its way was responsible for his rise to power and against which he knew he must continually be on guard, because as it sent him soaring, so could it send him crashing to disaster—which made these sessions so sweet to him. He must hide his brilliance from the rest of the world, how he was always a step in front of the rest, how he always knew what could happen and must wait . . . patiently, ready to leap into the right position at that half second before others saw the leap, so that it appeared that he had always stood firmly there.

Only his Lark knew how clever he was, only to her could he be frank.

They were both sad because his visits to the little house were less frequent now.

"Matters of state, sweetheart," he would murmur into that pretty ear; and she would sigh and cling to him and, even while she listened to the tales of his genius, she still longed for him to be an ordinary man, like the merchants who were her neighbours.

They had eaten and drunk well. The table in this house was more lavish than it had been a year before; the garments his wife and children wore, more splendid. He had talked to his children, listened to an account of their progress; had dismissed them; and had brought Mistress Wynter to this bedchamber where they had made love.

Now was the time for talk; so he lay relaxed and spoke of all that was in his mind.

"But when you are Pope, Thomas, how shall I be able to see you then?"

"Why, 'twill be easier then, my love," he told her. "A Pope is all-powerful. He does not have to fight his petty enemies as a Bishop does. Roderigo Borgia, who was Pope Alexander the

Sixth, had his mistress living near the Vatican; he had his children living with him and none dared tell him this should not be done . . . except those who lived far away. The power of the Pope is as great as that of the King. Have no fear. When I am Pope our way will be made easier."

"Then Thomas, how I wish you were Pope!"

"You go too fast. There are a great many steps, I can tell you, from tutor to King's almoner, from King's almoner to . . . My love, I have a piece of news for you. I have heard that I am to receive the Cardinal's hat from Rome."

"Thomas! Now you will be known as Cardinal Wolsey."

She heard the ecstasy in his voice. "The hat!" he whispered. "When it is brought to me, I shall receive it with great ceremony so all may know that at last we have an English Cardinal; and that is good for England. Cardinal Wolsey! There is only one more step to be taken, my love. At the next conclave . . . why should not an English Pope be elected to wear the Papal Crown?"

"You will do it, Thomas. Have you not done everything that you have set out to do?"

"Not quite all. If that were so I should have my family with me."

"And you a churchman, Thomas! How could that be?"

"I would do it. Doubt it not."

She did not doubt it.

"You are different from all other men," she said, "and I marvel that the whole world does not know it."

"They will. Now I will tell you of the new house I have acquired."

"A new house! For us, Thomas?"

"No," he said sadly. "It is for myself. There I shall entertain the King; but perhaps one day it will be your home . . . yours and the children's."

"Tell me of the house, Thomas."

" 'Tis on the banks of the Thames, well past Richmond. The Manor of Hampton. It is a pleasant place and belongs to the Knights of St. John of Jerusalem. I have bought the lease of this mansion and now I intend to make it my very own, for as it stands it suits me not. There I shall build a palace and it shall be a great palace, my sweetheart . . . a palace to compare with the palaces of Kings, that all the world shall know that if I wish to have a palace, I have the means to build me one."

"It will be some time before this palace is built as you wish it."

"Nay. I shall have them working well for me, sweetheart.

I am setting the most prominent members of the Freemasons to work for me, and who now would care to displease Cardinal Wolsey? I have decided that there shall be five courts about which the apartments will be built. I tell you, they will be fit for a King."

"Does the King know of this, Thomas? I mean, what will he say if a subject builds a palace to match his own?"

"He knows and shows great interest. I am well acquainted with our King, sweetheart. He likes not the display of wealth of certain noblemen who have the temerity to fancy themselves more royal than the Tudors, but with one whom he believes he has brought out of obscurity, it is a different matter. In Hampton Court Palace, my love, he will see a reflection of his own power. So I talk to him of the palace and he is of the opinion that I take his advice. But it is he, you know, who always takes mine."

Wolsey began to laugh, but Mistress Wynter trembled slightly and when he asked what ailed her, she said: "You have come so high, Thomas, perilously high."

"And you think—the higher the rise the greater the fall? Have no fear, my Lark, I am sure-footed enough to remain perilously high."

"I was fearing that you might be too high to remember us . . . myself and the children."

"Never. You shall see what I will do for our son . . . for you all. Remember, my prosperity is yours."

"And soon you will be leaving England again for France."

Wolsey was thoughtful. "I am not sure of that."

"But the King is going to war this year as last. The whole country talks of it."

"There are certain matters which set me wondering, my dear. When we were in Lille we made a treaty with Maximilian and Ferdinand to attack the French. We won two towns which were of the utmost importance to Maximilian, and we paid him thousands of crowns to work with us. It seemed to me at the time that Maximilian came very well out of that campaign—as Ferdinand did out of the previous one. What was in it for England? But the King was pleased, so it was necessary for his servant to be pleased. One thing I have learned: a man must never go against his King. So, because Henry is pleased, so must I seem to be. But I am uncertain. I believe that Henry will soon discover that Maximilian and Ferdinand are not the friends he believes them to be."

"Then there would be no war in France?"

"It might well be so. My dear one, imagine these two wily old men. They have great experience of statesmanship. Remember that Maximilian's son Philip, and Ferdinand's daughter, mad Juana, were married. Their sons are Charles and young Ferdinand. They have their eyes on Italy, not on France. They want Italy for young Ferdinand because Charles will have the whole of Spain and possibly the Austrian Empire, which includes the Netherlands. The King of France also has his eyes on Italy. 'Tis my belief that the English invasion of France is being planned by Ferdinand and Maximilian to put fear into Louis' heart, and that if they can make favourable terms with him regarding Italy they will be ready to leave their English allies to fight France alone. It was significant that after the capture of Thérouanne and Tournai Maximilian was very eager that hostilities should cease. He knew further battles would mean bitter losses and he did not wish to impoverish himself, but to be in a strong position to bargain with the French."

"And our King does not know this?"

"As yet he is a happy boy; he thinks with the mind of a boy. He trusts others because he is frank himself. He has had warning of Ferdinand's perfidy; yet he is prepared to trust him as ever."

"It is because Ferdinand is his father-in-law, perhaps."

"The Queen is a clever woman, I believe, but she is fast losing her influence. The King is enamoured of Lady Taillebois but Katharine does not know this. Lady Taillebois does not interest herself in politics. But she might not please the King for ever, and if there were a woman who made great demands on the King and sought to influence him . . . who knows what would happen."

"Thomas, I am alarmed by all this. It seems so dangerous."

"You have nothing to fear, my love. I will always protect you and our children."

"But Thomas, what if . . . ?"

She did not say it. It seemed sacrilege even to think of it. Thomas would always maintain his place. There was no man in England who was as clever as her Thomas.

*　　　*　　　*

The King paced up and down his apartment and with him was Charles Brandon, the newly created Duke of Suffolk. Suffolk, recently returned from Flanders, looked grim.

"So she'll not have you," Henry was saying.

"She was adamant in her refusals. You can be sure Maximilian has had a hand in this."

"An English Duke is match enough for a Duchess of Savoy!" growled Henry.

"Alas, Your Grace. She—or perhaps the Emperor—would not agree. And there is another matter."

Henry nodded. "Say on, Charles."

"There was a hesitancy in the Emperor's manner when, on your instructions, I tried to bring the negotiations for the Princess Mary's marriage to completion."

"Hesitation! What do you mean?"

"He was evasive. He seemed unwilling to make the final arrangements. Your Grace, it appears to me that the Emperor is one such as Ferdinand. He makes plans with us, and at the same time with others elsewhere."

Henry's brows were drawn together; he was thinking of the man who had placed himself under his banner and declared his willingness to serve the King of England.

"I cannot believe this," he shouted. "He served me well."

"He was paid well for doing so, Your Grace."

Henry's face darkened; but he could take more from Brandon than almost any other man.

"What means this change of front?"

"I know not, Your Grace, but let us be prepared."

Henry stamped angrily from the apartment, but he gave orders that preparations for war were to go on apace.

*       *       *

It was a week or so later when an envoy from France arrived to negotiate for those prisoners whom Henry had taken at the battles of Thérouanne and Tournai and who still remained in England.

The envoy asked if he might speak in private with the King and, when Henry received him—in Wolsey's presence—the envoy said: "I have words for Your Grace's ears alone."

Wolsey retired with dignity, knowing that the King would immediately pass on the news to him, and indeed having a shrewd notion as to what it must be.

When they were alone the envoy said to Henry: "Your Grace, I have a message from my master, the King of France. He wishes to warn you that King Ferdinand has renewed the truce he made with France, and that the Emperor Maximilian stands beside him in this."

"Impossible!" cried Henry. "This must be untrue."

"Your Grace will soon hear confirmation of this," said the envoy. "But my master, wishing to prepare you and to show you that he is willing to be your friend, determined to let you know of it as soon as the truce had been signed."

The veins stood out at Henry's temples; his face was purple and he cried: "The traitors! By God, I'll be revenged for this. My friends indeed! Base traitors both. They'll be sorry if these words you speak are truth. And if they are lies . . . then shall you be."

"I speak truth, Your Grace."

"By God!" cried Henry, and strode from the apartment; storming into Wolsey's quarters, he told him the news.

Wolsey, who was already prepared for it, received it calmly enough.

"What now?" demanded Henry.

"We know our false friends for what they are."

"That will not conquer France for us."

"A project which Your Grace will doubtless decide must be set aside for a while."

The King's eyes were glazed with anger, and in those moments he looked like a petulant boy who has been deprived of some much desired toy.

"Your Grace, what else had the envoy to say?"

"What else? Was that not enough?"

"Enough indeed, Sire. But I thought mayhap the King of France, showing his friendship in this way, might have further signs of friendship to show us."

Henry looked bewildered.

"Would Your Grace consider recalling the envoy? Perhaps a little delicate questioning with Your Grace's usual subtlety might reveal something of the mind of the King of France."

"What is this you are saying? Do you believe it possible that I might become the ally of the King of France!"

"Your Grace, the other powers of Europe have proved themselves no friends of yours."

" 'Tis true enough, by God."

"And Your Grace is now telling yourself, I know, that there can be no harm in hearing what this Frenchman has to say."

"Send for him," growled Henry.

In a short time the envoy stood before them.

Wolsey said: "Is it Your Grace's wish that I speak of those matters which you have explained to me?"

"Speak on," said Henry.

"It would seem," said Wolsey, "that the motive of the King of France is friendship towards his brother of England."

"That is my master's desire, Your Grace, Your Excellency."

"Then how would he show this friendship?"

"By making a peace with the English who shall be his friends, and forming an alliance which could not but bring dismay to those who have so clearly shown themselves the enemies of both countries. He says that to show his good faith he would be happy to make a marriage between France and England. As you know, Your Grace, Your Excellency, the King is without a wife. He is still of marriageable age. The marriage of the Princess Mary with the treacherous Hapsburg surely cannot now take place. The King of France would be happy to take the Princess as his bride."

Wolsey caught his breath. The King was astounded. This was a complete volte-face. But the treachery of Ferdinand and Maximilian rankled; and what better revenge could possibly be achieved than such a treaty, such a marriage? It would be France and England against Austria and Spain. Henry saw now that those two wily old men had wanted to set him fighting France while they turned their attention to Italy—thus widening the dominions of their grandsons.

It was all startlingly clear. And the revenge: this alliance, this marriage.

Wolsey was looking cautiously at the King. "His Grace will wish to have time to consider such a proposal," he said.

"That is so," said Henry.

The envoy was dismissed, and, placing his arm through that of Wolsey, Henry began to pace the apartment with him while they talked.

\* \* \*

The news was out and Katharine was bewildered. So once more her father had shown his treachery. He and Maximilian together had been profiting by the inexperience of the King of England and had used him shamelessly: Ferdinand in the conquest of Navarre, Maximilian for the capture of those two towns which were important to Netherlands trade. In addition Maximilian had received many English crowns as payment for his double dealing. They had endeavoured to win concessions from the King of France by informing him of imminent invasion by England so that he would be ready to make peace with them, almost at any price in order to be free to tackle the English invaders.

Louis however had had a plan of his own to outwit them: the French and English should forget old enmities and stand together as allies.

Caroz was bewildered; he did not know which way to turn; and, as on a previous occasion he saw that he would be in the position of scapegoat. He hurried to see Katharine and was met by Fray Diego Fernandez who informed him haughtily that the Queen was in no way pleased with his conduct of Spanish affairs.

Caroz, angry beyond discretion, pushed aside the priest and forced his way into the Queen's apartment.

Katharine met him coolly.

"Your Grace," he stammered, "this news . . . this alarming news. . . . The English are incensed against us."

"Against you and your master," said Katharine coldly.

"My . . . master . . . your Grace's father."

"There is nothing I have to discuss," said Katharine. "I dissociate myself from the instructions of the King of Spain."

Caroz was astonished, because he sensed the coldness in Katharine's voice when she spoke of her father.

"Do you understand," stormed Caroz, "that there is a possibility of a treaty of friendship between England and France?"

"These are matters for the King and his ministers," said Katharine.

"But our country. . . ."

"Is no longer my country. I count myself an Englishwoman now, and I put myself on the side of the English."

Caroz was shocked. He bowed and took his leave.

As he went from the Queen's apartments he saw Fray Diego who smiled at him insolently.

His recall to Spain shall be immediate, Caroz decided. It is he who has poisoned the Queen's mind against her father.

\*　　　　\*　　　　\*

The Princess Mary came hurrying into Katharine's apartments, her lovely eyes wild, her hair in disorder.

"Oh Katharine," she cried, "you have heard this news?"

Katharine nodded.

"I!" cried Mary. "To marry with that old man! He is fifty-two and they say he looks seventy. He is old, ugly and mean."

"I wish I could help you," said Katharine, "but I know of nothing I can do."

Mary stood clenching her hands. She was of a deeply passionate nature and had been greatly indulged by her brother. Her youth and beauty aroused his tenderness; and the fact that he was her guardian had always made him feel sentimental towards her, so that she had had her own way in all other matters and was furious that in this, the most important of all, she could not.

"I will not be used in this way. I will not!" she cried.

"Oh Mary," Katharine tried to soothe her, "it happens to us all, you know. We are obliged to marry the person who is chosen for us. We have no choice in the matter. We must needs obey."

"I'll not marry that old lecher," cried Mary.

"You'll be Queen of France."

"Who cares to be Queen of France! Not I . . . if I have to take the King with the crown."

"He will be kind to you. He has heard of your beauty and is very eager for the match."

"Lecher! Lecher! Lecher!" shouted Mary, and Katharine thought how like her brother she was in that moment.

"He will be gentle, perhaps kinder, more gentle than a younger man."

"Do I want gentleness! Do I want an old man drooling over my body!"

"Mary, I pray you be calm. It is the fate of us all."

"Did *you* have to marry a rheumaticky old man?"

"No, but I came to a strange land to marry a boy whom I had never seen."

"Arthur was handsome; he was young. And then you had Henry. Oh you fortunate Katharine!"

"You may be fortunate too. I am sure he will be kind to you, and kindness means so much. You were prepared to marry Charles, yet you did not know him."

"At least he is young." Mary's eyes blazed afresh. "Oh, it is cruel . . . cruel. Why should I, because I am a Princess, not be allowed to marry the man of my choice?"

Katharine knew that she was thinking of Charles Brandon. The whole Court knew of her feelings for that handsome adventurer; none more than Brandon himself who would dearly have liked to match her passion with his own. And now that it seemed he was not going to get Margaret of Savoy, he would doubtless be very happy to take the Princess of England.

Mary's defiance crumbled suddenly; she threw herself on to Katharine's bed and began sobbing wildly.

\*　　　　\*　　　　\*

Wolsey was directing the King's thoughts towards the French alliance. He could see great advantages there. He believed the King was willing enough; Henry had counted on the help of Ferdinand and Maximilian to enable him to win territories in France; he had memories of Dorset's disastrous campaign, and he had begun to see the dangers of tackling the conquest of France alone.

Wolsey was for ever at his ear, explaining without appearing to do so; carefully, skilfully planting those thoughts in the King's mind which he wished him to have.

Contemplating an expedition to France gave Wolsey nightmares. What if they should fail to maintain supplies? What if there should be disaster for the English? There had to be a scapegoat, and that might well be the almoner who had won such praise for his conduct of the previous campaign. No, Wolsey was determined that there should not be an expedition to France this year.

There was something else which made him long for the French alliance.

He had received information from the Vatican to the effect that the Holy Father would be pleased to see an alliance between France and England and trusted his newly created Cardinal would work to that end. It was very necessary to please the Pope. It was important that the Holy Father and his Cardinals in the Vatican should feel they had a good friend in Cardinal Wolsey. It would be remembered when the time for the next conclave arrived.

So each day Henry began to see more clearly the advantages of the suggested alliance; and one of the most important clauses would be the marriage treaty between the Princess Mary and Louis XII.

In vain did Mary storm; Henry was sorry, but England must come before his sister's whims.

He was truly sorry for her and his eyes were glazed with tenderness when she flung her arms about his neck and sought to cajole him.

"I would do what you ask, sister, if I could," he cried, "but it does not rest with me."

"It does. It does," she cried vehemently. "You could refuse this day, and that would be an end to the matter."

"Then there would be no alliance with the French."

"Who cares for alliance with the French?"

"We all must, sweet sister. It is a matter of policy. We have to stand against those two scoundrels. You cannot see how important this is because you are yet a girl, but it is a matter of state. Were it not, willingly would I give you what you ask."

"Henry, think of me—married to that old man!"

"I do, sweetheart, I do. But it must be. It is the duty of us all to marry for the good of our country."

"He is old . . . *old*. . . ."

"He is no worse than Charles. Charles looked to me like an idiot. By God, were I a maiden I'd as lief take Louis as Charles."

"Charles is at least young. Louis is . . . ancient."

"So much the better. You'll be able to twirl him round your pretty fingers. Ah, you'll get your way with the King of France, my sister, as you do with the King of England."

"But do I? When he will not grant me this one little thing?"

" 'Tis the one thing I cannot grant my dear sister. Be good, sweeting. Marry the man. He'll not live long."

Mary drew away from him and looked long into his face. He saw the new hope spring up in her eyes.

"Henry," she said slowly, "if I make this marriage, will you grant me one request?"

"That's my good sister," he said. "Have done with your tantrums—for if news of these reached Louis' ears he would not be pleased—and I'll grant whatsoever you request."

Mary took her brother's face between her hands.

"Swear this," she said.

"I swear," he answered.

Then she went on, speaking very slowly and distinctly: "I will marry old Louis; but when he dies, I have Your Grace's promise that I shall marry wheresoever I like for me to do."

Henry laughed.

"You have my promise."

Then she threw her arms about his neck and kissed him heartily on the lips.

Henry was delighted; she could always charm him, for his pride in this pretty sister—all Tudor, as he was fond of saying— was great.

Now the Court noticed that the Princess Mary had become resigned to the French marriage. There were no more displays of temper, no more tears of rage.

She allowed herself to be drawn into the preparations, and her manner was quiet and calculating yet a little aloof, as though she were looking far ahead, well into the future.

*       *       *

The summer was progressing. Henry was as deeply involved with Bessie as ever; he delighted in her, and familiarity did not pall.

He hated all Spaniards, he told himself; and he could not entirely forget that Katharine was one of them. She seemed to grow less attractive and, had it not been for the fact that she was pregnant, he could have come near to hating her at this further revelation of her father's treachery.

It was comforting to see Mary quieter and even showing an interest in the preparations for her wedding.

One day in the early autumn, when he was told that Caroz wanted to see him, he agreed to give the audience although he disliked the Spanish ambassador and had scarcely spoken to him since he had discovered that he had been betrayed by Ferdinand a second time.

Caroz came into his presence and Henry nodded briefly to him, without warmth.

"Your Grace is indeed kind to receive me. I have sought this interview for many days."

"I have been occupied with state matters which do not concern your master," the King answered coldly.

"It is a great grief to me that we are excluded from Your Grace's favour."

"It is a greater grief to me that I ever trusted your master."

Caroz bowed his head sorrowfully.

"My master seeks to recall the Queen's confessor, Fray Diego Fernandez."

Henry was about to say that this was a matter for the Queen, but he changed his mind. His conscience had been worrying him lately. He was spending a great deal of time in Bessie's company, and after a passionate night with her he often felt uneasy. During one of these uneasy periods he had told himself that Katharine had worked for her father rather than her husband, and this was another reason why she had forfeited the right to his fidelity.

Now he asked himself why he should consult Katharine about the return of her confessor. He did not like the man. He did not like any Spaniards at this time.

Bessie had been particularly enchanting last night and consequently the burden of his guilt this day was heavier.

He stuck out his lower lip petulantly.

"Then let the man be sent back to Spain," he said sullenly.

Caroz bowed low; he was exultant. The Queen could not

countermand the King's order; and he had the King's word that Fernandez should be sent back to Spain.

\* \* \*

Katharine was distraught. She had sent for her confessor and had been told that he was no longer at Court.

In desperation she summoned Caroz to her presence.

"What does this mean?" she demanded. "Where is Fray Diego?"

"On his way to Spain," replied Caroz, unable to restrain a smirk.

"This is impossible. I was not told of his departure."

"The orders were that he was to leave immediately."

"Whose orders?"

"Those of the King of Spain."

"The King of Spain's orders are invalid here at the Court of England."

"Not, I venture to point out, Your Grace, when they are also the orders of the King of England."

"What do you mean?"

"The King, your husband, ordered that Fray Diego should be sent back to Spain with all speed. He had no wish for him to continue to serve you as confessor."

Katharine hurried to the King's apartment with as much speed as she could, for her body was now becoming cumbersome.

Henry, who was with Compton mixing an ointment, turned with the pestle in his hand to stare at her.

She said curtly to Compton: "I would speak to the King alone."

Compton bowed and retired.

"What is the meaning of this?" demanded Henry.

"I have just heard that my confessor has been dismissed."

"Is that so?" said the King in a deceptively light tone.

"Dismissed," went on Katharine, "without any order from me."

"It is my privilege," Henry told her, and so disturbed was she that she did not see the danger signals, "to decide who shall and who shall not remain at my Court."

"My own confessor. . . ."

"A Spaniard!" Henry almost spat out the word. "May I tell you, Madam, that since I have had dealings with your father I do not trust Spaniards."

"He has been with me many years. . . ."

"All the more reason why he should return to his own country."

Katherine felt the tears in her eyes. Pregnancies were becoming more trying than they had been in the beginning, and her weakness often astonished her; usually she was not one to give way to tears.

"Henry . . ." she began.

"Madam," he interrupted, "do not seek to dictate to me. There have been spies enough at my Court. I would like to rid it of all Spaniards."

She caught her breath with horror.

"You have forgotten that I am . . ." she began.

But he cut in: "I do not forget. I know full well that you have been in league with your father, whispering in my ear, tempting me to this or that project . . . knowing all the while that it was to your father's benefit . . . and not to mine."

"Henry, I swear this to be untrue."

"Swear if you will. But who trusts a Spaniard?"

"You talk to me as though I were a stranger . . . and an enemy."

"You are a Spaniard!" he said.

She reached for the table to steady herself.

Evil rumours had been in the air of late. She had disregarded them as mere gossip: If the Queen does not give the King a child soon, he may decide that she is incapable of bearing children and seek a divorce.

She had thought at the time: How can people be so cruel? They make light of our tribulations with their gossip.

But now she wondered what had set such rumours in motion. When his eyes were narrowed like that he looked so cruel.

She turned away.

"I must go to my apartment," she said. "I feel unwell."

He did not answer her; but stood glowering while she walked slowly and in an ungainly manner from the apartment.

*          *          *

She was waiting now—waiting for the birth of the child which would make all the difference to her future. If this time she could produce a healthy boy, all the King's pleasure in his marriage would return. It was merely this run of bad luck, she told herself, which had turned him from her. So many failures. It really did seem that some evil fate was working against them. No wonder Henry was beginning to doubt whether it was possible for them to have a family; and because he was Henry, he would not say, Is it impossible for *us* to have children . . . but, for her? He would not believe that any failure could possibly come from himself.

She prayed continually: "Let me bear a healthy child. A boy, please, Holy Mother. But if that is asking too much, a girl would please, if only she may be healthy and live . . . just to prove that I can bear a healthy child."

In her apartments the device of the pomegranate mocked her. It hung on embroidered tapestry on the walls; it was engraved on so many of her possessions. The pomegranate which signified fruitfulness and which she had seen so many times in her own home before she had understood the old Arabic meaning.

How ironic that she should have taken it as her device!

She dared not brood on the possibility of failure, so she tried to prove to Henry that she was completely faithful to his cause. When the French ambassadors arrived she received them with outward pleasure and the utmost cordiality; she gave a great deal of time to the sad young Mary, helping her to live through that difficult time, cheering her, recalling her own fears on parting from her mother, assuring her that if she would meekly accept her destiny she would eventually triumph over her fears.

She was invaluable at such a time. Even Henry grudgingly admitted it and, because he knew that she was telling him that she had cut off her allegiance to her own people and was determined to work entirely for his cause, he softened towards her.

With the coming of that July the negotiations for the French marriage were completed and the ceremony by proxy was performed.

Mary, her face pale, her large eyes tragic, submitted meekly enough; and Katharine, who was present at the putting to bed ceremony, was sorry for the girl. Quietly she looked on while Mary, shivering in her semi-nakedness, was put to bed by her women, and the Duc de Longueville, who was acting as proxy for the King of France, was put to bed with her, he fully dressed apart from one naked leg with which he touched Mary. The marriage was then declared to be a true marriage, for the touching of French and English body was tantamount to consummation.

\*　　　　\*　　　　\*

In October of that year Mary was taken with great pomp to Dover, there to set sail for France. Katharine and Henry accompanied her, and Katharine was fearful when she saw the sullen look in Mary's eyes.

It was a sad occasion for Katharine—that stay at Dover Castle while they waited for storms to subside, for she could not help but remember her own journey from Spain to England and she understood exactly how Mary was feeling.

How sad was the fate of most Princesses! she thought.

She was eager to comfort her young sister-in-law, and tried to arouse Mary's interest in her clothes and jewels; but Mary remained listless except for those occasions when her anger would burst out against a fate which forced her to marry an old man whom she was determined to despise because there was another whom she loved. The marriage had done nothing at all, Katharine saw, to turn her thoughts from Charles Brandon.

They seemed long, those weeks at Dover. Henry strode through the castle, impatient to have done with the painful parting and return to London, for there could be no real gaiety while the Queen of France went among them, like a mournful ghost of the gay Princess Mary.

Again and again Katharine sought to comfort her. "What rejoicing there will be in Paris," she said.

But Mary merely shrugged her shoulders. "My heart will be in England," she said, "so I shall care nothing for rejoicing in Paris."

"You will . . . in time."

"In time!" cried Mary, and her eyes suddenly blazed wickedly. "Ah," she repeated, "in time."

There were occasions when she was almost feverishly gay; she would laugh, a little too wildly; she would even sing and dance, and the songs were all of the future. Katharine wondered what was in her mind and was afraid.

Her women doubtless had a trying time. Katharine had noticed some charming girls among the little band who were to accompany Mary to France. Lady Anne and Lady Elisabeth Grey were two very attractive girls and she was sure they were helping in upholding Mary's spirits.

One day when she went to Mary's apartments she saw a very young girl, a child, there among the women.

Katharine called to her and the little girl came and curtsied. She had big, dark eyes and one of the most piquantly charming faces Katharine had ever seen.

"What are you doing here, my little one?" she asked.

"Your Grace," answered the child with the dignity of a much

older person, "I am to travel to France in the suite of the Queen. I am one of her maids of honour."

Katharine smiled. "You are somewhat young for the post, it would seem."

"I am past seven years old, Your Grace." The answer was given with hauteur and most surprising dignity.

"It would seem young to me. Do you travel with any member of your family?"

"My father is to sail with us, Your Grace."

"Tell me the name of your father, my child."

"It is Sir Thomas Boleyn."

"Ah, I know him well. So you are his daughter . . . Mary, is it?"

"No, Your Grace. Mary is my sister. My name is Anne."

Katharine, amused by the precocity of the lovely little girl, smiled. "Well, Anne Boleyn," she said, "I am sure you will serve your mistress well."

The child swept a deep and somewhat mannered curtsey, and Katharine passed on.

## CHAPTER XII

## THE OPEN RIFT

WHEN MARY HAD sailed for France the Court returned to Richmond, and with the coming of the winter Katharine felt that she had regained a little of her husband's esteem which she had lost through the treachery of her father.

December was with them and plans for the Christmas festivities were beginning to be made. There were the usual whisperings, the secrets shared by little groups of courtiers, plans, Katharine guessed, for a pageant which would surprise her; there would doubtless be a Robin Hood or a Saracen Knight to startle the company with his prowess and later disclose himself to be the King. No round of gaiety would be complete without that little masquerade.

She felt old and tired, contemplating the excitement going on about her—like a woman among children. How was it possible for her to feel excitement about a pageant when she was so concerned with her own all-important and most pressing problem. Is it true, she asked herself, that I am growing old, far in advance of the King?

It was a cold day and she awakened feeling tired. This was proving a difficult pregnancy and she wondered whether she was less robust than she had been; an alarming thought, because she foresaw many pregnancies ahead of her, and if her health failed, how could she go on attempting to bear children? And if she did not, of what use was she to her King and country? The word Divorce was like a maggot in her brain.

Because she felt too tired to talk she dismissed her women and sat alone. She went to her prie-dieu and there she prayed, remaining on her knees for nearly an hour, begging, pleading that this time she might have a healthy child.

She rose and stood for some time before the embroidered tapestry on the wall, which portrayed her device of the pomegranate.

This time all will be well, she promised herself.

She thought she would take a walk in the gardens, and as she wished to be alone she went down by a rarely frequented spiral stone staircase.

As this part of the Palace was seldom used, it was very quiet here. She felt a curiosity about it and wondered why it had been neglected. She paused on the staircase to open a door, and saw a pleasant enough room. Entering, she found that the windows looked out on a courtyard in which grass grew among the cobbles. There was little sun in this part and she idly supposed that was why it was so rarely used.

She shut the door quietly and went on. Halfway down the staircase was another door and, as she passed this, hearing the sound of voices, she paused and listened. Surely that was Henry's voice.

She must be mistaken, for she had heard that he had gone off with the hunt that day. Impulsively she opened the door, and thus discovered what most members of the Court had known for many months. There could be no mistake. Bessie Blount, Lady Taillebois, was lying on a couch and Henry was with her. There could be no doubt whatever what they were doing: rarely could any have been discovered so completely *in flagrante delicto*. Katharine gave a gasp of horror.

Henry turned his head and looked straight at her, and in that second of time shame, fury, hatred flashed from his eyes.

Katharine waited for no more; she turned, shut the door, and stumbled back the way she had come. As she missed her footing and fell, the cold stone struck into her body, and she felt a sharp pain that was like a protest from the child; but she picked herself up and hurried on.

When she reached her own apartments she shut herself in.

One of her women came to her and asked if she were ill.

"I am merely tired," she said firmly. "I wish to be alone that I may rest."

\*　　　\*　　　\*

Henry came into the room; his face was scarlet and his eyes sparkled with anger.

He had been caught by his wife in an extremely compromising situation with another woman, and he was deeply ashamed of the figure he had cut in her eyes. When Henry was ashamed of himself he was angry, and because he had always come to terms with his conscience before he indulged in what might be considered sinful, he was always prepared to defend his virtue. Thus he was doubly angry when he was shamed, and as he could never be angry with himself the flood of that anger must be allowed to flow over someone else.

He stood glowering at her as she lay on her bed.

She did not attempt to rise as she would have done on any other occasion. For one thing she felt too ill and there was a dull nagging pain in her womb which terrified her.

He said: "Well, Madam, what have you to say?"

She was suddenly too tired to placate him, too weary to hide her anger. She was no longer the diplomatic Queen; she was the wronged wife.

"Should I have anything to say? Should not you be the one to explain?"

"Explain! Do you forget I am the King? Why should I be called upon to explain?"

"You are also my husband. What I saw . . . horrified me."

Henry was thinking of what she had seen and he grew hot with indignation—not with himself and Bessie for being thus together, but with Katharine for shaming them.

"Why so?" he asked, battling with the rage which threatened to make him incoherent.

"You ask that! Should I be delighted to see you behaving thus . . . with that woman?"

"Listen to me," said Henry. "I brought you to your present eminence. What were you when I married you? Daughter of the King of Spain. A man who neglected you and used you to trap me. Yet I married you. Against the advice of my ministers I married you . . . because I pitied you . . . because I thought you would make me a good wife . . . would give me children. And what have you given me? Still-born children! One son who lived for a few days! Madam, I am beginning to wonder whether you are incapable of bearing children."

"Is it for this reason that you dally thus shamelessly in daylight with the women of your Court?"

"This is but one woman," he said, "and her I love dearly. She gives me such pleasure, Madam, as is beyond your ken. I have given you the chance to bear me sons; I have considered your health; I have not disturbed your nights. And because, in my consideration for you, I have found another to allay those desires which methinks are natural to all men, you play the shrew."

"I see," said Katharine, "that I have been mightily mistaken. I thought you a virtuous man. I did not know you."

"Find me one more virtuous in this Court! I hear Mass regularly each day . . . and more than once a day. I have sought to please God and his saints. . . ."

"They must be delighted by such spectacles as I have just witnessed."

"You blaspheme, Madam."

"You commit adultery—by far the greater sin."

Henry's face was purple with rage.

"You forget your position, Madam."

Katharine rose from her bed and came to stand before him.

"I have never forgotten my position," she said. "I was ready to show my gratitude. I have spent long hours on my knees praying for a healthy child. Has it occurred to you that our failure might in some measure be due to yourself?"

"I understand you not," he said coldly.

"The sensual appetites of men when indulged, so I have heard, may make them sterile."

Henry was purple with rage. He was so furious that he could not speak for some seconds, and Katharine went on: "I know you have blamed me for our inability to get healthy children; knowing what I now know I am of the opinion that the cause may well come from you."

"This . . . is monstrous!" cried the King.

She turned away from him, for in that moment the pain of her body was greater than the pain of her mind. Her face was twisted with the effort to keep back her cry of agony.

Henry watched her and, guessing that the shock she had suffered might have brought about a premature birth, he swallowed his anger and going to the door began bellowing for her women.

When they came running, he said: "The Queen is ill. See to her."

Then he strode back to his own apartments; all who saw him scuttled away; even his dogs were aware of his moods and, instead of bounding towards him, they slunk after him keeping a good distance between themselves and that glittering angry figure.

\*　　　　\*　　　　\*

It was over—yet another failure.

It was no consolation to know that the child was male.

"Oh God," moaned Katharine, sick and weak in her bed, "have You deserted me then?"

She was ill for several weeks and when she rose from her bed the Christmas festivities were in full progress.

She joined them and the King was cool to her, but now there

was no longer anger between them. His attitude implied that she must accept with a good grace whatever she found in him; and since she was his Queen he would be at her side on public occasions.

But change had come to the Court. The Queen had aged visibly. Her body was no longer that of a young woman; it bore the marks of several pregnancies and had lost its shapeliness; her hair, still long and plentiful, was without that bright colour which had been so attractive and had done so much to lighten the somewhat heavy nature of her face; now that it was dull mouse-colour she looked much darker than before, and as her skin had become sallow she was thought of as a dark woman.

The King had changed too. He would never be so easily duped by his political enemies in future. He was still the golden, handsome King, but he was no longer a boy; he was a young man in the very prime of life. A certain bloom of innocence had been rubbed off. Now he led Bessie Blount in the dance and caressed her openly before his courtiers, no longer attempting to conceal the fact that he spent his nights with her. Often they would ride together to Jericho with a little company of friends and stay there, while Katharine remained behind at Richmond, Westminster or Greenwich.

Bessie was accepted as the chief mistress, and although there were others—little lights-o'-love who amused him for a while— none took Bessie's place.

The courtiers smiled. "It is natural," they said. "And since the Queen is so dull and has lost what beauty she had, and as she is fast becoming an old woman, who can blame young Henry?"

It was hurtful to Katharine, but she hid her feelings; yet she wondered whether she would be able to get a child now.

So much had happened in a year.

Now she spent most of her time sewing with her women, hearing Mass, praying in her own apartments, making pilgrimages to such places as the shrine at Walsingham.

Often she thought of those days when Henry had seemed contented with his wife. But it was not only the husband whom she had lost. She often remembered how, at one time when he had received foreign despatches, he brought them to her and they read them together. He never did this now.

There were two others who had supplanted her.

There was Cardinal Wolsey in state affairs, and in his bed there was Bessie Blount.

## CHAPTER XIII

# A VENETIAN EMBASSY AND A CARDINAL'S HAT

IT WAS NEW YEAR'S night and there must be entertainment at the Court to celebrate such an occasion; so the great hall of Westminster had been decorated with cloth of gold, and at night, by torchlight, it was a beautiful sight indeed.

The people had crowded in to watch the royal sport; and on such an occasion Henry liked to show his people that he lived in the splendour expected of a King.

Katharine was seated on a dais at one end of the great hall as she had sat so often before. About her were her ladies, and she was glad to have with her her dear Maria de Salinas who, with her husband, was paying a visit to the Court. Maria had heard of the King's open liaison with Elizabeth Blount and had condoled with Katharine about this. It was the way of Kings, she said, and not to be taken seriously. Why, even the people accepted the fact that the King must have his mistress.

Katharine was considerably comforted by Maria and, perhaps because of that, looked more like her old self on that night. She was magnificently dressed in rich blue velvet, and diamonds, sapphires and rubies glittered about her person.

While she sat there a messenger came to her in the costume of Savoy and begged to be allowed to speak to her. Katharine recognized one of the gentlemen of the Court and knew at once that this was part of the entertainment.

"Pray speak on," she said.

There was silence in the hall, and the Savoyard said in loud ringing tones but using a foreign accent: "Your Grace of England, there are without a band of dancers from Savoy. They have travelled far that they may enchant you with their dancing on this first night of the New Year. Have they your permission to enter and dance for the pleasure of the Court?"

"I beg you bring them in at once. They must perform for us."

Katharine sat back on her throne while the party were brought in. There at the head of them were two tall figures—whom she knew well. One was Henry, the other Brandon. They were masked, but beneath the mask it was possible to see the King's golden hair.

"Welcome, Gentlemen," said Katharine.

They bowed low; and as they did so Katharine's eyes began to sparkle, for this was as it had been in the old days, and it might mean that Henry was going to forget their differences and treat her once more as his wife.

When Henry spoke—and who could not recognize his voice— he said: "Most beautiful Queen of this fair land, we are strolling dancers from the land of Savoy. We would fain dance before you so that Your Grace may judge whether there are not as good dancers from Savoy as live in this fair land."

Katharine threw herself into the game. "You may try," she said, "but I must warn you, we have most excellent dancers in this land, and they are led by the King himself whom all agree none has ever equalled. If you would care to try your skill against us, do so. But I dare swear you will be dismayed when you see the King dance."

"We are happy, Your Grace, to put our skill to the test, and you shall be our judge."

Katharine signed to the musicians then and by the light of the torches the little party took its place before her. There were four men and four women, all in blue velvet and cloth of silver and their costumes were fashioned after the manner of Savoy.

The dancing began. It was a beautiful ballet outstanding on account of the high leaping of the leader.

There were murmurs in the crowd. "Can it be? Does he in truth out-jump the King? Where is his Grace? He should see the unusual skill of these men and in particular the leader."

Sitting back Katharine marvelled at the ability of all to enter so whole-heartedly into the game and to show such seeming innocence of the masquerade which all must have seen so many times before.

At length the dancing ceased and the dancers were all on their knees before the Queen's throne.

"I pray you," said Katharine, "unmask, that we may see your faces."

The dancers rose to their feet and Katharine kept her eyes on the leader while he, with a dramatic gesture, drew off his mask.

There was a gasp throughout the Court and then loud bursts of applause. Henry bowed to the Queen and turned about so that none should be in doubt as to his identity.

He has not grown up at all, thought Katharine; and she felt a little happier, for it was more pleasant to see the naïve boy taking the place of the brutal man.

He then stepped to the Queen's side and taking her hand kissed it, which drew more lusty cheers from the people.

Holy Mother of God, murmured Katharine to herself, can we really go back to the beginning? Can it really be as though our troubles never happened?

She was more than ready to meet him halfway.

She said so clearly that all might hear: "So it was Your Grace. I could not believe there was one to rival you, and yet it seemed that Savoyard could do so. I thank Your Grace for my good pastance."

Then boldly she rose and putting her hands to his face drew him down to her and kissed him.

For a few seconds she held her breath with apprehension, but he had returned her kiss, and the people cheered.

"Good Kate," he whispered, " 'tis all done in thy honour."

It seemed to the watchers then that something of the Queen's youth returned, as Henry sat beside her and they talked amicably.

That night they slept together. The need to get a child was as urgent as ever. It was a return to the old pattern; and there was, after all, to be another chance.

\*     \*     \*

It was shortly after the New Year revels when a messenger from France came to Westminster with an urgent despatch for the King.

Henry read the news and let out an exclamation of dismay. He had the messenger taken to the kitchens to be refreshed and sent at once for Wolsey.

"News!" he cried. "News from France. Louis is dead. He died on New Year's day."

Wolsey took the news calmly; he had not expected Louis to live long; a new bride, such as Mary, would not act as an elixir to such as he was, for Louis was Gallic and as such would ape the gallant no matter at what cost.

Wolsey smiled secretly thinking of the old man trying to play lover to that young and passionate girl.

"This means, Your Grace, that Francis of Angoulême will now be King of France unless. . . ."

"Exactly," said the King, "unless my sister is with child by the King; then Francis' long nose will be a little out of joint. I'll warrant the sly fellow is beside himself with anxiety. Imagine! For years he and his mother and doting sister have watched old Louis . . . waiting for him to die. Then the old man marries my

O

sister. 'Is she with child?' 'Is she not with child?' This is a fine joke."

"Let us hope, Your Grace, that the Queen of France *has* conceived. With one sister Queen of France and another Queen of Scotland, Your Grace would be most fortunately placed."

" 'Tis so. 'Tis so."

Henry smiled at Wolsey. He appreciated this servant, being fully aware that Wolsey possessed something which he himself lacked. He called it seriousness. He would come to it in time; but at this stage he did not want to devote all his energies to state affairs. He had discovered that he was not as completely devoted to war as he had imagined he would be. When he entered into a game he liked to know what the outcome would be. He wanted the shouts of wonder at his prowess. These did not always come in war. Even Ferdinand and Maximilian—those great warriors, who, all would admit, had had their share of victories—frequently suffered defeat and humiliation. Henry had not been prepared to go to war alone with France, and the reason was that he feared defeat.

He was indeed growing up and it was unfortunate for his peace of mind that, in spite of his vanity and frequent displays of naïvety, he was also intelligent. And this intelligence kept asserting itself—even as his conscience did—to disturb his peace.

Therefore he was grateful to Wolsey. That man had genius, and while he could place state affairs in those capable hands he could be at peace. He was ready to show his appreciation to Wolsey who must be well on the way to becoming one of the richest men in England—next to himself. Henry rejoiced in Wolsey's advancement; he was ready to abet it. His face softened at the sight of the man; he would put his arm about his shoulders as they walked in the gardens, so that all might realize the esteem in which he held his new Cardinal.

So now he said: "Well, Thomas, what's to be done?"

"There is nothing we can do but wait, Sire. All depends on whether the Queen of France carries the heir."

Henry nodded. "My poor sister! There she is, all alone in that country. And she will have to endure the period of mourning as a widow, shut into her darkened apartments where she will be most unhappy. I must send my envoy at once to France to convey my condolences . . . to my sister, to Francis . . ."

"And we will not add, Sire," said Wolsey with a smile, "that here we are praying that the Queen is with child."

The King laughed aloud and slapped Wolsey's shoulder.

"Nay, Thomas, we'll not mention the matter. I had thought that Suffolk might be the envoy on this occasion."

Wolsey was silent for a moment, and Henry's expressive mouth tightened. Wolsey was grateful for that mobile countenance which so often gave a hint of the King's desires before Henry uttered them.

Suffolk! pondered Wolsey. The Queen of France would be an excellent pawn in skilful hands. Were they going to throw her to Suffolk merely because her wanton body lusted after that man?

He followed Henry's thoughts. This was his sister Mary, his favourite sister who was gay and pretty; knowing how to flatter her brother she fostered his sentimentality towards her, and had lured him into a promise. "If I marry the King of France, when he is dead I shall marry whom I please." And Henry knew who pleased her.

He wanted to comfort her now, to say: Look, little sister, you are a widow in a foreign land; so I am sending you a gift to cheer you. And the gift was Suffolk.

Henry was telling himself that Brandon was a worthy envoy; and as he was ardently courting the Duchess of Savoy, in these circumstances sending him would merely be a gesture; no harm could come of it. Mary would have enough sense to know that there must be no dalliance with Suffolk while she might be carrying the heir of France within her.

In any case Henry had made up his mind.

So must it be, thought Wolsey, who was not going to commit the folly of going against the King in this matter and mayhap through it lose control of other and more important affairs. "If Your Grace is satisfied with Suffolk as your envoy to the Court of France, then so I am," he said.

\*       \*       \*

The Cardinal read the letter from Suffolk. He was gratified because the Duke had written to him. It indicated that this man understood that the one most likely to influence the King was Thomas Wolsey.

His Cardinal's hat had not yet arrived, but that was coming. He was growing more and more certain that one day he would gain the Papal crown; in the meantime he was content to govern England.

Suffolk had written that he and Mary had married.

Wolsey laughed aloud at the folly of the man. Then he

thought of his own folly with Mistress Wynter, and his laughter faded a little.

But to marry with the Princess so soon after the death of her husband! Moreover, was Brandon in a position to marry? There were some who maintained that he was already married; and he had certainly been involved in matrimonial tangles with three other women. The first was Elizabeth Grey, daughter of the Viscount of Lisle, who had been made his ward and whom he had contracted to marry. This lady had refused to marry him and the patent was cancelled. Later he had contracted to marry a certain Ann Brown, but before the marriage was celebrated he obtained a dispensation and married a widow named Margaret Mortymer, who was a relative of his. When he was weary of this woman he acquired a declaration of invalidity from the Church on the grounds of consanguinity, and it was said that later he went through a form of marriage with Ann Brown by whom he had had a daughter. Certainly his past did not bear too close a scrutiny and it was questionable whether he was in a position to marry again. Yet such was his fascination that not only had he charmed Mary but to some extent Henry as well.

Wolsey read the letter:

"The Queen would never let me be in rest until I had granted her to be married; and so now, to be plain with you, I have married her heartily, and have lain with her in so much I fear me lest she be with child. I am like to be undone if the matter should come to the knowledge of the King, my master."

He was asking Wolsey to break the news gently and to convey loving messages from Mary to Henry in the hope that he might be softened towards them and allow them to return home, which they longed to do.

Wolsey considered the matter. The King had provoked this situation. He had known how headstrong his sister was, and he had promised her that if she married Louis she should choose her next husband. Henry, Wolsey was sure, would feign anger at the news, but he would not be greatly disturbed. He loved his sister dearly and missed her, so would be glad to have her home. He missed Suffolk too, for that gay adventurer was one of the most amusing of his friends.

Therefore it was without much trepidation that Wolsey sought an audience and showed Henry the letter which he had received from Suffolk.

"By God's Holy mother!" ejaculated Henry. "So they are married—and she, like as not, with child. What if . . ."

"We should know, Your Grace, if the King of France was its father. I fear that is not so. Poor Louis, he could not get his wife with child."

For a moment there was deep silence, and to Wolsey's consternation he saw the healthy flush in the King's cheeks darken.

So, thought Wolsey, he is already beginning to wonder whether *he* is capable of begetting children. Is it so? One would have thought Elizabeth Blount might have shown some signs by now; and the Court was becoming so accustomed to Katharine's failures that they expected her miscarriages before they occurred.

Wolsey said quickly: "The King of France was too old to beget children."

The King breathed more easily. The danger was past, and Wolsey went on: "What are Your Grace's wishes in this matter?"

"I am deeply shocked," said Henry. "Punishment there must be. I am displeased with them . . . both."

But indeed he was not. He was already wishing they were at the Court. He indulged his pleasures so much that he put their gratification before matters of state. While Wolsey thought of the grand marriages which might have been arranged for Mary, Henry was thinking: Mary will be happy; and I shall be happy to have my sister with me again.

But as ever he was ready to listen to Wolsey's advice; and, when later Suffolk wrote to Henry begging to be allowed to come home and offering his body, knowing that he might be "put to death, imprisoned, or destroyed" for this great sin he had committed, Henry left it to Wolsey to suggest on what terms the erring couple might be allowed to return.

"Let them return to Your Grace the gift you made the Princess Mary of plate and jewels," suggested Wolsey; "let Suffolk undertake to pay by yearly instalments the expenses you incurred by the French marriage. Then it would seem that they had been adequately punished. All would know that none dares flout your Grace's wishes with impunity, and at the same time these two, for whom we all have great affection, could—after a short period—return to Court."

Henry was delighted with the solution.

Once again he was realizing how much he could rely upon his dear friend Wolsey.

\*　　　　\*　　　　\*

That young gay amorist, Francis of Angoulême, had leaped happily into the position which he and his family had coveted for himself for so long.

With what great joy he discovered that Mary Tudor was not with child; and, although he himself had cast lascivious eyes on this attractive English girl, the Suffolk marriage seemed a happy enough conclusion to that affair.

He was ambitious and energetic, and in the first weeks of his accession he was turning his eyes towards Italy.

It was during March of that year that a Venetian embassy arrived in England with the blessing of Francis.

The position of the Venetians in Europe was dictated by their trade. They were first and foremost traders and asked only to be allowed to continue to sell those goods for which they were famous. Since Maximilian had captured Verona, he had proved a serious handicap to Venetian trade, and the people of Venice believed that an alliance with France would enable them to regain Verona; and as France was aware that her power in Lombardy depended on Venetian friendship there was a *rapprochement* between the two.

It seemed important to Venice that England should strengthen her alliance with France, which should have been cemented by the marriage between Louis XII and the Princess Mary; but with Louis dead and his widow already the wife of English Brandon it seemed necessary to send an embassy to England.

So on a sparkling March day the Venetian embassy arrived, having been entertained most lavishly on the way by the new King of France.

Henry was on his mettle. He believed that Francis would have made a great effort to impress the Venetians with his grandeur and elegance, and was determined to outdo the King of France whom he had always believed to be his especial rival ever since he had heard that Marguerite of Angoulême—who had once been suggested as a bride for Henry—had declared her brother to be the handsomest, wittiest and most charming man in the world and one whom she would always love beyond any other.

So he was prepared. He was a sight so dazzling on that morning that even those who were accustomed to his splendour were astonished.

The Venetians had sailed up the Thames to Richmond in a barge which was gaily decorated with cloth of gold and silver. Before they entered the King's presence they were given bread and wine to sustain them, and then they were taken to the King's chapel to hear Mass.

When this was over they were led into the presence of the

King. The Palace had been decorated to receive them, and gold and silver cloth and tapestries had been hung in each apartment. In these rooms three hundred halberdiers, wearing silver breast plates, stood at attention, in order to impress the newcomers with the might of England. They were astonished because the halberdiers, who were chosen for their height, towered above the little Venetians, their fresh faces glowing in striking contrast to the swarthy ones of the men of Venice.

Then to the King's chamber where Henry waited to receive them. He was standing when they entered, leaning against his throne. He wanted them to receive an immediate impression of his great height, which they could not do if he sat. Henry was indeed an impressive figure; his purple velvet mantle was lined with white satin, and fell behind him in a train four yards long; this mantle was fastened across his massive chest by a thick chain made entirely of gold; his doublet was of satin, crimson and white in colour; and on his head was a cap of red velvet decorated with a white feather. About his neck was a gold collar with St. George picked out in fine diamonds; and below that another collar from which hung a round diamond the size of a big walnut; and from this diamond hung a large flawless pearl.

The Venetians blinked. Francis had been elegantly splendid, but Henry was more colourfully so.

Henry was delighted with the impression he so obviously created; the blue eyes, under the red hair which was combed straight about his head, sparkled; he held out a hand, the fingers of which seemed entirely covered by dazzling gems.

Henry welcomed the newcomers warmly, telling them how happy he was to have them at his Court. They would be in need of refreshment, so he had a banquet prepared for them, and when they had eaten they should see the joust which Henry believed had been perfected by his countrymen.

The Venetians, overwhelmed by the friendliness and the hospitality of the King, were then graciously received by members of the King's Council at the head of whom was the new Cardinal Wolsey whom they well knew to be the most important man in the realm.

They met the Queen—herself gorgeously attired and glittering with jewels; but they had heard rumours of the King's feelings towards his wife and they did not believe her to have any real influence with him now.

Henry led the way to the banquet where he surrounded himself by the leaders of the embassy and delightedly watched their incredulity at the dishes produced by his cooks and the ability of the English to consume large quantities of food.

He had no intention of talking of state matters; that would come later with Wolsey; but he was eager to know whether the newcomers were comparing him with Francis in their minds.

He was soon asking questions about his great rival.

"You have recently left the King of France; tell me, is he as tall as I am?"

"There can be very little difference in the height of the King of France and the King of England," was the answer. "Your Grace is a big man; and so is Francis."

"Is he a fat man, this young King of France?"

"No, Your Grace. He could not be called a fat man. Far from it. He is lean and lithe."

"Lean and lithe." Henry caressed his own plump thigh.

"What are his legs like?" demanded Henry.

The Venetians were puzzled; they looked at each other. What sort of legs had the King of France? To be truthful they had not taken particular note of his legs; but they recalled that they must be spare because of the leanness of the King's body.

"Spare legs, eh!" cried Henry. "Look at mine." He held up his legs to display the fine calf, well shaped, firm, the leg of an athletic man. "Has he a leg like that, eh?"

The Venetians were certain that the King of France had not a leg like that.

Henry laughed, well pleased. Then he threw open his doublet. "Look at this thigh," he said. " 'Tis every bit as firm and well shaped as my leg. Has the King of France a thigh like that?"

When the Venetians assured Henry that the thigh of the King of France could not be compared with the thigh of the King of England, he was delighted and felt full of affection towards them and Francis.

"Methinks," he said, "I am very fond of this King of France."

After the banquet Henry retired to prepare himself for the joust; and later this was held in the Palace courtyard.

Henry excelled even his previous exploits on that day, shivering many a lance; which was as it should be; and one by one his opponents went down before him.

He was extremely happy.

When he joined the Venetians to be congratulated he said: "I should like to joust with the King of France as my opponent."

But even as he spoke there was a shadow on his face. He was alarmed by this King on the other side of the water; he had heard so many tales of him, of his bravery, his wit and his lechery. He had scarcely been on the throne a week when he was talking of leading his armies to victory; and Henry had discovered that he himself had no great desire to place himself at the head of his armies.

What if he were to joust with Francis and Francis should win? Did Compton, Kingston and the rest go down before their King because they knew it was wise to do so?

"So," he growled, "the King of France thinks to make war on Italy. He will cross the Alps. Will his people love him, think you, since he plunges them into a war at the very beginning of his reign?"

Then he was angry because he had longed to bring conquests to his people; and this he had failed to do. He burst out: "He is afraid of me. Why, were I to invade his kingdom he would not be able to cross the Alps into Italy, would he? So you see, all depends on me. If I invade France, Francis cannot make war on Italy. If I do not, he can. You see, my friends, in these hands I hold the future of France."

The thought pleased him, and he was once more in good spirits.

Now to forget war and plan new entertainments to impress the visitors.

\*   \*   \*

That May was a happy month. Katharine rejoiced in the coming of spring which she had always loved in England. The dark winter was over; there were buds on the trees and wild parsley and stitchwort shone white in the hedges mingling with the blue of speedwell and ground ivy.

The season of renewal, she thought; and this year she had been happier than she had for some time, for it seemed to her that her relationship with Henry had been renewed and it was like the return of spring. She too had become wiser.

She had learned that she must accept her husband for the lusty young man he was, five years her junior; she must turn a blind eye on those flirtations which took place without too much secrecy; she must accept Elizabeth Blount as her maid of honour and her husband's chief mistress, and not care that he shared the bed of one because of his great desire to do so and of the other in order to serve the state and produce an heir.

She was full of hope that May. He visited her often; he was kind to her; she rarely saw an outburst of anger. She had learned how to avoid them.

O*

This then was May Day, and Henry was happy because the occasion called for one of those ceremonial pageants in which he delighted.

He came to the Queen's apartment early and he was already clad in green velvet—doublet, hose and shoes; and even his cap, which was sporting a jaunty feather, was of the same green.

"A merry good day to Your Grace," he called blithely. "I come to see if you will venture a-maying with me this morn."

"There is none with whom I would wish to go a-maying but Your Grace."

"Then Kate, your wish is granted. We leave at once. Come."

She was dressed in green velvet to match the King's, and because she was happy she had regained some of that youthful charm which had attracted him in the early days of their marriage.

So from the Palace of Greenwich they rode out to Shooter's Hill surrounded by members of the Venetian embassy and nobles of the Court, all gaily dressed to share in the maying.

When they reached the hill a party of men dressed as outlaws, led by one who was clearly meant to be Robin Hood, galloped up to them.

"Ho!" cried Henry. "What means this, and who are you who dare molest the King and Queen of England?"

Robin Hood swept off his hat; and Katharine recognized him through the mask as one of Henry's courtiers.

"Molest His Grace the King! That we would never do. The outlaws of the Forest respect the King even as do the gentlemen of the Court. Would Your Grace step into the good green wood and learn how the outlaws live?"

Henry turned to Katharine.

"Would Your Grace venture into the forest with so many outlaws?"

"My lord," answered Katharine, "where Your Grace ventured there would I fearlessly go."

Henry was delighted with her answer and Katharine thought: I begin to play his games as well as he does himself.

So into the forest they rode, and there they were taken to a sylvan bower made of hawthorn boughs, spring flowers and moss, where a breakfast of venison and wine was laid out.

"All for the pleasure of Your Graces," said Robin Hood.

The King expressed his delight and watched Katharine closely to see if she appreciated this surprise. She did not disappoint him.

They sat close like lovers and the King took her hand and kissed it.

He was happy; he knew that his sister Mary and her husband were on their way to England, and that pleased him. He was going to enjoy being very displeased with them and then forgiving them; and he was going to be very happy to have them near him once more.

The sun shone brilliantly, and after the feast when they left the wood, several beautiful girls in a vehicle which was decorated with flowers and drawn by five horses were waiting for them. The girls represented Spring and they sang sweetly the praise of the sweetest season of all, not forgetting to add a few paeans of praise to their goodly King and Queen.

And so the May Day procession rode back to Greenwich.

That was a happy day. The King was like a young lover again.

Within the next few days Katharine conceived once more; and this time she was determined that her child should live.

\*         \*         \*

That summer was a happy one. The knowledge that she was once more pregnant delighted Katharine and the King.

"Why, this time, sweetheart," said Henry, "our hopes shall not be disappointed. You have a goodly boy within you and he'll be the first of many."

Katharine allowed herself to believe this. She would not think of possible bad luck. This was her year.

In September there came news of Francis's victory. The King of France was hailed already as one of the greatest soldiers in history. Young, intrepid, he set out to perform the impossible and prove it possible.

Contrary to Henry's assertion that it depended on him whether or not France went into Italy, Francis—indifferent as to whether or not Henry made an attempt to invade France—had crossed the Alps with twenty thousand men, going from Barcelonnette to Salazzo, crossing passes which were no more than narrow tracks, accoutred as he was for war. That was not all. He had fought and won the resounding victory of Marignano.

Henry's anger when this news was brought to him was too great to hide.

He looked, said those who watched him at the time, as though he were about to burst into tears.

"He will have to face Maximilian," snapped out Henry.

"Nay, Your Grace. Maximilian now seeks friendship with my master," the French envoy answered.

"I assure you he is not seeking that friendship," snapped Henry. The envoy lifted his shoulders, smiled and remained silent.

"How many of France's enemies have fallen in battle?" demanded Henry.

"Sire, it is some twenty thousand."

"You lie. I hear from sources which I trust that it was but ten thousand."

Henry dismissed the envoy and sulked for several hours.

News of Francis's success with the Pope was brought to him. Leo hailed the young conqueror and when Francis had attempted to kiss his toe had lifted him in his arms and embraced him.

Leo, it was said, had promised to support Francis, and when Maximilian died—and there must then be an election to decide who should be the next Emperor—he promised to give Francis his support.

It was intolerable.

"Ha," cried Henry. "They will learn that wise men do not trust Frenchmen."

But even these events worked favourably for Katharine, for Ferdinand, knowing that the alliance between France and England was weakening, wrote to Henry in a most friendly fashion. He guessed how that young bantam, Henry, would be feeling and was determined to exploit the situation to the full.

Ferdinand did not like to see lack of good faith in families, he wrote. He thought fondly of his dear son and daughter. And to prove this he did an extraordinary thing; he sent Henry a collar studded with jewels, two horses caprisoned in the richest manner, and a jewelled sword.

Ferdinand, it was said, was either genuinely seeking Henry's friendship this time or in his dotage to send such gifts.

But it was very pleasant for Katharine, nursing the child in her womb, basking in the tenderness of her husband, enjoying the atmosphere of tolerance which had grown up about them—all this and reunion with her own country!

All will be well, thought Katharine. I am happy because I have learned to take life comfortably as it comes along; I no longer fight, I accept. Perhaps that is the lesson of life.

She did not greatly care. She busied herself with the preparations for her confinement.

She had never felt so calm and confident.

\*          \*

That September the Cardinal's hat arrived from Rome.

This, Wolsey assured himself, was the greatest moment of his life so far; but he was convinced that it was nothing compared with what was to come.

He determined that the country and the Court should be aware of his rising greatness; they should not be allowed to think that the arrival of a Cardinal's hat was an everyday affair.

He was a little angry with the Pope for sending an ordinary messenger, and he immediately sent word that he was to be detained as soon after disembarking as possible.

He announced to the City that a great procession was about to take place, and the people, who liked nothing so much as the pageantry provided by the Court and were only content with their own colourless lives because of it, turned out in their thousands.

Wolsey knew that Mistress Wynter and his children would be watching; and the thought added to his pleasure.

The Pope's messenger was persuaded to discard his simple raiment in exchange for one of fine silk; this he was happy to do, for the clothes were his reward for taking part in the ceremony.

Then he rode towards London, and was met at Blackheath by a great and vividly coloured procession made up of the members of the Cardinal's household. There they were, his higher servants and his lower servants, all aping their master, all giving themselves airs and strutting in a manner which implied: "We are the servants of the great Cardinal and therefore far above the servants of every nobleman in the land. Only the King's servants are our equals, and we wish the world to know it."

So through the City the hat was borne so that all might see it and marvel at it.

"It is being taken to the great Cardinal," said the citizens, "who is not only beloved by the people but by the Pope."

In his apartments at the Palace of Westminster Wolsey waited to receive the hat.

Taking it reverently in his hands he placed it in state upon a table on which tapers glowed.

He then declared that this was in honour of England and he would have all Englishmen under the King pay homage to the hat. None should consider himself too important to come forward and pay his homage in deep obeisance.

There was a murmuring among the Dukes and Earls of the realm; but Wolsey was creeping higher and higher in the King's favour, for Henry believed that he could not do without him if he were to pursue his life of pleasure. It gave him great content, when he hunted through the day, to think of friend Thomas grappling with state affairs. He believed in this man, who had come to his present position from humble beginnings. He had proved his genius.

Therefore Wolsey insisted that all those disgruntled noblemen —chief among whom was the Duke of Buckingham—should pay homage to his hat; and one by one they succumbed; so it was that Wolsey acquired at that time not only a Cardinal's hat but the hatred and envy of almost every ambitious man in the land.

What did he care! If Katharine believed this was her year, Thomas Wolsey knew it was his.

Before the year was out he could count his gains. Cardinal Wolsey, papal legate, Archbishop of York and Lord Chancellor of England, Prime Minister of State. Under the King he was the richest man in England, and many believed that his wealth might even be greater than Henry's. In his hands was the disposal of all ecclesiastical benefices; he held priories and bishoprics, among which were the rich ones of York and Durham, Bath and Hereford; he also held the Abbeys of St. Albans and Lincoln.

He had come as far as he could in this country; but he did not believe that was the end. His eyes were firmly fixed on Rome.

## CHAPTER XIV

# THE DEATH OF FERDINAND

FERDINAND WAS OFTEN thinking of his daughter in England. Indeed lately he had begun to ponder on the past, a habit he had never indulged in before. This may have been due to the fact that his health was rapidly declining. His limbs were swollen with dropsy, and, although he longed to rest them, he found it difficult to breathe within closed walls because of the distressing condition of his heart.

There were times when he had to battle for his breath, and then would come these sessions of reminiscence. His conscience did not trouble him. He had been a fighter all his life and he knew that the only way he could have preserved what he had, was to have fought and schemed for it.

He had heard an alarming rumour that Henry of England believed his wife to be incapable of bearing healthy children because not one of them so far had lived. Ferdinand knew the significance behind such rumours.

But Catalina is strong, he told himself. She is her mother's daughter. She will know how to hold her place.

It was not for him to worry about his daughter; his great concern was to keep the breath in his body.

There was one place where he felt more comfortable, and that was out of doors. The closeness of cities was intolerable to him, for the air seemed to choke him. He would not admit that he was old; he dared not admit it. If he did he would have young Charles closing in on him, eager to snatch the crown.

He could feel angry about young Charles. The boy did not know Spain, and did not even speak Spanish; he was Fleming from the top of his flaxen head to the toes of those—if he could believe reports—ungainly feet. He lacked the dignity of the Spaniard.

"If I could only put his brother Ferdinand in his place, how willingly would I do so." Ferdinand thought lovingly of his grandson who bore the same name as himself, and who had been as the son he had longed for. He had had the boy educated in the manner of a Spanish grandee, he himself supervising that education; he loved young Ferdinand.

His eyes glinted. Why should he not give his possessions to Ferdinand?

He laughed to picture the disapproving face of Ximenes who would remind him of his duty and that Charles was the heir, the elder of mad Juana's sons. Ximenes would rigidly adhere to his duty. Or would he? He had a great affection for young Ferdinand also.

But I have many years left to me, he assured himself, refusing to think of death. It was true he was nearly sixty-four years old— a good age—but his father had been long-lived and, but for this dropsy and the accursed difficulty in breathing, he would not feel his age. He had a young wife, and he still endeavoured to persuade her that he was young, yet he was beginning to wonder if the continual use of aphrodisiacs did not aggravate his condition.

As he sat brooding thus he was joined by the Duke of Alva who looked at him keenly and said: "Your Highness yearns for the fresh air of the country. Come to my place near Placencia. There are stags in plenty and good hunting."

Ferdinand felt young at the thought of the hunt.

"Let us leave this very day," he said.

When they came into the country he took deep breaths of the December air. Ah, he thought, this suits me well. I am a young man again in the country. He looked at Germaine who rode beside him. She was so fresh and youthful that it did him good to see her; yet his thoughts strayed momentarily to his wife Isabella who had been a year older than he was, and he felt a sudden desire to be back in those old days when he and Isabella had fought for a kingdom, and at times for supremacy over each other.

As usual the fresh air was beneficial and he found that if the day's hunting was not too long, he could enjoy it. Alva, concerned for his health, made sure that the hunt finished when the King showed signs of fatigue, and Ferdinand began to feel better.

In January he decided that he should travel on to Andalusia, for he was never one to neglect state duties for pleasure.

Perhaps the hunt had been too strenuous, perhaps the journey was too arduous, but Ferdinand was finding it so difficult to breathe that by the time his party reached the little village of Madrigalejo not far from Truxillo, he could not go on.

There was great consternation among his followers as there was no place worthy to provide a lodging for the King. Yet stop they must, and certain friars in the village came forward and said they had a humble house which they would place at the King's disposal.

The house was small indeed; rarely in his adventurous life had Ferdinand rested in such a place; but he knew that he could not go on, so he gasped out his gratitude to the friars, and allowed himself to be helped to a rough bed.

He looked round the small room and grimaced. Was this the place where the most ambitious man in Europe was to spend his last days on Earth?

Almost immediately he laughed at himself. His last days! He had never been easily defeated and he would not be now. After a little rest he would be ready to go on with his journey; he had learned one lesson; he would take more rest; he would give up his rejuvenating potions and live more as a man of his years must expect to live. If he curtailed his physical exercise he could direct state affairs from a couch. He thanked God that he was in possession of his mental powers.

But as he lay in that humble dwelling news was brought from the village of Velilla in Aragon. In this village was a bell which was said to be miraculous; when any major disaster was about to befall Aragon the bell tolled. Certain bold men had sought to stop the bell's tolling only to be dashed to death. The bell, it was said, rang and stopped of its own volition, when the warning had been given.

Now, said rumour, the bell of Velilla was tolling for the imminent death of great Ferdinand of Aragon.

So stunned by this were those about him that Ferdinand asked what ailed them; and one, unable to withstand the insistent interrogation, told Ferdinand that the bell of Velilla had given a warning of imminent disaster.

Ferdinand was horrified because until this moment he had not believed death could possibly come to him. To other men, yes; but in his youth he had seen himself as an immortal; such self-made legends died slowly.

But the bell was tolling . . . tolling him out of life.

He said: "I must make my will."

He thanked God . . . and Isabella . . . in that moment for Ximenes, because thinking of the tolling of the Velilla bell, his great anxiety was not for himself but for the good of his country. Ximenes he could trust. There was a man who was above reproach, above ambition, who would never give honours to his friends and family unless he honestly believed they deserved them. He remembered even now all he owed to Isabella, and he would serve Isabella's family with all his powerful ability.

Then Cardinal Ximenes, Archbishop of Toledo, should be

the Regent of Spain, until such time as his grandson was ready to rule it.

Ximenes would support Charles, he knew. Ferdinand grimaced. Oh, that I were not on my death-bed! Oh, that I might fight for a kingdom and bestow it on my grandson Ferdinand!

But this was a matter outside the control of a dying man. There was no question of the succession of Castile; as for the succession of Aragon and Naples they must fall to Juana—mad Juana, a prisoner in Tordesillas—and to her heirs. The Regency of Castile should go to Ximenes and that of Aragon to his dear son the Archbishop of Saragossa.

Ferdinand could smile wryly, and it seemed to him then that his first wife Isabella was at his bedside and that he snapped his fingers at her. "Yes, Isabella, my bastard son, my dear one on whom I bestowed the Archbishopric of Saragossa when he was six years old. How shocked you were, my prim Isabella, when you discovered his existence! But see, he is a good and noble boy, of sound good sense and beloved by the people. The Aragonese love my illegitimate son more than you did, Isabella."

He would not forget his grandson Ferdinand. He should have an annual income of fifty thousand ducats and a share in Naples. As for Germaine, she must be provided for. She should have thirty thousand gold florins, and five thousand should be added to that while she remained a widow. Would that be long? He pictured her—gay Germaine—with a husband who did not have to resort to potions. Jealous anger almost choked him and he had to restrain himself in order to get back his breath.

He saw a man standing at his bedside and demanded: "Who is there?"

Some of his servants came forward and said: "Highness, it is Adrian of Utrecht who has arrived here, having heard of the indisposition of Your Highness."

Ferdinand turned his face to the wall to hide his anger. Adrian of Utrecht, the chief adviser of his grandson Charles.

So, he thought, the carrion crows have arrived already. They sit and wait for the last flicker of life to subside. They are mistaken. I'm not going to die.

He turned and gasped: "Tell . . . that man to go. He has come too soon. Send him away."

So Adrian of Utrecht was forced to leave the house. But Ferdinand was wrong.

A few days later when his gentlemen came to his bed to wish him good morning, they found that he was dead.

## CHAPTER XV

# THE PRINCESS MARY

THE CHRISTMAS FESTIVITIES were over and Katharine was glad. She was expecting the child in February and was determined not to exhaust herself by over-exertion.

Henry continued tender. He was quite happy for her to be a mere spectator at those entertainments in which he played the central part. He could tell her solicitously that she was to retire to bed and rest; then he would be off to Elizabeth Blount or perhaps to some other young woman who had caught his passing fancy.

Katharine did not mind. She was patiently waiting.

That winter was a hard one—the coldest in living memory— and it was while the frost was at its worst, and the ice on the Thames so thick that carts could pass over it, that news was brought to Henry of the death of Ferdinand.

He received it with elation. Ferdinand, that old trickster, was dead. Henry would never have completely forgiven him for duping him as he had. It was the passing of an era; he knew that well. There would be a new ruler in Spain. Henry wanted to laugh aloud. It would be that boy whom he had met in Flanders —that slow-speaking young oaf, with the prominent eyes and the pasty skin. There would be one who was a complete contrast to Ferdinand.

He was far from displeased. Now he would turn his hatred and envy of the Spanish ruler to the King of France, that sly-eyed, fascinating creature who was bold and had begun his reign—as Henry had longed to do—by offering his people conquest.

But for the time being, Ferdinand was dead.

"This will be a shock to the Queen," he said to Wolsey when they discussed the news. "It would be better to keep it from her until after the child is born."

"Your Grace's thoughtfulness is equalled only by your wisdom."

"You agree, eh, she should not be told?"

"It would be unwise to tell her in her present state. There might be another disaster."

The King nodded. His eyes had become cunning. Wolsey followed his thoughts. Katharine had lost a powerful ally in her father. If the King should decide to repudiate her now, there would be no great power in Europe to be incensed by this treatment of her, for in place of a warlike and cunning father-protector she had only a young and inexperienced nephew.

Wolsey thought: Bear a healthy son, Katharine, or you will be in acute danger.

"I will let it be known," said Wolsey, "that on pain of Your Grace's displeasure, none is to tell the Queen of her father's death."

\*     \*     \*

It was on the 18th day of February of the year 1516, in the Palace of Greenwich, when Katharine's child was born.

Katharine came out of her agony to hear the cry of a child.

Her first thought was: "Then the child is alive."

She saw faces about her bed, among them Henry's. She heard a voice say: "The child is healthy, Your Grace. The child lives."

She was aware of a great contentment. How she loved that child! All my life I shall love it, she thought, if only for the joy it has brought me in this moment.

But why did they say "the child?"

"A . . . boy?" she asked.

The brief silence told her the answer before it came: "A bonny girl, Your Grace."

There was a faint intake of breath. But it was too much to hope for a boy and a child that lived.

Henry was beside her bed.

"We have a healthy child, Kate," he said. "And the next . . . why, that will be a boy."

Days of acute anxiety followed; she was terrified that events would take the same tragic course as on so many other occasions. But this little girl was different from the beginning; she lived and flourished.

When it was time for her christening it was decided that she should be called Mary after Henry's sister who, having returned to England and been publicly married to the Duke of Suffolk at Greenwich, was now installed high in the King's favour.

It was the Queen's great delight to watch over the Princess Mary. She loved her with deep devotion which could scarcely have been so intense but for all the disappointments which had preceded the birth.

Even the grief she suffered when she heard of her father's death, and the faint fear which, knowing something of the exigencies of state, this event must arouse in her, was softened, because at last she had her child, her healthy little Mary, the delight of her life.

\* \* \*

Katharine, playing with her daughter, knew that this was the happiest period of her life. The child was charming; she rarely cried but would lie solemnly in her cradle or in Katharine's arms.

Katharine would stand with the wet-nurse, Katharine Pole, and the governess, Margaret Bryan, wife of Sir Thomas Bryan, about the little Princess's cradle; and they made an admiring circle, while they watched the child playing with the gold pomander which had been a present from her Aunt Mary, now Duchess of Suffolk. The child seemed to love that ornament which later she might stuff with perfumes and wear about her waist, but which at the moment she liked to suck.

Henry would come in and join the circle. Then Katharine Pole and Margaret Bryan would draw back and leave the parents together.

Henry's eyes would be glazed with tenderness. This was his child and he told himself that more than anything on Earth he wanted children. He marvelled at those plump wrists, at the fingers, at the eyes which looked solemnly into his. He was delighted with the down of reddish hair on that little head, because it was his own colour.

Katharine watching him loved him afresh; they had something they could share now: this adorable little daughter.

"By God, Kate," murmured Henry, "we've produced a little beauty."

He wanted to hold her; and he was delighted when she did not cry as he picked her up. He would sit, looking a little incongruous, that big figure, glittering with jewels, holding the baby somewhat awkwardly yet so tenderly in his arms.

He insisted on having her brought to the banqueting hall or his presence chamber when his courtiers were present or when he was receiving foreign ambassadors.

"My daughter," he would say proudly, and take her in his arms, rocking her to and fro.

She never cried as most children would, but her large solemn eyes would stare at that big face at this time all suffused with tenderness and love.

The ambassadors would look on, admiring the baby, and the courtiers were continually discovering new likenesses to the King.

"She has the temper of an angel," said the Venetian ambassador.

"You are right there," cried Henry. "By God, Mr. Ambassador, this baby never cries."

Mary was almost perfect in the eyes of the King. If she had but been a boy she would have been quite so.

\* \* \*

Before Ferdinand's death he had recalled Caroz and sent in his place Bernardino de Mesa, a very different type from Caroz. De Mesa was a Dominican friar, quiet, seemingly humble but in truth one of the shrewdest of Spaniards. It was a master stroke for Ferdinand to have sent him because his outward meekness was just what was needed to offset Wolsey's arrogance and ostentation.

Ferdinand had realized too late that the Cardinal was the real ruler of England. However, de Mesa immediately began an attempt to repair the damage Caroz had done; and it was on de Mesa's suggestion that Ferdinand had sent Henry the handsome present.

But Ferdinand was dead; de Mesa would have a new master; Katharine was no longer interested in politics as her attention was focused on her daughter; but Wolsey favoured the Spanish ambassador because he was knowledgeable in that field which was one of the utmost interest to the Cardinal—the Papal Court.

De Mesa waited apprehensively for new policies. While Ximenes was Regent he imagined that there would be little change; but what would happen when young Charles took the reins of government, guided no doubt by his Flemish favourites?

De Mesa sought to speak to the Queen of these matters but Katharine had become half-hearted, since her father's perfidy and death had shocked her deeply.

She no longer wanted to feel herself a Spaniard; she had her daughter to absorb her; and all the time de Mesa was seeking to draw her attention to European politics she was thinking: How she grows! To think that we can dispense with Katharine Pole's services now! She will be easily weaned. Was there ever such a good tempered child? They say sweet temper means good health. Soon she will have her own household, but not yet. For a while her place will be in her mother's apartments.

She smiled absently at the Spanish ambassador, but she did not see him; she saw only the bright eyes of her daughter, the round, chubby cheeks and that adorable fluff of reddish hair on the top of the exquisite little head which so delighted the child's father.

And when Henry's sister, Margaret, Queen of Scotland, came to London to seek her brother's help against her enemies, Katharine's great interest was in discussing Margaret's children with her and trying to win her sister-in-law's admiration for the beloved little Princess.

## " 'PRENTICES AND CLUBS"

THE FOLLOWING SPRING there was disquiet in the streets of London.

During recent years many foreigners had settled there, and these people, being mostly exiles from their native lands—serious people who had fled perhaps for religious reasons—were by nature industrious. Day in, day out, they would be at their work, and so they prospered. There were Flemings who were expert weavers; Italians who were not only bankers but could make the finest armour and swords. The Hanseatic traders brought over leather, rope, wax, timber, nails and tar; and of course since the coming of Katharine to London to marry Prince Arthur there had always been Spaniards in London.

Life was hard for the citizens of London. During the cruel winter many had died of starvation in the streets and there had been rumblings of dissatisfaction all through the year.

With the coming of Spring the young apprentices gathered in the streets and talked of the injustice of foreigners' coming to their city and making a good living, while they and their kind lived in such poor conditions.

They themselves could not understand the joy some of these cordwainers and weavers, these glaziers and lacemakers found in the work alone. They did not seem to ask for pleasure as the apprentices did. They cared for their work with the passion of craftsmen, and those who lacked this skill were angry with those who possessed it.

They met in Ficquets Fields and near the Fleet Bridge, and talked of these matters.

There was one among them, a youth named Lincoln, who demanded: "Why should we stand by and see foreigners take away our livings? Why should we allow the foreigners to live in our city at all?"

The ignorant apprentices shook their fists. They had a leader; they craved excitement in their dull lives. They were ready.

So on May morning of the year 1517, instead of rising early to go and gather May flowers in the nearby countryside, the apprentices gathered together and, instead of the cry "Let's a-maying," there were shouts of " 'Prentices and Clubs!"

The revolt had begun.

The apprentices stormed into the city; there were hundreds of them and they made a formidable company. Through the streets of London they came, carrying flaming torches in their hands; they broke into the shops of the foreigners; they came out carrying bales of silk, the finest lace, jewels, hats, textiles.

When they had ransacked these shops and houses they set them on fire.

News was brought to the King at Richmond.

Henry was first angry; then alarmed. The people could always frighten him because he had a dread of unpopularity.

He decided to remain at Richmond until others had the revolt under control.

\*　　　\*　　　\*

Chaos reigned in London.

The under-sheriff of the city, Sir Thomas More, pitying the plight of the apprentices and knowing that they would be quickly subdued, went among them, risking his life, for tempers were running high, imploring them to stop their violence.

Wolsey meanwhile had taken the position in hand and had sent for the Earl of Surrey who arrived with troops and very soon had hundreds of people under arrest and others hanging from gibbets which had been quickly erected throughout the city.

Meanwhile Henry waited at Richmond, determined not to go into his capital until order was restored.

It was eleven days after the uprising that he rode into the city and took his place on a dais in Westminster Hall. With him came three Queens—Katharine, Mary—who had been Queen of France and was far happier to be Duchess of Suffolk—and Margaret, Queen of Scotland.

"Bring the prisoners to me," cried Henry, his brows drawn together in a deep frown, "that I may see these people who would revolt against me."

There was a sound of wailing from the spectators as the prisoners were brought in. There were some four hundred men and eleven women, all grimy from their stay in prison, all desperate, for they knew what had happened to their leaders and they expected the same fate to befall themselves; they even came with ropes about their necks; and in the crowd which had pressed into the Hall and clustered round it were the families of these men and women.

The King raged in his anger. They had dared rise against his merchants; they had burned the houses of his citizens; they deserved the worst death which men could devise.

His troops were stationed about the city; his guards surrounded him, and he was eager to show these people the might of the Tudor.

Wolsey came close to him. He said: "Your Grace, I beg of you in your clemency spare these men."

Henry's little eyes glittered. He hated them, those wild-eyed men and women. They had dared show criticism of his rule. Yet . . . they were the people. A King must always please his people.

He caught Wolsey's eye; the Cardinal was warning him: "It would be as well, Your Grace, to pardon these men. A fine gesture . . . here in the heart of your capital. A powerful King but a merciful one."

Yes, he knew. But here was the spirit of the masque again. He must play his part as he always had done.

He scowled at Wolsey and said: "These prisoners should be taken from here and hanged by the neck on gibbets prepared for them within the city."

Katharine was watching the faces of some of the women who had pressed into the hall. They were mothers, and some of these boys who stood there on the threshold of death, the halters round their necks, had been their babies.

It was more than she could bear. Stripping off her headdress so that her hair fell about her shoulders—as became a supplicant— she threw herself at the King's feet.

"Your Grace, I implore you, spare these prisoners. They are young. Let them grow to serve Your Grace."

Henry, legs apart, his fingers playing with the great pearl which hung about his neck, regarded her with assumed tenderness and said: "You are a woman, Kate, and soft. You know nothing of these matters. . . ."

Katharine turned to Mary and Margaret and they, seeing the appeal in her eyes and being moved themselves by the sight of those miserable prisoners and their sorrowing families, loosened their hair and knelt with Katharine at the King's feet.

Henry regarded them, and his eyes were a brilliant blue.

Three Queens knelt at his feet! What a spectacle for his people!

He appeared to consider.

Wolsey—the great Cardinal who, when he went abroad, rode

through the streets in a procession which rivalled that of a king's
—also appealed to Henry.

His appeal was a warning, but there was no need for the warning. Henry was about to make the grand gesture.

"I am not proof against such pleading," he declared. "And I
know full well that these foolish men and women now regret their
folly. They shall live to be my very good subjects."

There was a sudden shout of joy. The prisoners took the halters
from their necks and threw them high into the air.

Henry stood watching them—sons rushing into their mother's
arms, wives embracing husbands—a smug smile of pleasure on
his face.

As Katharine watched, the tears flowed down her cheeks.

## CHAPTER XVII

# THE KING TRIUMPHANT

LITTLE MARY WAS growing up to be a model child. She was now two years old and had her separate establishment at Ditton Park in Buckinghamshire. Katharine could not bear to be separated from the child, and consequently she spent a great deal of time in her daughter's nursery; and she contrived to be often at Windsor Castle so that the child could be ferried over to her there.

Katharine was going to supervise her education as Isabella had her children's. She was going to take her mother as an example; Mary should learn to love and depend on her mother as she, Katharine, had on hers.

Already Mary was showing great promise. She had a lively intelligence, could speak clearly and knew how to receive important personages. It was a constant delight to present them to her that she might charm them as she charmed her parents.

Henry was almost as devoted as Katharine. He enjoyed taking the child in his arms or on his knees and playing with her. Only occasionally would the frown appear between his eyes, and Katharine would know then that he was thinking: Why is this child not a boy?

Mary quickly showed an aptitude for music, and, young as she was, Katharine taught her how to play on the virginals. The Queen would sit with the little girl on her lap, the four feet long box in which the keyboard was set, placed on the table; and there the childish fingers would pick out the notes.

Her progress was amazing, and Henry as well as Katharine liked to show off her talent as much as possible.

What happy days they were; and to crown her pleasure, Katharine discovered that she was once more pregnant.

"Now we have a healthy girl, we must get us a boy," said Henry.

His tone was playful but there was a faint threat beneath it. He was determined to have a boy . . . from someone.

\*　　　\*　　　\*

Autumn had come and the King hunted all through the day and returned in the late afternoon to banquets and masques.

Katharine was spending the days in happy preoccupation with her domestic affairs. There was so much to occupy her days. She liked to sit sewing with her women; and it was her delight to embroider Henry's linen, and garments for little Mary. She had moved away from the sphere of politics and was happier for it.

Her hopes of bearing another healthy child were high. Mary was a joy in more ways than one. Not only was she her charming self but she was a promise of future children, a symbol which insisted that what could be done once could be done again.

This was the happiest of her pregnancies—apart from the first one. This time she could feel almost complacent.

"But let it be a boy," she prayed. "O Holy Mother, intercede for me and give me a boy."

She was seated at the table on the dais; the hunters had returned hungry from the forest, and Henry was in his place at the centre of the table where there was much jesting and laughter.

Elizabeth Blount was present. Katharine always looked for her among the guests, and she marvelled that Henry could have been faithful to a woman for so long. Elizabeth was, of course, a beauty; and she was entirely the King's. The marriage to Sir Gilbert Taillebois was one in name only. They could be certain of this. Sir Gilbert would not dare to be a husband to Elizabeth while she was the King's paramour.

Poor Gilbert! thought Katharine with some contempt. He stands by, like a cur, waiting for his master to throw the bone after he has finished gnawing it.

She felt no jealousy of Elizabeth; she felt nothing but this great desire to bear a son.

She did notice, however, that Elizabeth looked different tonight. She was even more attractive than usual. A diamond glittered at her throat. A gift from the King of course. She was dressed in blue velvet with cloth of silver, and those colours were very becoming to her fair beauty. She was subdued tonight. Had she perhaps noticed that the King was less attentive? Yet she seemed radiant. Had she another lover?

Katharine ceased to think of the woman. It was no concern of hers if Henry discarded a mistress, because there would be another if he dispensed with this one. She was not a giddy girl to look for faithfulness in a man such as Henry.

There was a burst of laughter at the table. The King had

made a joke. It must be the King's, for only his jokes provoked such abandoned laughter.

Katharine set her face into a smile, but she was not thinking of the King nor of Elizabeth Blount.

The child stirred suddenly within her.

"Holy Mother, give me a healthy child . . . a healthy male child."

\*         \*         \*

Henry's hand touched that of Elizabeth in the dance. She raised her eyes to his and smiled.

He pressed her hand warmly. He too had noticed the change in her tonight.

"But you are more fair than ever," he whispered.

"Your Grace . . ." Her voice faltered.

"Speak up, Bessie."

"There is something I must tell you."

"What is this?"

"I . . . wish to tell you as soon as we can be alone."

"You're frightened, Bessie. What's wrong?"

"I pray Your Grace. . . . When we are alone."

Henry narrowed his eyes, but she was whirled away from him in the dance.

\*         \*         \*

She was waiting for him in the ante-chamber where he had bidden her go.

"Slip away," he had said when their hands had touched again in the dance. "I will join you. None will notice us."

At one time she would have smiled at his belief that, when he did not wish to be noticed, he never was. As if everyone in the hall was not aware of the movements of the King! But tonight she was too preoccupied with her thoughts and fears.

He shut the door and stood looking at her.

"Well, Bessie?"

"Your Grace . . . I . . . we . . . I am with child."

Henry stared at her.

Then he began to laugh. "By God, Bessie," he cried, "I had begun to think you were a barren woman. When I considered all the nights we have been together . . . and no sign of a child. I began to wonder what was wrong with you . . . or . . ."

He frowned, as though admonishing himself.

He came towards her then, and there was a tender smile on his lips.

"Your Grace is not displeased . . .?"

Bessie was thinking: This will be the end. He will not want a pregnant woman. There will be someone else. Nothing will ever be the same again.

"Displeased!" He took her face in his hands and gently pinched her cheeks. "There's nothing could have pleased me more."

He seized her in his arms and held her so tightly that she would have cried out with the pain if she had dared. Then he swung her into his arms and held her up, looking at her.

Displeased! he was thinking. He had said that nothing could please him more; that was not true. If Bessie gave him a son he would be delighted, but a legitimate son was what he desired more than anything on Earth.

Now that Bessie carried their child he could look more closely at the fears which had been trying to intrude into his mind.

When there was failure to produce children it was natural to presume that something might be wrong with the would-be parents—both of them perhaps. Katharine was not barren. She could become pregnant; her failure lay in not giving birth to a healthy male child. Among her offspring there had been boys— but still-born, or, as in the case of the first, living only a few days.

If Bessie Blount bore a healthy child, it would prove, would it not, that the fault did not lie with him.

True there was Mary—but one living girl in all those pregnancies! It was almost as though God was against him in some way, as though He had said, you shall not have a male heir.

His high spirits began to overflow. He began dancing round the small chamber with Bessie in his arms.

Then he was sober suddenly. "We must take care of you, my Bessie," he said, lowering her gently to the ground. "We must cherish this little body of thine now that it shelters a royal child."

They returned to the ballroom and were covertly watched.

The King does not grow out of his love for Bessie Blount, it was whispered. See, he is as enamoured of her now as he was when he first saw her.

*          *          *

Katharine was in her daughter's apartments. Mary was seated at the table, propped up with cushions so that she was high enough to reach the virginals which had been placed on the table.

The plump little fingers were moving over the keys with a dexterity astonishing in one so young.

Katharine watched her. She was not yet three years old; surely there was not another child like her in the whole of the kingdom.

"My precious daughter," she murmured.

Glancing through the window she saw that the November mist was wreathed about the trees like grey ghosts; the ghosts of unborn children, she thought, and shivered.

She placed her hands on the child in her womb; and involuntarily the prayer rose to her lips. "A boy. Let it be a boy."

If I have a boy—as healthy, as bright as my little Mary, then Henry will be pleased with me. It is all he needs to make him happy. What need have I to concern myself with the Elizabeth Blounts of the Court if only I can have a healthy boy.

The child had finished her piece. Margaret Bryan clapped her hands, and the Duchess of Norfolk and her daughter, Lady Margaret Herbert, who were both in attendance on the little Princess, clapped with her.

Katharine rose to embrace her daughter and, as she did so, she felt the now familiar nagging pains begin.

She cried out in alarm. It was not the pains which frightened her. It was the grey mist out there. It looked like ghosts . . . ghosts of children who had made a brief appearance on Earth and then had gone away. It reminded her that this was but November and her child was not due to be born until the Christmas festivities should begin.

*          *          *

So it was over.

She lay frustrated, sick, weary and a little frightened. She heard voices which seemed to come from a long way off but which she knew were in her bedchamber.

"A daughter . . . a still-born daughter."

Oh my God, she thought, then You have forsaken me.

There were other voices, but these were in her mind.

"They say the King fears his marriage does not find favour in Heaven." "They say it is because he married his brother's wife." "They say it would not be difficult to end such a marriage . . . now, for the Queen's father is dead and there is no need to fear her nephew . . . he is but a boy. Why should the King fear him?"

She closed her eyes. She was too weak to care what became of her.

She thought: This was my last chance. I have tried so many times. We have one daughter. But where is the son he so desperately needs, where is the boy who could make him tender towards me?

*       *       *

He was standing by her bedside, and they were alone. When he had that look in his eyes, people slunk away from him. Even his dogs were aware of it. She had seen him often standing, legs apart, eyes blue fire, chin jutting forward—the sullen, angry boy. The dogs waited in corners and the clever men like Cardinal Wolsey were called away on urgent state matters.

Now they had left him with her; and she lay helplessly looking up at him.

She said: "I am sorry, Henry. We have failed once more."

"*We* have failed? I did my part. It is you who fail to do yours."

"I do not know where I failed, Henry."

Those were the wrong words. How easy it was to speak the wrong words.

"You would suggest that it is something in me!"

"I do not know what it is, Henry."

She thought he would strike her then.

O God, she thought, how much it means to him! How angry he is!

He had taken one step towards the bed and stopped; then he turned and began pacing the room. He was holding in his anger. He was hurt and bewildered. He had thought, after Mary, that they would get a son.

She knew that with each attempt she lost some charm for him. Each time she took to her bed in the hope of giving birth, she rose from it more wan, more listless; each time she left some of her youth behind.

She understood him well enough to know that these failures hurt him so much because they brought an insidious doubt into his mind. He would admit this to none, but she who had lived close to him for nine years knew him perhaps better than he knew himself, for he was a man who would never know himself well because he refused to look where it was not pleasant to do so.

Yet he could not drive the question from his mind. Is it in some measure due to me? Am I incapable of begetting a healthy son?

He could not bear that he should be anything but perfect. He loved himself so much.

Even in that moment she, who was so much wiser, was sorry for him. If she could, she would have risen from her bed and comforted him.

He had paused before the device which hung on the wall. The device of the pomegranate—the Arabic sign of fertility.

Oh, if I could but go back to the happy days in Granada before I had seen England, when my beloved mother was alive, I would never have chosen this as my device.

Henry began to laugh; and his laughter was not pleasant to hear.

He lifted his hand, and she thought that he was about to tear the device from the wall and trample on it. As though with difficulty he restrained himself; then, without another look at her, he strode from the room.

*        *        *

Henry rode out to a certain Priory, and with him he took only his most intimate friends. Compton and Bryan were among them, and they chatted and laughed gaily as they went along.

But Henry had not his heart in the raillery. He listened half-heartedly and there was a strained expression in his face. And after a while they fell silent.

Henry believed what was waiting for him at the Priory was of the utmost importance. He was praying, as he went along, for a sign. He would discuss his thoughts with no one, for as yet he was afraid of them; but if what he hoped should happen, then he might begin to reshape his life.

When they reached the Priory, he rode ahead of his friends into the courtyard, and grooms who clearly were expecting the important visitor hurried out to do them service.

Henry leaped out of the saddle; he was striding into the

building and as he did so he was met by two excited nuns; their faces under their black hoods were flushed and their eyes alight with excitement.

"What news?" demanded Henry.

"It is all over, Your Grace. Her ladyship is well and will be eager to see you."

"And . . . is there a child?"

"Yes, Your Grace, a bonny child."

Holy Mother of God, they torture me, thought Henry.

He shouted. "Boy or girl?"

"A bonny boy, Your Grace."

Henry gave a shout of triumph.

He called to Compton who was close behind him: "Did you hear that? A boy! Bessie has my boy!" Then he seized the nearest nun by the shoulder. "Take me to them," he cried. "Take me to Lady Taillebois and my son."

They led the way, running, for this was an impatient King.

He saw her on her pillows, her red gold hair spread about her as he had seen it so many times before. She was pale and triumphant. She was his beautiful Bessie who had given him what he wanted, now as she always had.

"Why, Bessie." He was on his knees by the bed. "So you've done it, eh, girl? You've come through it, eh?" He took her hand and kissed it loudly. "And the child? Where is he?" Suspicion shot up in his eyes. "Where is he, I say?"

A nun had appeared; she was holding a child.

Henry was on his feet, staring down at the burden in her arms

So small. So wrinkled. Yet a child. His child. He wanted to shout with joy. There was the faint down on that small head— and it was Tudor red.

Tears were in his eyes. The smallness of the child moved him; this little one, his son!

Then he thought, Holy Mother, how could you do this to me. . . . ? You give Bessie my son . . . when I want to give him my crown."

He took the child from the woman.

"Your Grace, have a care. He is young yet."

"Do you think to tell me to have a care for my own child? Let me tell you, woman, this child means as much to me as my crown. This is my son. By God, this boy shall know great honours. . . ." He was overcome with love for the child, with gratitude to Bessie, who had not only given him a son, but proved his capability to beget sons. He said rashly: "This child might have my crown."

Bryan and Compton exchanged glances.

The remarks of an exuberant father on beholding his son?

Mayhap. But both Bryan and Compton were wondering what effect the existence of this young child could have on the Queen.

\*         \*         \*

Henry had summoned the whole Court to that Manor which he had some time since bought for Bessie Blount. This was the occasion of the christening of his son.

It was to be a grand ceremony, for he would have everyone know that since he welcomed his son into the world with such joy, so must they all.

There was one guest at the ceremony whom many thought it was cruel to have asked. She had come, pale and resigned, looking like a middle-aged woman since her last pregnancy.

Poor Katharine! How sad it was that it was she who, out of so many pregnancies, had been only able to produce one daughter while Bessie Blount should give the King a healthy son.

She brought presents for the child. She showed no resentment for she had already learned that it was wise to hide her true feelings.

The King seemed unaware of the indignity he was heaping upon her; he seemed at that time unaware of her.

And when the name of the newly-born child was asked, it was Henry himself who answered in a deep, resonant voice which could be heard by all: "This child's name is Henry Fitzroy."

And as he spoke he looked at Katharine. She was startled; she had always known that there was cruelty in his nature; but now she read his thoughts: You see, I can get me a son. But not through my wife. Here is my boy . . . my healthy boy. Is it not strange that you should have tried so many times and failed? Is it because our marriage is frowned on in Heaven? Is it, my wife? My *wife*!

Now her nightmares had taken shape. They were no vague phantoms.

She saw the speculation in those blue eyes.

She thought: I am the Queen. None can change that. And she

would not meet his gaze for fear she should be tempted to look into the future.

She was here in the Manor he had bought for his mistress; she was attending the christening of his only son—and a son by that mistress.

For the present she was the Queen of England. She would not look beyond that.

*The King's Secret Matter*

## CHAPTER I

# THE CARDINAL'S REVENGE

KATHARINE, QUEEN OF ENGLAND, sat at her window looking down on the Palace gardens; her hands lay idly in her lap, her tapestry momentarily neglected. She was now approaching her thirty-fifth birthday, and her once graceful figure had grown somewhat heavy during the years of disappointing pregnancies; yet she had lost none of her dignity; the humiliation she was forced to suffer could not rob her of that serene assurance which reminded all who came into her presence that she was not only the Queen of England but the daughter of Isabella of Castile and Ferdinand of Aragon.

She wore the fashionable five-cornered hood which glittered with jewels, and from it hung a black mantilla, for although it was nineteen years since she had left her own country she still clung to certain customs and fashions of her native land; her gown was of blue velvet trimmed with sable; and as she sat, her feet gracefully crossed, her petticoat of gold-coloured satin was visible; at her throat were rubies, and similar jewels decorated the *cordelière* belt which encircled her thick waist and fell to her feet.

Now as she gazed out of the window the expression on her regular, though heavy, features was serious in the extreme; and the high forehead was wrinkled in a frown. The woman who was watching her felt compassion welling up within her, for she knew that the Queen was uneasy.

And the reason was obvious, thought Lady Willoughby who, as Maria de Salinas, had come with Katharine to England nineteen years before, and until her marriage to Lord Willoughby had never left her mistress's service; and even now returned to her whenever she found it possible to do so.

Katharine the Queen had anxieties enough.

If there could only be a male child, thought Maria. *One* male child. Is that too much to ask? Why is it denied her?

They had been so close to each other for so many years that there were occasions when they read each other's thoughts, and the Queen, glancing away from the gardens, caught Maria's pitying look and answered that unspoken thought.

"I have a feeling that it will never be, Maria," she said. "There have been so many attempts."

Maria flushed, angry with herself because she had betrayed

thoughts which could only bring further pain to her beloved mistress.

"Your Grace has a charming, healthy daughter."

Katharine's face became young and almost beautiful as it invariably did when her daughter, the five-year-old Princess Mary, was mentioned.

"She grows more beautiful as the months pass," murmured the Queen, smiling to herself. "She is so gay, so merry, that she has won her father's heart so certainly that I do believe that when he is with her he forgives her for not being a boy."

"No one could wish the Princess Mary to be other than she is," murmured Maria.

"No. I would not change her. Is that not strange, Maria? If it were possible to turn her into a boy I would not do so. I would not have her different in any way." The smile disappeared and she went on: "How I wish I could have her more often with me here at Greenwich."

"It is because the King is so eager that she shall enjoy the state which is due to her that he insists on her maintaining a separate household."

The Queen nodded and turned to her tapestry.

"We shall be leaving for Windsor shortly," she said; "then I shall have her ferried over from Ditton Park. I long to hear how she is progressing with the virginals. Did you ever know a child of five who showed such musical talent?"

"Never," answered Maria, thinking: I must keep her mind on Mary, for that will give her a respite from less pleasant matters.

But as she was reminding Katharine of that occasion when the King had carried his daughter down to the state apartments and insisted on the ambassadors of France and Spain paying homage to the little girl's rank and accomplishments, a shout from the grounds diverted the Queen's attention to other matters, and Maria noticed the momentary closing of the eyes which denoted that disgust she felt for what was happening down there.

It was a mistake, Maria told herself, for the Queen to hold aloof from the King's pastimes; and while she sympathized with Katharine and understood her mistress's revulsion, she felt that it was unwise of her to show such feeling. The King was a man who looked for adulation and, because it was almost always unstintingly given, he was quick to perceive when it was not; and merely by declining to accompany him to the arena, the Queen had doubtless offended him. True, she had pleaded indisposition; but the King, who was himself so rarely indisposed, was apt to regard the illness of others with scepticism and derision.

No, it was unfortunate that while the King, surrounded by his courtiers, was watching a bear being torn to pieces by his ban dogs, which had been kept hungry for hours in order to increase their ferocity, the Queen should be sitting over her tapestry with one faithful friend at her side.

More shouts followed, and the sound of trumpets came through the open window.

Katharine said: "The game will have ended. How thankful I am that I was not there to witness the death agony of some poor creature."

"We shall never grow accustomed to English sports, I fear," answered Maria. "After all these years we remain Spanish."

"Yet we are English now, Maria, by reason of our marriages. We both have English husbands, and Spain seems so very far away; yet I shall never forget the Alhambra and my mother."

"You would like to return to Spain, Your Grace?"

Katharine shook her head. "I did not want to after she had died. For me she *was* Spain. I do not think I could have endured life there after she had gone. There would have been too much to remind me. It is so many years since she died . . . yet for me she never died. She lives on in my heart and brings me comfort still. I say to myself, when I think of my own sweet daughter: Katharine of Aragon will be such a mother to the Princess Mary as Isabella of Castile was to Katharine of Aragon."

"She was both great and wise."

"There are times," went on Katharine, "when I wish with all my heart that she were here, that she had her apartments in this Palace and that I could go to her, tell her what perplexes me, so that out of her great wisdom she might tell me what to do."

What could even great Isabella tell her daughter? wondered Maria. How could she advise her to please that wayward husband of hers? She could only say, as so many at Court could say: Give him a son. Then you will be safe.

Katharine looked at the woman who for so long had been her dearest friend. She knows of my troubles, thought the Queen. It would be impossible for her not to know. Who in this Court does not know that the King is persistently unfaithful to his wife, that he is beginning to find her five years seniority distasteful, that he is dissatisfied because, although she has proved herself capable of becoming pregnant, she has also shown herself unable to bear him a healthy male child? Twelve years of marriage had resulted in several miscarriages and only one healthy child—a daughter.

She was not one to ask for sympathy; she knew it was dangerous

to confide in others. Yet Maria de Salinas was her very dear
friend and she believed there was no one in her life who loved her
more. It was a sad admission. Her husband no longer loved her;
she was fully conscious of that sad fact. Her mother who had loved
her dearly—even as she herself loved Mary—was long since dead.
Recently her father, the ambitious, parsimonious Ferdinand, had
died; but of course Ferdinand had never had much love to spare
for any one person, his possessions taking all the affection he had
to give; and to him she had merely been an important counter
in the game of politics which was his life. Mary loved her; but
Mary was a child.

God grant she never has to suffer as I have, thought the Queen
hastily.

But all would be well for Mary who was now heir to the throne,
because there was no Salic law in England. If there were no male
children born to her parents, and one day she ascended the
throne, she would be Queen in her own right, which was a very
different matter from being a King's Consort.

Katharine's mother had been a Queen in her own right and,
much as she had loved her husband, she had never forgotten it;
for although Ferdinand had often been unfaithful—there were
several illegitimate children to prove it—although she had accepted this as inevitable, forgiven him and remained his loving
and submissive wife, in state matters she had held rigorously to
her supremacy.

"Oh, Maria!" she sighed. "I am passing through troublous
times, and I feel . . . alone."

Maria went to Katharine and kneeling, buried her face in the
blue velvet. "Your Grace, while I live to serve you, you are never
alone."

"I know it, Maria . . . my very good friend. I love you dearly,
as you love me, and to no other would I speak of these matters.
But to you I will say this: I despair of getting a male child. There
is so little opportunity. The King rarely visits my bed. And since
the birth of a son to Elizabeth Blount his manner towards me
grows colder."

"That sly creature!" Maria said angrily.

"Nay, do not blame her. She was a shy girl, and he is her
King. He said, 'Come hither' and the girl has no more power to
resist than a rabbit facing a stoat. And she has given him this
son."

"I hear that she no longer pleases him."

The Queen shrugged her shoulders. "He has taken the boy
away to be brought up."

"In seclusion, Your Grace," said Maria quickly.

"But royally. If another woman should give him a son . . ."

Maria knew that the Queen was thinking of that catastrophe which she feared so much that she would not even speak of it. It was summed up in one dangerous word which was whispered throughout the Court: Divorce.

Impossible! Maria assured herself. Even Henry would never dare. How could he when the nephew of the Queen was not only King of Spain but Emperor of Austria, the greatest monarch of them all. No, it was all so much talk. Had the Queen been some humble princess, there might have been cause for fear; but the aunt of the Emperor was surely safe from all such indignities.

The Queen went on: "There is this new girl."

Maria waited.

"She was in France; he found her during that extravagant frolic. She is of a bad reputation and is known in the court of France as a wanton. I cannot understand him. But I have decided to send for the girl."

Maria trembled. She wanted to say: Oh . . . no . . . no. It is folly. Let the King have his women, and look the other way.

"She is the daughter of Thomas Boleyn. I believe he has two girls and a boy. The other girl is in France now and much younger, and is said to be more intelligent than her sister. It is to be hoped this is so. But I shall have something to say to this Boleyn girl."

"And His Grace . . . "

"His Grace was amused by her wantonness . . . as it appears many have been before."

"Your Grace, this affair has gone . . . "

"As far as it is possible to go. It would not surprise me if Mary Boleyn is not already with child . . . perhaps twins. Boys, I'll dare swear."

It was unlike the Queen to show such feeling, and Maria trembled afresh. Characteristically the Queen noticed the expression in Maria's face and was sobered by it—not because she feared for herself, but because she had troubled her friend.

"Have no fear, Maria," she said. "I shall dismiss this girl from the Court. I shall know how to deal with such a one. The King has amused himself with her, but she is no Elizabeth Blount. He will do nothing to detain her at Court. He will merely look about him and . . . find another."

"But if he will find another . . . "

"I understand your meaning, Maria. Why dismiss this girl? Simply because her reputation is so light. No, if the King must have a mistress it should be one who has not shared the beds of quite so many. I hear that she even included the King of France among her lovers, briefly, oh very briefly. Elizabeth Blount at least behaved decorously and she was connected with the Mount-joys. These Boleyns, I have heard, have descended from trade."

"Is that so, Your Grace? When one considers Thomas Boleyn that is surprising."

"Thomas Boleyn gives himself airs, indeed. A very ambitious man, Maria. I wonder he does not take this girl of his and put her into a convent. But I do assure you that I have not been mis-informed as to his origins, for when I heard of the King's . . . connection . . . with this girl I had enquiries made. One Geoffrey Boleyn was apprentice to a mercer in London . . . oh, it is a long time ago, I grant you, and he became rich; but he was a trades-man, no more, no less. Becoming Lord Mayor of London and buying Blickling Hall from Sir John Falstaff, and Hever Castle from the Cobbhams, does not alter that. So this family rose through trade and advantageous marriages. They are connected with the Ormonds, and Thomas's wife is Norfolk's daughter. But this girl . . . this Mary . . . is doubtless a throw-back to the days of trade."

How bitter she is, thought Maria; and how unlike herself. My poor Queen Katharine, are you becoming a frightened woman?

"It is a deplorable state of affairs when such people are allowed to come to Court," went on Katharine.

There was a brief silence and Maria took advantage of it to say that she had heard the Emperor might again visit England, and how she hoped this was true.

"I hope so too," said Katharine. "I think the King has changed the opinion he once held of my nephew."

"All who saw him on his visit to England were impressed by his serious ways and his fondness for Your Grace."

Katharine smiled tenderly. "I could not look on him without sadness, although it gave me so much pleasure to see him. He is indeed worthy of his destiny, but I could not help thinking of my sister."

Maria winced and wished she had not turned the conversation in this direction. There was so much tragedy in the life of the Queen that it seemed impossible to avoid it. Now in reviving her memories of her nephew's visit she had reminded her of her poor sister Juana, Charles's mother, who was insane and living out her sad life in the castle of Tordesillas and who would have been the ruler of Spain had she not lost her reason.

"Poor Juana," went on Katharine, "she was always wild, but

we never thought it would come to this. There are times when I can feel almost happy because my mother is dead. I always thought that the deaths of my brother and eldest sister shocked her so deeply that she went earlier to her tomb than she would otherwise have done. But if she were alive now, if she could see her daughters—one mad, the other tormented . . .''

Maria interrupted, forgetting that it was a breach of etiquette to do so, ''Your Grace's troubles will be over one day. You have a healthy daughter; there will surely one day be a son.''

And so they had arrived back at the matter of the moment; this was the subject which occupied the minds of all at Court. A son. Will there be a son born to the King and Queen? There must be . . . for, if there is not, the position of Queen Katharine in England will be uncertain.

The Queen had turned back to the window.

''They are coming now,'' she said, and picked up her tapestry.

The two women worked in silence for some moments while the sounds from without increased. Those of voices accompanied by laughter floated up to them, but they kept their eyes on the tapestry.

The King's voice was immediately recognizable; loud and resonant, it was that of a man who knew he only has to speak to achieve the result he wished. If he wanted laughter his courtiers gave it in full measure, with the required implication that his jokes were more witty than any other's; his frown was also more terrifying.

Katharine was thinking: Yet at heart he is only a boy. He plays at kingship. It is those about him who hold the power; men such as Thomas Wolsey on whom he depends more and more. An able man, this Thomas Wolsey, but an ambitious one, and the daughter of Ferdinand must know that ambition could warp a man's nature. But so far Wolsey's ambition was—like the King's strength—in check, and it seemed that Wolsey acted for the good of the state. Katharine had thought him her friend until recent months, when there were signs of a French alliance. Then she had not been so sure.

But it was not such as Thomas Wolsey whose company she most enjoyed. There were even now occasions when she could be at peace in the King's company; this was when he invited men such as Dr. Linacre or Thomas More to his private apartments for an intimate supper. In particular was Katharine drawn to Thomas More; there was a man whose gentle charm and astringent wit had made an instant appeal to her, but perhaps what she had admired most of all was that integrity which she sensed in the man. It was so rare a quality that all seemed to change when they came into contact with it; even Henry ceased to be the licentious young man and was a serious monarch, determined to increase his intellectual stature and work for the good of his people. It was small wonder that she looked forward with pleasure to those days when the King said: "Come, Master More, you shall sup with us tonight, and you may talk to us of astronomy, geometry or divinity; but willy-nilly we shall be merry with you."

And strangely enough they would be for, with Thomas More leading the conversation, however serious its nature, it must be merry.

But on this day such as Thomas More and Dr. Linacre would not be the King's companions.

She glanced out of the window. The King was leading his courtiers towards the Palace, and with him were his brother-in-law the Duke of Suffolk, William Compton and Thomas Boleyn.

Katharine's mouth tightened at the sight of the last.

Thomas Boleyn was the kind of man who would be delighted to offer his daughter to the King in exchange for honours. The honours were evidently being granted, and the man had been at the King's side during his meeting with the King of France—that ostentatious and vulgar display of the "Field of the Cloth of Gold"—and he remained there.

But not for long, vowed Katharine—unless he can hold his place by his own qualities and not through the lewdness of his daughter.

Wherever the King went there was ceremony. Now the heralds stationed at the doors were playing a fanfare—a warning to all those who had been within the Palace while the King was at sport to leap to attention. He would stroll through the Palace smiling graciously, if his mood was a good one; and it would seem that it was so now from the sound of his voice, and the laughter which followed his remarks.

She wondered whether he would go to his own apartments or come to hers. What did he wish now? Sweet music? Would he call for his lute and entertain the company with one of his own musical compositions? Would he perhaps summon Mary Boleyn and dismiss his courtiers? He was a young healthy animal and his whims and moods could change in a moment.

"He is coming here," she said, and she saw the faint flush begin in Maria's cheeks as the door was flung open.

The King stood on the threshold looking at his Queen and her attendant bent over their tapestry.

Maria rose immediately, as did Katharine, and they both made a deep curtsey as Henry came into the room chuckling, his fair face flushed, his blue eyes as bright as chips of glazed china with the sun on them; his golden beard jutting out inviting admiration; he had recently grown it because King François had one, and he believed that a golden beard was more becoming than a black one.

Beside him most other men looked meagre, and it was not merely the aura of kingship which made them so. It was true they fell away from him, giving him always the centre of the stage, for every word, every gesture which was made in his presence must remind him that he was the King whom they all idolized.

He was glittering with jewels. How he loved colour and display! And since he had returned from France he had worn brighter colours, more dazzling jewels. It was true that he did so with a hint of defiance; and Katharine knew that it would be a long time before he forgot the sly looks of the King of France, the caustic wit which, it had to be confessed, had set the King of England at a loss; that long nose, those brilliant dark eyes, had frequently seemed to hold a touch of mockery. The King of France was the only man who in recent years had dared snap his fingers at Henry and make sly jokes at his expense. Oh, the extravagant folly of that Field of the Cloth of Gold! All sham, thought Katharine, with two monarchs swearing friendship while hatred filled their hearts.

But Henry was not thinking of François now as he stood at the threshold of his wife's apartment. He was in a favourite position, legs apart—perhaps to display that fine plump calf; his jerkin was of purple velvet, the sleeves slashed and puffed; his doublet of cloth of gold decorated with pearls; on his head was a blue velvet cap in which a white feather curled and diamonds scintillated; about his neck was a gold chain on which hung a large pearl and ruby; the plump white fingers were heavily loaded with rings, mostly of rubies and diamonds.

It was small wonder that wherever he went the people shouted for him; unlike his father he was a King who looked like a King.

"How now, Kate?" he said; and she straightened herself to look into his face, to read the expression there—his was the most expressive face at Court—and Katharine saw that for this moment his mood was a benign one. "You've missed a goodly sight." He slapped his thigh, which set the jewels flashing in the sunlight.

"Then 'twas good sport, Your Grace?" answered Katharine, smiling.

"'Twas so indeed. Was it not?" He turned his head slightly and there was an immediate chorus of assent. "The dogs were game," he went on, "and the bear was determined to stay alive. They won in the end, but I've lost two of my dogs."

"Your Grace will replace them."

"Doubt it not," he said. "We missed you. You should have been at our side." His expression had changed and was faintly peevish. She understood. He had been with Mary Boleyn last night and was making excuses to himself for conduct which shocked him a little, even though it was his own. She knew that he was tormented periodically by his conscience; a strange burden for such a man to carry. Yet she rejoiced in the King's conscience; she believed that if he ever contemplated some dastardly act, it would be there to deter him.

"It was my regret that I was not," answered Katharine.

He growled and his eyes narrowed so that the bright blue was scarcely visible. He seemed to make a sudden decision, for he snapped his fingers and said: "Leave us with the Queen."

There was immediate obedience from those who had accompanied him into the apartment; and Maria de Salinas hurried to where the King stood, dropped a curtsey, and followed the others out. Henry did not glance at her; his lower lip was protruding slightly as the plump fingers of his right hand played with the great ruby on his left.

Katharine experienced a twinge of that apprehension which was troubling her more and more frequently nowadays. He had felt contented when he was watching his animals; when he had crossed the gardens and come into the Palace he had been happy. It was the sight of her sitting at her tapestry which had aroused his anger.

When they were alone he grumbled: "Here is a pleasant state of affairs. The King must sit alone and watch good sport because his Queen prefers not to sit beside him that people may see their King and Queen together."

"I believed I did not displease Your Grace in remaining in my apartment."

"You knew full well that I wished you to be beside me."

"But Henry, when I explained my indisposition, you seemed contented enough that I should remain in the Palace."

It was true; he had shrugged his shoulders when she had pleaded a headache; would she never learn that what he accepted at one time with indifference could arouse his anger at another?

"I liked it not," he growled. "And if this headache of yours was so distressing, do you improve it with the needle? Nay, 'twas our rough English sports that disgusted you. Come, admit it.

Our English games are too rough for Spanish ladies, who faint at the sight of blood. 'Tis so, is it not?''

"It is true that I find the torturing of animals distasteful."

"'Tis odd in one who comes from Spain where they make a religious spectacle out of torturing people."

She shuddered; the thought of cruelty was distasteful to her; she knew that during the reign of her revered mother the Spanish Inquisition had tortured heretics and handed them over to the Secular authorities to be burned to death. This she had often told herself was a matter of faith; those who suffered at the *autos-de-fé* in her native land did so because they had sinned against the Church. In her eyes this was a necessary chastisement, blessed by Holy Church.

She said quietly: "I do not care to witness the shedding of blood."

"Bah!" cried the King. "'Tis good sport. And 'twould be well that the people see us together. Like as not we shall be hearing that all is not well between us. Rumours grow from such carelessness, and such rumours would not please me."

"There are rumours already. I'll warrant the secret of your mistresses is not kept to the Court."

The King's ruddy face grew a shade darker and there was a hint of purple in it. She knew she was being foolish, knew that he was like an ostrich, that he fondly imagined that no one was aware of his infidelities or, if they were, looked upon them as a kingly game no more degrading than the hounding of animals to death.

"And is it meet that you should reproach me for seeking elsewhere what I cannot find in your bed?" he demanded.

"I have always done my best to please you there."

The eyes narrowed still more; the face was an even darker shade, the chin jutted out in a more bellicose manner; and only the beard prevented his looking like a boy in a tantrum.

"Then," he shouted, "let me tell you this, Madam. You have not pleased me there!"

She closed her eyes waiting for the onslaught of cruel words. He would not spare her because, with the guilt of his adultery heavy upon him, he had to find excuses for his conscience. He was talking to that now—not to her.

The tirade ended; a slightly pious expression crossed the scarlet face; the blue eyes opened wider and were turned upwards. His voice was hushed as he spoke.

"There are times, Kate, when I think that in some way you and I have offended God. All these years we have prayed for a boy and again and again our hopes have been disappointed."

And those words smote her ears like a funeral knell; the more so because they were spoken quietly in a calculating manner; he had momentarily forgotten the need to appease his conscience; he was planning for the future.

He had expressed that thought before, and always in that portentous manner, so that it sounded like the opening chorus, the prelude to a drama on which the curtain was about to rise.

So now she waited for what would follow. It must come one day. If not this day, the next. Perhaps a week might elapse, a month, a year . . . but come it would.

He was eyeing her craftily, distastefully, the woman who no longer had the power to arouse any desire in him, the woman who after twelve years of marriage had failed to give what he most desired: a son born in wedlock.

There was nevertheless still to be respite; for suddenly he turned on his heel and strode from the room.

But Katharine knew that the curtain was soon to rise.

\*     \*     \*

As the courtiers left the King and Queen together, many an understanding glance was exchanged. It was common knowledge that all was not well between the royal pair. Who could blame the King, said the gay young men, married to a woman five years older than himself—a woman who was over-pious and a solemn Spaniard—when he was surrounded by gay young English girls all eager for a frolic! It would have been different of course had there been a son.

There was one among the company whose smile was complacent. This did not go unnoticed. Edward Stafford, third Duke of Buckingham, had good reason to be delighted by this lack of royal fertility. Secretly Buckingham believed himself to be more royal than the Tudors, and there were many who, had they dared to express such an opinion, would have agreed with him.

Buckingham was a proud man; he could not forget that through his father he was descended from Thomas of Woodstock, son of Edward III, and that his mother had been Catherine Woodville, sister of Elizabeth Woodville who had married Edward IV. And who were the Tudors but a bastard sprig from the royal tree!

Never could Buckingham look on the King without this thought crossing his mind: There but for the chances of fate might stand Edward Stafford.

Such thoughts were only safe when locked in the secret places of the mind; and it was unwise to betray, even by a look, that they existed. Buckingham was a rash man and therefore, since he lived under Henry VIII, an unwise one.

The old Duke of Norfolk who was at his side, guessing his thoughts, whispered: "Caution, Edward."

As Buckingham turned to look at his friend a faint frown of exasperation appeared on his brow. Further resentment flared up in his mind against the King. Why should he have to be cautious lest the stupid young King should realize that he fancied himself in his place? If Henry had a spark of imagination, he would guess this was so.

Norfolk and Buckingham were intimate friends and there was a connection between the families because Buckingham's daughter had married Norfolk's son.

Buckingham smiled wryly. The old man would want no trouble to befall his friend and connection by marriage, and would be thinking that such trouble often embraced the whole of a family.

"Your looks betray your thoughts," whispered Norfolk. "There are those who are ready to carry tales. Let us go to your apartments where we shall be able to talk in peace."

Buckingham nodded and they disengaged themselves from the crowd.

"You should be watchful," murmured Norfolk as they mounted the staircase on their way to Buckingham's apartment.

Buckingham shrugged elegant shoulders. "Oh come," he said, "Henry knows that I'm as royal as he is. He doesn't need my careless looks to remind him."

"All the more reason for caution. I should have thought you would have been warned by the case of Bulmer."

Buckingham smiled reminiscently. It had been worth it, he decided; even though at the time he had suffered some uneasy moments.

But he was glad that he had shown his daring to the Court; there was no doubt of that when he had approached Sir William Bulmer, who was in the service of the King, and bribed him with an offer of better service in his own retinue. He had done this out of bravado, out of that ever persistent desire to show the King that he was of equal standing. Buckingham had never forgotten how Henry had sought to seduce his, Buckingham's, sister, as though she were some serving girl at the Court. Perhaps Henry also had not forgotten Buckingham's action in having the girl whirled out of his orbit by her enraged husband just at that moment when successful seduction seemed imminent. Buckingham had scored then. It was a glorious victory for a Duke to win over a King. And he had tried again with Bulmer. Not so successfully, for the King, no longer an uncertain boy, had summoned Bulmer to the Star Chamber and accused him of having deserted the royal service. Bulmer had cowered before the onslaught of the King's anger and had been kept on his knees until he despaired of ever being allowed to rise.

But at length Henry had relented, forgiven Bulmer and taken him back into his service. The affair, however, was meant to be a warning—chiefly to an arrogant Duke. Yet the Duke still thought his dangerous thoughts; and it was possible to read them in almost every gesture that he made.

"Ah, Bulmer," he mused now. "That man was a coward. He should have returned to me."

"It might have cost him his head," suggested Norfolk.

"I would rather lose my head than be known as a coward."

"Take care that you are not called upon to prove those words, Edward."

"Henry does not possess a surfeit of bravery," retorted Buckingham. "Look how he let my sister go."

"It would be a different state of affairs if that had happened today. Henry was a boy when he decided on your sister. I do believe that up to that time he had never been unfaithful to the Queen. Those days are over."

"He realized that we Staffords would not accept the insult."

"You deceive yourself. If he fancied your wife or mine he'd care not a jot for our families. The King is no longer a boy to be led. He is a man who will have what he wants and thrust aside all those who stand in his way."

"If he respects royalty he must include those who are as royal as he is."

"Henry sees only one point of view, his own. He is the King. The rest of us, be we Dukes or lords, are so far beneath him that he would have our heads, ay, and feel it was but his due, should the fancy take him. That is why I bid you to be cautious. Ha, here comes Wolsey, on his way to the royal apartments, I'll swear."

"The butcher's dog is for ever sniffing at the heels of his master," said Buckingham, without taking the precaution of lowering his voice.

Thomas Wolsey was making his way towards them, an impressive figure in his scarlet Cardinal's robes. He was a man of about forty-five, his expression alert, his face mildly disfigured by smallpox, and the lid of one eye hanging lower than the other, which gave an added expression of wisdom to his clever face.

Buckingham did not pause as he approached; his gaze became cold and he looked beyond the Cardinal as though he could not see the red-clad figure.

"A merry good day to you, gentlemen," said the Cardinal.

"Good day to you," answered Norfolk.

"I trust, my lords, you enjoyed good sport and that His Grace is happy because of it."

"The sport was fair enough," murmered Norfolk; but Buckingham, who had not spoken, was walking on.

Wolsey did not appear to have noticed; he inclined his head slightly and Norfolk did likewise, as Wolsey went on towards the King's apartments, the two Dukes on to Buckingham's.

"'Tis my belief he heard your words," said Norfolk.

"'Tis my hope that he did."

"Curb your pride, Edward. Will you never understand that he is forever at the King's side, ready to pour his poison in the royal ear?"

"Let him pour—if the King listens to the butcher's boy he is unworthy to be King."

"Edward . . . you fool! When will you learn? You already have an enemy in the Cardinal; if you love your life do not seek one in the King."

But Buckingham strode on ahead of Norfolk, so that the old man had to hurry to keep up with him; and thus they came to his apartments.

As they entered three men of his retinue who were conversing together bowed to him and his companion. These were Delacourt his confessor, Robert Gilbert his chancellor, and Charles Knyvet who was not only his steward but his cousin.

The Dukes acknowledged their greetings and when they had passed into Buckingham's private apartment he said: "My servants are aware of it. They know full well that their master might, by good chance, ascend the throne."

"I trust," put in Norfolk nervously, "that you have never spoken of such matters in their presence."

"Often," laughed Buckingham. "Why, only the other day Delacourt said to me: 'If the Princess Mary died, Your Grace would be heir to the throne.' Why, my friend, you tremble. Norfolk, I'm surprised at you."

"I never heard such folly."

"Listen to me," murmured Buckingham soothingly. "The King is not such a fool as to attack the nobility. He has too much respect for royalty to harm me. So set aside your fears. This much I tell you: I will be treated with the respect due to me. Now, what do you think the King is saying to his Queen at this moment?

He is upbraiding her for not accompanying him to watch the sport; but what he really means is that she is of no use to him since she cannot give him a son. I do believe he has begun to despair of ever getting a boy by her."

"But the boys he gets by others will not provide the heir to the throne."

Buckingham chuckled. "No. There'll be no heir—and is the Princess Mary really a healthy child? But the King would do well to forget his anxieties. He has good heirs in me and mine."

It was useless, Norfolk saw, to turn Buckingham from the subject which obsessed him; nevertheless he tried; and they talked awhile of the Field of the Cloth of Gold and the treaties which had been made with François Premier and the Emperor Charles.

Norfolk, who had not accompanied the royal party to France on that occasion, grumbled about the cost to which England had been put, and Buckingham agreed with him. The nobility would be on short commons for the next few months in order to pay for all the finery they had had to provide.

"And for what?" demanded Buckingham. "That our Henry might show François what a fine fellow he is! As if François could not match pageant with pageant!"

Norfolk sourly agreed. He had not stood in high favour with the King since Thomas Wolsey had risen to such eminence; he hated the Cardinal as much as Buckingham did, but he had had an opportunity of realizing the venom and power of the man, and he was too shrewd to take unnecessary risks.

Buckingham was in a rebellious mood that day and, being conscious that members of his retinue were hovering, and fearing some indiscretion might be uttered in their presence, in which he might be involved, Norfolk took his leave as soon as he could politely do so.

When he was alone Buckingham brooded on that favourite subject of his, which aroused such bitterness within him and which, try as he might, he could never succeed in dismissing from his mind. He could work himself to a fury over what he construed as an insult from anyone of lowlier birth than his own, and the very presence of Wolsey at Court seemed an affront.

Norfolk's warnings had only succeeded in intensifying his recklessness, and when Knyvet came to his apartment to ask his advice about some matter of his stewardship, the Duke said: "His Grace of Norfolk has been talking to me of the affair of William Bulmer."

"Ah, Your Grace," said Knyvet, "that man is now back in the King's service. Some say he had a lucky escape."

"Oh yes, he went back like a whipped cur. He would have done better to have remained with me. I shall not forget that he deserted me . . . when the time comes."

Knyvet looked startled. "It is not easy to disobey the King's command."

Buckingham lifted his shoulders. "At one time I believed the King was preparing to have *me* sent to the Tower for my part in that affair."

"Your Grace to the Tower!"

Buckingham nodded. "Kings do not last for ever," he mused. "My father learned that. He was in conflict with Richard III. But my father was no coward. He planned that when he was brought to the King he would have his dagger ready and plunge it into that false heart. I do assure you, cousin, that had an indignity been forced upon me, I should have been as ready to avenge the honour of my family as my father was."

Knyvet murmured: "Your Grace cannot mean . . ."

"And," interrupted Buckingham fiercely, "if the King were to die and the Princess were to die, I should take over the crown of this Kingdom, and none should say me nay."

Knyvet recoiled, which amused Buckingham. How terrified everyone was of being drawn into a conspiracy! Such fear in others spurred the Duke on to further recklessness. He said: "Is Hopkins, the monk, in the Palace today?"

"Yes, Your Grace."

"Then send him to me. I have heard that he can see into the future. I want him to look into mine."

"I will have him brought to Your Grace."

"With all speed," cried Buckingham.

He paced excitedly up and down his apartment while waiting for the monk; and when the man was brought to him he shouted so that several of his servants could not fail to hear him: "So, Hopkins, you are here. I want you to tell me what the future holds for me. I want you to tell me what chance I have of attaining the throne."

The monk shut the door and put his fingers to his lips. The face which peered out of his hood was shrewd. He took in the details of the apartment; the love of luxury was apparent. Here was a noble Duke who could do him much good in exchange for the prophecy he wanted. Hopkins knew that if he told the Duke that he would be more likely to end his days on a scaffold than on a throne (and one did not have to be a soothsayer to suspect that) he would be dismissed without reward. But such as this Duke would be ready to pay well for what he wanted to hear.

Hopkins looked long into that arrogant face, half closed his eyes and murmured: "I see greatness ahead for Your Grace."

"What sort of greatness?"

"All that you desire will be yours. I see a crown . . ."

A slow, satisfied smile spread across the Duke's face. This fellow has great and unusual powers, he told himself. It *shall* come to pass. Has he not prophesied that it shall?

So he presented the monk with a heavy purse; and from that moment his manner grew a shade more arrogant.

\*        \*        \*

In one of the privy gardens of the Palace a young man and woman sat on a wicker seat, their arms about each other. In the distance the shouts from the arena could be heard but both were oblivious of everything but the ardour of their passion.

The woman was plump and dark-haired; her body voluptuously curved; and the expression of her face, soft and sensuous, betrayed her nature. One glance was enough to see that she was one who had been endowed by nature with a deep appreciation and knowledge of fleshly pleasures; and her generous nature was one which wanted to share these. It was the secret of her great appeal to almost every man who saw her. And if they tired of her quickly it was because she could hold nothing back, but must give all that was demanded; so that in a short time there was little to learn of Mary Boleyn.

Since her early teens Mary had been in and out of more beds than she could remember. The Kings of England and France had been her lovers; so had the humblest officers of the Court. Mary was overflowing with desire which demanded appeasement and, being on such terms with pleasure and of a generous nature which never sought material gain, her favours had until this time been bestowed on most of those who asked for them.

Now she was in love and discovering that the emotions this young man aroused in her were of a different nature from those she had ever felt for any other person. She was still Mary, as uninhibited as a young animal in forest or jungle; lust was strong in her but it was tempered by affection, and when she thought of her future with her lover it was not only sharing his bed that filled her mind, but sharing his table, his fortune, and being a mother to the children they would have. This was a new and exciting experience for Mary Boleyn.

"And so," he was saying now, as his hands caressed the bare plump bosom, "we shall marry,"

"Yes, Will," she answered, her lips slightly parted, her eyes glazed, while she wondered whether they dared here in full daylight. If they were discovered and tales carried to the King . . . ! It was only a few nights ago that His Grace had summoned her to his bed. He might be somewhat angry if he knew of her love for Will Carey.

"And when shall I speak to your father?"

Mary was alarmed. She caught his hand and pressed it against her breast. It was so easy to lose oneself in a sensuous dream and forget reality. In truth she was more afraid of her father than of the King. The King might decide that it was a good idea that she married. It was often the case in relationships such as theirs. He had found a husband for Elizabeth Blount and there was always a possibility that a mistress might become pregnant, when the necessary hasty marriage could be a little undignified. No, she did not think the King would object to the marriage; though he might insist that husbandly activities were confined only to giving his wife his name. Mary would not be greatly perturbed. Could she imagine herself living in a house with Will, and not . . . The thought made her want to laugh.

But her father—approaching him was another matter.

Thomas Boleyn had never thought much of his daughter Mary until she had caught the King's eye. Now he was inclined to regard her with greater respect than he had even for his son George; and all knew how clever George was.

Strange that Mary should have been the one . . . with her wantonness which had earned her many a beating in the past . . . to have brought honours to the family. But if Will Carey went to her father and asked for his daughter's hand there would be trouble.

"He'll never give his consent," she said sadly.

"Why should he not?"

"You do not know my father, Will. He is the most ambitious of men, and of late he has risen high in the King's service."

"Does he not wish to see his daughter married?"

"Mayhap, but alas, Will, you have no money and are only a younger son of your father. To us such matters are of no moment because we love, and that is all we ask. But my father does not believe in love. He will never give his consent."

"Then what can we do?" Will asked in despair.

Mary took his face in her hands and kissed his lips. The kiss was full of invitation and promise. She was telling him that, even if they had to wait awhile for marriage, they had much to give each other in the meantime.

"I want to take you away from Court, Mary."

"And I want to go." She frowned. If the King sent for her, she must go to him. But it would really be Will with whom she wished to make love.

"What *can* we do about it? We must do something. I cannot wait for ever."

"Something will happen, Will, never fear. We will be patient . . . about marriage . . . and something will happen; you sée."

Will fell upon her in a storm of passion. She was the ideal mistress, never withholding, always ready to give. But he wanted to take her away that he might keep her all to himself and that no others might share the pleasures which she gave so wholeheartedly. He knew about the King, of course. He could never be sure, when she was not with him, whether she was with the King.

She soothed him as she well knew how and after a while she said: "I will speak to my father of your offer."

"And if he forbids us to meet?"

"No one could prevent our meeting, Will."

But Will was unconvinced.

"They are returning from their sport now," went on Mary. "My father will surely have been with the King. It may well be that his mood is a good one. Will, what if I spoke to him now?"

"But it is surely I who should speak to him, Mary."

She shook her head, imagining her father intimidating her lover. Will was a man who might easily be intimidated, and her father, who had always been formidable, had become more so during the years of success.

She withdrew herself from him, sighing regretfully. "Nay, Will," she said, "I will find him, and if the moment is a good one, speak to him. I know him better than you and if he shows signs of anger I shall know how to withdraw and pretend that our matter is of no importance."

"You will not let him dissuade you?"

"No one shall persuade me to give you up, Will."

He believed her, because he knew that she could be strong where her passions were concerned.

\*     \*     \*

Thomas Boleyn, taking a moment's respite in his private apartments of the Palace whither he had retired when the King dismissed the courtiers that he might be alone with the Queen, was confronted by his daughter, who asked to speak with him in private.

Graciously he granted this permission, for Mary had become

an important member of the household since the King had elevated her to the position of mistress.

Even so Thomas regarded her with faint distaste. Her dress was crumpled and her hair escaping from her headdress. Though, Thomas thought fleetingly, it may be the slut in her which appeals to the King. Yet although he was pleased with her, he was often anxious because he must constantly ask himself how long she would continue to hold the King's attention.

It was difficult to reconcile himself to the fact that Mary had sprung to such importance. She had always been the fool of the family. The other two were such a precocious pair. He had high hopes of George and it was his plan to bring him into prominence at Court at the earliest opportunity; he was sure that when that young man was a little older he would prove an amusing companion for the King. As for Anne, she was too young yet to make plans for. At the present time she was at the Court of France whence he heard news of her from time to time, and how her cleverness and charm pleased the King and Queen and members of their Court. But that the little slut Mary should have found favour with the King . . . was incredible.

"Well, my daughter?"

"Father, I have been thinking that it is time I married."

Thomas was alert. Had the King put this into her head? If so he would be following the normal procedure. The King would feel happier with a mistress who had a husband; it forestalled an undignified shuffling into marriage if the need to do so should arise. No doubt Henry had found some worthy husband for his favourite; and Thomas, even if he wanted to, would not be such a fool as to refuse his consent to a marriage suggested by the King.

"Perhaps you are right, Mary," he said. "Whom have you in mind?"

Mary smiled in what seemed to the practical Thomas a vacuous manner as she murmured: "It is William Carey, Father."

"William Carey! You cannot mean . . . No, you could not. I was thinking of Carey's son . . . a younger brother. . . . "

"It is that Will, Father."

Thomas was astounded and horrified. Surely the King would never suggest such a lowly match for a woman in whom he had been interested. It was an insult. The blood rushed to Thomas's face and showed even in the whites of his eyes. "The King . . ." he stammered.

"The King might not object to this marriage," Mary began.

"He has suggested it to you?"

"Oh . . . no! It is because Will and I have fallen in love."

Thomas stared at his daughter. "You must be mad, girl. You . . . have fallen in love with this Will Carey? A younger son of a family that can scarcely be called distinguished!"

"One does not think of family honours or wealth when one falls in love," said Mary simply.

"You have lost your wits, girl."

"I believe it is called losing one's heart," replied Mary with some spirit.

"The same thing, doubtless. Well, you may put this young man out of your mind. I want to hear no more of such nonsense. It may well be that, if you are patient, the King will suggest a good marriage for you. Indeed, it might be a good plan for you to make some light suggestions. Carefully, mind. Hint perhaps that marriage might be necessary . . ."

Mary bowed her head that he might not see the defiance which had sprung into her eyes. Hitherto she had been as easily swayed as a willow wand, but the thought of Will had stiffened her resistance. Strangely enough she was ready to put up a fight, to displease her father and the King, if need be, for the sake of Will Carey.

Thomas laid his hand on her shoulder; he had no doubt of her obedience. He was confident of his power when he looked back and saw how far he had come in the last years. He was forty-three years old, in good health, and his ambition was limitless. The King's pleasure in him was stressed by the fact that he had designated Sir Thomas Boleyn to play such a large part in making the arrangements for the Field of the Cloth of Gold; and now that Henry had favoured his daughter he was more grateful to Thomas than ever, because he had produced such a willing and comely girl. Mary had always been pliable, lacking the arrogance and temper of George and Anne.

Had he looked a little closer at Mary on that occasion he might have noticed that when her jaw was purposefully set, as it was at this moment, she bore a striking resemblance to her headstrong brother and sister.

But Thomas was too sure of his daughter, too sure of his ability to subdue her, to be alarmed.

He patted her shoulder.

"Now, my daughter, no more of this foolishness. There'll be a grand marriage for you, and now is the time to ask for it. I see no reason why you should not become a Duchess. That would please you, His Grace, and your family."

Still she kept her head lowered, and giving her a playful push he dismissed her.

She was glad to escape because of the overwhelming desire to tell him that she was no longer his puppet, nor the King's; Mary Boleyn in love, fighting for the future she desired, was as formidable as any young woman of spirit.

*     *     *

The great Cardinal was alone in his audience chamber, where he stood at the window looking out over the parkland of that most magnificent of his residences, Hampton Court. He could always find delight in this place which he regarded as essentially his own; for how different it had become in those years since he had taken over the lease from the Knights of St. John of Jerusalem and raised this impressive edifice to what it was at this time, built around five courts and containing 1500 rooms.

Here was opulence of a kind not seen even in the King's own palaces; the walls were hung with the finest tapestry which the Cardinal caused to be changed once a week; throughout the palace were exquisite pieces of furniture and treasures which proclaimed the wealth of their owner. The Cardinal was a man who liked to be constantly reminded of his possessions, for he had attained them through his own brilliance, and because he remembered humbler days he found the greater pleasure in them. He did not care that the people murmured and said that his court was more magnificent than that of the King; that was how he wished it to be. He often said to himself: "All that is Henry's is his because he is his father's son. All that is mine, is mine because I am Thomas Wolsey."

He encouraged ostentation. Let noblemen such as Norfolk and Buckingham sneer. They would sneer once too often. Let them make sly references to the butcher's shop in which they swore he had been born. What did he care? These men were fools; and Wolsey believed that one day he would triumph over all his enemies. He was determined to do so, for he was not the man to forget a slight.

He smoothed the crimson satin of his robes and caressed his tippet of fine sable.

Oh, it was good to be rich. It was good to have power and to feel that power growing. There was very little he wished for and did not possess, for he was not a man to seek the impossible. The greatest power in England, the Papal Crown . . . these were not impossibilities. And if he longed to install his family here in Hampton Court, to boast to the King of his son—his fine sturdy Thomas, named after himself, but known as Wynter—he accepted the impossibility of doing so. As a prelate he could not allow the fact of that uncanonical marriage of his to be known; he was therefore reconciled to keeping his family in the background while he could bestow honours on his son.

He was smiling to himself now because he knew of the activities which would be going on in the great kitchens. There was a special banquet this day; the King would be present in some disguise. Wolsey had not been specifically told that Henry would come; he had merely heard that a party of gentlemen from a far country planned to test the hospitality of Hampton Court, for they had heard that it vied with that to be enjoyed at the King's Court.

Wolsey laughed aloud. Such childish games! One among them would be the King, and the company must express its surprise when he discarded the disguise, and then the great delight and pleasure all felt in the honour of having their King with them.

"A game," mused Wolsey, "that we have played countless times and will doubtless play countless times again, for it seems that His Grace never tires of it."

But was His Grace tiring? Had there been an indication recently of a change in the King's attitude to life? Was he taking more interest in matters of state, a little less in masking?

The longer the King remained a pleasure-loving boy the greater pleased would the Cardinal be. Those workmanlike hands of his were the hands to hold the helm. He wanted no interference.

Let the golden boy frolic with his women. Wolsey frowned a little. Boleyn was growing somewhat presumptuous on account of that brazen girl of his; and the man was becoming a little too important. But the Cardinal could deal with such; it was the King's interference that he most feared; and while the King was concerned with a girl he could be expected to leave matters of state to his trusted Chancellor.

The guests were already arriving. He would not join them until the coming of the party of gentlemen in disguise, for that was beneath his dignity. His guests must wait for him to come among them, as at Greenwich or Westminster they waited for the King.

He knew that they would whisper together of the magnificence they saw about them, of the manner in which he dressed his servants, so that many of them were more richly clad than his guests. In the kitchens now his master cook, attired in scarlet satin with a gold chain about his neck, would be directing his many servants as though he himself was the lord of this manor; and that was how Wolsey would have it: that each man—from his steward who was a dean, and his treasurer who was a knight, to his grooms and yeomen of the pastry and his very scullery boys—should know, and tell the world by his demeanour, that it was better to be a page of the pantry in the household of Cardinal Wolsey than a gentleman steward in the house of any nobleman under the King.

As he brooded, his man Cavendish came to the door of the apartment and craved his master's indulgence for disturbing him, but a certain Charles Knyvet, late of the household of the Duke of Buckingham, was begging an audience with him.

Wolsey did not speak for a second. He felt a surge of hatred rise within him at the mention of the hated Buckingham. There was a man who had been born to wealth and nobility and who never failed to remind the Cardinal of it. It was in every look, every gesture and, often when he passed, Wolsey would hear the words: butcher's dog.

One day Buckingham was going to regret that he dared scorn Thomas Wolsey, for the Cardinal was not the sort to forget a grudge; all insults were remembered in order to be repaid tenfold; for that dignity which he had had to nurture, having cost him so much to come by, was doubly dear to him.

This was interesting. Knyvet to see him! He knew that the fellow was related to Buckingham—a poor relation—who had been in the Duke's employ until recently. There had been some difference of opinion between Master Knyvet and his rich relation, with the result that Knyvet had been dismissed from the ducal household.

So he came to see the Cardinal.

Wolsey regarded his hands thoughtfully. "You discovered his business?"

"He said it was for the ears of Your Eminence alone."

The Cardinal nodded; but he would not see the man—not at the first request. That would be beneath the dignity of the great Cardinal.

"Tell him he may present himself again," he said.

Cavendish bowed. The man was favoured. At least the Cardinal had not refused his request for an interview.

So Cavendish went back through the eight rooms, which had to be traversed before the Cardinal's private chamber was reached, and in which none who sought an audience might wait.

Now Wolsey could hear shouts on the river, the sound of music, and he decided it was time for him to leave his apartment and cross the park to the water's edge, there to receive the party, for it would contain one before whom even a great Cardinal must bow.

He made his way down his private staircase and out into the sunshine; standing at the river's edge he watched the boat approach the privy stairs. In it was a party of men dressed in dazzling colours, all heavily masked and wearing beards, some of gold wire, some of black. The Cardinal saw with some dismay that the masks, the false beards, and caps of gold and scarlet which covered their heads were all-concealing, and this was going to be one of those occasions when it was not easy to pick out the King.

Usually his great height betrayed him; but there were several who appeared to be as tall. A faint irritation came to the Cardinal, although he hastened to suppress it; one of the first steps to disfavour was taken when one betrayed a lack of interest in the King's pastimes. That was one of the lesser ways in which the Queen was failing.

"Welcome, gentlemen," he cried, "welcome to Hampton Court."

One of the masked men said in a deliberately disguised voice which Wolsey could not recognize: "We come from a strange land, and news of the hospitality of the great Cardinal has been brought to us, so we would test it."

"Gentlemen, it is my pleasure to entertain you. Come into the palace. The banquet is about to be served, and there are many guests at my table who will delight you as you will delight them."

"Are there fair ladies?" asked one.

"In plenty," answered the Cardinal.

One tall man with a black beard came to the Cardinal's side. "Fair ladies at the table of a Cardinal?" he murmured.

Wolsey spread his hands, believing he heard mockery in the voice. This disturbed him faintly for he fancied it might well be the King who walked beside him.

"My lord," he answered, "I give all I have to my guests. If I believe the company of fair ladies will enliven the occasion for them, then I invite fair ladies to my table."

"'Tis true you are a perfect host."

They had come to the gates of the palace beside which stood two tall yeomen and two grooms, so still that they looked like statues, so gorgeously apparelled that they looked like members of the nobility.

"Methinks," said the black-bearded man in an aside to one of his companions, "that we come not to the Cardinal's court but to the King's Court."

"It pleases me that you should think so, my lord," said Wolsey, "for you come from a strange land and now that you are in the King's realm you will know that a Chancellor could possess such a manor only if his master were as far above him as you, my lord, are above my grooms whom you so recently have passed."

"Then is the King's Court of even greater brilliance?"

"If it were but a hut by the river it would be of greater brilliance because our lord the King was therein. When you have seen him you will understand."

He was feeling a little uneasy. It was disconcerting to be unsure of the King's identity. The game was indeed changing when that golden figure could not be immediately discovered.

"It would seem that you are not only a great Cardinal but a loyal subject."

"There is none more loyal in the kingdom," replied Wolsey vehemently; "and none with more reason to be. All that I am, I am because of the King's grace; all that I possess comes from his mercy."

"Well spoken," said the black-bearded man. "Let us to your banquet table; for the news of its excellence has travelled far."

In the banqueting hall the guests were already assembled, and the sight was magnificent, for the great hall was hung with finest tapestry, and many tables were set side by side. In the place of honour was a canopy under which it was the Cardinal's custom to sit, and here he would be served separately by two of his chief servants. The brilliance of the gathering was dazzling, and the members of the Cardinal's retinue in their colourful livery contributed in no small way to the opulence of the occasion.

Wolsey's eyes were on the black-bearded man. "You shall be seated in the place of honour," he said.

"Nay, my lord Cardinal, it pleases us that you should take your place under the cloth of state and behave as though we were the humblest of your guests."

But as he took his place under the canopy the Cardinal's apprehension increased. Previously during such masquerades he had discovered the King immediately and acted accordingly. Irritated as he was, he forced himself to appear gracious and to behave as though this really was a party of foreign travellers who had come unexpectedly to his table.

But it was difficult. Who were behind those masks? Buckingham doubtless. Boleyn? Compton? Suffolk? All Henry's cronies and therefore casting wary eyes at a man of the people who had risen so far above them.

He signed to his servants to serve the banquet but his eyes ranged about the table. The napery was exquisite; the food as plentiful as that supplied at the King's table. Everything was of the best. Capons, pheasants, snipe, venison, chickens and monumental pies. Who but the Cardinal's cooks could produce such light pastry with the golden look? Peacocks, oysters, stags, bucks, partridges, beef and mutton. There were fish of many descriptions; sauces made from cloves and raisins, sugar cinnamon and ginger; and gallons of French wines with Malmsey, and muscadell —all to be drunk from fine Venetian glasses which were the wonder of all who saw them.

But while the company gave themselves to the appreciation of this banquet Wolsey continued uneasy, and suddenly he raised his voice and said:

"My friends, there is one among us who is so noble that I know it to be my duty to surrender my place to him. I cannot sit under this canopy in good spirit while he, who is so much more worthy than I, takes his place unrecognized at my table."

There was silence, and then one of the masked men spoke; and a great hatred seized Wolsey when he recognized the disguised voice as that of Buckingham. "My Lord Cardinal, there are many members of the nobility present."

"I speak of one," said Wolsey.

Then one of the masked men said in a muffled voice: "Since Your Eminence believes there is such a noble personage among us, you should remove the mask of that man that all may see him."

It was the invitation to unmask, always the great climax of these childish games.

The Cardinal stood up. "It shall be so!" he said. And he walked along the tables to that man with the black beard, and stood before him.

"Take off his mask if you believe it to be he," commanded a voice which was husky with suppressed laughter.

And Wolsey stretched up and removed the false beard and the mask, to disclose the features of Charles Brandon, Duke of Suffolk.

While he stared with dismay there was a shout of laughter and a tall figure rose and confronted Wolsey.

"So my lord Cardinal," he cried, removing his mask, "you would deny your King!"

Wolsey knelt and took Henry's hand.

"May God forgive me," he murmured.

Henry, his face scarlet with pleasure, his blue eyes sparkling, flung his gold wire beard from him. He began to laugh in that deep rumbling way which appeared to be infectious for the whole company laughed with him.

Thomas stood up and raised his eyes to the jovial giant.

"So Thomas, my friend, you did not know me."

"Your Grace, I have never seen you so perfectly disguised."

Henry slapped his satin thigh. "'Twas a good mask. And I'll applaud Suffolk. He led you astray, did he not. Yet I thought you would have seen he lacked that inch or so."

"But surely Your Grace stooped to deceive me?"

"Ha! Stoop I did. And 'twas effective."

"And I had thought I could find Your Grace anywhere . . . in any circumstances."

"So, friend Thomas, you offer me your seat of honour, eh?"

"Everything I have belongs to Your Grace. And now I would crave your indulgence and ask you to wait awhile before you sit to table. That which was served for a band of travellers is not what I would put before my King."

"How so, Thomas?"

"If Your Grace will excuse me I will send for my master cooks. When the King comes to Hampton Court that which is served must not only be fit for a King but fit for the King of England."

Henry's eyes gleamed with pleasure. There was never such a one as Thomas Wolsey. He could be trusted to rise to any occasion. Whether it was matching the wits of his great enemy, François Premier, or talking of treaties with the Emperor Charles, Wolsey was the man he wanted to have beside him. And in a mask such as this he could be as effective as at the Council table.

"Go to, Thomas," he said; and when Thomas gave a quiet order to his stewards the King's merry eyes watched the ceremonial arrival of Thomas's cooks in their scarlet velvet livery and golden chains.

"The fellows look as royal as myself," he said in an aside to Suffolk. But he enjoyed it. He admired Wolsey for living in this manner; it was a credit to his country and his King.

"We are honoured by the presence of the King," said Wolsey to his cooks. "Have this food removed; bring in new and scented napery; set new dishes on the tables. I wish for a banquet—not worthy to set before His Grace, for that would be impossible—but the best we can offer."

The cooks bowed and with ceremony left the hall followed by their clerks of the kitchens, surveyors of the dresser, clerks of the hall-kitchens and clerk of the spicery who followed the master cooks as Wolsey's gentlemen of the household followed him on his ceremonial journeys from Hampton to Westminster Hall.

Then the guests left the tables and Wolsey led the King to

another apartment; the banquet was postponed for an hour that
it might be made worthy of the King.

Nothing could have pleased Henry more, for the climax of his
game was that he should receive the homage due to him as King.
Buckingham might grumble to Norfolk that the butcher's cur
was vulgar in the extreme; but there was not a man present who
did not know that it was the red-clad figure which led the way
and that which was clad in jewelled cloth of gold followed,
because it was pleasant and easy to do so.

So it was with Wolsey that Henry walked in the hall of Hampton
Court, his arm laid heavily on the shoulder of the Chancellor
so that all could see—if they had ever doubted it—that he looked
upon Thomas Wolsey as his friend, that he rejoiced in the Cardinal's possessions because they were a symbol of how high a
humble man could rise in his service, that he saw Thomas's
glory as a reflection of his own power. Nothing the jealous near-
royals could do would alter that.

And when the food was prepared and the company reassembled
in the great banqueting hall, Henry took his place under the
canopy of state and all were merry as it pleased the King to be;
but Henry would have, seated on his right hand, his host and
friend, Thomas Wolsey.

He wanted all to know that he had great love for that man.

\*          \*          \*

The next morning when Knyvet again asked for an audience
with the Cardinal, Wolsey received him.

The Cardinal, in crimson damask on this morning, sat at his
table, his hands—very white in contrast to the crimson—spread
out before him.

"You have something to tell me?" he asked.

"My lord Cardinal, I have wrestled with my conscience . . ."

How they always wrestled with their consciences! As though
it was not the desire for revenge which so often brought them to
him!

"I am listening," said Wolsey.

"It concerns my Lord Buckingham."

"In whose service you are."

"In whose service I was, Your Eminence."

"So you are with him no longer?"

Wolsey's face was impassive but he was chuckling inwardly.
So the fool Buckingham had dismissed a man from his service
after having been indiscreet before him. The trouble with Buckingham was that he felt himself too important to need caution.

It might be that the time was near when he would learn that he misjudged that importance.

"A little difference between us, Your Eminence. The Duke has a hasty temper."

"I am sorry."

"Your Eminence, it is a matter of relief to me to be free of him. Although he is my cousin I must say that."

There was venom there. It might be usefully employed.

"And why have you come to see me?"

"Because I felt it my duty to do so."

"You wish to tell me something about the Duke?"

"Yes, Your Eminence."

"I am listening."

"I would have Your Eminence know that it is my duty to King and State which impels me to lay these matters before you."

"I accept that."

"Then I would say that my lord and cousin has uttered remarks against the King's Grace which seem to me treasonable."

"And what were these remarks?"

"Before the Princess Mary was born he claimed to be heir to the throne. Since Her Highness's birth he has said that should she die he would be the heir."

"Is that so?"

"Your Eminence, he has referred constantly to his noble birth and has made slighting remarks concerning the bastardy of a certain family."

Wolsey nodded encouragingly.

"Your Eminence, he has consulted a soothsayer who has told him that the crown will one day be his."

"It would seem that your cousin is a rash man, Master Knyvet."

"'Twould seem so, Eminence. You will remember that he lured Sir William Bulmer from the King's service into his."

"I remember the occasion well. The King was angry and declared he would have no servant of his hanging on another man's sleeve."

"Yes, Eminence, and my Lord Buckingham told me that had the King reprimanded *him* and sent him to the Tower, he would have asked for an audience with His Grace, and when it was granted would have stabbed the King and taken over the rule of this kingdom."

"His recklessness is greater than I believed it to be. Why was he such a fool as to dismiss a man to whom he had uttered such treasonable words?"

Knyvet flushed uncomfortably. "He accused me of oppressing the tenantry."

"And he dismissed you? And it was only when you were dismissed that you recognized these remarks of his as those of a traitor?"

Knyvet shivered and began to wish that he had not come to the Cardinal, but Wolsey had begun to smile as he laid a hand on the ex-steward's shoulder.

"My lord, I came to you because I felt it to be my duty . . ."

"It was indeed your duty. But what will be said of a man who only recognizes his duty when his master dismisses him from his service?"

"You would not find it difficult to prove the truth. I was not the only one who heard these remarks. There were Hopkins the monk, and my lord's confessor, Delacourt, and Gilbert his chancellor. My lord lacks caution and speaks his mind before his servants."

The Chancellor waved a hand, which was enough to tell Knyvet that he was dismissed.

Knyvet looked at him in amazement; he had often heard Buckingham sneer at Wolsey; surely, he reasoned, Wolsey should reward one who brought such evidence to him.

But the Cardinal's white hand was now at his lips suppressing a yawn; and there was nothing Knyvet could do but bow and retire with as much dignity as possible.

When he was alone the Cardinal took a tablet from a drawer and set it before him; then he began to write: "Hopkins the monk, Delacourt the confessor, Gilbert the chancellor."

It might be that he could use these men if and when a certain occasion arose.

*       *       *

The Queen had dismissed all her women with the exception of Maria de Salinas.

"I think, Maria," she said thoughtfully, "that when the woman comes in, you should go."

Maria bowed her head. She was sorry that the Queen had made up her mind to see this woman. It would have been better, she was sure, to ignore her. Moreover, if the woman went to the King and complained to him, what an undignified position the Queen would be in!

"You are thinking that I am being unwise?" Katharine demanded.

"Your Grace, who am I to think such thoughts?"

"I am not the King, Maria, in constant need of flattery. I like to hear the truth from my friends."

"I think, Your Grace, that the interview may be distasteful to you."

"There is so much that is distasteful to me," Katharine answered sadly.

"Your Grace, I hear voices without."

"She is come. When she enters, Maria my dear, leave at once."

A page entered and told the Queen that Mistress Boleyn was without and saying that she had come at the Queen's command.

"It is true. Bring her to me. Now Maria, you will go."

Maria curtseyed and went out as Mary Boleyn entered.

Mary came to stand before the Queen; she made a deep curtsey, raising her big, dark eyes fearfully to the Queen's face as she did so.

Mary shivered inwardly. How frozen she looked! No wonder Henry went elsewhere for his comforts. She would be a cold bed-fellow.

So this is the girl for whom he has neglected me! thought Katharine. She has the look of a slut. Why does he not choose someone more in keeping with his rank?

"Mistress Mary Boleyn, pray rise," said the Queen.

The girl straightened herself and stood forlornly waiting for what the Queen had to say.

"You are the centre of a most distressing scandal," began Katharine, and watching the slow flush mount to the girl's forehead, thought that it was some small comfort that she felt some shame. "It is unbecoming of you and . . . in those who share your misdemeanours."

Mary looked at her helplessly. She wanted to explain: It was at Ardres or Guisnes—she was not quite sure. She had noticed his eyes upon her; and she had known the meaning of the looks he gave her. Then he had caught her alone one day and when his hands had strayed over her body there was nothing she could do but say Yes. She would have said Yes to anyone who was as handsome and had such need of her. With the King, of course, there could be no thought of refusal. Did not the Queen understand this? Poor lady. Mary believed she really did not. She did not know the King very well then. She did not know the way of the Court.

But how explain? She hung her head for she was ashamed; and she was deeply sorry that she had caused the good and pious Queen distress. Strangely enough she had never thought of the Queen; she could never think of anything at such times but the need for gratification, and when it was over it was too late. Mary was not the sort to waste regrets on things which it was too late to change.

What was the Queen asking of her now? To refuse the King! Did anyone ever refuse the King?

Then an idea occurred to her. The Queen still had some power, even with the King. Although she was so old and the King was clearly tired of her, she was still a Princess of Spain and her nephew was the most important monarch in Europe.

Mary had wanted to tell the Queen that she was sorry, that she would willingly end her liaison with the King tomorrow if she could. But it was so difficult to explain. So Mary did the only thing possible; she burst into tears.

Katharine was quite unprepared for such a loss of control, and for a few moments did not know what to say to the girl.

"Your Grace," sobbed Mary. "I wish I were a good woman . . . but I'm afraid I'm not. I was made this way. And now that I want to marry Will . . . Oh dear, it is all so difficult, but I wish . . . oh how I wish . . ."

"You should control yourself," said the Queen coldly.

"Yes, Your Grace," said Mary, dabbing at her eyes.

"What is this talk of marriage?"

"I am in love, Your Grace, with Will Carey. He is a younger son, and my father does not find him a good enough match for me. He has . . . forbidden us . . ."

"I see. So this young man is willing to marry you in spite of the scandal you have brought on yourself."

"There would be no more scandal, Your Grace, if only I could marry Will. I want none but Will, and he wants none but me. If Your Grace would speak for us . . ."

A strange state of affairs, pondered the Queen. I send for her to reprimand her for her lewd conduct with the King, and she asks me to help her to marry with a young man whom she says she loves.

Yet there was something lovable about the girl. Katharine had never thought that she could feel a slight degree of tenderness towards any of her husband's mistresses, but she was finding that this could be so. Mary with her plump bosom that seemed to resent being restrained within that laced bodice, her tiny waist and her flaring hips, had the air of a wanton even when she was distressed as she was at this moment; and there was also a look of the slattern about her; and yet that gentleness, that desire to please, that certain helplessness was appealing.

How could he deceive me with such a one? Katharine asked

herself. Elizabeth Blount had been different—a young and beautiful virgin when he had first seen her; and their *affaire* had been conducted with decorum. But Katharine was certain that the King had not been this girl's first lover.

And for many nights he had not visited his wife because the creature had claimed his attention. This slut had been preferred to a princess of Spain; the daughter of Thomas Boleyn—who for all his airs had his roots in trade—had been preferred to the daughter of Isabella and Ferdinand!

There were so many questions she wanted to ask. She was jealous of this girl, because she knew that there would be such passion between her and the King as there never had been between the King and his wife. How did you manage to attract him? she wanted to ask. How did you manage to keep him? He went to you in spite of his conscience, in spite of the scandal which he hates. Yet he cannot bring himself to come to me when it is right and proper that he should, and it is his duty to give me the chance of bearing a son.

She ought to hate the girl, but it was impossible to hate her when she stood there, an occasional sob still shaking her body.

The Queen said: "So you have spoken to your father of this marriage?"

"Yes, Your Grace. He is against it."

"Why so?"

"Because Will is only a younger son."

"And do *you* not think that you might look higher?"

"I could not look higher, Your Grace, than the man I love."

Katharine was shaken. She had expected to find a calculating mind beneath that voluptuous exterior; but the girl's looks did not lie. She was indeed soft and loving.

"That is a worthy sentiment," murmured the Queen. "When I sent for you I had thought of dismissing you from the Court, of sending you back to your father's castle at Hever." The Queen half closed her eyes, visualizing the scene with Henry if she had dared to do this. "But," she went on, "since you speak to me of your love for this young man, and speak of it with sincerity, I feel that I should like to help you."

"Your Grace!" The babyish mouth was slightly open; the dark tearful eyes wide.

"Yes," said the Queen. "I can see that you need to be married. Your husband will then keep you out of mischief."

"And Your Grace will . . ."

"I will arrange for your marriage to Will Carey. The ceremony shall be here at Court and I myself will attend."

"Your Grace!"

There was no mistaking the joy in the girl's face.

Katharine held out her hand, Mary took it and pressed a damp hot face against it.

"You may go now," said the Queen graciously, and watched the girl depart.

A slut, she thought. And no virgin when he found her. Yet he desired her as he never did his wife.

Why should this be? Katharine asked herself passionately. Is there no hope left to me? What is the use of praying for a son when the King has given up all hope of begetting one? How can there be a son when he never comes to me, when he spends his manhood on girls such as Mary Boleyn?

\* \* \*

There were isolated moments in life, thought Katharine, which were sheer happiness; and what had happened in the past and what the future held could not touch them. As she sat watching her daughter Mary leaning against her father's knee while he instructed her in playing the lute, she assured herself that this was one of them.

The King's face was flushed and he was smiling; there was rare tenderness about his mouth; he dearly loved children, and he would have been a contented man if, instead of one small girl in the nursery, there were half a dozen—and more than one lusty boy among them.

But in this happy moment he was well pleased with his little daughter.

How enchanting she is! thought Katharine. How dainty! How healthy with that flush in her cheeks and her long hair falling about her shoulders! Why am I ever sad while I have my Mary?

"Ha!" boomed the King, "you are going to be a musician, my daughter. There is no doubt of that." He turned, smiling to Katharine. "Did you hear that? She shall have the best teacher in the land."

"She already has that," said Katharine meaningfully, and she went to the pair and laid her hand lightly on the King's shoulder. He patted that hand affectionately.

Holy Mother of God, the Queen prayed silently, if we had only one son, all would be well between us. Who would believe, witnessing this scene of domestic felicity, that he continually betrays me and that . . .

But she would not allow herself to say it even to herself. It was impossible. Only her enemies had whispered it because they hated her. They must have forgotten that she was of the House of Spain and that the Emperor was her own sister's son.

"Henry," went on Katharine, "I want to discuss her general education with you. I wish her to receive tuition in languages, history and all subjects which will be of use to her in later life."

"It shall be so," agreed Henry.

"I have been talking to Thomas More on this subject."

"A good fellow, Thomas More," murmured the King, "and none could give you better advice."

"His daughters, I have heard, are the best educated in England. He firmly believes that there should be no difference between the education of girls and boys."

The King's look of contentment faded; his lower lip protruded in an expression of discontent.

I should not have said that, thought Katharine. I have reminded him that while Thomas More has a son, he, the King, has none—at least not a legitimate son.

These pitfalls appeared on every occasion. Was there no escaping them?

The King was staring at Mary's brown curls, and she knew that he was thinking to himself: Why was this girl not a boy?

The little girl was extremely sensitive and this was not the first time that she had been aware of the discontent she aroused in her father. She lowered her eyes and stared at the lute in his hands. He frightened her, this big and glittering father, who would sometimes pick her up in his arms and expect her to shout with glee because he noticed her. She did shout, because Mary always tried to do what was expected of her, but the glee was assumed, and in her father's presence the child was never completely free from apprehension.

She longed to please him and applied an almost feverish concentration on her lessons, and in particular, her music; and because she knew that he liked to boast of her abilities, she was terrified that she would fall short of his expectation.

Those occasions when he smothered her with his exuberant affection were almost as alarming as when he showed his displeasure in her sex.

She had begun to ask herself: "Where did I fail? What could I have done to have made myself be born a boy?"

She took a swift glance at her mother. How glad she was that the Queen was present, for in the company of her mother she felt safer. If she could have had her wish they would have been together always; she would have liked to sleep in her mother's chamber, and stay with her the whole day long. Whenever she was afraid, she thought of her mother; and when they were alone together she was completely happy.

Now she raised her eyes and found her mother's gaze upon her. The Queen smiled reassuringly because she immediately sensed her little daughter's disquiet.

We must never show our differences in the child's presence, thought Katharine. But how long can I protect her from rumour? She already knows that her father constantly rages against the fate which made her a girl and not a boy.

The Queen said quickly: "Now that you have the lute in your hands, Henry, play us one of your songs, and sing to us."

The frown lifted from the King's brow. He was still boyish enough to be drawn from discontent by a treat. It was like offering a child a sweetmeat, and compliments were the sweetmeats Henry most desired.

"Since you ask me, Katharine, I will sing for you. And what of my daughter? Does she wish to hear her father sing?"

The little girl was alert. She said in a shy voice: "Yes, Your Grace."

"You do not sound quite certain," he growled.

The Queen put in hastily: "Mary is all eagerness, but a little shy of showing her pleasure." She held out her hand to the Princess who immediately ran to her.

Oh the comfort of those velvet skirts, the joy of hiding her face momentarily in them, of feeling that gentle, protective hand on her head! The Princess Mary looked up at her mother with adoration shining in her eyes.

The Queen smiled and held that head against her skirts once more. It would not be wise for her father to see that the love she had for her mother was greater than that which she had for him. Mary did not understand that he demanded always to be the most admired, the best loved.

"I do not look for shyness in my daughter," murmured the King. But his fingers were already plucking at the lute and he was singing his favourite song in a pleasant tenor voice.

The Queen settled herself in her chair and kept her arm about her daughter.

Snuggling up to her Mary prayed: "Please, Holy Mother of God, let me stay with my mother . . . always."

The song came to an end and the King stared before him, his eyes glazed with the pleasure he found in his own creation, while the Queen clapped her hands and signed to her daughter to do the same. Thus the King was appeased.

When their daughter had been returned to her governess,

Katharine said to the King: "Mary Boleyn has been to see me to plead for permission to marry."

The King did not speak for a moment. Then he said: "Is that so?"

"Yes. It seems that she wishes to marry a certain William Carey, who is a younger son and I fancy not to her father's liking."

"Thomas Boleyn wants a better match for the girl, I'll warrant."

"Thomas Boleyn is an ambitious man. I have promised to help the girl."

The King shrugged his shoulders. "The matter is in your hands."

"I had thought in the circumstances . . ."

He swung round on her, his eyes narrowed. What was she hinting? Was she reproaching him because he had found the girl attractive?

"In what circumstances?" he demanded.

She saw that she had strayed into one of those pitfalls which it was always so necessary to avoid. She should have murmured that, as the girl was of the Court and her father stood high in the King's favour, she had believed that she should first ask for the King's approval before consenting to her marriage.

But her natural dignity revolted. Was she not, after all, a daughter of the House of Spain? Should she allow herself to be treated as a woman of no importance? The recent interview with her daughter had reminded her of her own mother, and she believed that little Mary felt for her the same devotion that she herself had felt for Isabella of Castile. Isabella would never have lost her dignity over one of her husband's mistresses.

Katharine said coldly: "In view of the fact that the girl is—or was—your paramour . . ."

The King's face darkened. In his eyes sins seemed blacker when they were openly referred to. He might placate his conscience to some extent ("I am but a man. The girl was more than willing. My wife is sickly and after each pregnancy she grows more so. Providence sends me these willing girls, who, by God, lose nothing through the affair, that I may save my wife discomfort") but when his wife actually spoke of the matter with that smouldering resentment in her eyes she emphasized the unworthiness of his conduct. Therefore if he had been dissatisfied with her a moment before, as soon as she uttered those words he hated her.

"You forget to whom you speak, Madam," he said.

"Why should you think that? Is the girl then the mistress of others? I must say it does not surprise me."

"This girl's marriage is of no interest to me," cried Henry. "But your insolent accusations are, Madam, I would have you know. I have suffered much. I have been a loving husband. You forget how I brought you out of poverty . . . exile, one might say. You forget that against the advice of my ministers I married you. And how did you repay me? By denying me that which I longed for above all else. All these years of marriage . . . and no son . . . no son . . ."

"That is our mutual sorrow, Henry. Am I to blame?"

His eyes narrowed cruelly. "It is strange that you cannot bear a son."

"When Elizabeth Blount has done so for you?" she demanded.

"I have a son." He raised his eyes to the ceiling and his attitude had become pious. "As King of the realm and one whose task it is to provide his country with heirs I thought it my duty to see wherein the fault lay."

How could one reason with such a man? He was telling her now that when he had first seen that beautiful young girl and had seduced her, it was not because he had lusted after her, but only to prove to his people that, although his Queen could not give him a son, another could.

No, it was impossible to reason with him because when he made these preposterous statements he really believed them. He had to believe in the virtuous picture he envisaged. It was the only way in which he could appease his conscience.

He was going on: "I have prayed each day and night; I have heard Mass five times a day. I cannot understand why this should be denied me, when I have served God so well. But there is a reason."

Cunning lights were in his eyes; they suggested that he had his own beliefs as to why his greatest wish should have been denied him. For a moment she thought he was going to tell her; but he changed his mind, and turning, strode to the door.

There he paused, and she saw that he had made an effort to control his features. He said coldly: "If you wish to arrange the marriage of any of the Court women, you should consult me. This you have done and in this case I say I pass the matter into your hands."

With that he left her. But she was scarcely listening.

What plans was he making? What did he say of his marriage, behind locked doors in the presence of that man Wolsey?

A cold fear touched her heart. She went to her window and

looked out on the river. Then she remembered the visit of the Emperor and that he would come again.

Henry wanted the friendship of the Emperor, for England, even as she did.

He would not be so foolish as to dare harm, by word or deed, the aunt of the most powerful monarch in Europe.

\* \* \*

On a bleak January day Mary Boleyn was married to William Carey. The Queen honoured the bride and bridegroom with her presence, and the ceremony was well attended because Mary, on account of her relationship with the King, was a person of interest.

When Mary took the hand of her husband, there were whispers among those present. What now? they asked each other. Surely if the King were still interested in the girl he would have made a grander match for her than this. It could only mean that he had finished with her, and Mary—silly little Mary—had not had the wits to ask for a grand title and wealth as a reward for services rendered.

But Mary, as she passed among the guests, looked so dazzlingly happy that it appeared she had gained all she sought; and the same could have been said for Will Carey.

The Queen received the young couple's homage with something like affection—which seemed strange, considering how proud the Queen was and that the girl had lately been her rival.

The general opinion was that the King's affair with Mary Boleyn was over. The fact that Thomas Boleyn did not attend the ceremony confirmed this.

"I hear he has renounced her," said one of the ladies to the nearest gentleman.

"Small wonder!" was the reply. "Thomas was climbing high, doing his duty as complaisant father. He's furious with the girl and would have prevented the marriage if Mary had not won the Queen's consent."

"And the Queen readily gave it—naturally."

"Well, it is a strange affair, I grant you. This is very different from the Blount affair."

"What of that child?"

"Doubtless we shall hear news of him some day, unless of course the Queen surprises us all and produces that elusive male heir."

"Stranger things have been known to happen."

Many furtive glances were sent in the Queen's direction and

the whispered gossip went on, but Katharine gave no sign that she was aware of this.

She felt sure that there would be other mistresses. That had become inevitable since she no longer appealed to the King as a woman; and because she could not safely suffer more pregnancies he was not interested in her.

She had her daughter Mary, and Mary would one day be Queen because it was impossible for the King to have a legitimate son. It was sad, but it was something they must accept.

This at least, she told herself, is the end of the Boleyn affair.

\*       \*       \*

The King and Queen sat at the banquet table; about them were assembled all the great personalities of their Court, for this was a ceremonial occasion. On the King's right hand sat the Cardinal, and every now and then they would put their heads together to whisper something which was for their ears alone. The complacent expression on the Cardinal's face was apparent; there was little he liked more than these grand occasions when the King selected him from all others and showed his preference.

This was particularly delightful when the noblemen of the Court could look on and see the King's reliance on him; and on this occasion the Duke of Buckingham was present, and he made no secret of his distaste for the King's preference.

The musicians played as the sucking pig was brought in and ceased as it was placed on the table by the steward; homage to the dish was expressed by a respectful silence.

The King looked on the table with drowsy eyes; he had already partaken of many dishes and his face was flushed with wine. His bright blue eyes were slightly glazed as they rested on the group of young girls who sat together at some distance from him.

It seemed that he was no longer enamoured of Mary Boleyn and that others might hope to take her place.

The Cardinal was aware of the King's glances and rejoiced. He liked the King to have his pleasures. He had no desire for him to discover that statecraft could be more absorbing than the pursuit of women; when he did, that could mean a slowing down in Wolsey's rapid journey to the heights of power.

Wolsey wished his King to remain the healthy, active boy—the young man who could tire out five horses a day at the hunt, who could be an easy victor at the joust, who could beat all his opponents at a game of tennis; and whose thoughts ran on the pursuit of women.

Thomas More had said once: "If the lion knew his strength, it would be hard for any man to rule him."

No one knew the truth of this better than Wolsey. Therefore he planned to keep the lion unaware of his strength. At the moment he was so. Not through any lack of conceit but because it was so pleasant to be a figure of glory in the tiltyard, at the masques and balls, and to leave state matters to the efficient Cardinal. Why should he tire his eyes by studying state papers? Wolsey was the man for that. The King had often said with a rumbling laugh that a state document could bring a brighter shine to Wolsey's eyes than any wench could.

It pleased Henry that the shrewd Cardinal should be the perfect complement to the dazzling King. But the lion must not know his strength.

Wolsey looked about the company and his eyes came to rest on the Queen. There was one of whom he must be wary. Relations between them had been less cordial since the friendship of England with France, for, like the good Spaniard that she was, Katharine hated the French. She looked at Europe and saw the only two rulers of consequence there—François Premier and the Emperor Charles—and she knew that they must inevitably be the most bitter of enemies. Each fought for power and there would be continual strife between them. It was Katharine's great desire that England should be the ally of her nephew Charles; and she had blamed Wolsey for the *rapprochement* with François which had led to that fantastic spectacle at Guisnes and Ardres. She had been cool with him, a little arrogant, and would have to learn in time that none was allowed to show arrogance towards the great Cardinal—not even the Queen.

Rarely had the Cardinal felt so contented as he did at this banquet. He was climbing high and would go higher, never forgetting that the ultimate goal was the Papal chair, for once he had attained it he would be free from the whims of the King of England. Until then he must feign to submit to them.

He shall be kept in ignorance, thought Wolsey. Such blissful ignorance. Those bright blue eyes must be kept shining for conquest in the tiltyard and the ladies' chambers; they must not discover the delights of statecraft until the Cardinal had become the Pope.

The King's plump white hands were greasy with sucking pig; he called for music, and the minstrels began to play one of his songs, which could not fail to increase his good humour.

How easy to handle! thought Wolsey, and his eyes met those of Buckingham who gave him a haughty stare.

Buckingham turned towards Norfolk who was sitting beside him and made a comment which Wolsey knew was derogatory to himself. But Buckingham was a fool. He had spoken during the playing of the King's music.

"You do not like the song?" demanded Henry, his eyes suddenly narrowed.

"Your Grace," answered Buckingham suavely, "I was but commenting on its charm."

"It spoils the pleasure of others when you drown the music with your chatter," grumbled the King.

"Then," answered Buckingham, "would Your Grace allow the musicians to play it again that all may hear it in silence?"

Henry waved a hand and the tune was repeated.

Fool Buckingham! thought Wolsey. He was heading straight for trouble.

The Cardinal excelled at collecting information about those he wished to destroy. His spy ring was notorious throughout the Court. Did Buckingham think that because he was a noble duke —as royal as the King, as he loved to stress—he was immune from it?

The music over, the King rose from the banqueting table. On such an occasion it was the duty of one of his gentlemen to bring a silver ewer in which he might wash his hands. The duty was performed by noblemen of the highest rank, and on this occasion the task fell to the Duke of Buckingham.

The ewer was handed to Buckingham by one of his ushers; he took it and bowed before Henry who washed his hands as was the custom.

When the King had finished, the Cardinal, who had been standing beside Henry, put his hands into the bowl and proceeded to wash them.

For a few seconds Buckingham was too astonished to do anything but stand still holding the bowl. Then a slow flush spread from his neck to his forehead. He, the great Duke of Buckingham, who believed himself more royal than Henry Tudor, to hold the ewer for a man who had been born in a butcher's shop!

In an access of rage he threw the greasy water over the Cardinal's shoes, drenching his red satin robe as he did so.

There was silence. Even the King looked on astonished.

The Cardinal was the first to recover. He turned to Henry and murmured: "A display of temper, Your Grace, by one who thinks himself privileged to show such in your presence."

Henry had walked away and the Cardinal followed him.

Buckingham stood staring after them.

"'Tis a sad day for England," he muttered, "when a noble duke is expected to hold the ewer for a butcher's cur."

\* \* \*

In the King's private chamber, Henry was laughing.

"'Twas a merry sight, Thomas, to see you there with the water drenching your robes."

"I am delighted to have provided Your Grace with some amusement," murmured Wolsey.

"I have rarely seen you so astonished. As for Buckingham, he was in a rage."

"And in your presence!"

Henry clapped a hand on Wolsey's shoulder. "I know Buckingham. He was never one to hold in his temper. And when you . . . Thomas Wolsey . . . not a member of the nobility, dipped your hands into the bowl . . . "

"As Your Grace's Chancellor . . ."

"Buckingham pays more respects to a man's family tree than to his attainments, Thomas."

"Well I know it, for the man's a fool, and I thank the saints nightly that this realm has been blessed with a ruler who is of such wisdom."

The King smiled almost roguishly. "As for me, Thomas, I care not whether men come from butchers' shops or country mansions. I am the King, and all my subjects are born beneath me. I look down on one and all."

"Even on Buckingham!"

"Why do you say that, Thomas?"

"Because the Duke has strange notions about his birth. He fancies himself to be as royal as Your Grace."

The roguishness disappeared and a look of cruelty played about the tight little mouth. "You said Buckingham was a fool, Thomas. We are once again in agreement."

Now it was Thomas's turn to smile.

He believed the time had come to make an end of his enemy.

\* \* \*

The Cardinal allowed a few weeks to pass; then one day he came to the King in pretended consternation.

"What ails you, Thomas?" asked Henry.

"I have made discoveries, Your Grace, which I hesitate to lay before you, of such a shocking nature are they."

"Come, come," said the King testily; he was in a white silk

shirt and purple satin breeches, puffed and slashed, ready for a game of tennis.

"They concern my Lord Buckingham. I must regretfully advise your Grace that I believe him to be guilty of treason."

"Treason!"

"Of a most heinous nature."

"How so?"

"He lays claim to the throne and declares he will have it one day."

"What!" roared the King, tennis forgotten. There was one subject which filled him, as a Tudor, with alarm. That was the suggestion that anyone in the realm had a greater right to the throne than he had. His father had had to fight for the crown; he had won it and brought prosperity to England, uniting the houses of York and Lancaster by his marriage; but the hideous Wars of the Roses were not so far behind that they could be forgotten; and the very mention of a pretender to the throne was enough to rouse Henry to fury.

"I have long suspected him," the Cardinal soothed. "Hence his hatred of me and the enmity between us. This I should feel towards any who sought to harm Your Grace. I have made it my duty to test his servants, and I now have the results of these labours to lay before Your Grace."

"What are these results?"

"In the first place Buckingham feels himself to be as royal as your Grace."

"The rogue!" cried Henry.

"He has said that there is no bar sinister on his escutcheon."

Wolsey had the pleasure of seeing the red colour flame into the plump cheeks. "He has told his confessor, Delacourt, that if you were to die and the Princess Mary were to die, he would have the throne."

"By God!" cried the King. "He shall lose his head—for it is his just deserts."

"That is not all," went on the Cardinal. "I have learned that he consults a soothsayer, and that he has been told that one day he will mount the throne."

"And how can he do this? Tell me that. Does he think to go to war . . . with *me*!"

"He's a fool, Your Grace, but not such a fool as that. He knows the people love you and that you have your friends. Soothsayers often practise another trade. I have heard they are often well versed in the art of poison."

Henry was speechless for a few seconds. Then he burst out:

"We'll have him in the Tower. We'll have him on the rack. We'll have the truth from him. By God, his head shall be forfeit for what he has done."

"Your Grace," murmured the Cardinal, "we must build up a case against him. This I believe we can do."

"You mean we can send him to the scaffold?"

"Why should we not, if we can prove him guilty of treason?"

"He would have to be tried before his peers. Forget not, Thomas, that this is Buckingham; 'tis true that there is royal blood in his veins. You think his peers would judge him worthy of the traitors' death?"

"If the case were strong enough against him."

"Norfolk would be one of his judges. You know the bonds between them. He and his fellows would be loth to condemn one of such nobility. Had he raised an army against the Crown, that would be another matter. But it would seem that he has done nothing but prate."

"Against Your Grace!"

"Thomas, I understand you well. You serve me with all your heart. I brought you up, and you have had little but insults from these men. But they are the nobility; they make a shield around the throne. They have certain privileges."

"Your Grace, I concern myself only with the safety of my master." The Cardinal snapped his fingers. "I care not that for this shield. Your Grace, I crave pardon but I say this: You know not your strength. All men about the throne should tremble at your displeasure . . . be they scullions or noble dukes. This could be so. This must be so. You are our lord and our King."

For a few seconds the two men regarded each other. The Cardinal knew that this was one of the most significant moments of his career.

He was showing the young lion that the golden walls of his cage were only silken strands to be pushed aside whenever he wished. Yet looking at this man of turbulent passions, even then the Cardinal wondered what he had done. But he was vindictive by nature; and from the moment he had seen the greasy water splash his satin robes he had determined at all costs to have his revenge.

\*　　　\*　　　\*

The news spread round the Court.

"This cannot be," it was whispered. "What has he done, but talk? Who can prove that this and that was said? Who are the witnesses against him? A pack of disgruntled servants! This trial is a warning. Do not forget this is the noble Duke of Buckingham. He will be freed with a pardon and a warning."

But the King's anger against Buckingham was intense when he examined the evidence which his Chancellor had put before him.

His face was scarlet as he read the report of Buckingham's carelessly spoken words. It was infuriating that anyone should dare *think* such thoughts, let alone express them. And in the hearing of servants, so that those words could be repeated in the streets, in taverns, wherever men congregated! This was treason.

And what care I, thought Henry, if this be a noble duke! Am I not the King?

For the first time he had realized the extent of his power. He was going to show all those about him that none could speak treason against the King with impunity. He was greedy for blood —the blood of any man who dared oppose him. He could shed that blood when and where he wished; he was the supreme ruler.

Norfolk came to him in some distress. Henry had never felt any great affection for Norfolk. The Duke seemed so ancient, being almost fifty years older than the King; his ideas were set in the past, and Henry thought that the old man would have liked to censure him if he dared. He had been young and daring in the days of Henry's maternal grandfather, Edward IV, but those days of glory were far behind him.

"Well, well?" Henry greeted him testily.

"Your Grace, I am deeply disturbed by the imprisonment of my kinsman, Buckingham."

"We have all been deeply disturbed by the treason he has sought to spread," growled the King.

"Your Grace, he has been foolish. He has been careless."

"Methinks that he has too often repeated his treason to offer the excuse that he spoke in an unguarded moment. This is a plot . . . a scheme to overthrow the Crown, and there is one word for such conduct; that is treason. And I tell you this, my lord Duke, there is but one sentence which right-minded judges can pronounce on such a man."

Norfolk was startled. He knew the King was subject to sudden anger, but he had not believed that he could be so vehemently determined on the destruction of one who had been in his intimate circle and known as his friend. And for what reason? Merely a carelessly spoken word repeated by a dissatisfied servant!

Norfolk had never been noted for his tact; he went on: "Your Grace, Buckingham is of the high nobility."

"I care not how high he be. He shall have justice."

"Your Grace, he has erred and will learn his lesson. I'll warrant that after the trial he will be a wiser man."

"It is a pity that there will be so little time left to him to practise his new-found wisdom," said the King venomously.

Then Norfolk knew. Henry was determined on the death of Buckingham.

But even so, he could not let the matter end there. He and Buckingham were not only friends but connected by the marriage of his son and Buckingham's daughter. He thought of the grief in his family if Buckingham should die; moreover he must stand by the rights of the nobility. This was not rebellion against the King; Buckingham had not set out to overthrow the Crown. The King must be made to understand that, powerful as he was, he was not entitled to send the nobility to death because of a careless word.

"Your Grace cannot mean that you demand his *life*!"

The King's eyes narrowed. "My lord Norfolk," he said significantly, "do you also seek to rule this realm?" Norfolk flinched and Henry began to shout: "Get from here . . . lest you find yourself sharing the fate of your kinsman. By God and all His saints, I will show you, who believe yourselves to be royal, that there is only one King of this country; and when treason stalks, blood shall flow."

Norfolk bowed low and was glad to escape from the King's presence. He felt sick at heart. He had received his orders. Buckingham was to be judged guilty by his peers; he was to pay the supreme penalty.

The pleasure-loving boy King was no more; he had been replaced by the vengeful man.

*          *          *

He stood at the bar, the reckless Buckingham, facing the seventeen peers, headed by Norfolk, who were his judges. His arms folded, his head held high, he was ready to throw away his life rather than beg for mercy.

Old Norfolk could not restrain his tears. He wanted to shout: This is madness. Are we going to condemn one of ourselves to the scaffold on the evidence of his servants?

But Norfolk had received his orders; he had looked into those little blue eyes and had seen the blood-lust there. Insults to the King, though carelessly uttered, must be paid for in blood; for the King was all-powerful and the old nobility must realize that.

Calmly Buckingham heard the charges brought against him. He had listened to prophecies of the King's death and his own ascension to the throne; he had said that he would kill the King;

he had many times mentioned the fact that only the King and the Princess Mary stood between him and the throne.

He defended himself against these charges. He pointed out that none but his unworthy servants had been able to speak against him. Was the court going to take the word of disgruntled servants before that of the Duke of Buckingham?

But Wolsey had prepared the case against him skilfully; and moreover all seventeen of his judges knew that the King was demanding a verdict of guilty; and if any of them refused to give the King what he wanted, it would be remembered against them; and it was likely that ere long they would be standing where Buckingham now stood.

The old Duke of Norfolk might weep, but nevertheless when his fellow judges agreed that the prisoner was guilty he read the terrible sentence.

"Edward Stafford, third Duke of Buckingham, you are found guilty of treason." His voice faltered as he went on: "You shall be drawn on a hurdle to the place of execution, there to be hanged, cut down alive, your members to be cut off and cast into the fire, your bowels burned before your eyes, your head smitten off, your body to be quartered and divided at the King's will. May God have mercy on your soul."

Buckingham seemed less disturbed than Norfolk.

When he was asked if he had anything to say, he replied in a clear, steady voice: "My lord, you have said to me as a traitor should be said unto, but I was never a traitor. Still, my lords, I shall not malign you as you have done unto me. May the eternal God forgive you my death, as I do!" He drew himself to his full height and a scornful expression came into his eyes. "I shall never sue the King for my life," he went on. "Howbeit, he is a gracious Prince, and more grace may come from him than I desire. I ask you to pray for me."

They took him thence back to his prison of the Tower, and those who had gathered to watch his progress knew that he was condemned when they saw that the edge of the axe was turned towards him.

\*          \*          \*

Maria de Salinas, Countess of Willoughby, was with the Queen when she heard that the Duke of Norfolk was begging an audience.

Katharine had him brought to her at once, and the old man's grief distressed her because she guessed at once what it meant.

"I pray you be seated, my lord," she said. "I fear you bring bad news."

He gazed at her, and he seemed to be in a state of bewildered misery.

"Your Grace, I have come from the court where I have pronounced the death sentence, for treason, on the Duke of Buckingham."

"But this is impossible."

The old Duke shook his head. "Nay, Your Grace. 'Twas so."

"But to find him guilty of treason . . ."

"It was the King's wish."

"But his peers?"

The Duke lifted a trembling hand in resignation.

Katharine was indignant. She had known Buckingham to be arrogant, to have offended the Cardinal, to have been overproud of his royal connections, but these were venial sins; a noble duke was not condemned to the barbaric traitors' death for that.

"It is known what influence Your Grace has with the King," went on Norfolk. "I have come to plead with you to beg him to spare Buckingham's life. I am certain that this sentence will not be carried out. I am sure that the King means only to warn him. But if Your Grace would but speak to the King . . ."

"I promise you I shall do so," said Katharine.

The Duke fell to his knees and taking her hand kissed it.

"Maria," said Katharine, "send for my lord Surrey that he may look after his father."

The Duke shook his head. "My son is in Ireland, Your Grace. Despatched thither on the orders of the Cardinal." His lips curved ironically.

"The Cardinal doubtless thought to spare him the anxiety of his father-in-law's trial," the Queen suggested.

"He sent him away because he thought he might have spoken in his father-in-law's favour," Norfolk replied roughly.

Poor old man! thought Katharine. Buckingham is very dear to him and if this terrible sentence is carried out there will be mourning, not only among the Staffords, but the Howards also.

She shivered, contemplating the hideous ceremony of pain and humiliation. They could not do that to a noble duke!

She laid her hand lightly on Norfolk's shoulder. "Rise, my lord," she said. "I will speak to the King and implore him to show mercy."

"Your Grace is good to us," murmured Norfolk.

When he had gone, Maria looked sorrowfully at her mistress. "Your Grace . . ." she began.

Katharine smiled sadly at her dear friend. "I know what you

want to say, Maria. This is a dangerous matter. You want to advise me not to meddle."

Maria said quickly: "'Tis so."

"No harm can come to me if I plead for Buckingham. I am at least the King's wife, Maria."

Maria did not answer. She was afraid of the new trend of events, afraid of what effect it would have on her mistress.

"I shall go to the King at once," said Katharine. "I want to put those poor people out of their misery as quickly as possible."

There was nothing Maria could do; so, as Katharine left her apartment for the King's, she went to the window and stood looking broodingly out over the gardens.

\* \* \*

The Cardinal was with the King.

"What now, Kate?" asked Henry, mildly testy.

"I would have a word with Your Grace if you will grant me a few minutes."

"Say on," said Henry.

Katharine looked at the Cardinal who bowed and went with reluctance towards the door.

"Henry," said Katharine, catching her husband's sleeve, "I want you to show mercy to the Duke of Buckingham."

"Why so?" he demanded coldly.

"Because I believe that a warning will suffice to make him your very good friend in the future."

"So we are to allow traitors to live?"

"It was not treason in the accepted form."

"And what, I pray you, is the accepted form?"

"There was no rebellion. He did not take up arms against you."

"How can you know what methods he used against me? I believe he was planning to poison me."

"Henry, he would never do that. He was rash and foolish . . . but I do not think he would ever commit a crime like that."

"And what can you know of the schemes of such a rogue?"

"I knew him well. He it was who met me when I first came to England."

"I tell you this, Madam," roared the King. "Any who acts treason against me shall pay with his life—be he your dearest friend on Earth."

"But Henry, he is a noble duke . . . the highest in the land."

"So he believed. 'Twas his opinion of himself which brought him to where he is this day."

"His relations are the most powerful in the land," persisted Katharine. "His wife, the daughter of Northumberland; the Percys will not forget. His son married to Salisbury's daughter. This will alienate the Poles. His daughter is married to Norfolk's son. The Howards will grieve deeply. Then there are the Staffords themselves. Four of our noblest families . . ."

Henry moved a step nearer to his wife. "I forget none of this," he said. "And were my own brother—and I had one—guilty of treason, he should suffer a like fate."

Katharine covered her face with her hands. "Henry, shall a noble duke be taken out and barbarously killed before the eyes of the people!"

"The fate of traitors is no concern of mine. He was judged by his peers and found guilty."

Meanwhile the Cardinal waited anxiously in the ante-chamber. He knew that the Queen had come to plead for Buckingham. She must not succeed.

Moreover it was necessary that the Queen herself should learn her lesson from the fate of this man. Once she and the Cardinal had been good friends; but now, since the friendship with France, she had looked on him with suspicion. He had heard himself referred to as a butcher's boy in her hearing, and she had offered no reprimand to the speaker.

It was not only noble dukes who must be taught that it was unwise to lose the friendship of the Cardinal.

He picked up a sheaf of papers and looked at them. Then with determination he passed through the ante-room into the King's chamber.

"Your Grace," he said, "I crave your pardon for the intrusion. An important matter of state requires your attention . . ."

The Queen looked angry, but that was of small importance as the King was not displeased.

He was saying: "He shall die. But we will show mercy unto him. It shall be the executioner's axe in place of the sentence which you feel to be an insult to his nobility."

The Cardinal was not ruffled.

The method mattered little to him, as long as Buckingham died.

\*  \*  \*

On a bright May day the Duke was brought out from his lodging in the Tower to meet his death on the Hill.

There were many to watch this nobleman's last hour on Earth. There were many to sigh for him and weep for him. He had been arrogant and reckless; he had been harsh to some of his tenants, causing them great hardship with his enclosure laws; but it seemed cruel that this man, who was in his early forties, should have to walk out of his prison to face death on such a bright May morning. His good characteristics were remembered; he was a very religious man and had founded colleges. And now he was to die because he had offended the King and the Cardinal.

He met his death bravely, as all expected he would; and while his body was being taken to its burial place in Austin Friars, among those who thought of him were the King, the Queen and the Cardinal . . . the Queen with sorrow, the King with righteous indignation, and the Cardinal with deep pleasure which was however pricked by apprehension.

Buckingham would insult him no more, but the Cardinal was too shrewd a man not to know that he had paid a high price for his vengence.

A subtle change had crept into the King's demeanour. The lion was no longer couchant. He had risen; he was testing his strength.

And, when he had assessed the full measure of that power, who would be safe? A Queen? A Cardinal?

CHAPTER II

THE QUEEN'S ENEMY

In her apartments at Greenwich Palace the Princess Mary was being prepared by her women for a ceremonial occasion. They were all very excited and kept telling the little girl that she would be the target of all eyes on this occasion.

She wriggled beneath her headdress which seemed too tight.

"Be careful, my precious one," said her governess. "Remember, you must walk very slowly and as I have taught you."

"Yes," said Mary, "I will remember."

The women looked at her fondly. She was such a good child, rather too serious perhaps, but always eager to learn her lessons and please those about her.

Six-year-old Mary felt uncomfortable in the stiff gown, but she liked the dazzling jewels which decorated it; she pulled at the gold chain about her neck because it seemed so heavy.

"Careful, my lady. Hands down. That's right. Let me see the

sort of curtsey you will make to your bridegroom when you meet him."

Mary obediently made a deep curtsey, which was not easy in the heavy gown, and several of the women clapped their hands.

"Does she not look beautiful!" asked one of another.

"She's the most beautiful and the luckiest Princess in all the world."

Mary did not believe them, and knew that they were bribing her to behave in such a way that she would be a credit to them.

"What is the Emperor Charles like?" she asked.

"What is he like! He is tall and handsome and the greatest ruler in the world—save only your royal father, of course. And he loves you dearly."

"How is it possible to love people whom one does not know?" The child was too clever for them.

"Do you not love the saints?" her governess asked. "And do you know *them*? Have you seen them and talked with them? Thus it is with the Emperor Charles. He has come all across the seas to hold your hand and promise to marry you."

The little girl was silent, but there was nothing to fear, because her mother had told her that she was not to go away from her. Being affianced to the Emperor would make no difference at all; they would be together as before, she and her beloved mother.

Mary wished they could be together now, the two of them alone, in the royal nursery, bent over the books while she learned her Latin, and perhaps if her progress pleased her mother, to shut up the books and be allowed to sit at her feet while she told stories of those days when she was a little girl herself in far away Spain. There she had learned lessons in her nursery, but she had had sisters and a brother. How Mary wished that she had sisters and a brother. Perhaps only a brother would suffice. Then her father would not frown so when he remembered she was his only child and a girl.

No, there was no need to feel anxious about this coming ceremony. She had been affianced before. Strangely enough, although last time it had been to a French Prince, the ceremony had taken place in this very Palace; and she was not sure whether she remembered the occasion or her mother had told her about it and she thought she remembered; in any case it was vivid in her mind: Herself a little girl of two in a dress made of cloth of gold, and a cap of black velvet which was covered in dazzling jewels. There had been a man who had taken the place of her bridegroom-to-be because her bridegroom could not be present. He had only just been born, but he was very important because he was the son of the King of France, and her father had wanted to show his friendship for the King of France at that time. A diamond ring had been put on her finger; she was sure she remembered the difficulty she had had in trying to keep it on.

But that was four years ago, and now her father was no longer the friend of the King of France. She often wondered about that baby and whether he had been told that while he was in his cradle he was affianced to her; she wondered what he thought about it.

Now, of course, it might never have taken place; it was of no importance whatsoever.

What she did remember though, was her mother coming into her apartment and taking her in her arms and laughing with her, and weeping a little. "Only because I am so happy, my darling daughter," she had said.

The reason for the Queen's happiness was that there would be no French marriage. Instead there was to be a Spanish one. "And this makes me happy," said the Queen, "because Spain is my country; and you will go there one day and rule that country as the wife of the Emperor. My mother, your grandmother, was once the Queen of Spain."

So Mary had been happy because her mother was happy; and she shivered with horror to think that she might have been married to the little French boy; then she smiled with pleasure because instead she was to marry the Emperor who was also the King of Spain.

A page came into the apartment with the message for which Mary had been waiting.

"The Queen is ready to receive the Princess."

Mary was eager, as always, to go to her mother.

The Queen was waiting for her in her own private apartments and when the little girl came in she dismissed everyone so that they could be alone; and this was how Mary longed for it to be. She wished though that she was not wearing these ceremonial clothes, so that she could cling to her mother; she wished that she could sit in her lap and ask for stories of Spain.

The Queen knelt so that her face was on a level with her daughter's. "Why, you are a little woman today," she said tenderly.

"And does it not please Your Grace?"

"Call me Mother, sweeting, when we are alone."

Mary put her hands about her mother's neck and looked gravely into her eyes. "I wish we could stay together for hours and hours—the two of us and none other."

"Well, that will be so later."

"Then I shall think of later all the time the ceremony goes on."

"Oh no, my darling, you must not do that. This is a great occasion. Soon I shall take you by the hand and lead you down to the hall, and there will be your father and with him the Emperor."

"But I shall not go away with him yet," said Mary earnestly.

"Not yet, my darling, not for six long years."

Mary smiled. Six years was as long as her life had been and therefore seemed for ever.

"You love the Emperor, Mother, do you not?"

"There is no one I would rather see the husband of my dearest daughter than the Emperor."

"Yet you have seen him but little, Mother. How can you love someone whom you do not know?"

"Well, my darling, I love his mother dearly. She is my own sister; and when we were little she and I were brought up together in the same nursery. She married and went into Flanders, and I came to England and married. But once she came to England with her husband to see me . . ."

Mary wanted to ask why, if her mother loved her sister so much, she always seemed so sad when she spoke of her; but she was afraid of the answer, for she did not want any sadness on this occasion.

But into the Queen's eyes there had come a glazed look, and at that moment she did not see the room in Greenwich Palace and her little daughter, but another room in the Alcazar in Madrid in which children played: herself the youngest and the gravest; and Juana, in a tantrum, kicking their governess because she had attempted to curb her. In those days Juana had been the wild one; her sister had not known then that later she would be Juana the Mad. Only their mother, watching and brooding, had suffered cruel doubts because she remembered the madness of her own mother and feared that the taint had been passed on to Juana.

But what thoughts were these? Juana was safe in her asylum at Tordesillas, living like an animal, some said, in tattered rags, eating her food from the floor, refusing to have women round her because she was still jealous of them although her husband, on whose account she had been so jealous, was long since dead. And because Juana was mad, her eldest son Charles was the Emperor of Austria and King of Spain and, since the discoveries of Columbus, ruler of new rich lands across the ocean. He was the most powerful monarch in the world—and to this young man Mary was to be affianced.

R

"*I* wasn't here when Charles's mother came."

"Oh no, my darling, that was long, long ago, before you were born, before I was married to your father."

"Yet you had left your mother."

Katharine took the little face in her hands and kissed it. She hesitated, wondering whether to put aside the question; but, she reasoned, she has to know my history some day, and it is better that she should learn it from me than any other.

"I left my mother to come here and marry your uncle Arthur. He was the King's elder brother and, had he lived, he would have been the King, and your father the Archbishop of Canterbury. So I married Arthur, and when Arthur died I married your father."

"What was my uncle Arthur like, Mother?"

"He was kind and gentle and rather delicate."

"Not like my father," said the girl. "Did he want sons?"

Those words made the Queen feel that she could have wept. She took her daughter in her arms, not only because she was overcome by tenderness for her, but because she did not want her to see the tears in her eyes.

"He was too young," she said in a muffled voice. "He was but a boy and he died before he grew to manhood."

"How old is Charles, Mother?"

"He is twenty-two years old."

"So old?"

"It is not really very old, Mary."

"How many years older than I?"

"Now you should be able to tell me that."

Mary was thoughtful for a few moments; then she said: "Is it sixteen?"

"That is so."

"Oh Mother, it seems so many."

"Nonsense, darling; I am more than ten years older than Charles, yet you can be happy with me, can you not?"

"I can be so happy with you, Mother, that I believe I am never really happy when I am away from you."

The Queen laid her cheek against her daughter's. "Oh my darling," she said, "do not love me too much."

"How *can* I love you too much?"

"You are right, Mary. It can never be too much. I loved my mother so much that when I left her and when she left this Earth it seemed to me that she was still with me. I loved her so much that I was never alone."

The child looked bewildered and the Queen reproached herself for this outburst of emotion. She, who to everyone else was so calm and restrained, was on occasions forced to let her emotions flow over this beloved daughter who meant more to her than any other living person.

I frighten the child with my confidences, she thought, and stood up, taking Mary's hands in hers and smiling down at her.

"There, my love, are you ready?"

"Will you stand beside me all the time?"

"Perhaps not all the time, but I shall be there watching. And when you greet him I shall be beside you. Listen. I can hear the trumpets. That means they are close. We should be waiting to greet them. Come. Give me your hand. Now, darling, smile. You are very happy."

"Are you happy too, Mother?"

"Indeed, yes. One of the dearest wishes of my heart is about to be fulfilled. Now we are ready to greet my nephew, who will be my son when he is the husband of my beloved daughter."

She held the little hand firmly in hers; and together they descended to the hall for the ceremonial greeting.

*　　　*　　　*

As the royal cavalcade came from Windsor to Greenwich the people massed in their thousands to watch their King pass by. Loudly they cheered him, for he was a magnificent sight on horseback, and beside him the Emperor appeared a somewhat poor figure. The King of England was over six feet tall, his skin was pink and smooth as a boy's, his blue eyes were bright and clear, and he glowed with good health, so that in comparison the Emperor looked pallid and unhealthy. His teeth were prominent and none too white, and he breathed through his mouth which was perpetually ajar; his aquiline nose had a pinched look and the only colour in his face was the blue of his eyes. He was serious, whereas the King of England was gay; he smiled faintly while Henry roared forth his good humour.

But he seemed happy to be in England, and Henry was clearly pleased with him because of the contrast they made and the attention which was therefore called to his own many physical perfections.

As they rode along Henry was thinking of the masques and pageants with which he would impress this young man; but Charles was thinking of the loan he must try to wring from the English. As his father had been, he was perpetually in need of funds to maintain his vast Empire, and in his struggle with the King of France he needed money to pay his mercenaries.

E

He knew that he would have to pay a price for English gold and English support, and had at last decided that he would accept betrothal to the Princess Mary. He had come to this decision with some reluctance—not because he was against an English match, not that he did not believe the child to be un-usually accomplished; but it was distressing to contemplate her age and that he could not hope for an heir until at least eight years had passed. However, there was nothing to be done but accept the inevitable as graciously as he could, for he was fully aware that alliance with England was not only desirable but a necessity.

So as they rode along he listened to the King's conversation, laughed at his jokes and gave an impression to all who saw them that they were the best of friends.

In the cavalcade rode the Cardinal and, as always, his retinue was as magnificent as that of the King. He was wearing his red robes of taffety this day—the finest obtainable—and about his neck hung a tippet of sables; borne before him was the great seal, and one of the noblemen, whom he had deigned to take into his household, carried his Cardinal's hat on a cushion and was bareheaded to indicate the respect he had for it; behind him rode other gentlemen of his household and his higher servants in their red and gold livery.

Wolsey was uneasy during that ride. He felt that since the death of Buckingham the King had taken too great an interest in state affairs. He was inclined to meddle and he did not always want to follow in that direction in which Wolsey would have led him.

The Cardinal was no more sure of this quiet young man than he was of the flamboyant François. In fact he felt that it would be necessary to be even more wary of the Emperor. François was dashing, bold, reckless and lecherous; and a shrewd statesman could often guess which turning he would take. But this pale, serious young man, who was somewhat hesitant in speech and had an air of humility—which Wolsey knew to be entirely false— might be unpredictable and by far the shrewdest ruler of the three who were now so important in Europe.

Charles had had the foresight to recognize that, if he were to consolidate the alliance he wished for, he must first placate Wolsey, and for that reason he had promised the Cardinal a considerable "pension". The thought of vast sums being paid to him from the Imperial coffers was sweet, but some promises were made to be broken; and Wolsey was not certain whether Charles was to be relied on. He had also promised what was more important still: to use his influence at the Papal election, for the great goal of the Cardinal was the Papal crown since, possessing that, he would stand apart from kings, a ruler in his own right. He yearned for that crown.

There had been a disappointment early that year when Pope Leo X had died and a Papal election had taken place. Wolsey had felt that his chances of election were slender, but the promise of Imperial favour had sent his hopes soaring. He received only seven votes, and Adrian VI was elected.

This was not such a bitter disappointment as it might have been, for the Cardinal did not believe Adrian would live long and it seemed certain that another election would be held before many months had passed. If by that time Wolsey could show himself to be the true friend of the Emperor it might be that the promise of help would this time be fulfilled.

Perhaps he had no reason to feel disappointed; he was rising higher and higher in his own country and only last year Henry had presented him with the Abbey of St. Albans, doubtless to repay him for the money from his own pocket which he had spent on the recent embassy to Calais, whither he had gone to help settle differences between François and the Emperor.

And now the friendship with Charles was being strengthened and a treaty had been signed at Windsor in which Henry and Charles agreed on an invasion of France before the May of 1524.

This was where the King had shown himself inclined to meddle. Wolsey himself was not eager to go to war. War to him meant expense, for even with victory the spoils were often scarcely worth the effort made to obtain them. But war to Henry meant the glory of conquest, and it was as irresistible to him as one of the games he played with such *élan* at a pageant.

Still, a goodly pension from the Emperor, the promise of Imperial support at the next Papal election, and the need to fall in with the King's wishes—they were very acceptable, thought Thomas Wolsey as he rode on to Greenwich.

\*          \*          \*

At the door of the Palace stood the Queen holding the hand of her daughter.

The Emperor dismounted and went towards them. He knelt before his aunt and, taking her hand, kissed it fervently.

Mary looked on, and she thought she loved the Emperor— firstly because he was so delighted to see her mother and looked at her so fondly; secondly because her mother was so pleased with him; and thirdly because there was nothing in that pale face to alarm a six-year-old girl.

Now he had turned to greet Mary. He took her hand and stooped low to kiss it; and as he did so there was a cheer from all those watching.

The King could not allow them to keep the centre of the stage too long and was very quickly beside them, taking his daughter in his arms to the great delight of all who watched, particularly the common people. They might admire the grace of Charles, but they liked better the King's homely manners. Henry knew it, and he was delighted because he was now the centre of attention and admiration.

So they went into the Palace, Mary walking between her father and mother while the Emperor was at the Queen's side.

Katharine felt happy to have with her one who was of her own family, although Charles did not resemble his mother in the least, nor was he, with his pallid looks, like his father who had been known as Philip the Handsome.

A momentary anxiety came to Katharine as she wondered whether Charles resembled his father in any other way. Philip had found women irresistible, and with his Flemish mistresses had submitted the passionate Juana to many an indignity, which conduct it was believed had aggravated her madness.

But surely there was no need to fear that her daughter would be submitted to similar treatment by this serious young man.

"I am so happy to have you with us," she told her nephew.

"You cannot be more delighted than I am," replied Charles in his somewhat hesitant way; but Katharine felt that the slight stammer accentuated his sincerity.

Henry said: "After the banquet our daughter shall show Your Imperial Highness how skilful she is at the virginals."

"It would seem I have a most accomplished bride," replied Charles and when, glancing up at him, Mary saw he was smiling at her with kindliness, she knew he was telling her not to be afraid.

So into the banqueting hall they went and sat down with ceremony, when good English food was served.

The King looked on in high good humour. He was pleased because he and the Emperor were going to make war on François, and he had sworn vengeance on the King of France ever since he, Henry, had challenged him to a wrestling match only to be ignobly thrown to the ground by that lean, smiling giant.

He was even pleased with Katharine on this occasion. She had played her part in bringing about the Spanish alliance; for there was no doubt that the Emperor was more ready to enter into alliance with an England whose Queen was his aunt than he would otherwise have been.

Henry caught the brooding eye of his Cardinal fixed on the pale young man.

Ha! he thought, Wolsey is uncertain. He is not enamoured of our nephew. He looks for treachery in all who are not English. 'Tis not a bad trait in a Chancellor.

He thought of how Wolsey had bargained when they had made the treaty. A good servant, he mused, and one devoted to the interests of his King and country.

Enough of solemnity, he decided, and clapped his hands. "Music!" he cried. "Let there be music."

So the minstrels played, and later Mary sat at the virginals and showed her fiancé how skilful she was.

"Is it possible that she is but six years old!" cried Charles.

And the King roared his delight.

"I think," said the Emperor, "that with one so advanced it should not be necessary for me to wait six years for her. Let me take her with me. I promise you she shall have all the care at my court that you could give her at yours."

Katharine cried in alarm: "No, no. She is too young to leave her home. Six years is not so long, nephew. You must wait six years."

Charles gave her his slow, kindly smile. "I am in your hands," he said.

Mary who had been listening to this conversation had grown numb with terror. Six years was a life-time, but he wanted to take her now. This young man no longer seemed so kindly; he represented a danger. For the first time in her life she became aware that she might be taken from her mother's side.

Katharine, who was watching her, noticed her alarm and knew the cause. She said: "It is past the Princess's bed time. The excitement of Your Excellency's visit has exhausted her. I ask your leave for her to retire to her apartments."

Charles bowed his head and Henry murmured: "Let her women take her to bed, and we will show our nephew some of our English dances."

So Mary was taken away while the royal party went into the ballroom; and soon the King was dancing and leaping to the admiration of all.

Katharine slipped away when the revelry was at its height and went to her daughter's apartment, where she found Mary lying in her bed, her cheeks still flushed, her eyes wide open.

"Still awake, my darling?" Katharine gently reproved.

"Oh, Mother, I knew you would come."

Katharine laid a hand on the flushed forehead. "You are afraid you will be sent away."

Mary did not answer but her small body had begun to tremble.

"It shall not be, my little one," went on the Queen.

"The Emperor said . . ."

"He meant it not. It was to compliment you that he spoke those words. It is what is called diplomacy. Have no fear, you shall not leave me for a long, long time . . . not until you are old enough to want to go."

"Mother, how could I ever want to go from you?"

Katharine lifted the little hand and kissed it.

"When you grow up you will love others better than your Mother."

"I never shall. I swear I never shall."

"You are too young to swear eternal love, my darling. But I am here now. I slipped away from the ball because I knew you would be fretting."

Katharine lay on the bed and held the child in her arms.

"Oh Mother, you love me, do you not?"

"With all my heart, sweeting."

"And I love you with all of mine. I never want to go away from England, Mother . . . unless you come with me."

"Hush, my sweetheart. All will be well. You will see."

"And you will not let the Emperor take me away?"

"No . . . not for years and years . . ."

The child was reassured; and the Queen lay still holding her daughter fondly in her arms, thinking of a young girl in Spain who had been afraid and had told her mother that she wished to stay with her for ever.

This is the fate of royal children, she told herself.

The comfort of her mother's arms soothed Mary and soon she slept. Then Katharine gently disengaged herself; the Queen must not stay too long from the ball.

\*     \*     \*

The King was momentarily contented. He was at war with France and he dreamed of being one day crowned in Rheims. His temper was good. He spent more time than he ever had engaged on matters of state, and the Cardinal, seated beside him, explaining when the need arose to do so, was feeling certain twinges of uneasiness.

He had been forced to support the war somewhat against his wishes; yet he was too wily to let anyone know that he was against it. The King wished it and Wolsey had no intention of arousing Henry's anger by seeming lukewarm about a project which so pleased the King.

Henry had inherited the wealth which his miserly father had so carefully accumulated; but he had spent lavishly and already the treasury was alarmingly depleted.

"Nothing," said the Cardinal, "absorbs wealth as quickly as war. We shall need money if we are to succeed in France."

The King waved a plump hand. "Then I am sure there is no one who can raise it more ably than my good Chancellor."

So be it, thought Wolsey. But the levying of taxes was a delicate matter and he suspected that the people who were obliged to pay them would blame, not their glittering charming King, but his apparently mean and grasping Chancellor.

There was talk of the King's going to France with his army, but although Henry declared his eagerness to do this, nothing came of it. His adventures abroad with his armies in the earlier years of his reign had not been distinguished although he had thought they had at the time. Much as Henry would have enjoyed riding through the streets of Paris, a conqueror, and even more so returning home to England as the King who had brought France to the English dominions, he was now wise enough to realize that even hardened campaigners did not always succeed in battle, and that he was a novice at the game of war. Failure was something he could not bear to contemplate. Therefore he felt it was safer to wage war on the enemy with a strip of channel between himself and the armies.

François Premier was a King who rode into battle recklessly; but then François was a reckless fellow. He might win his successes, but he also had to face his defeats.

So Henry put aside the plans for a personal visit to the battlefields. But war was an exciting game played from a distance, and Wolsey must find the money to continue it.

*       *       *

These were happy days for the Queen. Her husband and her nephew were allies and they stood together against the King of France whom she believed to be more of a menace to Christianity than the Turk. François, already notorious for his lecherous way of life, must surely come to disaster; and since her serious-minded nephew had the power of England beside him she was certain that Charles was invincible.

She had her daughter under the same roof with her and she herself supervised her lessons.

R*

Mary was docile and happy as long as her mother was with her. The King left Katharine alone, it was true, but she believed that even he had ceased to fret for a son, and accepted the fact that their daughter Mary was heir to the throne; and one day when she married Charles she would be the Empress of Austria and the Queen of Spain as well as the Queen of England. That matter was happily settled.

She was constantly seeking the best method of teaching her daughter, and one day she summoned Thomas More to her that she might discuss with him the manner in which his own daughters were educated.

As usual she found great pleasure in his company. She talked a little about the war but she saw that the subject was distressing to him—which was to be expected, for he was a man to whom violence was abhorrent—so she turned the conversation to his family, which she knew could not fail to please him.

She told him of her desire that the Princess Mary should receive the best education in all subjects which would be of use to her, and Thomas said: "Has your Grace thought of consulting Juan Luis Vives?"

"I had not until this moment," she said, "but now that you mention him I believe he is the man who could help me in the education of the Princess. I pray you, bring him with you and come to see me at this hour tomorrow." When Thomas had left her she wondered why she had not thought of Vives before. He had so much to recommend him. In the first place he was one of her own countrymen and she felt that, as her daughter was after all half Spanish and would be the wife of the King of Spain, there must be a Spanish angle to her education.

Both Erasmus and Sir Thomas More had called her attention to Juan Luis Vives, and those two were men whose intellectual abilities had won the admiration of the world. Vives was a man, said Thomas, forced by poverty to hide his light under a bushel. He was living at Bruges in obscurity; he had published very little of his writings and few people had ever heard of him. Erasmus would bear him out, for Vives had studied Greek with him at Louvain. It was Thomas's opinion that Vives should be brought to England and encouraged by the Court, for there was little his native Valencia or the city of Bruges could offer him.

Katharine, out of her great admiration for Thomas, had immediately sent money to Vives with a letter in which she explained her interest in his work. It had not been difficult to persuade Henry—with the help of Thomas More—that Vives would be an ornament to the English Court; and Henry, who, when he was not masking or engaged in sport, liked occasionally to have conversation with men of intellect (François Premier boasted that his Court was the most intellectual in Europe and Henry was eager to rival it) very willingly agreed that Vives should be given a yearly pension.

Thus in gratitude Vives dedicated his book, *Commentaries on Saint Augustine* to Henry, which so delighted the King that he called him to England to lecture at the college which Wolsey had recently founded at Oxford.

This had happened some years before, but Vives made a point of spending a certain part of each year in England with his friends and patrons; and it so happened that he was in London at this time. So the very next day he arrived in the company of Thomas More for an interview with the Queen regarding her daughter's education.

Katharine received them in her private apartment and they sat together at the window overlooking the Palace gardens as they talked.

"You know, Master Vives, why I have commanded you to come to me?" asked Katharine.

"My friend has given me some idea of what Your Grace desires," Vives answered.

"My daughter's education is a matter which is of the utmost importance to me. Tell me how you think this should be arranged."

"Sir Thomas and I are of one opinion on the education of young people," said Vives.

"It is true," added Thomas. "We both believe that it is folly to presume that a girl's education is of less importance than that of a boy."

"It is but natural," went on Vives, "that an intelligent girl may come to a better understanding of Latin and Greek than a boy who is not possessed of the same intelligence."

"I would have my daughter educated in scholarly subjects, but at the same time I wish her to learn the feminine arts," answered Katharine.

"In that I am in full agreement with Your Grace," said Vives.

"What more charming sight," mused Thomas, "than a girl at her embroidery?"

"Or even at the spinning wheel working on wool and flax," added Vives. "These are excellent accomplishments, but Your Grace has not summoned me to discuss them."

"I am going to appoint you my daughter's tutor," the Queen

told Vives, "and I wish you immediately to draw up a list of books for her to read."

Vives bowed his head. "I will go to my task with the utmost pleasure, and I can immediately say that I think the Princess should read the New Testament both night and morning, and also certain selected portions of the Old Testament. She must become fully conversant with the gospels. She should, I believe, also study Plutarch's *Enchiridion*, Seneca's *Maxims*, and of course Plato and Cicero." He glanced at his friend. "I suggest that Sir Thomas More's *Utopia* would provide good reading."

The Queen smiled to see the look of pride on Thomas's face, thinking that his few vanities made him human, and therein lay the secret of his lovable nature.

"And what of the *Paraphrase* of Erasmus?" asked Thomas quickly.

"That also," agreed Vives. "And I think the Princess should not waste her time on books of chivalry and romance. Any stories she might wish to read for her entertainment should either be sacred or historical, so that her time is not wasted in idleness. The only exception I would make is the story of Griselda, which contains such an excellent example of patience that the Princess might profit from it."

Katharine said: "I can see that you will be an excellent tutor, but we must remember that she is but a child. Her life must not be all study. There must be some pleasure."

Vives looked surprised; to him the greatest pleasure was in study, and he believed the Princess to be the most fortunate of children, having such a plan of study made for her.

Thomas laughed. "I'll swear the Lady Mary, who so loves her music, will find time to escape to it from her books now and then. I know my own daughters . . ." (Katharine noticed the look of pride when he spoke of his daughters, which was even more marked than when he spoke of his books) ". . . are proficient in Greek and Latin but they find time to be merry."

"Yours is a merry household," answered the Queen.

And she found that she was comparing the King and Thomas More—two fathers who could not be more unlike. She had seen Thomas in company with his eldest daughter, Margaret, had seen them walk, their arms entwined, had heard the girl's unrepressed laughter ringing out as she scolded her father in an affectionate way. It was impossible to imagine Mary and Henry thus.

What a fortunate man, this Thomas More; what a fortunate family!

"There is much merriment at Court," answered Thomas gravely.

But he understood of course—he was a man who would always understand—and a great tenderness touched his face; the Queen knew that it expressed the compassion he felt for her little daughter, who would study alone—not as Thomas's family did—and would be taught by the somewhat stern though excellent Vives instead of merry Thomas.

Somewhere from the grounds she heard the sound of laughter, and glancing down saw a group of young people. They made a charming picture on the grass in their brightly coloured clothes, and there was one girl among them who appeared to be the centre of attraction. She was dark-haired, dark-eyed, somewhat sallow of complexion and, although not a beauty, certainly striking. She seemed to have more vitality than any other member of the group and was quite clearly taking the attention of the young men from the other girls who were present.

"A high-spirited party," said the Queen; and Vives and Thomas More glanced out of the window. "That girl seems familiar but I do not recall who she is. Surely that is Thomas Wyatt with her—and Henry Percy."

"The girl is Thomas Boleyn's daughter, Your Grace," Thomas told her.

Then Katharine knew of whom the girl reminded her. It was Mary Boleyn. The resemblance was slight, otherwise she would have realized immediately. This girl had an air of dignity and assurance, and pride too—all qualities in which Mary had been dismally lacking.

"This is the second girl, I believe," said the Queen.

"Recently home from France on account of the war," explained Thomas.

"Doubtless her father is looking for a place at Court for her," said the Queen.

"He will find it," replied Thomas, "not only for Anne but for his George also."

"I trust," said the Queen, "that this Anne is not like her sister in her morals, and that George does not bear too strong a resemblance to his father."

"From what I have seen of them," Thomas answered, "I should say they are a dazzling pair."

"Well then, I suppose we must resign ourselves," said the Queen with a smile, "for it seems the Boleyns have come to Court."

\* \* \*

The Cardinal had shut himself in his private apartments at Hampton Court; seated at the window from which he could see the river, he was waiting for a message which was all-important to him, for it would tell him whether his greatest ambition was realized or not.

The pale November sun shone wanly on the river. He thought: I shall miss Hampton Court; I shall miss England.

He would miss his family too; but he would find means of seeing them. He would have young Thomas in Rome with him, because he would very quickly overcome all difficulties. He thought of Rodrigo Borgia, Alexander VI, who, while living in the Vatican, had yet arranged to have his children with him; for a Pope was as powerful as a King; and once he was supreme in the Vatican, the frowns of unpredictable Henry would be of little moment to him.

Yet, he mused, I shall not forget my own country, and it will be a good day for England when an Englishman takes the Papal Crown.

How long the waiting seemed! He would see nobody. He had told his secretaries that he was to be disturbed only by messengers from abroad because he was working on important matters of state.

But soon the messenger must come.

He began to pace the apartment because he could no longer bear to stare at the river.

His chances were good. On the death of Leo X when Adrian VI had been elected, his hopes had been slender. Why should the Cardinals have elected a comparative newcomer to their ranks, an Englishman who had not previously worked closely with the Vatican? That election had taken place at the beginning of the year, and Adrian's tenure of the Papacy had indeed been a short one for in September news had come to England of his death, and for the next two months the Cardinal had given less thought to affairs in England; his mind was on what would happen at the next conclave.

Since the election of Adrian and his death the Emperor Charles had visited England, and he had become more aware than he had been before of the important part played by the Cardinal in the foreign policy of England. To win Wolsey's approval of the alliance he had offered large sums of money, a pension no less; but Wolsey had begun to grow uneasy because none of these sums of money had yet been paid; and he could get no satisfaction as to when they would be from Louis de Praet, who was now Charles's Ambassador in England.

Money was needed to prosecute the war, was the excuse, and Wolsey was angry to contemplate the riches which were being squandered on useless battlefields in Europe, riches which could have been used not only to make the country prosperous but would have enabled him to increase his personal treasures.

But there was one concession which Charles could make and would cost him little in money; and this was what the Cardinal needed more than anything else in the world: His influence at the Conclave. The powerful Emperor, of whom every Cardinal would stand in awe, had but to make it known that he wished to see an English Pope in the Vatican and that those who depended on his bounty were to give their vote to Cardinal Wolsey, and the Papal crown would be won.

This the Emperor could do. He would do it. He must . . . since he had failed to supply the pension.

"If he does not . . ." said Wolsey aloud, but he did not continue.

He would not face the possibility of failure. The Emperor could and would.

The Cardinal's unpopularity throughout the country was growing, and people looked on sullenly when he paraded the streets on his way to Westminster. He went in all his splendid pomp, but that did nothing to appease the people's anger, but rather increased it. They were openly murmuring against him.

He had always known, during his brilliant career, when it was time to move on, so now he was aware that he had reached the pinnacle of power in England, and that it was time to take the final step to Rome. It must be now, for there might not be another opportunity.

This war will end in failure, he thought. And when there are failures, scapegoats are sought. Who would make a better scapegoat, in the eyes of the people, than the opulent Cardinal?

He was alert because he had seen a boat pulling up at the privy stairs, and he guessed it could be his messenger.

He tried to curb his impatience; he was so eager to go down to meet the man, but, as much as he longed to, he must remember his position and his dignity.

How long it seemed to take for him to cross the park! Now he had entered the palace. Soon the usher would come to his door.

I must be calm, he told himself. I must show no excitement, no eagerness.

Cavendish was at the door.

"A messenger is without, Your Eminence. He asks that he may be brought at once to your presence."

"A messenger?" He was sure the beating of his heart disturbed the red satin of his robe. "Let him wait . . . no, on second thoughts I will see him now."

Cavendish bowed low. Now he would be traversing the eight rooms to that one in which the messenger waited . . . the all-important messenger. It seemed an hour before he was standing on the threshold of the room.

"You have a message for me?" he said.

"Your Eminence," said the man and held out a roll of parchment.

As Wolsey took it it seemed to burn his fingers, but still he restrained himself.

"You may go now to the kitchens. Tell them I sent you and you are to be refreshed."

The man bowed and was gone; so at last he was alone.

He tore at the parchment, his trembling fingers impeding him; he felt dizzy and it was some seconds before he read the words which danced like black demons on the parchment scroll.

He stared at them and tried to force them by his dominant will to reform themselves into what he wished to read.

But of what use was that? The result was there for him to see and there was nothing he could do to alter it.

"Cardinal de' Medici has been elected the new Pope of Rome, Clement VII."

Never since the days of his obscurity had he known a defeat like this. Disappointed he had been when Adrian was elected; but then he had been sure that there would shortly be another conclave, and he had needed the time to consolidate his forces.

But when would he have another chance? Perhaps never.

This was the darkest moment of his life so far. He had come such a long way; he could not believe in failure. Was he to fail with the very peak of achievement in sight? It seemed so.

Then a burning rage took possession of him. It was directed against one man—a sly pallid youth who had promised so much and done so little, who had seemed perhaps a little simple in his humility. But there was no real humility behind those mild blue eyes. A wily statesman lurked there, a statesman who believed he could best outwit his rivals by deceiving them with their belief in his own incompetence.

Wolsey spoke softly to himself: "The Emperor has done this. He has refused me the Papal crown as he has the pensions he promised me. He shall regret it, as all those shall who become the enemies of Thomas Wolsey."

\* \* \*

All through the winter Wolsey successfully hid his rancour against the Emperor while he was waiting for his opportunity. Determined to break the friendship between Henry and Charles, he kept a sharp watch on Katharine for, since her nephew was his enemy, she must be also.

He asked the King's permission to introduce a new woman to the Queen's intimate circle, and Henry, delighted to do his Chancellor a favour, agreed that the woman should become one of the Queen's maids of honour.

Katharine did not like the woman, but she was enjoying her new peaceful existence too much to protest. She need not see much of her; and in any case she was so completely wrapped up in her daughter that she had little time for anything or anyone else. Vives's curriculum was certainly a strenuous one and sometimes she thought Mary spent too much time in study; however the little girl was a willing pupil and, to help her, Katharine herself studied with her and commanded some of the ladies of the Court to do likewise.

Being so pleasantly engaged she scarcely noticed the woman and thus gave her excellent opportunities for hiding herself when the Spanish Ambassador called and had conversations with the Queen; nor was it difficult to find a means of conveying those letters, which the Queen wrote to her nephew, to Wolsey before they were sent to Spain.

As for the Cardinal, he had always been able to wait for revenge and, as he had never favoured the Spanish policy and had always thought that alliance with the French would be a better alternative, he began to plan to this end.

The winter passed; there were good reports of the progress of the war, but no material gains came the way of the English; and the King preferred to forget what was happening on the Continent in the Christmas and New Year Revels.

During these Katharine was aware on several occasions of Thomas Boleyn's daughter Anne who always seemed to be in the centre of a merry and admiring group, with either Wyatt or Henry Percy at her side. Katharine had noticed the King, glowering at these young people as though their high spirits annoyed him. Could it be that he was angry because he was no longer quite so young; was he tiring of pageants and masques?

*                    *                    *

All through the spring and summer there was news of the war, but none of it good. Wolsey was trying to raise money; the

Emperor was still making promises to pay, not only what he had borrowed, but Wolsey's pension.

That is money we shall likely never see, thought Wolsey; but he did not tell the King this because Henry was at the moment eager to maintain his alliance with Charles, and his hatred of François was as strong as ever.

One summer's day Dr. Linacre, the King's physician, begged an audience of the Queen, and when he came into her presence he brought a bouquet of beautiful roses.

Katharine congratulated him warmly because she knew that he had recently brought this rose to England, and had succeeded in making it grow in English soil.

The doctor was delighted and as he bowed low before her Katharine smiled at his enthusiasm and held out a hand to take the roses.

"They are beautiful," she cried.

"I knew Your Grace would think so. I have come to ask permission of you and the King to present you with trees I have grown."

"I am sure His Grace will be delighted."

"I had doubts that they would grow in our soil. Our climate is so different from that of Damascus."

"And you have succeeded magnificently. I know the King will be as pleased as I am to accept these trees."

"I have called it the Damask Rose," said the doctor.

"An excellent name, and so explicit."

She was still admiring the roses when the King entered the apartment. The peaceful atmosphere was immediately disturbed for the King's face was of that faintly purplish tinge which nowadays indicated anger, and his eyes ice-blue, his mouth tight.

"Your Grace," began the doctor, who could think of nothing but the pleasure his roses gave him and, he believed, must give all those who looked at them, "I have been showing the Queen the new Damask Rose."

"Very pleasant," said the King shortly.

"Dr. Linacre wishes to present us with trees too," said the Queen.

"They will be some of the first to be planted in this country, Your Grace," went on the doctor. "I shall count it an honour . . ."

"We thank you," said the King. He took one of the roses in his hand and studied it, but Katharine knew that he gave it little attention. "It is indeed beautiful. We accept the trees. They shall be tended with care, and I am sure give us pleasure for many years to come."

The doctor bowed and asked the Queen's permission to take some of the roses to the Princess Mary. Katharine gave that permission willingly and the doctor took his leave.

When he had gone, Henry walked to the window and stood glowering out.

Katharine knew that it was on occasions like this when his dogs and all wise men and women kept their distance from him, but she was his wife and must know what disturbed him, so she asked: "Does aught ail you, Henry?"

He turned and she noticed how his lower lip jutted out.

"Oh, 'tis naught but the folly of young Percy."

"Northumberland's son?"

"Yes, Henry Percy. The young fool has been presumptuous enough to promise marriage to one of the girls of the Court."

"And you cannot grant permission for this marriage?"

"Northumberland's is one of the most noble families in the land," growled Henry.

"Is the girl whom he has chosen so lowly?"

"She is not of his rank."

"So far below him then?"

"It is Thomas Boleyn's girl."

"Oh?" The Queen thought of the girl as she had seen her about the Court—a flamboyant personality, one made to attract attention to herself, decidedly French in manners and style of dressing. Indeed since the beginning of the French wars, when the girl had come to England, fashions had been changing and becoming more French, which was strange when it was considered that the English were at war with that country. "I have noticed her often," went on the Queen. "She seems to be one who attracts attention to herself. I have seen Percy with her and Wyatt also."

"Wyatt is married so he could not make a fool of himself," muttered the King.

"Thomas Boleyn has risen in your favour in the last years, Henry. Is the girl so very much below Percy?"

"Come, come, he is the eldest son of Northumberland. His father will never consent to the match."

"But the girl's mother is a Howard and . . ."

Henry made an irritable gesture, wriggling his shoulders like a petulant boy. "Northumberland is coming to Court to forbid his son to have anything to do with the girl. Indeed she is pledged already to marry the son of Piers Butler. As to Percy, he is to marry Shrewsbury's girl—Mary Talbot . . . a suitable match."

Katharine stared sadly before her. She was sorry for the lovers.

"I thought the Boleyn girl to be well educated, and she has a certain dignity."

The King turned on her angrily. "'Tis a most unsuitable match. The Cardinal has already reprimanded that young fool Percy and made him see his folly. 'Tis a pity he ever took service with the Cardinal, since it has brought him into close contact with the girl."

"Percy will be docile," said the Queen. She remembered him as she had last seen him at the side of that vital, glowing girl, and she had seen what a contrast they made—she so full of life, he so gentle, weak almost. She was certain there would be no rebellion from Percy.

"He had better be," said the King. "In any case he's banished from Court and has been ordered not to see the girl again. His duty now is to marry Mary Talbot as soon as possible, and we shall see that that is done."

"Ah well, Henry, then the matter will be settled. But I am surprised that you should feel so strongly about it."

"You are surprised!" The King's eyes were fierce. "Let me tell you that the welfare of the young people at my Court is my greatest concern."

"I know it well."

The King strode from her apartment; and she continued to wonder why he should have been so incensed by such a trivial matter.

She saw Anne Boleyn a few days later, and all the sparkle seemed to have gone out of her. She was dejected and sullen.

Poor girl! pondered the Queen. She is heartbroken at the loss of her lover.

She wondered whether to send for her and offer her comfort; but decided that would be unwise, and tantamount to acting against the wishes of the King.

A week passed and she remembered that she had not seen the girl; so she asked one of her women if Anne Boleyn was still at Court.

"No, Your Grace," was the answer, "she has returned to Hever Castle on the King's command."

Banished from Court! And simply because she accepted Percy's offer of marriage.

The King's anger was unaccountable.

\*     \*     \*

As the Cardinal bent over the documents on his table his usher entered and told him that a merchant of Genoa was craving an audience with His Eminence.

"What is his business?" asked the Cardinal.

"He would tell me nothing, Eminence, except that he had merchandise to show you which he would show no other, and that he felt sure you would be willing to grant him an interview if you would but look at the nature of the articles he has to lay before you."

Wolsey was thoughtful. Was he right when he fancied there was a hint of subtlety in the merchant's words? What was the nature of the merchandise he wished to show? Could it be information—secret information?

A year ago he would have had the merchant told that he might call again; since his defeat at the Papal election he had added that to his caution which he had subtracted from his dignity.

"Bring the man to me," he said.

Cavendish retired and returned in a few moments with a dark-skinned man who carried a bag in a manner to suggest that what it contained was very precious indeed.

"You may leave," Wolsey told Cavendish; and as soon as he was alone with the Genoese, the man set down his bag and said: "My lord Cardinal, I am not merely a merchant. I come on behalf of one who is eager to negotiate with you."

"And who is that?"

"The Duchesse of Savoy."

The Cardinal was silent. He knew that in truth this man was a messenger from François Premier, because, in everything François did, his mother, Louise of Savoy, was firmly behind him. Therefore if this man did indeed come from the Duchesse, it was tantamount to coming from the King of France.

At last Wolsey spoke. "For what purpose are you here?"

"My lady Duchesse knows full well the perfidy of the Emperor, which Your Eminence has so recently had reason to deplore. She believes that England would be happier in friendship with the King of France than with this perfidious Emperor. She knows that the King of England is deeply involved with the Emperor, that the Princess Mary is the Emperor's betrothed; but she feels that a greater understanding could be possible between France and England if Your Eminence and she were friends. She sends you letters which I bring to you; and if it should please Your Eminence to answer these letters, your reply can be safely trusted to my care."

"Your credentials?" asked the Cardinal.

The merchant opened his bag and produced papers which Wolsey studied.

These told him that he was in the presence of Giovanni

Joachino Passano, a man whom he could trust; Passano was in England as a merchant and would carry on that trade. If the Cardinal could find lodgings for him it would make their meetings easier to arrange and he would be always at his disposal as the go-between for correspondence between France and England.

The Cardinal was thoughtful.

He was determined to end the war, the cessation of which was necessary for England's solvency; he was equally determined to show the Emperor that he could not neglect his promise to Thomas Wolsey with impunity. Secret communications with France would be useful at this moment.

"I shall lodge you in London with a servant of mine in whom I have the utmost trust," he said. "As a merchant of Genoa it will be understood that you are constantly travelling between London and the Continent. I shall study these papers you have brought to me and it may be that I shall wish you to carry my answers to the Duchesse."

"If that is so, Your Eminence, I shall be at your service."

"Let me see the articles you have brought with you to sell."

For the next ten minutes the Cardinal examined the exquisite cloth which the merchant showed him; then he summoned one of his pages and told him to send in a certain servant, one who did not live in the Cardinal's intimate entourage but had his lodgings in London.

When this man arrived he said to him: "Here is Giovanni Joachino Passano, a merchant from Genoa, who has brought me rich cloth. I wish him to return to Genoa in due course to bring me more, but for the time being he needs lodgings in London. Take him into your house, that he may be near at hand when I wish to give him my orders."

The servant was delighted to be so selected and assured the Cardinal that the Genoese merchant should have the best room in his house, and all the respect deserved by one whose merchandise pleased the Cardinal.

Wolsey nodded his approval in a manner which implied good services would not be forgotten.

And so the agent of Louise of Savoy—who was naturally the servant of François Premier—had his lodgings in London; and the Cardinal often called him to Hampton Court, where they would remain together and alone, sometimes for hours at a time.

\*  \*  \*

The King came riding to Greenwich from Hever Castle where he had been spending a night as the guest of Sir Thomas Boleyn.

As soon as he reached the Palace he summoned the Cardinal to his presence.

He greeted Wolsey with the pleasure he habitually bestowed upon his favourite minister, but there was a change in his manner which baffled the Cardinal.

He seemed almost subdued, which was rare in Henry; he looked more like a boy than ever and there was a certain gentleness about him which the Cardinal had never seen before.

"'Twas pleasant in the country," he said. "I declare Boleyn's castle of Hever is a restful place in which to spend a night."

That was strange also. When had Henry ever asked for restfulness?

"Your Grace took but a small party with you?"

"'Twas enough. I declare, Thomas, I am weary of ceremony on every occasion."

"'Tis pleasant for Your Grace to escape now and then; and may I say that it is doubly pleasant for your servant to see you again."

"Good Thomas," murmured the King, but the Cardinal felt that his attention was elsewhere.

Was this a good time to let him know that it might not be difficult to make peace with France, to whisper in the royal ear those first drops of poison regarding the Emperor? It seemed likely while he was in this gentle mood.

"Boleyn entertained me royally at his castle," went on Henry musingly. "I thought I would show my gratitude by granting him certain land. You might see what we could do for him."

"It shall be so, Your Grace."

"I had thought of elevating him to the peerage . . . as Viscount Rochford."

"This would take time, Your Grace."

"Yes, yes," said Henry testily. "But it is in my mind to do so."

"He is a fortunate man to have found such favour in Your Grace's eyes, particularly as his daughter so recently offended you."

"Ah . . . the girl." The King began to smile. "A haughty wench, Thomas. I saw little of her during my stay at Hever."

"She was absent from her home?"

"Indisposed."

"Your Grace was doubtless glad not to be bothered by the presence of the girl, preferring the company of her father."

"Bold," mused Henry, "and haughty."

"Your Grace believes this indisposition to have been sulks on account of banishment from Court. The saucy wench should be clapped into prison for behaving so."

"Nay nay," said the King. "I do not disturb myself with the vagaries of girls. I believe her to have declared she will be revenged on you, Thomas."

Thomas laughed. "Should I tremble, Your Grace?"

"I notice she has flashing black eyes and the look of a witch. She blames you for sending Percy back to his father."

"She should blame Percy for being so easily persuaded, or herself for choosing such a lover."

"As usual, Thomas, you speak good sense."

Wolsey bowed his head in appreciation of the compliment and went on: "Your Grace, I confess I am disturbed about the war."

"Ah yes." The King seemed reluctant to end the discussion of his trip to Hever.

"I do not trust the Emperor."

"I begin to agree with you, Thomas."

"We have been pouring our resources into war and have so far not gained a foot of French soil. If Your Grace considers our expenditure . . ."

"I am considering it, Thomas, considering it with great sadness."

"Look at the progress the Emperor has made. He has driven the French from Italy. But what gain to us is that? He has strengthened his frontiers in the Netherlands and Spain. That is good . . . for the Emperor. I would say, Your Grace, that in Charles we have another such as Maximilian."

Henry nodded and his face darkened, as he remembered how he had been duped by Charles's grandfathers—the Emperor Maximilian and Ferdinand of Aragon.

"I had hoped much from the rising of the Duke of Bourbon against François," said Henry.

"And we hoped in vain, Your Grace."

"Well, Thomas, what can we do?"

"I should be ready to forget all that we have spent on this enterprise and put out feelers for a separate peace with France."

The King's frown sent a shiver of alarm through the Cardinal. Fleetingly he wondered what Henry's reaction would be if he discovered that Giovanni Joachino Passano paid regular visits to him, not to sell him cloth but to carry letters back and forth between the chief of the King's ministers and the mother of François. One thing was certain; he was playing a dangerous game.

The King was like a child who had set his heart on a certain glittering bauble; in this case the conquest of France. Such a project was an impossibility—Wolsey knew.

"Despatches from the Emperor have been increasingly gloomy, Your Grace."

Henry stuck out his lower lip like a petulant child.

"I have poured money into this project," he began.

"And the Emperor asks for more, Your Grace. He says that unless we provide it the entire enterprise may be fruitless. It would appear now that even the Pope . . ." Wolsey's voice was faintly bitter . . . "whom he helped to elect, is uncertain of him!"

"Ah, the Pope!" said Henry, and an alert expression had crept into his face. He knew it had been a bitter disappointment to Wolsey that he was not elected, and he wondered how he himself would have fared, robbed of the services of his Chancellor. It seemed to him in that moment that there was a tinge of disloyalty in the Cardinal's disappointment. "You were over-eager to leave us, Thomas," he said with a trace of petulance.

"Solely that I could have worked for England from the Vatican."

Henry was sorry for his suspicions. "I believe that to be so," he said. "Well, it did not happen as we wished it, Thomas. But Clement is a good friend to you and to me."

"He could not be the friend of one and not the other," said Wolsey.

"'Tis true," answered the King. "And I rejoiced when he confirmed your Legateship for life, and gave you the Bishopric of Durham."

"Your Grace is good to me."

"Well, you have a King and a Pope as your good friends, Thomas; I wonder which you value the more."

"Your Grace does not need me to answer that question."

Henry smiled well pleased, and the Cardinal knew that no rumours had reached him concerning the French spy in their midst.

"Then Your Grace would not be prepared to think of peace?"

"Thomas, there is one reason why I stand firmly with the Emperor and, no matter what our losses, there I shall remain. Do not forget that he is betrothed to the Princess Mary. While he adheres to that promise we must forgive him if he breaks some others."

The Cardinal then understood that he must continue to work in secret.

\*　　　\*　　　\*

The Queen and her daughter sat with some of the women of the Court busily working with their needles. As they bent over their work one of their number read to them from Thomas More's *Utopia*; this was a custom which Katharine remembered from the days of her childhood, when her mother had sought to have the hands usefully employed while the mind was exercised.

Katharine's life was becoming increasingly busy. She spent a great deal of time with her daughter, whose education was, she believed, in constant need of her supervision. Her daughter was her greatest joy, and while she had her with her she could not be unhappy. Mary was now nine years old and it was distressing to remember that in three more years she would be expected to leave her home and go to the Court of the Emperor. Three years was such a short time. But I must not be selfish, thought the Queen. My daughter will be a great Queen, and it is not for me to regret that which is necessary to make her so.

Nevertheless, she wished to have her with her at every moment of the day, so that none of the time which they could spend together would be lost.

Now they were working on small garments which would be given to the poor women who had babies and no means of clothing them. Katharine was alarmed by the growing poverty among some classes in England; she knew that many people were wandering from town to town, village to village, homeless, sleeping in barns and under hedges, working when they could, eating when they could; and, as was inevitable in these circumstances, now and then stealing or starving to death.

Thomas More, when he came to her intimate suppers, had on several occasions spoken of his growing anxiety about the new conditions in England. He had pointed out that the prosperity of the upper classes was in some measure responsible for the poverty of the lower. There was a great demand for fine cloth which meant that many of the landowners, deciding to keep more sheep, took small-holdings from the men who had hitherto farmed them, and turned them into grazing land. The land which had been rented to them lost, turned out of their cottages, hundreds of these small farmers had become vagabonds.

Thomas More had said that the enclosing of land had so far affected no more than about five per cent of the entire population but he felt that to be a great deal.

Katharine was therefore doing all she could to right this evil, and she had appointed her Almoner to distribute funds from her own purse to the poor. She set aside a regular portion of her income for charity and took a great pleasure in providing the needy with clothes and food. Thus, temporarily, she abandoned the tapestry which she delighted to work and set herself and her women making garments for the poor.

Thus they were sitting together when a page entered to tell the Queen that the Seigneur de Praet, the Emperor's ambassador in England, was without and begging an audience.

As it was rarely that she had an opportunity of seeing her nephew's ambassador, she said that she would receive him at once; and this meant the dismissal of all present.

Seeing the look of disappointment in Mary's face she took the child's hand in hers and kissed it. "Go along now for your practice on the virginals," she said. "When the Seigneur has left I will come and hear how you are getting on."

Mary smiled and curtseyed; and the Queen's eyes remained on her until she had disappeared. Almost before the ladies had all left the apartment the Seigneur de Praet was being ushered in.

Katharine received him with graciousness although she did not feel the same confidence in him as she could have had in an ambassador of her own nationality. But the Seigneur, as a Flemish nobleman, was preferable, in Charles's eyes, to a Spaniard. Katharine had to remember that Charles was more Fleming than Spaniard because he had spent very little time in Spain and had been brought up in Flanders, so it was natural of course, that he should choose Flemings rather than Spaniards to represent him.

The Seigneur was a very grand gentleman and he had already been unwise enough to show his lack of respect for Cardinal Wolsey on account of the latter's humble birth. It seemed incredible to him that he should be expected to treat with one who, so rumour had it, had spent his infancy in a butcher's shop.

As for the Queen, he found her so Spanish in some ways, so English in others, that he had never felt on very easy terms with her. Moreover whenever he had sought an interview he had always found it difficult to reach her; and he suspected the reason. The Cardinal contrived this—and for what cause? Because, for all his outward protestations, he was no friend of the Emperor.

Now de Praet was excited because he had made an important discovery and was determined at all costs to lay it before the Queen. Strangely enough on this occasion he had found no difficulty in reaching her.

As Katharine welcomed him and he bent over her hand, one of the women who had been in the sewing party slipped away unnoticed from the group of women who had just left and went swiftly into the ante-room adjoining the Queen's apartment.

There she took up her stand near the door and very quietly lifted the latch so that it was slightly ajar without seeming to be so.

"Your Grace," said de Praet, "it is a great pleasure to find myself at last in your presence."

"You have news for me from the Emperor?"

"No, but I have discovered treachery which I must immediately lay before you. Our enemy is working against us. Your Grace knows whom I mean."

"The French?"

"*They* work continually against us. I was referring to one nearer at home who, while he pretends to be our friend and supports the King's war, is in fact working against us." He lowered his voice and whispered: "The Cardinal."

"Ah!" said Katharine.

"It does not surprise you."

"Nothing the Cardinal did would surprise me."

"What can be expected . . . He was not born to this."

"Do not let us underestimate his skill," said the Queen. "He is a brilliant man. It is for this reason that we must be very wary of him."

"Your Grace will be surprised when I tell you that I have discovered he is in secret negotiations with the French."

"Without the King's knowledge!"

"That I cannot say, Your Grace, but he is a traitor to my master and your nephew. There is a certain merchant from Genoa, now lodging with one of his servants, and this man is a regular go-between for François and Wolsey."

"It is impossible!"

"Not with such a one. I can tell you we should never have trusted him."

"The King knows nothing of this, I am sure."

De Praet lifted his shoulders. "It is impossible to know what the King knows, how far Wolsey works in conjunction with His Grace, how far on his own account."

"Should not the King be told of Wolsey's action?"

"If the King is already aware of these negotiations with France —and we must not lose sight of this—we should be playing into their hands by telling them of our discovery."

Katharine was horrified. It seemed to her that Charles's ambassador was drawing her towards a controversy in which she might well, by supporting her nephew, be obliged to work against her husband. This was reminiscent of those days of humility before her marriage to Henry when her father, Ferdinand, had used her in his negotiations with Henry's father.

She said quickly: "I fear my nephew has made promises which he has not kept."

"The Emperor is engaged in bitter war and needs all the money he can find to prosecute that war; he has little to spare for bribes."

"He has accepted loans and has not repaid them," Katharine reminded him.

"He will . . . in due course. Your Grace knows that he is a man of honour."

"I am sure of that."

"Then Your Grace will write to the Emperor and tell him of these discoveries? He should be warned."

"I could not work against the King."

"This would not be so. You would merely be telling him of the Cardinal's perfidy. Your Grace, it is imperative that he should be aware of this. I myself shall write and tell him, and to stress the urgency of the situation I beg of you to do the same."

"I will write to him," said the Queen.

De Praet bowed. "If you would do so with all speed I believe you would be doing your nephew a great service."

"I will do so without delay."

"Then I shall take leave of you that you may lose no time. I do assure Your Grace that the matter is urgent."

As soon as he had left her she went to her table and took up writing materials, carefully considering what she would say to her nephew. She began by imploring him to be frank with her husband, to let him know exactly how the war was progressing, and above all not to make promises unless he was sure he could keep them. She added that the Cardinal was aggrieved because he believed that with the Emperor's help he might have achieved the Papacy. She implored Charles to be aware of Wolsey who was as vindictive as he was ambitious. There were rumours that he was already pondering the desirability of a *rapprochement* with the enemy. Charles must not make the mistake of so many who believed that because of Wolsey's humble origins he lacked ability; rather should he believe that the Cardinal possessed a shrewd and brilliant brain; for the more lowly his beginnings, the greater must be his brilliance, since he had come so far.

Carefully she sealed the letter and summoned a page.

One of her women was coming towards her, having slipped unseen from the ante-room wherein she had overheard the conversation between Katharine and de Praet.

"I want a page to take this to the courier," said Katharine.

"If Your Grace will allow me I will take it to him."

Katharine handed the letter to the woman, who took it not to the courier, but to another of the Cardinal's spies. It was not difficult to find one as the Cardinal had them placed in the most strategic positions in the Court, and one of these was undoubtedly the Queen's household.

"Take this with all speed to the Cardinal," she instructed.

Then she joined the ladies who were stitching together and listening to *Utopia*.

\*        \*        \*

The Cardinal read the Queen's letter which she had addressed to her nephew. So it was known that he was in negotiation with the French! He did not relish the Queen's comments about himself; but they did not surprise him for he had long suspected that she regarded him as an enemy.

It would be unfortunate if his negotiations with Louise of Savoy through Passano were made known to the King by Charles's ambassador. He did not think this was likely, because his spies were thick about the ambassador and all his correspondence came to Wolsey before it went overseas. It was not difficult to reconstruct the ambassadorial seal; and the Cardinal had felt it was a matter of common sense that he should ascertain what de Praet was writing to his master at such a time.

If the letters contained news which Wolsey did not wish Charles to receive they were destroyed; only those which were innocuous went through. De Praet was scarcely a subtle ambassador; Charles must realize this. He would have been wiser to have chosen a Spaniard rather than a Fleming. The Cardinal had always had more respect for the solemn subtleties of the Spaniards than for the brash *bonhomie* of the Flemish.

De Praet concerned him but little for if he became dangerous some means could be found to remove him; it was the Queen with whom his thoughts were occupied. She would be an enemy of some consequence. He would never lose sight of the fact that she was not only the King's wife and mother of the heir to the throne, but also the aunt of the Emperor. Relations between the King and the Queen were not of the best; but still she was the Queen and as such wielded a certain influence.

She was therefore a potential enemy to be watched with the utmost diligence; and as the Cardinal had always believed in crippling the power of those who he feared might harm him, he began to think frequently about the Queen.

In the meantime he burned the letter which she believed was on its way to the Emperor, and decided to be ready for the first opportunity which came his way.

It came soon, as he expected it would.

He had been going over the cost of the war with Henry, a subject which never failed to make the King angry. Wolsey could see that it would not be difficult to wean him from the Emperor, and that it was only the hope of marrying Mary to Charles that caused him to remain Charles's ally.

"This marriage is of such importance," murmured Wolsey. "And it should be taking place within three years. The Queen already mourns because her daughter will have to go away. Alas, daughters must leave their royal homes; which is always so sad for those who love them. With sons . . ."

The King was startled. Few people were bold enough to mention the subject of sons in his presence. He looked at the Cardinal who was staring idly before him.

Wolsey went on as though to himself: "I do not altogether despair."

"What's this?" growled Henry.

Wolsey made a show of appearing startled. "Your Grace, I crave your pardon. My thoughts ran on. It is unforgivable in your presence, but I forgot . . ."

"Of what do you not despair?"

Wolsey pretended to hesitate. Then as the King frowned he went on: "It is a matter which occupies my thoughts day and night."

"What is?"

"Your Grace's happiness; Your Grace's contentment."

The King looked slightly mollified but he said sullenly: "You speak in riddles."

"Louis XII did it satisfactorily. Your Grace's sister Margaret did it in Scotland . . ."

Light dawned in the King's face; the little eyes were suddenly ablaze with interest. There was no need to ask what his Chancellor meant, because the people he had mentioned had rid themselves of unwanted spouses.

"Well," said Henry as Wolsey did not go on, "what have you in mind?"

"I have spoken too soon," murmured Wolsey. "I am certain there must be a way . . . I am certain that we can find it. But so far I cannot see it clearly."

"Thomas," said the King almost tenderly, "I have known you but once fail to reach your objective and that was when you did not get the Papal Crown."

"I relied on false friends then, Your Grace. It is a good lesson to have learned. Henceforth let us rely on none but ourselves."

Henry nodded.

"And you say there is a way out for me?"

"I shall not rest," said the Cardinal, "until I see Your Grace the sire of a healthy boy . . . nay, not one, but several."

"How is this possible?"

"As it has been possible for others."

"Divorce!" whispered Henry.

"Your Grace, let us make this our secret matter. Let us keep it constantly in our minds. That is what I do when a problem baffles me. Leave it there . . . maturing, one might say. It so often happens that after a while the answer presents itself."

The King grasped his Chancellor's hand.

"You bring me that which I had almost lost, Thomas. You bring me hope."

The Cardinal returned that affectionate smile. "It shall come to pass because Your Grace can only know contentment when he gives his country what it most needs."

"How well you know me, Thomas."

"It may be necessary for Your Grace to harden his heart. You will remember how nobly you married your brother's widow. Your brother's widow . . ." he repeated emphatically.

"I know full well," replied Henry. "But I tell you this, Thomas, though I am a man with feelings most tender, I am a King also." The little mouth was prudish suddenly. "And I would not consider the fine feelings of Henry Tudor if my duty to my kingdom dictated that I should overcome them."

"Then, Your Grace, let us bring our minds to bear on it . . . and for a time . . . this shall be our secret matter."

The King was excited and well pleased.

So the battle had begun, the Cardinal told himself. Let those who set themselves against Thomas Wolsey beware—even though they be queens.


## CHAPTER III

# THE JILTING OF MARY

THE King glanced at his confessor, John Longland the Bishop of Lincoln, and shook his head gloomily. He had confessed his sins and received absolution; but he did not dismiss the Bishop who waited, believing that the King had not confessed all that was on his conscience.

"Your Grace has something else to tell me?"

"A certain matter hangs heavily upon my conscience," began the King.

"It appears so, Your Grace."

"Then I will tell you, for it may well be that you can find some comfort to offer me. I would have you turn to the twentieth chapter of Leviticus, and you will see what disturbs me."

The Bishop took his bible and turned to that chapter.

"I pray you read verse twenty-one," said the King.

The Bishop read: "'And if a man shall take his brother's wife, it is an unclean thing; he hath uncovered his brother's nakedness; they shall be childless.'" He stopped reading and was silent, not daring to make comment.

Then Henry said: "You see! You have read that. Does it not state clearly God's will? They shall be childless . . . and in all these years . . ."

Seeking to comfort the King, the Bishop said quickly: "God cannot be displeased with Your Grace. He has given you the Princess Mary."

"A girl!" snarled the King. "I think of those sons which were born to us. Born dead. Again and again God gave us signs of His displeasure . . . and we heeded them not. We went on living . . . in sin."

"Your Grace distresses himself unduly. There may yet be a son."

"There will be no son," Henry shouted.

"Your Grace, there was a dispensation. There is no need for Your Grace to feel anxious."

The King's eyes narrowed. He snapped: "There is every need. This burden of sin lies heavy on my conscience. I, who have lived as near to God as a man can live . . . I who have heard Mass five times a day . . . have confessed my sins regularly and have always obtained absolution . . . I, the King, have offended against the laws of God. I have lived for all these years with a woman who is not my wife in the eyes of God. So He tells me this . . . He denies me my son. Do you not see that while I live thus there will never be a son!"

"Your Grace, let us pray for God's help."

Henry could have cuffed the Bishop. He was no Thomas Wolsey. He was anxious to please the King but he lacked the Chancellor's wits. He thought to please him by assuring him that he had nothing to fear, that his marriage was legal.

Fool! Fool! he thought. Then he remembered the Chancellor's injunctions: As yet it is our secret matter.

He went on to his knees, and while the Bishop prayed he

thought: Thomas is right. Good Thomas. 'Tis a delicate matter. There is the Emperor to be thought of. He will never stand aside and see his aunt repudiated. We have to go carefully. So . . . caution for a while.

When they rose from their knees, the Bishop said: "Your Grace is unduly concerned; I shall re-double my prayers that you may be blessed with a son."

And the King's feelings were under such control that instead of roaring "Fool" at the man, he merely murmured: "I thank you, Bishop. I too shall pray."

*　　　*　　　*

In his private chamber at Hampton Court the Cardinal was reading the letters which de Praet had written to the Emperor. There was matter therein which if laid before the King could bring about the man's downfall.

Had the time come to expose the ambassador to the King?

Wolsey was for prompt action. François and Louise were restive, and they were anxious for an immediate secret alliance with the English against the Emperor. An end, thought Wolsey, to this senseless war. What could be more desirable?

Although his spies worked well for him, there must be occasions when it was impossible to learn all that passed between the Queen and her nephew's ambassador.

The case against the Queen must necessarily move slowly. But, thought Wolsey, you are doomed, Madam. You have yet to discover that. But I shall find a French Princess for Henry, and then the bonds with your perfidious nephew will be cut for ever.

What of Mary? Well, that marriage was three years away and more royal marriages were proposed than celebrated.

He wished that he could take de Praet's letters to Henry and say: You see how your ally's ambassador works against you. You see what an opinion he has of your Chancellor who cares more for your welfare than his own.

He was sure Henry would be furious; and then would be the time to bring forward those French ambassadors, whom he had waiting in hiding, that they might treat with Henry.

Yet how could he go to the King and say, My spies bring me the ambassador's letters; I have a method of breaking the seals and resealing them so expertly that none could guess they have been tampered with. Might not the King question the honour of his Chancellor? Of course he could explain that what he had done had been in the interest of the State; but it was never wise to expose one's methods too freely.

Wolsey had an idea. The city gates were closed each evening, and if any foreigner tried to pass through them he would be arrested by the watch and brought before a royal officer. If the Cardinal gave orders that any letters found on suspected persons were to be brought to him personally, and if he could delay de Praet's courier until the gates of the city had been closed, it was certain that the letters found on that courier would find their way to his table. It was almost certain too that those letters would contain words which would not please the King. And what more reasonable than that the Cardinal, so assiduous in the protection of the King's realm, should read those letters in person, and lay them before his master?

It was the way to deal with the matter and not difficult, with so many spies surrounding the ambassador, to waylay his courier and prevent his attempting to leave the city until after the gates were closed; and as the man did not know the city's laws the plot worked as smoothly as Wolsey could have hoped. In a very short time the courier had been arrested by the watch as he attempted to leave the city, searched, and the letters found. They now lay on Wolsey's table.

Luck was with him. Both the King and Wolsey were referred to in these documents in a manner which was slighting, and Wolsey could scarcely wait to reach the King's apartments.

"A matter of some importance, Your Grace."

The King waved a hand and those men who had been with him immediately departed leaving Henry alone with his Chancellor.

Wolsey quickly told Henry what had happened and as he laid the documents before him, was delighted to see the rich colour flood the plump cheeks and the eyes blaze with anger.

"I had long suspected him," said Wolsey; "and now Providence has enabled me to lay evidence of this man's perfidy before Your Grace."

"He shall go to the Tower!"

"A foreign ambassador, Your Grace?"

"By God, this is treason."

"As he is an ambassador of the Emperor, might I suggest that we place guards at the door of his house and forbid him to leave?"

"Let it be done!" commanded the King.

*　　　*　　　*

The Seigneur de Praet stood before the Cardinal in the latter's private chamber at Hampton Court. The Flemish nobleman looked with something like scorn at the red satin garments of the Chancellor; he had felt incensed, as he disembarked at the privy stairs and walked across the grass, at the sight of that magnificent edifice; but when he had entered the place and seen the gloriously apparelled servants, the valuable treasures in every room, he had said to himself: Is it possible that a man of the people could own so much? He was resentful, believing possessions and honours to be the prerogative of the nobility.

It was easy when he was not in the presence of Cardinal Wolsey to sneer at his origins; when he stood before him he could not help being conscious of the man's intellectual power; the rather protruding brown eyes of the man of the people seemed to look into his mind, discovering his secret thoughts, to suggest that the reason he clung to the importance of his noble birth was because, knowing himself at a mental disadvantage, he sought to flaunt every little asset he possessed.

Archbishop of York, Cardinal, Papal Legate and Chancellor. So many great titles for one man to hold—and he a man who had risen from the people. In spite of one's prejudices, one must feel in awe of such achievements.

He was received almost haughtily by the Cardinal's stewards. They would make His Eminence aware of the Seigneur's arrival. Had His Eminence summoned him to Hampton Court? Because if this was not so, they doubted whether they could disturb His Eminence at such an hour.

This was an insult. It did not occur to him that it might be intended. He presumed the servants to be ignorant of his standing.

"Tell the Cardinal," he said in his haughtiest manner, "that the Ambassador of His Imperial Highness, The Emperor of Austria and the King of Spain, calls upon him at his own wish."

He was kept waiting for fifteen minutes and then, fuming with rage, was led through the eight splendid rooms to the Cardinal's private apartment. Wolsey was seated at his table and did not rise when the ambassador entered.

What can one expect of a butcher's son? de Praet asked himself.

Wolsey continued to study the paper before him for a few seconds until de Praet said angrily: "I have come as you asked me to, my Lord Cardinal."

"Oh, yes," said Wolsey, laying aside the paper with what appeared to be reluctance. "I have bad news for you, Mr. Ambassador."

There was insult in the title and de Praet felt the blood rushing to his face. Was he, the Emperor's ambassador, to be kept standing while the Cardinal remained sitting at his desk! He might be a servant come to receive a reprimand.

"Bad news!" he cried. "What bad news is this?"

"Your courier was arrested last night and certain documents were taken from him."

"My courier! This is an insult to the Emperor."

"It happened quite naturally," explained the Cardinal. "He delayed his departure until the gates of the city were closed. As you may know, the law says that all foreigners, attempting to enter or leave the city after the gates are closed, are arrested and searched."

"But he should have left before that. What delayed him?"

The Cardinal lifted his shoulders and smiled. "It is useless to ask me to keep an eye on your servants, Seigneur. This is what has happened. The letters you have written to the Emperor were brought before me. I had no recourse but to read them. We have to be very careful when dealing with those whom we believe to be spies. As it so happened I considered the contents of those letters treasonable, and I saw that it was my duty to lay them before the King."

De Praet was startled. He remembered the frankness with which he discussed the King and Cardinal in his letters to his master; he remembered the slighting comments he had made about them both—particularly this man who was now smiling blandly at him.

"His Grace," went on Wolsey, "was much displeased. It seemed to him that we have been harbouring an enemy in our midst."

De Praet shouted: "You have done this. You had the man arrested. It is a plot."

"And the letters? Shall you say that I wrote those treasonable documents?" Wolsey demanded with a smile.

"They were intended for the Emperor."

"I did not expect for a moment that they were intended for the King and myself."

"I shall go to the King," said de Praet. "I have evidence against you, Master Wolsey. I know that you have been receiving a spy from France. I know that you are working to destroy the alliance between the King and the Emperor. The King does not know the Cardinal whom he trusts. If he did he would not trust him. But he shall know. I have the evidence. I shall go back to my house; and when I have collected this evidence, which shall bear out my word, I will lose no time in going to the King and laying before him all I have discovered."

Wolsey continued to smile, and the ambassador turned and walked quickly out of the apartments. The Cardinal went to the window and watched him hurrying across the grass to his boat.

"Helpful of him to explain his intentions in such detail," he murmured to himself, and then called his stewards to him and began to give orders.

De Praet cursed the slowness of his boat as he was rowed back to London. His indignation increased as he rehearsed what he would say to the King.

When he reached his house he went in and collected certain documents which he had kept in a safe place, and made a careful list of all the people he would call as witnesses against the Cardinal.

Then he was ready to set out for Greenwich. But as he attempted to leave his house two guards barred his way. He saw then that many of them were stationed about his house.

"What is the meaning of this?" he demanded fiercely, but his fierceness had no effect on the guards.

"Begging Your Excellency's pardon," said one of them, "you are not to leave this house."

"Who dares to restrict the Imperial ambassador?"

"The King, Your Excellency."

De Praet was so angry that for a moment he could find no words to express his indignation; but as he grew a little calmer he realized that he was defeated. They called him the King's prisoner, but he was in truth that of the Cardinal.

Yet, he reflected, in this country that was one and the same thing.

*          *          *

With satisfaction Wolsey presented himself to the King.

"The spy is a prisoner in his lodging," he said. "He can do little harm now."

"Let him remain so," said Henry, who was still smarting from the references to himself in the ambassador's correspondence; accustomed to flattery he was always surprised when he did not receive it, and on those rare occasions when he discovered disparaging comments had been made about him he never failed to be deeply shocked.

This was the moment to drive home the advantage, and Wolsey murmured: "It may be that Your Grace will see fit to acquaint our own ambassador with your horror. It is for the Emperor to send us an ambassador, not a spy."

"I shall write to Dr. Sampson and command him to express my displeasure to the Emperor."

"Your Grace is wise. It is as well that he should be acquainted with your displeasure. In this campaign he has had all the advantages."

Henry scowled but he believed that what Wolsey said was true.

"Your Grace," went on the Chancellor, "as you know, I am ever watchful and I have discovered that there are in England at this moment emissaries from France."

The King's face flamed, and Wolsey with great temerity continued before he could speak: "If Your Grace would but see these men there would be no necessity to commit yourself in any way. But in view of the manner in which the Emperor has behaved towards us, I personally see little harm in listening to these men. It may be that Your Grace, in his greater wisdom, has some reason for not wishing to see them. If that is so, then I shall see that they are sent back to France without delay."

"Were it not for the betrothal to our daughter, Thomas, I should be seeking a way out of this alliance."

"We must remember the importance of this match," agreed Wolsey. "But could we not say that this is a matter apart? If we listened to the French we could then perhaps use their desire for friendship to extract some advantage from the Emperor. Your Grace knows full well that we have had little so far."

"I know it well." The King hesitated. "I see no harm in listening to what these men have to say."

Wolsey consolidated his gains before the King had time to withdraw.

"I beg of Your Grace to come to Hampton Court; I shall send for the men, and if you see them there it will make less talk than if they came to Greenwich."

The King was agreeable. He was beginning to take a deep interest in Hampton Court, and the Cardinal had thought somewhat uneasily that occasionally he saw an acquisitive gleam in the blue eyes. "I will come to your fair manor, Thomas," he said. "I confess to a fondness for the place." His eyes narrowed slightly. "And there's something else, I confess. My own palaces look a little less grand, less like the residences of a King, after my visits to Hampton Court."

"I have furnished the place that it might be a refuge for Your Grace at any time it is your pleasure and my delight that you visit it."

"Then let us see these men from France at Hampton, Thomas."

Victory! thought the Cardinal. But in a measure uneasy victory. The King had changed since Buckingham's execution. Often one had the feeling that he was eager to prove the power he had over all men—including his dear friend and counsellor, Thomas Wolsey.

\*          \*          \*

The King paced up and down his bedchamber. He was alone, which was rare for him; but he had wished it so. He was not at ease. He did not want to see these messengers from France; what he wanted was news of the Emperor's victory, to hear that the fair land of France was conquered and that the King of England was invited to go to Rheims to receive the crown he longed for.

But to make peace would mean an end of that dream.

He hated the King of France as, he believed, he could never hate Charles. François was bold and witty; handsome and clever; he was a rival as Charles—pallid, without good looks, serious—could never be. So while Henry hated François he could only distrust Charles. Not that he did not distrust François also. But the Emperor was young, his wife's nephew and therefore his own. Charles had called Henry Uncle when he was in England and deferred to his advice. Not that he had taken it. He was sly, full of pretence; but he was young and when they were together Henry could patronize him. When he was with François he had to summon all his wits and then be outwitted.

It seemed to him that he had reached a stage of his life when all that he longed for most was denied him. He wanted the crown of France and cynical François stood between him and it; he wanted a son and Katharine stood between him and that goal; he wanted a young girl who had caught his imagination, and she flouted him, telling him that he, being married, was in no position to make advances to her.

So he, the King, was frustrated of his three greatest desires. It was a state of affairs which he had not thought possible.

He knew the position in Europe was so bad that it could not continue; and if he did not win France this year, perhaps he would win it some other year. He would never give up hope. The matter of getting a son was more urgent. He was not old by any means, but being thirty-four years of age he was no longer a boy. He was impatient for sons. Yet he remained married to Katharine—if it was a marriage. His conscience was telling him that it was not, and that the sooner he made this known to his people the more pleased God would be with him. But Thomas Wolsey was to be trusted and he had said: Wait.

And then the girl. He had seen her at the Court, and had been maddened at the thought of her marrying Percy—maddened with the foolish young man for thinking to take what the King desired, and with the girl herself for agreeing to the marriage; then he had seen her in her father's garden at Hever, where she had treated him not as the King but as a would-be lover who did not please her. He should have been angry; he should have had the girl sent to the Tower; but a strange softness, which he had never felt before, had come to him. He had merely allowed himself to be so treated, which was wonderfully mysterious.

He had ridden away from Hever, still thinking of her and—although he was surprised at himself for doing so—had visited the place again and again . . . not as a King honouring a subject but as a humble suitor cap in hand.

Yet she continued to resist him. So here again he was frustrated.

A king must not consider his own personal desires, he told himself. I must not think of her but of these men who come from François.

He stood at the window looking out on the river, but he did not see it because instead he saw a garden at Hever and in it the most fascinating young woman he had ever known.

There was a bustle below, and as he turned from the window, roughly jolted from his dream of Hever, the Cardinal came into the room.

The King was surprised by his unceremonious entry, and by the fact that his cap was somewhat askew. The pockmarked face was as pale as ever but the brown eyes gleamed so that Henry knew the Cardinal came to announce some matter of importance.

"Your Grace . . . news . . ."

Wolsey was breathless and the King saw that behind him stood a man who was obviously travel-stained and looked as though he had ridden far.

"What news?" demanded the King who, in spite of the excitement, was still faintly bemused by memories of the bold and haughty girl who had dared repulse him.

"From the battlefield, Your Grace. The Imperial troops have routed the French at Pavia. The French army is destroyed and François himself is the Emperor's prisoner."

Henry clapped his hands together and his great joy showed in his face.

At last the vision of Hever was replaced by one of a handsome, golden-haired, golden-bearded King receiving the crown at Rheims.

"This is news which gives me the greatest pleasure. It is certain . . . ? There has been no mistake?"

The Cardinal turned to the travel-stained man behind him, who came forward and bowed low before the King.

"Your Grace, this is true. The King of France has been taken prisoner at Pavia and is now the Emperor's captive."

Henry laid his hand on the man's shoulder. "You are as welcome as the Angel Gabriel was to the Virgin Mary!" he declared. "Why, Thomas," he went on, turning to the Cardinal, "this is the best news we have had for many a long day."

Wolsey bowed his head as though in assent; and while the King fired questions at the messenger he slipped away to send his own messenger to meet the French emissaries. He wished them to be told that the King could not see them as he had hoped to on this day.

*          *          *

"Now," Henry wrote to the Emperor Charles, "is the time for us to invade France jointly. Let us meet in Paris. Let France be handed to me that it may come under the domination of England. I shall then have the greatest pleasure in accompanying Your Imperial Highness to Rome where I shall see you crowned."

He was so delighted that he went about the Court in high good humour. He was jubilant with Katharine, for was it not her nephew who had captured the King of France? Had not she helped to strengthen the bonds between the two countries? Their daughter was the affianced bride of the Emperor who was now more powerful than ever. When she married him and had her first son, that son should be proclaimed the future King of England, lord of Ireland and Wales, and now . . . France. This boy would be the greatest monarch in the world, for he would also inherit Spain, Austria, the Netherlands, Naples, Sicily and the recently discovered dominions of the New World. This would be a boy with Tudor blood in his veins. Perhaps it was not so important that *he* had no son when his grandson would be a monarch such as the world had never seen before.

He was gay and jovial with his Queen—although he could not bring himself to share her bed. The memories of a laughing girl, ho would not be put out of his mind, prevented that.

As for the girl herself, who had more respect for her own virtue than the King's royalty, she should be dismissed from his mind. There would be other girls at his Court only too eager to comfort him for her loss.

Those were good days, spent chiefly in making plans for his coronation in France.

Katharine was delighted; at last she could share the King's pleasure. He liked to walk with her in the gardens of the Palace, his arm in hers while he made plans for his journey to France.

But Henry could not forgive Charles's ambassador for the manner in which he had written of himself and the Chancellor, and de Praet was still kept a prisoner in his house. In vain did Katharine plead for him; in vain did she ask permission for the man to come and see her. Henry became sullen when she mentioned these matters, and replied shortly that he would not tolerate spies in England, even Spanish spies. And finally, when the dispirited de Praet asked for leave to return to his own country and Henry gave it, Katharine was not allowed to see him before he left; she consoled herself however that never had Henry's friendship for Charles been so firm as it was at this time, so that the fact that Charles had no ambassador in England did not seem so important as it would have been a short time ago.

*        *        *

When the Emperor read Henry's letter he raised his eyebrows in dismay.

Henry crowned in Rheims King of France! Himself crowned in Rome! The English King had no idea of the situation.

Charles had taken the French King prisoner, it was true, and that was a success; the army which had served with François was disbanded, but that did not constitute all the men at arms in France. Charles himself had suffered enormous losses; his army was only in slightly better condition than that of the French; moreover he had no money to pay his mercenaries.

Charles was a realist. He knew that the Italian princes, who had had to submit to him, did so with great unwillingness, that the Pope was watching his movements with anxiety. His mercenaries had demanded the spoils of battle as he could not pay them, and as a result the countryside had been ravaged as the troops passed through; and as the sullen people were ready to revolt against the conqueror, this was no time to talk of crowning ceremonies. Henry seemed to think that war was a game and that the winner received all the spoils of victory. Had he not learned yet that in wars such as this there were often very little spoils?

The Emperor was weary of battle. He had the upper hand now; François was in prison in Madrid, and while he was there it would be possible to make him agree to humiliating terms. It was a matter of taking what he could; but it was totally unrealistic to imagine that he could take France and hand it to his ally as though it were a particularly fine horse or even a castle.

"When will my uncle grow up?" he sighed.

There was another matter which was disturbing him. He was twenty-four years of age and affianced to Mary who was nine.

He was tired of waiting, and his ministers had implied that the people of Spain were eager for an alliance with Portugal.

His cousin, Isabella of Portugal, was of a marriageable age at this present time, and her dowry was nine hundred thousand golden ducats. How useful such a sum would be! And Mary's dowry? He had had it already in loans from her father, and he knew that to take Mary would merely be to wipe off the debts he had incurred in the war.

He wanted a wife now . . . not in three years' time. In three years' time he might have a lusty son. When he went to war he would have a Queen to leave in Spain as his regent. Moreover Portugal had always been closely allied with Spain. The people wanted one of their own as their Queen, not a strange little girl who, although half Spanish, would seem to them wholly English.

True, he had given his promise, but his grandfathers had made promises when it was expedient to do so; and when state policy demanded that those promises should be broken, they broke them. Charles was sorry because his aunt would be hurt and the King of England would be angry. But he did not greatly care for the King of England. A strip of Channel divided them and they had always been uneasy allies.

Wolsey had turned against him he knew from the few letters he had received from de Praet; and he was certain that he had not received all that de Praet had written. Wolsey was a wily fellow and it was unfortunate that they should be enemies, but that must be accepted.

He could not simply jilt Mary, but he could make a condition that her parents would find it impossible to fulfil. Suppose he demanded that she be sent at once to Spain? He knew his aunt would never agree to part with her daughter at this stage. He would demand half as much again as Henry had already paid towards the cost of the war, knowing that this would be refused. But these would be the terms he would insist on if he were to carry out his part of the bargain.

The Portuguese ambassador was waiting to see him; he would have to have something to tell him when he came. He must decide whether there should be discussions between the two countries regarding the betrothal of himself and Isabella.

He therefore sent for a gentleman of his entourage, and while he was waiting for him he wrote a letter which, on account of the news it contained, he put into code.

When the Knight Commander Peñalosa was shown into his presence, he signed to him to be seated.

"I have a letter here which you are to take to England. It is in code, so you must go at once to de Praet who will decode it for you. Then you will read the contents and discuss with de Praet and the Queen the best manner of putting the proposals it contains to the King of England. De Praet will then inform me of the King's reception of this news. This is of the utmost importance. You must leave at once."

Peñalosa left with the letter and prepared to set out for England, while Charles received the Portuguese ambassador.

By the time Peñalosa reached England, de Praet had left and there was no one who could decode the letter. Peñalosa sought an audience with the Queen, but the Cardinal, who was more watchful of her than ever, had so surrounded her with his spies that Peñalosa was never allowed to see her except in public. If Katharine's eyes alighted on him by chance she had no notion that he was an important messenger from her nephew.

\* \* \*

Katharine was with her women engaged in that occupation which so frequently occupied her—the making of clothes for the poor—when the storm broke.

The King strutted into her apartment and one wave of his hands sent her women curtseying and scuttling away like so many frightened mice.

"Henry," Katharine asked, "what ails you?"

He stood, legs apart, that alarming frown between his brows, so that she felt her spirits sink. She knew that he had come to tell her of some great disaster.

In his hand he carried a document, and her heart began to beat rapidly as she recognized her nephew's seal.

"You may well ask," said the King ominously.

"It is news from the Emperor?"

"It is, Madam. News from the biggest scoundrel that ever trod the soil of Europe."

"Oh no . . . Henry."

"Oh yes, Madam. Yes, yes, yes. This nephew of yours has insulted us . . . myself, you and our daughter."

"The marriage . . ."

"There will be no marriage. Our daughter has been tossed aside as though she were of no importance . . . tossed aside for what he believes to be a better match."

"It is impossible."

"So you would doubt my word."

"No, Henry, but I am sure there is some explanation."

"There is explanation enough. This treacherous scoundrel

believes that he can serve himself better by marriage with his cousin of Portugal. He has already possessed himself of Mary's dowry in loans . . . which will never be repaid. Now his greedy hands are reaching out for his cousin's ducats."

"But he is promised to Mary."

Henry came close to her and his eyes looked cruel. "When have your family ever respected their promises? I should have understood. I should have suspected. I do not forget how your father deceived me again and again. And Maximilian . . . this Charles's grandfather . . . he deceived me in like manner. I am deceived every way I turn. Spain! I would to God I had never heard of that country. What have I ever had from Spain? Broken promises . . . my treasury rifled . . . lies . . . lies . . . lies and a barren wife!"

"Henry . . . I implore you . . ."

"You would implore me? What would you implore, Madam? That I say thank you to this nephew of yours? Thank you for deceiving me. Thank you for jilting my daughter. I'd as lief thank you, Madam, for all the sons you have not given me!"

"That was no fault of mine," she said with spirit. "I have done my best."

"No fault of yours? Then whose fault, Madam? You know I have a healthy son. It is more than you have. All those years and one daughter . . . and that daughter, jilted . . . by *your* nephew."

For the moment tears came to his eyes—tears of self pity. All that he desired was denied him. The crown of France; the sons; the marriage of his daughter to the greatest monarch in Christendom; the favours of a sprightly young girl who persistently avoided him. Why was the King so frustrated?

His conscience gave him the answer. Because you have offended God. You have lived with a woman who is not your wife because she was first the wife of your brother. You will never know good fortune while you live in sin, for God will continue to turn his face from you.

He hated her then—this woman with her sagging shapeless body. How different from that other! This woman who could no longer arouse the slightest desire within him. The woman whose nephew had betrayed him and their daughter.

It was difficult to hold in the words, to remember that as yet it was the secret matter.

But how he hated her!

She flinched before the cruelty in his eyes; she saw the brutal curve of his mouth. Thus had he looked when he had determined to send Buckingham to the scaffold.

He was controlling himself; she knew that. He was holding in the words he longed to utter. She almost wished that he would speak so that she might know what thoughts were in the secret places of his mind.

He forced himself to leave her; he went straight to his apartments and summoned Wolsey.

He would be revenged on Charles. He could not reach the Emperor, but the aunt should suffer for the nephew. None should treat him so scurvily and escape. Charles should learn that he, Henry, cared nothing for the House of Spain and Austria. Had Charles forgotten that there was one member of that House who was completely in his power?

"Come, Wolsey," he growled, while he waited for his Chancellor. "We'll make peace with France; we'll have a French Prince for Mary. We'll form an alliance to make His Imperial Highness tremble. We shall show you, Master Charles, that we care naught for you and yours! A plague on the House of Spain and Austria—and all those who belong to it!"

\*     \*     \*

That June day a ceremony took place in Bridewell Palace and the King had commanded all the high officials of the Court to attend: he was particularly anxious that Peñalosa, who was the only ambassador Charles had in England at the time, should be present at the ceremony and send an account of it to his master.

The hero of this occasion was a small boy, six years old. He was handsome, and his pink and gold Tudor beauty both delighted and exasperated Henry.

Every time he looked at the boy he said to himself: Why could he not have been my legitimate son!

Henry had ceased to think of the boy's mother; she had been handsomely rewarded for giving the King a proof of his ability to beget sons. Manors in Lincolnshire and Yorkshire had been bestowed on her, so she would have no cause to regret those days when she had been the King's mistress.

Henry had watched with smouldering eyes while this handsome boy was created a Knight of the Garter; and now this even more significant ceremony was taking place.

He came to stand before the King; on either side of him were the leading Dukes of England—Norfolk and Suffolk.

But this boy, thought Henry, shall take precedence over all. For I would have all understand that he is my son and living proof of the fact that I can get sons with other women—though not with my wife.

Holy Mother of God, he prayed as he watched; I see my fault. I live in sin with my brother's wife and for that reason my union is not blessed with sons. How could it be when in the eyes of God it is a sinful union!

Now proud Norfolk and Suffolk had taken a step backwards that the newly created Duke might stand alone as one whose titles would henceforth set him above them; he would now be known as the first peer of the land, and his titles were impressive: Henry Fitzroy, Duke of Richmond and Somerset, Lord High Admiral of England, Wales, Ireland, Normandy, Gascony and Aquitaine, Knight of the Garter, and first peer of England.

There was a buzz of excitement throughout Court circles which extended to the streets of the city.

Even in the taverns the importance of the ceremony was understood.

"This means one thing: The King, despairing of sons by his wife, honoured Elizabeth Blount's boy."

"Note the significance of that title—Richmond," it was whispered. "The King's father was Duke of Richmond before he became King. Depend upon it, the King has decided that that boy shall one day wear the crown."

"It is not possible while Mary lives."

"If the King decrees, it will be possible. None will dare gainsay him. And this ceremony is to prepare his people for what he intends to bring about."

"The people would not accept the boy while Mary lives."

"The people will accept what the King wishes. It is better not to argue against the King. Remember Buckingham."

The name of Buckingham could still send shivers through most bodies.

And so it was generally agreed that the ceremony at Bridewell was a first step in the direction the King intended to go as regards his illegitimate son.

*     *     *

Katharine who could often suffer in silence on her own account could not do so on her daughter's.

She faced the King boldly on the first opportunity when they were alone and declared her horror and fear at the recognition given to Henry Fitzroy.

"You forget," Henry told her coldly, "that the Duke of Richmond is my son."

"Should you be so proud to call him so?"

"Yes, Madam. Proud I am and always shall be. For his birth

gave me the answer I sought. It is no fault of mine that I have no legitimate son."

"And so you had this one merely to prove this?" she asked with a trace of sarcasm rare in her.

"I did," said Henry who had told himself this was the case, so frequently that he believed it.

"This is an insult to our daughter. Has she not been insulted enough?"

"By your nephew . . . yes. This is no insult to Mary. I still accept her as my daughter." A cunning look came into his eyes. "She is a girl and her position may not be so different from that of the little Duke."

This was going too far; it was betraying the secret matter. He must be cautious. Katharine did not construe his words as he had meant them. She thought only that he planned to set this illegitimate son before his daughter because of his sex.

"You cannot mean you would set aside our daughter for a . . . bastard!"

His eyes narrowed. He wanted to speak of what was in his mind. He was never one for secrets. He wanted her to know that although she was a daughter of the hated House of Spain, because she had previously married his brother it might well be that she had no legitimate hold on him.

"Mary is a girl," he said sullenly.

"There is no reason why she should not make as good a monarch as a man. My own mother . . ."

The King snapped his fingers. "I have no wish to hear of your sainted mother. And know this, if I decide that any man, woman or child in this kingdom shall be elevated . . ." His eyes were even more cruel suddenly . . . "or set down, this shall be done and none shall be allowed to stand in my way."

"I wonder," said the Queen, "that you allowed our daughter to keep the title, Princess of Wales. Why did you not take that away from her and bestow it on your bastard? Then there could have been no doubt of your intentions."

He looked at her in silent hatred for a few seconds; then fearing that he would be unable to keep from her all the plans which were fermenting in his mind, he left her.

\*　　　\*　　　\*

Wolsey was waiting for him in his apartment. The Chancellor saw the flushed face and angry looks and guessed that Henry had been listening to Katharine's reproaches.

"Your Grace looks displeased," he murmured.

"'Tis the Queen. I have never known her so bold . . . so care-less of my feelings."

"The Queen is afraid, Your Grace. She has her qualms about the marriage, even as you do. Perhaps more so."

"She could not be more uneasy."

Wolsey lowered his voice. "She knows, Your Grace, whether or not the marriage with your brother was consummated."

"You think this is a sign of her guilt?"

"The guilty are often those who feel most fear, Your Grace."

"You are right, Thomas. And her boldness astonished me."

"She is surrounded by women who urge her to behave thus. The Queen herself should be . . . malleable."

Henry's lower lip jutted out. "There's strength beneath that gentleness, Thomas."

"Your Grace is right as usual, but that strength is, shall we say, given support by some of those women about her."

The King looked questioningly at Wolsey.

"There is the Countess of Salisbury for one. She has ever been close to the Queen. Lady Willoughby is another. Women like that chat in secret, talking of wrongs, urging resistance."

"They shall be banished from Court."

"May I suggest, Your Grace, that we move with care? We do not want to rouse too much sympathy in . . . the wrong quarters."

"You mean that there would be those to take her side against *me*!"

"Among the people, Your Grace. And some men of the Court, in secret. Let Lady Willoughby be sent away from Court. As for Lady Salisbury . . . If Your Grace will trust this matter to me, and commission me to deal with the Queen's household, I will see that those women likely to influence her are removed from her side."

"Do that, Thomas. By God, she must understand that I'll not stand by and accept her reproaches. She had the temerity to suggest that I might soon take Mary's title of Wales that I might give it to young Henry."

"The Queen may well wean the Princess's affection from Your Grace."

The King looked at his Chancellor; and for a few moments they both remained thoughtful.

\*          \*          \*

This was the most cruel blow of all. Katharine had been so stunned when she heard the news that she could not believe it was true.

All the humiliations, all the uneasiness of the past years had been forgotten when she was in the presence of her daughter; her only joy in life had been wrapped up in the child. The love between them was intense, as deep and abiding as that which Katharine had shared with her own mother.

In all her troubles she had been able to tell herself: "I have my daughter."

And now Mary was to be taken away from her.

She did not weep. This was too great a sorrow to be assuaged by tears. She sat limply staring before her while her dearest friend, Maria de Salinas, Countess of Willoughby, sat beside her, desperately seeking for words which would comfort her.

But there was no comfort. Maria herself would not long be at the Queen's side. She was to leave Court, and she believed she knew why.

One of the Queen's women had recently been dismissed from the Court and she had confessed to Maria that the reason was because she had declined to act as the Cardinal's spy. His idea was clearly to remove from the Queen's side all those who would not work for him against her.

What did it all mean? Maria asked herself. Should I try to warn her? If only I could stay with her to comfort her.

But now Katharine could think of nothing but her daughter.

"Why should she be taken from me?" she demanded passionately. "When she marries it may be necessary for her to leave me. There cannot be many years left to us. Why must I lose her now?"

"I think, Your Grace," said Maria, desperately seeking a reason that might soothe the Queen, "that the King wishes her to go to Wales so that the country may know she is still Princess of the Principality and heir to the throne."

The Queen brightened at that suggestion. "It may be so," she said. "The people did not like his elevating the bastard."

"That is the answer, Your Grace. You can depend upon it, she will not stay long. It is merely a gesture. I feel certain that is the reason."

"I shall miss her so much," said the Queen.

"Yes, Your Grace, but perhaps it is well that she should go."

Katharine said: "There is one consolation; Lady Salisbury is going with her as her governess. I cannot tell you how that cheers me."

One more friend, thought Maria, to be taken from the Queen's side.

Katharine rose suddenly and said: "I shall go to my daughter now. I would like to break this news to her myself. I trust that she has not already heard it. Stay here, Maria. I would be alone with her."

In the Princess's apartments the little girl was seated at the virginals; one or two of her attendants were with her. When the Queen entered they curtseyed and moved away from the Princess who leaped from her chair and threw herself into her mother's arms.

"That was well played," said the Queen, trying to control her emotion.

She smiled at the attendants and nodded. They understood; the Queen often wished to be alone with her daughter.

"I was hoping you would come, Mother," said the Princess. "I have learned a new piece and wanted to play it to you."

"We will hear it later," answered Katharine. "I have come to talk to you."

She sat on a stool near the virginals, and Mary came to stand beside her while the Queen put her arm about her daughter.

"You have heard no rumours about Wales?" asked the Queen.

"Wales, Mother? What sort of rumours?"

The Queen was relieved. "Well, you know you are Princess of Wales and it is the custom for the Prince or Princess to visit the Principality at some time."

"We are going to Wales then, Mother?"

"You are going, my darling."

Mary drew away from her mother and looked at her in startled dismay.

"Oh, it will not be for long," said the Queen.

"But why do you not come with me?"

"It is the wish of your father that you go alone. You see, *you* are the Princess of Wales. *You* are the one the people want to see."

"You must come too, Mother."

"My darling, if only I could!"

"I will not go without you." For a moment Mary looked like her father.

"My darling, your father has commanded you to go."

Mary threw herself against her mother and clung to her. "But it is so far away."

"Not so very far, and you will come back soon. We shall write to each other and there will be the letters to look forward to."

"I don't want to go away from you, Mother . . . ever."

The Queen felt the tears, which she had so far managed to keep in check, rising to her eyes.

"My love, these partings are the fate of royal people."

"I wish I were not royal then."

"Hush, my darling. You must never say that. We have a duty to our people which is something we must never forget."

Mary pulled at the rings on her mother's fingers but Katharine knew she was not thinking of them. "Mother," she said, "if I were to plead with my father . . ."

The Queen shook her head. "He has decided. You must go. But do not let us spoil what time is left to us in grieving. Time will pass, my darling, more quickly than you realize. I shall hear of you from your governess and tutors, and you will write to me yourself. You see I shall have all that to live for."

Mary nodded slowly. Poor child! thought the Queen. She has learned to keep her feelings in check. She has learned that the fate of Princesses can often be cruel and that one thing is certain, they must be accepted.

"You will go to Ludlow Castle," said the Queen trying to speak brightly. "It is a beautiful place."

"Tell me about when you were there, Mother."

"It was long . . . long ago. I went there with my first husband."

"My father's brother," murmured Mary.

"It was so long ago," said the Queen, and she thought of those days when she had been married to the gentle Arthur who was so different from Henry; Arthur who had been her husband for scarcely six months.

"Tell me about the castle," said Mary.

"It rises from the point of a headland," the Queen told her, "and is guarded by a wide, deep fosse. It is grand and imposing with its battlemented towers; and the surrounding country is superb . . . indeed some of the best I have ever seen."

The Princess nodded sadly.

"You will be happy there," murmured Katharine, putting her lips to Mary's forehead. "We shall not be very far away from each other, and soon you will come back to me."

"How soon?" asked Mary.

"You will be surprised how soon."

"I would rather know. It is always so much easier to bear if you know how long. Then I could count the days."

"My darling, you will be happy there. When I left my mother, the ocean separated us. This is not the same at all."

"No," said Mary slowly. "It is not the same at all."

"And now, my love, go to the virginals. Play the piece which you wished me to hear."

Mary hesitated and for a moment Katharine feared that the child would lose her hold on that rigid control. But obediently she rose, went to the virginals, sat down and began to play; and as she did so, the tears, which would no longer be kept back, rolled silently down her cheeks.

## CHAPTER V

# THE PRINCESS AT LUDLOW CASTLE

THE Princess Mary was melancholy in the Castle of Ludlow and the Countess of Salisbury was alarmed on her account. The only thing which could bring the child out of that languid indifference as to what went on around her was a letter from her mother.

Each day she told the Countess how long they had been at Ludlow; and she would ask wistfully if there were any news of their returning to her father's Court.

"All in good time," the Countess would say. "With the passing of each day we are a little nearer to our return."

The Princess rode often in the beautiful woods close to the castle; she had to admit that the country was some of the fairest she had ever seen; but it was clear that when she was separated from her mother she could not be happy, and the Countess feared that her health would be affected by her melancholy.

Great plans were afoot for the celebrations of Christmas, The New Year and Twelfth Night.

"There will be plays, masques and a banquet . . . just as at your father's Court," the Countess told her.

"I wonder whether my mother will come," was all the Princess could say.

It was true that she had a certain interest in her lessons; she worked hard at her Latin and her music and sometimes she would chuckle and say: "My mother will be surprised that I have come so far. I shall write to her in Latin, and when she comes I shall play all my new pieces."

The Countess was grateful that she had this interest in her Latin and music, and made the most of it. There had been rumours which had come to the Countess's notice before she left Court and, although she could not believe there was much truth in them, they made her very uneasy. The fact that the Queen had married the King's brother could have no effect on the present marriage. The Pope had given the necessary dispensation, and during all the years the King and Queen had been married there had never before been any suggestion that the marriage might not be legal.

She was a wise woman, and in her fifty-two years she had seen much tragedy. None understood, more than she did, the Tudors's fierce determination to fight off all those who threatened to take the crown from them. It was natural that the King wanted to make sure of the Tudor succession. Desperately he needed a son, and Katharine had failed to give it to him.

There were times when Margaret Pole, Countess of Salisbury, wished that she were not a Plantagenet and so near to the throne. She had lived through troublous times. Her maternal grandfather had been that Earl of Warwick who had been known as the Kingmaker; her father had been the Duke of Clarence, brother of Richard III, who had been imprisoned in the Tower and there, it was believed, had been drowned in a butt of malmsey. She had been a young child when that had happened and it had made a deep and terrible impression on her; ever after she had been aware of the insecurity of life and the favour of Kings; and it seemed to her that those who lived nearest the throne had the most to fear. That was why she often thought with deep compassion of the Queen, and now as she sat with her royal charge she could grow quite melancholy wondering what the future held for her. Only recently tragedy had struck at her family through her youngest child, Ursula, wife of Henry Stafford, son of the Duke of Buckingham whose life had recently come to an end on the block.

Henry VIII had occasionally been kind to her family; she had fancied that he wanted to make amends to them for his father's murder of her brother Edward who, as the Earl of Warwick, had been a menace to the throne. But how long would that favour last? She believed now that she was regarded with suspicion by Wolsey because of her close friendship with the Queen.

If Katharine could have been with her in Ludlow she would have been almost happy. It was peaceful here and seemed so far from the world of ambition. And how happy little Mary would have been if the Queen were here! But as the weeks stretched into months the love between the governess and her charge grew deeper and did—so the Countess fervently hoped—compensate in some measure for the child's loss of her mother.

Margaret tried to replace that mother, and it was a great joy to her to know that the times of the day to which Mary looked forward more than any other were those when she and the Countess were alone together; and the little girl, released from her lessons which Margaret often felt were too much for her, would sit at the Countess's feet and demand to hear stories of her life.

And when Mary said: "My mother used to tell me stories of the days when she was a girl in Spain . . ." Margaret knew that the substitution had taken place in the child's mind; and she wrote to the Queen telling her of these pleasant hours which seemed to give consolation to Mary for her exile.

Through Margaret's description of her family Mary began to know the Pole children so well that they seemed to be her intimate friends. There was Henry, Lord Montague, who had followed the King to France to the Field of the Cloth of Gold. Margaret did not tell the child of the anxiety she had suffered when Henry had been arrested at the time of the trial of the Duke of Buckingham because his father-in-law was a connection of the Duke's; in any case he had been speedily released, and very soon afterwards had been restored to favour, being among those noblemen who had greeted the Emperor Charles on his arrival in England. The Countess would talk of her sons, Arthur, Reginald, Geoffrey and her daughter Ursula, with such loving detail that the Princess knew that these quiet hours were as enjoyable to the Countess as they were to her.

But it was of Reginald that Mary liked best to hear; Reginald was learned and deeply religious, and Mary had always felt that to give lifelong devotion to religion was the best way of living. Therefore Reginald became her hero.

The Countess told how she had always meant him to go into the Church and how eager he had been to follow that calling, although he had not yet taken holy orders.

"There is no better man in the world than my Reginald," said Margaret proudly, and Mary began to believe her.

"When he was a boy at Oxford he astonished his tutors," the fond mother declared. "In truth I think they began to realize that he was more clever than they. He became a Dean at Wimborne though still a layman. He held many posts, and then he decided to go to Padua, and that is where he is now. The King, your father, is pleased with him and there is great hospitality in his house there. Scholars flock to see him. He thinks it is because he is a kinsman of the King."

"But it is really because of his noble character," Mary asserted.

"I believe that to be so. Mary, I think he will soon be coming to England."

Mary clasped her hands in ecstasy. "And will he come to Ludlow?"

"Come to see his mother! Of a certainty he will. You do not know my Reginald."

"I do," declared the Princess.

And after that they often spoke of his coming and when Mary awoke in the mornings she would say to herself: "Will there be news from my mother today?" And then: "Is Reginald now on his way to the Castle?"

It was only these hopes which made the separation tolerable. But the months passed and there was no news of Mary's joining her mother; and Reginald continued to stay in Italy.

\*     \*     \*

Henry cut himself off from communication with his Queen, and she rarely saw him. She lived quietly, working on her garments for the poor, reading religious books, going to Mass, praying privately. Her great joy was writing letters to her daughter, but what a difficult task this was when she must suppress her fierce longing, and not convey her fears that the long absence was stifling that deep affection they had for each other!

Henry was growing impatient. He had begun to wonder whether Wolsey was working as wholeheartedly for him as he had once believed. Wolsey was a man who had seen that his own pockets were well lined; and should a king feel such gratitude towards a man who in his service had grown as rich as surely only a king should be?

Wolsey was constantly whispering caution, and Henry was becoming a little uncertain of the game the Chancellor was playing. There was a new faction springing up at Court, and at the centre of this was George Boleyn whom the King found a fascinating young man, largely because he was the brother of Anne.

Anne remained at Hever, but she should not do so for long. Henry had already shown his favour to the family by raising Sir Thomas to the peerage, so that he now bore the title of Viscount Rochford. He had even given poor Will Carey, Mary's husband, a post at Court as gentleman of the Privy Chamber. He was certain that soon the haughty girl would give in to his pleading, and stop talking about her virtue.

But at the same time it was this Boleyn faction which was making him doubt Wolsey. He sent for his Chancellor in order to discuss a matter which was of great concern to them both at this time: the marriage of the Princess Mary.

When Wolsey entered, the King did not greet him with the affectionate look which the Chancellor usually received from him. Wolsey was acutely aware of the King's changing attitude towards him and it was doubly alarming because he was not sure of its origin.

"I have news from France," said Henry. "It seems that François is rejecting our offer of my daughter."

Wolsey nodded gravely. Here was one matter on which they were in agreement; they shared the desire for a marriage between Mary and a member of the royal French family. Nothing would disturb the Emperor more; at the same time if Mary were to marry into France she would very soon be sent to that country; and if the King were about to rid himself of the Queen, Mary's presence in England could prove an embarrassment. There was no need to speak of this matter. Each knew that it was well to the fore in the mind of the other.

The King took a document from his table which had been sent to him from Louise of Savoy who was her son's Regent while he, François, remained the Emperor's prisoner in Madrid.

"Read it," commanded the King; and Wolsey read that the Duchesse of Savoy could not express sufficient regret that the marriage between her son and the Princess Mary was not possible. She knew that the Princess of England excelled all other Princesses; she had heard nothing but good of her character, her attainments and her beauty. Alas, a tragic fate had befallen her son; he was in the hands of the Emperor and harsh terms were being imposed on him. Not the least harsh of these—in view of the offer of the Princess's hand from England—was that he should marry the Emperor's sister Eleanora whom Emanuel of Portugal had recently left a widow. It seemed likely that the King of France would have to comply with this unless Eleanora refused to marry him.

The Duchesse however hoped that this might not make an end of their desire for a French-English alliance. She had grandsons. She was certain that François would welcome the Princess Mary as the wife of his son Henri, Duc d'Orléans.

"Well," the King demanded, "what do you think of this proposition?"

"A fair one. Marriage to young Henri would, in truth, be more suitable than marriage with François."

"A second son," murmured the King.

"Eldest sons sometimes die," Wolsey reminded him.

"That's so," replied the King, himself a second son. He was thoughtful for a while. "The child is young . . . not yet ten years of age. There is time. But it shall be a French match for her."

"I am in full agreement with Your Grace."

"I rejoice to hear it." Was it his imagination, wondered

Wolsey, or was there a trace of sarcasm in the King's voice. The little blue eyes swept over the rich satin robes. "We shall be having French ambassadors here soon, I doubt not. When they come it would be well for them to be entertained at Hampton Court."

"Hampton Court is, as always, at Your Grace's command."

"These foreigners . . ." mused Henry. "They do not think they are at Court until they are received at Hampton. Is it meet a subject should possess such a palace?"

Wolsey quickly saw the meaning behind the words. He had always gambled. He gambled now.

"There is only one reason why a subject could possess such a palace," he answered quickly, "and that is that he can put it into the hands of his King."

Suddenly the peevish animosity died in the King's face and the old affection was back there. The blue eyes were so bright that Wolsey was not sure whether it was tears of friendship or covetousness which he saw there.

The Chancellor felt a catch of fear at his heart; it was as though he were running towards danger; and that only by throwing his most valued possessions to his pursuers could he stave off the evil moment of disaster. He was playing for time. He believed that he could regain his power over the King . . . given time. If he could arrange a divorce for Henry, get him married to a French Princess, put an end to unprofitable wars—then he would be able to rout all his enemies. But he needed time.

The King put his own construction on those words.

"A goodly gift," he said, "from a loyal subject to his affectionate master. I would not offend you, Thomas, by refusing your handsome gift. But you shall live on there . . . you shall entertain these foreigners there . . . in my name, eh? Then they will no longer sing in the streets: 'The King's Court or Hampton Court . . .' for from now on Hampton Court *is* the King's Court."

Wolsey bowed his head and taking the King's hand kissed it. He was glad to hide his face for a few seconds; the loss of his most cherished possession was a blow, and he found it difficult to hide the sorrow he was feeling.

\*          \*          \*

The days were dreary to Katharine, one so much like another. She had no friend in whom she could confide. Maria de Salinas was no longer at Court; Margaret Pole was in Ludlow with Mary; and, saddest of all, there was no mention of Mary's returning.

The women who surrounded her, she knew, were not her true friends, but had been put there by her enemy, Wolsey, to spy on her. She saw the King frequently but never in private; he was courteous to her but she fancied that he was afraid to meet her eye and always seemed relieved when he parted from her.

On one or two occasions she had mentioned their daughter, to which he invariably replied with prompt finality: "It pleases me that she now has her own Court in her own Principality. She will learn something of government there in Ludlow."

She wanted to protest: She is only a child. At least allow me to go and stay with her there.

But she knew that it was impossible to speak of such things in public, and there was never an opportunity of doing so in private.

She guessed that there was a mistress—perhaps several. Light-o'-loves, she thought contemptuously; and as she could not discuss this matter with the women who surrounded her, who would report to their master every word she said, she was silent.

She knew that negotiations were going forward with a view to a French alliance for Mary. She prayed that this might not be carried through. What she dreaded more than anything was alliance with France because she longed to restore friendship between her nephew and her husband. She believed that, if only Charles could explain in person, or if only he had a good and efficient ambassador, Henry would understand that he had been forced to do what he had done. None could be more disappointed at his rejection of Mary than she was. Had it not been the dearest dream of her life that her nephew and daughter should marry? But Charles was no longer very young and it was understandable that he should feel the need to marry without delay. She did not believe that Charles had wantonly deceived her husband; it was pressure of circumstances—and that must at times afflict every head of state—which had made him do so.

She wrote many letters to Charles—cautiously worded—for she could not be sure that they would reach him. A little spice was added to those dreary days by this game of outwitting the Cardinal, whom she had now begun to regard as her greatest enemy.

And one day in the spring of that long year a letter from her nephew was smuggled to her and she felt a great triumph, as at least one of hers had reached him. That made her feel that she had some friends at the English Court.

Charles wrote that he was sending a new ambassador to England, Don Iñigo de Mendoza, who would be travelling through France and should arrive in England not long after she received this letter. He knew, of course, that Wolsey was doing his utmost to make a French alliance for Mary and that Katharine would agree with him that such an alliance would be fatal to their interests. He believed that she would find Mendoza more to her liking than ambassadors from Flanders, and it was for this reason that he was sending a Spaniard to England.

When Katharine read this letter she felt the tears of joy rushing to her eyes. Mendoza was coming. A Spaniard, one with whom she could converse in her native tongue. She even knew Iñigo. He had been her mother's favourite page, and she had seen him often riding in the entourage when Isabella had gone from town to town visiting her dominions, her family with her, as she had insisted whenever possible. Perhaps they would talk of Granada and Madrid, of the days of Isabella's greatness.

Katharine closed her eyes and thought of her early life in Spain, when she had never been forced to suffer the humiliation she had endured since coming to England, when she had been surrounded by the love of her family and, most of all, that of her mother.

"Oh Holy Mother," she murmured, "how sad life becomes when the greatest joy it has to offer is in remembering the past."

\*        \*        \*

Through the spring and summer Katharine awaited the arrival of Mendoza in vain. A little news did seep through to her and eventually she discovered that the French were determined to delay the arrival of the Spanish ambassador in England until a French embassy had been able to arrange for the marriage of Mary with the Duc d'Orléans.

They had promised Mendoza free passage through France, but shortly after he had set foot on that land he was arrested as a foreign spy and put into prison where he remained for months without trial.

Katharine was in despair because plans for the French marriage were going forward, although she did console herself that the matter could not be viewed with any certainty. François had been released from his prison in Madrid but he had only been allowed to go home if he promised on oath to send his two sons to Madrid as hostages for his good faith in carrying out the terms Charles had imposed on him. Thus the little boy who was betrothed to Mary was now the Emperor's prisoner in his father's stead.

Katharine was reminded now of those days between the death of her first husband, Arthur, and her marriage with Henry, when she lived through the uneventful yet dangerous months. Unable to be lulled by a false feeling of security and with dreadful premonition always in her mind that a storm was soon to break about her, she waited, knowing that when it did come it would contain an element of the unexpected, to face which she would need every scrap of courage she possessed.

It was December of that year when Mendoza arrived in London, but by that time she knew it was too late to stop the negotiations with France.

The first action of Mendoza was to beg an audience of the Queen. This she granted and he came speedily to her apartments.

She received him with emotion because of the memories of early and happier days he brought with him.

"It gives me great pleasure to see you," she told him.

"I cannot express to Your Grace my pleasure in being here. I have found the delay almost intolerable."

She looked at him closely and saw what those months in a French prison must have done to him; but, of course, when she had seen him in her mother's entourage he had been nothing but a boy. She was forgetting how many years ago that was.

This was not the time to waste on reminiscences and she said: "There is much we have to say to each other. I am seriously alarmed about the relations between my nephew and this country."

"The Emperor greatly desires to put them back on a friendly footing."

"The King is incensed on account of his treatment of Mary."

"Your Grace is also displeased."

"It was of course a bitter disappointment to me."

"The Emperor was pressed hard by the people of Spain, and he needed money from Portugal."

"I know . . . I know. But let us talk of what we shall do to put matters right between Spain and England. I must tell you that the Cardinal is my most bitter enemy. I am surrounded by his spies and I know not whom I can trust. You will know that he is the most powerful man in England."

Mendoza nodded. "We shall have to make sure that he cannot interfere with our correspondence as he did with de Praet's."

At that moment a page appeared at the door. Katharine looked at him in surprise, because she had given orders that she was not to be disturbed.

The page's look was apologetic, but before he could speak he was thrust aside and a red-clad figure came into the room.

"My lord Cardinal!" cried the Queen.

"Your Grace . . . Your Excellency . . . I come on the King's orders."

"What orders are these?" demanded Katharine haughtily.

"He requests the Imperial Ambassador to come to his apartment without delay."

"His Excellency called to see me . . ." the Queen began.

The Cardinal smiled at her whimsically. "The King's command," he murmured.

"His Excellency will call on the King within an hour."

"The King's orders are that I shall conduct him to his presence with all speed."

Katharine felt exasperation. She turned to the Ambassador and said rapidly in Spanish: "You see how it is. I am constantly overlooked."

But there was nothing to be done and the Ambassador must leave at once for the King's apartment, having achieved nothing by his visit to the Queen.

Katharine, with resignation, watched him go, knowing that future meetings between them would be difficult to arrange, and that when they talked together they would never be sure who overheard them; they must remember that anything they wrote to the Emperor would almost certainly be first censored by the Cardinal.

\*      \*      \*

Two wonderful events befell the Princess Mary.

It was strange, she reflected afterwards, that she should have waited for these things to happen and that they should have followed so swiftly on one another.

She was in one of her favourite haunts on a tower looking out over the battlements. The country was so beautiful that she found great peace merely by looking at it. She enjoyed riding in the woods with a party from her suite; during the warm days they had picnicked on the grass, and that was pleasant; but one of the most pleasurable occupations was kneeling up here on a stone seat inside the tower and looking out over the hills. This was her favourite view, for below in all its beauty was the valley of the Teme with the Stretton Hills forming a background.

She had been here so long that she was beginning to believe she would never leave the place; and yet every day she awoke with the thought in her mind: Will it be today?

Sometimes she let her fancy wander, imagining that a party of riders appeared in the valley, that she watched as they came nearer; and seeing the royal standard, knew that her mother had come.

It was nearly eighteen months since they had been parted.

How fortunate that I did not know how long it would be! she thought. If I had, I should never have been able to endure it.

But all through those months hope had been with her, and she often prayed that whatever happened to her she would always be able to hope.

She had grown considerably in the months of separation. Her mother would see a change. She had learned a great deal; she could write Greek and Latin very well now, and could compose verses in these two languages. As for her music, that had improved even more.

One day, as she knelt in her favourite position, she did see a party of riders in the valley. She stared, believing in those first moments that she was dreaming, so often she had imagined she saw riders.

She kept her eyes on the party and as it came nearer she saw that it was a group of men and that they were making straight for the Castle. She watched until they were within its walls before she turned from the battlements and went to her own apartments, knowing that she would soon be told who the newcomers were.

It was the Countess herself who came into Mary's apartment and, in all the eighteen months during which they had been in Ludlow Castle, Mary had never seen the Countess so radiant.

"Your Highness," she cried, "I have wonderful news. There is someone who is most eager to meet you. I want your permission to present him to you at once."

And there he was, in the room; tall, handsome, obviously of the nobility, austerely dressed though not in clerical robes, he seemed godlike to Mary.

"My son Reginald," went on Margaret, "who is also your humble servant."

He knelt before Mary and she smiled at him as she bade him rise. "Welcome," she said. "I feel I know you already because we have talked of you so often, your mother and I."

"Yes," agreed Margaret. "Her Highness insisted on hearing tales of my family."

"I found those tales interesting," said Mary. She turned to Margaret. "I trust they are busy in the kitchens preparing a welcoming banquet."

In that moment she felt grown up, the mistress of the Castle, Margaret noticed, and a wild hope was born in her mind.

She said: "I will leave my son with you while I go to the kitchens. I want to give orders myself for, as Your Highness says, this is a special occasion and we wish everyone within the Castle to know it."

Mary scarcely noticed that she had left. She went to the ornate chair which was kept especially for her and sat down, signing for Reginald to be seated too.

"We live somewhat simply here," she told him, "when compared with my father's Court. I pray you tell me about your stay on the Continent."

"It has been a very long one," he answered. "It is five years since I left England. A great deal can happen in five years; I have lived in Padua and Rome, and I have now come to complete my studies at Sheen . . . in the Carthusian monastery there."

"How wonderful! Your life is dedicated to God."

"All our lives are dedicated to some purpose," he replied. "I was fortunate to be able to choose the way I should go. My mother wanted me to go into the Church. I was very happy to do this but I have not yet taken Holy Orders."

"Have you come straight here from Rome?"

"Oh no, I visited London first and presented myself to Their Graces."

"You have seen my mother!"

"Yes, I saw her and when I told her that I should visit my mother at Ludlow she begged me to commend her to you and to tell you that she sends her dearest love."

Mary turned away for a moment, overcome by her emotion. Even the arrival of this man who had played a part in her dreams could not stifle her longing for her mother.

She asked questions about the Court. He did not tell her of the plans for a French marriage, nor of the speculations as to the efforts the Queen and the new Spanish ambassador would make to prevent this. He thought her charming, but a child; and yet during that first interview he was made aware of her serious turn of mind and that she had long ago put away childish things.

When Margaret returned and found them, absorbed in each other, and saw her son's interest in the child and Mary's in him— for Mary was unable to disguise the change his coming had made, and during the whole of her stay at Ludlow she had not looked so joyous—she said to herself: "Foreign matches seem to come to nothing. Why should not Mary marry my son?"

Oh, but how handsome he was! Twenty-seven years old, yet he looked younger; his gentle, noble nature had left his face unlined. There was in him the nobility of the Plantagenets, and the resemblance to his ancestor, Edward IV, was at times marked. It would strengthen the crown if Tudor and Plantagenet were joined together, thought Margaret. And she was glad that Reginald had not yet taken Holy Orders.

During the next days the two of them were continually together. They rode out of the Castle, surrounded by the Princess's attendants naturally, but they were always side by side, a little apart from the rest of the cavalcade. She played on the virginals for his pleasure; and there were balls and banquets as well as masques in Ludlow Castle.

The Princess Mary was growing pretty, for the sternness and slight strain, which had prevented her being so before, had left her; her pale cheeks were flushed and she was less absorbed in her lessons than she had been.

It was not possible, thought Margaret, for an eleven-year-old child to be in love with a man of twenty-seven, but Mary's feelings were engaged and she was ready to idealize the man who for so long had figured in her reveries.

And as though the tide of Mary's fortune had really turned, a week or so after the arrival of Reginald Pole, Margaret came to her apartment one day holding a letter in her hand.

Mary's heart leaped with excitement because she saw that it bore the royal seal.

"I have news from Court," she said. "We are to prepare to leave at once for London."

"Oh . . . Margaret!"

"Yes, my love. We have waited so long, have we not. But did I not tell you that if we were patient it would come? Well, here it is."

Mary took the letter and read it. Then she said slowly: "And Reginald . . . will he come with us?"

"There would be no point in leaving him in Ludlow. He will surely accompany us on the journey."

Mary looked as though she were about to dance round the room; then she remembered her dignity, and smiling she said in a clear, calm voice: "I am well pleased."

CHAPTER V

# THE KING'S CONSCIENCE

EACH morning when Cardinal Wolsey awoke, he would immediately be conscious of a black cloud of depression. He was not quite certain what it meant, but it was no phantom left over from a nightmare. It was real and it was hanging over him; each day it seemed to take him a little longer to assure himself that he could overcome any difficulties which might present themselves.

On this morning he awoke early and lay listening to the birds singing their songs in the trees of Hampton Court Gardens.

Once he could have said to himself: All this is mine. Those trees, that grass, this magnificent palace and all it contains. But that glory was of the past. He had lost some of his treasures; he must hold firmly to what he had.

Each day, it seemed to him, he was more and more unsure of the King's temper.

Yesterday Henry had looked at him slyly and murmured that he had heard from Mistress Anne Boleyn's lips that she had no love for My Lord Cardinal.

Why should he care for the malicious words of a careless girl? He would know how to deal with Anne Boleyn if she were ever important enough to demand his attention. At the moment she was amusing the King.

"Let be, let be," murmured Wolsey. "I like the King to amuse himself with women. While he does so it keeps him from meddling in state affairs."

And it was true that of late the King was paying less attention to state affairs; although of course, in a manner characteristic of him, he would think the "secret matter" the biggest state affair of all. To rid himself of Katharine, to take a new French Princess to be his bride . . . a French bride for the King; a French bridegroom for the Princess Mary . . . what heavier blow could be struck at the Emperor?

The King was eager that they should begin working out the details of his separation from Katharine. The difficulty was that, if the King's marriage was no true marriage, what then of the Princess Mary? A bastard? Would François Premier want to betroth his son to a bastard?

The situation was full of dangers. Not that he did not believe he could overcome them; but he wished the attitude of the King had not changed towards him.

He had thrown Hampton Court to his master, and one would have thought that such a gift was something to remember for as long as they both should live; but the King did not seem to think so, for although he now proudly referred to "my palace at Hampton," his attitude to the Cardinal had not grown more kindly.

There was no doubt about it; the King must be placated. And what he was demanding was the end of his marriage.

Wolsey rose from his bed and within an hour of his rising he was receiving Richard Wolman, who had been Vicar of Walden in Essex and Canon of St. Stevens in Westminster until the King, recently, had made him his chaplain, since when he had lived at Court.

When Richard Wolman stood before the Cardinal, Wolsey said: "I have sent for you that we may discuss the delicate matter of the King's conscience."

Wolman bowed his head.

"You know of this matter," stated Wolsey.

"His Grace has mentioned it to me on several occasions."

"Then you should go to him and accuse him of living in sin. Tell him that you think that as a sinner of nearly eighteen years' standing he should put himself before his Archbishop and the ecclesiastical Court to answer the charges which you have brought against him."

Richard Wolman turned pale. "Cardinal . . . you cannot mean . . . Why, the King would . . ."

Wolsey laughed, and lately his laughter was tinged with bitterness. "The King will frown at you, stamp his feet and show rage. But he'll not forget those who serve him . . . as he wishes to be served. Go now and be thankful that you have been chosen to serve the King . . . and yourself."

Wolman bowed his head. "You can be assured of my obedience," he said.

"That is well," answered Wolsey. "Lose no time. The King grows impatient."

\*     \*     \*

The King narrowed his eyes and studied his chaplain.

"Speak up!" he barked. "Speak up!"

"Your Grace, it is in all humility I bring this charge against you."

"You bring a charge against me!" The voice was fierce but

there was a note of eagerness in it. He was like a tame lion going through his tricks.

"Your Grace, it is after much meditation and prayer . . ."

"Get on! Get on!" said Henry impatiently.

"I have been considering Your Grace's marriage, and I come, with much fear and trembling, as Your Grace's chaplain to . . . to charge you with living in sin for eighteen years with a woman who cannot be your wife."

"What! This is monstrous!"

Henry stamped his foot and gave such a good imitation of genuine anger, that Wolman began to tremble. "Your Grace," he said, "I crave your pardon. If I have offended you . . ."

"*If* you have offended me! You come here and charge me . . . and who has more earnestly endeavoured to lead a godly life? . . . you charge *me* with . . . immorality."

Wolman fell to his knees. He was thinking: This is a plan of the Cardinal's to ruin me. What a fool I was to allow myself to be persuaded. This is the end of my career at Court, perhaps on Earth.

"I crave Your Grace's pardon. I spoke carelessly. If Your Grace will overlook . . ."

"Silence!" thundered the King. Then his voice softened suddenly. "If my chaplain has a criticism of my conduct I am not the man to turn a deaf ear to that criticism."

"It was presumptuous of me, Your Grace. I pray you forget . . ."

"Alas, I cannot forget. How could I forget a matter which for so long has given me many troublous thoughts?"

Great relief swept over Wolman. This was no trick. In coming here and making the accusation he had served the King and the Cardinal as they wished to be served.

"Get up," went on Henry. "Now you have spoken, and right glad I am to have this matter brought into the light of day. I married a woman who was my brother's wife, and in the Book of Leviticus we are told that this is a sin in the eyes of God. I have been shown God's displeasure. I have been denied a male heir. What are you and your ecclesiastics prepared to do in this matter?"

Wolman, completely restored to confidence, began to outline Wolsey's plan. "Your Grace will know that I have talked of this matter with His Eminence the Cardinal."

Good Thomas, thought Henry. Acquisitive, avaricious he might be, but he could be relied upon to work out a plan of action which would bring the King his desires.

"The Cardinal feels it will be necessary to summon Your Grace before a Council led by himself and the Archbishop of Canterbury."

The King nodded. He could rely on Thomas; as for Archbishop Warham, he was a timid fellow and could be trusted to do as his King commanded.

"There," went on Wolman, "the matter would be discussed, and if the Council found that Your Grace had never in truth been married . . ."

The King interrupted: "I should then be free to marry."

"It would be necessary doubtless to have the matter confirmed in Rome."

The King nodded. Clement was a good friend to him and Wolsey. He felt jubilant.

He clapped his hand on Wolman's shoulder. "You have been bold," he said, with a twinkle in his eyes, "thus to accuse me. But we ever like bold men even when they upbraid us for our sins."

\*      \*      \*

Gabriel de Grammont, Bishop of Tarbes, led his train into the King's apartment, where Henry, with Wolsey, Warham and several of his most eminent ministers, was waiting to receive them.

Wolsey was delighted because he felt that at last the alliance with France was secure. This would mean war with the Emperor. Wolsey visualized a Europe rising in unison against that young man. Henry had recently received an appeal from Clement who implored him to stand against the Emperor; if he did not, declared the Pope, Charles would shortly be the universal monarch. The Italian countryside had been devastated by his troops, and there was only one course of action: England, France, and the Vatican must stand against the conqueror. The letter had come at an opportune moment and Henry had been deeply impressed by it. And when Wolsey had pointed out: "We must stand by Clement now, for it may be that shortly we shall wish him to stand by us" Henry understood, and was as eager as his Cardinal for the French alliance.

So they had helped the Pope by sending Sir John Russell to Rome with money which would enable Clement to pay his troops and assist in the garrisoning of the City. His Holiness, when he heard English help was on the way, had called a blessing on the English King and Cardinal, and had said that their friendly action had restored him from death to life.

The moment was certainly ripe to apply to him for the Bull which would confirm that the marriage between the King of England and the Emperor's aunt was not valid and that therefore the King of England was free to marry where he wished.

Henry listened to the French Ambassadors outlining the terms of the new alliance which would mean certain war with the Emperor. François was not the man who would sit down under defeat; he would want to regain all that he had lost; he was waiting for his turn to impose harsh terms on Charles.

Henry nodded shrewdly. He knew that his people had always regarded the French as their natural enemies; and that since the coming of Katharine to England they favoured the Spanish alliance. Katharine had contrived to endear herself to the people, because they thought her serious and virtuous and there were many who had profited from her charities. Henry was a little disturbed that she had made such a good impression, but the people must be forced to understand the desirability of getting a male heir. When they realized that the important men of the Church, backed by the Pope himself, considered the King's marriage unlawful, they would be as eager as he was to accept it as no marriage at all. They would look forward to the pageantry a royal marriage would mean.

Henry pictured it: His bride beside him in the Palace of the Tower of London where she would come before her Coronation; he saw the glittering crown on her head; he saw her sitting beside him in the tiltyard, all haughtiness gone, only gratitude and love for him who had lifted her to such eminence. And the face he saw beneath the crown, the eyes that smiled at him with a faint hint of mockery, were not those of some stranger from France but a well-known young lady, a well-loved one, one who had haunted him ever since he had first seen her at Court and who had beguiled him in the gardens of her father's castle of Hever.

"By God!" he whispered to himself. "Why not?"

He could hear her voice, high-pitched and imperious: "Your wife I cannot be, both in respect of mine own unworthiness and because you have a queen already. Your mistress I will not be."

And, strangely enough, he who had never been humble was so before this girl; he, who had looked upon the gratification of his desires as his Divine right, was content to wait and plead.

He had to rouse himself from his reverie to listen to the Frenchmen; and when he did so the words of Grammont startled him.

"There is one point which I feel compelled to raise at this time," he was saying. "Rumours are circulating concerning the King's marriage. My master would wish to know whether it is certain that the Princess Mary is the legitimate daughter of the King."

Sudden anger flamed in Henry's eyes to be replaced by immediate exultation.

If the legitimacy of the Princess Mary was in question, who could blame him for his determination to have the circumstances of his marriage examined?

He forced a look of intense sadness into his face and glanced towards Wolsey, who said quietly: "We heed the Bishop's words. Little good can come of discussing that matter further at this stage."

*        *        *

Katharine watched her daughter riding into the Palace of Richmond and she thought: This is one of the happiest moments of my life.

How radiant the child looked! How she had grown! Was she as happy as her mother was by this reunion?

Mary came forward ceremoniously, her eyes lowered. It is because she fears her emotions, Katharine decided. What a Queen she will make when her time comes.

With Mary came her governess, Margaret Pole, Countess of Salisbury, and Margaret's son Reginald, both good friends of the Queen. So here was further cause for rejoicing.

Now her daughter knelt before her, and Katharine, who could stand on ceremony no longer, raised her up and embraced her

"My dearest daughter . . ."

"Oh Mother, it has been so long."

"Soon we shall be alone, my darling, and able to talk freely to each other."

"That will be wonderful, Mother."

She has not changed towards me, thought Katharine exultantly. How foolish of me to fear that she would.

She turned reluctantly from her daughter to greet Margaret. "I thank you for the good care you have taken of my daughter."

"To serve Your Grace and Her Highness is my pleasure," answered Margaret formally, but the gleam in her eyes was certainly not formal.

"And your son is here too." She smiled at Reginald. "That gives me great pleasure."

So they entered the Palace, and as soon as possible Katharine took her daughter to her private apartments that they might be alone.

"I have longed for this," she told Mary.

"Oh, Mother, if you could only know how much I longed to see you. I used to kneel in the turret watching for a party of riders which would be you and your suite on the way to the Castle."

"My dear child . . . and I never came!"

"No, but I always hoped. I never knew before how important hope is. One goes on being disappointed and loses it for a while, and then . . . there it is again."

"You have learned an important lesson, my dearest."

"And one day, Mother, Reginald came. That was a consolation."

"Ah, I noticed that there was friendship between you."

"Is he not wonderful, Mother? He is so clever and yet so kind. I think he is the gentlest man I ever knew."

Katharine smiled. "And you liked his gentleness?"

"So much, Mother. With him I felt at peace. And after he had been with us a short time the message came that I was to return to you. We shall not be parted again."

Katharine did not answer. It was her duty to prepare her daughter to receive the French ambassadors who would carry news of her beauty, accomplishments and deportment to the King of France.

And if this marriage were to take place within a year . . . or very little longer . . . Mary would be sent to France, for there could be no excuse for keeping her at home any longer. Katharine felt she could not endure another separation.

"You are sad, Mother," said Mary. "Is it this marriage they are arranging for me which makes you so?"

The Queen nodded. "But we will not think of unpleasant things. It could not happen for a very long time. I will tell you this: I will do everything in my power to postpone, nay prevent it."

Mary threw herself into her mother's arms and cried passionately: "Yes, please do. Do not let them send me away from you again. Why could I not marry in my own country?"

Katharine stroked her daughter's hair.

"Because, my darling, you would have to marry someone who is as royal as yourself."

"There are people here who are as royal as I am."

Katharine felt a twinge of alarm. Such words, when applied to one of the King's subjects, could be dangerous. Buckingham had used them too often.

"Edward IV was Reginald's ancestor and mine also. So Reginald is as royal as I am."

The Queen was silent, thinking: Then has she thought of Reginald as a husband?

The idea excited Katharine. And why not? It was true Reginald Pole had Plantagenet blood in his veins. Surely it was a better policy to arrange marriages rather than executions for those whose royalty could be a threat to the crown.

If Mary married Reginald Pole, she could remain in England. Katharine visualized a happy future with her daughter never far from her side. She pictured herself with Mary's children who would take the place in her heart of those she had never had. If only it could be. If only she could prevent this French alliance!

"Yes," she said slowly, "Reginald Pole has royal blood in his veins. I am glad that you feel affection for him because I know him to be a good man, and his mother is one of my dearest friends."

Mary was astute enough to read the promise in those words. She embraced her mother in sudden ecstasy as though, thought Katharine, she believes me to be all-powerful.

But let her think that, because it makes her happy; and we must be happy in these hours of reunion.

*　　　*　　　*

Later Katharine sat with her dear friend Margaret Pole and they were alone together, which gave pleasure to them both.

Katharine was saying: "This is one of the happiest days of my life. I have dreamed of it ever since Mary went away."

"As she has too," added Margaret.

"It pleases me that she and Reginald should be drawn to each other."

"They have indeed become good friends. The Princess is such a serious child that the difference in their ages is scarcely noticeable. My son considers her to be one of the most highly educated ladies it has been his pleasure to meet,"

"Your son has not taken Holy Orders?"

"No, he has not done so yet."

"Does he intend to?"

"I think he is eager to study more before he does so. That is why he is going to the Carthusians at Sheen."

The Queen smiled and a thought came to Margaret which she had had before; then it had seemed a wild dream, but it did not seem so now because she believed she read the Queen's thoughts correctly.

Katharine went on: "The French marriage does not please me."

"But the King and the Cardinal . . ."

"Oh yes, the Cardinal leads the King the way he wishes him to go."

Margaret was surprised that the Queen should speak so frankly; then she realized that Katharine did so because the bond between them was a little closer even than it had been before.

"I shall not allow Mary to receive the French ambassadors tomorrow," went on the Queen. "I shall make the excuse that she is too weary after her long journey from Ludlow. Depend upon it, I shall do all in my power to prevent this proposed marriage. Nor do I despair of so doing. Monarchs are fickle, and François more fickle than most. Mary was betrothed to this boy once before, you remember. There was great enthusiasm . . . even a ceremony . . . and then a few years later it was as though that ceremony had never taken place."

"The Princess is sensitive. One does not care to think of her in a foreign court. And I believe that that of the French is the most licentious in the world."

The Queen shuddered. "How I should like to make a match nearer home for her. There are more worthy men in England than across the seas."

The two women had drawn closer together; they were not Queen and subject merely, not only lifelong friends; they were two mothers discussing the future of the children who meant everything in the world to them.

\*     \*     \*

While the Queen sat with Margaret Pole, Iñigo de Mendoza called at the Palace and asked for an interview with her. It was imperative, he declared, that he see Her Grace without delay.

When the message was brought to the Queen, Margaret, without being bidden to do so, left her presence and Mendoza was ushered in.

Katharine saw from his expression that he was extremely agitated, and his first words told her why.

"The Cardinal is working to separate you and the King; he has called together certain bishops and lawyers that they may secretely declare the marriage to be null."

Katharine could not speak. She knew that the King no longer desired her; that his disappointment at the lack of a male child continued to rankle. But to cast her off as a woman who had been living with him all these years outside the sanctity of marriage, was unthinkable. Such a thing could not happen to a Daughter of Spain.

"I fear I have given you a great shock," said the ambassador. "But it is a matter which must be faced quickly. This must not be allowed to happen."

"It is the Cardinal who has done this," said the Queen. "He has long been my enemy."

"He could not have done it without the King's consent," the ambassador reminded her.

"The King is a careless boy at heart. He is tired of me . . . so he allows Wolsey to persuade him that he should be rid of me."

"Your Grace, we must act immediately."

"What can we do if the King has decided to rid himself of me?"

"We can do our best to prevent him."

"You do not know the King. All that he desires comes to him. He takes it as his Divine right."

"He may have his will with his own subjects, but Your Grace is of the House of Spain. Have you forgotten that the Emperor is the son of your sister?"

"They care little for the Emperor here now," said Katharine wearily.

"Your Grace," the ambassador replied almost sternly, "they will have to care."

Katharine covered her eyes with her hand. "So this is the end," she said.

"The end! Indeed it is not. Your Grace, if you will not fight for yourself, you must fight for your daughter."

"Mary! Of course . . . she is involved in this." The Queen had dropped her hand, and the ambassador saw how her eyes flashed. "Are they saying that Mary is a bastard?"

"If the marriage were declared null, that is what I fear she would be called, Your Grace."

"That shall never be," said the Queen firmly.

"I knew Your Grace would say that. I beg of you, be as calm as you can, for it is calmness we need if we are to outwit those who work against us. It would be helpful, I am sure, if you could behave as though you know nothing of this which is being called the King's Secret Matter. The only help we can hope for must be from the Emperor and in view of existing relations our task is made difficult. I beg Your Grace to speak of this matter to no one until we have found a means of conveying the news to my master, your nephew."

"This we must do without delay."

"Your Grace is right. But to send a letter might be to act rashly. I feel sure that everything that leaves my hands is in danger of falling into those of the Cardinal's spies. We must find a messenger who will go to the Emperor with nothing written down, who will tell him by word of mouth what is happening here in England. Let us discover such a man, who must be humble enough not to excite suspicion, yet loyal enough to keep his secrets until he arrives in Spain."

The Queen, knowing that the ambassador spoke wisely, agreed.

"I will call on you tomorrow," he told her. "By then I hope to have some plan. In the meantime I trust Your Grace will give no sign that we have wind of the King's Secret Matter."

When Mendoza left her, Katharine sat for a long time, very still, an expression of melancholy amplifying the lines on her face.

Such a short while ago she had felt so happy because her daughter was returned to her. Now her happiness had been shattered, for she knew that the greatest calamity which could befall her was threateningly near.

"There are times," she murmured, "when I think God has deserted me."

\* \* \*

As Henry prepared to set out for the Cardinal's Palace of York Place, a complacent smile played about his mouth, and his eyes were gleaming with satisfaction in which humour mingled.

It was an amusing situation when a King was summoned to appear before a court, charged with immorality. He believed that those lawyers and men of the Church must be telling themselves that here was the most tolerant King on Earth. He might have had them all clapped into the Tower for their presumption. But what had he done? Meekly accepted the summons to appear before them and hear his case thrown from the prosecuting to the defending counsels like a ball in a game.

He was certain that the outcome of the case would be that he was found guilty, after which there would be nothing to do but his penance for his sins, receive absolution and marry again that he might do his duty to his country and give it a male heir. The Pope would be called in to have the dispensation, which Julius II had given, declared invalid, but he need have no qualms about that; Clement was the friend of England. It had been a clever stroke to answer his appeal for help against the Emperor. Wolsey was to be commended for his far-sightedness.

So the King set out for York Place in high spirits.

As he stepped from his barge he studied the Palace and thought how grand it looked. It was the town residence of the Archbishops of York and thus it had passed into Wolsey's possession; but the Cardinal had added a magnificence to it which it had not possessed before, and although it may have lacked the grandeur of Hampton Court it was a very fine palace. Henry's eyes smouldered a little as he surveyed it. Hampton Court was now his, yet he felt a little resentful that a subject should possess such a residence as that of York Place.

He was slightly mollified when he entered and was received by the Cardinal who exchanged with him a secret look which was meant to imply that the stage was set and in a very short time they would have achieved their desire.

At the end of a hall on a dais Wolsey took his place beside William Warham, Archbishop of Canterbury.

Among those gathered in the hall were John Fisher, the Bishop of Rochester, who was said to be one of the wisest and saintliest men in England, Dr. Bell who was to be the King's Counsel, and Dr. Wolman who was to state the case against Henry's marriage.

Dr. Wolman opened the proceedings against the King.

"Henry, King of England, you are called to this archiepiscopal court to answer a charge of living in sin with your brother's wife . . ."

Henry listened with the shocked appearance of a man who, in his innocence, has been caught up in a sinful intrigue, and when Wolman had stated the case against the King's marriage Dr. Bell rose to speak for him.

His Grace had, it was well known, married his brother's widow, but it was said that the marriage of Prince Arthur and the Infanta Katharine had never been consummated. The reigning King, Henry VII, had expressed his desire that this consummation should not take place on account of the bridegroom's youth and delicate state of health. And when he died, six months after the marriage, Katharine had stayed in England and in the year 1509 had married their sovereign lord. A dispensation had been received from Pope Julius II, and it was the defence's case that the King had married in good faith and that it had not occurred to him that his marriage could be anything but legal. Then the Bishop of Tarbes had made a suggestion, and it became clear that this was the result of some pernicious rumour he had heard. It was the King's desire to stand by the finding of this court, but he was going to ask them to say that his marriage to Katharine of Aragon was a legal one.

Henry's eyes narrowed as he studied Dr. Bell, but Wolsey had assured him that they could trust Bell. He must put the King's case in such a manner that it would appear to be a case for the defence. But Bell would know how to act when the moment came.

Wolman was on his feet; he did not think the marriage could have remained unconsummated during the six months the married pair lived together. It would be remembered that they travelled to Ludlow with their own Court and there made merry together. If the marriage had been consummated then, Katharine of Aragon had been the wife of the King's brother in actual fact, and Wolman maintained that the marriage was illegal.

When it was Henry's turn to speak he did so with apparent sincerity, for he had convinced himself that it was solely because he wished to stand unsullied in the eyes of God and his subjects that he was glad the matter had been brought to light.

"I can but rejoice that this matter has been brought into the light of day," he told the court. "Lately it has much troubled my conscience. I could not understand why our prayers should be unanswered. The Queen's persistent ill health has been a matter of great concern to me, and I trust you learned gentlemen will unravel this delicate matter that I may peacefully return to my wife or—which will cause me much sorrow—declare that our marriage was no marriage and our union must end without delay."

William Warham listened intently. He lacked the guile of Wolsey and he was coming to the end of an arduous life. He was in his seventies and often it seemed to those about him that he was failing. He was simple enough to believe that the reason for this enquiry was the fact that the Bishop of Tarbes had raised the question of the Princess's legitimacy. He was anxious to give the matter his most careful attention with the hope that he might lead the members of this court to come to the right conclusion.

The details of the King's marriage were discussed at length; Katharine's arrival in England was recalled, followed by her marriage to Arthur which had lasted only six months.

"If that marriage was consummated," said Warham, "then the Queen has most certainly been the wife of Prince Arthur, and the King could be said to have taken his brother's wife."

"Which," sighed the King, "according to the Holy Word is an unclean thing. Such unions shall be childless, says the Bible. And behold a son has been denied me."

"But there was a dispensation from the Pope," put in the Bishop of Rochester. "I think Your Grace should not reproach yourself."

"The Pope would have been under the impression that the marriage had not been consummated, when he granted the dispensation," said Wolman. "If it could be proved that the marriage *had* been consummated, then clearly there could be no marriage between the King and Katharine of Aragon."

"I think," persisted Rochester gently, "that the King should suppress his qualms, for there seems little doubt that his marriage is a good one and that the Bull, which legalized it, was sufficient to do so."

Henry studied John Fisher, Bishop of Rochester, from beneath lowered lids. He found it hard to hide his animosity. A curse on these saintly men who expressed their opinions with freedom even before their rulers. Fisher was the Queen's confessor and clearly her partisan. Wolsey should not have included the man in this court. It was folly to have done so.

Warham was weak and growing simple in his old age. Warham could be handled. But the King was not sure of Fisher.

By God, he thought, I'll have him in the Tower, beloved of the people though he may be, if he dares to stand out against me.

"My lords," Wolsey was saying, "I beg of you to come to a quick decision in this case, for the matter is grievous to the King. His Grace is perplexed. If you decide that his union is unlawful, remember it will be necessary for him to part from the Lady Katharine at once, and this will afford him great sorrow for, though he be not in truth her husband, he has a husband's affection for her."

Warham's gentle grey eyes were sad. He was thinking of the Queen who would be deeply disturbed if she knew what was happening at York Place.

Henry was now on his feet telling the court how devoted he was to his wife, how there was no other motive in his heart but the desire to free himself from a sinful union that he might live in peace with God. Katharine had been his wife for eighteen years, and he had found in her all he had hoped to find in a wife.

"Save in one thing!" His voice thundered. "And that, gentlemen, is this matter which is of the utmost importance to my kingdom. Our marriage has not been as fruitful as we wished. We have but one daughter. Again and again it seemed that my wife would produce the son for whom we prayed each night and day; but we were disappointed. It is not until now—when the Bishop of Tarbes comes to my kingdom with his revealing enquiry —that I see the divine pattern of these continual misfortunes. Ah, gentlemen, if you decide that my marriage is no marriage, if I must part with her . . . whom I love dearly and have always regarded as my wife . . . then your King will be the most unhappy of men. For the Lady Katharine is of such virtue, such gentleness and humility, possessed of all the qualities pertaining to nobility; and if I were to marry again—and it were not a sin to marry *her*—she is the woman I would choose above all others."

As he spoke he seemed to see a vital young face laughing at him, mocking him. There was more than a trace of mockery in Anne. It was part of her witchery and it enslaved him.

He found himself answering her in his thoughts: Well, 'tis for our future. Were I to tell these Bishops of my need for you, they would never understand. Poor old fellows, what could they know of what is between us two!

But the mood passed quickly, and in a few moments he was believing all he said. The little mouth, which had grown slack as he thought of Anne, tightened and became prim. I should never have thought of casting off Katharine but for the continued gnawing of my conscience, he told himself; and he immediately believed it. Katharine was the woman he had insisted on marrying eighteen years ago; it was not because her body had grown shapeless, her hair lacked lustre, and that she provoked no physical desire in him that he would be rid of her. It had nothing to do with the most fascinating woman he had ever known, who still kept aloof and would not submit to him, yet maddened him with her promises of what would be his if she were his wife. No, he told himself sternly, Anne was apart from this. He loved Anne with every pulse of his body; his unsatisfied desire was becoming more than he could endure; and since he had discovered that no other woman would suffice in her place, he was making secret plans now to give Anne what she wanted. (By God, she asks a high price for herself, a crown no less. But worth it, my beauty!) Yet, he assured himself, but for the demands of conscience he would never have questioned his marriage to Katharine. It was solely because he feared he was living in sin, and must quickly cease to do so, that he was here before his bishops and lawyers this day.

"This matter cannot be settled in any haste," said Warham. "The findings of the court must be examined."

Henry fidgeted. He was almost on his feet. He wanted to shout at them: You idle fellows Time to examine your findings! What do you want with that? I tell you I want a divorce, and, by God, a divorce I shall have or clap every man of you into the Tower.

But in time he saw the horror which was dawning in the Cardinal's eyes and restrained himself with difficulty.

So the court was adjourned.

\*       \*       \*

The King was with the Cardinal when the messengers arrived; these were messengers with no ordinary tidings; they demanded that they be taken with all speed to the King's presence, assuring those who tried to detain them that it would go ill with them if the news they carried were kept from the King an instant longer than it need be.

When this message was brought to Henry he said: "Let them come to me at once."

They came in, travel-stained and breathless from their haste, their eyes alight with the excitement of those who have news which is such as is heard once in a lifetime.

"Your Grace . . . Your Eminence . . ." The words then began to tumble out. "Bourbon's troops have attacked Rome. The city is in the hands of savage soldiery. The Pope has escaped with his life by shutting himself up in the Castle of St. Angelo. The carnage, Your Grace, Your Eminence, is indescribable."

Henry was horrified. The Pope a prisoner! Rome in the hands of lewd and savage soldiers! Never had such a disaster befallen Christendom.

The Constable of Bourbon, the declared enemy of the King of France, was siding with the Emperor, and his army it was which had launched this attack on Rome. Bourbon himself was dead; indeed, he had had no desire to attack Rome; but his army was reduced to famine; there was no money with which to pay them; they demanded conquest and would have killed him if he had stood in their way.

So on that fateful May day this ragged, starving, desperate army had marched on Rome.

Bourbon had been killed in the attack but his men did not need him. On they had rushed, into Rome.

Never had men and women seen such wanton destruction; the fact that this was the city of Rome seemed to raise greater determination to destroy and desecrate than men had ever felt before.

The invaders stormed into the streets, killing men, women and children who were in their way; they battered their way into the palaces and great houses; they crammed food into their starving mouths; they poured wine down their scorching throats. But they had not come merely to eat and drink.

They invaded the churches, seizing the rich ornaments, images, vases, chalices which were brought into the streets and piled high into any means of conveyance the marauders were able to snatch. Every man was determined to have his pile of treasures, to reward himself for the months of bitter privation.

During those five terrible days when the soldiers were in possession of Rome, they determined that every woman should be raped and not a single virgin left in the city. The greatest amusement was afforded them by the nuns who had believed that their cloth would protect them. Into the convents burst the soldiers. They caught the nuns at prayer and stripped them of those robes which the innocent women had thought would protect them. Horror had pervaded the convents of Rome.

In the streets wine ran from the broken casks, and satiated soldiers lay in the gutters exhausted by their excesses. Priceless tapestry and gleaming utensils which had been stolen from altars and palaces and thrown from windows were lying in the street. The soldiers were mercenaries from Spain, Germany and Naples; and to the desecration of Rome each brought the worst of his national characteristics. The Germans destroyed with brutal efficiency; the Neapolitans were responsible for the greatest sexual outrages; and the Spaniards took a great delight in inflicting subtle cruelty.

It was not enough to commit rape and murder; others must join in their fun. So they brought monks and nuns together, stripped them of their robes and forced the monks to rape the nuns, while these vile soldiers stood by applauding and mocking.

Never had such sights been seen in Rome, and the people who had managed to escape with their lives cried out in great lamentation, declaring that if God did not punish such wickedness it must be believed that He did not trouble Himself about the affairs of this world.

This was the story the messengers brought to the King on that May day, and to which he listened in increasing anger and horror.

He sent the messengers away to be refreshed, and when they had gone he turned to the Cardinal.

"This is the most terrible tale I ever heard."

"And doubly so," answered Wolsey, "coming at this time."

Henry was startled. While he was listening to the tale of horror he had forgotten his own predicament.

Wolsey went on: "The Pope a prisoner in the Castel Sant' Angelo! Although Bourbon led the attack on Rome, the Pope is now the Emperor's prisoner. Your Grace will see that, being the prisoner of the Emperor, he will not be in a position to declare invalid the dispensation regarding the Emperor's aunt."

"By God, I see what you mean," said Henry. "But he will not long be a prisoner. It is monstrous that the Holy Father should be treated so."

"I am in agreement with Your Grace. But I fear this will mean delay."

The King's mouth was petulant. "I weary of delay," he murmured.

"We must act quickly, Your Grace, and there are two tasks which lie ahead of us. We must send an embassy to France without delay in order that we may, with the help of our ally, liberate the Pope from this humiliating situation."

"Who will go on such an embassy?"

"It is a delicate matter, in view of what is involved," said Wolsey.

"You must go, Thomas. None could succeed as you will. You know all that is in my heart at this time; and you will bring about that which we need."

Wolsey bowed his head. "I will begin my preparations at once, Your Grace."

"You spoke of another task."

"Yes, Your Grace. The Queen will have heard rumours of our court of enquiry. I think she should be told of Your Grace's conflict with your conscience."

"And who should tell her this?" demanded Henry.

Wolsey was silent and Henry went on sullenly: "I see what is in your mind. This should come from no lips but my own."

\*          \*          \*

The Princess Mary was seated in her favourite position on a stool at her mother's feet, leaning her head against the velvet of Katharine's skirt. She was saying how happy she was that they could be together again, and that the long sojourn at Ludlow seemed like a nightmare.

"Oh Mother," cried the Princess, "is there any more news of my marriage?"

"None, my darling."

"You would tell me, would you not. You would not try to shield me . . . because, Mother, I would rather know the truth."

"My dearest, if I knew of anything concerning your marriage I should tell you, because I believe with you that it is well to be prepared."

Mary took her mother's hand and played with the rings as she used to when she was a baby.

"I fancied you seemed distraught of late. I wondered if there had been some evil news . . ."

Katharine laid her hand on her daughter's head and held it firmly against her. She was glad Mary could not see her face.

Evil news! she thought. The most evil news that could be brought to me! Your father is trying to cast me off.

But she would not tell Mary this, for who could say how the girl would act? She might be foolhardy enough, affectionate enough, to face her father, to upbraid him for his treatment of her mother. She must not do that. Henry could never endure criticism, more especially when he was doing something of which he might be ashamed. He could harm Mary as certainly as he could harm Katharine. Indeed, thought the Queen, my daughter's destiny is so entwined with mine that the evil which befalls me must touch her also. Better for her not to know of this terrible shadow which hangs over us. Let her be kept in ignorance for as long as possible.

"There is no further news of your marriage," said the Queen firmly. "Nor do I think there will be. These friendships with foreign countries are flimsy. They come and go."

"It would be so much better if I were married to someone at home here," said Mary.

"Perhaps that may happen," replied the Queen soothingly. "Who shall say?"

Mary turned and lifted a radiant face to her mother. "You see Mother, not only should I marry someone who was of my own country . . . speaking my own language, understanding our ways . . . but I should be with you. Imagine, for evermore we should be together! Perhaps I should not always live at Court. Perhaps I should have a house in the country; but you would come and visit me there . . . and often I should be at Court. When my children are born you would be beside me. Would that not be so much happier than our being separated and your hearing the news through messengers?"

"It would be the happiest state which could befall us both."

"Then you will tell my father so?"

"My darling, do you think I have any influence with your father?"

"Oh . . . but you are my mother."

The Queen's brows were drawn together in consternation and, realizing that she had let a certain bitterness creep into her voice, she said quickly: "Kings are eager to make marriages of state for their sons and daughters. But depend upon it, Mary, that if I have any influence it shall be used to bring you your heart's desire."

They were silent for a while and the Queen wondered whether Mary was really thinking of Reginald Pole when she talked of marriage, and whether it was possible for one so young to be in love with a man.

While they sat thus the King came into the apartment. He was alone, which was unusual, for he rarely moved about the Palace without a little cluster of attendants. He was more sombrely clad than usual and he looked like a man with a private sorrow.

The Queen and Princess rose, and both curtseyed as he approached.

"Ha!" he said. "So our daughter is with you. It is pleasant to see you back at Court, daughter."

"I thank Your Grace," murmured Mary.

"And you play the virginals as well as ever, I believe. You must prove this to us."

"Yes, Your Grace. Do you wish me to now?"

"No . . . no. I have a matter of some importance to discuss with your mother, and I am going to send you away. Go and practise on the virginals so that you will not disappoint me when you next show me your progress."

As Mary curtseyed again and went away, Katharine was thinking: What can I say to him now, knowing what I do? How can anything ever be the same between us again?

As soon as Mary had left them, Henry turned to her, his hands clasped behind his back, on his face an expression of melancholy, his mouth tight and prim, the general effect being that before Katharine stood a man who had forced himself to a painful duty.

He began: "Katharine, I have a grievous matter to discuss with you."

"I am eager to discuss that matter with you," she answered.

"Ah," he went on, "I would give half my kingdom if by so doing I could have prevented this from happening."

"I pray you tell me what is in your mind."

"Katharine, you were poor and desolate when I married you; you were a stranger in a strange land; you were the widow of my brother, and it seemed that there was no home for you in the country of your birth nor here in the country of your adoption."

"I shall never forget those days," she answered.

"And I determined to change all that. I was young and idealistic, and you were young too, then, and beautiful."

"Both qualities which I no longer possess."

The King turned his eyes to the ceiling. "That could be of no importance in this matter. But it seems that learned men . . . men of the Church . . . have examined our marriage . . . or what we believed to be our marriage . . . and they have found that it is no true marriage."

"Then they deceive you," she said fiercely.

"As I told them. But they are learned men and they quote the law to me. They read the Bible to me and tell me that I have sinned against God's laws. We have both sinned, Katharine."

"This makes no sense," retorted Katharine. "How could we have sinned by marrying?"

"It is so clear to me now. It is in the Bible. Read it, Katharine. Read the twenty-first verse of the twentieth chapter of Leviticus. Then you will see that ours was no true marriage and that for all these years we have been living in sin."

Katharine stared at him blankly. This was no surprise to her, but to hear it from his own lips, to see that stubborn determination which she knew so well, light up his eyes, shocked her more deeply than she had ever been shocked before.

"I know," went on the King, "that this is a matter which distresses you, even as it distresses me. I will admit to a temptation to turn my back on this, to scoff at my critics, to say, Let us forget that I married my brother's wife. But I can hear the voice of God speaking to me through my conscience . . ."

"When did your conscience first begin to trouble you?" she asked.

"It was when I heard the suggestion made by the Bishop of Tarbes; when he questioned Mary's legitimacy."

At the mention of her daughter, Katharine's bravado crumpled; she looked older suddenly and a very frightened woman.

"You see," went on the King, "much as this distresses me, and indeed it breaks my heart to consider that we can no longer live together . . ."

"Which we have not done for some time," she reminded him. "We had ceased to be bedfellows before your conscience was troubled."

"Your poor state of health . . . my consideration for you . . . my fears that another pregnancy would be beyond your strength . . ."

"And your interest in others . . ." murmured Katharine.

But Henry went on as though he had not heard her: "What a tragedy when a King and Queen, so long married, so devoted to each other, should suddenly understand that their marriage is no marriage, and that they must separate. I have given this matter much thought. I have said to myself, What will become of her? For myself, I have not cared. But for you, Katharine . . . you whom I always, until this time, thought of as my wife . . ." He paused, pretending to be overcome by his emotions.

She wanted to shout at him that she despised him, that she knew it was not his conscience that was behind this dastardly plot but his desire for a new wife. She wanted to say: How dare you cast insults at a Princess of Spain? And what of our daughter? Will you, merely that you may satisfy your lust in the sanctity of a marriage bed, cast me off and proclaim our daughter a bastard!

It was the thought of Mary which was unnerving her. Her usual calm had deserted her; she could feel her mouth trembling so that it would not form the words she wanted to utter; her limbs were threatening to collapse.

Henry went on: "Knowing your serious nature, your love of the Church and all it stands for, it seemed to me that you would wish to enter a convent and there pass the rest of your days in peace. It should be a convent of your choosing and you should be its abbess. You need have no fear that you would lose any of the dignity of your rank . . ."

A voice within her cried: Do you think you could strip me of that? You have insulted me by telling me that I lived with you for all these years when I was not your legal wife; and now you dare tell me—the daughter of Isabella and Ferdinand—that you will not rob me of my rank!

But the words would not come and the hot tears were spilling over and running down her cheeks.

Henry stared at her. He had never seen her thus. That she, who had always been so conscious of her dignity and rank, should weep, was something he had not considered.

It horrified him.

"Now, Kate," he said, "you must not weep. You must be brave . . . as I would fain be. Think not that I cease to love you. Love you I always shall. The Bishops may say what they will; you may not be my wife in the eyes of God but always I shall love you as I did in those days when you were so poor and lonely and I lifted you up to share my throne. Do not grieve. Who knows . . . they may find that there is naught wrong with our marriage after all. Kate, Kate, dry your eyes. And remember this: For the time being this is our secret matter. We do not want it bruited abroad. If I could but come to terms with my conscience I would snap my fingers at these Bishops, Kate. I'd have them clapped into the Tower for daring to hint . . ."

But she was not listening. She did not believe him. She did not see the virtuous, religious man he was trying to show her; she saw only the lustful King who was tired of one wife and wanted another.

Her tears fell faster, and convulsive sobs shook her body.

Henry stood awhile, staring at her in dismay; then he turned abruptly and left her.

CHAPTER VI

# THE QUEEN AND THE CARDINAL IN DANGER

WHEN the Queen had recovered from her grief she sent for Mendoza.

"All that we feared has come to pass," she told him. "The King is determined to rid himself of me. He has told me that his conscience troubles him because learned men have assured him that we are not truly married."

"So it has gone as far as that!" muttered Mendoza. "We shall need a strong advocate to defend Your Grace . . ."

"Where should I find one here in England? she asked.

"Your Grace can trust none of the King's subjects. We must immediately appeal to the Emperor."

"I will write to him with all speed."

Mendoza shook his head. "It is very doubtful that any appeal from you would be allowed to reach him."

Katharine stared helplessly at the ambassador.

"Or," he continued, "any appeal from me either. The Cardinal's spies will be doubly vigilant. We must smuggle a messenger out of the country, and it must be done in such a way that no suspicion is attached to him."

"What a sad state of affairs when I am denied a lawyer to defend me."

"Let us be hopeful," answered Mendoza, "and say that the King knows that he has such a poor case that he dare not allow a good lawyer to defend you. Is there any member of Your Grace's household whom you trust completely?"

Katharine thought awhile and then said: "He must be a Spaniard for he will have to travel into Spain to reach the Emperor. I can only think of Francisco Felipez who has been in my service for twenty-seven years. I am sure he is to be trusted."

"An excellent choice. He should leave for Spain as soon as possible. But he should carry nothing in writing and it should seem that you do not send him but that he wishes to go of his own accord."

"I will summon him and together we will form some plan."

"It would be unwise for Your Grace to send for him now while I am here. I am certain that we are being closely watched. Indeed, it may be unwise to send for him at all, because it will doubtless be suspected that you will try to get a message through to the Emperor. If Your Grace could seize an opportunity of speaking to him when he is performing some duty—just whispering a word to him when no one will notice—that would be the best plan. Then if he expresses a desire to see his family, it will not appear that he is on Your Grace's business."

"How I hate this intrigue! I feel like a prisoner in the Tower rather than a Queen in her Palace."

The ambassador looked at her sadly. He wondered what might have befallen her, standing in the King's way as she did, had she not been the aunt of the Emperor.

\*          \*          \*

Francisco Felipez presented himself to the King and asked if he might speak to him in private.

Henry granted this request, thinking that the man came with some message from the Queen, but as soon as they were alone Felipez said: "Your Grace, I am in great distress. My mother is dying and wishes to give me her blessing. I have come to ask your permission to go to her."

"You are a servant of the Queen," said Henry. "Have you not asked her for this licence?"

Felipez looked uneasy. "I have, Your Grace."

"Well?"

"And she has refused it."

The King's blue eyes were wide with astonishment.

"Why so?" he demanded.

"She believes that I do not speak the truth."

"And has she reason to believe this?"

"None, Your Grace."

"This is unlike the Queen. I have always thought her to be most considerate of her servants."

"The Queen has changed. She accused me of seeking to leave her, as all her servants would do in time."

"But why should she say such a thing?"

The man hesitated, but Henry insisted that he should continue. "Your Grace, the Queen says that, since you are displeased with her, all her servants will find excuses to leave her."

"I fear the Queen is suffering from delusions," said Henry. "It grieves me that she should have so little thought for her servants. You did well to come to me. I will grant your licence; I will do more. I will give you a safe-conduct through France which will make your journey so much easier."

Felipez fell to his knees, tears of gratitude in his eyes.

"We see you are pleased," said Henry gruffly. "I will give you your licence now."

"How can I thank Your Grace?" stammered the man.

But Henry waved a hand and went to the table. He wrote for a while, then handed the man a document.

"This will suffice," he said. "You need have no fear that you will be intercepted. I trust that you will reach your mother in time."

When Felipez had gone, Henry thought: There is a man who, should he return to England, will be my servant, not the Queen's.

It was some days later when Henry remembered the incident and mentioned it in a letter he wrote to the Cardinal who was now in France.

The Cardinal's answer came back promptly.

"This man but feigns to visit his sick mother. Your Highness will realize that it is chiefly for disclosing your secret matter to the Emperor and to devise means and ways of how it may be impeached. I pray Your Grace to ascertain whether this man has left England and, if he has not, to stop him. If he has left, I will, if it be in my power, have him intercepted in his journey across France, for if this matter should come to the Emperor's ears, it should be no little hindrance to Your Grace."

When Henry read that letter he was furious. He had been foolish not to see through the ruse. What a cunning woman the Queen had become! He should have seen through her deception. And because the Cardinal had seen at once, and because had the Cardinal been in England the licence would never have been granted, Henry, perversely, felt irritated with the Cardinal.

There was another reason which made him uneasy when he thought of the Cardinal. There were certain matters which he had withheld from his minister. Anne hated Wolsey and she was gradually persuading Henry to hate him.

Anne had said: "If the Cardinal knew of our desires he would work against us. Never have I forgotten the time when he treated me as though I were the lowest serving wench—and all because Henry Percy had spoken for me."

"But, sweetheart, if any man can get me my divorce, that man is the Cardinal," Henry had insisted.

Anne had agreed with that. They should use the Cardinal, for he was a wily man; she did not deny that. But he believed that the purpose of the divorce he was trying to arrange was that Henry might marry Renée, daughter of Louis XII, not Anne Boleyn.

So there were secrets which the King had kept from the

Cardinal, and during recent months it had often been necessary to deceive him. Once there had been complete accord between them, but this was no longer so, and now Henry was irritated to think of those secrets; he might have despised himself for his duplicity, but as he could not do that, he gave vent to his feelings in his dislike of Wolsey.

He brushed the man out of his thoughts and had the Court searched for Francisco Felipez. He could not be found. It seemed that he had left England several days before.

*　　　*　　　*

The King sent for one of his secretaries, Dr. William Knight. This was a man whom he trusted and who had already shown himself a worthy ambassador, for Henry had often sent him abroad on state business.

William Knight was a man of some fifty years and Henry had chosen him for his wisdom and experience.

"Ah, my good William," said the King as soon as Dr. Knight entered his apartment, "you have been in my service many years, and I have great faith in you; that is why I now assign to you the most important task of your life."

William Knight was surprised. He stammered: "Your Grace knows that whatever task is assigned to me I will perform with all my wits."

"We know it, William. That is why we are entrusting you with this matter. You are to leave at once for Rome, travelling through France of course."

"Yes, Your Grace."

"And when you reach Rome you must find some means of seeing the Pope. I wish this matter of the divorce to be hastened. I chafe with the delay. I wish you to ask the Pope to give Cardinal Wolsey the power to try our case here in England. And there is one other matter. As soon as the divorce is settled I shall marry—immediately. I consider it my duty to marry and I have chosen the Lady Anne Boleyn to be my wife."

William Knight did not answer. He had heard rumours of course. He knew that the Boleyn faction had great influence with the King, but had not realized that the matter had gone so far and that the King could possibly contemplate marriage with Thomas Boleyn's daughter while Wolsey was in France—not exactly negotiating for a marriage with the Princess Renée, but surely with this in mind.

"There is one matter," went on the King, "which gives me great concern. I fear there may be an obstacle to my union with the Lady Anne, owing to a relationship I once had with her sister, Mary. Because of the existing canon law a close relationship has been established between the Lady Anne and myself, and in order that this be removed there would have to be a dispensation from the Pope. Your mission in Rome is that you request the Pope, beside giving Wolsey permission to try the case, to give you the dispensation which would enable me to marry the Lady Anne with a free conscience.''

William Knight bowed. ''I will set out for Rome at once,'' he told the King, ''and serve Your Grace with all my heart and power.''

Henry slapped his secretary's shoulder.

''Begone, good William. I look to see you back ere long. Bring me what I wish and I'll not forget the service you have rendered. But, by God, make haste. I chafe against delay.''

\*　　　\*　　　\*

Wolsey had set out for France, travelling to the coast with even more than his usual pomp. His red satin robes, his tippet of sables, made him a dazzling figure in the midst of his brilliant cavalcade; he held himself erect and glanced neither to right nor left, because he knew that the looks of those who had gathered to see him pass would be hostile. At one time he would have scorned them; he did so no longer; he, the proud Cardinal, would have eagerly welcomed one kindly smile, would have been delighted with one friendly word.

He thought as he rode along that he was like a man climbing a mountain. He had come far over the grassy slopes which had been easy to scale; but now the top was in sight and he had to traverse the glacial surface to reach it. He had come so far that there was no going back; and he was on the treacherous ground where one false step could send him hurtling into the valley of degradation.

All about him were his servants in their red and gold livery. Where the crowd was thick his gentlemen ushers cried out: ''On, my lords and masters, on before. Make way for my Lord's Grace.''

Even he who had been wont to pass each day from York Place or Hampton to Westminster Hall in the greatest pomp had never travelled quite so magnificently as he did at this time. Now he rode as the King's vicar-general, and as he went through the City and over London bridge, through Kent on his way to the sea, he could not help wondering how many more such glorious journeys there would be for him; and what the next journey would be, and whether the people would come from their houses to watch Wolsey pass by.

Yet even though his heart was heavy with foreboding, he could enjoy this ostentatious display. Here he was the central figure among nine hundred horsemen, seated on his mule with its trappings of crimson velvet and stirrups of copper and gilt. In his hand he held an orange, the inside of which had been removed and replaced with unguents and vinegar which would be proof against the pestilential air. Delicately he sniffed it when he passed through the poor villages and from the corner of his eye saw the ragged men and women who had come out to stare at him. Before him were carried two enormous crosses of silver and two pillars, also of silver, the great seal of England and his Cardinal's hat, that all might realize that he was not merely the great Cardinal, as his red robes proclaimed him, but the Chancellor and the richest man in England—under the King.

He proposed to make two calls on his way to Dover. One should be at Rochester and the other at Canterbury, that he might confer with the Archbishops, Fisher and Warham. The King had commanded him to do this for Henry was unsure of those two. It was Warham who had wanted time to consider the findings of the court. If this had not been so, it might have been declared, before the news of the Sack of Rome reached London, that the marriage was invalid. As for Fisher, since he was the Queen's confessor, Henry suspected him of being the Queen's friend.

So the Cardinal halted at Rochester and there was received in the Bishop's palace.

When they were alone together Wolsey said tentatively that he believed the Bishop was not fully informed of the King's Secret Matter and that the King was eager that this should be remedied. He then went over the old ground to stress the suggestion made by the Bishop of Tarbes and the King's consequent misgivings.

Fisher listened gravely, and his compassion for the Queen was intensified by all he heard.

"I fear," said Wolsey, "that when His Grace broached the matter to the Queen she became hysterical, much to the King's displeasure."

"I am sorry to hear it," answered Fisher.

"As her confessor," Wolsey replied, "you might bring her to a mood of submission. His Grace feels that you have much influence with her and that you might remind her of the comfort to be found in a life of seclusion."

The Bishop nodded and, when the Cardinal had left him, he was on his knees for a long time praying for the Queen.

Then on to Canterbury to see Warham and to hint to him that Henry would expect no opposition to the divorce; and, sure that he was bringing Warham to the right state of mind, he continued on his way.

And so to France, there to pass through the countryside, to be gaped at and watched in silence as he proceeded along the road to Paris.

There was nothing lacking in the welcome given him by François and Louise. Pageants and balls were arranged for his pleasure; plays were enacted before him; and all of a greater wit and subtlety than those he was accustomed to witness at the Court of England. François insisted on showing him some of the fine building he was carrying out; building was one of the French King's passions and almost as important to him as the pursuit of women. Wolsey was enchanted by the superb architecture he saw in France, and dreamed of rebuilding some of his own residences in England. This made him think of Hampton Court which was no longer his and, because when he had been obliged to throw that mansion to the King it had been a gesture which marked the change in their relationship, he was depressed; and it occurred to him then that he would never be able to plan new additions to his palaces.

But his skill was still with him. He completed the treaty with France and gave a pledge that Mary should marry the Duc d'Orléans. As yet he could do little but hint of the King's marriage with the Princess Renée, because it was scarcely diplomatic to discuss the proposed marriage of a man who was not yet recognized as a bachelor in the eyes of the world. But François could understand a hint better than most; and naturally he was fully aware of the King's Secret Matter, and he gave hint for hint; he would welcome a marriage between the Princess Renée and the King of England, once the latter was free to take a wife.

Wolsey was resting at Compiègne when Dr. Knight caught up with him. The Cardinal was surprised to see his fellow countryman and received him warmly, eager to know on what business he had come to France.

Dr. Knight had received no instructions not to inform Wolsey of his mission; he believed that the Cardinal was perfecting the more difficult negotiations with François while he, Knight, had the simpler task—for it would be simple once he could reach the Pope—of requesting the required dispensation and asking permission for Wolsey to conduct the enquiry into the divorce.

When the two men were alone together, Knight explained: "The King decided, soon after you had left, that he would send me to Rome. I am now on my way there."

Wolsey was startled and depressed. If the King was not keeping him informed of all the measures he was taking, it was a bad sign.

"What is your mission in Rome?" he asked, hoping to sound casual.

"In the first place to get the permission of His Holiness for you to try the case."

Wolsey gave a great sigh of relief. It was reasonable that such a request should not come from him personally, and he immediately saw the point of the King's engaging Knight for this commission.

"And in the second place?" he asked.

"Oh . . . a simple matter. The King's conscience worries him regarding a previous connection with Mary Boleyn."

"With Mary Boleyn!"

"It seems the girl was his mistress at one time."

"And his conscience worries him . . ."

"I confess I was a little surprised. It is true that family has been giving itself airs of late but I did not know the King was infatuated so much as to consider marriage."

"Please explain," said Wolsey calmly.

"Since the King proposes to marry Anne Boleyn he requires a dispensation on account of his sexual conduct with her sister."

Wolsey was speechless for a few seconds. Somewhere close by a bell began to toll, and it seemed to him that the bell tolled for Cardinal Wolsey.

He soon recovered his poise. He was eager that Knight should not guess how deep the rift was between him and the King.

"The King's conscience is ever active," he said lightly.

"He is cautious now—eager that when he marries again it shall be a true marriage and that he runs no risk of offending the Deity and thus be deprived of a male heir."

Wolsey nodded, eager to be alone with his thoughts.

When Knight had left him he sat for a long time staring before him. He had come to France, and one of his missions was to hint at a French marriage for the King. The King knew this. And yet . . . all the time they had discussed this matter together he had been contemplating marriage with Anne Boleyn.

"That black-eyed witch!" muttered Wolsey; and suddenly so much was clear to him. He knew why the King had slowly but certainly turned his back on him. Mistress Anne had commanded him to do so. Mistress Anne hated the Cardinal who had upbraided her as though she were a humble serving wench at the time when Percy had tried to marry her. Vengeance had blazed from those proud eyes and he had laughed, because he could not believe that he—the great Cardinal—had anything to fear from a foolish girl.

Now this girl was constantly at the King's side; she had bewitched him so completely that, unsuitable as the marriage was (and to think he had declared her not good enough for Percy!) he was determined to marry her. It was desire for this blackeyed girl, not his miserable conscience, that had set this matter in motion. And the most powerful person at Court was now Anne Boleyn, the declared enemy of the Cardinal.

It had happened under his very eyes and he had not seen it. He had been blind—he who had come so far because he had always seen a move ahead of all others. But he was old and tired now and he was afraid.

What now? he asked himself; and once more he heard the tolling of the bell.

He wanted to pray then, for help, for guidance.

I shall overcome this, as I have all other obstacles. I shall make this woman sorry that she proclaimed herself my enemy.

He seemed to hear mocking laughter, and he thought it sounded like Buckingham's laughter. Buckingham had lost his head; it had not been difficult to teach him a lesson, and he was one of the foremost noblemen in the land. Should he fear a woman —and one whose claims to nobility were slight?

No, he was not afraid.

Yet he wanted to pray and suddenly realized that he could not do so. All he could do was sink to his knees and talk of his fear, ask for the power to triumph over his enemies. But that did not seem like a prayer.

He rose. He would return to England and there he would see the King; and now there would be no secrets between them. He was no longer deceived by the King's attitude to the Lady which he had believed to be similar to that which he had felt towards many another.

This was different. This was something the King had never felt before, and it explained the change in their relationship.

Wolsey must tread very warily. Always before he had triumphed; why should he not triumph again?

Tomorrow he would leave for England, his mission completed. He would retire and after a good night's rest he would be refreshed.

U

He went to the window to look out on the peaceful scene below, and as he stood there he saw that someone had drawn a sketch on the woodwork with a piece of charcoal.

It was not pretty. There was a gallows and there was something lifelike about the figure which hung from it. The Cardinal's robes had been roughly but effectively sketched.

Who had done that? Someone in his suite? Someone who hated him and took a vicious delight in making such a sketch where, more likely than not, his eyes would alight on it.

The Cardinal took his kerchief and was about to rub it away. Then he hesitated. No. It would be a sign of weakness. Let it remain; let others see it. He was accustomed to abuse. It had always been his from the start of the climb, yet it had had little effect on his success. If it had not then, why should it now?

So he went to bed; but he slept ill that night. He dreamed of a black-eyed woman who, for the King's delight, was drawing charcoal sketches of a Cardinal swinging on the gallows.

*        *        *

The Queen's barge sailed from Greenwich to Richmond, and all along the banks the people stood cheering her as she passed. The Princess Mary was with Katharine; she could scarcely bear the girl to be out of her sight, and her greatest fear was that they would be separated.

"God bless the Queen!" shouted the people. "God bless the Princess Mary!"

Katharine acknowledged their greetings and the Princess did the same. It was comforting to go among these people, for everywhere they showed their pleasure in her. Henry might talk in hushed tones of his Secret Matter, but he was the only one who believed it was a secret, and the King's desire for a divorce was discussed in every tavern along the river. Almost without exception the people were on the side of the Queen. The women were fierce in championing her cause.

"A pretty state of affairs," they grumbled, "when a man tires of his wife and says she is not his wife that he may be free to choose a younger woman. If this is marriage, then save us from it!"

Since Queen Katharine had come to England, the English had felt the Spaniards to be their friends, and their natural enemies the French; some believed the latter to be a species of monkey and that many of them had tails which their fine clothes hid.

And the villain behind it all was the Cardinal. They had always hated the Cardinal. "Who was the Cardinal?" they had often asked each other. "No better than you or I. Did you know his father was a butcher?"

Who imposed taxes to fight wars which no one wanted? The Cardinal.

Who lived like a king although he was the son of a butcher? Who made treaties with France because France paid him well to do so? Who was responsible for all the poverty in the country? Who chopped off the head of the noble Duke of Buckingham because he had thrown dirty water over his shoes? The answer to all these questions was Wolsey.

They thought of him as they had seen him so many times, riding through the streets on his mule which was caparisoned in scarlet and gold, sniffing his orange as though he disdained them and feared contamination with them.

The King has been led astray by him. The King was jovial, fond of sport; the King was young and easily led. Wolsey had wanted to make an alliance with the French, so he had made the King doubt the validity of his marriage to Katharine of Aragon; and the Princess Mary—the dear little Princess Mary—was proclaimed a bastard!

"Long live Queen Katharine!" cried the people. "Queen Katharine for ever!"

To the barge came the sound of singing and Katharine took heart as she heard it, for it proclaimed the love of the people for the Princess Mary whom they regarded as the heir to the throne.

> *"Yea, a Princess whom to describe*
> *It were hard for an orator.*
> *She is but a child in age,*
> *And yet she is both wise and sage—*
> *And beautiful in flavour.*
>
> *Perfectly doth she represent*
> *The singular graces excellent*
> *Both of her father and mother.*
> *Howbeit, this disregarding,*
> *The carter of York is meddling*
> *For to divorce them asunder."*

In that song was not only their love of their Princess and their determination to support Katharine's cause but their hatred of Wolsey, Archbishop of York, whom they sometimes referred to as a carter, sometimes a butcher.

"Long live the Princess Mary!" cried the people; and Mary lifted a hand in acknowledgment of the greeting and smiled in her eager but dignified way which never failed to please them.

And so they came to the oddly shaped turrets of Richmond which glowed in the sunshine like inverted pears.

In the quiet of her apartments Bishop Fisher was waiting for Katharine who had summoned him thither.

"My lord," she said, when they were alone, "it pleases me that you have come. I have need of your counsel."

"I pray Your Grace to calm yourself. Wolsey visited me on his way to the coast. He told me how distressed you were after your interview with the King."

"I fear I lost control."

"We must pray for greater control."

"Sometimes I could hope that death would come to me."

"When we die, Your Grace, is a matter for God to decide."

"I know it is wrong of me, but there are times when I feel that life is too bitter to be borne."

"And you pray that this cup might pass from you," murmured the Bishop. "There is one, Your Grace, who needs you now. You must not forget that this matter concerns your daughter."

"It is that which breaks my heart."

"We are not defeated yet."

"My lord, you say *we*. Does that mean that you will stand beside me?"

"I will pray with you and for you."

She looked at him searchingly. "I have always felt you to be my friend as well as my confessor. I know you to be a good man. But I am well acquainted with the King's nature. He is a boy at heart, but boys can be selfish, my lord Bishop. They stretch out greedy hands for that which they want, and because they are boys, lacking the experience of suffering, they do not think what pain may be caused to those who stand in their way."

The Bishop looked at her sadly. He believed she did not understand her husband if she thought of him merely as a boy who had been led into temptation. The Bishop had looked at the King and seen the cruelty behind the jovial mask. He prayed that this gentle woman would never be forced to see her husband in a different light from the one in which she saw him now.

"You will need courage," said the Bishop. "Let us pray for courage."

They prayed and when they rose from their knees the Queen said: "I shall not go into a convent. That is what they are trying to force me to do."

"It is what they hope you will do."

"I know. But I shall never do it. There is my daughter to fight for; and let me tell you this, my lord Bishop: I shall never agree to be put aside, and the reason is that, if I did so, they would brand my daughter with bastardy. That is something I shall never allow to happen."

John Fisher bowed his head. He believed that the Queen's decision was the right one and a brave one. He had seen the vicious determination in the King's face; he had seen the shrewd cunning in Wolsey's. Could this gentle woman defend herself against them; and what would be the result to herself . . . and to those who supported her?

She had made her choice and he knew that she would not diverge from it. John Fisher too made his choice.

She would not have many friends when the King abandoned her; but he, John Fisher, Bishop of Rochester, would be one of them.

\*     \*     \*

The Queen was delighted when Mendoza brought her the news.

"Felipez did his work well," he said. "I have heard from the Emperor, and he sends notes for you and for the King. I know that His Grace was not pleased with his, as it reproved him for his treatment of you and expressed shock and indignation."

The Queen clasped her hands together. "I knew I could trust Charles," she cried. "He is immersed in his wars, but when a matter of vital importance arises, such as this, he would always stand by his family. His support will make all the difference in the world."

"I am in agreement with Your Grace," said Mendoza. "And we should not forget that the Pope, without whom the marriage cannot be declared invalid, is at your nephew's mercy. Here is the letter he sends to you."

Katharine took it eagerly and as she read it a smile of triumph touched her lips.

Charles was horrified; he was shocked beyond measure. It would seem that the King of England had forgotten, so long had his wife been in England, that she was a daughter of the House of Spain. He was sending Cardinal Quiñones, the General of the Franciscans, to Rome with all speed; he would look after her affairs there; and she could trust her nephew to watch over her cause and help her. Clement VII, still in Castel Sant' Angelo, was too wise a man to flout the wishes of the Emperor.

Katharine put her lips to the letter. "God bless you, Charles," she murmured. "Families should stand together always."

She felt the tears touch her eyes, for she was reminded suddenly of Charles's mother, running wildly round the nursery in the days when they were children, trying to quarrel with her sisters and brother; and their mother drawing the rebellious child to her and explaining that sisters and brothers should never quarrel; they must always stand together against the rest of the world if need be.

Oh to be a child again! thought Katharine. Oh to be back there in Madrid, in Granada, in Valladolid . . . under the loving wing of that best and wisest of mothers . . . never to grow up, never to leave the nest!

Then she thought of her own daughter. Had she remained a child herself she would never have had Mary.

She laughed at her folly. She should feel exultant because Charles had answered her cry for help.

\*        \*        \*

The Cardinal had returned to England, and, hearing that the King was in residence at Greenwich, he sent his messenger to the Palace to tell Henry of his arrival and ask where His Grace would wish to receive him.

Henry was in good spirits when the messenger arrived; a pageant was being enacted before him and it had been the work of Anne Boleyn, her brother George and some of the bright young poets who were members of their set. Henry was finding these young people far more to his taste than the older men and women. Moreover Anne was the leader of the group, and where Anne was, there Henry wished to be.

Anne, imperious in her beauty and fully aware of the hold she had over the King, bold, flamboyant and arrogant, had already taken upon herself the role of Queen which she expected shortly to be hers in fact. She seemed to delight in shocking those about her by taking such liberties that the King would never have tolerated from anyone else and yet meekly accepted when coming from her.

So when the messenger asked where and when His Grace would wish to receive the newly returned Cardinal, it was Anne who answered in her sprightly way: "Where should the Cardinal come except where the King is?"

There was a breathless silence. Would the King endure such boldness even from her? Was she suggesting that the Cardinal—still the greatest of the King's ministers—should come into the ballroom, travel-stained as he must be? Was she ordering him to come in as though he were some lackey?

Apparently in the King's eyes she could do no wrong, for he laughed aloud and said: "That's true enough!" and repeated: "Where should the Cardinal come except where the King is?"

"Your Grace will receive him here!" said Wolsey's messenger, aghast.

"You heard His Grace's command," answered Anne sharply.

So the messenger bowed himself from their presence and went to Wolsey who, with the stains of travel on his red satin robes and sweat on his brow, a little breathless from the journey, very weary, hoping for a little time in which to bathe himself, change his linen and rest awhile that he might collect his thoughts and frame his conversation with the King, listened in astonishment.

"To go straight to his presence! You have not heard aright," he insisted.

"Your Eminence, it is the King's command, given through the Lady Anne, that you should go to him at once."

The Lady Anne! So she was with him. She was already the Queen of England in all but name. And that would come, for the King demanded it. And he, poor fool, had helped to sow the seeds of that desire for divorce in the fickle mind; he, who had had dreams of a French alliance, a permanent bulwark against the Emperor, had helped to bring the Lady Anne—his most bitter enemy—to where she now stood.

He could do nothing but obey; so, weary, conscious of his unkempt appearance, he went into the ballroom and made his way to the King.

It was as he had feared. There stood the King, and beside him the Lady Anne. The others had moved away leaving the three of them together.

"Your Grace . . . my lady . . ."

The King's eyes were not unkind; but they showed he was absentminded; their blue was shining with pleasure in his companion, desire for her; even as they stood, his hand caressed her shoulder.

And she smiled at Wolsey—the enemy's smile, the smile of one who inflicts humiliation and rejoices. It was as if she were saying to him: Do you remember Anne Boleyn who was not good enough for Percy? Do you remember how you berated her as though she were some slut from the kitchens? This is the same Anne Boleyn who now stands beside the King, who says, You shall come to us now! and whom you dare not disobey.

"I trust you have good news for us, Thomas," said the King.

"The mission went well, Your Grace."

But Henry scarcely saw his minister. Good news meant for him one thing. When could he go to bed with this woman, accompanied by a good conscience?

This was a more dangerous moment than any the Cardinal had yet passed through; he felt now as he had felt when he had heard the bell's tolling at Compiègne, when he had seen the charcoal drawing of a Cardinal hanging on the gallows. No, his apprehension went deeper than that.

He knew that this day there were two people in England who were in acute danger. And if one of these was Katharine the Queen, the other was Cardinal Wolsey.

## CHAPTER VII

# THE KING PENITENT

THROUGH the winter which followed, Katharine tried to ignore her fears. She continued to live much as she had lived before; her days were made up of sewing, reading, prayers, listening to music and playing an occasional game of cards with her maids.

There was one of these maids of honour who commanded her attention; she could no longer be blind to the position of Anne Boleyn in the Court. At the centre of all the tourneys and masques was this woman, and her constant companions were her brother, Thomas Wyatt and some of the other bright men of the younger artistic set. They wrote plays and pageants which they acted for the King's pleasure; and it was, during those fateful winter days, as though there were two groups—one which revolved round the Queen and the other round Anne; it was in Anne's that the King was to be found.

Often Katharine would absent herself from some entertainment because her dignity would not allow her to see the King treating Anne Boleyn as though she were already the Queen.

She herself did not show by her demeanour that she regarded this woman as different from any other of her maids of honour; she made herself seem blind to the fact that the King was chafing against his marriage to her and made no secret of his desire for Anne.

As for Anne, imperious as she might be to all others, including the King, she was subdued by the dignity of the Queen; and because of Katharine's restraint there were no difficult scenes between them. Henry avoided his wife as much as possible; they shared no part of their private life. He had said that he regarded himself as a bachelor and that while he deplored the necessity of waiting until he was publicly announced to be that, nothing could prevent him from regarding himself as one.

Only once did Katharine show that she knew Anne was trying to usurp her position; that was during a game of cards. Anne had dealt, and Katharine said: "My Lady Anne, you have good hap to stop at a king; but you are not like others, you will have all or none."

Anne had seemed a little shaken by this comment and had played her hand badly, but Katharine remained serene, and those who watched said: "She believes that the King will come to his senses, that he will realize it is impossible for him to cast her off."

Yet that evening when she was alone she thought of the imperious young beauty, with her flashing dark eyes and her exotic clothes, her grace, her manner of holding herself as though she already wore a crown on her head, and she dared not look too far into the future.

Sometimes she felt so alone. There was her daughter who meant everything to her, but she did not care to speak to Mary of this trouble. She hoped that Mary knew nothing of it; the child was too sensitive.

As long as we are together, she told herself, I suppose I can endure anything. But I shall stand out firmly against a convent, for Mary's sake.

She considered those who might help her. Mendoza would stand beside her but he was only an ambassador and no theologian. His word would carry little weight in this country. Warham was an honest man, but he was old and very much in awe of Wolsey and the King. The women who had been her friends had been sent away from her. How comforting it would have been to have talked with Maria de Salinas! Luis Vives had left England after having been told sharply by Wolsey that he would be wise not to meddle in the King's affairs. Vives was a scholar who was eager to avoid conflict, so perhaps he had thought it as well to leave while he could do so.

Thomas More came to see her. He did not speak of what was known as the King's Secret Matter, but managed to convey to her the assurance that he was her friend.

John Fisher, to whom she confessed her sins, also came and brought comfort.

U*

"I have been warned," he told her, "not to meddle in the King's matter, but if I can be of use to Your Grace I shall continue to disobey those orders."

"I thank God for your friendship," Katharine told him.

"Let us pray for courage," answered the Bishop; and they prayed together.

Often during those winter months when her spirits were at their lowest, she thought of Fisher and More, and felt happier because they were not far away, and although they might not have much influence in this matter with the King, they were her friends.

With the spring came news from Rome. The Pope had appointed Lorenzo Campeggio, Cardinal of Santa Anastasia, to come to England to decide the case in conjunction with Cardinal Wolsey.

\*          \*          \*

There was consternation at Court. It was June and the heat was oppressive. One day a man walking by the river suddenly fell and lay on the bank and, when certain passers-by paused to see what ailed him, it was clear that he was a victim of the sweating sickness.

The same day several more people died in the streets; the epidemic had come to London.

Periodically this scourge returned, killing people in their thousands, and when it appeared in the big cities such as London it brought panic with it for it was in the hot and fetid streets that the sickness was more quickly passed from one to another.

Henry was disturbed when the news was brought to him. He was at Greenwich and he decided that he would stay there for a few days and not journey to Westminster through the infected city even by barge.

It was his gentleman of the bedchamber, William Carey, who had brought him the news. He had been gracious to Will Carey because Anne expected him to be so to all her relations, and Will was in need of advancement, having very little money of his own. Moreover Henry was not displeased to favour the man, for he still thought affectionately of Will's wife Mary, although he now heartily wished that she had never been his mistress, since there was a possibility that this might make it necessary for him to procure a dispensation on her account.

"The sweat is claiming more victims, Your Grace," said Will. "I saw several people lying in the streets as I came through the city."

The King's eyes narrowed. "I do not know," he said gloomily, "why this pestilence should visit my country every now and then. I do believe that there are some of my subjects who are of the opinion that it is sent to us when we have in some way offended God."

"Ah, it may be so, Your Grace."

Will was thinking that the King referred to his living in sin with Katharine and, because Mary had told him that they must always stand by Anne who had stood by them so magnificently, he added: "It may be that when your Grace's matter is settled the sickness will pass."

"It may well be, it may well be," murmured the King.

But he was uneasy. He had ceased to co-habit with Katharine these many months, so he could no longer be said to be living in sin; it was strange that God should have sent the sweat now that he had realized his sinful way of life and was seeking to rectify it.

In common with most he believed that pestilences were a sign of Divine anger. Then, in spite of his desire to break away from Katharine, God had sent a pestilence to his Kingdom.

His expression was sullen, and Will, who by living near to him had learned when to remain silent, said no more. Indeed Will himself was experiencing a strange shivering fit which had nothing to do with being in the presence of the King. When Henry had strolled to the window and stood looking out on the river accompanied by certain of his gentlemen, Will seized the opportunity to leave the royal apartments.

Before he had time to reach his own quarters he felt the dreaded sweat on his body.

\* \* \*

"Your Grace, the sweat is in the Palace."

Henry heard the dreaded words and stared at the man who was speaking to him.

"One of Your Grace's gentlemen has succumbed to the sickness. He is dead."

Henry shouted: "Who?"

"Will Carey, Your Grace."

Will Carey! He had been speaking to the man only a few hours before.

Henry was trembling. "Leave me," he said.

Will Cary dead! Will was a man whom he had favoured because of his relationship to Anne. And he was the first victim in the Palace, the King's own Palace.

Mary would be left a widow with her two young children, and Anne would be seeking help for her ere long, for she was ever zealous regarding the needs of her family.

But even as he thought of Anne his terror caught up with him. Now he must face the truth. Why was he seeking to rid himself of Katharine? Was it indeed because he feared he had lived in sin all these years, or was it because he was tired of Katharine and wanted a new wife?

He half closed his eyes and set his mouth into the familiar prim lines, but he could not hold that expression because he was thinking of Anne, Anne in black velvet, in scarlet and gold, Anne stretching out her arms to him, no longer holding him off. It was no use; there were times when even he could not deceive himself.

He sent for Wolsey; he believed then that in times of peril he would always send for Wolsey.

The Cardinal came from Hampton in his barge. He made no concessions to the plague, beyond the orange which he carried more as an elegant gesture than out of fear. Wolsey had little concern for the sweat; he had other and more pressing matters with which to occupy himself.

"We are deeply disturbed by this pestilence," said the King. "It seems that the Almighty is displeased with us."

The Cardinal asked: "For what reason does Your Grace think God is displeased?"

"I will admit," answered the King, "that I have thought with much eagerness of my approaching marriage."

Wolsey looked grim. Let the King's conscience worry him. It was well that it should. If he lusted after Anne Boleyn, let him regard that as a sin.

"That may well be," said Wolsey.

The King looked startled, but the Cardinal's expression was as gloomy as his own.

"It is true that I am not in actual fact married to Katharine," went on the King almost defiantly.

Wolsey spread his hands. "Perhaps, Your Grace, it would be well, until we have proved that the marriage with the Lady Katharine is no true marriage, if Your Grace continued to live the life of a bachelor."

A hot flush spread itself across Henry's features as he muttered: "I have heard Mass each day . . . more than once. I have confessed each day . . ."

"None knows Your Grace's piety better than I, but it may be that is not enough."

"Not . . . enough!"

"It may be that it would be wise at this stage to send the Lady Anne back to her father's castle."

Henry looked so angry for a few moments that Wolsey felt he had gone too far. But after a while the King nodded. He was clearly very frightened.

"Mayhap you are right," he said.

An easy victory, thought the Cardinal; and that day the Lady Anne Boleyn was sent to her father's castle at Hever.

As for Henry, he changed his mode of life. He made several wills; he was often in the Queen's company when they conversed like good friends, and he would sit with her watching her at her tapestry; when she went to a religious service in the chapel, he would accompany her and none appeared to be more devout than the King. It would seem that he had dismissed Anne Boleyn and returned to the Queen in all but one respect; he would not share her bed.

How virtuously he lived during those hot summer weeks! Soon after Carey's death he insisted that the Court leave Greenwich, and first they went to Eltham and then farther away from the City. Henry kept his physicians beside him; he was in terror that he might become a victim of the sickness.

He made Dr. Butts talk to him of plasters and lotions which might serve, in less severe cases, to save the lives of victims. His greatest pleasure was to concoct these cures with the doctor, and he even made a plaster of his own and gave the recipe to apothecaries that they might make it for their customers. It was said to be efficacious in mild cases and was known as The King's Own Plaster.

Still further news came of death. When his old friend Sir William Compton died, Henry was deeply distressed. He remembered how, on his first illness, after his return from France, when an ulcer had appeared on his leg, he and Compton had made plasters together, for Compton had also suffered with an ulcer.

And now . . . Compton was a victim of the sweat!

The Cardinal, who was so busy with his affairs at Hampton, was surprised by the King's conscience which insisted that at this time he part with Anne Boleyn by sending her home to Hever while he himself posed as a virtuous husband to Katharine, although not sharing her bed. Wolsey wondered whether Henry admitted to himself that he avoided this because he found her unattractive or whether he told himself that he still believed she was not his wife.

But although he had sent Anne away, Henry wrote loving

letters to her, erotic letters, telling her of his need of her, hinting at what the future held for them both. As though God, being so busy watching him at confession and Mass, did not see the sly little notes which were sent behind His back.

At one time the Cardinal might have rejoiced in this characteristic of the King's; now he knew how dangerous it might prove. So Wolsey was one who was too concerned with his own affairs to be worried by the possibility of death through the sweating sickness.

Nor was Katharine afraid. If death came she would be ready to welcome it, for life had little to offer her. Many people were dying, and accounts of deaths came every day, but she had few friends to lose. She thanked God that Maria de Salinas was in the country far from risk of infection, and Margaret Pole was with Mary who had also been sent out of danger.

Meanwhile the King lived his ostentatiously virtuous life and longed for the epidemic to pass.

But one day there came news from Hever which threw the King into a panic: Anne was a victim of the sweating sickness.

Henry threw aside his penitence and sat down at once to write a letter to her.

Her news had made him desolate. He would willingly share her sufferings. He could not send her his first physician because the man was absent at this time and he feared delay, so he was sending her his good Dr. Butts. She must be guided by Dr. Butts. He longed for her, and to see her again would be greater comfort to him than all the most precious jewels in the world.

Then he settled himself to wait. It was no use. He could no longer pretend. He could no longer sit with the Queen and listen to her conversation; he had to face the truth. He wanted Anne. He would have Anne.

So his conscience—on which he could almost always rely to do what was required of it—began greatly to trouble him once more concerning his marriage with his brother's widow. If the sickness had been a sign of God's anger, that anger was the result of his living in sin with Katharine, and the sooner he was free of her the better pleased would he—and God—be. Why was that Cardinal Campeggio taking such a long time to arrive? Wolsey was a laggard. Why had he not arranged matters better than this?

He waited for news from Hever. He could think of nothing but his need of her. And when that news came, and it was good news, he was full of joy for many days, taking it that, since his darling's life was spared, this was a sign of heavenly approval for their union.

He no longer sat with Katharine; there was no longer need to confess so regularly, to pray so long.

The sickness was abating; Anne had recovered; soon she would be with him.

But where was Campeggio? And what was the sluggish Wolsey doing to bring him his heart's desire?

<br>

CHAPTER VIII

## THE MARRIAGE BRIEF

CARDINAL LORENZO CAMPEGGIO arrived in London in October. It was three months since he had set out from Rome, and he had been expected long before. Wolsey received him at York Place where he arrived inconspicuously, much to Wolsey's disgust, for even now, anxious as he was, he hated to miss an opportunity of giving the people a display of his magnificence. Wolsey would have preferred to go out with his household about him—his silver crosses, his pillars of silver, his seal and his Cardinal's hat—and to have a ceremonial meeting with his fellow Cardinal in public.

Campeggio had other ideas and had kept his arrival a secret until he came quietly to York Place.

Wolsey embraced him and gave orders for apartments to be made ready for the distinguished visitor. "The best we have to offer. Your Eminence, we have long awaited this pleasure."

Campeggio winced as Wolsey took his hands. "I suffer agonies from the gout," he told his host; and indeed it was obvious that he spoke the truth. When Wolsey looked into that pale face with the lines of pain strongly marked on it, he assured himself that here was a man who would not be difficult to lead. Surely one who suffered as Campeggio did would be more concerned with resting his weary limbs than fighting Katharine's battle.

"We shall do our utmost to make you comfortable here," Wolsey told him; "and we shall put the best physicians at your service."

"There is little physicians can do for me," mourned Campeggio. "My friend, there are days when I am in such pain that I cannot bear the light of day. Then I ask nothing but to lie in a dark room and that no one should come near me."

"Yours must have been a grievously painful journey."

Campeggio lifted his shoulders despairingly. "There were times when it was impossible for me to ride; even travelling in a litter was too much for me. Hence the delay."

Wolsey was not so foolish as to believe that Campeggio's gout was the only reason for the delay. He guessed that the Pope, in his very delicate position, would not be eager to proclaim the marriage of the Emperor's aunt invalid. Clearly Clement was playing for time. Campeggio's gout had been very useful; and doubtless would be in the future.

"The King," Wolsey told Campeggio ,"is most eager to have this matter settled."

"So I believe." Campeggio shook his head sadly. "It is not good for the Church," he went on. "Whatever the outcome, His Holiness will not feel easy in his mind."

"But if the King's marriage is no marriage . . ."

"His Holiness is horrified at the thought that the King of England and the Infanta of Spain may have been living in sin for eighteen years."

"It should not be a difficult matter," insisted Wolsey, "to prove that owing to the Queen's previous marriage, that with the King cannot be legal."

"I cannot agree," Campeggio retorted. "It may well prove a most difficult matter."

Wolsey understood then that the Pope was not going to grant a divorce, because he was too much in awe of the Emperor; and Wolsey believed that Clement had sent Campeggio, who was as much an expert in vacillation as he was himself, to conduct the case with very definite orders that nothing must be settled in a hurry, and before any decision was reached the Vatican must be informed.

The King would be infuriated by the delay, and if he were disappointed in the manner in which the case was conducted, he would blame Wolsey.

*       *       *

When Campeggio had recovered from the strain of his journey, he went, accompanied by Wolsey, to Greenwich to see the King.

Henry received him with outward cordiality but inward suspicions. He did not like the appearance of Campeggio—the Legate was unhealthy; he looked pale and tired; his limbs were swollen with the gout which had so lengthened his journey across France. Could not Clement have sent a healthy man! the King grumbled to himself. Moreover there was a shrewd look in the fellow's eyes, a certain dignity which Henry believed was meant to remind him that he was a servant of the Pope and served no other.

By God, thought the King, there has been delay enough.

"Welcome, welcome," he said; and bade Campeggio be seated with Wolsey beside him.

When Henry had offered condolences for the Legate's sufferings he plunged into the real reasons for his being in England.

"There has been much delay," he said, "and I wish the proceedings to begin at once."

"As soon as possible," murmured Campeggio. "But I would like to say that if we could settle this matter without much noise it would please His Holiness."

"I care not how it is settled, provided it *is* settled," said the King.

"His Holiness begs Your Grace to consider the effect of a divorce on your subjects."

Wolsey watching closely saw the danger signals leap up in the King's eyes. He said quickly: "His Holiness has no need to ask His Grace to do that. His Grace's one great concern is the wellbeing of his subjects, and it is for their good that he seeks freedom from this alliance which has proved a barren one."

Henry threw a grateful glance at his Chancellor.

"Then," went on Campeggio, "I am sure I have an acceptable solution. His Holiness will examine the dispensation made by his predecessor, Julius II, and adjust it, making a new dispensation in which there can be no manner of doubt that the marriage between Henry Tudor and Katharine of Aragon is lawful."

Wolsey dared not look at the King because he knew that Henry would be unable to contain his rage.

"So I have waited three months to hear that!" spluttered Henry. "It may well be that I know more of this matter than any other person. I have grappled with my conscience, and it tells me this: never . . . never . . . shall I find favour in the sight of God while I continue to live with a woman who is not my wife in His eyes."

"Your Grace knows more of the matter than any theologian, it seems," said Campeggio with a faint smile.

"That is so!" thundered Henry. "And all I want of you is a decision whether or not that marriage is valid."

Campeggio, who had a wry sense of humour, murmured: "I gather that what Your Grace wishes is a decision that the marriage is *not* valid."

"His Grace has suffered much from indecision," added Wolsey.

"The indecision of others," retorted Campeggio. "I see that there is no uncertainty in his mind. Now His Holiness is most eager that there should be an amicable settlement of this grievous matter, and my first duty will be to see the Queen and suggest to her that she retire into a convent. If she would do this and renounce her marriage, His Holiness would then without delay declare the marriage null and void. It would be her choice, and none could complain of that."

Henry's anger was a little appeased. If Katharine would but be sensible, how simply this matter could end. What was her life outside convent walls that she could not make this small sacrifice? She could live inside a convent in much the same manner as she did outside. It seemed to him a little thing to ask.

"She might be told," he suggested, "that if she will retire to a convent, her daughter shall not suffer but shall be next in succession after my legitimate male heirs. There, you see how I am ready to be reasonable. All I ask is that she shall slip quietly away from Court into her convent."

"I will put this matter to her," replied Campeggio. "It is the only solution which would please the Holy Father. If she should refuse . . ."

"Why should she refuse?" demanded Henry. "What has she to lose? She shall have every comfort inside convent walls as she does outside."

"She would have to embrace a life of celibacy."

"Bah!" cried the King. "She has embraced that for several months. I tell you this: I have not shared her bed all that time. Nor would I ever do so again."

"Unless of course," murmured Campeggio rather slyly, "His Holiness declared the marriage to be a true one."

The King's anger caught him off his guard. "Never! Never! Never!" he cried.

Campeggio smiled faintly. "I see that an angel descending from Heaven could not persuade you to do what you have made up your mind not to do. My next duty is to see the Queen."

\*          \*          \*

Katharine received the two Cardinals in her apartments where Campeggio opened the interview by telling her that he came to advise her to enter a convent. Wolsey, watching her closely, saw the stubborn line of her mouth and knew that she would not give way without a struggle.

"I have no intention of going into a convent," she told him.

"Your Grace, this may be a sacrifice which is asked of you,

but through it you would settle a matter which gives great distress to many people."

"Distress?" she said significantly. "To whom does it bring greater distress than to me?"

"Do you remember what happened in the case of Louis XII? His wife retired to a convent and so made him free to marry again."

"I do not intend to follow the example of others. Each case is different. For myself I say that I am the King's wife, and none shall say that I am not."

"Does Your Grace understand that unless you comply with this request there must be a case which will be tried in a court?" Wolsey asked.

She turned to Wolsey. "Yes, my lord Cardinal, I understand."

"If you would take our advice . . ." began Wolsey.

"Take your advice, my lord? I have always deplored your voluptuous way of life, and I know full well that when you hate you are as a scorpion. You hate my nephew because he did not make you Pope. And because I am his aunt you have turned your venom on me, and I know that it is your malice which has kindled this fire. Do you think I would take advice from you?"

Wolsey turned to Campeggio and his expression said: You see that we have a hysterical woman with whom to deal.

"Your Grace," interposed Campeggio, "I would tell you that, if you allow this case to be tried in the light of day, it may well go against you, in which event your good name would suffer grievous damage."

"I should rejoice if this case were brought into the light of day," replied Katharine, "for I have no fear of the truth."

Campeggio's hope of an easy settlement of this matter was fast evaporating. The King was determined to separate from the Queen; and the Queen, in her way, was as stubborn as the King.

He still did not abandon hope of forcing her into a convent. If he could get her to admit that her marriage with Arthur had been consummated, he believed he could persuade her to go into a convent. He had summed up her character. She was a pious woman and would never lie in the confessional even though, for her daughter's sake, she might do so outside it.

He said: "Would Your Grace consider confessing to me?"

She did not hesitate for a moment. "I should be happy to do so."

Campeggio turned to Wolsey who said immediately: "I will take my leave."

He went back with all haste to the King to tell him what had taken place at the interview; and Campeggio and Katharine went into the Queen's private chamber that she might confess to him.

When she knelt the Legate from Rome asked the fatal question: "Your Grace was married to Prince Arthur for some six months, from November until April; did you never during that time share a bed with the Prince?"

"Yes," answered Katharine, "I did."

"On how many occasions?"

"We slept together only seven nights during those six months."

"Ah," said Campeggio, "and would you tell me that not once during those seven nights . . ."

Katharine interrupted: "Always he left me as he found me—a virgin."

"And this you swear in the name of God the Father, the Son and the Holy Ghost?"

"This I swear," said Katharine emphatically.

He sighed, knowing that she spoke the truth; the gout was beginning to nag and he longed for the peace of a dark room. He could see that this case was not going to be settled without a great deal of trouble; nothing, he decided, must be settled quickly. The situation in Europe was fluid. It would go ill with him and the Holy Father if they granted Henry his wish and then found that the whole of Christendom was in the hands of the Emperor.

\*         \*         \*

Henry was furious when he learned of Katharine's determination not to go into a convent.

He summoned Wolsey, and the Chancellor came apprehensively, wondering in what mood he would find the King. He was not kept long in doubt. Henry was striding up and down his apartment, his little eyes seeming almost to disappear in the folds of puffy flesh; an unhealthy tinge of purple showed in his cheeks.

"So the Queen will not go into a convent!" he roared. "She does this out of perversity. What difference could it make to her? As for your gouty companion, I like him not. I think the pair of you put your heads together and plot how best you can cheat me of my rights."

"Your Grace!"

"Ay!" said the King. "Cardinals! They fancy they serve the Pope." His eyes narrowed still further. "They shall discover that the Pope has no power to protect them from the wrath of a King!"

"Your Grace, I admit to sharing your disappointment in Campeggio. He seems to delight in delay. I have reasoned with him. I have told him of your Grace's wishes. I have reminded him that when the Holy Father was in distress he came to you, and how out of your benevolence . . ."

"'Tis so," interrupted the King. "I sent him money. And what good did it do? You advised it, Master Wolsey. You said: 'We will help him now and later he will help us.' Whom do you serve —your King or your Pope?"

"With all my heart and soul, with all the powers that God has given me, I serve my King."

The King softened slightly. "Then what are we to do, Thomas? What are we to do? How much longer must I go on in this sorry state?"

"When the case is heard, Your Grace, we shall have the decision of the court . . ."

"Presided over by that man . . . he has his orders from Clement, and I may not like those orders."

"Your Grace, you have your own Chancellor to fight for you."

"Ah, Thomas, if they had but let you try this case as I so wished!"

"Your Grace would have been free of his encumbrances ere now."

"I know it. I know it. But this waiting galls me. There are times when I think I am surrounded by enemies who plot against me."

"Clement is uncertain at this time, Your Grace. I hear that he is not enjoying good health. The Sack of Rome and his imprisonment have shocked him deeply. It may be that he will not be long for this world."

Henry looked at his Chancellor and suddenly he burst out laughing.

"Ha!" he cried. "If we had an English Pope there would not be all this trouble for the King of England; that's what you're thinking, eh Thomas?"

"An English Pope would never forget that he owed his good fortune to an English King."

Henry clapped his hand on Wolsey's shoulder.

"Well," he said, "we'll pray that Clement may see the light or . . . fail to see aught else. He's shaking in his shoes, that Holy Father of ours. He fears to offend Charles and he fears to offend me, so he sends his gouty old advocate and says: 'Do nothing . . . promise nothing . . . wait!' By God and all His saints, I cannot think how I endure him and his master's policy."

"We shall win our case, Your Grace. Have no fear of it. Remember that your Chancellor will sit with Campeggio, and while he is there Your Grace has the best advocate he could possibly procure."

"We shall find means of winning our case," said Henry darkly. "But it grieves me that the Queen should have so little regard for the fitness of this matter as to refuse our request. Why should she refuse to go into a convent! What difference could it make to her?" His eyes narrowed. "There are times when I wonder if she does this to spite me; and if she is so determined to do me harm, how can we know where such plans would stop? I have my enemies. It might be that they work against me in secret. If the Queen were involved with them in some plot against me . . ."

Henry fell silent. He could not continue even before his Chancellor; and to Wolsey his words and the secretive manner in which he said them were like a cold breeze on a hot summer's day. The climate of the King's favour was growing very uncertain.

Wolsey could not have much hope for the Queen's future peace if she did not comply with the King's desires. Perhaps she was unwise. Perhaps life in a convent, however abhorrent it seemed to her, would be preferable to what her life would be were she to arouse the full fury of the King's displeasure.

*       *       *

Since the Queen refused to enter a convent, Campeggio realized that there would have to be a court case; and as this was so it was impossible to deny Katharine the advisers who would be granted to any defendant in such circumstances.

Accordingly William Warham and John Fisher, Archbishops of Canterbury and Rochester respectively, were appointed her leading counsel; the Bishop of London, Cuthbert Tunstall and Henry Standish, Bishop of St. Asaph's, joined them with John Clerk, the Bishop of Bath and Wells. It was arranged that as the Queen was a foreigner she should not rely entirely on Englishmen for her defence, and Luis Vives and one of her confessors, Jorge de Athequa, were appointed with two Flemings. The Flemings and Vives were abroad, and it seemed unlikely that they would be of much use to her; and she was shrewd enough to know that, with the exception of John Fisher, those who had been chosen to support her cause would be in great fear of offending the King.

Preparations for the hearing were going forward and Campeggio looked on with some misgivings. His great plan was to postpone the hearing on any pretext whatsoever, as he dreaded being forced to give a judgment while the affairs of Europe were so unsettled. His gout provided him with a good excuse, and there were whole days when he shut himself in a darkened room while the servants assured all callers that he was too ill to see them.

One day when Katharine was with her chaplain, Thomas Abell, the priest said to her: "Your Grace, the Imperial ambassador desires urgent speech with you, and he wishes to come before you disguised as a priest as he is fearful that, if he comes undisguised, that which he has to say to you will be overheard."

Katharine was torn between her anger that she could not receive her nephew's ambassador without fear of being overheard, and apprehension as to what new schemes were afoot.

She looked at Thomas Abell, and wondered how far she could trust him. He had not been long in her service but she could say that during that time he had served her well. She decided that she had such need of friends that she must accept friendship when it was offered, without looking too suspiciously at it.

"He has asked my assistance in this matter," went on Thomas Abell, "and being eager to serve Your Grace I told him I would do what I could."

"Then bring him to me in my chapel," she said. "I will speak to him there."

So it was that Iñigo de Mendoza came to her robed as a priest, a hood concealing his features, and as, there in the chapel, he knelt beside her, she realized at once that he was deeply excited.

"Your Grace," he said, "the best of news! Do you remember a de Puebla who once served your father here in England?"

"I remember him well," Katharine answered. "He is long since dead."

"But his son who is now a chaplain lives, and he has found an important document among his father's papers."

"What document is this?"

"It is a brief of the same date as the Bull of Dispensation granted by Julius II, but this goes more deeply into the matter, and if we could lay our hands on the original—which is among the archives in Madrid—we could show without doubt that your marriage with the King is legal."

"You have this?"

"I have the copy of it which de Puebla has given me. I propose to put it into the hands of your defending counsel."

"Then pray do this," said the Queen.

"I trust none of them save Fisher and I am afraid that, as this case is being heard in England, there will be scarcely a man here who would stand against the wishes of the King. What we must work for is to have the case tried in Rome. Then we could hope for justice. At least we have this document, which I have brought to you. Your best plan would be to give it to Fisher. Tell him that it is but a copy and that the original is in Spain. I think we shall see some consternation among our enemies."

Katharine took the document and studied it. She was immediately aware of its importance and her spirits rose as Mendoza took his leave and left her in the chapel.

\*　　　\*　　　\*

The King, pacing up and down his apartment, stopped to glare at his Chancellor.

"It seems that everyone conspires against me! When is this hearing to take place? When am I to be granted my divorce? With others, these matters are settled in a matter of weeks. With me they must last for years. And why? Because those who should serve me, bestir themselves not at all."

The Cardinal's thoughts were miles away . . . in Rome. Heartening news had been brought to him a few days before. Clement had suffered a great shock, his health was declining, and it was believed that he could not recover.

Let this be granted to me, prayed the Cardinal. Here is the way out of danger, the path which will lead me to new power. My day is over in England. I am going down . . . down . . . The King grows tired of his Thomas Wolsey who once so pleased him, since Anne Boleyn pours poison into his ear. My great mistake was when I made an enemy of that woman. She will not believe that it was at the King's command that I berated her, that I told her she was not worthy to marry into the House of Northumberland. But she blames me; and she has determined to destroy me.

Once it might have been said: Thomas Wolsey's will is the King's will. That was no longer so, but it was true to say that that which Anne Boleyn desired, the King desired also, for at this time his one wish was to please her.

The woman was a witch. None other could so completely have bemused the King.

So he *must* become the new Pope. He prayed at every possible moment of the day, and often during sleepless nights, for this mercy. But he was not the man to trust to prayer. He had climbed high, he had often said to himself, through the actions of Thomas Wolsey rather than of God. Now Thomas Wolsey must continue to fight. He had asked François for his help, and François had promised to give it. But would the French King prove as unreliable as the Emperor? Wolsey had sent Gardiner to Rome with a list of Cardinals and bags of gold. No expense was to be spared, no bribe was to be considered too much. He would spend all he had to win at the next Conclave, because this time he knew he was not only fighting for power; he was fighting for his life.

So his thoughts wandered during the King's tirade, and fervently he hoped that soon he would be free of the unpredictable moods of the King of England.

But the King's next words were so startling that Wolsey's thoughts were diverted from his hopes of the next Conclave.

"This brief that is in the Queen's hands. We must get it. Warham tells me that it is worked out in such detail that it gives no shadow of a doubt that the marriage is a true one."

"This . . . brief?" murmured Wolsey.

The King was too excited to show his impatience. "Warham has brought this news. He says that through de Puebla's son this document has reached the Queen. It is enough to win the case for her."

Wolsey was alert. He had to remember that the Papal Crown was not yet his; Clement was not even dead; he must not lose his grip on the power he possessed in England. He must show himself as eager as he ever was to work for the King.

He asked a few searching questions and then he said: "But, Your Grace, this is not the original document. It is only a copy."

"But the original document is in Spain."

"First," went on the Chancellor, "we shall declare our belief that the paper which the Queen holds will be considered a forgery unless she produces the original. Therefore she must write immediately to the Emperor imploring him to forward the original to her here."

"And when it comes . . . if indeed it be as the copy?"

"It will come to her counsel," said Wolsey with a smile. "We shall not have any difficulty in laying our hands on it when it is in England."

Henry smiled slyly.

"And," went on Wolsey, "when it is in our possession . . ." He lifted his hands in a significant gesture. "But, Your Grace will see that we must get that brief, and our first step is to persuade the Queen to write to her nephew, urging him to send the document to her."

"I shall order her to do this without delay," said the King.

"Your Grace," Wolsey began tentatively and hesitated.

"Yes, yes?" said the King impatiently.

"It would be well if the Queen wrote on the advice of her

counsel. Allow me to send for Warham and Tunstall. They will not hesitate to obey Your Grace."

Henry nodded and his eyes were affectionate once more. By God, he thought, this man Wolsey has much skill. Then he frowned. He greatly wished that Anne did not dislike the Chancellor so. He had told her that Wolsey was working for them, but she would not believe it. He was her enemy, she said, whose great desire was to marry the King to a French Princess, and now that he knew the King would have none other than Anne Boleyn he sought to delay the divorce with all the means in his power.

There were times when Henry agreed with Anne; but when he was alone with his Chancellor he was sure she was wrong. He did wish that there was not this hatred between two for whom he had such regard.

"Do that," he commanded.

"We must watch Fisher," said Wolsey. "There is a man whom I do not trust to serve Your Grace."

"He's one of these saints!" cried the King. "I know full well his kind, that which declares: 'I would give my head for what I believe to be right.' Master Fisher should take care. He may one day be called on to prove his words. And now . . . send Warham and Tunstall to me. By God, we'll have that document in our hands before many weeks have passed. As for Master Campeggio, you may tell him this: If he delays much longer he will have to answer to me."

Wolsey bowed his head; he could not hide the smile which touched his lips. Campeggio cared not for the King of England, because he answered to one master only—a man who, in his own kingdom, was more powerful than any king.

It was pleasant to brood on Papal power.

Wolsey's lips were mocking; he was praying for the death of Clement and that the result of the next Conclave might bring him freedom from an exacting master and the utmost power in his own right.

\*       \*       \*

Katharine received her advisers and as they stood in a semi-circle about her she looked at each man in turn: Warham, Fisher, Tunstall, Clerk and Standish. They were eagerly explaining to her what she must do and Warham was their spokesman.

"It is clear, Your Grace, that the copy of this document cannot be accepted as of any importance. We must have the original. And we know full well that its contents are of the utmost importance to Your Grace's case."

"Do you suggest that I should write to the Emperor, asking for it?"

"It is the only discourse open to Your Grace."

"And you are all in agreement that this is what I should do?"
There was a chorus of assent, only Fisher remaining silent.

She did not comment on this, but she understood. The Bishop of Rochester was warning her that on no account must the document be brought to England.

"The King grows impatient," went on Warham, "for until this document is produced the case cannot be opened. He declares that Cardinal Campeggio is delighted by the delay, but His Grace grows weary of it. Your Grace should with all speed write to the Emperor imploring him to send this document to you here in England."

"Since we have a good copy here," she asked, "why should that not suffice?"

"A copy is but a copy which could well be a forgery. We must have the original. For your sake and that of the Princess Mary, Your Grace, I beg of you to write to the Emperor for the original of this document."

She looked at Fisher and read the warning in his eyes. He was a brave man. He would have spoken out but he knew—and she knew—that if he did so he would shortly be removed from her Council of advisers and no good would come of that. But his looks implied that on no account must she write to Spain for the document and that it was false to say that the copy would have no value in the court. This was a ruse to bring the original document to England and there destroy it, since it would prove an impediment to the King's case.

She answered them boldly: "Gentlemen, we have here a very fair copy. That will suffice to show the court. It is well, I believe, that the original should remain in the Emperor's keeping. I shall not send to Spain for it."

The men who were pledged to defend her left her, and she saw from Fisher's looks that she had acted correctly.

But when they had gone she was afraid. Hers was a pitiable position, when she could not trust her own Council.

*         *         *

Katharine stood before the Royal Council which was presided over by the Chancellor. Wolsey studied her shrewdly. Poor, brave woman, he thought, what hope does she think she has when she attempts to stand against the King's wishes?

"Your Grace," said the Chancellor, "I have to tell you that

I speak for the King and his Council. Are we to understand that you refuse to write to the Emperor asking him to return that brief which is of the utmost importance in this case?"

"You may understand that. There is a good copy of the brief which can be used in the court; and I see no reason why the original should not remain for safe keeping in the hands of the Emperor."

"Your Grace, you will forgive my temerity but, in refusing to obey the King's command, you lay yourself open to a charge of high treason."

Katharine was silent and Wolsey saw that he had shocked her. Now she would perhaps begin to realize the folly of pitting her strength against that of the King and his ministers who, more realistic than she was, understood that not to obey meant risking their lives.

"Your Grace," went on Wolsey soothingly, "I have prepared here a draft of a letter which the King desires you to copy and send to the Emperor."

She held out her hand for it and read a plea to her nephew that he despatch the brief with all speed to England as it was most necessary for her defence in the pending action.

She looked at the Chancellor, the man whom she had begun to hate because she considered him to be the instigator of all her troubles. He was ruthless; he had to procure the divorce for the King or suffer his displeasure and he did not care how he achieved that end. She did not doubt that when the brief came to England it would be mislaid and destroyed, for it was the finest evidence she could possibly have.

"So I am certain," went on the Chancellor, "that Your Grace will wish to comply with the King's desire in this matter."

She bowed her head. She could see that she would have to write the letter, but she would write another explaining that she had written under duress. She felt desolate, for it seemed that she depended so much on that pale aloof young man who might so easily consider her troubles unworthy of his attention.

Wolsey read her thoughts and said: "Your Grace must swear not to write to the Emperor any other letter but this. If you did so, that could only be construed as high treason."

She saw her predicament. She had to give way, so she bowed before the power of her enemies.

\*　　\*　　\*

As she knelt in her chapel, a priest came and knelt beside her.

"Your Grace," whispered Mendoza, "the brief must not come to England."

"You know I must write to my nephew," she replied. "I am being forced to it, and I gave my word that I would write no other letter to him."

"Then we must find a means of communicating without letters."

"A messenger whom we could trust?"

"That is so. Francisco Felipez did good service once."

"Perhaps he would be suspect if he did so again."

"Is there anyone else in your suite whom you could trust?"

"There is Montoya. He is a Spaniard, and loyal. But I do not think he would be so resourceful as Felipez."

"Then let us chance Felipez. This time he should not ask for permission, as the matter is very dangerous. Let him leave at once for Spain, with nothing in writing. When he reaches the Emperor he must explain to him how dangerous it would be to send the brief to England as it would almost surely be destroyed."

"Felipez shall leave at once," said the Queen. "He will then have a good start of the messenger with the letter."

"Let us pray for the success of his journey," murmured Mendoza. "But later. Now there is not a moment to be lost."

\*         \*         \*

The Cardinal, brooding on his affairs in his private apartments at York Place, was interrupted by the arrival of a man who asked permission to speak with him on a private matter.

Wolsey received the man at once, for he was one of his spies in the Queen's household.

"Your Eminence," said the man, "Francisco Felipez disappeared from the Queen's household yesterday. I have made one or two enquiries and it seems he was seen riding hard on the road to the coast."

Wolsey rose and his eyes glowed with anger.

So the Queen, for all her outward resignation, was putting up a fight. Her man must not reach the Emperor, as the King's hopes of procuring a divorce could well depend on that brief. He would not rest—nor would the King—until it was in their hands.

Felipez must be stopped before he reached Madrid.

\*         \*         \*

The Queen was seated with a few women while she worked with her needle and one of them read aloud. She was anxious that there should be no change in her routine.

Yet she was not listening to the reader; her thoughts were with her nephew. Felipez would have reached him by now; he would be explaining all that was happening to the Emperor's aunt in England, and the urgent need for Charles to hold that brief in safe keeping, so that it could be shown to the Pope if there were any attempt to declare her marriage invalid.

Charles was a man of honour; he had the utmost respect for family ties, and he would see that to treat her as Henry was planning to do was an insult to Spain. He would understand, as soon as Felipez explained to him, that the King's ministers were not to be trusted. She blamed the King's ministers—chief of them Wolsey. She could never for long see Henry as the monster he sometimes appeared to be. He had been led astray, she believed. He was young in heart and spirit; he was lusty and sensual and she had never greatly pleased him physically; she was too religiously minded and the sexual act to her was only tolerable as the necessary prelude to child-bearing. Henry had always seemed to her like a boy; those childish games which he had once played at every masque, when he had disguised himself and expected all to be so surprised when the disguise was removed, were symbolic. He had not grown up; he was easily led astray. He was still the chivalrous knight who had rescued her from humiliation when he was eighteeen years old. Never would she forget those early days of their marriage; always she would remember that he it was who had rescued her. At this time he was in the thrall of the wicked minister, Wolsey, and he was bemused be the black-eyed witch named Anne Boleyn.

If she could live through these troublous days, if she could bring Henry to a sense of duty, she was sure that they would settle down happily together. This was what she prayed for.

But in the meantime she must continue the fight against the machinations of those about him and the inclinations of his own youthful desires.

There was a commotion below her window and, setting aside her work, she went to it and looking out, saw a man limping into the Palace; his arm was bandaged and it was clear that he had recently met with an accident.

She stood very still, clenching her hands, for she had recognized the man as Francisco Felipez, who should at this time be in Spain.

She turned to the group of women and said: "I think that one of my servants has met with an accident. One of you must go below and bring him to me at once. I would hear what has befallen him."

One of them obeyed and Katharine said to the others: "Put away the work for today and leave me."

When Francisco Felipez came to her her first emotion was relief to see that he was not seriously hurt.

"You have been involved in an accident?" she asked.

His expression was apologetic. "I was riding through France, Your Grace, and in the town of Abbeville I was set upon by foot-pads. They knocked me unconscious and rifled my pockets." He grinned ruefully. "They found nothing to interest them there, Your Grace. So they left me with a broken arm which meant that I was unable to ride my horse. A merchant bound it for me and helped me to return to England."

"My poor Francisco," said the Queen, "you are in pain."

"It is nothing, Your Grace. I can only regret that I had to delay so long before returning to you, and that I was unable to continue my journey because of my inability to ride."

"I will send you to my physician. Your arm needs attention."

"And Your Grace has no further commission for me?"

Katharine shook her head. She understood that he had been seen to leave England, that the nature of his mission had been guessed, that he had been incapacitated by the Cardinal's men, and that the hope of conveying an understanding of her peril to the Emperor was now slight.

\*      \*      \*

The Cardinal sat with his head buried in his hands. He had been reading despatches from Rome, and had learned that Clement, after seeming near to death, was making a remarkable recovery. The position at the Vatican was more hopeful and it seemed as though the Pope had taken a new grip on life. It followed that the chances of a Conclave in the near future were gradually but certainly fading; and the Cardinal's position in England had worsened.

Each day the King viewed him with more disfavour after listening to the complaints of Anne Boleyn. Continually Henry chafed against the delay. Had there ever, he asked himself, been such procrastination over such a simple matter? Other Kings, when they needed to rid themselves of unwanted wives, procured a dispensation and the matter was done with. But he, Henry Tudor, who had always until now, taken what he wanted, was balked at every turn.

And what could his faithful servant do to hasten the decision when Campeggio had clearly been advised by the Pope to avoid a trial of the case if possible, and if not to use every means to delay bringing matters to a head! Wolsey was powerless to work without Campeggio; and the Pope and the King were pulling in opposite directions.

One of his most trusted servants entered the apartment, and the Cardinal, startled, withdrew his hands.

"I suffer from a headache," Wolsey explained.

"A pressure of work, Your Eminence," was the answer.

"Can it be so? I have suffered from a pressure of work, Cromwell, for as long as I can remember."

Thomas Cromwell sighed sympathetically and laid some documents before the Cardinal. In a lesser degree Thomas Cromwell shared his master's uneasiness, for people in the Court and in the City were beginning to show their dislike of him, which was entirely due to the fact that he was the Cardinal's man.

He thought of himself as a parasite feeding on the abundance of the Cardinal; and if Wolsey fell, what would happen to Cromwell?

Could Wolsey stand out against all the powers that fought against him? There could not be a man in England who had more enemies. Norfolk and Suffolk were watching like vultures; so was Lord Darcy; and the Boleyn faction, which was daily growing stronger, was standing by eagerly waiting for the kill.

The King? The King was Wolsey's only hope. Henry still admired the cleverness of his minister and was loth to part with his favourite. That was Wolsey's hope . . . and Thomas Cromwell's.

Now suppose the Lady Anne lost a little of her influence over the King; suppose she gave way to his pleadings and became his mistress; suppose Henry made the natural discovery that Anne was very little different from other women . . . then Wolsey might yet retain his hold on the King. That was if the French alliance provided all that Wolsey and Henry hoped for. But François was an unreliable ally—even as Charles had been.

So many suppositions, thought Thomas Cromwell, for a Cardinal's fate to depend on, and the fate of his lawyer who had risen because he was in his service hung with that of his master.

It was nearly six years before that Thomas Cromwell had set up in Gray's Inn and had been called to work for the Cardinal. He had helped to suppress certain small monasteries in order to promote colleges at Ipswich and Oxford in which the Cardinal was interested, and there had been complaints about the manner in which he, Cromwell, and his colleague, John Allen, had set about this business, but the Cardinal had protected them from trouble.

Wolsey had been pleased with him, and since then all his legal business had gone into Thomas Cromwell's hands. Thus it was that a lawyer could rise from obscurity to greatness; but Thomas Cromwell was too shrewd not to know that a man could as easily fall as rise.

He had come a very long way from his father's blacksmith's shop, although his father was a man of enterprise and had been a fuller and shearer of cloth in addition to his trade as black-smith. Thomas had intended to go farther, and after a some-what wild youth, which had resulted in a term of imprisonment and flight from the country, he had, following a period spent abroad, returned sobered, with the intention of making his fortune.

He had every reason to be pleased with what he had done until he suddenly understood that the Cardinal's good fortune was turning sour.

"These are troublous times," murmured Cromwell.

"You speak truth," answered the Cardinal grimly.

"Your Eminence," went on Cromwell, "what in your opinion will be the King's answer if the Pope refuses to grant his divorce?"

Wolsey's body seemed to stiffen. Then he said slowly: "The King will have only one course of action. He will accept his fate, and give up all plans for remarriage."

"Your Eminence has noticed, no doubt, that there are many Lutheran books entering the country."

"I know it. Since that man Luther set the new doctrines before the world there seems no way of preventing these books from coming here. They are smuggled in; they are read, talked of . . ."

"Is it true, Your Eminence, that the King himself is interested in these ideas?"

Wolsey looked up sharply at the thickset lawyer, with the big head which seemed too close to his shoulders; at the strong jaw and thin lips which made his mouth look like a trap, at the cold expression, the gleaming, intelligent dark eyes.

"How did you know that he was?" demanded Wolsey. "Has he told you this?"

Cromwell smiled deprecatingly to indicate his humility. That smile said: Would the King confide in Thomas Cromwell? "No, Your Eminence," he answered. "But the Boleyns are interested. I believe the Lady passed a book to the King and told him he must read it. And he, being told he must, obeyed."

Wolsey was silent.

Cromwell leaned forward slightly and whispered: "What if

the King should so dislike the Pope that he became more than a little interested in heresy?"

"He never would," declared Wolsey. "Is he not Defender of the Faith?"

"He was a fierce foe of Luther at the time that title was bestowed on him. But times change, Eminence."

Once more Wolsey looked up into that cold, clever face. He had a great respect for the lawyer's intelligence.

"What mean you, Cromwell?" he asked.

Cromwell shrugged his shoulders. "That the Lady and her friends might give their support to Lutheranism, seeing thereby a way to dispense with the services of the Pope."

"I think not," said the Cardinal, rising and smoothing the red folds of his robe as though to remind himself and Cromwell of the importance of Rome. "The King has always been devoted to the Church."

Cromwell bowed and Wolsey said: "I must go now to His Grace. I have a matter of some importance to discuss with him."

The lawyer walked from the apartment at the side of the Cardinal, his manner obsequious. He was thinking that Wolsey was growing old and that old men lost their shrewdness. Then his problem was pressing down upon him: What will Cromwell do when Wolsey has fallen? When would be the time for the parasite to leave his host? And where would he find another?

Cromwell's eyes glinted at the thought. He would leap up, not down. Was it such a long jump from a Cardinal to a King?

*          *          *

The Cardinal had summoned Thomas Abell, the Queen's chaplain, to appear before him and the King.

"He will be here in a few minutes, Your Grace," Wolsey told Henry.

"And you think he is the man for this mission?"

"I am sure we could not find a better, Your Grace, for since he is the Queen's chaplain, the Emperor will think he acts for the Queen."

"It seems a marvellous thing," said Henry peevishly, "that there should be this delay. When . . . when . . . when shall I be granted what I wish? How much longer must I live in this uncertainty?"

"As soon as we have the brief safely in our hands the case can be opened. But let us not despair of the Queen's entering a convent."

"She is a stubborn woman," grumbled the King.

"I know, Your Grace, but she pins hope to this brief. Once it is in *our* hands her case will crumble."

A page entered to say that Thomas Abell was without.

"Send him in," commanded Wolsey.

Thomas Abell bowed low before the King.

"Now to our business," said Henry.

"It is His Grace's wish," said the Cardinal, "that you should leave at once for Spain. You are to go to the Emperor and hand him a letter from the Queen. He will give you a certain document, and this you are to bring to His Grace with all speed."

"Your Grace, Your Eminence," said Thomas Abell, "gladly would I serve you, but I must tell you that I have little Spanish and I fear that would be an impediment to me in this mission."

Henry looked at Wolsey who said quickly: "You shall take a servant and interpreter with you."

"Then I shall set out with all speed. There is a man in the Queen's household who would make a good servant and is moreover a Spaniard. I refer to Montoya. If this man could accompany me I should have no qualms in setting out immediately."

"Let it be so," said the Cardinal. "You should leave tomorrow, and in the meantime it is His Grace's wish that you should have no communication with the Queen. You must carry with you, apart from this one, no letters from the Queen to the Emperor. To do this would incur the King's displeasure and, as you know, you could then be accused of high treason."

Thomas Abell said he understood, and withdrew in order to make his preparations for the journey, while Wolsey summoned Montoya that the importance of his journey might be impressed upon him.

When he left the King and the Cardinal, Thomas Abell was thoughtful. He was to carry a letter from the Queen to the Emperor, and this letter was to be given him by the Cardinal. He was not to take any other message from the Queen to her nephew. It therefore seemed to him that the letter which he carried, although in the Queen's hand-writing and purporting to express her wishes, had no doubt been written under duress.

Thomas Abell was a deeply religious man. His position at Court had by no means increased his ambitions, which were not for worldly gain. He was a man who cared passionately for causes; and it seemed to him that the Queen's cause was more worthy than the King's.

There had been a moment, as he confronted the King and Cardinal, when he had almost refused to obey their orders. No, he wanted to say, I refuse to work against the Queen in this matter of the divorce.

That would doubtless have been construed as high treason and he might have been hustled to the Tower. Such a possibility would not have deterred him in the least. Indeed, he had a secret longing for a martyr's crown. But it had occurred to him that by accepting this commission he might serve the Queen's cause more effectively than by refusing it.

He obeyed the instructions and did not see the Queen before he left, her letter safely in his scrip; the voluble Montoya riding beside him.

They travelled across France and the journey was tedious; but there was much to talk of as they went, for Montoya was well versed in what was known throughout the Court as the Secret Matter; he filled in gaps for Abell; so that long before they came into Spain, the chaplain knew that the Queen had been forced to write the letter he carried, that she knew that, once the brief left the Emperor's safe keeping, her case was lost, that she had tried to reach him by means of Franciso Felipez who had been set upon and all but killed by the Cardinal's men.

So Abell made up his mind; and when he reached Spain and was taken into the Emperor's presence, with Montoya to translate, he told the Emperor that the Queen had been forced to write the letter asking for the brief, and that unless the Emperor kept the original in his hands the Queen would have no redress; he had, moreover, worked out a plan that a notorially attested copy, which would be valid in any court, should be made and the original kept in safety in Spain.

The Emperor listened gravely and thanked the chaplain, who he saw was his aunt's very good friend. He assured Abell that the copy should be made and he himself would ensure that the original brief would be kept in the royal archives at Madrid.

Abell was delighted with the success of his mission and, while he waited for the copy of the brief to be made, he started to write a book in which he set out the Queen's case; and the more he worked, the clearer it became to him that the King based his desire for a divorce on false premises.

Abell now had a cause for which he was ready to give his life.

He was eager to return to England, there to hand the copy of the brief to Wolsey, and complete his book which he would eventually publish, no matter what the consequences should be.

## CHAPTER IX

# "COME INTO THE COURT"

HENRY was growing more and more disturbed. He had noticed the change towards him in the people's attitude. When he rode in the streets there was no longer the spontaneous outburst of cheering; and the approval of the people had always been very dear to him. Anne was growing restive; she continually complained and accused him of making promises which he was unable—or unwilling—to keep. The knowledge of his impotence in this matter infuriated Henry.

Moreover the popularity of the Queen had increased since the plan for the divorce had become known. If she appeared at a balcony crowds would collect and shout: "Long live our Queen!" as though to remind all who heard them—including the King— that they would not allow her to be cast aside for the sake of Anne Boleyn. Anne herself had on one or two occasions been in danger from the people. They called her the "whore" and shouted that they'd "have no Nan Bullen as their Queen!"

Moreover the copy of the brief had arrived, and that was useless for Henry's purpose while the original was in the Emperor's keeping. The Pope, weak in health and weak in purpose, vacillated between the King and the Emperor, desperately trying to placate first one, then the other.

But the Emperor was nearer at hand and more formidable, so Clement had declared that, since Campeggio seemed unable to proceed with the trial in England, the whole matter had better be referred to Rome.

"Tried in Rome!" shouted the King. "A fine state of affairs. What hope should I have of obtaining a divorce if the matter were tried in Rome under the whip of the Emperor!"

No. There must be no more delay. They must go ahead with the trial even though the brief did remain in the Emperor's hands. He must rely on Wolsey who knew full well, the King malevolently reminded himself, that if the case did not go in the King's favour Master Cardinal would have a great deal for which to answer.

In the meantime he could not endure his unpopularity with the people and sought to remedy this by making a public pronouncement of his difficulties. He therefore called together as many of the burgesses of London who could be squeezed into the great hall of Bridewell Palace, led by the Lord Mayor, aldermen and many from the Inns of Court; and on a dull November Sunday afternoon he took his place on a dais and endeavoured to put his case before them.

Henry was always at his best when he played a part, because his belief in the part of the moment was absolute.

He was a glittering figure, standing there on the dais, the light filtering through the windows making his jewels scintillate; he was exceedingly handsome, standing in his characteristic attitude, legs apart—which made him look so broad and sturdy—his glittering hands folded across his blue and gold doublet.

He surveyed the crowd before him with the benevolent eyes of a father-figure, for he had already assured himself that what he wanted was for their good rather than his own.

"My friends," he cried, "there is much disquiet throughout the land because up to this time God has denied me my greatest wish—to give you the heir who would naturally follow me. This matter has for some time gravely disturbed my conscience, and I doubt not that there have been many evil rumours in the streets concerning it."

He went on to remind his audience of the prosperity they had enjoyed under his rule.

"My beloved subjects, it is a matter of great concern to me that one day I must die and be no longer with you. So I wish to leave you one, whom I have trained to take the burden of kingship from my shoulders, one on whose head I could contemplate the placing of my crown and die happy. There are some among you who may remember the horror of civil war. If this country were to be plunged into like horror on my death, my friends, my dear subjects, I believe I should have lived in vain. I wish to live in friendship with France and so I plan to marry my daughter to a French Prince. I wish also to live in friendship with the Emperor Charles, for I know full well that this country's disagreements with him have caused certain hardship to some of our people."

There was grave nodding among the assembly. The clothiers had cried out again and again that they could not live if they could not sell their cloth in the Flemish markets.

"It was during the negotiations for my daughter's marriage that a point was made which has caused me great perturbation. The French ambassador, the Bishop of Tarbes, has raised the question of my daughter's legitimacy. It was a point which I could not ignore since, my friends, this matter had for some time given me cause for uneasiness. I have since consulted bishops and lawyers, and they have assured me that I have, for all the years that I have believed the Lady Katharine to be my wife, been living in mortal sin.

"Ah," went on Henry, "if it might be adjudged that the Lady Katharine is my lawful wife, nothing could be more pleasant or acceptable to me, both for the clearing of my conscience, and for her own good qualities, and conditions which I know her to be in. For I assure you all that beside her noble parentage she is a woman of gentleness, humility and buxomness; yea, and of all good qualities pertaining to nobility she is without comparison. So that if I were to marry again I would choose her above all women. But if it be determined in judgment that our marriage is against God's law, then shall I sorrow, parting from so good a lady and a loving companion. These be the sores that vex my mind. These be the pangs which trouble my conscience, for the declaration of which I have assembled you together. I beg of you now go your ways, and in doing so form no hasty judgments on your Prince's actions."

The meeting was over. Henry left the hall, and those who had assembled to hear him went into the streets where they stood about in little groups talking; but the theme of their conversation was still sympathy for the Queen.

\* \* \*

Iñigo de Mendoza, who had learned of the King's oration at Bridewell, sat down to communicate with his master.

"There is nothing I can do here," he wrote, "to further the Queen's cause. The King is determined to have an end of this matter and there will be a trial. The Queen's chances of receiving justice at the hands of the judges are slight. She needs an ambassador who is also a lawyer. I therefore implore Your Excellency to recall me from a post which I have not the ability to fulfil."

All through the winter Mendoza awaited his recall.

It came at the end of the spring, when it had been decided to open the Court at Blackfriars for the hearing of the King's Matter, which was no longer secret.

\* \* \*

There could be no more delay. The summons had been sent both to the King and the Queen, and the Legatine Court was to be set up in Blackfriars on the 16th day of June.

Katharine, who during this most difficult time had not changed her mode of life, was with her daughter when the summons came.

Poor little Mary! She was fully aware of the troubles between her parents and how she herself was affected. She had lost her healthy looks and had grown nervous, starting with dismay when any messengers appeared; she still kept her feelings under control, but there were occasions when she would throw herself into her mother's arms and without a word demand to be comforted.

Now as the scroll was handed to her mother Mary began to tremble.

The Queen dismissed the messenger, but she did not look at the scroll. She laid it aside, telling herself that she would study it when her daughter was no longer with her. But although Mary tried to play the virginals, she was thinking of the scroll and her fingers faltered so that Katharine knew that it was useless to try to keep the secret from her.

"You must not fret, my darling," she said.

"Mother," answered the Princess, turning from the instrument, "if you are in truth not married to the King then I am but a bastard, is that not so?"

A hot flush touched the Queen's pale face. "It is wrong even to question it," she answered. "I will not allow it. You are the legitimate daughter of the King and myself, the only heir to the throne."

"Yes, I know that to be true, Mother; but there may be some who insist it is not so, and if they should succeed, what would become of us?"

The Queen shrugged her shoulders. "They cannot succeed . . . if there is justice."

"There is not always justice, is there, Mother?"

The Queen did not answer and Mary went on: "I was talking to Reginald of this matter. He said that no matter what the verdict of the court was, he would never call anyone but you the Queen of England, and none heir to the throne but myself."

"So we have some friends," said Katharine. "Why should we not have justice too?"

"Perhaps because our friends will not be in the court? That is what you are afraid of, Mother. Your friends are not allowed to stay with you here, so why should they be allowed to act as judges?"

"I think I have some friends."

"But, Mother, what is important is that we are not separated. That is why, when I am frightened, I remind myself that if they say you are no true Queen, then I cannot be the true heir. So that if you are sent away I shall go with you."

"My darling . . . my darling," said the Queen with a sob in her voice; and Mary ran to her and knelt at her feet.

"Is that all you care about then?" asked Katharine.

"I do not care what they say of me," came Mary's muffled answer, "if they will but let me stay with you for ever. If I am a bastard the French Prince will not want me. We shall go away from Court, Mother, you and I, and we shall stay quietly somewhere in the country, and there will be no talk of my going over the sea to marry." She laughed on a high, hysterical note. "For who will want to marry a bastard!"

"Hush! Hush!" admonished the Queen.

"Oh, but you are afraid, Mother."

"No . . . no . . . ."

"If you are not afraid, why do you not open the scroll?"

"Because we are together now and I do not see you as often as I wish. So matters of state can wait."

"We are both thinking of it, Mother. We do not escape it by ignoring it."

The Queen smiled and, going to where she had laid the scroll, picked it up and read it. Mary ran to her and stood before her, anxiously scanning her mother's face.

"It is a summons to appear at Blackfriars," she said.

"A summons? Should the Queen be summoned?"

"Yes, Mary. For the King will be summoned also."

"And at this court they will decide . . ."

Katharine nodded. "They will decide."

Mary kissed her mother's hand. "All will be well," she said. "If they decide one way you will be the King's wife and we shall be as we were. If the other, we shall go away together, away from the Court, away from the fear of a royal marriage in a strange country. Oh, Mother, let us be happy."

"Yes, let us be happy while we are together."

And she tried to set aside the gloom which hung about her. She did not believe, as Mary did, that if her marriage were proved invalid she and her daughter would be allowed to slip away quietly into oblivion. But she did not tell Mary this. Why disturb the child's peace of mind, and how could she know how long such peace would be enjoyed?

\*     \*     \*

The Queen came to Campeggio's apartment. She felt desolate; she scarcely knew this man, and yet it was to him she must go.

She had confessed to John Fisher on the previous day and they had taken advantage of their privacy to discuss the coming trial. She had not asked Fisher to come to her for this purpose, because she knew that Wolsey's spies were all about her and, although it was reasonable that she should ask the advice of a man who had been chosen to defend her, she did not want to put John Fisher in any danger, for she knew he was an honest man who would speak his mind even though his views were not those of the King and Cardinal.

It was Fisher who had advised her to see Campeggio in the vain hope that she might be able to persuade the Legate to have the case tried in Rome.

Campeggio, who could feel the beginning of an attack of the gout, was irritated by the arrival of the Queen. If only she had shown good sense she would be in a convent by now and he would be back in Italy where he belonged. He had used his delaying tactics, on Clement's command, for as long as he had been able, but it was impossible to hold out any longer against the King's desire. What he must do now was prevent the case from reaching any conclusion, for he was certain that the King would not allow it to be said that there had never been any impediment to the marriage, and Clement dared not so offend the Emperor as to grant the divorce.

A delicate situation, especially so since his fellow Legate was Cardinal Wolsey whose own fate depended on giving the King what he wanted—and quickly.

Thus he felt irritated by the Queen who could so easily have solved the problem for them all by giving up her life outside convent walls.

"Your Grace . . ." he murmured, bowing with difficulty.

"I regret that you are in pain," said the Queen with genuine sympathy.

"I am accustomed to it, Your Grace."

"I am sorry for all who suffer," said the Queen. "I have come to ask you not to hold this court. I have lodged an appeal to His Holiness and have high hopes that the case will be heard outside England—where I might have a greater chance of justice."

"Your Grace," Campeggio pointed out, "His Holiness has already appointed two Legates. This is tantamount to having your case tried in Rome."

"I am surprised that you should have so small an opinion of my intelligence as to push me aside with such a comment," Katharine retorted scornfully. "If this case is tried in England all the advantages will be the King's. Have you forgotten who one of the Legates is?"

"The matter has not slipped my memory, Your Grace."

"Wolsey!" she cried. "The man whom I have to thank for all my troubles. I have always abhorred his way of life, which is not that of a priest. He hates my nephew because he did not help him to become a Pope."

"You should pray to God," Campeggio told her. "He would help you to bear your trials."

"And who," cried Katharine, "would dare to pronounce a verdict contrary to the King's wishes?"

"I would, if the findings of the court should show me clearly that the King was wrong."

"The findings of the court!" snapped Katharine. "Do you not know that there cannot be more than one or two men who would dare give a decision which the King did not want? So you can rely with certainty on the findings of the court!"

"Let us pray," said Campeggio.

They did so, but Katharine could only think of the fate which was waiting for her and her daughter.

What will become of us? she asked herself. And then she prayed that whatever disaster should befall her, her daughter should remain unscathed.

\*　　　\*　　　\*

There was tension in the great hall at the Blackfriars Palace. The case had begun.

Never had those assembled seen anything quite like this before.

Seated on chairs covered by cloth of gold and placed at a table over which was hung a tapestry cloth sat the Legates, Cardinals Campeggio and Wolsey. On the right of the table was an ornate chair with a canopy over it; this was in readiness for the King who was expected to appear in a few day's time; on the left hand side of the table was a chair as rich but lacking the canopy, which was meant for the Queen.

Henry did not appear in person but sent two proxies. Katharine, however, arrived in the company of four Bishops and several of her women.

As Katharine entered there was a stir in the court, for she was not expected until that day when the King would be there. She did not go to the chair which was intended for her, but to the table where she stood before the Legates. There was a hushed silence in the court as she began to speak.

"My lords, I come to make a protest against this court and to ask that the case may be transferred to Rome."

Katharine was conscious of the malevolent gaze of Wolsey and the peevish one of Campeggio. To the first she was an enemy to be ruthlessly removed; to the second she was an irritation, the woman who might, by going into a convent, have saved him so much trouble and allowed him to rest his gouty limbs in a more congenial climate. The sight of those two men filled Katharine with further apprehension and an immense determination to fight for her future and that of her daughter.

"Why does Your Grace object to this court?" Wolsey asked coldly.

"I object because it is hostile to me," replied the Queen. "I demand to be tried by unprejudiced judges."

Campeggio appeared to be shocked; Wolsey looked pained, but Katharine went on boldly: "This case has been referred to Rome; in due course it could be tried there; the verdict must have the sanction of the Holy Father. I protest against this matter's being tried here."

Wolsey rose and said: "Your Grace is misinformed." And Campeggio added: "Your Grace can be assured that justice shall be done, and I urgently pray you to take confidence in the members of this court who serve none but justice."

Katharine turned away and, holding her head high, left the court followed by her train.

It was useless, she was telling herself. There was nothing she could do to prevent the trial.

She could only go back to her apartments and wait until that day when she, with Henry, must appear in person before the Legatine court.

\*          \*          \*

"Henry, King of England, come into the court!" The cry rang out in the great hall of Blackfriars.

Henry was seated under the canopy, and above him on the dais were the two Cardinals, magnificent in their robes of scarlet. At the foot of this dais were the Bishops and officers of the court, with William Warham, Archbishop of Canterbury, at their head. There sat the counsellors of the two opposing parties; Dr. Bell and Dr. Sampson for the King, and the Bishop of Rochester and the Bishop of St. Asaph's for the Queen.

The voice of the crier, calling the King, silenced the whispers. Those who were present could not help but marvel that the King and Queen could be called into court as though they were common people.

This, it was murmured, shows the power of Rome. Only the Pope would dare summon the King of England to appear in court in his own country. Since we were ruled by one of the Pope's cardinals—our butcher's son—England has been but a vassal of Rome.

Henry himself felt a wave of anger to be so summoned. He would have refused to attend this trial; he would have stated that he had no intention of accepting any verdict but the one he wanted; but the people must be placated; they were already murmuring against the injustice done to his Queen. It was part of his policy to say: "Reluctant I am to part from her whom I believed to be my wife, but I do so on the orders of the Church." Therefore what could he do but submit himself to the jurisdiction of the Church, making sure, of course, that his Cardinal understood how the verdict must go.

So he answered in a voice devoid of rancour: "Here I am, my lords."

"Katharine, Queen of England, come into the court."

Katharine stood up, crossed herself, and to the astonishment of the Bishops and officers of the court, made her way to the chair in which Henry sat. She knelt before him and began to speak in a ringing voice which could be heard all over the hall.

"Sir, I beseech you, for all the love there has been between us, and for the love of God, let me have right and justice. Take pity on me and have compassion for me, because I am a poor stranger born outside your dominions. I have here in this court no unprejudiced counsellor, and I appeal to you as the head of justice within your realm. Alas! Wherein have I offended you? I take God and all the world to witness that I have been to you a true, humble and obedient wife, ever conformable to your will and pleasure. I have been pleased and contented with all things wherein you had delight and dalliance. I loved all those you loved, only for your sake, whether they were my friends or mine enemies. These twenty years I have been your true wife, and by me you have had divers children, although it has pleased God to call them out of this world, which has been no fault of mine. I put it to your conscience whether I came not to you as a maid. If you have since found any dishonour in my conduct, then I am content to depart, albeit to my great shame and disparagement; but if none there can be, then I beseech you, thus lowlily, to let me remain in my proper state."

There was a hush in the court as she paused for breath. She had at the beginning of the hearing stated that fact which was the crux of the matter. Her marriage to Prince Arthur had been no true marriage; she had stated before this court that she had been a virgin when she married Henry.

The King flinched a little; his face was stern; he did not look at his kneeling wife, but stared straight before him.

"The King, your father," went on Katharine, "was accounted

in his day a second Solomon for wisdom, and my father, Ferdinand, was esteemed one of the wisest kings that had ever reigned in Spain; both were excellent princes, full of wisdom and royal behaviour. They had learned and judicious counsellors and they thought our marriage good and lawful. Therefore it is a wonder to me to hear what new inventions are brought up against me, who never meant aught but honestly."

Again she paused. Campeggio moved in his chair to ease his painful limbs. She makes her own advocate, he thought; where could she have found a better? It will not be easy for them to find against her.

He was pleased with her. It was what he wished, for Clement's orders were that the court should come to no decision.

"You cause me to stand to the judgment of this new court," continued the Queen, "wherein you do me much wrong if you intend any kind of cruelty; you may condemn me for lack of sufficient answer, since your subjects cannot be impartial counsellors for me, as they dare not, for fear of you, disobey your will. Therefore most humbly do I require you, in the way of charity and for the love of God, who is the just Judge of all, to spare me the sentence of this new court, until I be advertised in what way my friends in Spain may advise me to take. And if you will not extend to me this favour, your pleasure be fulfilled, and to God do I commit my cause."

Katharine stood up and all in the court saw that there were tears on her cheeks. The Bishops looked on grimly, not daring to show their sympathy in the presence of the King, who still sat staring stonily before him; but in the body of the hall many a kerchief was applied to an eye and secret prayers for the Queen were murmured.

She took the arm of her receiver-general and instead of making her way back to her seat she began to move through the crowd towards the door.

The crier was in consternation. He called: "Katharine, Queen of England, come again into the court."

But Katharine did not seem to hear and, staring before her, her eyes misted with tears, she continued towards the door.

"Your Grace," whispered the receiver-general, "you are being called back to the court!"

"I hear the call," answered the Queen, in tones which could be heard by those about her, "but I heed it not. Let us go. This is no court where I may have justice."

"Katharine, Queen of England, come again into the court!" shouted the distracted crier.

But Katharine passed out of the court into the sunshine.

The Queen had gone, and Henry was fully aware of the impression she had made.

He rose and addressed the assembly. He spoke with conviction and considerable powers of oratory; he was well practised in this speech for he had uttered it may times before. He explained that he had no wish to rid himself of a virtuous woman who had always been a good wife to him. It was his conscience which urged him to take action. It had been put to him by learned men—bishops and lawyers—that he was living in sin with a woman who had been his brother's wife. The twenty-first verse of the twentieth chapter of Leviticus had been brought to his notice, and it was for this reason that he—determined to live at peace with God—had decided to ask learned men whether he was truly married. If the answer was in the affirmative he would rejoice, for there was none who pleased him as did the woman who had been his wife for twenty years; but if on the other hand it were shown to him that he was living in sin with her, then, much as this would grieve him, he would part with her.

After Katharine's speech the King's sounded insincere. It was a fact that the whole court and country knew of his passion for Anne Boleyn, and that it was this woman's desire to share his crown before allowing him to become her lover which was, if not the only motive for bringing the case, an important one.

However, Henry, believing in what he said while he said it, did manage to infuse a certain ring of truth into his words.

When he had finished speaking Wolsey rose to his feet, came to the chair in which Henry was sitting and knelt there.

"Your Grace," he said, "I beseech you to tell this assembled court whether or not I have been the first to suggest you should part from the Queen. Much slander has been spoken against me in this respect and there are many who feel that, should this be truth, I am no fit person to sit as Legate in this case."

The King gave a short laugh and cried: "Nay, my Lord Cardinal, I cannot say you have been the prime mover in this matter. Rather have you set yourself against me."

Wolsey rose from his knees and bowed to the King. "I thank your Grace for telling this court that I am no prejudiced judge."

Wolsey returned to his seat and Warham, Archbishop of Canterbury, rose to produce a scroll which he told the court contained the names of the Bishops who had agreed that an enquiry into the matter of the King's marriage was necessary. He then began to read out the names on the scroll.

When he came to that of John Fisher, Bishop of Rochester,

Fisher rose from the bench and cried: "That is a forgery, for I have signed no such document."

Henry, who was growing more and more impatient at the delay and wondering when the judges would declare his marriage null and void—which he had believed they would quickly do—was unable to restrain himself. "How so?" he cried irritably. "Here is your name and seal."

"Your Grace, that is not my hand or seal."

Henry's brows were lowered over his eyes. Once he had loved that man Fisher. It was such men who, in the days of his youth, he had wished to have about him. Thomas More was another. They had never flattered him as blatantly as other people did and when he did wring a word of praise from them it was doubly sweet. John Fisher had at one time been his tutor—a gentle kindly man with whom it had been a pleasure for an exuberant youth to work with now and then.

But now Fisher was on the Queen's side. He was the Queen's counsel. He did not approve of a divorce. He believed that, having married Katharine and been disappointed in her, his King should yet remain her faithful husband.

What did Fisher know of the needs of a healthy man who was in the prime of life?

As he glowered at his one-time tutor, Henry hated the tall, spare figure. The fellow looks as though he spends his time shut in a cell, fasting, he thought derisively. No matter what love I had for him it shall be forgotten if he dares oppose me in this matter. He will have to learn that those who cross me do so at the peril of their lives.

And now what was this matter of a forgery?

Warham was saying: "This is your seal."

Fisher retorted: "My Lord, you know full well this is not my seal. You know that you approached me in this matter and I said that I would never give my name to such a document."

Warham could see the King's anger mounting. Warham was all for peace. He did not think that Fisher realized the full force of the King's passion in this matter. Perhaps Fisher was too honest to understand that when the King was being driven by his lust he was like a wild animal in his need to assuage it. Warham tried to end the matter as lightly as possible.

"You were loth to put your seal to this document, it is true," he murmured. "But you will remember that in the end we decided that I should do it for you."

"My lord," said Fisher, "this is not true."

The King shifted angrily in his seat. Warham sighed and put

down the document; it was a gesture which meant that no good could come of pursuing that matter further.

"We will proceed with the hearing," Wolsey announced. Henry sat sullenly wondering what effect Fisher had already had on the court. By God, he thought, that man's no friend of mine if deliberately he flouts me in order to serve the Queen.

But all would be well. Katharine had been right when she had said that few in this court would dare disobey him. They would not; and thus they would give him the verdict he was demanding. What difference would one dissenting voice make?

But he hated the dissenters. He could never endure criticism. And when it came from someone whom he had once admired, it was doubly wounding.

He scarcely heard what was being said about him until it was Fisher's turn to make his speech for the Queen.

"Those whom God hath joined together, let no man put asunder . . ."

As soon as Fisher had finished speaking, Henry rose from his seat.

He had had enough for one day. The session was over.

\*          \*          \*

The days passed with maddening slowness for the King. It was a month since the trial had begun and still no conclusion had been reached. Each day the counsels for the King and those for the Queen argued their cases; and it was clear that Fisher alone was determined to do his utmost to win a victory for the Queen.

Campeggio was in despair, for although he applied his delaying tactics whenever possible he could see that he could not extend the proceedings much longer, and, in view of the evidence he had heard, he knew that if he made a decision it would have to be in favour of the King.

This he could not do, as his strict orders from the Pope were that he should give no definite verdict.

Understanding the motives behind his fellow Legate's methods Wolsey was depressed; he knew that Campeggio's one desire was to prolong the action of the court until he could suitably disband it.

This was the state of affairs when the Cardinal was summoned to the King's presence.

Henry was purple with anger, and striding up and down the apartment waving papers in his hands. He did not speak as Wolsey approached, but merely thrust the papers at the Cardinal.

Wolsey read the news and felt sick with horror. François had suffered defeat in Italy and a peace was to be made between him and the Emperor. Margaret, Regent of the Netherlands, who was the Emperor's aunt, and Louise of Savoy, the mother of François, had arranged this peace which was consequently called The Ladies' Peace. It was natural that Clement should at the same time sign a treaty with the Emperor.

"And," cried Henry, glowering at his Chancellor, "these matters are settled and we are told nothing of them until they are completed. It seems to me that our French ally is as treacherous as our Spanish ones. Why is it that we are always betrayed?"

"Your Grace," stammered Wolsey, who was near exhaustion and whose mind had been concentrated on the King's divorce, "this will mean that Campeggio will never give us the verdict we want."

"This trial is nothing but a mockery!" roared the King. "Is it not marvellous that I should be made to wait so long for that which others have for the asking?"

"Circumstances have moved against us, Your Grace. But for the sack of Rome . . ."

"Do not give me your buts . . ." cried the King. "Give me freedom to marry, that I may provide my kingdom with an heir."

"It would seem, Your Grace, that we should make another appeal to the Queen. If she would but retire to a convent, I am certain that Clement would immediately grant the divorce. All we need is her consent to do so, nay her desire to do so. The Emperor himself would not object to that."

"She must be made to see reason," insisted the King.

"Your Grace, have I your permission to make one more appeal to her?"

"Do so, without delay."

Wolsey was relieved to escape from the King, and immediately went to Campeggio's apartments, and there made the suggestion that they should go to the Queen and endeavour to show her what a benefit she would confer, not only on herself, but on all others, if she would retire to a nunnery.

\*        \*        \*

The two Cardinals went by barge to Bridewell where the Queen at that time had her lodging. She was sitting with some of her women, working on her embroidery, for, she had said, she was so melancholy at this time that working with bright colours raised her spirits.

When she heard that the Cardinals had called on her, she

went to greet them with skeins of red and white silk hanging about her neck.

"Your Grace," said Wolsey, "we crave your pardon for disturbing your peace, and pray you to give us a hearing."

"Gladly will I do so," she answered, "but I cannot argue with such as you. I am not clever enough." She touched the skeins about her neck. "You see how I pass my time, and my maids are not the ablest counsellors, yet I have no others in England. And Spain, where there are those on whom I could rely, is far away."

"Take us into your privy chamber," said Wolsey, "and there we will show you the cause of our coming."

"My Lords," answered the Queen, "if you have anything to say, speak it openly before these folk, for I fear nothing that can be alleged against me, but I would all the world should see and hear it. Therefore speak your minds openly, I pray you."

Wolsey was uneasy and had no desire to speak before the women, so he began to explain his mission in Latin, but Katharine interrupted.

"Pray, my good lord, speak to me in English, for I can, thank God, speak and understand English, though I do know some Latin."

So there was nothing to be done but to speak to her in the presence of her women in English, and Wolsey said: "Your Grace, if you will consent to the divorce you shall lack nothing you desire in riches and honours. If you should desire to go into a convent, which would be a seemly setting for your devout manner of living, you shall have all that you require there. The King will place the Princess Mary next in order of succession to the issue of his second marriage."

"My lords," said Katharine, "I could not answer you suddenly, for I have no one to advise me."

Campeggio said: "Cardinal Wolsey and I would gladly give you the advice you need."

"Then now come to my private chamber and there we will speak of these matters," she said.

So the two Cardinals and the Queen retired together, and she told them once more that she had no wish to enter a convent, that the Princess Mary was the true heir to the throne, that she herself was indeed married to the King, for she had never in truth been wife to his brother; and this she would maintain no matter what befell her.

It was clear to the Cardinals that they could not make her change her decision, so they left her, Wolsey in deep melancholy, Campeggio determined to bring a speedy end to the case.

"This matter," said Wolsey as they stepped into the barge, "must be settled without delay. We must give our judgment, and, on what we have heard, how can we help but decide in the King's favour?"

Campeggio shook his head. "I am not satisfied that we have heard all the truth. The Queen is right when she says this is a prejudiced court. Nay, there is one course open to us. We must refer the matter to His Holiness."

"The King will never stomach further delay."

"This matter," answered Campeggio, "is not in the King's hands."

Wolsey did not answer. He envied Campeggio his freedom. He would return to Rome where he had only to answer to the Pope and by delaying judgment he had carried out his orders. But Wolsey . . . he had served the King, and each day Henry's displeasure and dissatisfaction increased.

So slowly they sailed along the river—Campeggio would leave the barge for his lodgings and the rest for which his limbs were crying out, but Wolsey must return to the King and once more report failure.

*          *          *

Campeggio arrived at the court. He took his place beside Wolsey, but as the proceedings were about to open, he rose and addressed the company.

"This court is under the jurisdiction of Rome," he announced, "and the holidays have begun in Rome. Therefore this court is closed until the holidays are over. We shall reassemble here on October the first."

There was a gasp of astonishment. Wolsey was as startled as the rest, and his brown eyes looked like great marbles in his pallid face. True, he had been expecting something like this, but not so soon. He knew, of course, that Campeggio would never open the court again; that his one idea was to return to Italy and not come back. He had done his duty. He had opened the court of enquiry and had kept it going for a month; now he sought this excuse to close it; and meanwhile the state of affairs in Europe had steadied themselves, giving Clement some indication of which side he must take.

This was disaster at home and abroad. Wolsey's French foreign policy had failed, for the Emperor and François were now friends, and neither felt much affection for England. So he had failed in that, and the people would be more against him than ever. He had also failed the King. He had promised him divorce, yet he was no nearer getting it than he had been more than a year ago.

Suffolk, Henry's brother-in-law, who had been working zealously in the King's cause, suddenly clenched his fist and hammered it on the table.

"England was never merry," he declared, "since we had Cardinals among us."

And as he spoke he glared at Wolsey who could not resist reminding him of that occasion when Suffolk had married Henry's sister Mary and had appealed for the Cardinal's help to placate the King. "Had it not been for one Cardinal," he said, "you my Lord Suffolk, might have lost your head, and with it the opportunity of reviling Cardinals."

The court broke up, and Wolsey was smiling as he saw Suffolk's crestfallen face. Norfolk was watching him with hatred too. So was Darcy. But they dared not speak against him. He was still the most powerful man in the land—under the King; and while he had the King's support, his enemies were powerless to touch him.

The King had already heard the news when Wolsey reached him.

Henry was alone and the Cardinal was surprised to see that his face was pale rather than scarlet as might have been expected. The eyes were as cold as ice.

"So," he said, "the Pope's man has closed the court."

Wolsey bowed his head in assent.

"And all these weeks have been wasted. He never meant to settle this matter. Meanwhile I am left uncertain."

"Your Grace, the Papal Legate has from the beginning practised procrastination to a fine degree."

"You need not tell me this. And the Queen has refused once more to enter a convent!"

"It is so, Your Grace."

The little blue eyes were narrowed. "I'll warrant she wishes me dead," he said.

Wolsey was startled. "Your Grace . . ." he began.

Henry was scowling. His Chancellor had not the sharp wits which had once been his.

"It would not surprise me," went on Henry, "if there should be a plot afoot to kill both me and you."

"Is it so, Your Grace?" Wolsey was waiting for orders and the King was satisfied.

"If such a plot should be discovered," went on the King, "and it was found that the Queen had a part in it . . ." The little mouth was cruel, the eyes ruthless . . . "she should not expect to be spared," he added.

Wolsey was thinking: Queen Katharine, you are a fool. Why did you not take yourself off to a convent? There you would have been safe. This is a man who takes what he wants, no matter who stands in his way. And you, Queen Katharine, now stand most dangerously in his path.

The King went on: "This is a matter which should be laid before the Council. They will be prepared to act if evidence is brought before them. You will see to this, for I hold it to be of great importance to our safety . . . yours and mine."

Wolsey bowed his assent.

He was vaguely troubled by his conscience, which over the years of good living he had learned to stifle.

So it has come to this, he thought. Katharine, you are in acute danger . . . and so am I.

## CHAPTER X

## THE FALL OF WOLSEY

NEVER in the whole of her life had Katharine felt so desolate and alone.

She lay on her bed, the drawn curtains shutting her in a small world of temporary peace. What will become of me? she asked herself, as she had continued to do since the Council's document had been brought to her. But she was not really thinking of what would become of herself; for there was one other whose safety was of greater concern to her than that of any other living person. She knew what it meant to be alone and friendless. What if such a fate befell her daughter?

"Holy Mother, help me," she prayed. "Guide me through this perilous period of my life."

The evil suggestion was afoot that she was trying to work some ill on the King and the Cardinal. Did they truly think that she—who never willingly harmed the humblest beggar—would try to poison the King and his chief minister? They had wronged her wilfully—at least the Cardinal had; she believed him to be the prime mover against her, and still saw Henry as an innocent boy who could be led. How could they honestly believe that she, a pious woman, could think for one moment of committing murder?

This was another plot of course to drive her into a convent.

Lying in her bed she thought of the comfort of a bare-walled cell, of the pleasant sound of bells, of escape from a world of intrigue. It attracted her strongly.

She sat up in her bed and once more read the scroll which she had been clutching in her hands as she lay there.

It informed her that she had not shown as much love for the King as she ought; that she appeared too often in the streets, where she sought to work on the affections of the people. She showed no concern for the King's preoccupation with his conscience, and the King could only conclude that she hated him. His Council therefore was advising him to separate from her at bed and board and to take the Princess Mary from her.

To take the Princess Mary from her!

If they had not added that, they might have frightened her into a convent. But while she had her daughter to think of she would never retire into oblivion.

Attached to the document was a note in Wolsey's hand. He had written that the Queen was unwise to resist the King, that the Princess Mary had not received the blessing of Heaven and that the brief which was held by the Emperor was a forgery.

"What will become of me?" she repeated. Whatever the future held, she would never allow them to frighten her into a convent, which would be tantamount to admitting that her marriage with the King was no true marriage. Never would she forget the slur this would cast on Mary.

She threw aside the scroll and lay down again, closing her eyes tightly, and said: "Let them do with this body what they will. Let them accuse me of attempting to murder the King and the Cardinal. Let them make me a prisoner in the Tower. Let them send me to the scaffold. Never will I allow them to brand Mary a bastard."

\*　　　\*　　　\*

Even greater than the Queen's sufferings were those of the Cardinal, for he lacked Katharine's spiritual resignation and constantly reproached himself for his own blindness which, looking back, he could see had brought him to that precipice on which he now stood; he mourned all that he had lost, and there was none of Katharine's selflessness in his grief.

Henry had left London with the Court without seeing him, and was now at Grafton Manor, that beautiful palace which was situated on the borders of the shires of Buckingham and Northampton, and had once been the home of Elizabeth Woodville.

Anne Boleyn was with the King, and Anne was now Queen of England in all but name; moreover she ruled the King as Katharine had never done. It was Anne who had suggested that Henry should leave Greenwich without informing his Chancellor; a procedure which but a few months before would have been unthinkable.

And now there had been no summons for him to go to Grafton; he had to beg leave—he, the mighty Cardinal—to accompany Campeggio who must pay his respects to the King before leaving the country.

What a sad and sorrowful journey it was, through London, where the people came out to see him pass! He travelled with his usual pomp but it seemed an empty show now, for the humblest beggar could not feel more fearful of his future than the great Cardinal of England.

Campeggio rode in silence beside him; his gout, he believed, had not improved since his sojourn in England and he was glad to be leaving and rid of a tiresome and delicate task; yet he had time to be sorry for his fellow Cardinal.

Poor Wolsey! He had worked hard to bribe his way into the Vatican . . . and failed. The Emperor had failed him; François had failed him; and now, most tragic of all, his own sovereign was being pressed to discard him. What then, when the whole world stood against him?

Optimism had never been far below the surface of Wolsey's nature; it was to this quality that, in a large measure, he owed his success. He believed that when he saw the King, Henry would remember how, over so many years, they had worked together, and he would not leave him unprotected and at the mercy of his enemies who were even now massing against him. Lord Darcy had already drawn up a list of his misdeeds in order that he might be impeached. They would be saying of him that he had incurred a *præmunire* because he had maintained Papal jurisdiction in England. He had failed to give the King the divorce he needed, and his enemies would be only too ready to declare that he had served not the King but the Pope. Norfolk and Suffolk had always hated him; and now they were joined by the powerful Boleyn faction headed by Anne herself, who ever since he had berated her for daring to raise her eyes to Percy, had been his enemy and had sought to destroy him with a vindictiveness only paralleled by Wolsey's own hounding of those who he considered had humiliated him.

It was the case of Buckingham repeating itself; only on this occasion the victim was the Cardinal himself.

And so they came to Grafton. There was revelry in the Manor, for Anne Boleyn and her brother George were in charge of the entertainments; and none knew how to amuse the King as they did. There would be hunting parties by day—the woods about Grafton had been the hunting ground of kings for many years—and the Lady would accompany the King and show him in a hundred ways how happy he would be if only he could discard the ageing Katharine and take to wife her brilliant, dazzling self.

The arrival of the Cardinals was expected and several of the King's household were assembled to welcome them. Campeggio was helped from his mule and led into the Manor to be shown the apartments which had been made ready for him; but no one approached Wolsey, and he stood uncertain what to do, a feeling of terrible desolation sweeping over him. For one of the rare occasions in his life he felt at a loss; it was no use assuming his usual arrogance because it would be ignored; he stood aloof, looking what he felt: a lonely old man.

He became aware that no preparation had been made for him at the Manor and that he would be forced to find lodgings in the nearby village. Such an insult was so intolerable and unexpected that he could not collect his wits; he could only stand lonely and silent, aware of little but his abject misery.

A voice at his side startled him. "You are concerned for a lodging, my lord?"

It was a handsome youth whom he recognized as Henry Norris, and because he knew this fellow to be one of those who were deeply involved with the Boleyns and formed part of that admiring court which was always to be found where Anne was, Wolsey believed that he was being mocked.

"What is that to you?" he asked. "I doubt not that lodgings have been prepared for me."

"My lord, I have reason to believe that they have not."

Only when Wolsey looked into that handsome face and saw compassion there, did he realize how low he had fallen. Here he stood, the great Cardinal and Chancellor, close friend of the King, seeking favours from a young gentleman of the Court who, such a short time before, had been wont to ask favours of him.

"I pray you," went on Henry Norris, "allow me to put a lodging at your disposal."

The great Cardinal hesitated and then said: "I thank you for your kindness to me in my need."

So it was Henry Norris who took him to a lodging in Grafton, and but for the compassion of that young man there would have been no place for him at the King's Court.

\*       \*       \*

There was excitement at Grafton. The Cardinal was in the Manor but all knew that no lodging had been prepared for him. That was on the orders of the Lady Anne, who commanded all, since she commanded the King. Now she would command Henry to dismiss his Chancellor, and all those who had hated the Cardinal for so long and had yearned to see his downfall were waiting expectantly.

Henry knew this, and he was disturbed. He had begun to realize that his relationship with the Cardinal had been one based on stronger feelings than he had ever experienced before in regard to one of his ministers; and much as he wished to please Anne, he could not bring himself lightly to cast aside this man with whom he had lived so closely and shared so much.

Anne insisted that Wolsey was no friend to the King because he worked for the Pope rather than Henry. And, she ventured to suggest, had the Cardinal so desired, the divorce would have been granted by now.

"Nay, sweetheart," replied Henry, "I know him better than you or any other man. He worked for me. 'Twas no fault of his. He made mistakes but not willingly."

Anne retorted that if Norfolk or Suffolk, or her own father had done much less than Wolsey they would have lost their heads.

"I perceive you are not a friend of my lord Cardinal, darling," Henry answered.

"I am no friend of any man who is not the friend of Your Grace!" was the reply, which delighted Henry as far as Anne was concerned but left him perplexed regarding Wolsey.

And now he must go to the presence chamber where Wolsey would be waiting with the other courtiers. He could picture the scene. The proud Cardinal in one corner alone, and the groups of excited people who would be watching for the King's entry and waiting to see the Cardinal approach his master—to be greeted coldly or perhaps not greeted at all.

Henry tried to work up a feeling of resentment. Why should he be denied his divorce? Why had not Wolsey procured it for him? Was it true that when the matter had been first suggested the Cardinal had intended a French marriage? Was it possible that, when he had known that the King's heart was set on Anne, he had worked with the Papal Legate and the Pope against the King?

Scowling, Henry entered the presence chamber and it was as he had believed it would be. He saw the expectant looks on the faces of those assembled there—and Wolsey alone, his head held high, but something in his expression betraying the desolation in his heart.

Their eyes met and Wolsey knelt, but the sight of him, kneeling there, touched Henry deeply. A genuine affection made him forget all his resolutions; he went to his old friend and counsellor and, putting both his hands on his shoulders, lifted him up and, smiling, said: "Ha, my lord Cardinal, it pleases me to see you here."

Wolsey seemed bemused as he stood beside the King, and Henry, slipping his arm through that of his minister, drew him to the window seat and there sat, indicating that Wolsey should sit down beside him.

"There has been too much friendship between us two for aught to change it," said Henry, his voice slurred with sentiment.

And the glance Wolsey gave him contained such gratitude, such adoration, that the King was contented, even though he knew Anne would be displeased when she heard what had happened. But there were certain things which even Anne could not understand and, as he sat there in the window seat with Wolsey beside him, Henry recalled the security and comfort which, in the past, this clever statesman had brought to him.

"Matters have worked against us," continued Henry, "but it will not always be so. I feel little sorrow to see your fellow Cardinal depart; he has been no friend to us, Thomas."

"He obeyed orders from Rome, Your Grace. He served the Pope; it was not enough that one of the Legates worked wholeheartedly for his King."

Henry patted Wolsey's knee. "It may be," he said darkly, "that we shall win without the Pope's help."

"His Holiness would give it, but for his fear of the Emperor."

"He's a weak fellow, this Clement. He sways with the wind."

"His position is so uncertain since the sack of Rome."

Henry nodded, and Wolsey went on, his spirits rising: "If Your Grace will grant me an audience in the morning, before I must depart with Campeggio, we could discuss the matter further. There are many ears cocked to listen here, many eyes to watch."

"'Tis so," said Henry nodding, and rising he put his arm once more through that of his Chancellor, and went with him back to the group of his gentlemen who were standing some distance from them.

\*　　　　\*　　　　\*

What comfort to rest his weary limbs in the bed for which he must be grateful to young Norris! How simple to explain the neglect!

It had happened without the King's knowledge. Naturally he would have believed that preparations were made for his Chancellor, for his dear friend the Cardinal. It was his enemies who had sought to degrade him. He was fully aware of the existence of them. When had he ever been without them?

As he stretched out blissfully he told himself that he had been unduly worried. He had suffered misfortunes, but he was as strong now as he had ever been and, while the King was his friend, he was invincible.

How he had misjudged his King! Hot tempered, selfish, hypocritical, capable of extraordinary blindness where his own faults and desires were concerned, yet Henry's heart was warm for those who had been his friends; and while that friendship could be relied on, there was nothing to fear. All that he, Wolsey, had done to serve his King was worth while. He would not regret the loss of Hampton Court; the gift was a symbol of the love between them which was indestructible. Nothing could change it . . . not even the vindictiveness of Anne Boleyn.

And tomorrow, thought Wolsey, we shall be alone together. Before I ride away with Campeggio on our way to the coast, I shall have had my intimate talk with Henry. All misunderstandings will be cleared away and it will be as it was in the old days when there was perfect accord between us. I will procure the divorce for him, but by that time, Mistress Anne Boleyn, he will have recovered from his infatuation. You have declared yourself my enemy; I declare myself yours. It shall be a French Princess for His Grace.

Tomorrow . . . Tomorrow . . . thought Wolsey, and slept. It was the most peaceful night he had enjoyed for a long time.

"A good bed, Norris," he murmured, when he awoke and saw that it was daylight. "I'll not forget you."

He rose and found that it was later than he had at first thought; but there was plenty of time to see the King before he left with Campeggio. In excellent spirits he dressed and, as he was about to make his way to the King's apartments, he met Henry Norris.

"I thank you for a good night's lodging," he said.

"Your Eminence looks refreshed," was the answer.

Wolsey patted the young man's shoulder. "I shall not forget your goodness to me. Now I go to seek the King."

Norris looked surprised. "His Grace left early this morning in the company of the Lady Anne."

Wolsey could not speak; he felt a lump in his throat which seemed as though it would choke him.

"They have gone off with a party for a day's hunting," continued Norris. "They'll not be back till dusk."

It was like arriving at this place and finding no lodging prepared for him. She was the cause of that; and she was the cause of this. Doubtless she had heard of the King's display of friendship and determined that there should be no more.

So he must leave with Campeggio, and that interview from which he had hoped so much would never take place. His defeat seemed as certain as it had been on his arrival.

In the palace they would be saying: Perhaps his fall is not as imminent as we hoped . . . but it is coming. Look at the warning shadows.

\*　　　\*　　　\*

These were uneasy months. The King stormed through the Court sometimes like a bewildered, angry bull, at others like a peevish boy. Why was a divorce denied him? Why was he so provoked?

He was politician enough to know the answer. It was because the Emperor was more powerful at the Vatican than the King of England, and the woman the King wished to put aside was the Emperor's aunt; it was as simple as that.

"Yet I will have my way!" declared the King.

In the Boleyn circle he had met a man who interested him because, although of somewhat obscure origins, he expounded original ideas. This man was a certain Thomas Cranmer, a scholar who had passed through Cambridge and had there become acquainted with Stephen Gardiner and Richard Fox. This man, Cranmer, had, during the course of conversation, which naturally enough turned on the main topic of the day, expressed original views on the way in which the King might obtain a divorce in spite of the continued vacillation of the Vatican.

"It is clear," Cranmer had said, "that the Pope is reluctant to grant the divorce because he fears the Emperor. Is it not time that the King looked for a solution to his Matter outside the Vatican?"

Gardiner and Fox had suggested that he should explain how

this could be done; to which Cranmer made answer that he believed the King should first make the universities see the reason behind his desires, and then appeal to enlightened opinion. Was England always going to remain a vassal of the Holy See?

Dr. Cranmer had voiced these opinions in other circles, and it was for this reason that the Boleyns had taken him under their protection and were making it known that Dr. Cranmer was a man of new, startling and brilliant ideas.

When Gardiner and Fox told the King of Cranmer's suggestion, Henry had listened intently and, as he did so, his expression lightened; he cried out: "By God, that man hath the right sow by the ear! Who is he? Let him be brought to me. I would talk with such a one."

So Cranmer had been brought forward and Henry had not been disappointed by their discourse, which had started a new train of thought in his mind.

The Queen's melancholy was lifted a little by the arrival of the new Imperial ambassador. This was Eustache Chapuys, an energetic Spaniard who had not been in England long before Katharine realized that here she had a stronger champion than she had had in Mendoza. Of humble beginnings, he had none of the aristocrat's preoccupation with his own nobility and was not constantly looking for slights. His family had, with some struggle, managed to send him to the University of Turin, and from there he had begun to make his fortune. He was now forty years old and this opportunity to work for the Queen against the divorce seemed to him like the chance of a lifetime; he was determined to succeed.

However, arriving in England he had discovered that it was very difficult to speak in private with the Queen, who very quickly warned him that she was spied on at all times, and implored him to be very wary of Wolsey. He understood at once that this was no exaggeration. As for the King, he met the new ambassador with reproaches, complaining that by withholding the Papal brief the Emperor had done a grave injury, not only to his but to Katharine's cause.

"If," Henry had said, "I could have been assured that the brief was genuine, I should, at this time be living with the Queen, for that is what I wish beyond all things, and it is solely because my conscience tells me that to resume marital relations with the Emperor's aunt would be to live in sin, that I refrain from doing so. Yet, since the Emperor will not release the brief I must conclude that he knows it to be a forgery and is afraid to submit it to the light of day."

"Your Grace," Chapuys had answered, "I myself can assure you that the brief is no forgery and that the copy you received in England is exact in every detail. Your conscience need disturb you no more."

Henry had been angry with the ambassador, and this was not a good beginning to their relationship; but at least he would understand that in the new ambassador he had a worthy adversary, and Katharine a good friend.

So Katharine's hope increased, because she believed that her case would be tried in Rome, and there she would have justice. She was convinced that all that was necessary to make Henry send Anne Boleyn back to Hever and turn to his true wife was an order from Rome.

But how sad she was in the Palace, where Anne ruled as though she were Queen, and Katharine was only at the King's side on the most formal occasions! The humiliation she could have endured; but it was Anne's decree that the Princess Mary should not be present at Court, and because Anne commanded this, Mary was kept away.

She fears the King's affection for my daughter, Katharine decided; and there was a little comfort in that belief. But how she longed for the child's company. On those rare occasions when she was with the King she sought to lead the conversation to their daughter's absence in an endeavour to arouse a desire in him to have her with them.

But he was sullenly pursuing Anne, and Katharine often wondered whether his dogged determination to have his way was as strong as his desire.

One day when he had supped in her apartments she seized an opportunity to whisper to him: "Henry, would you not like to see our daughter here?"

"She is well enough where she is."

"I miss her very much."

"Then there is no reason why you should not go to her."

"To go to her would be to leave you. Why cannot we all be together?"

He was silent and turned away from her. But she could not control her tongue. "As for myself," she went on, "I see so little of you. I am often alone, neglected and forsaken. Who would believe that *I* was the Queen? I must brood on my wrongs continually."

"Who forces you to do so?" demanded Henry. "Why do you not count your blessings?"

"My blessings! My daughter not allowed to come to me! My

husband declaring he has never been my husband and seeking to marry another woman!"

"If you are neglected," said Henry, his voice rising, "that, Madam, is your affair. There is no need for you to remain here if you wish to go. Do I keep you a prisoner? I do not. You may go whither you like. As for the way I live . . . it is no concern of yours, for learned men have assured me that I am not your husband."

"You *know* that you are my husband. You know that I was a virgin when I married you. You choose to forget that now. But, Henry, do not rely on your lawyers and doctors who tell you what they know you want to hear. They are not my judges. It is the Pope who will decide; and I thank God for that."

Henry's eyes narrowed. He was thinking of recent conversations with Cranmer, Gardiner, Fox and Anne, and he said slowly and deliberately: "If the Pope does not decide in my favour, I shall know what to do."

She flashed at him: "What could you do without the Pope's approval?"

Henry snapped his fingers and his lips scarcely moved as he replied, though the words smote clearly on Katharine's ear: "This I should do, Madam. I should declare the Pope a heretic and marry when and whom I please."

\*          \*          \*

The Cardinal was taking a solitary tour through York Place, knowing that it was doubtless the last time he would do so. Here were stored many of his treasures which almost rivalled those which had been in Hampton Court when he had lost that mansion to the King.

He stood at the windows but he did not see the scenes below; he leaned his heated head against the rich velvet hangings, as he glanced round the room, at the tapestries and pictures, at the exquisite furniture which he had so treasured.

In the pocket of his gown was the communication he had received from the King. The Lady Anne, it seemed, had set her heart on York Place. She would have no other house in London. Therefore the King asked the Cardinal to offer this up to her.

Hampton Court . . . and now York Place! One by one his treasures were being stripped from him. Thus it would be until he had nothing left to give but his life. Would they be content to leave him that?

He knew that a Bill of Indictment had been registered against him; he knew the hour could not be long delayed when Norfolk and Suffolk would arrive to demand that he give up the Great Seal.

The days of greatness were over. The fight for survival had begun.

He did not have long to wait. Smug, smiling, like dogs who had at last been thrown the titbits for which they had been begging, Norfolk and Suffolk arrived to demand the delivering up of the Great Seal.

He received them with dignity in the beautiful hall, surrounded by rich treasures which he must soon surrender. His dignity was still with him.

"I would see the King's handwriting on this demand," said Wolsey, "for how may I know you come at his command if I do not?"

Norfolk and Suffolk flushed and looked at each other. Neither was noted for his quick wits. Then Suffolk spluttered: "You know full well that we come on the King's command."

"How should I know, when there is no written order from him?"

"Then is it a surprise to you that you should be asked to hand back the Seal?"

"This is not a question of my emotions, my lords, but of your authority to take the Seal from me. I shall not give it to you unless you bring me a written order from the King."

The Dukes were angry but they had never been able to argue successfully with Wolsey.

"Come," said Suffolk, "we will return in a very short time with what he demands."

And they left him. It would be a short time, Wolsey knew. But there was a small hope within him. The King had not wished to put his name to a demand for the Great Seal. He had turned his back on Wolsey, but at least he had not joined the pack who were waiting to tear the old minister to pieces.

\*     \*     \*

The Cardinal was in great terror. It was not the fact that Norfolk and Suffolk had returned to take the Seal from him, with a written command from the King. That, he had known, was inevitable. It was not that he was ordered to leave York Place for Esher, an empty house which belonged to his bishopric of Winchester. It was the knowledge that his physician had been taken to the Tower where he might be put to the question, and betray secrets which could mean disaster to Wolsey if they were ever told to the King.

He had been desperate. He had seen disaster coming and had

Y

sought to win back all he had lost in one desperate throw. His enemy was Anne Boleyn and he had determined to be rid of her, knowing that if he could do this, he could quickly win back the King's regard.

As a Cardinal he was in a position to have direct communication with the Pope, and he had made use of his advantages by advising the Pope to insist that the King send Anne from the Court or face excommunication. This had seemed to him to offer a solution of his troubles, because if the King dismissed Anne he, Wolsey, would very quickly return to his old position. If the King did not dismiss Anne but defied the Pope, Wolsey calculated that opinion in the country would be split; the situation would be dangerous for England; and the King would quickly realize that there was only one man strong enough to save the country from disaster; that man was Wolsey.

This had been his plan, and it had been made not for the good of the country, not for the good of the King, but for the salvation of Wolsey.

He had failed in his attempt; yet it was not that failure which disturbed him, but the knowledge that his weak physician may have confessed this secret and that the King might soon be aware of what he had done.

What hope would there be for him then? Banishment to Esher! It would not end there.

The grim shadow of the Tower lay before him; he could see himself walking from his prison with the executioner beside him and the blade of the axe turned towards him.

Now outside York Place and all along the banks of the river the people were assembling; craft of all description crowded the river. It was a holiday for them. They believed they were gathering to watch Wolsey on his way to the Tower.

He would pass out of York Place with all the pomp and ceremony with which he had been wont to make his journey from Hampton to Westminster. There would no longer be the Great Seal to proclaim him Chancellor. But he still had his Cardinal's hat and his magnificently attired entourage. He would have his fool beside him, his cooks and stewards, his ushers and secretaries, as though the journey from York Place to Esher was no different from many another journey he had taken.

But he felt sick and weary. Thomas Cromwell was with him, and Cromwell's dejection was clear to see. Was he mourning for the downfall of a friend, or asking himself what effect the loss of an influential benefactor would have? Who could say? And what did it matter now?

So out of York Place he came to take barge for Putney. Soon they would be counting the treasures there, and delightedly laying before the King and the Lady the lists of valuables, the costly booty. York Place was following Hampton Court; and Esher lay before him, an empty house where he would endeavour to keep his state until perhaps he was called to an even less comfortable lodging.

He was making up his mind what he would do. There were two courses open to him. It was no use appealing to Parliament, which was under the influence of Norfolk; but he could take his case to the law courts. There he had a fair chance of winning, because he was still the wiliest statesman in the land. But it would never do to win. The King would never forgive that. There was one object which he must keep in mind; one preoccupation which must be his to the exclusion of all else. He must keep his head upon his shoulders. He knew what he must do. He would admit that he had incurred a *præmunire* and he would ask the King, in payment for his sins, to take all that he possessed.

He smiled wryly, thinking of those bright blue eyes alight with acquisitiveness. While Henry studied the lists of possessions which would fall into his eager hands he might spare a little kindness for his one-time Chancellor and favourite minister. He might say: "Good Thomas, he always knew what would please me best."

Disembarking at Putney he continued his journey away from the glories of the past into the frightening unknown future. The people watched him sullenly. This was an occasion for which they had long waited.

"His next journey will be to the Tower!" they cried.

And some raised their voices, because there was now no need to fear: "To the scaffold with the butcher's cur!"

But as he rode through the muddy streets on his way to Esher he was met by Sir Henry Norris, the young man who had given him a lodging at Grafton.

He was moved by the sight of the young man, and he found that he could be touched more deeply by discovering that there were some in the world who did not hate him than by anything else. He realized that, apart from that little family which he kept shut away from his public life and of whom during the last busy years he had seen very little, he had tender thoughts for no one and had used all who came within his orbit in the manner in which they could serve him best. Therefore a sign of friendship from any of these people seemed a marvellous thing.

Thus with Norris. But it was more than his friendship that Norris had to offer on this day.

"Your Eminence," he said, "I come from the King. He sent you this as a token of the friendship which he still feels towards you in memory of the past."

Norris was holding out a ring which Wolsey had seen many times on the King's finger, and when he recognized it the tears began to fall down the Cardinal's cheeks. There had been some true friendship between them then. He had been more than a wily minister to his King.

If I could but reach him, thought Wolsey. Oh Lord, give me one half hour alone with him and I will make him listen to me and share my opinions. There was never ill-feeling between us that was not engendered by that black night-crow. Give me a chance to talk to him . . .

But it was too late. Or was it? Here was the ring . . . the token of friendship.

He must show his gratitude to this young man, so he dismounted and embraced Norris; then he knelt in the mud to give thanks to God because his King had sent him a token of friendship. He could not remove his hat easily because the ribbon was too tightly tied, so he tore the ribbon and knelt bareheaded while Norris looked on embarrassed, and the crowds watched in bewilderment.

The Cardinal had no thought for them. Henry had sent him a token, and with the token—hope.

He gave Norris an amulet—a gold cross and chain—and, wondering what gift he could send to the King which would convey the depth of his gratitude, he saw his Fool standing by and he called to him.

"Go with Sir Henry Norris to the King," he said, "and serve him as you have served me."

The Fool looked at him with mournful eyes and shook his head.

"What means this?" asked Wolsey. "It is better to serve a King than a Cardinal; did you not know that, Fool?"

He was expecting some merry retort, but none came. Instead the man said: "I serve none but my master."

And as he stood there, his satin robes spattered with the mud of the streets, the ring warm on his finger, the Cardinal was once more astonished to find that he who had cared for nothing but ambition had yet found one or two who would serve him for love.

"You are indeed a fool," he said.

"The Cardinal's Fool, not the King's Fool," was the answer.

Wolsey signed to him to go, but the Fool knelt and clung to the red satin robes until it was necessary to call six yeomen to drag him protesting away.

The strangeness of that street scene, thought Wolsey, as he rode on to Esher, will remain with me for as long as I live.

\* \* \*

In the manor house at Esher there were neither beds, cups, cooking utensils nor sheets.

Wolsey entered the hall and stared about him in dismay at the emptiness. His servants gathered round him wonderingly. Thomas Cromwell moved towards an embrasure and looked out of the window, his eyes alert, his trap-like mouth tight. What now? he was asking himself. Need the end of Thomas Wolsey be the end of Thomas Cromwell?

The Cardinal asked that all his servants should be brought into the hall, and there he addressed them.

"As you see, we have come to a house which is empty of food and furniture. We must bestir ourselves and borrow for the needs of myself and one or two servants. For the rest of you, I advise you to return to your homes. It may well be that in three or four weeks I shall have cleared myself of the charges which are being brought against me; then I shall return to power and call you back to me. Now you must go for, as you see, you cannot stay here."

Across that room the eyes of Cromwell met those of Wolsey.

Cromwell took five pounds in gold from his purse and said: "There are many among us who owe what they have to the Cardinal. There was a time when great blessings flowed from him. Now we see him stripped of his possessions, his home this manor in which there is nowhere to lay his head. It is my hope that many here will follow my example and add to this sum, so that some comfort may be bought for His Eminence during the time which may elapse before he returns to favour."

And before the Cardinal's astonished eyes certain members of his household came forward and laid what sums of money they could afford beside that set down by Cromwell.

Then his servants busied themselves and went out to borrow beds and cooking utensils from neighbouring houses; and there was activity in the manor of Esher.

So, until a call came for him to go elsewhere, he would live there surrounded only by those lower servants who were necessary to look after his physical comforts.

The others—the ambitious men—rode away from Esher; and

among them was Thomas Cromwell, who had made up his mind
to try his fortune in the King's Court.

*          *          *

There was time, in the weeks which followed, to review his
life, to reproach himself with having strayed far from the road of
self-denial, to do penance because his ambition had destroyed
him first spiritually and now physically.

He was a sick man. He scarcely slept, and when he did he was
constantly awakened by nightmares. During his stay at Esher,
in much discomfort, he had suffered from dropsy. The house was
damp as well as ill-furnished, and he had appealed to the King
to allow him to move nearer to London where the air, suiting him
better, might help him to throw off his malaise. Henry was still
kind to him, though refusing all requests to receive him in
audience. Was there some softness in the King's nature which
told him that once he and his ex-chancellor were in each other's
company all would be forgotten but the friendship they had once
had for each other? Was that why the King so stubbornly refused
that much-desired interview?

Well, he was alone, shorn of his power; no longer did men come
to him seeking favours. But the King had allowed him to move to
the lodge in Richmond Park, had sent him another ring with his
portrait and had demanded that Anne Boleyn also send him a
token of her esteem. An empty gift from the Lady, but showing
that even she dared not disdain the Cardinal too harshly in the
King's presence. Henry had also sent Dr. Butts, with orders that
his good physician's commands were to be obeyed.

But Wolsey had not been allowed to stay in Richmond.
Norfolk and Suffolk saw to that. Wolsey smiled wryly to hear
how disturbed those two were, and how they had put their
ducal heads together to plan how to keep him and the King
apart. And so he had returned to his house at Southwell for the
summer months and attempted to live there in some state. But
Norfolk would not leave him in peace and insisted that he go to
York.

How painfully he travelled, a sad and lonely exile! Yet he
was enjoying a hitherto unknown popularity with the people,
and many came to him to ask his blessing.

And so he came to Cawood which was but twelve miles from
the city of York, his destination. There he stayed awhile, con-
firming and blessing people who asked this service of him, in his
obscurity living like a man of the Church, as in the role of statesman he had never done before.

Yet always he waited for a word from the King, a sign that Henry was ready to welcome him back. He was a sick man, and there was but one elixir which could restore him to health; it was what he had fought for and won, and now knew he could never live happily without: The King's favour.

\*        \*        \*

Henry missed his Wolsey.

Often he would shout at those who served him: "It was never thus in the Cardinal's day."

His new Chancellor was Thomas More, a man for whom he had a deep affection; but More was no Wolsey. He never considered his own comforts nor those of his King. More, who was a lawyer, was a thousand times more a churchman than the Cardinal had ever been, but saintly men made uneasy companions and More had taken office only on condition that he was not asked to act in the matter of the divorce. Henry was aware that Thomas More was one of those who believed him to be truly married to Katharine. It was small wonder that he yearned for his accommodating Wolsey.

But his enemies were pleading for the Cardinal's blood. It did not please them that he should merely be sent into exile. They wanted to see him lay his head on the block.

There was Anne who would not rest until Wolsey was dead. She was scornful, her black eyes flashing. How often had she cried: "If my father or my lords Norfolk and Suffolk had done half what he has done they would have lost their heads."

Henry wanted to explain to Anne: We were more than King and statesman. We were friends. I have sent him from me. Let that suffice.

There was Norfolk for ever whispering in his ear. When the King was a little anxious about an ulcer on his leg, which refused to heal, it was Norfolk who cried:

"Your Grace, the Cardinal suffered from the great pox. Is it to be wondered at? Your Grace knows the life he led. Yet knowing that the pox was with him he came to Your Grace, blowing upon your noble person with his perilous breath."

"Nay," said the King. "This ulcer of mine has naught to do with Wolsey."

"And, Sire, did you know that he spoke often of 'The King and I' as though there was no difference in your rank?"

"We were friends," said Henry with a smile, "and when I was a young man and given to pleasure, he taught me much."

"Did Your Grace know that he had as mistress the daughter

of a certain Lark, and by her had two children . . . a son and daughter?"

"A son," said the King wistfully. "So even Wolsey had a son."

"I heard that he married the woman off to give her and her children a name. The boy received great benefits."

The King nodded. He was not to be shocked or moved to anger against his minister.

But there came a day when news was brought to him by both Norfolk and Suffolk.

"Your Grace, the Cardinal's Italian physician, Dr. Augustine Agostini has made an important statement."

"What statement is this?"

"He tells us that the Cardinal suggested to the Pope that he should command you to put aside the Lady Anne and return to the Lady Katharine and, if you failed to do this, to excommunicate you."

Henry's face grew purple with anger.

"Then he is indeed guilty," he said. "He has indeed incurred a *præmunire*."

"Worse still, Your Grace. He deserves the traitor's death, for what he has done could be called high treason."

The King nodded. He was distressed; but before he had time to allow his feelings to soften, the warrant for the Cardinal's arrest was put before him and signed.

Norfolk and Suffolk were delighted. No more need they fear the anger of the Cardinal. His days were numbered.

\*       \*       \*

In the Cardinal's lodgings at Cawood there was peace. Wolsey sat at supper. He felt comforted, contemplating that soon he would arrive in York and there, he promised himself, he would endeavour to spend his last months—he was sure it would not be more—in pious living.

As he supped he became aware of a commotion in the house, and then of footsteps on the stairs, and when the door was thrown open, to his astonishment he saw a man who had once been in his service: young Northumberland. He rose somewhat hastily from the table and went forward to embrace the young man who, he believed, had come on a visit of friendship. In those first seconds he forgot that this was the young man whom once, in the days of his power, he had sternly berated for contemplating marriage with Anne Boleyn.

"My friend," he cried, "it gives me great pleasure to see you here . . ."

But as he approached, Northumberland drew himself up and did not take the Cardinal's outstretched hands.

He looked down at the old man and said in a voice so soft that it could scarcely be heard: "My lord Cardinal, I come to arrest you on a charge of high treason."

"My dear boy . . ." began Wolsey.

But Northumberland's face was expressionless; he looked down on Wolsey, without emotion, without pity.

And as he stood there, the Cardinal saw others come into the room, and he knew that what he had dreaded for so long was about to happen.

\* \* \*

The painful journey back to London began.

There was time to brood, and he thought of Anne's arranging that Northumberland should be sent to arrest their enemy. Poor, pallid Northumberland, doubtless he would not have been willing, for he had ever lacked Anne's spirit. It would have been an ill match. She should have thanked the Cardinal for breaking it. But how like her, to send Northumberland, she, who resembled himself, and never forgot a slight, and demanded payment in full—with interest.

So, because of her, he was riding back to London, and his constant prayer now was that he would never reach that city. In his dreams he was passing along the dark river and through the traitor's gate; he was placing his head on the block. Was that to be the end of the journey?

There were many halting places as he could not travel far at one time. His dropsy had grown worse, and he suffered from dysentery and mental discomfort. He was an old, tired man, and he longed to rest his weary limbs; how could he travel quickly towards a cold bed in a dismal cell, there to live a few weeks under the shadow of the axe?

So far have I risen, he mused, that there is a long way to fall.

When he arrived at Sheffield Park the Earl of Shrewsbury welcomed him as though he were still the chief minister. He rested there awhile, for he was exhausted and it was physically impossible to ride on.

It was at Sheffield that messengers came from the King, and to his horror Wolsey saw that at the head of them was Sir William Kingston, the Constable of the Tower. This could mean only one thing: Kingston had come himself to take him straight to the fortress; and in spite of Kingston's assurances that Henry still thought of the Cardinal as his friend, Wolsey was seized with violent illness, and all those about him declared that from that moment he lost his desire to live and began to yearn for death.

In the company of Kingston he travelled down to Leicester, blessing the people as he went. How differently they felt about him now. They no longer called him "butcher's cur" because they were no longer envious of him. They pitied him. They had learned of the pious life he had led in exile, and they regarded him as the holy man his garments proclaimed him.

The party drew up at the Abbey; it was dusk and servants with torches hurried out to welcome them. The Abbot, knowing who his guest was, came forward to salute the Cardinal and receive his blessing; but as Wolsey tried to dismount, his limbs gave way and he collapsed at the Abbot's feet.

"Your Eminence," cried the Abbot, trying to raise him, "welcome to Leicester. Your servants rejoice to have you with us for as long as you can rest here."

With the help of the Abbot the Cardinal rose to his feet; he was trembling with fatigue and sickness.

"Father Abbot," he said, "methinks I shall stay with you for ever, for hither I have come to lay my bones among you."

Alarmed, the Abbot gave orders that the Cardinal should be helped to his room. His usher, George Cavendish, was at his side; indeed, he had been with him through his triumphs and his trials, and nothing but death could part them.

"Stay near me, George," murmured the Cardinal. "You know as I do, that now it will not be long."

Cavendish discovered that he was weeping silently but the Cardinal was too exhausted to notice his tears.

For a day and a night he lay in his room, unable to move, unaware of time. He slept awhile and awoke hungry and asked for food, which was brought to him.

He partook of the food almost ravenously and then paused to ask Cavendish what it was he ate.

"'Tis a cullis of chicken, my lord, which has been made especially for you in order to nourish you."

"And you say we have been here a day and a night; then this will be St. Andrew's Eve."

"'Tis so, Your Eminence."

"A fast day . . . and you give me chicken to eat!"

"Your waning strength needs it, Eminence."

"Take it away," said Wolsey. "I will eat no more."

"Your Eminence needs to regain his strength."

"Why George? That I may be well enough to travel to the block?"

"Your Eminence . . ." began Cavendish in a faltering voice.

"You should not distress yourself, George, for I feel death near, and death coming now is merciful to me. Go now. I believe my time is short and I would see my confessor."

He made his confession; and afterwards he lay still like a man who is waiting patiently though with longing.

Kingston came to his bedside and Wolsey smiled at him quizzically, remembering how the sight of the man had filled him with fear before.

"Your Eminence will recover," said Kingston.

"No, my lord. For what purpose should I recover?"

"You are afraid that I come to take you to the Tower. You should cast aside that fear, because you will not recover while it is with you."

"I would rather die in Leicester Abbey, Kingston, than on Tower Hill."

"You should cast aside this fear," repeated Kingston.

"Nay, Master Kingston, you do not deceive me with fair words. I see the matter against me, how it is framed."

There was silence in the room; then Wolsey spoke quietly and firmly, and Kingston was not sure that he addressed himself to him.

"If I had served God as diligently as I have done the King, He would not have given me over in my grey hairs."

He closed his eyes, and Kingston rose and left the chamber. At the door he met George Cavendish and shaking his head said: "Your master is in a sorry state."

"I fear he will not last long, my lord. He is set on death. He thought to die ere this. He said that he would die this morning and he even prophesied the time. He said to me: 'George, you will lose your master. The time is drawing near when I shall depart this Earth.' Then he asked what time it was and I told him 'Eight of the clock.' 'Eight of the clock in the morning,' he said. 'Nay it cannot be, for I am to die at eight of the clock in the morning.'"

"He rambled doubtless."

"Doubtless, my lord, but he seemed so certain."

"Well, eight of the clock passed, and he lives."

Kingston went on, and Cavendish entered the Cardinal's chamber to see if he lacked anything. Wolsey was sleeping and seemed at peace.

Cavendish was at his bedside through the night and the next morning—when he died.

As the Cardinal drew his last breath, the faithful usher heard the clock strike eight.

## CHAPTER XI

# THE LAST FAREWELL

THOMAS CROMWELL was on his way to an appointment with the King. His eyes were gleaming with excitement; he had proved to himself that it was possible for an astute man to profit by disaster, to make success out of failure, for, incredible as it seemed, out of the decline of Wolsey had come the rise of Thomas Cromwell.

Yet he had remained the friend of Wolsey until the end. He wanted men to know that he was a true friend; and he and the Cardinal had been too closely attached for him to break away when Wolsey was in danger. As Member of Parliament for Taunton he had pleaded Wolsey's case in the Lower House and so earned the Cardinal's gratitude and at the same time the admiration even of his enemies.

He was a shrewd and able man. No one could doubt that; and it was said that if he could work so well for one master, why should he not for another. The son of a blacksmith, he must be possessed of outstanding ability to have come so far, a feat which was only outrivalled by that of Wolsey himself.

Shortly after Wolsey's death Cromwell was made a Privy Councillor, not, naturally, of the same importance as Norfolk or Thomas Boleyn, who was now the Earl of Wiltshire, but a man who had already found his way into that magic circle in which limitless opportunity was offered.

It was not long before Cromwell had attracted the attention of the King. Henry did not like the man personally but the shrewdness, the alert mind, the humble origins, all reminded him of Wolsey, and he was already beginning to regret the loss of the Cardinal and remembered those days when, in any difficulty, he summoned his dear Thomas to his side.

Therefore he was more ready than he might otherwise have been to take notice of Cromwell. Thus came Cromwell's opportunity—a private interview with the King.

When he was ushered into the presence, the King pondered wistfully: The fellow lacks the polish of Wolsey!

But he remembered that Wolsey had singled out this man and that fact counted in his favour. Cromwell had been a good friend to Wolsey in the days of his decline; so he was capable of loyalty.

The King waved his hand to indicate that Cromwell might dispense with ceremony and come to the point.

"Your Grace, I have long considered this matter of the Divorce . . ."

Henry was startled. The man was brash. Others spoke in hushed tones of this matter; they broached it only with the utmost tact. Cromwell looked bland, smug almost; as though he were playing a game of cards and held a trump in his hand.

"You are not alone in that," said Henry with a hint of sarcasm which did not appear to be noticed by Cromwell, whose dark eyes burned with enthusiasm as he leaned forward and gazed intently at the King.

"Your Grace is debarred from success in this matter by the cowardly ways of your advisers. They are afraid of Rome. They are superstitious, Your Grace. They fear the wrath of the Pope."

"And you do not?"

"Sire, I am a practical man unmoved by symbols. I fear only my King."

"H'm! Go on, go on," he urged, slightly mollified.

"It has been a marvel to me that Your Grace's advisers have not seen what must be done, ere this. Thomas Wolsey was a Cardinal; it was natural that he should have been in awe of Rome. But those men who now advise Your Grace are not Cardinals. Why should they so fear the Pope?"

It was strange for Henry to have questions fired at him. He did not care for the man's crude manners, but the matter of his discourse had its interests.

"At this time," went on Cromwell, "it would seem that England has two heads—a King and a Pope. Furthermore, since the Pope denies the King that which he desires, it appears that the Pope holds more power in England than the King."

Henry was beginning to frown, but Cromwell went on quickly: "As a loyal subject of the King this pleases me not at all."

"The power of Kings is temporal," murmured Henry.

"I would wish to see my King holding supreme power, temporal and spiritual."

Henry was startled, but Cromwell continued blithely: "I cannot see why our King should not dispense with the Church of Rome. Why should not the Church of England stand alone with the King as its Supreme Head? Would it be necessary then for the King to plead in Rome for what he needs?"

Henry was aghast. He had often said that he would declare the Pope a heretic, that if the Pope would not grant him a divorce he would find some other means of getting it; but this man was proposing a more daring step than he had ever taken. He was suggesting that the Church should sever its connections with Rome; that the King, not the Pope, should be Supreme Head of the Church.

The King listened and his eyes burned as fiercely as those of Cromwell.

"In a few years," Cromwell told him, "I could make Your Grace the richest and most powerful King in Christendom . . . but not while you remain a vassal of the Pope."

It was astounding. It meant more than the Divorce. The King was shaken. There was so much to consider. If only Wolsey were here . . . but Wolsey would never work for the severance of England from Rome. Wolsey had been a Cardinal, his eyes constantly on the Papal Crown; he had even pleaded guilty to attempting to set up Papal jurisdiction in England. New times needed new ideas. Wolsey's day was gone and a new era was beginning.

When Henry at length dismissed Cromwell he was telling himself that Cromwell, like Cranmer, had the right sow by the ear.

*         *         *

Katharine at Richmond was unaware of the great schemes which were absorbing the King and his new ministers. Mary was with her, and she was determined to enjoy the hours she spent with her daughter. Mary was now fifteeen years old, an age when many girls were married; but the question of Mary's marriage had been shelved; how could it be otherwise when there was so much controversy about her birth?

During these days Katharine seemed possessed of a feverish desire to make the most of each hour they spent together; each day when she arose she would wonder whether some command would be given and her daughter taken from her. She knew that Henry was as devoted to Anne as ever; that they had taken over York Place and, like a newly married pair, were exulting in all the treasures they found there.

The palace had ceased to be known as York Place, which had been its name as the town residence of the Archbishops of York; it was now the King's palace and, because of the reconstructions which had been made in white stone, it was called White Hall.

Now Wolsey had gone, Katharine felt that she was rid of her greatest enemy. She could tell herself that in good time the Pope would give the only possible verdict, and when Henry realized that their marriage was accepted as valid, he must, for the sake of reason and his good name, accept her as his wife. So she allowed herself to be lulled into a certain peace which Mary's presence made it possible for her to enjoy.

Reginald Pole was in England and it was delightful when he came to visit them, which he did very frequently. He was their friend and staunch supporter. One day, mused Katharine, why should he not be consort of the Queen? What a brilliant adviser Mary would have! What a tender, gentle husband!

"That is what I want for her," the Queen told her friend, Maria de Salinas, who, now that she was a widow, had come back into the Queen's service. "A tender, gentle husband, that she may never be submitted to the trials which I have had to bear."

Katharine and Mary were sitting together over the Latin exercise when a page entered the apartment to tell them that Reginald was without and begging an audience.

Mary clasped her hands together in delight, and Katharine could not reprove her. Poor child, let her not attempt to curb her pleasure by hiding it. Katharine said with a smile: "You may bring him to us."

Reginald came in and the three of them were alone together. Mary took both his hands when he had bowed first to the Queen and then to herself.

"Reginald, it seems so long since we saw you."

He smiled at her youthful exuberance. "It is five days, Your Highness."

"That," said Mary, "is a very long time for friends to be apart."

"We have so few friends now," Katharine quickly added.

"You have more than you know," Reginald replied seriously. "Many of the people are your friends."

"They greet us warmly when we go among them," Mary agreed. "But we have few friends at Court whom we can trust. I believe they are afraid of . . ." Mary's lips tightened and she looked suddenly old, ". . . of . . . that woman," she finished.

Katharine changed the subject. "Reginald, something has happened, has it not?"

"Your Grace has a penetrating eye."

"I can see it in your expression. You look . . . perplexed."

Reginald took a document from the pocket of his doublet and handed it to the Queen. While she studied it he turned to Mary who laid her hand on his arm. "Reginald," she said, almost imploringly, "you are not going away?"

"I do not know," he said. "So much depends on the King."

"Please do not go away."

He took her hand and kissed it. "If I followed my own will I would never go away."

"Nor if you followed mine," said Mary.

Katharine lowered the document and looked from one to the other. The sight of them together frightened her while yet it pleased her. If only it *could* be, she thought; yet how can it?

"So the King has offered you the archbishopric of York or Winchester," she said.

Mary caught her breath in dismay. If he became an Archbishop he would take Holy Orders and marriage would be outside his power. Mary loved him with all the force of her serious young nature. She had dreamed that they would go away from Court, quietly with her mother to where they might forget such hateful matters as divorce, such hateful words as bastard, where they would never even think of the Lady who hated them so much and was determined to keep them apart. In her youthful innocence she dreamed of the three of them leaving Court in secret, going out of the country to Padua or some such place which Reginald knew well.

"These offices became vacant on the death of the Cardinal," Reginald explained, "and someone is needed to fill them."

"It is a great honour," the Queen said almost listlessly.

"It is one, I have told him, that I cannot accept."

The relief in the apartment was great. Mary laughed aloud and took Reginald's hand. "I am glad," she cried. "I could not bear to think of your stepping into the Cardinal's shoes."

"Nor I," he said. "But that is not all. In my refusal of this offer I implored the King not to be deluded by his ministers and his passion for a wanton woman. I am summoned to his presence in White Hall."

Mary was horrified; although her father had shown her affection at times, she had never conquered her fear of him. Katharine was equally afraid. She knew the climate of the King's temper. He was fond of Reginald, but when the people of whom he was fond ceased to agree with him he could easily hate them. She thought of the tenderness he had once shown to her; and she believed that his hatred of her was the greater because of it.

"Oh, Reginald," she murmured, "have a care."

"You should not have mentioned us," said Mary imperiously.

"I believed I must say what I felt to be right."

Katharine turned to her daughter and said gently: "We must all speak and act according to our consciences."

"I came to see you before I presented myself to the King," said Reginald. And both understood that he had come because this might, in view of the seriousness of the occasion, be the last time he could visit them. Neither of them spoke, and he went on: "I should go now. I dare not keep the King waiting."

He kissed their hands, and Mary suddenly forgot the dignity due to her rank as, like a child, she flung her arms about him; and Katharine was too moved to prevent her.

When he had gone, Mary began to weep, silently.

"My darling, control yourself," murmured the Queen, putting an arm about her.

But Mary merely shook her head. "What cruel times we live in," she whispered. "What cruel and perilous times!"

\* \* \*

When Reginald left the Queen and the Princess he took a barge to White Hall. He knew full well that the archbishopric had been offered him as a bribe. He was of royal blood and the friend of the Queen and the Princess; the King was hinting: "Come, work with me, and here is an example of the prizes which shall be yours."

That was why in refusing the offer he had told the King that he firmly believed in the royal marriage and implored his kinsman not to imperil his soul by attempting to deny it.

The result: A summons to White Hall.

As he entered the palace he thought of the great Cardinal who had once occupied it; and all this splendour had been passed to the King—a mute appeal . . . "all my possessions in exchange for my life . . ." What an example of the worth of treasures upon Earth!

Reginald uttered a prayer for the Cardinal's soul as he made his way to the gallery whither the King had summoned him.

I enter the Palace of White Hall a free man, he thought; how shall I leave it? It was very possible that he would do so with a halberdier on either side of him and thence take barge to the Tower.

Before he reached the gallery he met his elder brother, Lord Montague, who, having heard of the summons, was waiting for him.

As soon as Montague saw Reginald, he drew him into an anteroom and cried: "You are a fool. Do you want us all to lose our heads?"

"News travels fast," Reginald replied. "So you know I have refused York and Winchester."

"And have sought to teach the King his business at the same time."

"The archbishoprics were offered as a bribe; it was necessary to explain why I could not take either of them."

"It was enough to refuse and thereby offend the King; but to add criticism of his conduct . . . are you mad, brother?"

"I do not think so," answered Reginald, "unless it be madness to speak one's mind."

"That could be a very good definition of mental disorder," said Montague; and he turned away from his brother, who went on to the gallery.

Henry was expecting him and he was not kept waiting long. The King stood, massive in his jewelled garments, and for a few seconds while Reginald bowed he glared at him through half-closed eyes.

"So, sir," said Henry at length, "you think so little of my gifts that you haughtily refuse them!"

"Not haughtily, Your Grace."

"Do not dare contradict me. How dare you tell me what I should do! Is the King to take orders?"

"No, Sire, but perhaps advice."

"You young coxcomb, so *you* would presume to advise *me*!"

"Sire, I would plead with you on behalf of the Queen and the Princess Mary."

"You would be wise to keep your mouth shut."

"Nay, Your Grace, I hold that a wise man is one who speaks out of his love for the truth and not out of expediency."

Henry came closer to him, and his scarlet glowing cheeks were close to Reginald's pale ones.

"Is it wise then to gamble with your head?"

"Yes, Sire, for the sake of truth."

"The sake of truth! You dare to come to my presence in the manner of a father confessor . . . you whom I could send to the block merely by signing my name?"

"I come not as a father confessor, Your Grace, but as a humble kinsman of you and the Princess Mary."

"Ha," interrupted Henry, "so you prate of your royal blood. Take care that you do not think too highly of it. Mayhap you remember what befell a certain Duke of Buckingham?"

The sight of Reginald's calm face incensed the King; this was largely because here was another of those men, like Fisher and More, whose approval meant so much to him. They were men of integrity and he needed their approval and support. They maddened him when they would not give it.

"I remember well, Sire," Reginald answered.

"And the memory does not help you to change your views?"

"No, Your Grace."

The King's mood altered suddenly. "Now listen. I am asking you to come down from the seat of judgment. I am assured by learned men that I am not truly married to the Lady Katharine. I need the help of men such as you. You could write a treatise for me; you could explain the need of my severance from the Lady Katharine and my remarriage. I command you to do this. You are a man whom people respect; your word would carry much weight." He laid a hand on Reginald's shoulder affectionately. "Come now, Reginald, my dear cousin. Do this for love of me."

"Sire, on any other matter I would serve you with all my heart, but . . ."

"But!" Henry shrieked, pushing Reginald from him. "It would seem you forget to whom you speak."

"I forget not," answered Reginald. "But I crave Your Grace to excuse me in this matter."

Henry's hand flew to his dagger. "Do you not know that it is high treason to disobey the King?"

Reginald was silent.

"Do you?" cried the King. "By God, if you do not I shall find means to teach you." He called for a page, and when the young man appeared he shouted: "Send Lord Montague to me without delay."

The page departed and in a few moments Reginald's brother came hurrying into the gallery.

Henry shook his fist at Montague. "By God," he cried, "I'll have every member of your family clapped into the Tower. I'll brook no more insolence from you."

Montague stammered: "Your Grace, pray tell me what any member of my family has done to displease you."

Henry pointed at Reginald. "This brother of yours should be kept in better order. He dares to come here and meddle in my affairs. I'd have you know, Montague, that I have a way with meddlers."

"Yes, Your Grace; on behalf of my family I offer my deepest regrets. . . ."

"Take him away," shouted Henry, "before I lose my patience, before I order him to be sent to the Tower."

"Yes, Your Grace."

They bowed and left the irate Henry glaring after them, thinking: By God, 'twere better if Master Reginald had never come back to England.

When they were alone Montague turned indignantly to his brother.

"You . . . *fool*!" he cried.

"I will say to you, brother, what I have said to the King. Is it foolish to adhere to what one believes to be the truth?"

"Indeed you are a fool, having been at Court, to ask such a question. A man is a fool who attempts to wrestle with kings. I thought he would commit you to the Tower without delay."

"I believe he was contemplating the effect it would have on certain of his subjects if he did."

"You are calm enough. Do you seek a martyr's crown?"

"I hope never to perjure my soul for the sake of my head." said Reginald quietly.

He left his brother, who was filled with apprehension. Reginald was thinking of the King's suggestion that he should write a treatise. He would; but it would not put forward the reasons why the King should separate from Katharine; instead it would show why the marriage was a true one.

\*    \*    \*

When he was left alone Henry's anger abated a little. He began to think of the earnest young man whom he had threatened. He liked Reginald. He had always admired him; he knew him to be learned and pious; and now he had proved himself to be no coward.

Why could such men not see the truth about this marriage? Why did all the men he most respected set themselves against him?

He had tried to win the approval of Chancellor More but he could not do so. More was a clever lawyer and knew how to back out of any discourse that grew uncomfortable for him. What Henry most wanted was for Thomas More to work with him in all matters, and especially that of the divorce. He wanted Reginald Pole to do the same.

Brooding on these matters he sent once more for Reginald and his brother Montague, and when they stood before him he smiled at them in a friendly fashion.

"It is not meet," he said, "for kinsmen to quarrel."

"Sire, you are indeed gracious," said Montague.

Reginald did not speak, and Henry went on: "I am overwrought. These are troublous times. It may be that I appeared more angry towards you two than I felt."

"We rejoice to hear it," said Montague, and Reginald echoed those words.

"Come," said Henry, stepping between them and slipping an arm through one of each, "we are kinsmen and friends. Reginald

here has his own ideas as to what is right and what is wrong. I
will not say that he is alone in this, although many learned men
would not agree with him—nor can I, much as I should long to.
Remember this: I have to answer to my conscience. Oh, I
respect those who have views and do not hide them and are not
afraid to say 'This I think,' or 'With that I disagree.' I take all
that has been said in good part."

"Thank you, Your Grace," said Reginald with real emotion
in his voice.

Henry's tones softened and he turned almost pleadingly to
Reginald. "Why, if you could bring yourself to approve of my
divorce, no one would be dearer to me than you."

Montague was looking appealingly at his brother; but Reginald
remained silent.

Henry released their arms and patted both brothers in a gesture
of dismissal.

"Forget it not," he said.

\*          \*          \*

During the warm June weather the Court rode from Greenwich to Windsor. The Queen was in the party with her daughter
and Maria de Salinas; and the King rode gaily with the Lady
Anne. In the party Cranmer and Cromwell also rode.

There was a new confidence about the Lady, as there was
about the King. All noticed this except the Queen and her
daughter, for the former believed firmly that nothing could be
settled without the sanction of the Pope, and the latter fitted her
mood to that of her mother.

There were grave rumours everywhere and the whole Court
was expecting that the King's patience would not last much
longer.

Henry brooded as he rode. Why should I endure this continual
frustration? he asked himself. He looked at the glowing face of
Anne beside him and he longed to be able to soothe his troublesome conscience by telling the world that she was not his mistress
but his wife.

But events were moving fast. Cranmer had now obtained the
opinions of the universities of Europe regarding the divorce,
and had discovered several who believed it was expedient.
Henry had made up his mind that when they reached Windsor
he would ask the Queen to allow the matter to be judged in an
English court.

Once that took place he would have the desired result in a
matter of days. Who in England would dare to go against him?

He could count the dissenters on the fingers of one hand. More, Fisher, Reginald Pole. There were others, more obscure men whom he did not consider to be of much importance. It was different in the case of those three. The public looked to them for guidance.

A plague on them! he thought. Why must they put obstacles in my path?

As they came to Windsor, the King looked with pleasure at the forest. There would be good hunting, and there was little he liked better than a day in the open; then to return to good feasting and masking, and later to retire between the sheets with the right bedfellow.

She had succumbed at last and he wondered what he would do were she to become pregnant. Then, by God, he told himself, I would make them act.

Oddly enough she did not. But he would not spoil his pleasure by brooding on that. When they could be free in their love, when she could dispense with her fretful questions as to how much longer he would allow the delay; when he could take her with a good conscience . . . ah, then their union would be blessed with healthy boys.

They entered the castle, and the Queen retired with her little court and the King retired with his.

It would seem there are two queens at this Court, grumbled some of the courtiers; but most of them knew to which Court they should attach themselves . . . if they sought advancement. The Lady's bright black eyes missed little, and any attention to the Queen or the Princess Mary was noted.

The Queen in her apartments was attended by her few ladies. She was not so much afraid of spies as she had been in the days of Wolsey; and she was very happy to have her daughter and Maria with her.

She prayed on her arrival and in her prayers, as always, asked that the King might be turned from his sad and evil scheme and come back to her.

Mary was in her own apartment, her women preparing her for the banquet, when Henry came to see the Queen. Her women went scuttling away at a look from him, and Katharine cried: "Oh, Henry, how pleased I am that you should come to see me. It is a rare honour."

"I would come often enough if I could but satisfy myself that you were in truth my wife."

"Henry, I do not think that deep within your heart you believe that I am not."

It was wrong, of course. She should not say such things; but there were occasions when the bitterness was too much to be hidden.

He ignored her words as though he had not heard them. He said: "Dr. Cranmer has procured the opinions of the universities. There are many who believe we should be formally divorced."

"Ah, Henry, you have many friends. I alas have few."

"I think you too have friends," he said. "Now I am going to ask you to give me something."

"There is little I would deny you."

"I ask only sweet reasonableness."

"I try always to be reasonable."

"Then I am sure you will agree that this matter has continued too long, and it is time it were brought to an end. I want to refer it to the arbitration of four English prelates and four nobles."

Her expression was stony. "No," she said.

"Katharine, you call this reasonableness?"

"I do. A court in this country is unnecessary. It is a waste of time, for any court you set up would decide in your favour."

"This is nonsense."

"Henry, have done with hypocrisy. You know it to be truth. May God grant you a quiet conscience."

"You talk to me of a quiet conscience when you know it to be perpetually disturbed by this matter."

"Let it speak for itself, Henry. Do not provoke it with your desire, but let it say what it knows to be truth. Abide by it. Come back to me and then I think your conscience need never trouble you again on this matter."

"Never!" cried the King.

She answered his obstinacy with her own.

"Never will I abide by any decision except that of Rome."

The King gave her a murderous glance before he strode out of her apartment.

\*　　　\*　　　\*

Henry called Norfolk and Suffolk to him and when they were alone said: "I fear the Queen hates me."

The Dukes looked alert. They had heard this statement from the King's lips before this, and they knew that it was meant to be the prelude to some action which he was willing himself to take.

Henry went on: "I believe she delights in my discomfiture,

that she seeks to prolong it; that, knowing herself not to be my wife, she is determined to proclaim to the world that she *is*. I believe that she is seeking to lure my subjects from me."

"That," said Suffolk, "would amount to treason."

"Much as it pains me to admit it, I must agree," replied Henry. "Eustache Chapuys is nothing but a spy. I believe that it is the Emperor's desire to bring about a civil war in England, to split the country and to set the Queen and the Princess Mary at the head of the rebels."

"This is indeed treason," declared Norfolk.

"I have seen some of the letters which Chapuys has written to his master. In them he states that the English people are against a divorce and it would not surprise him if they rose in protest. They have full sympathy for the Queen, he writes significantly. I believe that the Spanish ambassador, with the help of the Queen, is ready to raise an insurrection."

"Your Grace, should he not be arrested?" asked Norfolk.

Henry raised a hand. "This is a delicate matter. Although Katharine is no true wife to me, for many years I believed her to be so."

Henry was thinking of the discontent among the people who, when Katharine's barge sailed up or down river, lined the banks to cheer her. To put Katharine under arrest would be to turn their sympathy into fury and the desire to protect their Queen. Moreover, he did not believe for one moment that Katharine would ever put herself at the head of an insurrection. How lacking in subtlety were these two! Wolsey would have grasped his meaning immediately.

"Nay," went on Henry, "she is no wife to me, but I confess to a certain tenderness. I would be lenient with her."

"But Your Grace will not continue to be in her company," said Norfolk, who was a little sharper than Suffolk and had at last begun to follow the King's train of thought.

"I fear the time has come when we must part . . . finally," Henry replied.

"I am in full agreement," Suffolk put in. "Your Grace should separate yourself from the Lady Katharine both at bed and board. It would not be safe for you to do otherwise."

A look of sadness came into the King's face. "After so many years . . ." he murmured.

But the Dukes were now aware of the part they were expected to play, and Suffolk said sternly: "Your Grace would do well not to think of a woman with whom you have for so long been living in sin."

Henry laid a hand on his brother-in-law's arm. "You do well to remind me."

His eyes were vindictive suddenly because he was remembering her obstinacy and how quickly this case could have been settled but for that. He went on: "'Tis my belief that she sets my daughter Mary against me."

Suffolk piped up dutifully: "Your Grace, should not the Princess Mary be taken from her?"

"That might be wise," answered the King, looking at Norfolk.

The Duke was well aware of what was expected of him. He spoke vehemently. "Above all, the Princess Mary should be removed from the Lady Katharine. That I consider to be of the greatest importance."

"Thank you, my friends," said the King. "You echo the thoughts which my tenderness would not let me utter. But since this is your advice, and I know it to be based on sound good sense, I will accept your decision."

*      *      *

Mary came into the Queen's apartments, her face pale, her eyes frightened.

"Mother," she cried, even before Katharine had had time to sign to the women to leave them, "I am to go away from you."

Katharine took her daughter's hands and found that they were trembling. "Be calm, my precious."

"I am to go to Richmond. Those are my father's orders."

"Well, you will go to Richmond and soon I shall come to you there."

"Suppose you cannot?"

"But why . . . *why* ?"

"I do not know . . . except that it is a feeling I have. I was told to prepare to leave at once. Why, Mother? What harm am I doing them here? Do I prevent his . . . his . . . being with that odious woman?"

"Hush, my love. Go to Richmond. I will find means of coming to you there."

Mary had begun to shiver. "Mother, I am afraid. Reginald is writing his treatise and it is all for us. I tremble for Reginald. I do not believe he understands what this could mean."

"He understands, my darling."

"Then he does not seem to care."

"Reginald is a good man, a brave man. He could not be so if he trimmed his opinions to the prevailing wind. Do not fear for him, my child; for the only thing we should fear in life is our own wrong-doing. Go to Richmond, as your father commands. Think of me, pray for me . . . as I shall for you. You will be in my thoughts every minute of the day, and rest assured that as soon as I am able I shall be at your side."

"But Mother, what harm are we doing him . . . by being together? Does he not know that this is the only joy that is left to us?"

"My darling, be brave."

"There is tension in the Castle. Something is about to happen. Mother, I have a terrible fear that, if I leave you now, I shall never see you again."

"You are overwrought. This is merely another parting."

"Why . . . why . . . should there be these partings? What harm are we doing?"

"It is the second time you have spoken of harm. No one thinks we are doing harm, my love."

"They do, Mother. I see it in their looks. Our love harms him in some way and he is afraid of it. I cannot leave you. Let us go away together." Mary drew away from her mother. Her eyes were brilliant with sudden hope and speculation. "I will send for Reginald. I will ask him to take us with him to Italy. There the Pope will give us refuge—or perhaps the Emperor will."

Katharine laughed gently, and drawing her daughter to her stroked her hair.

"No, my love," she said. "That would profit us little. We are in your father's hands, but nothing can harm us if we do our duty. It matters little what becomes of our bodies, as long as our souls are pure. Go to Richmond and remember that there I am with you as I am when we are close like this, for you are never absent from my thoughts."

"Oh, Mother, if I could but rid myself of this fear . . ."

"Pray, my child. You will find comfort in prayer."

They embraced and remained together until one of Mary's women came to say that her party was ready to leave for Richmond, and the King's orders were that they were to depart at once.

At the door Mary turned to look at her mother, and so doleful was her expression that it was as though she looked for the last time on the beloved face.

\*          \*          \*

How she missed Mary! It was but a few days since she had left, but it seemed longer. She had had no opportunity of appealing to the King as she had not since been in his company alone.

He treated her with cool detachment, and she noticed that never once did he allow his eyes to meet her own; she was aware of the speculative glances of the courtiers; they knew more than she did and they were alert.

One morning she was awakened early by sounds below; she heard the whisper of voices as she lay in her bed, and afterwards the sound of horses' hoofs. People were arriving at the Castle, she supposed, and because she was weary after a sleepless night, she slept again.

In the early morning when two of her women came to awaken her, they brought her a message from the King, which told her that Henry was leaving Windsor and when he returned he wished her to be gone. Since she was not his wife and had no thought for his comfort he desired never to see her again.

She read the message twice before she grasped the full importance of it. Then she said: "I wish to see the King without delay."

"Your Grace," was the answer, "the King left Windsor with a hunting party at dawn. He is now on his way to Woodstock."

She understood. He had slunk away without telling her he was going; he had not even wanted to say goodbye. But soon he would be returning to Windsor, and when he did so he expected to find her gone. More than that, he had expressly commanded that she *should* be gone.

"It matters not where I go," she murmured, "I am still his wife. Nothing will alter that."

Maria came to her, for the news had reached her as soon as it had the Queen. She understood that Katharine was now forsaken.

"Where does Your Grace wish to go now?" she asked.

"What does it matter where I go?" retorted Katharine; and she wondered with increasing pain whether the King had determined, not only to live apart from her, but also to separate her from their child.

She recovered her dignity. She had some friends even in England; and she was sure that the Pope would give his decision in her favour. Her nephew would support her. The battle was not yet lost.

She said calmly: "We will go to my manor of the Moor in Hertfordshire; there I shall rest awhile and make plans for my future."

That day they left Windsor, and Katharine knew that she had reached yet another turning point in her life.

## CHAPTER XII

# POISON AT THE BISHOP'S TABLE

JOHN FISHER, Bishop of Rochester, faced the gathering of Bishops.

He was deeply disturbed, he said, because of a certain request with which he could not comply. The King was asking the Church and clergy to accept him as Supreme Head of the Church of England, and he, John Fisher, could not understand how that could be. There was and had always been one Head of the Church, and that was His Holiness the Pope. He did not see how, by making the claim to this title, it could be the King's.

The Bishops listened with averted eyes. The King had issued what he called this request, yet it was not in truth a request but a command. So many of them who owed their positions to the King, dared not contemplate what might become of them should they not bow to his will.

John Fisher seemed oblivious of his danger. This was an impossible thing, he urged them. They could not, with good consciences, change the law of the Church which had existed through the ages.

Warham, Archbishop of Canterbury, fidgeted uneasily as he listened. That head would be severed from the gaunt body before long, he was sure, if Fisher did not curb his tongue. Oh, that I should have lived so long! he thought. I am too old and tired now to navigate such dangerous waters. What will become of us all?

Alas, for him, as Archbishop of Canterbury, he could not remain silent.

Supreme Head of the Church! he mused. This is a break with Rome. There has never been anything like it in this country's ecclesiastical history. Nothing will ever be the same again. It is an impossible thing. And yet the King commanded it; and Warham knew well that it would go hard for those, like Fisher, who attempted to oppose it.

Fisher was looking at him now. "And you, my lord Archbishop . . . ?"

Everything that he said would be reported to the King. One word spoken which should have been left unsaid was enough to send a man to the block. I am too old, he thought, too old and tired.

He heard his voice speaking the carefully chosen words. "It

is my belief that we might accept the King as Supreme Head of the Church as far as the law of Christ allows . . ."

Beautifully noncommittal, certain to give offence to none. He was aware of Fisher's scornful eyes. But all men were not made to be martyrs.

One of the Bishops added that His Grace, fearing that the Supreme Head of the Church was a title which might not be acceptable to some of the clergy, had modestly changed it to: Supreme Head . . . after God.

Warham felt his lips curved in a smile of cynicism. So Henry was prepared to accept only the domination of God. He was safe enough, for he could expect no opposition to his desires from that direction. His conscience would always stand a firm bulwark between him and God.

Fisher was on his feet again but Warham silenced him.

"We have heard the views of the Bishop of Rochester," he said, "and now I would ask the assembled company if they are prepared to accept the King as Supreme Head of the Church, as I am . . . as far as the law of Christ allows."

There was silence. Heads were downcast in the rows of benches.

"Your silence I construe as consent," said Warham. He did not look at Fisher who must understand that one voice raised against the King's command was of little matter when so many were in agreement. Fisher should learn wisdom; there were times when silence was salvation.

\*     \*     \*

The Bishop of Rochester lived humbly in his London residence, but his doors were kept open and there was always a meal to be given to any who called on him when there was food on his table.

Perhaps his guests were not so many since the meeting of the Bishops. Those who wished him well deplored his outspokenness; some sought to advise him; but there were few who wished it to be said that they were in agreement with him.

It was a few days after the meeting when his cook, Richard Rouse, returning to the kitchens after shopping in the markets, was met by a stranger who asked for a word with him.

Richard Rouse was flattered, for beneath the disguise of a merchant he recognized a person of the quality. The cook was a man of ambition; he had not been long in the service of the Bishop and he was proud to be employed by a man of such importance; he did not see why he should not rise in his profession; the house of an Archbishop might be his next appointment; and after that—why should he not serve the King?

The stranger took him to a tavern where they sat and drank awhile.

"I have heard that you are an excellent cook," Rouse was told. "And that your services are not appreciated in that household in which you serve."

"My master is a good one."

"Any cook can call a master good who has a poor palate. The Bishop might be eating stinking fish in place of the excellent dishes you put before him. He would know no difference."

"His thoughts are on other matters," sighed Rouse.

"That's a tragedy for a good cook. Such a master would never sing his praises in the right quarters."

"I fear so."

"How would you like to work in the royal kitchens?"

There was no need for Rouse to answer, but he did. "It is the ambition of my life."

"It need not be so far away."

"Who are you?" Rouse demanded.

"You will discover, if you are a wise man."

"How can I convince you of my wisdom?"

"By taking this powder and slipping it into the Bishop's broth."

Rouse turned pale.

"I thought," said his companion contemptuously, "that you were an ambitious man."

"But this powder . . ."

"It is calculated to improve the flavour of the broth."

"The Bishop will not notice that the flavour is improved."

"Others at his table might."

Rouse was afraid, but he would not look at his fear. He tried to find an explanation of the stranger's conduct which would be acceptable to him. The man wanted to help him to a place in the King's kitchens because he believed his talents were wasted on the Bishop of Rochester; therefore he was giving him a new flavouring which would make people marvel at the broth he put before them. Perhaps at the table would be one of the King's higher servants . . . That was a very pleasant explanation. The only other was one he had no wish to examine.

He was a man who was always hoping for a great opportunity; he would never forgive himself if, when it came, he was not ready to take it.

\*       \*       \*

The Lord Chancellor brought grave news to the King.

Henry studied Thomas More with affectionate impatience.

Here was a man who might have done so much in moulding public opinion, because if it could be said "Sir Thomas More is of the opinion that my marriage is no true marriage," thousands would say "This matter is beyond me, but if Sir Thomas More says this is so, then it must be so, for he is not only a learned man, but a good man."

But Thomas was obstinate. His smile was sunny, his manner bland, and his wit always a joy to listen to. But whenever Henry broached the matter of the divorce Thomas would have some answer for him to which he could not take offence and yet showed clearly that Thomas was not prepared to advance his cause.

Now Thomas was grave. "The Bishop of Rochester is grievously ill, Your Grace."

Henry's heart leaped exultantly. Fisher had become a nuisance; he always looked as if he were on the point of death. Henry was sentimental enough to remember his old affection for the man, but his death would be a relief. He was another of those obstinate men who did not seem to care how near they approached danger to themselves as long as they clung to their miserable opinions.

"He has been ailing for some time," the King answered. "He is not strong."

"Nay, Your Grace, he became ill after partaking of the broth served at his table."

"What's this?" cried Henry, the colour flaming into his face.

"He was seized with convulsions, Your Grace, and so were others at his table. It would seem that there has been an attempt to poison him."

"Have his servants been questioned?"

"Your Grace, his cook has been arrested and under torture confesses that a white powder was given him by a stranger with instructions to put it into the Bishop's broth. He declares he was told it would but improve the flavour."

Henry did not meet his Chancellor's eyes.

"Has he confessed on whose instructions he acted?"

"Not yet, Your Grace."

Henry looked at his Chancellor helplessly. He was thinking of a pair of indignant black eyes, of a lady's outbursts of anger because of the dilatoriness which she sometimes accused the King of sharing; he thought of her ambitious family.

What if the cook, put to the torture, mentioned names which must not be mentioned?

Yet the Chancellor was looking at him expectantly. He could

not take this man into his confidence as he had that other Chancellor.

Oh, Wolsey, he thought, my friend, my counsellor, why did I ever allow them to drive a wedge between us? Rogue you may have been to some extent, but you were my man, and we understood each other; a look, a gesture, and you knew my mind as these men of honour never can.

He said: "Poisoning is the worst of crimes. If this fellow is guilty he must pay the full penalty of his misdeeds. Let him be put to the torture, and if he should disclose names, let those names be written down and shown to none other but me."

Sir Thomas More bowed his head. There were times when Henry felt that this man understood every little twist and turn of his mind; and that made for great discomfort.

He glanced away. "I will send my best physician to the Bishop," he said. "Let us hope that his frugal appetite means that he took but little of the poisoned broth."

The Chancellor's expression was sorrowful. Fisher was a friend of his—they were two of a kind.

Death is in the air, he thought as he left the King's presence.

\*       \*       \*

Crowds were gathered in Smithfield to watch the death of Richard Rouse. The name of the cook who had longed for fame and fortune was now on every tongue. He would be remembered for years to come because it was due to him that a new law had been made.

Several people who had sat at the Bishop's table had died; the Bishop himself remained very ill. Poisoning, said the King in great indignation, was one of the most heinous crimes a man could commit. And, perhaps because he would have been so relieved to know the Bishop was dead, he felt it his duty to show the people how much he regretted this attempt on the old man's life. The severest punishment man could conceive must be inflicted on the poisoner. After some deliberation the new law had come into being. The death penalty for poisoners from henceforth was that they should be hung in chains and lowered into a cauldron of boiling oil, withdrawn and lowered again; this to be continued until death.

And so the crowds assembled in the great square to see the new death penalty put into practice on the cook of the Bishop of Rochester.

Richard Rouse, who had to be carried out to the place of

execution, looked very different from the jaunty man who had spoken to a stranger in a tavern such a short time before.

He was crippled from the rack, and his hands, mangled by the thumbscrews, hung limply at his sides.

With dull eyes he looked at the chains and the great cauldron under which the flames crackled.

There was silence as he was hung in the chains and lifted high before he was lowered into the pot of boiling oil. His screams would be remembered for ever by those who heard them. Up again his poor tortured body was lifted and plunged down into the bubbling oil. And suddenly . . . he was silent. Once again he was lowered into that cauldron, and still no sound came.

People shuddered and turned away. Voices were raised in the crowd. "Richard Rouse put the powder into the broth, but who in truth poisoned those people who had sat at the Bishop's table?"

It was recalled that the Bishop had been one who had worked zealously for the Queen. Now he was only alive because of his frugal appetite, although even he had come close to death. Who would wish to remove the Bishop? The King? He could send the Bishop to the Tower if he wished, merely by giving an order. But there were others.

A cry went up from Smithfield: "We'll have no Nan Bullen for our Queen. God bless Katharine, Queen of England!"

## CHAPTER XIII

# KATHARINE IN EXILE

IN the castle of Ampthill Katharine tried to retain the dignity of a Queen. Her routine was as it had always been. She spent a great deal of time at prayer and at her needlework, reading and conversing with the women she had brought with her and in particular with Maria, the only one in whom she had complete trust; only to Maria did she refer to her troubles, and to the fact that she was separated from the King.

Each day she waited for some news, for she knew that in the world outside Ampthill events were moving quickly towards a great climax.

She could not believe that Henry would dare disobey the Pope; and she was certain that when Clement gave the verdict

in her favour, which he must surely do, Henry would be forced
to take her back.

She had one desire to which she clung with all the fervour of
her nature; only this thing mattered to her now. She had lost
Henry's affection for ever; she was fully aware of that. But Mary
was the King's legitimate daughter, and she was determined that
she should not be ousted from the succession, no matter what it
cost her mother.

"I will sign nothing," she told Maria. "I will not give way an
inch. They can have me murdered in my bed if they will; but I
will never admit that I am not truly married to Henry, for to do
that would be to proclaim Mary a bastard."

The great joy of her life was in the letters she received from
Mary. What if the final cruelty were inflicted and that joy denied
her! How would she endure her life then?

But so far they both had their letters.

Her faithful Thomas Abell had been taken from her when he
had published his book, setting forth his views on the divorce.
She had warned him that he risked his life, but he cared nothing
for that; and when they had come to take him away, he had gone
almost gleefully. It was well that he should, he told her, for many
would know that he was in the Tower, and why.

News came to Ampthill. The Pope had at last decided to act,
and he summoned Henry to Rome to answer Queen Katharine's
appeal; he must, was the Holy Father's command, appear in
person or send a proxy.

Henry's answer had been to snap his fingers at the Pope. Who
was the Pope? he demanded. What had the Pope to do with
England? The English Church had severed itself from Rome.
There was one Supreme Head of the Church of England (under
God) and that was His Majesty King Henry VIII.

This was momentous. This was telling the world that the rumour, that the Church of England was cutting itself free from
Rome, was a fact.

But all this was paled by news of her daughter. Margaret Pole
was with Mary still, and for that Katharine was grateful;
Reginald had been sent to Italy, and Katharine knew that, much
as Margaret loved her son, she was relieved that he was out of
England, for it was growing increasingly unsafe to be in England
and to disagree with the King.

Margaret wrote: "Her Highness the Princess has been ailing
since she parted from Your Grace. It has grieved me deeply to
watch her. She has had so little interest in life and her appetite
is so poor. Constantly she speaks of Your Grace, and I know that

if you could be with her she would be well. She has had to take
to her bed . . ."

The Queen could not bear to think of Mary, sick and lonely,
longing for her as she herself longed for Mary.

"What harm can we do by being together?" she demanded of
Maria. "How dare he make us suffer so! He has his woman.
Does our being together prevent that? Why should he be allowed
to make us suffer so, merely that he may appease his conscience
by telling himself—and others—that I plot against him with my
daughter?"

But there was no comfort for Maria to offer her mistress, and
at times Katharine came near to hating her husband.

Then she would throw herself on to her knees and pray.

"Forgive me, oh Lord. Holy Mother, intercede for me. He has
been led into temptation. He does not understand how he tortures
his wife and daughter. He is young . . . bent on pursuing pleasure,
led away by bad counsellors. . . ."

But was this true? Was he so young? Who was it who had
determined that no one should stand in the way of divorce? Who
but Henry himself? Once she had blamed Wolsey, but Wolsey
was dead, and this persecution persisted and had indeed intensified.

She sat down to write to him, and wrote as only a mother could
write who was crying for her child.

"Have pity on us. My daughter is pining for me, and I for her.
Do not continue in this cruelty. Let me go to her."

She sent the letter to him without delay, and then began the
weary waiting for his reply.

But the days passed, the weeks passed, and there was no
answer from the King.

*       *       *

Stirring news came from Court. Sir Thomas More, unable to
evade the great issue any longer, had resigned the Chancellor-
ship rather than fall in with the King's wishes.

Katharine prayed long for Thomas More when she heard that
news, prayed for that pleasant family of his who lived so happily
in their Chelsea home.

William Warham died; some said that like Wolsey he was
fortunate to finish his life in a bed when he was but a few short
steps from the scaffold. He was eighty-two years old and in the
last weeks of his life had been issued with a writ of *præmunire*—
a small offence but one by which he had shown he had not
accepted the King as Supreme Head. Perhaps the old man was

forgetful; perhaps he had not understood that it was necessary now to receive the King's permission in all matters concerning the Church as well as the state. He had behaved according to procedure *before* the severance from Rome. These were dangerous times and the King was jealous of his new authority.

Fortunate Warham, who could take to his bed and die in peace.

Dr. Cranmer became the new Archbishop of Canterbury. Henry need fear no opposition from him; he was the man who, with Thomas Cromwell, had worked more than any to extricate the King from the tyranny of Rome.

Lord Audley was now Chancellor in place of Sir Thomas More, and gradually the King was ridding himself of the men who might oppose him.

John Fisher had recovered from the poison and was still living, but he was very frail. Katharine prayed for him and often trembled for him.

She heard that the King had honoured Anne Boleyn by making her Marchioness of Pembroke and that he planned to take her to France with him as though she were his Queen.

This was humiliating in the extreme because it seemed that François and the French Court were now ready to accept Anne Boleyn as Queen of England.

But all these matters seemed insignificant when the news came from Margaret Pole that Mary had recovered and was almost well again.

"Still grieving for Your Grace, but, I thank God, growing stronger every day."

"If I could but see her," sighed the Queen. "I would cease to fret on account of anything else which might happen to me."

\*     \*     \*

On a January day in the year 1533 the King rose early. There was a grim purpose about him, and those who lived close to him had noted that during the last months a change had crept over him. The strong sentimental streak in his nature had become subdued and in its place was a new cruelty. He had always flown into sudden rages but these had quickly passed; now they often left him sullen and brooding. All those men whose duty it was to be in contact with him knew they must tread warily.

The little mouth had a strong determination about it on that morning. This was a day to which he had looked forward for six years, and now that it had come, the thought occurred to him that it was less desirable than it had seemed all those years ago.

Waiting had not enhanced his emotions; perhaps they had grown stale; perhaps his main thought as he prepared himself for what was about to take place was one of triumph over great odds rather than the climax of years of devotion.

He was going to make his way to an attic in the west turret of White Hall, not so much as a doting bridegroom as a man who has made up his mind to some action; and, even though it seemed less desirable to him than it had previously, he was determined to carry it out simply because it had been denied him and he was eager to show that he was a man who would allow no one to say him nay.

When he was ready he said to one of his gentlemen: "Go and seek my chaplain, Dr. Rowland Lee, and tell him that I wish him to celebrate Mass without delay. Bring him to me here."

Dr. Rowland Lee, who had hastily dressed himself, came to the King in some surprise, wondering why he had been sent for at such an early hour of the morning.

"Ah," said the King who had dismissed all but two of his grooms—Norris and Heneage. "I wish you to celebrate Mass in one of the attics. Follow me."

The little party made their way to the attic and very shortly were joined by two ladies, one of whom was Anne Boleyn, Marchioness of Pembroke, and the other her train bearer, Anne Savage.

Henry turned to Dr. Lee. "Now," he said, "marry us."

The doctor was taken aback. "Sire . . ." he stammered. "I . . . could not do this."

"You could not do it? Why not?"

"I . . . I dare not, Sire."

The blue eyes were narrowed; the cruel lines appeared about the mouth. "And if I command you?"

"Sire," pleaded Dr. Lee, "I know that you went through a ceremony of marriage with Queen Katharine, and although I am aware of your Secret Matter I could not marry you unless there was a dispensation pronouncing your marriage null and void."

For one second those assembled thought the King would strike his chaplain. Then suddenly his mood changed; he slipped his arm through that of the man, drew him away and whispered: "Perform this ceremony and you shall be rewarded with the See of Lichfield."

"Your Grace, Your Majesty . . . I dare not . . ."

It took a long time, thought the King, for these dunderheads to learn who was the Supreme Head of the Church. He was impatient, and he could see that this fellow was so immersed in the old laws of the Church that he could not cast them aside easily. Yet this ceremony must take place. Anne was with child. What if that were a *boy* she carried! There could be no more delay. It would be disastrous if Anne's boy should be declared illegitimate.

He made a decision. "You need have no fear. The Pope has pronounced himself in favour of the divorce and the dispensation is in my keeping."

Dr. Lee drew a deep sigh of relief.

"I crave Your Grace's pardon. Your Grace will understand . . ."

"Enough," interrupted Henry. "Do your work."

And in the lonely attic at White Hall, Henry VIII went through a ceremony of marriage with Anne Boleyn, while Norris, Heneage and Anne Savage stood by as witnesses.

\* \* \*

The King sent for the newly appointed Archbishop of Canterbury.

Thomas Cranmer, who had come so far since the Boleyns had brought him to the King's notice, was very eager that his royal benefactor should not regret having raised him so high.

When they were alone Henry explained to his Archbishop what he expected of him. There were many in England who clung to old ideas, and he was going to have every man who held any position of importance sign an oath which would declare his belief in the supremacy of the King. But that was for later. There was this tiresome matter of the divorce.

*He* knew himself never to have been married to Katharine, and he had been surrounded by rogues and vacillating fools—until now, he hoped.

The matter was urgent. He considered himself already married to Queen Anne, and he was certain that he had God's blessing because the marriage was already promising fruitfulness. He must have a speedy end to the old matter though, and it was the duty of the new Archbishop of Canterbury to see that this was so.

The Archbishop was nothing if not resourceful.

"The first step, Your Grace, is a new law to make it illegal for appeals in ecclesiastical causes to be carried out of the kingdom to Rome."

The King nodded, smiling. "I see where this will lead us," he said.

"And when this becomes a law of the land, it would be meet

for the Archbishop of Canterbury to ask Your Grace's leave to declare the nullity of the marriage with Katharine of Aragon."

The King, continuing to smile, slipped his arm through that of his Archbishop. "It is a marvellous thing," he murmured, "that all the wise and learned men who argued this matter did not think of this before."

And when Cranmer had left him, he continued to think of Cranmer, whose ideas had been so useful to him. Cromwell and Cranmer, they were two men who had suddenly sprung into prominence and, because their ideas were fresh and bold, with a few sharp strokes they were cutting the bonds which for so many years had bound him.

He would not forget them.

\*      \*      \*

It was a bright April day when Katharine heard the news. It came to her in a letter from Chapuys. Now that she was exiled she did receive letters more freely than she had when she had been at Court surrounded by Wolsey's spies, and so was in constant touch with the Spanish ambassador.

Often she thought that, had her nephew sent her a man with the energy of Eustache Chapuys some years ago, she might have had the advantage of very valuable advice. Chapuys was indefatigable. She had a great admiration for him; she knew that he was of humble origin and that he had come to England hoping to achieve fame and fortune; yet, when he had heard of the wrongs done to her, he had thrown himself so wholeheartedly into her cause that he had become the most ardent champion it had ever been her good fortune to have. Alas, she thought, luck was never with me, for he came too late.

Now she read his letter and the news it contained startled her.

The King, wrote Chapuys, had secretly gone through a form of marriage with the Concubine who was shortly to be proclaimed Queen. The fact was that she was with child by the King and Henry was taking no chances of the child's being branded illegitimate. Therefore, Katharine would shortly receive a summons to appear before a court which Cranmer was about to open at Dunstable. On no account must she answer that summons. Nevertheless they would conduct the court without her; but her absence would cause some discomfiture and delay; and owing to the recent law that ecclesiastical cases must be settled in England and not referred to Rome, they could be sure that Cranmer would pronounce the marriage null and void. She would see, of course, that there would then be no need of a dispensation from the Pope, because such a dispensation was unnecessary as the King would accept the ruling of Cranmer's court, which would be that Katharine and the King had never truly been married.

She sighed as she read these words.

She would obey Chapuys's instructions. He was one of the few people she could trust; and when the summons came for her to appear at Dunstable, following quickly on Chapuys's warning, she ignored it.

But her absence could not prevent the court's being opened and the case tried.

On the 23rd of May Cranmer declared that the marriage between King Henry VIII and Katharine of Aragon was invalid, and that the Queen of England was no longer Katharine but Anne.

The weary waiting was over. The matter had been settled simply by cutting the knot which bound England to the Church of Rome. There need no longer be talk of the divorce, for a divorce was not necessary between people who had never been married.

*     *     *

News came to Ampthill of the coronation of Queen Anne. Great pomp there had been in the streets of London; Katharine heard of how Anne had ridden in triumph under a canopy of state in purple velvet lined with ermine. A Queen at last! All the nobility had attended her coronation; they dared do no other; but the people in the streets had shown less enthusiasm than was usual on such occasions. Royal pageants were the highlights of living to them; they always welcomed them, especially when the King ordered that wine should flow in the conduits; but on this occasion there were few cheers.

Katharine's women tried to cheer her as they sat at their needlework.

"They say, Your Grace, that there was scarcely a cheer as she rode through the city."

Katharine nodded, and Maria who sat beside her knew that the Queen was remembering her own coronation: coming to the Tower from Greenwich, dressed in white embroidered satin, a coronal set with many glittering stones on her head, her long hair hanging down her back: remembering the ardent looks of Henry, who had insisted on marrying her against the advice of his ministers. In those days she had believed that nothing could happen to spoil their happiness.

"I heard," said one of her women, "that my lord of Shrewsbury declared he was too old to shout for a new Queen. He also said that the new Queen was a goggle-eyed whore; and many people heard him cry 'God save Queen Katharine who is our own righteous Queen!'"

Katharine shook her head. "Do not repeat such things," she warned.

"But, Your Grace, I had it on the best authority. It is true the people do not like Queen Anne. Many of them say they will not have her as their Queen."

"You should pray for her," answered Katharine.

Her women looked at her in astonishment.

"Pray for Nan Bullen!"

"Once," said the Queen, "I rode through the streets of London, the Queen, the King's chosen bride. He faced opposition, you know, to marry me." She had dropped her needlework into her lap and her eyes were misty as she looked into the past. "And look you, what I have come to. It may not be long before she is in like case."

There was silence, and the Queen took up her work and began to sew.

It was clear to all that Katharine's thoughts were far away; and when the sewing was over, and rising from her chair she was about to go to her private chapel, she tripped and fell, driving a pin into her foot.

Maria and others of her ladies helped her to her bed, and in the morning her foot was swollen and it was necessary to call her physician.

During the next days she remained in her bed. She had developed a cough which would not leave her in spite of the warm summer weather. And as she lay she wondered what steps the new Queen would take to further her discomfiture, for she was sure this would come. She pictured Anne, riding through the streets filled with sullen people. Ambitious, haughty and bold, Anne would certainly take measures to show the people that she was their new mistress.

Katharine did not have to wait long.

She was still in bed on account of the accident to her foot, and her cough had not improved, when her women came to tell her that a party of men had come from the King, and at their head was Lord Mountjoy.

Lord Mountjoy! He had once been her chamberlain and a very good servant to her; she was pleased then to hear that he it was who had been chosen to convey the King's wishes to her.

But when he was brought into her presence she realized quickly that her one-time servant was now the King's man.

"Your Grace," he told her, "you will know that at the court at Dunstable your marriage to the King was declared null and void by the Archbishop of Canterbury, and leave was given both to you and the King to marry elsewhere."

She bowed her head. "I have been informed of this."

"You will know also that the coronation of Queen Anne has also taken place."

Katharine nodded once more in acquiescence.

"The King decrees that, as it is impossible for there to be two Queens of England, you will henceforth be known as Princess of Wales since you are the widow of his brother Arthur, Prince of Wales."

Katharine raised herself on her elbow. "I am the Queen of England," she said, "and that is my title."

"But Your Grace knows that the Lords spiritual and temporal have declared the marriage invalid."

"All the world knows by what authority it was done," retorted Katharine. "By power, not justice. This case is now pending in Rome and the matter depends not on judgment given in this realm, but in the Court of Rome, before the Pope, whom I believe to be God's vicar and judge on Earth."

"Madam, you speak treason," said Mountjoy.

"It is a sorry state," answered the Queen mournfully, "when truth becomes treason."

Mountjoy handed her the documents he had brought with him from the King and, glancing at them, she saw that throughout she was referred to as the Princess Dowager.

She called Maria to bring her a pen and boldly struck out the words Princess Dowager wherever they occurred.

Mountjoy watched her in dismay, and as he did so he remembered the occasion of her coronation and how she had always been a just mistress to him.

"Madam," he said, pleading, "I beg of you to take care. It would be a grievous thing if you were charged with high treason."

She smiled at him. "If I agreed with your persuasions, my Lord Mountjoy, I should slander myself. Would you have me confess that I have been the King's harlot these twenty-four years?"

Mountjoy felt unnerved, and could not proceed as he had been instructed to do. Katharine sensed this and softened towards him.

"Do not distress yourself," she said, "I know full well that you do what you have been commanded to do."

Mountjoy went on to his knees. "Madam," he said, "should I be called upon to persecute you further, I should decline to do so . . . no matter what the consequences."

"I thank you, Lord Mountjoy, but I would not have you suffer for me. Take these papers back to the King. Tell him that I am his wife now as I was on the day he married me. Tell him also that I shall not accept the title of Princess Dowager because my title is Queen of England. That I shall remain until my death."

Apprehensively Mountjoy went back to Court.

*          *          *

Disturbed by Mountjoy's account of what had happened, Henry decided that Katharine should be sent farther from London and commanded that she move her household from Ampthill to Buckden, there to take up residence in a palace which belonged to the Bishop of Lincoln. In the summer, when Katharine arrived, this place was charming, offering views over the fen country; Katharine had yet to discover how damp and bleak it could be in winter and what a disastrous effect it would have on her health.

She was extremely unhappy to move because, not only was she to change her place of residence, but she was also to lose certain members of her household. She had had too many friends at Ampthill, and they had upheld her in her sauciness, said the King. She could manage with a smaller household at Buckden; and one of the first to be dismissed should be Maria de Salinas who had always been her strong partisan from the days when she had first arrived in England. The edict had been that all those who refused to address her as the Princess of Wales should be dismissed. Katharine promptly forbade anyone to address her by any title but that of Queen.

She was desolate to lose Maria. This was the bitterest blow of the entire upheaval, and those who watched their farewell wept with them.

Katharine's stubborn determination was a source of great irritation to the King, but he was fully aware that the people who lived in the villages surrounding her were her fervent supporters, and he had heard that when she had travelled from Ampthill to Buckden the way along which she had passed had been crowded with people who shouted: "Long live the Queen!"

She was an encumbrance and an embarrassment to him but he

knew he must treat her with care. Therefore he finally allowed her a few servants—though he firmly refused to allow Maria to be one of them—whom he excused from taking an oath to address her as the Princess of Wales; and with this smaller household, Katharine lived at Buckden.

There was one fact for which she was thankful. Her chaplain, Dr. Abell, who had written against the divorce, had been released from prison and allowed to come back to her. The man was too obscure, Henry decided, to be of much importance.

At Buckden Katharine endeavoured to return to the old routine. Her life was quiet, and she spent a great deal of time in her chamber which had a window looking into the chapel. She seemed to find great comfort in sitting alone in this window-seat.

She busied herself with the care of the poor people living close by who had never known any show such solicitude for their well-being before. There was food to be had at the palace for the hungry; the Queen and her ladies made garments for those who needed them; and although Katharine was far from rich she set aside a large part of her income for the comfort of the poor.

"A saint has come among us," said the people; and they declared they would call no other Queen but Katharine.

Henry knew what was happening and it angered him, for it seemed to him that all those who admired the Queen were criticising him; he could not endure criticism. But there was one matter which occupied his thoughts day and night. Anne was about to give birth to their child.

A son, he told himself exultantly, will put an end to all trouble. Once I have my son there will be such rejoicing that no one will give much thought to Katharine. It will be a sign that God is pleased with me for discarding one who was not in truth my wife, and taking another.

A son! Night and day he prayed for a lusty son; he dreamed of the boy who would look exactly like himself. He himself would teach him—make a man of him, make a King of him. Once he held that boy in his arms everything would be worth while, and his people would rejoice with him.

\*          \*          \*

It was September of that fateful year 1533 when Anne was brought to bed.

Henry could scarcely contain his excitement, and had already invited François to be the boy's sponsor. His name? It should be

Henry . . . or perhaps Edward. Henry was a good name for a King. Henry IX. But that was years away, of course. Henry VIII had many years before him, many more sons to father.

Queen Anne suffered much in her travail. She was as anxious as the King. Was there a certain apprehension in her anxiety? The King was still devoted to her—her passionate and possessive lover—but now that she had time for sober reflection she could not help remembering his indifference to the sufferings of his first wife. Once he had been devoted to Katharine; she had heard that he had ridden in pageants as Sir Loyal Heart; and his loyalty was then for Katharine of Aragon—short-lived loyalty. Was he a man whose passions faded quickly? He had been her devoted admirer for many years, but was that due to his faithfulness or a stubborn determination to have his will which her cleverness in keeping him at bay had inflamed?

A son will make all the difference, the new Queen told herself. Holy Mother of God, give me a son.

\*         \*         \*

The cry of a child in the royal apartments! The eager question, and the answer that put an end to hope.

"A girl, Your Majesty, a healthy girl."

The bitterness of disappointment was hard to bear, but the child was healthy. The King tried to push aside his disappointment.

Anne looked strangely humble in her bed, and he was still in love with her.

"Our next will be a boy, sweetheart," he told her.

And she smiled in agreement.

So they rejoiced in their daughter, and called her Elizabeth.

\*         \*         \*

Margaret Pole was anxious concerning the Princess Mary who had never seemed to regain her full strength since her parting from her mother. Margaret knew that she brooded a great deal and was constantly wondering what would happen next.

Mary was no longer a child; being seventeen years of age, she was old enough to understand the political significance of what was happening about her. There was a strong streak of the Spaniard in her, which was natural as, before their separation, she had been so close to her mother.

Mary was restless, delicate, given to fits of melancholy. And what else could be expected? Margaret asked herself. What a tragedy that a child should be torn from her mother's side when the bond between them was so strong, and when her position was so uncertain with her father.

But for Queen Anne, Margaret often thought, Henry would not have been unkind to his daughter. She was his child and he was eager to have children, even girls. But those occasional bursts of fondness were perhaps the very reason why Anne would not allow Mary at Court. Could it be that the new Queen was afraid of the influence Mary might have on her father?

It was so very tragic, and Margaret, while she thought fearfully of her own son Reginald who had offended the King, continually asked herself how she could make Mary's life brighter.

Mary liked to play the lute or the virginals, for music was still her favourite occupation; but Margaret fancied as she listened to her that she played listlessly and there was a melancholy note in her music.

"Play something lively, something to make us feel gay," Margaret suggested.

But Mary turned on her almost angrily: "How can I feel gay when I am not allowed to see my mother, when I know she is not in good health and mayhap has no one to care for her?"

"If I could write to her and tell her that you are cheerful, that would do her much good, I am sure."

"You could not deceive her. How could I be cheerful when I long to see her as I know she does me?" Mary rose from the virginals and came to stand by her companion. "What will happen to us now that the Concubine has a child? They will say this Elizabeth comes before me, I'll swear."

"How could they do that?"

"You know full well they could do it. They have said my mother's marriage was no marriage. That means one thing. The bastard Elizabeth will be declared heir to the throne until they get themselves a boy." Mary's face grew hard and stern. "I pray they never get a boy."

"Your Highness . . . my dear Princess . . . forgive me, but . . ."

"I must not say such things! I must pray, I suppose, that the Concubine may be fruitful! I must pray that there is peace in this land, even though to bring this about I must declare my mother lived in sin with the King and I am therefore a bastard!"

"My dear . . . my dear . . ."

Mary walked away to the window. "Reginald was brave," she cried, clenching her hands. "He was strong. He did not care if he offended my father. He would not have cared if they had cut off his head."

"He would have died a martyr's death and we should have been left to suffer," answered Margaret soberly. "Let us thank God that he is out of the country at this time."

"There is a party riding into the courtyard," said Mary.

Margaret rose swiftly and came to her side.

"They come from the Court," she said. "I recognize those women as of *her* suite."

"We want none of the Concubine's household here," Mary cried.

"You must receive them, Your Highness, and hear their business."

"I will not," Mary said firmly and went out of the room.

It was not Mary however whom they had come to see, but the Countess. Two women were brought to her and they stated their business briefly.

The Lady Mary was no longer heir to the throne, for her mother was the Princess Dowager and had never been the King's true wife. Certain jewels were in her possession which were the property of the crown. It was necessary now that these jewels be handed to them, for they were messengers from the King and Queen and had papers to prove this. The Lady Mary's jewels now belonged to the Princess Elizabeth, and it was Margaret Pole's duty to give them up.

Margaret stood very still; she had grown pale.

"I know the jewels to which you refer," she said. "They are the property of the Princess Mary and I should be failing in my duty if I gave them up."

"They are no longer the property of the Lady Mary. Here is an order from the Queen."

Margaret studied the order. But I do not consider Anne to be the Queen, she said to herself. I shall certainly not give up the Princess Mary's jewels.

So she remained stubborn, and the next day when the party rode away from Beauleigh, Mary's jewels remained behind.

When Mary heard what had happened she praised her governess.

"Let them do what they will to us," she said. "We will stand out against them."

"They will be back," said Margaret apprehensively.

Mary held her head high as she declared: "They know I am the true heir to the throne. They must. I shall never stand aside for this young Elizabeth."

But how could they hold out against the King and Queen? They could show defiance for a while, but not for long.

Queen Anne, in her new power, would not allow Margaret Pole and Mary to flout her wishes. Shortly afterwards a command came from the King: The Countess of Salisbury was discharged from her duty as governess to the Lady Mary and the pension paid to her in that capacity would immediately cease.

When Mary heard the news she was stricken with grief.

"Not you too!" she cried. "I have lost my mother and Reginald . . . you are all that is left to me."

"I will stay with you," answered Margaret. "I shall have no pension but I have money of my own. We shall not allow a matter of my pension to part us."

Then Mary threw herself into her governess's arms. "You must never . . . *never* leave me," she said solemnly.

But it was not to be expected that the Queen would allow Margaret to remain with Mary after she had dared refuse to obey a command. She would make the King see what a danger Mary could be. It was clear that she was truculent by her refusal to return what did not really belong to her. Queen Anne had a child to fight for now, and she was determined that her Elizabeth, not Katharine's Mary, should be regarded as heir to the throne.

Margaret saw that she had acted foolishly. What were a few jewels compared with real friendship, devotion and love? What would happen to Mary when she had no one to protect her? How would the news that Mary's governess had been dismissed affect Katharine, who had admitted often that she could feel some comfort knowing that Mary was with her very dear friend?

The edict came. Margaret Pole, Countess of Salisbury, was to leave the household of the Lady Mary, who herself was to be sent from Beauleigh to Hunsdon, where she would live under the same roof as her half-sister, the Princess Elizabeth. And to remind her that she was not the King's legitimate daughter, and therefore not entitled to be called Princess, she should live in humble state near the magnificence of Anne's baby daughter.

Bitterly they wept. They could not visualize parting, so long had they been together.

"One by one those whom I love are taken from me," sobbed Mary. "Now there is no one left. What new punishment will they inflict upon me?"

*     *     *

Eustache Cupuys had asked for a private interview with the King.

"Your Majesty," said the Spanish ambassador, "I come to

you because I can speak with greater freedom than can any of your subjects. The measures you have taken against the Queen and her daughter, the Princess Mary, are very harsh."

Henry glowered at him, but Chapuys smiled ingratiatingly.

"I speak thus, Your Majesty, because it is my great desire to see harmony between you and my master."

"There would be harmony between us but for the fact that you are continually writing to him of his aunt's misfortunes. If his aunt and her daughter were no more . . . that would be an end of our troubles."

Alarm shot into the ambassador's mind. Henry was not subtle. The idea had doubtless entered his head that life would be more comfortable if Mary and Katharine were out of his way. The Queen must be warned to watch what she ate; the Princess Mary must also take precautions. Chapuys's mind had been busy with plans for some time. He dreamed of smuggling the Princess Mary out of the country, getting her married to Reginald Pole, calling to all those who frowned on the break with Rome and the new marriage with Anne Boleyn to rise against the King. He visualized a dethroned Henry, Mary reigning with Reginald Pole as her consort, and the bonds with Rome tied firmly once more. Perhaps the King had been made aware of such a possibility. He was surrounded by astute ministers.

He must go carefully; but in the meantime he must try to make matters easier for the Queen and Princess.

"If they died suddenly Your Majesty's subjects would not be pleased."

"What mean you?" Henry demanded through half closed eyes.

"That there might well be rebellion in England," said the ambassador bluntly.

"You think my subjects would rebel against *me*!"

Eustache Chapuys lifted his shoulders. "Oh, the people love Your Majesty, but they love Queen Katharine too. They may love their King, but not his new marriage."

"You go too far."

"Perhaps I am over-zealous in my desires to create harmony between you and my master."

Henry was thinking: The man's a spy! I would to God we still had Mendoza here. This Chapuys is too sharp. We must be watchful of him.

He was uneasy. He did know that the people were grumbling against his marriage. They never shouted for Anne in the streets; and he was aware that when Katharine appeared they let her know that she had their sympathy.

"I come to ask Your Majesty," went on Chapuys, "to show a little kindness to Queen Katharine, if not for her sake for the sake of the people. There is one thing she yearns for above all others: To see her daughter. Would Your Grace now allow them to meet?"

"No," said the King firmly.

"Then would Your Grace give me permission to visit the Queen?"

"No, no, no!" was the answer.

The Spanish ambassador bowed, and the King signified that the audience was over.

It was unfortunate that Katharine's request should come when Henry was pondering the insinuations of Chapuys. She was finding Buckden very damp and unhealthy. She suffered from rheumatism and gout, and she asked the King to allow her to move to a house which would offer her more comfort.

Henry read her request frowning, and sent for Suffolk.

He tapped the letter and said: "The Queen complains again. Buckden is not to her liking. She asks permission to leave."

"And Your Majesty has decided that she may leave?"

"I was turning over in my mind where she might go."

"There is Fotheringay, Your Majesty. That could be put at her disposal."

Henry thought of the castle on the north bank of the river Nen in Northamptonshire. Its situation was notoriously unhealthy, but it was far enough away not to give cause for concern.

"Let it be Fotheringay," said Henry.

\*     \*     \*

When Katharine heard that she was to go to Fotheringay she cried out in protest.

"It is even more unhealthy than Buckden!" she said. "Is it true that the King wishes to see an end of me?"

She was weary of living and she was certain that if she went to Fotheringay she would not be long for this world. It was a comforting thought, but immediately she dismissed it. What of Mary? She visualized her daughter, shorn of her rank, forced to live under the same roof as Anne Boleyn's daughter, doubtless expected to pay homage to the child. It was intolerable. She must live to fight for Mary. Chapuys was full of ideas; he was constantly writing to her. He was ready to go to great lengths in her cause and that of the Princess Mary. And here she was, weakly welcoming death.

She would certainly not go to Fortheringay.

"I will not leave Buckden for Fotheringay," she wrote to the King, "unless you bind me with ropes and take me there."

But Henry was now determined to move her and, since she would not accept Fotheringay, he declared that she should go to Somersham in the Isle of Ely.

"As this place is no more acceptable to me than the Castle of Fotheringay," she wrote, "I will remain where I am."

But the King had decided that she should go to Somersham, for there she could live with a smaller household. Moreover he knew that she was far from well, and Somersham, like Fotheringay, was unhealthy. If Katharine were to die a natural death, and he could cease to think of her and the effect she was having on his popularity, he would enjoy greater peace of mind.

He sent Suffolk down to Buckden with instructions to move the Queen and certain members of her household to Somersham.

\* \* \*

The Duke of Suffolk had arrived at Buckden and was asking audience of the Princess Dowager. Katharine, walking with difficulty, received him in the great hall.

"My lady," said Suffolk, bowing, but not too low, making a difference in the homage he would give to a Queen and one who was of less importance than himself, "I come on the King's orders to move you and your household to Somersham."

"I thank you, my lord Duke," answered Katharine coldly, "but I have no intention of leaving Buckden for Somersham."

Suffolk inclined his head. "My lady, I fear you have no choice in this matter as it is the King's order that you should move."

"I refuse this order," retorted Katharine. "Here I stay. You see the poor state of my health. Buckden does not serve it well, but Somersham is even more damp and unhealthy. I shall not leave this house until one which pleases me is found for me."

"My lady, you leave me no alternative . . ."

She interrupted him: ". . . but to go back to the King and tell him that I refuse."

"That is not what I intended, my lady. I have orders from the King to move you, and I at least must obey my master."

"I'm afraid your task is impossible, my lord, if I refuse to go."

"There are ways, Madam," answered the Duke, "and these must needs be adopted in the service of the King."

Katharine turned and, leaving him, retired to her apartments. She expected him to ride off to tell the King what had happened, but he did not do this; and sitting at her window waiting to see him leave, she waited in vain. Then suddenly from below she heard unusual noises, and before she could summon any of her women to ask what was happening, one came to her.

"Your Grace," said the woman, "they are moving the furniture. They are preparing to take it away. Already the hall is being stripped bare."

"This is impossible!" said the Queen. "They cannot turn me out of Buckden without my consent."

But she was wrong, because this was exactly what Suffolk had made up his mind to do.

Secretly Suffolk was ashamed of this commission and wished that the King had chosen some other to carry it out; it was particularly distasteful to him, because he had, on the death of the King's sister Mary, recently married the daughter of Maria de Salinas who was such a close friend of the Queen. But his bucolic mind could suggest no other way of disguising his distaste than by truculence. Moreover he had orders to move the Queen from Buckden, and he did not care to contemplate what the King would say if he returned to Court and explained that he had been unable to carry out his task.

Katharine went to the hall and saw that what she had been told was correct. The tapestries had already been taken down from the walls, and the furniture was being prepared for removal.

Angrily she confronted Suffolk. "How dare you move my furniture without my consent?" she demanded.

He bowed. "The King's orders are that it and you should be removed."

"I tell you I shall not go."

She left him and went up to her bedchamber. Several of her faithful women were there, and she locked the door on herself and them.

Suffolk followed her and stood outside the door begging her to be reasonable.

She would not answer him and, realizing that it was no use arguing with a locked door, Suffolk went back to the hall.

"Go into all the rooms save those of the Queen's private apartments, which are locked against us," he commanded. "Dismantle the beds and pack all that needs to be packed. We are moving this household to Somersham."

The work went on while Katharine remained in her own apartments; but Suffolk and his retinue had been seen arriving, and it was not long before news of what was happening within the manor house was spread throughout the villages. As the crowd outside grew, Suffolk, who had posted his guards about the house, was soon made aware that the Queen's neighbours were gathering to protect her. It was a silent crowd, watching from a distance; but it was noted that many of the men carried choppers and billhooks; and Suffolk, who had never been noted for his quick wits, was uneasy. Here was a humiliating situation: the Queen locked in her own apartments with a few of her faithful servants; he and his men dismantling the house, preparing to move; and outside, the Queen's neighbours gathering to protect her! Suffolk knew that if he attempted to remove the Queen by force there would be a battle. He could imagine Henry's fury when news of this reached his ears.

Yet something must be done; but the winter evening was near and he could do nothing that night, so he called a halt to his men. They should see about their night quarters and making a meal. They were prepared for this for they had not expected to complete their task in one day and night.

In the morning, Suffolk told himself, I shall work out a plan. He thought wistfully of the Christmas revelry which would be taking place at the Court. The new Queen and her admirers would certainly arrange a lively pageant. There would be fun for those at Court, while he had to spend his time in this gloomy mansion, trying to persuade an obstinate woman to do something which she had sworn not to do.

But in the morning the situation was the same. Katharine remained in her own apartments, waited on by her faithful servants who treated the invaders as though they did not exist.

Meanwhile by daylight the crowds waiting outside seemed to be more formidable—young, strong countrymen with their ferocious-looking billhooks. If he attempted to force a way through them Suffolk knew there would assuredly be a clash.

More than ever he wished himself back at Court; but he could see only one possible course. He must write to the King and tell him the circumstances; he would be cursed for an incompetent fool, but that was better than being responsible for a fight between the King's soldiers and the Queen's protectors. Suffolk was shrewd enough to know that such an incident might be the spark to start a civil war.

Already the King was preoccupied with fears of a rebellion which might seek to set his daughter Mary on the throne.

Yet he was undecided. He put off writing to the King, telling himself that Katharine might relent. She was after all an ageing woman, a lonely woman who had suffered the greatest humiliation possible. Perhaps those yokels waiting outside to defend her would grow tired. So Suffolk decided to wait.

For five days he waited and still Katharine's door remained

locked. She took her food in her own apartments and would not open her door to Suffolk.

His patience ended. He went to her door and hammered on it.

"If you do not come out, I shall take you by force," he shouted.

"You would have to do that," was Katharine's answer. "Break down my door if you will. Bind me with ropes. Carry me to your litter. That is the only way you will get me to move from this house."

Suffolk swore in his angry uncertainty. There were spies in this household. They were carrying tales to those waiting people so that everything that was happening in this house was known. He was sure that the Queen's neighbours were sending word to friends miles away, and that the ranks about the house were swelling.

He dared not take her by force. He and his men would be torn to pieces if he did.

He returned to the hall, looked gloomily at the dismantled room; then he wrote to the King, to Cromwell and to Norfolk, explaining the Queen's obstinacy and his fear of mob violence from the crowd which now seemed to be some thousands.

He despatched the letters and prepared to depart himself.

He saw Thomas Abell coming from the Queen's apartments and called to him.

"So, sir priest, you are still here with the Princess Dowager."

"As you see, my lord Duke."

"And upholding her in her obstinacy as you ever did," snarled Suffolk.

"The Queen is a lady of stern ideals."

"The Queen? There is but one Queen of England. That is Queen Anne."

"There is but one Queen, my lord; and I say that Queen is Queen Katharine."

"By God," cried Suffolk, "you speak high treason." He shouted to his men. "Take this priest. He will leave with us as our prisoner."

He summoned all those servants, who were not with Katharine, to his presence and forthwith arrested several of them. At least he would not go back to London empty handed. Then he was ready to leave. He glanced round the castle which looked as though it had been sacked by invading soldiery—which in some measure it had—before he rode out into the courtyard and gave the order to depart.

The crowds parted for them to pass; no one spoke, but the looks were sullen.

Katharine came down from her private apartments and gazed in dismay at the havoc in her house. But when she heard that some of her servants had been taken prisoner, among them the faithful Abell, she ceased to care about the state of her dwelling. She thought of Abell going back to the discomfort of the Tower, where he might be submitted to torture as he had been before, and a feeling of utter desolation took possession of her.

Will there be no end to this persecution? she asked herself. Then she began to weep, for the strain of the last days had been greater than she had realized while they were happening; and although when confined to her room, unsure of whether she would be removed by force, she had not wept, now she could not prevent herself from doing so.

Two of her women came and stood with her.

"Your Majesty, pray return to your bed. There is more comfort there."

She did not answer but held her kerchief to her streaming eyes.

"A curse on Anne Boleyn," said one of the women.

Katharine lowered her kerchief and turned her stern gaze on the speaker. "Nay," she said. "Hold your peace. Do not curse her. Rather pray for her. Even now the time is coming fast when you shall have reason to pity her and lament her case."

She turned slowly and mounted the stairs to her apartment. Her women looked after her in wonderment. Then they shivered, for she spoke with the voice of a prophet.

CHAPTER XIV

## IN THE CASTLE OF KIMBOLTON

KATHARINE continued to live in her private apartments, and the rest of the castle remained as Suffolk's men had left it: the tapestries unhung, the furniture dismantled.

Every day Katharine expected to receive a command from the King to leave Buckden for some place of his choice, but Henry was too occupied by affairs at Court to concern himself with her.

There was about this life an air of transience. She scarcely left her apartments, and heard Mass at the window of her bedroom which looked down on the chapel; her food was cooked by her bedroom fire, and those who served her, living closer to her, began to find love of her mingling with the respect she had always inspired.

The winter was bitter and she often felt, during those rigorous weeks when she lay shivering in her bed, that she could not live long in this condition. Her great concern was for her daughter who she knew, through Chapuys, was as much in danger as she was herself.

Chapuys wrote to her that she must take care what she ate, and that her meals should be cooked only by her most trusted servants because he believed that in high quarters there was a plot to remove both her and the Princess Mary.

This threat did not diminish when in the March of that year Clement at last gave his verdict, declaring that the marriage of Henry VIII and Katharine of Aragon was valid in the eyes of God and the Church.

"Too late!" sighed Katharine. "Five weary years too late!"

She knew that Clement's verdict could do her and Mary no good now, but could only increase the wrath of her enemies among whom she knew in her heart—but she tried hard not to admit this—was the King, her husband.

In May of that year the King ordered her to leave Buckden for Kimbolton Castle in Huntingdonshire; and this time she obeyed.

\*     \*     \*

The reign of terror had begun. There were certain stubborn men who refused to take the Oath of Supremacy, and the King was no longer the carefree boy who was eager only for his pleasure.

His marriage with Anne was turning sour. Where was the boy for whom he had dared so much? Where was the tender passion he had once felt for Anne?

In Kimbolton Castle was the woman whom many still called his Queen. He was waiting impatiently for her death which surely could not be long delayed. The last years of anxiety and living in damp houses had ruined her health, he had heard; yet she clung as stubbornly to life as she had to her determination not to enter a nunnery.

A plague on obstinate women . . . and obstinate men.

He knew that Chapuys was dangerous, and he had refused again and again the ambassador's requests to see Katharine. How did he know what was being planned in secret? Was it true that plans were afoot to smuggle Mary from the country and marry her to Reginald Pole, that traitor who dared tell him . . . his King . . . that he disapproved of his conduct?

A plague on all men and women who risked their lives for a cause which was not the King's. They should see whither that road led.

Mary was as obstinate as her mother, refusing to travel with her baby sister, declaring that she was a Princess and would answer to no other title, continually pleading to see her mother; now she was most inconveniently ill, and it was being whispered that she had been poisoned.

Katharine wrote to him from Kimbolton: "Our daughter is ill. You cannot keep her from me now. I beg of you, allow me to see her. Do you remember how long it is since I did so? What joy does this cruelty bring you?"

The King's eyes narrowed as he read that appeal. Let them meet! Let them plot together! Let them smuggle notes to sly Chapuys . . . plans to get Mary abroad, married to Pole—a signal doubtless for their friends in England to rise against him!

"Never!" he cried.

\*          \*          \*

Those who did not obey the King should suffer the supreme penalty. In April of that bloodstained year five Carthusian monks were brought for trial and found to be guilty of high treason. Their crime: They refused to sign the Oath declaring the King to be Supreme Head of the Church.

"Let them understand," growled Henry, "what it means to disobey the King. Let all who plan like disobedience look on and see."

In that May the tortured bodies of these five martyrs were brought out of their prison for execution. The degrading and horrible traitors' death was accorded them and they were dragged on hurdles to Tyburn, hanged, cut down alive, their bodies ripped open and their bowels and hearts impaled on spears and shown to the spectators, that all might understand what happened to those who disobeyed the King.

In June more monks of the Charterhouse were brought to Tyburn and similarly dealt with. And a few days later John Fisher, Bishop of Rochester, was brought from his prison to die the traitors' death. Fortunately for him, there were some for whom it was expedient to show leniency; so the King said he would be merciful. Not for the bishop, whom some of the King's misguided subjects loved, the barbarous death accorded to the Carthusians; Fisher was allowed to die by means of the executioner's axe.

In July Sir Thomas More was brought from the Tower of

London, where he had been for fifteen months, and he too laid his head upon the block.

When Katharine heard of the death of these old friends she shut herself into her chamber and remained there alone.

She still could not believe that the gay young husband who had married her in the days of her humiliation was in truth the brutal murderer of good men. She still clung to the belief that it was those about him who urged him to these deeds. Now she feigned to believe it was Anne Boleyn, as once she had believed it was Wolsey.

Yet in her heart she knew that he was all-powerful; more so than ever now that he had cut himself off from the Pope.

John Fisher! she sighed. Thomas More! My dear friends . . . and the King's! How could he murder two such men?

But she knew. And she wondered: Who will be next?

She was very fearful for her daughter . . . and herself.

\*        \*        \*

The winter had come again, and Katharine knew with certainty that she could not live through it. She was now so feeble that she must keep to her bed for days at a time; and some premonition told her that her end was near.

Once more she appealed to Henry.

"I do not think I have long to live. I pray you permit our daughter to come to me. You surely cannot prevent her from receiving my last blessing in person."

She was hopeful when she had despatched that appeal because she persisted in believing that Henry was not so cruel as he seemed.

But this plea, like others, was unanswered, and she now understood that she would never see her beloved daughter again in this life.

Chapuys, hearing of the Queen's condition, was alarmed and went at once to the King. He was shocked to see the hopeful expression in the King's face. The man is a monster, he thought angrily.

"I ask Your Majesty's permission to visit the Queen at Kimbolton," he said.

Henry ignored the request, and began to speak of affairs in Europe. François would not rest until Milan was his; and could he win Milan without the help of England?

Chapuys did not answer. Instead he said: "I have heard from the Queen's physician that she is near death. She implores you to allow her to see her daughter."

"It is a matter which I could not decide without consulting my council." Henry took Chapuys by the shoulders and studied him intently. "The Emperor ignores his interests when he meddles in matters which are outside his concern. If he refuses my friendship, why should I not make an alliance with an ally who is eager to be my friend?"

"Your Majesty cannot believe the Emperor would ever abandon Queen Katharine while she is alive."

A smile of complacency crossed the King's face. "Then perhaps it is not important. She will not live long."

"It is for this reason that I ask your permission to visit her."

Henry shrugged his shoulders. She was dying; she could not long be an encumbrance to him.

"Go to her if you wish," he said. "But there shall be no meeting between her and the Lady Mary."

Chapuys did not wait, for fear that the King might change his mind. He left Henry's presence and with all speed set out for Kimbolton.

\* \* \*

Chapuys knelt by her bed and his heart was touched by the sight of her. The skin was tightly drawn across her bones; her hair, once so beautiful, hung limp and lustreless. Talking exhausted her. But she brightened at the sight of him; and when she saw his distress she told him not to weep, for, as he would see, death held no terrors for her, and since she was parted from her daughter life had little to offer.

Then she pushed aside her grievances and wished to hear news of her daughter and to give instructions as to what was to happen after her death.

"I have so little to leave," she said. "A few furs, a few jewels . . . but they are hers; and she will love them, more because they were mine than because of their value. When you see her, tell her that I loved her dearly and that had it not been for my delight in her I doubt I could have borne my sorrows. Oh, my dear friend, I fear I have brought great suffering to this country. Worthy men have died and others have endangered their souls. Yet I am Henry's wife, and how could I deny that?"

Chapuys tried to soothe her, and it was gratifying to him to know that he brought her some comfort. He looked round the room, at the few candles, at the rushes on the floor. A humble room to provide the death chamber of Isabella's daughter.

But his visit so comforted her that she seemed to recover.

\* \* \*

It was six o'clock on New Year's Day when a small party of weary travellers arrived at the gate of the Castle. At their head was a woman who declared that they were half dead with fatigue and implored to be given shelter.

The gate-keeper told her that none could be admitted to the Castle unless carrying a written permission from the King to do so; but the woman wept and begged him not to leave her without shelter in this bitter January night.

The gate-keeper was touched by the piteous spectacle the travellers presented, and consented to allow their leader to see Sir Edmund Bedingfeld whom the King had appointed steward to Katharine, but who was in fact her jailor.

When the woman was in his presence, her hooded cloak wrapped tightly about her shivering body, she entreated him to allow her to warm herself at a fire, and she was taken into the hall of the Castle.

"Tell me," she said as she stretched her white hands to the blaze, "is the Princess Dowager still alive?"

"She is," was the answer.

"I had heard that she was dead," said the woman sombrely.

"I fear she soon may be."

"I pray you let me see her."

"Who are you?"

"I have letters to prove my identity."

"Then show them to me."

"This I will do in the morning. They are now in the possession of my women."

"I should need to see them," said Bedingfeld, "before I could allow you to visit the Princess Dowager."

The woman went to her two servants who were standing some distance away, but instead of speaking to them she suddenly ran to the staircase and began to mount it.

Bedingfeld was so astonished that he could only stare after her, and in those few seconds she took the opportunity to get well ahead.

"Who is your mistress?" he demanded of the women; but they shook their heads and would not answer; and by that time the woman was at the top of the first flight of stairs and had come upon one of the Queen's maids.

"Take me to the Queen. I am a friend whom she will wish to see."

Bedingfeld cried: "Halt, I say."

The maid did not listen to him and turning began to run, while the visitor followed her.

The door of Katharine's bedchamber was thrown open and the maid cried: "Your Majesty, Lady Willoughby has come to see you."

Then the Queen tried to raise herself, and Maria de Salinas ran to the bedside, threw herself on her knees and embraced her.

When Bedingfeld entered the room he saw the two women in each other's arms. He saw the tears on the Queen's wasted cheeks; he heard her say: "So Maria, you came to me; so I am not to die alone. I am not abandoned like some forgotten beast."

The Queen's eyes met his over the head of her faithful Maria, and she said: "Leave us. My dear friend has braved much to come to me. I command you to leave us together."

And Bedingfeld turned quietly and shut the door.

\*     \*     \*

There were not many days left; and Maria de Salinas did not leave the Queen's bedside. She told Katharine of how she had made the perilous journey unknown to anyone, because she had determined to be with her mistress.

"Oh Maria, how happy you have made me," sighed the Queen. "The pity of it, there is little time left for us to be together."

"Nay," cried Maria, "you will get well now that I am here to nurse you."

"I am beyond nursing," replied the Queen; "yet not so far gone that I cannot rejoice in your dear presence."

Maria refused to leave the Queen's bedchamber, and during the days that followed she it was who nursed her and sat by her bed talking to her.

There were times when Katharine forgot that she was in her bed in dreary Kimbolton, and believed that she was in the Alhambra at Granada, that she wandered through the Court of Myrtles, that she looked down from her window on to the Court-yard of Lions; and that beside her there was one, benign and loving, her mother Isabella. Maria sitting at her bedside could speak of those days and, with Maria's hand in hers, they spoke the language of their native Castile; and it seemed to Katharine that the pains of her body and the sorrows of her life in England slipped away from her. Here was sunshine and pleasure amid the rosy towers; she saw the sign of the pomegranate engraved on the walls—the symbol of fertility which she had taken as her own, she forgot with what irony, because the years had slipped away and she was young again.

Maria watched her with startled eyes, for she knew that Katharine's life was ebbing away.

She sent for the priests and Extreme Unction was given. And at two o'clock in the afternoon of the 7th of January 1536 Katharine died.

\*       \*       \*

When the news was brought to Henry he was jubilant.

"Praise be to God," he cried. "We are delivered from the fear of war. Now I shall be able to treat with the French, for they will be fearful that I shall make an alliance with the Emperor."

There was another reason for his pleasure. She had been a perpetual embarrassment to him while there were men to believe she was still his wife.

He dressed himself in yellow from head to foot and wore a waving white plume in his cap, declaring that the revelries were to continue because there should be no period of mourning for a woman who had never been his wife.

Queen Anne followed his example and dressed in yellow. Like the King she was relieved by the death of Katharine; but there was a shadow across her relief. She was aware—as were many at Court—how the King's eyes would light with speculation as they rested on a certain prim but sly maid of honour whose name was Jane Seymour.

Now there was a feverish gaiety about the King and his Queen. Death was waiting round the corner for so many. But through the Court strode the King, the little Elizabeth in his arms, demanding admiration for his daughter. Some wondered what the fate of that other daughter would be, remembering a time when he had walked among them with Mary in his arms.

"On with the dance!" cried the King; and the musicians played while the company danced with abandon.

Queen Katharine was dead; More was dead; Fisher was dead. They formed part of the procession of martyrs.

Dance today! was the order of the Court, for who could know what tomorrow would hold? Whose turn would come next?